Praise for *The Last Coyote*

"Recalls no one so much as Raymond Chandler . . . Ambitious, skillful, and moving . . . An intricate and clever mystery."

—*Los Angeles Times*

"Connelly is one of a handful of crime writers who are raising the hard-boiled detective genre to a new level . . . adding substance and depth to modern crime fiction."

—*The Boston Globe*

"Connelly has created a smart, tough, independent, and dedicated cop in Harry Bosch."

—*The Seattle Times*

"Tough, taut writing."

—*The New York Times Book Review*

"Grabs you and shakes you—and it feels great."

—*Kirkus Reviews*

"A powerful book that will further Connelly's growing reputation as a skillful and imaginative writer."

—*Houston Chronicle*

"Edgar-winning Connelly smoothly mixes Harry's detecting forays with his therapy sessions to dramatize how, sometimes, the biggest mystery is the self."

—*Publishers Weekly*

"Harry examines his past, acknowledges the damage, and sets out to heal himself. It's heady territory for a cop novel, but Edgar winner Connelly handles it with style and grace."

—*Booklist*

"Prose that cuts to the quick . . . A masterfully written interwoven plot and gripping suspense."

—*Library Journal*

Praise for *Trunk Music*

"A terrific new police procedural."

—*The New York Times Book Review*

"A jazzy, funky roller coaster of a book . . . Connelly has it all working together here: skillful dialogue, solid plotting, nuances of race, and a pace that will keep readers gasping to keep up. . . . His best yet."

—*Publishers Weekly*

"Truly one of the year's best entertainments."

—*Booklist*

"Compelling . . . Connelly displays a wonderful atmospheric feel for the posh and the poor. . . . The last pages bring things to a shocking end that should satisfy Connelly's growing audience."

—*The Washington Post*

"For those seeking the kind of action that takes more turns than a roulette wheel, *Trunk Music* is a sure bet."

—*People* magazine

"A fictional delight."

—*St. Paul Pioneer-Press*

"*Trunk Music* is Connelly at his best, skewering the superficial Hollywood society, the hoods, the good guys and bad girls, the bureaucratic tyrants who would rather fill in the right form than get to the truth."

—*Orlando Sentinel*

"Former *Los Angeles Times* police reporter Michael Connelly is rapidly becoming the best procedural crime writer around. . . . *Trunk Music* has a rich, full-bodied plot."

—*Arizona Daily Star*

THE LAST COYOTE
TRUNK MUSIC

St. Martin's paperback titles by Michael Connelly

The Black Echo
The Black Ice
The Concrete Blonde
The Last Coyote
Trunk Music

THE LAST COYOTE
TRUNK MUSIC

Michael Connelly

St. Martin's Griffin ✖ New York

www.stmartins.com

ISBN 0-312-35377-4
EAN 978-0-312-35377-3

The Last Coyote was originally published by Little, Brown & Company in 1995.

Trunk Music was originally published by Little, Brown & Company in 1997.

First St. Martin's Griffin Edition: October 2005

10 9 8 7 6 5 4 3 2 1

THE LAST COYOTE

This is for Marcus Grupa

THE LAST COYOTE

Any thoughts that you'd like to start with?"

"Thoughts on what?"

"Well, on anything. On the incident."

"On the incident? Yes, I have some thoughts."

She waited but he didn't continue. He had decided before he even got to Chinatown that this would be the way he would be. He'd make her have to pull every single word out of him.

"Could you share them with me, Detective Bosch?" she finally asked. "That is the purpose of—"

"My thoughts are that this is bullshit. Total bullshit. That's the purpose. That's all."

"No, wait. How do you mean, bullshit?"

"I mean, okay, I pushed the guy. I guess I hit him. I'm not sure exactly what happened but I'm not denying anything. So, fine, suspend me, transfer me, take it to a Board of Rights, whatever. But going this way is bullshit. ISL is bullshit. I mean, why do I have to come here three times a week to talk to you like I'm some kind of—you don't even know me, you don't know anything about me. Why do I have to talk to you? Why do you have to sign off on this?"

"Well, the technical answer is right there in your own statement.

Rather than discipline you the department wants to treat you. You've been placed on involuntary stress leave, which means—"

"I know what it means and that's what's bullshit. Somebody arbitrarily decides I'm under stress and that gives the department the power to keep me off the job indefinitely, or at least until I jump through enough hoops for you."

"Nothing about this was arbitrary. It was predicated on your actions, which I think clearly show—"

"What happened had nothing to do with stress. What it was about was . . . never mind. Like I said, it's bullshit. So why don't we just cut through it and get to the point. What do I have to do to get back to my job?"

He could see the anger flare behind her eyes. His total disavowal of her science and skill cut to her pride. Quickly the anger was gone, though. Dealing with cops all the time, she had to be used to it.

"Can't you see that all of this is for your own welfare? I have to assume the top managers of this department clearly see you as a valued asset or you wouldn't be here. They'd have put you on a disciplinary track and you'd be on your way out. Instead, they are doing what they can to preserve your career and its incumbent value to the department."

"Valued asset? I'm a cop, not an asset. And when you're out there on the street nobody's thinking about incumbent value. What does that mean, anyway? Am I going to have to listen to words like that in here?"

She cleared her throat before speaking sternly.

"You have a problem, Detective Bosch. And it goes far beyond the incident that resulted in your being placed on leave. That's what these sessions are going to be all about. Do you understand? This incident is not unique. You have had problems before. What I am trying to do, what I have to do before I can sign off on your return to duty in any capacity, is get you to take a look at yourself. What are you doing? What are you about? Why do these problems happen to you? I want these sessions to be an open dialogue where I ask a few questions and you speak your mind, but with a purpose. Not to harass me and my profession or the leadership of the department. But to talk about you. This is about you in here, no one else."

Harry Bosch just looked at her silently. He wanted a cigarette but would never ask her if he could smoke. He would never acknowledge in front of her that he had the habit. If he did, she might start talking about oral fixations or nicotine crutches. He took a deep breath instead and looked at the woman on the other side of the desk. Carmen Hinojos was a small woman with a friendly face and manner. Bosch knew she wasn't a bad person. He'd actually heard good things about her from others who had been sent to Chinatown. She was just doing her job here and his anger was not really directed at her. He knew she was probably smart enough to know that, too.

"Look, I'm sorry," she said. "I should not have started with that kind of open question. I know that this is an emotional subject with you. Let's try to start again. By the way, you can smoke if you'd like."

"Is that in the file, too?"

"It's not in the file. It didn't need to be. It's your hand, the way you keep bringing it up to your mouth. Have you been trying to quit?"

"No. But it's a city office. You know the rules."

It was a thin excuse. He violated that law every day at the Hollywood Station.

"That's not the rule in here. I don't want you to think of this as being part of Parker Center or part of the city. That's the chief reason these offices are away from that. There are no rules like that here."

"Doesn't matter where we are. You're still working for the LAPD."

"Try to believe that you are away from the Los Angeles Police Department. When you are in here, try to believe that you're just coming to see a friend. To talk. You can say anything here."

But he knew she could not be seen as a friend. Never. There was too much at stake here. Just the same, he nodded once to please her.

"That's not very convincing."

He hiked his shoulders as if to say it was the best he could do, and it was.

"By the way, if you want I could hypnotize you, get rid of your dependency on nicotine."

"If I wanted to quit, I could do it. People are either smokers or they're not. I am."

"Yes. It's perhaps the most obvious symptom of a self-destructive nature."

"Excuse me, am I on leave because I smoke? Is that what this is about?"

"I think you know what it's about."

He said nothing else, remembering his decision to say as little as possible.

"Well, let's continue then," she said. "You've been on leave . . . let's see, Tuesday a week?"

"Right."

"What have you been doing with your time?"

"Filling out FEMA forms mostly."

"FEMA?"

"My house was red-tagged."

"The earthquake was three months ago. Why have you waited?"

"I've been busy. I've been working."

"I see. Did you have insurance?"

"Don't say 'I see,' because you don't. You couldn't possibly see things the way I do. The answer is no, no insurance. Like most everybody else, I was living in denial. Isn't that what you people call it? I bet you had insurance."

"Yes. How bad was your house hit?"

"Depends on who you ask. The city inspectors say it's totaled and I can't even go inside. I think it's fine. Just needs some work. They know me by name at Home Depot now. And I've had contractors do some of it. It'll be done soon and I'll appeal the red tag. I've got a lawyer."

"You're living there still?"

He nodded.

"Now that's denial, Detective Bosch. I don't think you should be doing that."

"I don't think you have any say about what I do outside my job with the department."

She raised her hands in a hands-off manner.

"Well, while I don't condone it, I suppose it serves its purpose. I think it's good that you have something to keep you occupied. Though I'd much rather it be a sport or a hobby or maybe plans for a trip out of town, I think it's important to keep busy, to keep your mind off the incident."

Bosch smirked.

"What?"

"I don't know. Everybody keeps calling it the incident. It kind've reminds me of how people called it the Vietnam conflict, not the war."

"Then what would you call what happened?"

"I don't know. But incident . . . it sounds like . . . I don't know. Antiseptic. Listen, Doctor, let's go back a minute. I don't want to take a trip out of town, okay? My job is in homicide. It's what I do. And I'd really like to get back to it. I might be able to do some good, you know."

"If the department lets you."

"If you do. You know it's going to be up to you."

"Perhaps. Do you notice that you speak of your job as if it's a mission of some sort?"

"That's about right. Like the Holy Grail."

He said it with sarcasm. This was getting intolerable and it was only the first session.

"Is it? Do you believe your mission in life is to solve murders, to put bad people in jail?"

He used the shoulder hike to say he didn't know. He stood up and walked to the window and looked down on Hill Street. The sidewalks were crowded with pedestrians. Every time he had been down here they were crowded. He noticed a couple of Caucasian women walking along. They stood out in the sea of Asian faces like raisins in rice. They passed the window of a Chinese butcher shop and Bosch saw a row of smoked ducks hanging whole, by their necks.

Farther up the road he saw the Hollywood Freeway overpass, the dark windows of the old sheriff's jail and the Criminal Courts building behind it. To the left of that he could see the City Hall tower. Black construction tarps hung around the top floors. It looked like some kind of mourning gesture but he knew the tarps were to hold debris from falling while earthquake repairs were made. Looking past City Hall, Bosch could see the Glass House. Parker Center, police headquarters.

"Tell me what your mission is," Hinojos said quietly from behind him. "I'd like to hear you put it in words."

He sat back down and tried to think of a way to explain himself but finally just shook his head.

"I can't."

"Well, I want you to think about that. Your mission. What is it really? Think about that."

"What's your mission, Doctor?"

"That's not our concern here."

"Of course it is."

"Look, Detective, this is the only personal question I will answer. These dialogues are not to be about me. They are about you. My mission, I believe, is to help the men and women of this department. That's the narrow focus. And by doing that, on a grander scale I help the community, I help the people of this city. The better the cops are that we have out on the street, the better we all are. The safer we all are. Okay?"

"That's fine. When I think about my mission, do you want me to shorten it to a couple sentences like that and rehearse it to the point that it sounds like I'm reading out of the dictionary?"

"Mr.—uh, Detective Bosch, if you want to be cute and contentious the whole time, we are not going to get anywhere, which means you are not going to get back to your job anytime soon. Is that what you're looking for here?"

He raised his hands in surrender. She looked down at the yellow legal pad on the desk. With her eyes off him, he was able to study her. Carmen Hinojos had tiny brown hands she kept on the desk in front of her. No rings on either hand. She held an expensive-looking pen in her right hand. Bosch always thought expensive pens were used by people overly concerned with image. But maybe he was wrong about her. She wore her dark brown hair tied back. She wore glasses with thin tortoiseshell frames. She should have had braces when she was a kid but didn't. She looked up from the pad and their eyes locked.

"I am told this inci—this . . . situation coincided with or was close to the time of the dissolving of a romantic relationship."

"Told by who?"

"It's in the background material given to me. The sources of this material are not important."

"Well, they are important because you've got bad sources. It had nothing to do with what happened. The dissolving, as you call it, was almost three months ago."

"The pain of these things can last much longer than that. I know this is personal and may be difficult but I think we should talk about this. The reason is that it will help give me a basis for your emotional state at the time the assault took place. Is that a problem?"

Bosch waved her on with his hand.

"How long did this relationship last?"

"About a year."

"Marriage?"

"No."

"Was it talked about?"

"No, not really. Never out in the open."

"Did you live together?"

"Sometimes. We both kept our places."

"Is the separation final?"

"I think so."

Saying it out loud seemed to be the first time Bosch acknowledged that Sylvia Moore was gone from his life for good.

"Was this separation by mutual agreement?"

He cleared his throat. He didn't want to talk about this but he wanted it over with.

"I guess you could say it was mutual agreement, but I didn't know about it until she was packed. You know, three months ago we were holding each other in bed while the house was shaking apart on the pad. You could say she was gone before the aftershocks ended."

"They still haven't."

"Just a figure of speech."

"Are you saying the earthquake was the cause of the breakup of this relationship?"

"No, I'm not saying that. All I'm saying is that's when it happened. Right after. She's a teacher up in the Valley and her school got wrecked. The kids were moved to other schools and the district didn't need as many teachers. They offered sabbaticals and she took one. She left town."

"Was she scared of another earthquake or was she scared of you?"

She looked pointedly at him.

"Why would she be scared of me?"

He knew he sounded a little too defensive.

"I don't know. I'm just asking questions. Did you give her a reason to be scared?"

Bosch hesitated. It was a question he had never really touched on in his private thoughts about the breakup.

"If you mean in a physical way, no, she wasn't scared and I gave her no reason to be."

Hinojos nodded and wrote something on her pad. It bothered Bosch that she would make a note about this.

"Look, it's got nothing to do with what happened at the station last week."

"Why did she leave? What was the real reason?"

He looked away. He was angry. This was how it was going to be. She would ask whatever she wanted. Invade him wherever there was an opening.

"I don't know."

"That answer is not acceptable in here. I think you do know, or at least have your own beliefs as to why she would leave. You must."

"She found out who I was."

"She found out who you were, what does that mean?"

"You'd have to ask her. She said it. But she's in Venice. The one in Italy."

"Well, then what do you think she meant by it?"

"It doesn't matter what I think. She's the one who said it and she's the one who left."

"Don't fight me, Detective Bosch. Please. There is nothing I want more than for you to get back to your job. As I said, that's my mission. To get you back there if you can go. But you make it difficult by being difficult."

"Maybe that's what she found out. Maybe that's who I am."

"I doubt the reason is as simplistic as that."

"Sometimes I don't."

She looked at her watch and leaned forward, dissatisfaction with the session showing on her face.

"Okay, Detective, I understand how uncomfortable you are. We're going to move on, but I suspect we will have to come back to this issue. I want you to give it some thought. Try to put your feelings into words."

She waited for him to say something but he didn't.

"Let's try talking about what happened last week again. I understand it stemmed from a case involving the murder of a prostitute."

"Yes."

"It was brutal?"

"That's just a word. Means different things to different people."

"True, but taking its meaning to you, was it a brutal homicide?"

"Yes, it was brutal. I think almost all of them are. Somebody dies, it's brutal. For them."

"And you took the suspect into custody?"

"Yes, my partner and I. I mean, no. He came in voluntarily to answer questions."

"Did this case affect you more than, say, other cases have in the past?"

"Maybe, I don't know."

"Why would that be?"

"You mean why did I care about a prostitute? I didn't. Not more than any other victim. But in homicide there is one rule that I have when it comes to the cases I get."

"What is that rule?"

"Everybody counts or nobody counts."

"Explain it."

"Just what I said. Everybody counts or nobody counts. That's it. It means I bust my ass to make a case whether it's a prostitute or the mayor's wife. That's my rule."

"I understand. Now, let's go to this specific case. I'm interested in hearing your description of what happened after the arrest and the reasons you may have for your violent actions at the Hollywood Division."

"Is this being taped?"

"No, Detective, whatever you tell me is protected. At the end of these sessions I will simply make a recommendation to Assistant Chief Irving. The details of the sessions will never be divulged. The recommendations I make are usually less than half a page and contain no details from the dialogues."

"You wield a lot of power with that half page."

She didn't respond. Bosch thought for a moment while looking at her. He thought he might be able to trust her but his natural instinct and experience was that he should trust no one. She seemed to know his dilemma and waited him out.

"You want to hear my side of it?"

"Yes, I do."

"Okay, I'll tell you what happened."

Bosch smoked along the way home but realized that what he really wanted was not a cigarette, but a drink to deaden his nerves. He looked at his watch and decided it was too early to stop at a bar. He settled for another cigarette and home.

After negotiating the drive up Woodrow Wilson, he parked at the curb a half block from the house and walked back. He could hear gentle piano music, something classical, coming from the home of one of his neighbors but he couldn't tell which house. He didn't really know any of his neighbors or which one might have a piano player in the family. He ducked under the yellow tape strung in front of the property and entered through the door in the carport.

This was his routine, to park down the street and hide the fact that he lived in his own house. The house had been red-tagged as uninhabitable after the earthquake and ordered demolished by a city inspector. But Bosch had ignored both orders, cut the lock on the electric box, and had been living in it for three months.

It was a small house with redwood siding that stood on steel pylons anchored in the sedimentary bedrock folded and formed as the Santa Monica Mountains rose out of the desert during the Mesozoic and Cenozoic eras. The pylons had held true in their moorings during the quake, but the overlying house had shifted atop them, breaking partially free of the pylons and seismic bolts. It slid. All of about two inches. Still, it was enough. Though short on distance the slide was long on damage. Inside, the woodframe house flexed and window and door frames lost their square. The glass shattered, the front door became terminally closed, frozen in a frame that had canted to the north with the rest of the house. If Bosch wanted to open that door, he would probably need to borrow the police tank with the battering ram. As it was, he'd had to use a crowbar to open the carport door. Now that door served as the main entrance to his home.

Bosch had paid a contractor five thousand dollars to jack the house up and then over the two inches it had moved. It was then put down in its proper space and rebolted to the pylons. After that, Bosch was content to work as time allowed on reframing windows and interior doors himself. The glass came first and in the months after that he reframed and rehung the interior doors. He worked from books on carpentry and often had to do individual projects two and three times until he had them reasonably correct. But he found the work enjoyable and even therapeutic. Working with his hands became a respite from his job in homicide. He left the front door as it was, thinking that somehow it was fitting, that it was a salute to the power of nature. And he was content to use the side door.

All of his efforts did not save the house from the city's list of condemned structures. Gowdy, the building inspector who had been assigned to this section of the hills, kept it red-tagged as condemned, despite Bosch's work, and so began the hiding game in which Bosch made his entrances and exits as surreptitiously as a spy's to a foreign embassy. He tacked black plastic tarps over the inside of the front windows so they would emit no telltale light. And he always watched for Gowdy. Gowdy was his nemesis.

In the meantime, Bosch hired a lawyer to appeal the inspector's edict.

The carport door granted entry directly into the kitchen. After he came in, Bosch opened the refrigerator and retrieved a can of Coca-Cola, then stood in the doorway of the aging appliance letting its breath cool him while he studied its contents for something suitable for dinner. He knew exactly what was on the shelves and in the drawers but still he looked. It was as if he hoped for the surprise appearance of a forgotten steak or chicken breast. He followed this routine with the refrigerator often. It was the ritual of a man who was alone. He knew this also.

On the back deck Bosch drank the soda and ate a sandwich consisting of five-day-old bread and slices of meat from plastic packages. He wished he had potato chips to go with it because he would undoubtedly be hungry later after having only the sandwich for dinner.

He stood at the railing looking down at the Hollywood Freeway, near capacity now with the Monday-evening commute. He had gotten out of downtown just before the crest of the rush-hour wave had broken. He would have to guard against going overtime on the sessions with the police psychologist. They were scheduled for 3:30 P.M. on Mondays, Wednesdays and Fridays. Did Carmen Hinojos ever let a session go over? he wondered. Or was hers a nine-to-five mission?

From his vantage on the mountain, he could see almost all northbound lanes of the freeway as it cut through the Cahuenga Pass to the San Fernando Valley. He was reviewing what had been said during the session, trying to decide whether it was a good or bad session, but his focus drifted and he began to watch the point where the freeway came into view as it crested the pass. Absentmindedly, he would choose two cars that came over about even with each other and follow them through the mile-long segment of the freeway that was visible from the deck. He'd pick one or the other and follow the race, unknown to its drivers, until the finish line, which was the Lankershim Boulevard exit.

After a few minutes of this he realized what he was doing and spun around, away from the freeway.

"Jesus," he said out loud.

He knew then that keeping his hands busy would not be enough while he was away from his job. He went back inside and got a bottle of Henry's from the refrigerator. Right after he opened the beer the phone rang. It was his partner, Jerry Edgar, and the call was a welcome distraction from the silence.

"Harry, how's things in Chinatown?"

Because every cop secretly feared that he or she might one day crack from the pressures of the job and become a candidate for therapy sessions at the department's Behavioral Sciences Section, the unit was rarely spoken of by its formal name. Going to BSS sessions was more often referred to as "going to Chinatown" because of the unit's location there on Hill Street, several blocks from Parker Center. If it became known about a cop that he was going there, the word would spread that he had the Hill Street blues. The six-story bank building where the BSS was located was known as the "Fifty-One-Fifty" building. This was not its address. It was the police radio code number for describing a crazy person. Codes like this were part of the protective structure used to belittle and, therefore, more easily contain their own fears.

"Chinatown was great," Bosch said sarcastically. "You ought to try it some day. It's got me sitting here counting cars on the freeway."

"Well, at least you won't run out."

"Yeah. What's going on with you?"

"Pounds finally did it."

"Did what?"

"Stuck me with somebody new."

Bosch was silent a moment. The news gave him a sense of finality. The thought that maybe he would never get his job back began to creep into his mind.

"He did?"

"Yeah, he finally did. I caught a case this morning. So he stuck one of his suckups with me. Burns."

"Burns? From autos? He's never worked homicide. Has he ever even worked CAPs?"

Detectives usually followed one of two paths in the department. One was property crimes and the other was crimes against persons. The latter included specializing in homicide, rape, assault and robbery. CAPs detectives had the higher-profile cases and usually viewed property crime investigators as paper pushers. There were so many property crimes in the city that the investigators spent most of their time taking reports and processing the occasional arrest. They actually did little detective work. There was no time to.

"He's been a paper guy all the way," Edgar said. "But with Pounds that doesn't matter. All he cares about is having somebody on the homicide table who isn't going to give his shit back to him. And Burns is just the guy. He probably started lobbying for the job the minute the word went out about you."

"Well, fuck him. I'm gonna get back to the table and then he goes back to autos."

Edgar took his time before answering. It was as if Bosch had said something that made no sense to him.

"You really think that, Harry? Pounds ain't going to stand for you coming back. Not after what you did. I told him when he told me I was with Burns that, you know, no offense but I'd wait until Harry Bosch came back and he said if I wanted to handle it that way, then I'd be waitin' until I was an old man."

"He said that? Well, fuck him, too. I still got a friend or two in the department."

"Irving still owes you, doesn't he?"

"I guess maybe I'll find out."

He didn't go further with it. He wanted to change the subject. Edgar was his partner but they had never gotten to the point where they completely confided in each other. Bosch played the mentor role in the relationship and he trusted Edgar with his life. But that was a bond that held fast on the street. Inside the department was another matter. Bosch had never trusted anyone, never relied on anyone. He wasn't going to start now.

"So, what's the case?" he asked, to divert the conversation.

"Oh, yeah, I wanted to tell you about it. This was weird, man. First the killing's weird, then what happened after. The call out was to a house on Sierra Bonita. This is about five in the A.M. The citizen reports he heard a sound like a gunshot, only muffled-like. He grabs his deer rifle out of the closet and goes outside to take a look. This is a neighborhood that's been picked clean lately by the hypes, you know? Four B and Es on his block alone this month. So, he was ready with the rifle. Anyway, he goes down his driveway with the gun—the garage is in the back—and he sees a pair of legs hanging out of the open door of his car. It was parked in front of the garage."

"He shoots him?"

"No, that's the crazy thing. He goes up with his gun but the guy in his car is already dead. Stabbed in the chest with a screwdriver."

Bosch didn't get it. He didn't have enough of the facts. But he said nothing.

"The air bag killed him, Harry."

"What do you mean, the air bag killed him?"

"The air bag. This goddamn hype was stealing the air bag out of the steering wheel and somehow the thing went off. It inflated instantly, like it was supposed to, and drove the screwdriver right into his heart, man. I've never seen anything like it. He must've been holding the screwdriver backwards or he was using the butt-end to bang on the wheel. We haven't exactly figured out that part yet. We talked to a guy at Chrysler. He says that you take the protective cover off, like this dude had, and even static electricity can set the thing off. Our dead guy was wearing a sweater. I don't know, could've been it. Burns says it's the first death by static cling."

While Edgar chuckled at his new partner's humor, Bosch thought about the scenario. He remembered a department info bulletin going out on air bag thefts the year before. They had become a hot commodity in the underground market, with thieves getting as much as three hundred dollars apiece for air bags from unscrupulous body shops. The body shops would buy them for three hundred and turn around and charge a customer nine hundred to install one. That was double the profit derived when ordering from the manufacturer.

"So it goes down as accidental?" Bosch asked.

"Yeah, accidental death. But the story ain't over. Both doors of the car were open."

"The dead guy had a partner."

"That's what we figure. And so if we find the fucker we can charge him. Under the felony homicide law. So we had SID laser the inside of the car and pull all the prints they could. I took 'em down to Latents and talked one of the techs into scanning them and running them on the AFIS. And bingo."

"You got the partner?"

"Dead bang. That AFIS computer has got a long reach, Harry. One of the nets is the U.S. Military Identification Center in St. Louis. We got a match on our guy outta there. He was in the Army ten years ago. We got his ID from that, then got an address from the DMV and picked him up today. He copped on the ride in. He's gonna go away for a while."

"Sounds like a good day, then."

"Didn't end there, though. I haven't told you the weird part yet."

"Then tell me."

"Remember I said we lasered the car and took all the prints?"

"Right."

"Well, we got another match, too. This one on the crime indexes. A case outta Mississippi. Man, all days should be like this one was."

"What was the match?" Bosch asked. He was growing impatient with the way Edgar was parceling out the story.

"We matched prints put on the net seven years ago by something called the Southern States Criminal Identification Base. It's like five states that don't add up in population to half of L.A. Anyway, one of the prints we put through today matched the doer on a double homicide in Biloxi all the way back in 'seventy-six. Some guy the papers there called the Bicentennial Butcher on account he killed two women on the Fourth of July."

"The car's owner? The guy with the rifle?"

"Damn right. His fingerprints were on the cleaver left in one girl's skull. He was a bit surprised when we came back to his house this afternoon. We said, 'Hey, we caught the partner of the guy who died in your car. And by the way, you're under arrest for a two-bagger, motherfucker.' I think it blew his mind, Harry. You shoulda been there."

Edgar laughed loudly into the phone and Bosch knew, after only one week of being grounded, how much he missed the job.

"Did he cop?"

"No, he kept quiet. You can't be that stupid and get away with a double murder for almost twenty years. That's a nice run."

"Yeah, what's he been doing?"

"Looks like he's just been laying low. Owns a hardware on Santa Monica. Married and has a kid and a dog. A total reform case. But he's going back to Biloxi. I hope he likes southern cooking 'cause he won't be coming back here anytime soon."

Edgar laughed again. Bosch said nothing. The story was depressing because it was a reminder of what he was no longer doing. It also reminded him about what Hinojos had asked about defining his mission.

"Got a couple of Mississippi state troopers comin' out tomorrow," Edgar said. "Talked to them a little while ago and they are happy campers."

Bosch didn't say anything for a while.

"Harry, you still there?"

"Yeah, I was just thinking about something . . . Well, it sounds like a hell of a day of crime fighting. How's the fearless leader taking it?"

"Pounds? Jesus, he's got a hard-on over this the size of a Louisville slugger. You know what he's doing? He's trying to figure out a way to take credit for all three clearances. He's trying to put the Biloxi cases on our rate."

It didn't surprise Bosch. It was a widespread practice among department managers and statisticians to add positive credit to crime clearance levels whenever and wherever possible. In the air bag case, there was no actual murder. It was an accident. But because the death occurred during the commission of a crime, California law held that an accomplice to the crime could be charged with his partner's death. Bosch knew that based on the partner's arrest for murder, Pounds intended to add a case to the murder clearance chart. He would not balance this by adding a case to the murder occurrence chart because the death by air bag was an accident. This little statistical two-step would result in a nice little boost for the Hollywood Division's overall homicide clearance rate, which in recent years had continually threatened to dip below fifty percent.

But unsatisfied with the modest jump this accounting deception would provide, Pounds intended to boldly add the two Biloxi murders to the clearance chart as well. After all, it could be argued, his homicide squad did clear two more cases. Adding a total of three cleared cases to one side of the chart without adding any to the other would likely give a tremendous boost to the overall clearance rate—as well as to the image of Pounds as a detective bureau commander. Bosch knew that Pounds was probably delighted with himself and the accomplishments of the day.

"He said our rate would jump six points," Edgar was saying. "He was a very pleased man, Harry. And my new partner was very pleased he had pleased his man."

"I don't want to hear any more."

"I didn't think so. So what are you doing to keep busy, besides counting cars on the freeway? You must be bored stiff, Harry."

"Not really," Bosch lied. "Last week I finished fixing the deck. This week I'll—"

"Harry, I'm telling you, you're wasting your time and money. The inspectors are going to find you in there and kick you out on your ass. Then they'll tear the place down themselves and hand you the bill. Your deck and the whole house will be in the back of a dump truck then."

"I hired a lawyer to work on it."

"What's he gonna do?"

"I don't know. I want to appeal the red tag. He's a land use guy. He said he can work it out."

"I hope so. I still think you ought to tear it down and start over."

"I didn't win the lotto yet."

"The feds've got disaster loans. You could get one and—"

"I've applied, Jerry, but I like my house the way it is."

"Okay, Harry. I hope your lawyer works it out. Anyway, I gotta go. Burns wants to have a beer over at the Short Stop. He's there waiting."

The last time Bosch had been at the Short Stop, a hole-in-the-wall cop bar near the academy and Dodger Stadium, it had still had I SUPPORT CHIEF GATES bumper stickers on the wall. For most cops, Gates was a dying ember of the past, but the Short Stop was a place where old-liners went to drink and remember a department that no longer existed.

"Yeah, have fun over there, Jerry."

"Take care, man."

Bosch leaned against a counter and drank his beer. He came to the conclusion that Edgar's call had been a cleverly disguised way of telling Bosch that he was choosing sides and cutting him loose. That was okay, Bosch thought. Edgar's first allegiance was to himself, to surviving in a place that could be treacherous. Bosch couldn't hold that against him.

Bosch looked at his reflection in the glass of the oven door. The image was dark but he could see his eyes in the shadow and the line of his jaw. He was forty-four years old and in some ways looked older. He still had a full head of curly brown hair but both the hair and the mustache were going to gray. His black-brown eyes seemed to him tired and used up. His skin had the pallor of a night watchman's. Bosch was still leanly built but sometimes his clothes hung on him as if they had been issued at one of the downtown missions or he had recently been through a bad illness.

He broke away from his reflection and grabbed another beer out of the refrigerator. Outside on the deck, he saw the sky was now brightly lit with the pastels of dusk. It would be dark soon, but the freeway below was a bright river of moving lights, its current never ebbing for a moment.

Looking down on the Monday night commute, he saw the place as an anthill with the workers moving along in lines. Someone or some force would soon come along and kick the hill again. Then the freeways would fall, the houses would collapse and the ants would just rebuild and get in line again.

He was bothered by something but was not quite sure what it was. His thoughts swirled and mixed. He began to see what Edgar had told him about his case in the context of his dialogue with Hinojos. There was some connection there, some bridge, but he couldn't get to it.

He finished his beer and decided that two would be enough. He went to one of the lounge chairs and sat down with his feet up. What he wanted to do was give everything a rest. Mind and body. He looked up and saw the clouds had now been painted orange by the setting sun. They looked like molten lava moving slowly across the sky.

Just before he dozed off a thought pushed through the lava. Everybody counts or nobody counts. And then, in the last moment of clarity before sleep, he knew what the connecting ribbon that had run through his thoughts had been. And he knew what his mission was.

In the morning Bosch dressed without showering so he could immediately begin work on the house and blank out the lingering thoughts from the night before with sweat and concentration.

But clearing the thoughts away was not easy. As he dressed in old lacquer-stained jeans, he caught a glimpse of himself in the cracked mirror over the bureau and saw that his T-shirt was on backward. Printed across his chest on the white shirt was the homicide squad's motto.

OUR DAY BEGINS WHEN YOUR DAY ENDS

It was supposed to be on the back of the shirt. He pulled it off, turned it and put it back on. Now in the mirror he saw what he was supposed to see. A replica of a detective's badge on the left breast of the shirt and the smaller printing that said LAPD HOMICIDE.

He brewed a pot of coffee and took it and a mug out to the deck. Next he lugged out his toolbox and the new door he had bought at Home Depot for the bedroom. When he was finally ready and had the mug filled with steaming black coffee, he sat on the footrest of one of the lounge chairs and placed the door on its side in front of him.

The original door had splintered at the hinges during the quake. He had tried to hang the replacement a few days earlier but it was too large to fit the door jamb. He figured he needed to shave no more than an eighth of an inch off the opening side to make the fit. He set to work with the plane, moving the instrument slowly back and forth along the edge as the wood peels fell away in paper-thin curls. Occasionally he would stop and study his progress and run his hand along the area of his work. He liked being able to see the progress he was making. Few other tasks in life seemed that way to him.

But still, he could not concentrate for long. His focus on the door was interrupted by the same intrusive thought that had haunted him the night before. Everybody counts or nobody counts. It was what he had told Hinojos. It was what he had told her he believed. But did he? What did it mean to him? Was it merely a slogan like the one on the back of his shirt or was it something he lived by? These questions mingled with the echoes of the conversation he'd had the night before with Edgar. And with a deeper thought that he knew he had always had.

He took the plane off the door edge and ran his hand along the smooth wood again. He thought he had it right and carried it inside. Over a drop cloth in an area of the living room he had reserved for woodworking, he ran a sheet of small-grain sandpaper over the door edge until it was perfectly smooth to his touch.

Holding the door vertically and balancing it on a block of wood, he eased it into the hinges and then dropped the pins in. He tapped them home with a hammer and they went in easily. He had oiled the pins and hinges earlier and so the bedroom door opened and closed almost silently. Most important, though, was that it closed evenly in the jamb. He opened and closed it several more times, just staring at it, pleased with his accomplishment.

The glow of his success was short-lived, for having completed the project left his mind open to wander. Back out on the deck the other thoughts came back as he swept the wood shavings into a small pile.

Hinojos had told him to stay busy. Now he knew how he would do it. And in that moment he realized that no matter how many projects he found to take his time, there was one job he still had to do. He leaned the broom against the wall and went inside to get ready.

The LAPD storage facility and aerosquad headquarters known as Piper Tech was on Ramirez Street in downtown, not far from Parker Center. Bosch, in a suit and tie, arrived shortly before eleven at the gate. He held his LAPD identification card out the window and was quickly waved in. The card was all he had. The card, along with his gold badge and gun, had been taken from him when he was placed on leave the week before. But it was later returned so that he could gain entry to the BSS offices for the stress therapy sessions with Carmen Hinojos.

After parking, he walked to the beige-painted storage warehouse that housed the city's history of violence. The quarter-acre building contained the files of all LAPD cases, solved or unsolved. This was where the case files came when nobody cared anymore.

At the front counter a civilian clerk was loading files onto a cart so that they could be wheeled back into the expanse of shelves and forgotten. By the way she studied Bosch, he knew it was rare that anyone ever showed up here in person. It was all done by telephones and city couriers.

"If you're looking for city council minutes, that's building A, across the lot. The one with brown trim."

Bosch held up his ID card.

"No, I want to pull a case."

He reached into his coat pocket while she walked up to the counter and bent forward to read his card. She was a small black woman with graying hair and glasses. The name tag affixed to her blouse said her name was Geneva Beaupre.

"Hollywood," she said. "Why didn't you just ask for it to be sent out in dispatch? There ain't no hurry on these cases."

"I was downtown, over at Parker . . . I wanted to see it as soon as I could, anyway."

"Well, you got a number?"

From his pocket he pulled a piece of notebook paper with the number 61-743 written on it. She bent to study it and then her head jerked up.

"Nineteen sixty-one? You want a case from—I don't know where nineteen sixty-one is."

"It's here. I've looked at the file before. I guess there was someone else clerking here back then, but it was here."

"Well, I'll look. You're going to wait?"

"Yeah, I'll wait."

This seemed to disappoint her but Bosch smiled at her in the most friendly way he could muster. She took the paper with her and disappeared into the stacks. Bosch walked around the small waiting area by the counter for a few minutes and then stepped outside to smoke a cigarette. He was nervous for a reason he could not exactly place. He kept moving, pacing.

"Harry Bosch!"

He turned and saw a man approaching him from the helicopter hangar. He recognized him but couldn't immediately place him. Then it hit him: Captain Dan Washington, a former Hollywood patrol skipper who was now commander of the aerosquadron. They shook hands cordially and Bosch immediately hoped Washington did not know of his ISL situation.

"Howzit going in the 'wood?"

"Same old same old, Captain."

"You know, I miss that place."

"You're not missing much. How is it with you?"

"Can't complain. I like the detail but it's more like being an airport manager than a cop, I guess. It's as good a place to lay low as any other."

Bosch recalled that Washington had gotten into a political scrap with the department weight and taken the transfer as a means of survival. The department had dozens of out-of-the-way jobs like Washington's, where you could lay up and wait for your political fortunes to change.

"What're you doing over here?"

There it was. If Washington knew Bosch was on leave, then admitting he was pulling an old case file would be admitting he was violating the leave order. Still, as his position in the aerosquad attested, Washington was not a straight-line company man. Bosch decided to run the risk.

"I'm just pulling an old case. I got some free time and thought I'd check a few things."

Washington narrowed his eyes and Bosch knew that he knew.

"Yeah . . . well, listen, I gotta run, but hang in there, man. Don't let the book men get you down."

He winked at Bosch and moved on.

"I won't, Captain. You either."

Bosch felt reasonably sure Washington wouldn't mention their meeting to anybody. He stepped on his cigarette and went back inside to the counter, privately chastising himself anyway for having gone outside and advertised that he was there. Five minutes later he started hearing a squeaking sound coming from one of the aisles between the stacks. In a moment Geneva Beaupre appeared pushing a cart with a blue three-ring binder on it.

It was a murder book. It was at least two inches thick, dusty, and with a rubber band around it. The band held an old green checkout card to the binder.

"Found it."

There was a note of triumph in her voice. It would be the major accomplishment of her day, Bosch guessed.

"Great."

She dropped the heavy binder on the counter.

"Marjorie Lowe. Homicide, 1961. Now . . ." She took the card off the binder and looked at it. "Yes, you were the last to take this out. Let's see, that was five years ago. You were with Robbery-Homicide then . . ."

"Yes. And now I'm in Hollywood. You want me to sign for it again?"

She put the card down in front of him.

"Yes. Put your ID number there, too, please."

He quickly did as he was told and he could tell she was studying him as he wrote.

"A lefty."

"Yeah."

He slid the card back across the counter to her.

"Thanks, Geneva."

He looked at her, wanting to say something else, but decided it might be a mistake. She looked back at him and a grandmotherly smile formed on her face.

"I don't know what you're doing, Detective Bosch, but I wish you good luck. I can tell it's important, you coming back to this after five years."

"It's been longer than that, Geneva. A lot longer."

Bosch cleared all the old mail and carpentry books off the dining room table and placed the binder and his own notebook on top of it. He went to the stereo and loaded a compact disc, "Clifford Brown with Strings." He went to the kitchen and got an ashtray, then he sat down in front of the blue murder book and looked at it for a long time without moving. The last time he'd had the file, he had barely looked at it as he skimmed through its many pages. He hadn't been ready then and had returned it to the archives.

This time, he wanted to be sure he was ready before he opened it, so he sat there a long time just studying the cracked plastic cover as if it held some clue to his preparedness. A memory crowded into his mind. A boy of eleven in a swimming pool clinging to the steel ladder at the side, out of breath and crying, the tears disguised by the water that dripped out of his wet hair. The boy felt scared. Alone. He felt as if the pool were an ocean that he must cross.

Brownie was working through "Willow Weep for Me," his trumpet as gentle as a portrait painter's brush. Bosch reached for the rubber band he had put around the binder five years earlier and it broke at his touch. He hesitated only another moment before opening the binder and blowing off the dust.

The binder contained the case file on the October 28, 1961, homicide of Marjorie Phillips Lowe. His mother.

The pages of the binder were brownish yellow and stiff with age. As he looked at them and read them, Bosch was initially surprised at how little things had changed in nearly thirty-five years. Many of the investigative forms in the binder were still currently in use. The Preliminary Report and the Investigating Officer's Chronological Record were the same as those presently used, save for word changes made to accommodate court rulings and political correctness. Description Boxes marked NEGRO had sometime along the line been changed to BLACK and then AFRICAN-AMERICAN. The list of motivations on the Preliminary Case Screening chart did not include DOMESTIC VIOLENCE or HATRED/PREJUDICE classifications as they did now. Interview summary sheets did not include boxes to be checked after Miranda warnings had been given.

But aside from those kinds of changes, the reports were the same and Bosch decided that homicide investigation was largely the same now as back then. Of course, there had been incredible technological advances in the past thirty-five years but he believed there were some things that were always the same and always would remain the same. The legwork, the art of interviewing and listening, knowing when to trust an instinct or a hunch. Those were things that didn't change, that couldn't.

The case had been assigned to two investigators on the Hollywood homicide table. Claude Eno and Jake McKittrick. The reports they filed were in chronological order in the binder. On their preliminary reports the victim was referred to by name, indicating she had immediately been identified. A narrative on these pages said the victim was found in an alley behind the north side of Hollywood Boulevard between Vista and Gower. Her skirt and undergarments had been ripped open by her attacker. It was presumed that she had been sexually assaulted and strangled. Her body had been dropped into an open trash bin located next to the rear door of a Hollywood souvenir store called Startime Gifts & Gags. The body was discovered at 7:35 A.M. by a foot patrol officer who walked a beat on the Boulevard and usually checked the back alleys at the beginning of each shift. The victim's purse was not found with her but she was quickly identified because she was known to the beat officer. On the continuation sheet it was made clear why she was known to him.

Victim had a previous history of loitering arrests in the Hollywood. (See AR 55-002, 55-913, 56-111, 59-056, 60-815 and 60-1121) Vice Detective Gilchrist and Stano described victim as a prostitute who periodically worked in the Hollywood area and had been repeatedly warned off. Victim lived at El Rio Efficiency Apts. located two blocks northerly of crime scene. It was believed that the victim had been currently involved in call girl prostitution activities. R/O 1906 was able to make identification of the victim because of familiarity of having seen victim in the area in previous years.

Bosch looked at the reporting officer's serial number. He knew that 1906 belonged to a patrolman then who was now one of the most powerful men in the department. Assistant Chief Irvin S. Irving. Once Irving had confided to Bosch that he had known Marjorie Lowe and had been the one who found her.

Bosch lit a cigarette and read on. The reports were sloppily written, perfunctory, and filled with careless misspellings. In reading them, it was clear to Bosch that Eno and McKittrick did not invest much time in the case. A prostitute was dead. It was a risk that came with her job. They had other fish to fry.

He noticed on the Death Investigation Report a box for listing the next of kin. It said;

Hieronymus Bosch (Harry), son, age 11, McClaren Youth Hall. Notification made 10/28-1500 hrs. Custody of Department of Public Social Services since 7/60—UM. (See victim's arrest reports 60-815 and 60-1121) Father unknown. Son remains in custody pending foster placement.

Looking at the report, Bosch could easily decipher all of the abbreviations and translate what was written. UM stood for unfit mother. The irony was not lost on him even after so many years. The boy had been taken from a presumably unfit mother and placed in an equally unfit system of child protection. What he remembered most was the noise of the place. Always loud. Like a prison.

Bosch remembered McKittrick had been the one who came to tell him. It was during the swimming period. The indoor pool was frothing with waves as a hundred boys swam and splashed and yelled. After being pulled from the water, Harry wore a white towel that had been washed and bleached so many times that it felt like cardboard over his shoulders. McKittrick told him the news and he returned to the pool, his screams silenced beneath the waves.

Quickly leafing through the supplemental reports on the victim's prior arrests, Bosch came to the autopsy report. He skipped most of it, not needing the details, and settled on the summary page, where there were a couple of surprises. The time of death was placed at seven to nine hours before discovery. Near midnight. The surprise was in the official cause of death. It was listed as blunt-force trauma to the head. The report described a deep contusion over the right ear with swelling but no laceration that caused fatal bleeding in the brain. The report said the killer might have believed he strangled the victim after knocking her unconscious but it was the coroner's conclusion that she was already dead when the killer wrapped Marjorie Lowe's own belt around her neck and tied it off. The report stated further that while semen was recovered from the vagina there were no other injuries commonly associated with rape.

Rereading the summary with an investigator's eyes, Bosch could see the autopsy conclusions only muddied the waters for the original two detectives. The initial assumption based on the appearance of the body was that Marjorie Lowe was the victim of a sex crime. That raised the specter of a random encounter—as random as the couplings of her profession—leading to her death. But the fact that strangulation occurred after death and that there was no convincing physical evidence of rape raised another possibility as well. They were factors from which it could also be speculated that the victim had been murdered by someone who then attempted to disguise his involvement and motivation in the randomness of a sex crime. Bosch could think of only one reason for such misdirection, if that had been the case. The killer knew the victim. As he moved on, he wondered if McKittrick and Eno had made any of the same conclusions he had made.

There was an eight-by-ten envelope next in the file which was marked as containing crime scene and autopsy photos. Bosch thought about it a long moment and then put the envelope aside. As with the last time he had pulled the murder book out of the archives, he couldn't look.

Next was another envelope with an evidence inventory list stapled to it. It was almost blank.

EVIDENCE RECOVERED
Case 61-743

Latent fingerprints taken from leather belt with silver sea shells. SID report no. 1114 11/06/61

Murder weapon recovered—black leather belt with sea shells attached. Property of victim.

Victims clothing, property. Filed w/ evidence custodian—Locker 73B LAPDHQ
   1 blouse, white—blood stain
   1 black skirt—torn at seam
   1 pair black high heel shoes
   1 pair black sheer stockings, torn
   1 pair undergarments, torn
   1 pair gold colored earrings
   1 gold colored hoop bracelet
   1 gold chain necklace w/cross

That was it. Bosch studied the list for a long time before jotting the particulars down in his notebook. Something about it bothered him but he couldn't draw it out. Not yet. He was taking in too much information and he would have to let it settle some before the anomalies floated to the surface.

He dropped it for the moment and opened the evidence envelope, breaking the seal of a red tape that had cracked with age. Inside was a yellowed print card on which two complete fingerprints, from a thumb and an index finger, and several partials had been taped after being lifted with black powder from the belt. Also in the envelope was a pink check card for the victim's clothes, which had been placed in an evidence locker. The clothes had never been retrieved because a case had never been made. Bosch put both items aside, wondering what would have happened to the clothing. In the mid-sixties Parker Center had been built and the department moved out of the old headquarters. It was long gone now, falling to the wrecking ball. What happened to the evidence from unsolved cases?

Next in the file was a group of summary reports on interviews conducted during the first days of the investigation. Most of these were of people with peripheral knowledge of the victim or the crime. People like other residents in the El Rio Apartments and other women in the same profession as the victim. There was one short summary that caught Bosch's eye. It was from an interview conducted three days after the murder with a woman named Meredith Roman. She was described in the report as an associate and sometime roommate of the victim. At the time of the report she also lived in the El Rio, one floor up from the victim. The report had been typed up by Eno, who seemed to be the clear-cut winner in illiteracy when comparing the reports of the two investigators assigned to the case.

Meredith Roman (10-9-30) was interviewed at length this date at her apartment in the El Rio Efficiencies where she lived one floor above the victim's apartment. Miss Roman was able to provide this detective with very little useful information in relation to the activities of Marjorie Lowe during the period of the last week of live.

Miss Roman acknowledged that she has engaged in prostitutional acts while in the company of the victim on numrus occassion in the previous eight years but she has no booking record to date. (later confirmed) She told the undersigned detective that such engagements were skeduled by a man named Johnny Fox, (2-2-33) who resides at 1110 Ivar in Hollywood. Fox, age 28, has no records of arrests but vice intelligence confirms he has been a suspect previously in cases of pandering, malicious assault and sales of heroin.

Miss Roman states that the last time she saw the victim was at a party on second floor of the Roosevelt Hotl on 10/21. Miss Roman did not attend party with victim but saw her there momentarily for a short conversation.

Miss Roman states that she now has plans to retire from the business of prostitution and leave Los Angeles. She stated that she will provide detectives with a forwarding adress and telephone number so that she can be contacted if necessary. Her demenor was corperative with the undersigned.

Bosch immediately looked through the summaries again for the report on Johnny Fox. There was none there. He flipped to the front of the binder to the Chronological Record and looked for an entry that would indicate whether they had even talked to Fox. The CR was just a log of one-line entries with references to other reports. On the second page he found a single notation.

11-3 800-2000 Watched Fox apt. No show.

There was no other mention of Fox in the record. But as Bosch read through the CR to the end, another entry caught his eye.

11-5 940 A. Conklin called to skedule meeting.

Bosch knew the name. Arno Conklin had been a Los Angeles district attorney in the 1960s. As Bosch remembered it, 1961 was too early for Conklin to have been DA, but he would still have been one of the office's top prosecutors. His interest in a prostitute's murder seemed curious to Bosch. But there was nothing in the binder that held an answer. There was no summary report of a meeting with Conklin. Nothing.

He noted that the misspelling of the word *schedule* in the CR entry had been made earlier in the summary of the Roman interview typed by Eno. Bosch concluded from this that Conklin had called Eno to set the meeting. However, the significance of this, if any, he didn't know. He wrote Conklin's name down at the top of a page in his notebook.

Getting back to Fox, Bosch could not understand why he was not located and interviewed by Eno and McKittrick. It seemed that he was a natural suspect—the victim's pimp. Or, if Fox had been interviewed, Bosch could not understand why there was no report in the murder book on such a key part of the investigation.

Bosch sat back and lit a cigarette. Already, he was tense with the suspicion that things were amiss with the case. He felt the stirring of what he knew was outrage. The more he read the more he believed the case had been mishandled from the start.

He leaned back over the table and continued flipping through the pages of the binder while he smoked. There were more meaningless in-

terview summaries and reports. It was all just filler. Any homicide cop
worth his badge could churn out reports like these by the dozens if he
wanted to fill a binder and make it look like he'd done a thorough investigation. It appeared that McKittrick and Eno were as skilled at it as the
best. But any homicide cop worth his badge could also tell filler when he
saw it. And that's what Bosch saw here. The hollow feeling in his stomach grew more pronounced.

Finally, he came to the first Follow-Up Homicide Investigation Report. It was dated one week after the murder and written by McKittrick.

Homicide of Marjorie Phillips Lowe remains open at this time,
no suspects identified.

Investigation at this time has determined that victim was engaged
in prostitution in the Hollywood area and may have fallen victim to a
customer who committed the homicide.

Preliminary suspect John Fox denied involvement in the incident
and has been cleared at this time through fingerprint comparison and
confirmation of alibi through witnesses.

No suspects at this time have been identified. John Fox states that
on Friday, 11/30 at approximately 2100 hours the victim left her residence at the El Rio Apts. to go to an unknown location for the purposes of prostitution. Fox states the arrangement was made by
victim and he was not made privy to it. Fox siad it was not unusual
practice for victim to make arrangements for liaissons without his
knowledge.

Victim's undergarment was found with body in ripped condition.
Noted, however, a pair of stockings also belonging to the victim
showed no tears and were believed to possibly have been removed
voluntarily.

Experience and instinct of investigators leads to the conclusion
that the victim met with foul play at the unknown location after voluntarily arriving and possibly removing some clothing. The body
was then transported to the trash bin in the alleyway between Vista
and Gower, where it was discovered the following morning.

Witness Meredith Roman was reinterviewed this date and asked to amend her earlier statement. Roman informed this investigator that it was her belief that the victim had gone to a party in Hancock Park the night previous to the discovery of her body. She could provide no address or name of party at the location. Miss Roman said her plan was to attend with victim but on the previous evening she was assaulted by John Fox in a dispute over money. She could not attend the party because she believed a bruise on her face made her unpresentable. (Fox readily acknowledged striking Roman in subsequent telephone interview. Roman refused charges.)

Investigation is termed at standstill as no further leads have been provided at this time. Investigators are currently seeking the aid of vice section officers in regard to knowledge of similar incidents and/or possible suspects.

Bosch read the page again and tried to interpret what was really being said about the case. One thing that was clear from it was that regardless of whether there was an interview summary report in the binder, Johnny Fox had obviously been interviewed by Eno and McKittrick. He had been cleared. The question Bosch now had was, why did they not type up a summary report, or had it been typed up and later removed from the murder book? And if so, who removed it and why?

Lastly, Bosch was curious about the lack of any mention of Arno Conklin in the summary or any other report save for the investigative chronology. Maybe, Bosch thought, more than just the Fox interview summary had been lifted from the binder.

Bosch got up and went to his briefcase, which he kept on the counter near the kitchen door. From it he took his personal phone book. He didn't have a number for LAPD archives so he called the regular records number and was transferred. A woman answered after nine rings.

"Uh, Mrs. Beaupre? Geneva?"

"Yes?"

"Hello, this is Harry Bosch. I was there earlier today to pick up a file."

"Yes, from Hollywood. The old case."

"Yes. Could you tell me, do you still have the checkout card there at the counter?"

"Hold the line. I already filed it."

A moment later she was back.

"Yes, I have it here."

"Could you tell me, who else has checked this binder out in the past?"

"Why would you need to know that?"

"There are pages missing from the file, Mrs. Beaupre. I'd like to know who might have them."

"Well, you checked it out last. I mentioned that be—"

"Yes, I know. About five years ago. Is there any listing of it being taken out before that or since then? I didn't notice when I signed the card today."

"Well, hold the line and let me see." He waited and she was back quickly. "Okay, I've got it. According to this card, the only other time that file was ever taken out was in 1972. You're talking way back."

"Who checked it out back then?"

"It's scribbled here. I can't—it looks like maybe Jack . . . uh, Jack McKillick."

"Jake McKittrick."

"Could be."

Bosch didn't know what to think. McKittrick had the file last but that was more than ten years after the murder. What did it mean? Bosch felt confusion ambush him. He didn't know what he had been expecting but he'd hoped there would have been something other than a name scribbled more than twenty years ago.

"Okay, Mrs. Beaupre, thanks very much."

"Well, if you've got missing pages I'm going to have to make a report and give it to Mr. Aguilar."

"I don't think that will be necessary, ma'am. I may be wrong about the missing pages. I mean, how could there be missing pages if nobody's looked at it since the last time I had it?"

He thanked her again and hung up, hoping his attempt at good humor would persuade her to do nothing about his call. He opened the refrigerator and looked inside while he thought about the case, then closed it and went back out to the table.

The last pages in the murder book were a due diligence report dated November 3, 1962. The department's homicide procedures called for all unsolved cases to be reviewed after a year by a new set of detectives with an eye toward looking for something that the first set of investigators might have missed. But, in practice, it was a rubber stamp process. Detectives didn't relish the idea of finding the mistakes of their colleagues. Additionally, they had their own case loads to worry about. When assigned DDs, as they were called, they usually did little more than read through the file, make a few calls to witnesses and then send the binder to archives.

In this case, the DD report by the new detectives, named Roberts and Jordan, drew the same conclusions as the reports by Eno and McKittrick. After two pages detailing the same evidence and interviews already conducted by the original investigators, the DD report concluded that there were no workable leads and the prognosis for "successful conclusion" of the case was hopeless. So much for due diligence.

Bosch closed the murder book. He knew that after Roberts and Jordan had filed their report, the binder had been shipped to archives as a dead case. It had gathered dust there until, according to the checkout card, McKittrick pulled it out for unknown reasons in 1972. Bosch wrote McKittrick's name under Conklin's on the page in the notebook. Then he wrote the names of others he thought it would be useful to interview. If they were still alive and could be found.

Bosch leaned back in his chair, realizing that the music had stopped and he hadn't even noticed. He checked his watch. It was two-thirty. He still had most of the afternoon but he wasn't sure what to do with it.

He went to the bedroom closet and took the shoebox off the shelf. It was his correspondence box, filled with letters and cards and photos he had wished to keep over the course of his life. It contained objects dated as far back as his time in Vietnam. He rarely looked in the box but his mind kept an almost perfect inventory of what was in it. Each piece had a reason for being saved.

On top was the latest addition to the box. A postcard from Venice. From Sylvia. It depicted a painting she had seen in the Palace of the Doges. Hieronymus Bosch's "The Blessed and the Damned." It showed an angel escorting one of the blessed through a tunnel to the light of heaven. They both floated skyward. The card was the last he had heard from her. He read the back.

Harry, thought you'd be interested in this piece of your namesake's work. I saw it in the Palace. It's beautiful. By the way, I love Venice! I think I could stay forever! S.

But you don't love me, Bosch thought as he put the card aside and began to dig through the other pieces in the box. He wasn't distracted again. About halfway through the box he found what he was looking for.

The midday drive out to Santa Monica was long. Bosch had to take the long way, the 101 to the 405 and then down, because the 10 was still a week away from being reopened. By the time he got into Sunset Park it was after three. The house he was looking for was on Pier Street. It was a small Craftsman bungalow set on the crest of a hill. It had a full porch with red bougainvillea running along the railing. He checked the address painted on the mailbox against the envelope that contained the old Christmas card on the seat next to him. He parked at the curb and looked at the card once more. It had been addressed to him five years earlier, care of the LAPD. He had never responded to it. Not until now.

As he got out he could smell the sea and guessed that there might be a limited ocean view from the house's western windows. It was about ten degrees cooler than it had been at his home and so he reached back into his car for the sport coat. He walked to the front porch while putting it on.

The woman who answered the white door after one knock was in her mid-sixties and looked it. She was thin, with dark hair, but the gray roots were beginning to show and she was ready for another dye job. She wore thick red lipstick, a white silk blouse with blue seahorses on it over navy blue slacks. She readily smiled a greeting and Bosch recognized her, but he could see that his own image was completely alien to her. It had been almost thirty-five years since she had seen him. He smiled back anyway.

"Meredith Roman?"

She lost her smile as quickly as she had found it before.

"That's not my name," she said in a clipped tone. "You have the wrong place."

She moved to close the door but Bosch put his hand on it to stop her. He tried to be as unthreatening about it as he could. But he could see panic starting in her eyes.

"It's Harry Bosch," he said quickly.

She froze and looked Bosch in the eyes. He saw the panic go away. Recognition and memories flooded her eyes like tears. The smile came back.

"Harry? Little Harry?"

He nodded.

"Oh, darling, c'mere." She drew him into a tight hug and talked in his ear. "Oh, so good to see you after—let me look at you."

She pushed him back and held her hands wide as if appraising a roomful of paintings at once. Her eyes were animated and sincere. It made Bosch feel good and sad at the same time. He shouldn't have waited so long. He should have visited for reasons other than the one that brought him here now.

"Oh, come in, Harry. Come in."

Bosch entered a nicely furnished living room. The floor was red oak and the stucco walls were clean and white. The furniture was mostly matching white rattan. The place was light and bright but Bosch knew he was there to bring darkness.

"Meredith is no longer your name?"

"No, Harry, not for a long time."

"What do I call you?"

"My name is Katherine. With a K. Katherine Register. Spelled like the cash register but you pronounce it *ree* as in reefer. That's what my husband used to say. Boy, he was so straight. Outside of me the closest that man ever came to something illegal was to say the word."

"He *used* to say that?"

"Have a seat, Harry, for crying out loud. Yes, used to. He passed away five years ago last Thanksgiving."

Bosch sat down on the couch and she took the chair across the glass coffee table.

"I'm sorry."

"It's okay, you didn't know. You never even knew him and I've been a different person for a long time. Can I get you something? Some coffee or maybe something stronger?"

It occurred to him that she had sent him the card on the Christmas soon after her husband's death. He was hit with another wave of guilt for not having responded.

"Harry?"

"Oh, uh, no, I'm fine. I . . . do you want me to call you by your new name?"

She started laughing at the ridiculousness of the situation and he joined in.

"Call me any damn thing you want." She laughed girlishly, a laugh he remembered from a long time before. "It's great to see you. You know, to see how, uh . . ."

"I turned out?"

She laughed again.

"I guess so. You know, I knew you were with the police because I had read your name in some of the news stories."

"I know you knew. I got the Christmas card you sent to the station. That must have been right after your husband died. I, uh, I'm sorry I never wrote back or visited. I should have."

"That's okay, Harry, I know you're busy with the job and a career and all . . . I'm glad you got my card. Do you have a family?"

"Uh, no. How about you? Any children?"

"Oh, no. No children. You have a wife, don't you, a handsome man like you?"

"No, I'm alone right now."

She nodded, seeming to sense that he wasn't here to reveal his personal history to her anyway. For a long moment they just both looked at each other and Bosch wondered what she really thought of his being a cop. The initial delight in seeing each other was descending into the uneasiness that comes when old secrets come close to the surface.

"I guess . . ."

He didn't finish the thought. He was grappling for a way into the conversation. His interviewing skills had deserted him.

"You know, if it's not too much trouble, I'd take a glass of water."

It was all he could think of.

"Be right back."

She got up quickly and went to the kitchen. He heard her getting ice out of a tray. It gave him time to think. It had taken him an hour to drive to her house but he hadn't given one thought to what this would be like or how he would get to what he wanted to say and ask. She came back in a few minutes with a glass of ice water. She handed it to him and put a round coaster made of cork on the glass-topped coffee table in front of him.

"If you're hungry, I can bring out some crackers and cheese. I just didn't know how much time you—"

"No, I'm fine. This is great, thanks."

He saluted her with the glass and drank half of it, then put it down on the table.

"Harry, use the coaster. Getting rings out of the glass is murder."

Bosch looked down at what he had done.

"Oh, sorry."

He corrected the placement of his glass.

"You're a detective."

"Yes. I work in Hollywood now . . . Uh, but I'm not really working right now. I'm on sort of a vacation."

"Oh, that must be nice."

Her spirits seemed to lift, as if she knew there was a chance he was not here on business. Bosch knew it was time to get to the point.

"Uh, Mer—uh, Katherine, I need to ask you about something."

"What is it, Harry?"

"I look around here and I see you have a very nice home, a different name, a different life. You're no longer Meredith Roman and I know you don't need me to tell you that. You've got . . . I think what I'm saying is the past may be a difficult thing to talk about. I know it is for me. And, believe me, I don't want to hurt you in any way."

"You're here to talk about your mother."

He nodded and looked down at the glass on the cork coaster.

"Your mother and I were best friends. Sometimes I think I had almost as much a hand in raising you as she did. Until they took you away from her. From us."

He looked back up at her. Her eyes were looking hard at distant memories.

"I don't think a day goes by that I don't think about her. We were just kids. Having a good time, you know. We never thought either of us could get hurt."

She suddenly stood up.

"Harry, come here. I want to show you something."

He followed her down a carpeted hallway and into a bedroom. There was a four-poster bed with light blue coverings, an oak bureau and matching bedside tables. Katherine Register pointed to the bureau. There were several photos in ornate stand-up frames on top. Most of them were of Katherine and a man who seemed much older than she was in the photos. Her husband, Bosch guessed. But she pointed to one that was to the right side of the grouping. The photo was old, its color faded. It was a picture of two young women with a tiny boy of three or four.

"I've always had that there, Harry. Even when my husband was alive. He knew my past. I told him. It didn't matter. We had twenty-three great years together. You see, the past is what you make of it. You can use it to hurt yourself or others or you can use it to make yourself strong. I'm strong, Harry. Now, tell me why you came to visit me today."

Bosch reached for the framed photo and picked it up.

"I want . . ." He looked up from the photo to her. "I'm going to find out who killed her."

An undecipherable look froze on her face for a moment and then she wordlessly took the frame out of his hands and put it back on the bureau. Then she pulled him into another deep embrace, her head against his chest. He could see himself holding her in the mirror over the bureau. When she pulled back and looked up at him he saw the tears were already down her cheeks. There was a slight tremor in her lower lip.

"Let's go sit down," he said.

She pulled two tissues out of a box on the bureau and he led her back to the living room and to her chair.

"Do you want me to get you some water?"

"No, I'm fine. I'll stop crying, I'm sorry."

She wiped at her eyes with the tissues. He sat back down on the couch.

"We used to say we were the two musketeers, both for one and one for both. It was stupid, but it was because we were so young and so close."

"I'm starting from scratch with it, Katherine. I pulled the old files on the investigation. It—"

She made a dismissing sound and shook her head.

"There was no investigation. It was a joke."

"That's my sense of it, too, but I don't understand why."

"Look, Harry, you know what your mother was." He nodded and she continued. "She was a party girl. We both were. I'm sure you know that's the polite way of saying it. And the cops really didn't care that one of us ended up dead. They just wrote the whole damn thing off. I know you're a policeman now, but that's the way it was then. They just didn't care about her."

"I understand. Things probably are not too much different now, believe it or not. But there has to have been more to it than that."

"Harry, I don't know how much you want to know about your mother."

He looked at her.

"The past made me strong, too. I can handle it."

"I'm sure it did . . . I remember that place where they put you. McEvoy or something like—"

"McClaren."

"That's it, McClaren. What a depressing place. Your mother would come home from visiting you and just sit down and cry her eyes out."

"Don't change the subject, Katherine. What is it I should know about her?"

She nodded but hesitated for a moment before continuing.

"Mar knew some policemen. You understand?"

He nodded.

"We both did. It was the way it worked. You had to get along to go along. That's what we called it anyway. And when you have that situation and she ends up dead, it's usually best for the cops to just sweep it under the rug. Let sleeping dogs lie, as they say. You pick the cliché. They just didn't want anyone embarrassed."

"Are you saying you think it was a cop?"

"No. I'm not saying that at all. I have no idea who did it, Harry. I'm sorry. I wish I did. But what I'm saying is, I think those two detectives that were assigned to investigate this knew where it could lead. And they weren't going to go that way because they knew what was good for them in the department. They weren't stupid in that way and like I said, she was a party girl. They didn't care. Nobody did. She got killed and that was that."

Bosch looked around the room, not sure what to ask next.

"Do you know who the policemen she knew were?"

"It was a long time ago."

"You knew some of the same policemen, didn't you?"

"Yes. I had to. That was the way it worked. You used your contacts to keep you out of jail. Everybody was for sale. Back then, at least. Different people wanted different forms of payment. Some of them, money. Some of them, other things."

"It said in the mur—the file that you never had a record."

"Yes, I was lucky. I was picked up a few times but never booked once. They always turned me loose once I could make a call. I kept a clean record because I knew a lot of policemen, honey. You understand?"

"Yes, I understand."

She didn't look away when she said it. All these years in the straight life and she still had a whore's pride. She could talk about the low points of her life without flinching or batting an eye. It was because she had made it through and there was dignity in that. Enough to last the rest of her life.

"Do you mind if I smoke, Harry?"

"No, not if I can."

They took out cigarettes and Bosch got up to light them.

"You can use that ashtray on the side table. Try not to get ashes on the rug."

She pointed to a small glass bowl on the table at the other end of the couch. Bosch reached over for it and then held it with one hand while he smoked with the other. He looked down into it as he spoke.

"The policemen you knew," he said, "and who she probably knew, you don't remember any names?"

"I said it was a long time ago. And I doubt they had anything to do with this, with what happened to your mother."

"Irvin S. Irving. Do you remember that name?"

She hesitated a moment as the name rolled around in her mind.

"I knew him. I think she did, too. He was on the beat on the Boulevard. I think it would have been hard for her not to know him . . . but I don't know. I could be wrong."

Bosch nodded.

"He was the one who found her."

She hiked her shoulders in a what's-that-prove gesture.

"Well, somebody had to find her. She was left out there in the open like that."

"What about a couple of vice guys, Gilchrist and Stano?"

She hesitated before answering.

"Yes, I knew them . . . they were mean men."

"Would my mother have known them? In that way?"

She nodded.

"What do you mean that they were mean? In what way?"

"They just . . . they just didn't care about us. If they wanted something, whether it was a little piece of information you might have picked up on a date or something more . . . personal, they just came and took it. They could be rough. I hated them."

"Did they—"

"But could they have been killers? My feeling at the time, and now, is no. They weren't killers, Harry. They were cops. True, they were bought and paid for, but it seemed everybody was. But it wasn't like it is today where you read the paper and you see some cop on trial for killing or beating or whatever. It's—sorry."

"It's okay. Anybody else you can think of?"

"No."

"No names?"

"I put that all out of my mind a long time ago."

"Okay."

Bosch wanted to take out his notebook but he didn't want to make this seem like an interview. He tried to remember what else he had read in the murder book that he could ask about.

"What about this guy Johnny Fox?"

"Yes, I told those detectives about him. They got all excited but then nothing ever happened. He was never arrested."

"I think he was. But then he was let go. His fingerprints didn't match the killer's."

She raised her eyebrows.

"Well, that's news to me. They never told me anything about any fingerprints."

"On your second interview—with McKittrick, you remember him?"

"Not really. I just remember that there were police, you know? Two detectives. One was smarter than the other, that's what I remember. But I don't remember which one was which. It seemed like the dumber one was in charge and that was par for the course in those days."

"Well, anyway, McKittrick talked to you the second time. In his report he said you changed your story and you told about this party in Hancock Park."

"Yes, the party. I didn't go because that . . . Johnny Fox hit me the night before and I had a bruise on my cheek. It was gorgeous. I played around with makeup but I couldn't do anything about the swelling. Believe me there wasn't much business in Hancock Park for a party girl with a knot on her face."

"Who was having the party?"

"I don't remember. I don't know if I even knew whose party it was."

Something about the way she answered bothered Bosch. Her tone had changed and it came across as almost a rehearsed answer.

"Are you sure don't remember?"

"Of course, I'm sure." Katherine stood up. "I think I'm going to get some water now."

She took his glass to refill and left the room again. Bosch realized that his familiarity with the woman, his emotion in seeing her again after so long, had blocked most of his investigative instincts. He had no feel for the truth. He could not tell whether there was more to what she was telling him or not. He decided he had to somehow steer the conversation back to the party. He thought she knew more than she had said all those years ago.

She came back with two glasses filled with ice water and placed his back down on the cork coaster. Something about the way she was so careful about putting the glass down gave him a knowledge about her that had not come through in her spoken words. It was simply that she had worked hard to attain the level she was at in life. That position and the material things it brought with it—like glass coffee tables and plush carpets—meant a lot to her and were to be taken care of.

She took a long drink from her glass after sitting down.

"Let me tell you something, Harry," she said. "I didn't tell them everything. I didn't lie, but I didn't tell them everything. I was afraid."

"Afraid of what?"

"I became afraid on the day they found her. You see, I'd gotten a call that morning. Before I even knew what had happened to her. It was a man, but a voice I didn't recognize. He told me if I said anything I would be next. I remember, he said, "My advice to you, little lady, is to get the hell out of Dodge.' Then, of course, I heard the police were in the building and had gone to her apartment. Then I heard she was dead. So I did what I was told. I left. I waited about a week until the police said they were done with me, then I moved to Long Beach. I changed my name, changed my life. I met my husband down there and then years later we moved here. . . . You know, I've never been back to Hollywood, not even to drive through. It's an awful place."

"What was it that you didn't tell Eno and McKittrick?"

Katherine looked down at her hands as she spoke.

"I was afraid, you see, so I didn't tell everything . . . but I knew who she was going to see there, at the party. We were like sisters. Lived in the same building, shared clothes, secrets, everything. We talked every morning, had our coffee together. We had no secrets between us. And we were going to go to the party together. Of course, after that . . . after Johnny hit me, she had to go alone."

"Who was she going to meet there, Katherine?" Bosch prompted.

"You see that is the right question but the detectives never asked that. They only wanted to know whose party it was and where it was. That didn't matter. What was important was who was she going to meet there and they never asked that."

"Who was it?"

She looked away from her hands and to the fireplace. She stared at the cold, blackened logs left from an old fire the way some people stare mesmerized by a burning fire.

"It was a man named Arno Conklin. He was a very important man in the—"

"I know who he was."

"You do?"

"His name came up in the records. But not that way. How could you not tell the cops this?"

She turned and looked at him sharply.

"Don't you look at me that way. I told you I was scared. I'd been threatened. And they wouldn't have done anything with it anyway. They were bought and paid for by Conklin. They wouldn't go near him on just the word of a . . . call girl who didn't see anything but knew a name. I had to think of myself. Your mother was dead, Harry. There was nothing I could do about it."

He could see the sharp edges of anger in her eyes. He knew it was directed at him but more toward herself. She could list all her reasons out loud but inside Bosch thought she paid a price every day for not having done the right thing.

"You think Conklin did it?"

"I don't know. All I know is that she'd been with him before and there was never anything violent. I don't know the answer to that."

"Any idea now who called you?"

"No, none."

"Conklin?"

"I don't know. I didn't know his voice anyway."

"Did you ever see them together, my mother and him?"

"Once, at a dance at the Masonic. I think it was the night they met. Johnny Fox introduced them. I don't think Arno knew . . . anything about her. At least, then."

"Could it have been Fox who called you?"

"No. I would've recognized his voice."

Bosch thought a moment.

"Did you ever see Fox again after that morning?"

"No. I avoided him for a week. It was easy because I think he was hiding from the cops. But after that I was gone. Whoever called me, he put the fear of God in me. I left town for Long Beach the day the cops said they were done with me. Packed one suitcase and took the bus . . . I remember, your mother had some of my clothes in her apartment. Things that she had borrowed. I didn't even bother to try to get them. I just took what I had and left."

Bosch was silent. He had nothing else to ask.

"I think about those days a lot, you know," Katherine said. "We were in the gutter, your mother and I, but we were good friends and we had fun in spite of it all."

"You know, all my memories . . . you're in a lot of them. You were always there with her."

"We had a lot of laughs in spite of everything," she said wistfully. "And you, you were the highlight of it all. You know, when they took you away from her, it nearly killed her right then . . . She never stopped trying to get you back, Harry. I hope you know that. She loved you. I loved you."

"Yes, I know that."

"But after you were gone, she wasn't the same. Sometimes I think what happened to her was sort of inevitable. Sometimes I think it was like she had been heading toward that alley for a long time beforehand."

Bosch stood up, looking at the sorrow in her eyes.

"I better go. I'll let you know what happens."

"I'd like that. I'd like to stay in touch."

"I'd like that, too."

He headed toward the door knowing that they wouldn't stay in touch. Time had eroded the bond between them. They were strangers who shared the same story. On the outside step he turned and looked back at her.

"The Christmas card you sent. You wanted me to look into this back then, didn't you?"

She brought out the faraway smile again.

"I don't know. My husband had just died and I was taking stock, you know? I thought about her. And you. I'm proud of how I turned out, Little Harry. So I think about what there could have been for her and you. I'm still mad. Whoever did this should . . ."

She didn't finish but Bosch nodded.

"Good-bye, Harry."

"You know, my mother, she had a good friend."

"I hope so."

Back in his car Bosch took his notebook out and looked at the list.

Conklin
McKittrick & Eno
Meredith Roman
Johnny Fox

He drew a line through Meredith Roman's name and studied those left on it. He knew that the way he had ordered the names was not the same order in which he would attempt to interview them. He knew that before he could approach Conklin, or even McKittrick and Eno, he needed more information.

He took his phone book out of his coat pocket and his portable from his briefcase. He dialed the Department of Motor Vehicles law enforcement line in Sacramento and identified himself to the clerk as Lieutenant Harvey Pounds. He gave Pounds's serial number and asked for a license check on Johnny Fox. After checking his notebook, he gave the appropriate date of birth. As he did this he ran the numbers and figured that Fox was now sixty-one years old.

As he continued to wait he smiled because Pounds would have some explaining to do in about a month. The department had recently begun to audit use of the DMV trace service. Because the *Daily News* had reported that cops all over the department were secretly doing the traces for friendly reporters and private detectives with liberal expense accounts, the new chief had cracked down by requiring all calls and computer link-ups to DMV to be documented on the newly implemented DMVT form, which required attribution of traces to a specific case or purpose. The forms were sent to Parker Center and then audited against the list of traces provided each month by the DMV. When the lieutenant's name showed up on the DMV list in the next audit and there was no corresponding DMVT form, he'd get a call from the auditors.

Bosch had gotten the lieutenant's serial number off his ID card one day when Pounds had left it clipped to his jacket on the coatrack outside his office. He'd written it down in his phone book on a hunch that one day it would come in handy.

The DMV clerk finally came back on the line and said there was no driver's license presently issued to a Johnny Fox with the birth date Bosch had provided.

"Anything close?"

"No, honey."

"That's Lieutenant, miss," Bosch said sternly. "Lieutenant Pounds."

"That's Ms., Lieutenant. Ms. Sharp."

"And I bet you are. Tell me, Ms. Sharp, how far back does that computer run go?"

"Seven years. Anything else?"

"How do I check the years before that?"

"You don't. If you want a hand records search you drop us a letter, Loo-ten-ANT. It will take ten to fourteen days. In your case, count on the fourteen. Anything else?"

"No, but I don't like your demeanor."

"That makes us even. Good-bye."

Bosch laughed out loud after flipping the phone closed. He was sure now that trace wouldn't get lost in the process. Ms. Sharp would see to that. The name Pounds would probably be on the top of the list when it came in to Parker Center. He dialed Edgar's number on the homicide table next and caught him before he had left the bureau for the day.

"Harry, what's up?"

"You busy?"

"No. Nothing new."

"Can you run a name for me? I already did DMV but I need some-body to do the computer."

"Uh . . ."

"Look, can you or can't you? If you're worried about Pounds, then—"

"Hey, Harry, cool it. What's wrong with you, man? I didn't say I couldn't do it. Just give me the name."

Bosch couldn't understand why Edgar's attitude enraged him. He took a breath and tried to calm down.

"The name's John Fox. Johnny Fox."

"Shit, there's going to be a hundred John Foxes. You got a DOB?"

"Yeah, I got a DOB."

Bosch checked his notebook again and gave it to him.

"What'd he do to you? Say, how you doing?"

"Funny. I'll tell you later. You going to run it?"

"Yes, I said I'll do it."

"Okay, you got my portable number. If you can't get through, leave me a message at home."

"When I can get to it, Harry."

"What, you said nothing's happening."

"Nothing is, but I'm working, man. I can't be running around doing shit for you all the time."

Bosch was stunned into a short moment of silence.

"Hey, Jerry, fuck you, I'll do it myself."

"Look, Harry, I'm not saying I'm—"

"No, I mean it. Never mind. I don't want to compromise you with your new partner or your fearless leader. I mean after all, that's what it's about, isn't it? So don't give me this shit about working. You're not working. You're about to go out the door for home and you know it. Or wait a minute, maybe it's drinks with Burnsie again tonight."

"Harry—"

"Take care, man."

Bosch flipped the phone closed and sat there letting the anger work out of him like heat from the grill of a radiator. The phone rang while it was still in his hand and he immediately felt better. He flipped it open.

"Look, I'm sorry, okay?" he said. "Forget it."

There was a long silence.

"Hello?"

It was a woman's voice. Bosch felt immediately embarrassed.

"Yes?"

"Detective Bosch?"

"Yes, I'm sorry, I thought it was someone else."

"Like who?"

"Who is this?"

"It's Dr. Hinojos."

"Oh." Bosch closed his eyes and the anger came back. "What can I do for you?"

"I was just calling to remind you that we have a session tomorrow. Three-thirty. You will be there?"

"I don't have a choice, remember? And you don't have to call to remind me about our sessions. Believe it or not, I have an appointment calendar, a watch, an alarm clock, all of that stuff now."

He immediately thought he had gone over the top with the sarcasm.

"Sounds like I caught you at a bad time. I'll let—"

"You did."

"—you go. See you tomorrow, Detective Bosch."

"Good-bye."

He snapped the phone closed again and dropped it on the seat. He started the car. He took Ocean Park out to Bundy and then up toward the 10. As he approached the freeway overpass he saw the eastbound cars on top weren't moving and the on ramp was jammed with cars waiting to wait.

"Fuck it," he said out loud.

He went by the freeway ramp without turning and then under the overpass. He took Bundy up to Wilshire and then headed west into downtown Santa Monica. It took him fifteen minutes to find street parking near the Third Street Promenade. He had been avoiding multi-level parking garages since the quake and didn't want to start using them now.

What a walking contradiction, Bosch thought as he prowled for a parking spot along the curb. You live in a condemned house the inspectors claim is ready to slide down the hill but you won't go into a parking garage. He finally found a spot across from the porno theater about a block from the Promenade.

Bosch spent the rush hours walking up and down the three-block stretch of outdoor restaurants, movie theaters and shops. He went into the King George on Santa Monica, which he knew was a hangout for some of the detectives out of West L.A. Division, but didn't see anybody he knew. After that, he ate pizza from a to-go joint and people-watched. He saw a street performer juggling five butcher knives at once. And he thought he might know something about how the man felt.

He sat on a bench and watched the droves of people pass him by. The only ones who stopped and paid attention to him were the homeless, and soon he had no change or dollar bills left to give them. Bosch felt alone. He thought about Katherine Register and what she had said about the past. She had said she was strong but he knew that comfort and strength could come from sadness. That was what she had.

He thought about what she had done five years ago. Her husband dead, she had taken stock of her life and found the hole in her memories. The pain. She had sent him the card in hopes he might do something then. And it had almost worked. He had pulled the murder book from the archives but hadn't had the strength, or maybe it was the weakness, to look at it.

After it got dark he walked down Broadway to Mr. B's, found a stool at the bar and ordered a draft with a Jack Daniels depth charge. There was a quintet playing on the small stage in the back, the lead on tenor saxophone. They were finishing up "Do Nothing Till You Hear from Me" and Bosch got the idea he had come in at the end of a long set. The sax was draggy. It wasn't a clean sound.

Disappointed, he looked away from the group and took a large swallow of beer. He checked his watch and knew he'd have clear driving if he left now. But he stayed. He picked the shot up and dropped it into the mug and drank deeply from the brutal mix. The group moved into "What a Wonderful World." No one in the band stepped up to sing the words but, of course, nobody could touch Louis Armstrong's vocals if they tried. It was okay, though. Bosch knew the words.

> I see trees of green
> Red roses, too
> I see them bloom
> For me and you
> And I think to myself
> What a wonderful world

The song made him feel lonely and sad but that was okay. Loneliness had been the trash can fire he huddled around for most of his life. He was just getting used to it again. It had been that way for him before Sylvia and it could be that way again. It would just take time and the pain of letting her go.

In the three months since she had left, there had been the one post-card and nothing else. Her absence had fractured the sense of continuity in his life. Before her, his job had always been the iron rails, as dependable as the sunset over the Pacific. But with her he had attempted to switch tracks, the bravest jump he had ever made. But somehow he had failed. It wasn't enough to keep her and she was gone. And now he felt he had run clear off the tracks. Inside, he felt as fragmented as his city. Broken, it seemed at times, at every level.

He heard a female voice from nearby singing the words of the song. He turned to see a young woman a few stools away, her eyes closed as she sang very softly. She sang only to herself but Bosch could hear.

> I see skies of blue
> And clouds of white
> The bright blessed day
> The dark sacred night
> And I think to myself
> What a wonderful world

She wore a short white skirt, a T-shirt and a brightly colored vest. Bosch guessed she wasn't older than twenty-five and he liked the idea that she even knew the song. She sat straight, her legs crossed. Her back swayed with the music of the saxophone. Her face was framed by brown hair and was turned upward, her lips slightly apart, almost angelic. Bosch thought she was quite beautiful, so totally lost in the majesty of the music. Clean or not, the sound took her away and he admired her for letting it. He knew that what he saw in her face was what a man would see if he made love to her. She had what other cops called a getaway face. So beautiful it would always be a shield. No matter what she did or what was done to her, her face would be her ticket. It would open doors in front of her, close them behind her. It would let her get away.

The song ended and she opened her eyes and clapped. No one else had applauded until she began. Then everyone in the bar, Bosch included, joined in. Such was the power of the getaway face. Bosch turned and flagged the bartender for another shot and beer. When it was down in front of him he took a glance over at the woman, but she was gone. He turned and checked the bar's door and saw it closing. He'd missed her.

On the way home he worked his way up to Sunset and took that all the way into the city. Traffic was sparse. He had stayed out later than he had planned. He smoked and listened to the all-news channel on the radio. There was a report about Grant High finally reopening in the Valley. It was where Sylvia had taught. Before going to Venice.

Bosch was tired and guessed that he probably wouldn't pass a breath test if stopped. He dropped his speed to below the limit as Sunset cut through Beverly Hills. He knew the cops in BH wouldn't cut him a break and that would be all he'd need on top of the involuntary stress leave.

He turned left at Laurel Canyon and took the winding road up the hill. At Mulholland he was about to turn right on red when he checked the traffic from the left and froze. He saw a coyote step out of the brush of the arroyo to the left of the roadway and take a tentative look around the intersection. There were no other cars. Only Bosch saw this.

The animal was thin and ragged, worn by the struggle to sustain itself in the urban hills. The mist rising from the arroyo caught the reflection of the street lights and cast the coyote in almost a dim blue light. And it seemed to study Bosch's car for a moment, its eyes catching the reflection of the stoplight and glowing. For just a moment Bosch believed that the coyote might be looking directly at him. Then the animal turned and moved back into the blue mist.

A car came up behind him and honked. Bosch had the green light. He waved and made the turn onto Mulholland. But then he pulled to the side. He put the car in park and got out.

It was a cool evening and he felt a chill as he walked across the intersection to the spot where he had seen the blue coyote. He wasn't sure what he was doing but he wasn't afraid. He just wanted to see the animal again. He stopped at the edge of the drop-off and looked down into the darkness below. The blue mist was all around him now. A car passed behind him and when the noise receded he listened and looked intently. But there was nothing. The coyote was gone. He walked back to his car and drove on Mulholland to Woodrow Wilson Drive to home.

Later, as he lay in his bed after more drinks and with the light still on, he smoked the last cigarette of the night and stared up at the ceiling. He'd left the light on but his thoughts were of the dark, sacred night. And the blue coyote. And the woman with the getaway face. Soon all of those thoughts disappeared with him into the dark.

Bosch got little sleep and was up before the sun. The last cigarette of the night before had nearly been his last for all time. He had fallen asleep with it between his fingers, only to be jolted awake by the searing pain of the burn. He dressed the wounds on two fingers and tried to return to sleep, but it wouldn't take him. His fingers throbbed and all he could think of was how many times he had investigated the deaths of hapless drunks who had fallen asleep and self-immolated. All he could think of was what Carmen Hinojos would have to say about such a stunt. How was that for a symptom of self-destruction?

Finally, as dawn's light began to leak into the room he gave up on sleep and got up. While coffee brewed in the kitchen he went into the bathroom and rebandaged the burns on his fingers. As he taped the fresh gauze on, he glanced at himself in the mirror and saw the deep lines under his eyes.

"Shit," he said to himself. "What's going on?"

He had black coffee on the back deck while watching the silent city come awake. There was a crisp chill in the air and the earthy smell of eucalyptus was rising from the tall trees down in the pass. The marine fog layer had filled the pass and the hills were just mysterious silhouettes in the mist. He watched the morning begin for nearly an hour, fascinated by the show he had from his deck.

It wasn't until he went back inside for a second cup that he noticed the red light flashing on his phone machine. He had two messages that had probably been left the day before and that he hadn't noticed after coming in last night. He pressed the play button.

"Bosch, this is Lieutenant Pounds calling on Tuesday at three thirty-five. I have to inform you that while you are on leave and until your, uh, status with the department is decided, you will be required to return your vehicle to the Hollywood Division garage. I have here that it is a four-year-old Chevrolet Caprice, tag number one-adam-adam-three-four-zero-two. Please make arrangements immediately to have the car turned in and checked out. This order is per *Standard Practices Manual* citation three dash thirteen. Violation could result in suspension and/or dismissal. Again, this is an order from Lieutenant Pounds, now three thirty-six on Tuesday. If there is any part of this message that you do not understand, feel free to contact me at the office."

The machine reported the message had actually been left at 4 P.M. Tuesday, probably right before Pounds had gone home for the day. Fuck him, Bosch thought. The car's a piece of shit anyway. He can have it.

The second message was from Edgar.

"Harry, you there? It's Edgar . . . Okay, listen, let's forget about today, okay? I mean it. Let's just say I was a prick and you were a prick and we're both pricks and forget it. Whether it turns out you are my partner or you were my partner, I owe you a lot, man. And if I ever act like I forgot that, hit me alongside the head like you did today. Now, to the bad news. I checked everything on this Johnny Fox. I got exactly nothing, man. That's from the NCIC, DOJ, DPP, Corrections, National Warrants, everything. I ran the works on him. Looks like this guy is clean, if he's alive. You say he doesn't even have a DL so that makes me think maybe you got a phony name there or maybe this guy ain't among the living. So, that's that. I don't know what you're up to but if you want anything else, give a call . . . Oh, and hang in there, buddy. I'm ten-seven after this so you can reach me at home if—"

The message cut off. Edgar had run out of time. Bosch rewound the tape and poured his coffee. Back on the deck he mulled over the whereabouts of Johnny Fox. When he had gotten nothing on the DMV trace, Bosch had assumed Fox might be in prison, where driver's licenses weren't issued or needed. But Edgar had not found him there nor had he found his name on any national computer that tracks criminals. Now Bosch guessed that Johnny Fox had either gone straight or, as Edgar had suggested, was dead. If Bosch was betting, he'd take the latter. Men like Johnny Fox didn't go straight.

Bosch's alternative was to go down to the Los Angeles County Hall of Records and look for a death certificate but without a date of death it would be a needle in the haystack search. It might take him days. Before he'd do that, he decided, he'd try an easier way, the *L.A. Times.*

He went back inside to the phone and dialed a reporter named Keisha Russell. She was new on the cop beat and still struggling to find her way. She had made a subtle attempt to recruit Bosch as a source a few months earlier. The way reporters usually did that was to write an inordinate number of stories on a crime that did not merit such intense attention. But the process put them in constant contact with the detectives on the case and that allowed them the chance to ingratiate themselves and hopefully procure the investigators as future sources.

Russell had written five stories in a week about one of Bosch's cases. It was a domestic violence case in which a husband had disregarded a temporary restraining order and gone to his separated wife's new apartment on Franklin. He carried her to the fifth-floor balcony and threw her off. He went over next. Russell had talked to Bosch repeatedly during the stretch of stories. The resultant dispatches were thorough and complete. It was good work and she began to earn Bosch's respect. Still, he knew that she hoped that the stories and her attention would be the building blocks of a long reporter/investigator relationship. Since then not a week had gone by that she didn't call Bosch once or twice to bullshit, pass along departmental gossip she had picked up from other sources, and ask the one question all reporters live and die by: "Anything going on?"

She answered on the first ring and Bosch was a little surprised she was in so early. He was planning on leaving a message on her voice mail.

"Keisha, it's Bosch."

"Hey, Bosch, how you doing?"

"Okay, I guess. I guess you heard about me."

"Not everything, but I heard you went on temporary leave. But nobody would tell me why. You want to talk about it?"

"No, not really. I mean, not now. I have a favor to ask. If it works out, I'll give you the story. That's the deal I've made in the past with other reporters."

"What do I have to do?"

"Just walk over to the morgue."

She groaned.

"I mean the newspaper morgue, right there at the *Times*."

"Oh, that's better. What do you need?"

"I've got a name. It's old. I know the guy was a dirtbag in the fifties and at least the early sixties. But I've lost track of him after that. Thing is, my hunch is that he's dead."

"You want an obit?"

"Well, I don't know if this is the type of guy the *Times* would write an obituary on. He was strictly small time, near as I can tell. I was thinking that there might be a story, you know, if his death was sort of untimely."

"You mean like if he got his shit blown away."

"You got it."

"Okay, I'll take a look."

She seemed eager, Bosch sensed. He knew that she thought that by doing this favor she would be cementing their relationship in place and it would only pay dividends in the future. He said nothing that would dissuade her of this.

"What's the name?"

"His name is John Fox. He went by Johnny. Last I have a trace on him is 1961. He was a pimp, general piece of trash."

"White, black, yellow or brown?"

"General piece of white trash, you could say."

"You have a birth date? It will help narrow it down if there's more than one Johnny Fox in the clips."

He gave it to her.

"Okay, where you going to be?"

Bosch gave her his portable phone number. He knew that would set the hook. The number would go right onto the source list she kept in her computer like gold earrings in a jewelry box. Having the number where he could be reached at almost any time was worth the search in the morgue.

"Okay, listen, I've got a meeting with my editor—that's the only reason I'm in this early. But after, I'll go take a look. I'll call you as soon as I have something."

"If there is something."

"Right."

After Bosch hung up he ate some Frosted Flakes from a box he took out of the refrigerator and turned on the news radio. He had discontinued the newspaper after the earthquake in case Gowdy, the building inspector, happened by early and saw it out front, a clue that someone was inhabiting the uninhabitable. There was nothing much in the top of the news summary that interested him. No homicides in Hollywood, at least. He wasn't missing out on anything.

There was one story after the traffic report that caught his attention. An octopus on display at a city aquarium in San Pedro had apparently killed itself by pulling a water circulation tube out of its tank fitting with one of its tentacles. The tank emptied and the octopus died. Environmental groups were calling it suicide, a desperate protest by the octopus against its captivity. Only in L.A., Bosch thought as he turned the radio off. A place so desperate even the marine life was killing itself.

He took a long shower, closing his eyes and holding his head directly under the spray. As he was shaving in front of the mirror after, he couldn't help but study the circles under his eyes again. They seemed even more pronounced than earlier and fit nicely with the eyes cracked with red from his drinking the night before.

He put the razor down on the edge of the sink and leaned closer to the mirror. His skin was as pale as a recycled paper plate. As he appraised himself, the thought he had was that he had once been considered a handsome man. Not anymore. He looked beaten. It seemed that age was gripping him, beating him down. He thought that he resembled some of the old men he'd seen after they were found dead in their beds. The ones in the rooming houses. The ones living in refrigerator boxes. He reminded himself more of the dead than the living.

He opened the medicine cabinet so the reflection would go away. He looked among the various items on the glass shelves and chose a squeeze bottle of Murine. He put in a heavy dose of the eye drops, wiped the excess spill off his face with a towel and left the bathroom without closing the cabinet and having to look at himself again.

He put on his best clean suit, a gray two-piece, and a white button-down shirt. He added his maroon tie with gladiator helmets on it. It was his favorite tie. And his oldest. One edge of it was fraying but he wore it two or three times a week. He'd bought it ten years earlier when he was first assigned to homicide. He pegged it in place on his shirt with a gold tie tack that formed the number 187—the California penal code for homicide. As he did this, he felt a measure of control come back to him. He began to feel good and whole again, and to feel angry. He was ready to go out into the world, whether or not it was ready for him.

Bosch pulled the knot of his tie tight against his throat before pulling open the back door of the station. He took the hallway to the rear of the detective bureau and then the aisle between the tables toward the front, where Pounds sat in his office behind the glass windows that separated him from the detectives he commanded. Heads at the burglary table bobbed up as he was noticed, then at the robbery and homicide tables. Bosch did not acknowledge anyone, though he almost lost a step when he saw someone sitting in his seat at the homicide table. Burns. Edgar was there at his own spot, but his back was to Bosch's path and he didn't see Harry coming through the room.

But Pounds did. Through the glass wall he saw Bosch's approach to his office and he stood up behind his desk.

The first thing Bosch noticed as he got closer was that the glass panel that he had broken just a week before in the office had already been replaced. He thought it was strange that this could happen so quickly in a department where more vital repairs—such as replacing the bullet-riddled windshield of a patrol car—normally took a month of red tape and paper pushing. But those were the priorities of this department.

"Henry!" Pounds barked. "Come in here."

An old man who sat at the front counter and took calls on the public line and gave general directions jumped up and doddered into the glass office. He was a civilian volunteer, one of several who worked in the station, mainly retirees that most cops referred to collectively as members of the Nod Squad.

Bosch followed the old man in and put his briefcase down on the floor.

"Bosch!" Pounds yelped. "There's a witness here."

He pointed to old Henry, then out through the glass.

"Witnesses out there as well."

Bosch could see that Pounds still had deep purple remnants of broken capillaries under each eye. The swelling was gone, though. Bosch walked up to the desk and reached into the pocket of his coat.

"Witnesses to what?"

"To whatever you're doing here."

Bosch turned to look at Henry.

"Henry, you can leave now. I'm just going to talk to the lieutenant."

"Henry, you stay," Pounds commanded. "I want you to hear this."

"How do you know he'll remember it, Pounds? He can't even transfer a call to the right table."

Bosch looked back at Henry again and fixed him with a stare that left no doubt who was in charge in the glass room.

"Close the door on your way out."

Henry made a timid glance back at Pounds but then quickly headed out the door, closing it as instructed. Bosch turned back to Pounds.

The lieutenant slowly, like a cat sneaking past a dog, lowered himself into his seat, perhaps thinking or knowing from experience that there might be more safety in not being at a face-to-face level with Bosch. Harry looked down and saw that there was a book open on the desk. He reached down and turned the cover to see what it was.

"Studying for the captain's exam, Lieutenant?"

Pounds shrank back from Bosch's reach. Bosch saw it was not the captain's exam manual but a book on creating and honing motivational skills in employees. It had been written by a professional basketball coach. Bosch had to laugh and shake his head.

"Pounds, you know, you're really something. I mean, at least you're entertaining. I gotta give you that."

Pounds grabbed the book back and shoved it in a drawer.

"What do you want, Bosch? You know you're not supposed to be in here. You're on leave."

"But you called me in, remember?"

"I did not."

"The car. You said you wanted the car."

"I said turn it in at the garage. I didn't say come in here. Now get out!"

Bosch could see the rosy spread of anger on the other man's face. Bosch remained cool and took that as a sign of a declining level of stress. He brought his hand out of his pocket with the car keys in them. He dropped them on the desk in front of Pounds.

"It's parked out by the drunk tank door. You want it back, you can have it. But you take it through the checkout at the garage. That's not a cop's job. That's a job for a bureaucrat."

Bosch turned to leave and picked up his briefcase. He then opened the door to the office with such force that it swung around and banged against one of the glass panels of the office. The whole office shook but nothing broke. He walked around the counter, saying, "Sorry about that, Henry," without looking at the old man, and then headed down the front hall.

A few minutes later he was standing on the curb on Wilcox, in front of the station, waiting for the cab he had called with his portable. A gray Caprice, almost a duplicate of the car he had just turned in, pulled up in front of him and he bent down to look in. It was Edgar. He was smiling. The window glided down.

"You need a ride, tough guy?"

Bosch got in.

"There's a Hertz on La Brea near the Boulevard."

"Yeah, I know it."

They drove in silence for a few minutes, then Edgar laughed and shook his head.

"What?"

"Nothing . . . Burns, man. I think he was about to shit his pants when you were in there with Pounds. He thought you were gonna come outta there and throw his ass outta your chair at the table. He was pitiful."

"Shit. I should've. I didn't think of it."

Silence came back again. They were on Sunset coming up to La Brea.

"Harry, you just can't help yourself, can you?"

"I guess not."

"What happened to your hand?"

Bosch held it up and studied the bandage.

"Ah, I hit it last week when I was working on the deck. Hurt like a son of a bitch."

"Yeah, you better be careful or Pounds is going to be on you like a son of a bitch."

"He already is."

"Man, he's nothing but a bean counter, a punk. Why can't you just leave it alone? You know you're just—"

"You know, you're beginning to sound like the shrink they're sending me to. Maybe I should just sit with you for an hour today, what you say?"

"Maybe she's talking some sense to you."

"Maybe I should've taken the cab."

"I think you should figure out who your friends are and listen to them for once."

"Here it is."

Edgar slowed in front of the rental car agency. Bosch got out before the car was even stopped.

"Harry, wait a minute."

Bosch looked back in at him.

"What's going on with this Fox thing? Who is the guy?"

"I can't tell you now, Jerry. It's just better this way."

"You sure?"

Bosch heard the phone in his briefcase start to ring. He looked down at it and then back at Edgar.

"Thanks for the ride."

He closed the car door.

The call was from Keisha Russell at the *Times*. She said she'd found one small story in the morgue under Fox's name but she wanted to meet with Bosch to give it to him. He knew it was part of the game, part of making the pact. He looked at his watch. He could wait to see what the story said. He told her he'd buy her lunch at the Pantry in downtown.

Forty minutes later she was already in a booth near the cashier's cage when he got there. He slipped into the opposite side of the booth.

"You're late," she said.

"Sorry, I was renting a car."

"They took your car, huh? Must be serious."

"We're not going to talk about that."

"I know. You know who owns this place?"

"Yeah, the mayor. Doesn't make the food bad."

She curled her lip and looked around as if the place were crawling with ants. The mayor was a Republican. The *Times* had gone with the Democrat. What was worse, for her, at least, was that the mayor was a supporter of the Police Department. Reporters didn't like that. That was boring. They wanted City Hall infighting, controversy, scandal. It made things more interesting.

"Sorry," he said. "I guess I could've suggested Gorky's or some more liberal establishment."

"Don't worry about it, Bosch. I'm just funnin' with ya."

She wasn't more than twenty-five, he guessed. She was a dark-complected black woman who had a beautiful grace about her. Bosch had no idea where she was from but he didn't think it was L.A. She had the touch of an accent, a Caribbean lilt, that maybe she had worked on smoothing out. It was still there, though. He liked the way she said his name. In her mouth, it sounded exotic, like a wave breaking. He didn't mind that she was little more than half his age and addressed him only by his last name.

"Where you from, Keisha?"

"Why?"

"Why? Because I'm interested is all. You're on the beat. I wanna know who I'm dealing with."

"I'm from right here, Bosch. I came from Jamaica when I was five years old. I went to USC. Where are you from?"

"Right here. Been here all my life."

He decided not to mention the fifteen months he spent fighting in the tunnels in Vietnam and the nine in North Carolina training for it.

"What happened to your hand?"

"Cut it working on my house. Been doing odd jobs while I'm off. So, what's it been like taking Bremmer's place on the cop beat? He'd been there a long time."

"Yeah, I know. It's been difficult. But I'm making my way. Slowly. I'm making friends. I hope you'll be one of my friends, Bosch."

"I'll be your friend. When I can. Let's see what you got."

She brought a manila file up onto the table but the waiter, an old bald man with a waxed mustache, arrived before she could open it. She ordered an egg salad sandwich. He ordered a well-done hamburger and fries. She frowned and he guessed why.

"You're vegetarian, right?"

"Yes."

"Sorry. Next time you pick the place."

"I will."

She opened the file and he noticed she had several bracelets on her left wrist. They were made of braided thread in many bright colors. He looked in the file and saw a photocopy of a small newspaper clipping.

Bosch could tell by the size of the clip that it was one of the stories that gets buried in the back of the paper. She passed it over to him.

"I think this is your Johnny Fox. The age is right but it does not describe him like you did. White trash, you said."

Bosch read the story. It was dated September 30, 1962.

CAMPAIGN WORKER VICTIM OF HIT AND RUN
By Monte Kim, *Times* Staff Writer

A 29-year-old campaign worker for a candidate for the district attorney's office was killed Saturday when he was struck by a speeding car in Hollywood, the Los Angeles police reported.

The victim was identified as Johnny Fox, who lived in an apartment on Ivar Street in Hollywood. Police said Fox had been distributing campaign literature supporting district attorney hopeful Arno Conklin at the corner of Hollywood Boulevard and La Brea Avenue when he was cut down by the speeding car as he crossed the street.

Fox was crossing the southbound lanes of La Brea about 2 P.M. when the car struck him. Police said it appeared Fox was killed on impact and his body was dragged for several yards by the car.

The car that hit Fox slowed momentarily after the collision but then sped away, police said. Witnesses told investigators the car proceeded south on La Brea at a high rate of speed. Police have not located the vehicle and witnesses could not provide a clear description of the make and model year. Police said an investigation is continuing.

Conklin campaign manager Gordon Mittel said Fox had joined the campaign only a week ago.

Reached at the district attorney's office, where he is in charge of the special investigation branch under retiring DA John Charles Stock, Conklin said he had not yet met Fox but regretted the death of the man working for his election. The candidate declined further comment.

Bosch studied the clip for a long moment after reading it.

"This Monte Kim, is he still at the paper?"

"Are you kidding? That's like a millennium ago. Back then the news-room was a bunch of white guys sitting around in white shirts and ties."

Bosch looked down at his own shirt, then at her.

"Sorry," she said. "Anyway, he's not around. And I don't know about Conklin. A little before my time. Did he win?"

"Yeah. I think he had two terms, then I think he ran for attorney general or something and got his ass handed to him. Something like that. I wasn't here then."

"I thought you said you've been here all your life."

"I went away for a while."

"Vietnam, right?"

"Right."

"Yeah, a lot of cops your age were there. Must've been a trip. Is that why you all became cops? So you could keep carrying guns?"

"Something like that."

"Anyway, if Conklin's still alive, he's probably an old man. But Mit-tel's still around. Obviously, you know that. He's probably in one of these booths eating with the mayor."

She smiled and he ignored it.

"Yeah, he's a big shot. What's the story on him?"

"Mittel? I don't know. First name on a big downtown law firm, friend of governors and senators and other powerful people. Last I heard, he's running the financing behind Robert Shepherd."

"Robert Shepherd? You mean that computer guy?"

"More like computer magnate. Yeah, don't you read the paper? Shep-herd wants to run but doesn't want to use up his own money. Mittel is doing the fund-raising for an exploratory campaign."

"Run for what?"

"Jesus, Bosch, you don't read the paper or watch TV."

"I've been busy. Run for what?"

"Well, like any egomaniac I guess he wants to run for president. But for now he's looking at the Senate. Shepherd wants to be a third-party candidate. Says the Republicans are too far right and the Democrats too left. He's right down the middle. And from what I hear, if anybody can get the money together for him to do the third-candidate dance, it's Mittel."

"So Mittel wants to make himself a president."

"I guess. But what are you asking me about him for anyway? I'm a cop reporter. You're a cop. What's this have to do with Gordon Mittel?"

She pointed to the photocopy. Bosch became aware that he might have asked too many questions.

"I'm just trying to catch up," he said. "Like you said, I don't read the papers."

"That's *paper*, not papers," she said smiling. "I better not catch you reading or talking to the *Daily Snews*."

"Hell hath no fury like a reporter scorned, right?"

"Something like that."

He felt assured that he had deflected her suspicions. He held up the photocopy.

"There was no follow-up to this? They never caught anybody?"

"I guess not or there would be a story."

"Can I keep this?"

"Sure."

"You feel like taking another walk back to the morgue?"

"For what?"

"Stories about Conklin."

"There will be hundreds, Bosch. You said he was DA for two terms."

"I only want stories from before he was elected. And if you have the time, throw in stories on Mittel, too."

"You know, you're asking a lot. I could get in trouble if they knew I was doing clip searches for a cop."

She put on a fake pout and he ignored that, too. He knew what she was driving at.

"You want to tell me what this is about, Bosch?"

He still didn't say anything.

"I didn't think so. Well, look, I've got two interviews to do this afternoon. I'm going to be gone. What I can do is get an intern to get the clips together and leave it all for you with the guard in the globe lobby. It will be in an envelope so nobody will know what it is. Would that be okay?"

He nodded. He'd been to Times Square before on a handful of occasions, usually meetings with reporters. It was a block-sized building with two lobbies. The centerpiece of the lobby at the First and Spring entrance was a huge globe that never stopped rotating, just as the news never stopped happening.

"You'll just leave it under my name? Won't that get you in trouble? You know, like you said, being too friendly with a cop. That's got to be against the rules over there."

She smiled at his sarcasm.

"Don't worry. If an editor or somebody asks, I'll just say it's an investment in the future. You better remember that, Bosch. Friendship is a two-way street."

"Don't worry. I never forget that."

He leaned forward across the table so he was up close to her face.

"I want you to remember something, too. One of the reasons I'm not telling you why I need this stuff is because I'm not sure what it means. If anything. But don't you get too curious. Don't you go making any calls. You do that, and you might mess things up. I might get hurt. You might get hurt. Got it?"

"Got it."

The man with the waxed mustache appeared at the side of the table with their plates.

I noticed you arrived early today. Am I to take that as a sign that you want to be here?"

"Not especially. I was downtown having lunch with a friend, so I just came over."

"Well, it's good to hear you were out with a friend. I think that is good."

Carmen Hinojos was behind her desk. The notebook was out and open but she sat with her hands clasped together in front of her. It was as if she was going out of her way to make no move that could be construed as threatening to the dialogue.

"What happened to your hand?"

Bosch held it up and looked at the bandages on his fingers.

"I hit it with a hammer. I was working on my house."

"That's too bad. I hope it's okay."

"I'll live."

"Why are you so dressed up? I hope you don't feel you have to do that for these sessions."

"No. I . . . I just like following my routine. Even if I'm not going to work, I got dressed like I was."

"I understand."

After she made an offer of coffee or water and Bosch declined, she got the session going.

"Tell me, what would you like to talk about today?"

"I don't care. You're the boss."

"I'd rather that you not look at the relationship in that way. I'm not your boss, Detective Bosch. I'm just a facilitator, someone to help you talk about whatever you want, whatever you want to get off your chest."

Bosch was silent. He couldn't think of anything to volunteer. Carmen Hinojos drummed her pencil on her yellow tablet for a few moments before taking up the slack.

"Nothing at all, huh?"

"Nothing comes to mind."

"Then why don't we talk about yesterday. When I called you, to remind you of our session today, you obviously seemed upset about something. Was that when you hit your hand?"

"No, that wasn't it."

He stopped but she said nothing and he decided to give in a little bit. He had to admit to himself that there was something about her that he liked. She was not threatening and he believed she was telling the truth when she said she was there only to help him.

"What happened when you called was that I had found out earlier that my partner, you know, my partner before all of this, had been paired up with a new man. I've been replaced already."

"And how'd that make you feel?"

"You heard how I was. I was mad about it. I think anybody would be. Then I called my partner up later and he treated me like yesterday's news. I taught that guy a lot and . . ."

"And what?"

"I don't know. It hurt, I guess."

"I see."

"No, I don't think you do. You'd have to be me to see it the way I did."

"I guess that's true. But I can sympathize. Let's leave it at that. Let me ask you this. Shouldn't you have expected your partner to be paired up again? After all, isn't it a department rule that detectives work in pairs? You are on leave for a so-far-unknown period of time. Wasn't it a given that he'd get a new partner, whether permanent or otherwise?"

"I suppose."

"Isn't it safer to work in pairs?"

"I suppose."

"What is your own experience? Did you feel safer the times you were with a partner on the job as opposed to those times when you were alone?"

"Yes, I felt safer."

"So what happened was inevitable and inarguable, yet still it made you angry."

"It wasn't that it happened that brought it on. I don't know, it was the way he told me and then the way he acted when I called. I really felt left out. I asked him for a favor and he . . . I don't know."

"He what?"

"He hesitated. Partners don't do that. Not with each other. They're supposed be there for each other. It's supposedly a lot like a marriage, but I've never been married."

She paused to write some notes, which made Bosch wonder what had just been said that was so important.

"You seem," she said while still writing, "to have a low threshold for the toleration of frustrations."

Her statement immediately made him angry but he knew that if he showed it then he would be confirming her statement. He thought maybe it was a trick designed to elicit such a response. He tried to calm himself.

"Doesn't everybody?" he said in a controlled voice.

"I suppose, to a degree. When I reviewed your records I saw that you were in the Army during the Vietnam War. Did you see any combat?"

"Did I *see* any combat? Yes, I saw combat. I was in the middle of combat, too. I was even under it. Why do people always ask, did you *see* combat, like it was a goddamn movie they took you to over there?"

She was quiet for a long time, holding the pen but doing no writing. It seemed like she was simply waiting for the sails of his anger to lose the wind. He waved his hand in a gesture he hoped told her that he was sorry, that it was behind him, that they should move on.

"Sorry," he said, just to make sure.

She still didn't say anything and her stare was beginning to weigh on him. He looked away from her to the bookshelves along one wall of the office. They were filled with heavy, leather-bound psychiatry texts.

"I am sorry to intrude on such an emotionally sensitive area," she finally said. "The reason—"

"But that's what this is all about, right? What you have is a license to intrude and I can't do anything about it."

"So, then, accept it," she said sternly. "We've been over this before. To help you we have to talk about you. Accept it and maybe we can move on. Now, as I was saying, the reason I mentioned the war was that I wanted to ask you if you are familiar with post-traumatic stress syndrome. Have you ever heard of it?"

He looked back at her. He knew what was coming.

"Yes, of course. I've heard of it."

"Well, Detective, in the past it's primarily been associated with servicemen returning from the war but it's not just a war or post-war problem. It can happen in any kind of stressful environment. Any kind. And I have to say I think that you are a walking, talking example of this disorder's symptoms."

"Jesus . . . ," he said, shaking his head. He turned in his seat so he wasn't looking at her or her bookcase. He stared at the sky through the window. It was cloudless. "You people sit up here in these offices and have no idea . . ."

He didn't finish. He just shook his head. He reached to his neck and loosened his tie. It was like he couldn't get enough air into his chest.

"Hear me out, Detective, okay? Just look at the facts here. Can you think of anything more stressful to be in this city during the last few years than a police officer? Between Rodney King and the scrutiny and villainy that brought, the riots, fires, floods and earthquakes, each officer on this force has had to write the book on stress management and, of course, mismanagement."

"You left out killer bees."

"I'm being serious."

"So am I. It was on the news."

"With all that's happened and gone on in this city, with every one of these calamities, who is in the middle every time? The police officers. The ones who have to respond. The ones who can't stay at home, duck down and wait until it's over. So let's go from that generalization to the individual. You, Detective. You have been a front-line contender with all

of these crises. At the same time you've had your real job to contend
with. Homicide. It's one of the highest-stress jobs in the department. Tell
me, how many murders have you investigated in the last three years?"

"Look, I'm not looking for an excuse. I told you before that I did
what I did because I wanted to. It had nothing to do with riots or—"

"How many dead bodies have you looked at? Just answer my question, please. How many dead bodies? How many widows did you break
the news to? How many mothers did you tell about their dead children?"

He brought his hands up and rubbed his face. All he knew was that he
wanted to hide from her.

"A lot," he finally whispered.

"More than a lot . . ."

He exhaled loudly.

"Thank you for answering. I'm not trying to corner you. The point
of my questions and the treatise on the social, cultural and even geologic
fragmentation of this city is that what I'm saying here is that you've been
through more than most, okay? And this doesn't even include the baggage you might still have from Vietnam or the loss of the romantic relationship. But whatever the reasons, the symptoms of stress are showing.
They are there, plain as day. Your intolerance, your inability to sublimate
frustrations, most of all your assault on your commanding officer."

She paused but Bosch didn't say anything. He had a feeling she wasn't
finished. She wasn't.

"There are other signs as well," she continued. "Your refusal to leave
your damaged home can be perceived as a form of denial of what is happening around you. There are physical symptoms. Have you looked at
yourself in the mirror lately? I don't think I need to ask to know that
you're drinking too much. And your hand. You didn't hurt yourself with
a hammer. You fell asleep with a cigarette in your hand. That is a burn
and I'd bet my state license on it."

She opened a drawer and took out two plastic cups and a bottle of
water. She filled the cups and pushed one across the desk to him. A peace
offering. He watched her silently. He felt exhausted, unrepairable. He
also couldn't help but be amazed by her at the same time she was so ex-
pertly cutting him open. After she took a sip of water she continued.

"These things are all indicative of a diagnosis of post-traumatic stress syndrome. However, we have one problem with that. The word *post* when used in such a diagnosis indicates the time of stress has passed. That's not the case here. Not in L.A. Not with your job. Harry, you are in a nonstop pressure cooker. You owe yourself some breathing room. That's what this leave is all about. Breathing room. Time to recoup and recover. So don't fight it. Grab it. That's the best advice I can give you. Grab it and use it. To save yourself."

Bosch breathed out heavily and held up his bandaged hand.

"You can keep your state license."

"Thank you."

They rested a moment until she continued in a voice meant to soothe him.

"You also have to know you are not alone. This is nothing to be embarrassed about. There has been a sharp increase in incidents of officer stress in the last three years. Behavioral Sciences Services just made a request to the City Council for five more psychologists. Our caseload went from eighteen hundred counseling sessions in 1990 to more than double that last year. We've even got a name for what's going on here. The blue angst. And you have it, Harry."

Bosch smiled and shook his head, still clinging to what denial he had left.

"The blue angst. Sounds like the name of a Wambaugh novel, doesn't it?"

She didn't answer.

"So what you're saying is that I'm not going to get my job back."

"No, I'm not saying that at all. All I am saying is that we have a lot of work ahead of us."

"I feel like I've been broken down by the world champ. You mind if I call you sometime when I'm trying to get a confession out of a hump who won't talk to me?"

"Believe me, just saying that is a start."

"What do you want me to do?"

"I want you to want to come here. That's all. Don't look at it as a punishment. I want you to work with me, not against me. When we talk I want you to talk about everything and nothing. Anything that comes to mind. Hold back nothing. And one other thing. I'm not telling you to completely cut it out, but you have to cut back on the drinking. You have to have a clear mind. As you obviously know, the effects of alcohol stay with an individual long after the night they were consumed."

"I'll try. All of it. I'll try."

"That's all I ask. And since you suddenly seem so willing, I have another thought. I have a cancelation of a session tomorrow at three. Can you make it?"

Bosch hesitated, didn't say anything.

"We seem to finally be working well and I think it will help. The sooner we get through with our work, the sooner you should be able to get back to your work. What do you say?"

"Three?"

"Yes."

"Okay, I'll be here."

"Good. Let's get back to our dialogue. Why don't you start? Whatever you want to talk about."

He leaned forward and reached for the cup of water. He looked at her as he drank from it, then put the cup back on the desk.

"Just say anything?"

"Anything. Whatever is happening in your life or mind that you want to talk about."

He thought for a long moment.

"I saw a coyote last night. Near my house. I . . . I was drunk, I guess, but I know I saw him."

"Why was that significant to you?"

He tried to compose the proper answer.

"I'm not sure . . . I guess there's not too many left in the hills in the city—least near where I live. So whenever I see one, I get this feeling that it might be the last one left out there. You know? The last coyote. And I guess that would bother me if it ever turned out to be true, if I never saw one again."

She nodded as if he had scored some point in a game he wasn't sure how to play.

"There used to be one that lived in the canyon below my house. I'd see him down there and—"

"How do you know it was a he? And I think you called the one you saw last night a he. How are you sure?"

"I'm not sure. I guess I don't even know. It's just a guess."

"Okay. Go on.".

"Um, he—it—lived down there below my house and I used to see him from time to time. After the earthquake it was gone. I don't know what happened to it. Then I saw this one last night. Something about the mist and the light out there . . . it looked like its coat was blue. He looked hungry. There is something . . . they're kind of sad and threatening at the same time. You know?"

"Yes, I do."

"Anyway, I thought about him when I got in bed after I got home. That was when I burned my hand. I fell asleep with the cigarette. But before I woke up I had this dream. I mean, I think it was a dream. Maybe like a daydream, like I was still kind of awake. And in it, whatever it was, the coyote was there again. But it was with me. And we were in the canyon or on a hill or something and I wasn't really sure."

He held up his hand.

"And then I felt the fire."

She nodded but didn't say anything.

"So what do you think?" he asked.

"Well, interpretation of dreams is not something I do often. Frankly, I'm not sure of its value. The real value I think I see in what you just told me was the willingness to tell me. It shows me a one-eighty-degree turn in your approach to these sessions. For what it's worth, I think it's clear you identify with the coyote. Perhaps, there are not many policemen like you left and you feel the same threat to your existence or your mission. I don't really know. But look at your own words. You called them sad and threatening at the same time. Could that be you also?"

He drank from his cup before answering.

"I've been sad before. But I've found comfort in it."

They sat in silence for a while, digesting what had been said. She looked at her watch.

"We still have some time. Is there anything else you want to talk about? Maybe something related to this story?"

He contemplated the question for a while and took out a cigarette.

"How much time do we have?"

"As long as you want. Don't worry about the time. I want to do this."

"You've talked about my mission. You told me to think about my mission. And you said the word again just a minute ago."

"Yes."

He hesitated.

"What I say here is protected, right?"

She furrowed her brow.

"I'm not talking about anything illegal. What I mean is, whatever I tell you in here, you're not going to tell people, right? It won't get back to Irving."

"No. What you tell me stays right here. That's an absolute. I told you, I make a single, narrowly focused recommendation for or against return to duty that I give to Assistant Chief Irving. That's it."

He nodded, hesitated again and then made his decision. He would tell her.

"Well, you were talking about my mission and your mission and so on and, well, I think I've had a mission for a long time. Only I didn't know it, or I mean . . . I didn't accept it. I didn't acknowledge it. I don't know how to explain it right. Maybe I was afraid or something. I put it off. For a lot of years. Anyway, what I'm telling you is that I've accepted it now."

"I'm not sure I'm following you. Harry, you have to come out and tell me what you're talking about."

He looked down at the gray rug in front of him. He spoke to it because he didn't know how to say it to her face.

"I'm an orphan . . . I never knew my father and my mother was murdered in Hollywood when I was a kid. Nobody . . . there never was any arrest made."

"You're looking for her killer, aren't you?"

He looked up at her and nodded.

"That's my mission right now."

She showed no shock on her face, which in turn surprised him. It was as if she expected him to say what he had just said.

"Tell me about it."

Bosch sat at his dining room table with his notebook out and the newspaper clips that Keisha Russell had had a *Times* intern gather for him sitting in front of him in two separate stacks. One stack for Conklin stories and one for Mittel stories. There was a bottle of Henry's on the table and through the evening he had been nursing it like cough syrup. The one beer was all he would allow himself. The ashtray, however, was loaded and there was a pall of blue smoke around the table. He had placed no limit on cigarettes. Hinojos had said nothing about smoking.

She'd had plenty to say about his mission, though. She'd flatly counseled him to stop until he was better emotionally prepared to face what he might find. He told her that he was too far down the road to stop. Then she said something that he kept thinking about as he drove home and it intruded even now.

"You better think about this and make sure it's what you want," she said. "Subconsciously or not, you may have been working toward this all your life. It could be the reason you are who you are. A policeman, a homicide investigator. Resolving your mother's death could also resolve your need to be a policeman. It could take your drive, your mission, away from you. You have to be prepared for that or you should turn back."

Bosch considered what she had said to be true. He knew that all his life it had been there. What had happened to his mother had helped define everything he did after. And it was always there in the dark recesses of his mind. A promise to find out. A promise to avenge. It was never anything that had been spoken aloud or even thought about with much focus. For to have done that was to plan and this was no part of a grand agenda. Still, he was crowded with the feeling that what he was doing was inevitable, something scheduled by an unseen hand a long time ago.

His mind put Hinojos aside and focused on a memory. He was under the surface of the water, eyes open and looking up toward the light above the pool. Then, the light was eclipsed by a figure standing above, the image murky, a dark angel hovering above. Bosch kicked off the bottom and moved toward the figure.

Bosch picked up the bottle of beer and finished it in one pull. He tried to concentrate again on the newspaper clips in front of him.

He had initially been surprised at how many stories there were about Arno Conklin prior to his ascendance to the throne of the district attorney's office. But as he started to read through them he saw most of the stories were mundane dispatches from trials in which Conklin was the prosecuting attorney. Still, Bosch got somewhat of a feel for the man through the cases he tried and his style as a prosecutor. It was clear that his star rose both in the office and the public's eyes with a series of highly publicized cases.

The stories were in chronological order and the first dealt with the successful prosecution in 1953 of a woman who poisoned both her parents and then stored their bodies in trunks in the garage until neighbors complained about the smell to the police a month later. Conklin was quoted at length in several articles on the case. One time he was described as the "dashing deputy district attorney." The case was one of the early forerunners of the insanity defense. The woman claimed diminished capacity. But judging by the number of articles, there was a public furor over the case and the jury only took a half hour to convict. The defendant received the death penalty and Conklin's place in the public arena as a champion of public safety, a seeker of justice, was secured. There was a photo of him talking to the reporters after the verdict. The paper's earlier description of him had him down perfectly. He was a dashing man. He wore a dark three-piece suit, had short blond hair and was cleanshaven. He was lean and tall and had the ruddy, All-American look that actors pay surgeons thousands for. Arno was a star in his own right.

There were more stories about more murder cases in the clips after that first one. Conklin won every one of them. And he always asked for—and got—the death penalty. Bosch noticed that in the stories from the later fifties, he had been elevated in title to senior deputy district attorney and then by the end of the decade to assistant, one of the top jobs in the office. It was a meteoric rise to have taken place in only a decade.

There was one report on a press conference in which DA John Charles Stock announced he was placing Conklin in charge of the Special Investigations Unit and charging him with cleaning up the myriad vice problems that threatened the social fabric of Los Angeles County.

"I've always gone to Arno Conklin with the toughest jobs," the DA said. "And I go to him again. The people of the Los Angeles community want a clean community and, by God, we will have it. To those who know we are coming for you, my advice is, move out. San Francisco will have you. San Diego will have you. But the City of Angels won't have you!"

Following that there were several stories spread over a couple of years with splashy headlines about crackdowns on gambling parlors, pipe dens, whorehouses and the street prostitution trade. Conklin worked with a task force of forty cops comprised of loaners from all departments in the county. Hollywood was the main target of "Conklin's Commandos," as the *Times* dubbed the squad, but the scourge of the law came down on wrongdoers all over the county. From Long Beach to the desert, all those who labored for the wages of sin were running scared—at least according to the newspaper articles. Bosch had no doubt that the vice lords Conklin's Commandos were targeting operated business as usual and that it was only the bottom feeders, the replaceable employees, that were getting the hook.

The last Conklin story in the stack was on his February 1, 1962, announcement that he would run for the top spot in the district attorney's office on a campaign of renewed emphasis on ridding the county of the vices that threatened any great society. Bosch noted that part of the stately speech he delivered on the steps of the old downtown courthouse was a well-known police philosophy that Conklin, or his speechwriter, had apparently appropriated as original thought.

People sometimes say to me, "What's the big deal, Arno? These are victimless crimes. If a man wants to place a bet or sleep with a woman for money, what's wrong with that? Where's the victim?" Well, my friends, I'll tell you what's wrong with that and who the victim is. We're the victim. All of us. When we allow this kind of activity to occur, when we simply look the other way, then it weakens us all. Every one of us.

I look at it this way. These so-called little crimes are each like a broken window in an abandoned house. Doesn't seem like a big problem, right? Wrong. If nobody fixes that window, pretty soon kids come along and think nobody cares. So they throw a few rocks and break a few more windows. Next, the burglar drives down the street and sees the house and thinks nobody around there cares. So he sets up shop and starts breaking into houses while the owners are at work.

Next thing you know, another miscreant comes along and steals cars right off the street. And so on and so on. The residents start to see their own neighborhood with different eyes then. They think, Nobody cares anymore, so why should I? They wait an extra month before cutting the grass. They don't tell the boys hanging on the corner to put the cigarettes out and go back to school. It's gradual decay, my friends. It happens all across this great country of ours. It sneaks in like weeds in our yard. Well, when I'm district attorney the weeds are coming out by the roots.

The story ended by reporting that Conklin had chosen a young "firebrand" from his office to manage his campaign. He said that Gordon Mittel would resign from the DA's office and begin work immediately. Bosch reread the story and immediately became transfixed by something that hadn't registered during his first read. It was in the second paragraph.

For the well-known and not-press-shy Conklin, it will be his first run for public office. The 35-year-old bachelor and Hancock Park resident said he has planned the run for a long time and has the backing of retiring DA John Charles Stock, who also appeared at the press conference.

Bosch turned the pages of his notebook back to the list of names he had written before and wrote "Hancock Park" after Conklin's name. It wasn't much but it was a little piece of verification of Katherine Register's story. And it was enough to get Bosch's juices going. It made him feel that at least he had a line in the water.

"Fucking hypocrite," he whispered to himself.

He drew a circle around Conklin's name in the notebook. He absentmindedly kept circling it as he tried to decide what he should do next.

Marjorie Lowe's last known destination was a party in Hancock Park. According to Katherine Register, she was more specifically going to meet Conklin. After she was dead, Conklin had called the detectives on the case to make an appointment but any record of the interview, if any occurred, was missing. Bosch knew it was all a general correlation of facts but it served to deepen and solidify the suspicion he had felt from the night he had first looked through the murder book. Something was not right about the case. Something didn't fit. And the more he thought about it, the more he believed Conklin was the wrong piece.

He reached into his jacket, which was on the chairback behind him, and took out his small phone book. He took it into the kitchen, where he dialed the home line of Deputy District Attorney Roger Goff.

Goff was a friend who shared Bosch's affection for the tenor saxophone. They'd spent many days in court sitting side by side during trials and many nights in jazz bars side by side on stools. Goff was an old-line prosecutor who had been with the office nearly thirty years. He had no political aspirations inside or outside of the office. He just liked his job. He was a rarity because he never tired of it. A thousand deputies had come in, burned out, and gone on to corporate America during Goff's watch, but he stayed. He now labored in the criminal courts building with prosecutors and public defenders twenty years his junior. But he was still good at it and, more important, still had the fire in his voice when he stood before a jury and called down the outrage of God and society against those in the defendant's chair. His mixture of tenacity and plain fairness had made him a legend in downtown legal and law enforcement circles. And he was one of the few prosecutors Bosch had unconditional respect for.

"Roger, Harry Bosch."

"Hey, goddamnit, how you doing?"

"I'm fine. What are you up to?"

"Watching the tube like everybody else. What're you doing?"

"Nothing. I was just thinking, you remember Gloria Jeffries?"

"Glo—shit, of course I do. Let's see. She's . . . yeah, she's the one with the husband got quaded in the motorcycle accident, right?"

Recalling the case, it sounded as if he were reading it off one of his yellow tablets.

"She got tired of caring for him. So one morning he's in bed and she sits on his face until she smothers him. It was about to go by as a natural but a suspicious detective named Harry Bosch wouldn't let it go. He came up with a witness who Gloria had told everything to. The clincher, the thing that got the jury, was that she told the wit that when she smothered him, it was the first orgasm the poor devil had ever been able to give her. How is that for a memory?"

"Damn, you're good."

"So what about her?"

"She's raising up at Frontera. Getting ready to. I was wondering if you'd have time to write a letter."

"Fuck, already? What was that, three, four years ago?"

"Almost five. I hear she's got the book now and goes to the board next month. I'll write a letter but it'd be good if there was one from the prosecutor, too."

"Don't worry about it, I got a standard in my computer. All I do is change the name and the crime, throw in a few of the gruesome details. The basic line is that the crime was too heinous for parole to be considered at this time. It's a good letter. I'll send it out tomorrow. It usually works charms."

"Good. Thanks."

"You know, they gotta stop giving the book to those women. They all get religion when they're coming up. You ever go to one of those hearings?"

"A couple."

"Yeah, sit through a half a day of them if you have the time and aren't feeling particularly suicidal sometime. They sent me out to Frontera once when one of the Manson girls was up. See, with the big ones like that they send a body out instead of a letter. So, I went out and I sat through about ten of these things waiting for my girl to come up. And let me tell you, everybody's quoting Corinthians, they're quoting Revelations,

Matthew, Paul, John three-sixteen, John this, John that. And it works! It goddamn works. These old guys on the board eat that shit up. Plus I guess they're all sitting up there getting thick in their pants having all these women groveling in front of them. Anyway, you got me started, Harry. It's your fault, not mine."

"Sorry about that."

"It's okay. So what else is new? Haven't seen you in the building. You got anything coming my way?"

It was the question Bosch had been waiting for Goff to get to so he could nonchalantly steer the conversation toward Arno Conklin.

"Ah, nothing much. It's been slow. But, hey, let me ask you, did you know Arno Conklin?"

"Arno Conklin? Sure, I knew him. He hired me. What are you asking about him for?"

"Nothing. I was going through some old files, making room in one of the cabinets, and I came across some old newspapers. They were pushed into the back. There were some stories about him and I thought of you, thought it was about when you started."

"Yeah, Arno, tried to be a good man. A little high and mighty for my taste, but I think he was a decent man overall. Especially considering he was both a politician and a lawyer."

Goff laughed at his own line but Bosch was silent. Goff had used the past tense. Bosch felt a heavy presence push into his chest and he only realized then how strong the desire to avenge could be.

"He's dead?"

He closed his eyes. He hoped Goff wouldn't detect the urgency he had let slip into his voice.

"Oh, no, he's not dead. I meant, you know, when I knew him. He was a good man then."

"He's still practicing law somewhere?"

"Oh, no. He's an old man. Retired. Once a year they wheel him out at the annual prosecutors banquet. He personally hands out the Arno Conklin Award."

"What's that?"

"Some piece of wood with a brass plate on it that goes to the administrative prosecutor of the year, if you can believe that. That's the guy's legacy, an annual award to a so-called prosecutor who doesn't set foot inside a courtroom all year. It always goes to one of the division heads. I don't know how they decide which one. Prob'ly whoever got his or her nose farthest up the DA's ass that year."

Bosch laughed. The line wasn't that funny but he was also feeling the relief of learning that Conklin was still alive.

"It's not funny, Bosch. It's fucking sad. Administrative prosecutor, whoever heard of such a thing? An oxymoron. Like Andrew and his screenplays. He deals with these studio people called, get this, creative executives. There's your classic contradiction. Well, there you go, Bosch, you got me going again."

Bosch knew Andrew was Goff's roommate but he had never met him.

"Sorry, Roger. Anyway, what do you mean, they wheel him out?"

"Arno? Well, I mean they wheel him out. He's in a chair. I told you, he's an old man. Last I heard he was in some full-care retirement home. One of the classy ones in Park La Brea. I keep saying I'm going to see him one day, thank him for hiring me way back when. Who knows, maybe I could put in a word for that award or something."

"Funny guy. You know, I heard that Gordon Mittel used to be his frontman."

"Oh, yeah, he was the bulldog outside the door. Ran his campaigns. That's how Mittel got started. Now that's one mean—I'm glad he got out of criminal law and into politics, he'd be a motherfucker to come up against in court."

"Yeah, I've heard," Bosch said.

"Whatever you've heard, you can double it."

"You know him?"

"Not now and not then. I just knew to keep clear. He was already out of the office by the time I came in. But there were stories. Supposedly in those early days, when Arno was the heir apparent and everybody knew it, there was a lot of maneuvering. You know, to get next to him. There was one guy, Sinclair I think his name was, that was set to run Arno's campaign. Then one night the cleaning lady found some porno shots under his blotter. There was an internal investigation and the photos proved to be stolen from another prosecutor's case files. Sinclair was dumped. He always claimed he was set up by Mittel."

"Think he was?"

"Yes. It was Mittel's style . . . But who knows."

Bosch sensed that he had said and asked enough to pass it off as conversation and gossip. Anything further and Goff might get suspicious about the call.

"So what's the deal?" he asked. "You zipped up for the night or you want to go by the Catalina? I heard Redman's in town to do Leno. I'd bet you the cover charge that he and Branford drop by to sit in on the late set."

"Sounds tempting, Harry, but Andrew's making a late dinner now and I think we're just going to stay at home tonight. He's counting on it. You mind?"

"Not at all. Anyway, I'm trying not to bend the elbow so much lately. I need to give it a rest."

"Now that, sir, is quite admirable. I think you deserve a piece of wood with a brass plate on it."

"Or a shot of whiskey."

After hanging up Bosch sat back down at the desk and wrote notes on the highlights of the conversation with Goff into his notebook. Next he pulled the stack of clips on Mittel in front of him. These were more recent clips than those on Conklin because Mittel had not made a name for himself until much later. Conklin had been his first step up the ladder.

Most of the stories were just mentions of Mittel as being in attendance at various galas in Beverly Hills or as host of various campaign or charity dinners. From the start he was a money man, a man politicians and charities went to when they wanted to cast their nets into the rich enclaves of the Westside. He worked both sides, Republican, Democrat, it didn't seem to matter. His profile grew, though, when he started working for candidates on a larger scale. The current governor was a client. So, too, were a handful of congressmen and senators from other western states.

A profile written several years earlier—and apparently without his cooperation—ran under the headline THE PRESIDENT'S MAIN MONEY MAN. It said Mittel had been tapped to round up California contributors for the president's reelection war chest. It said the state was one of the cornerstones of the national campaign's funding plan.

The story also noted the irony that Mittel was a recluse in the high-profile world of politics. He was a backstage man who abhorred the spotlight. So much so that he had repeatedly turned down patronage jobs from those he'd helped elect.

Instead, Mittel elected to stay in Los Angeles, where he was the founding partner of a powerful financial district law firm, Mittel, Anderson, Jennings & Rountree. Still, it seemed to Bosch that what this Yale-educated lawyer did had little to do with law as Bosch knew it. He doubted Mittel had been inside a courtroom in years. That made Harry think of the Conklin award and he smiled. Too bad Mittel had quit the DA's office. He might've been in line for it someday.

There was a photo that ran with the profile. It showed Mittel at the bottom of the steps of Air Force One greeting the then president at LAX. Though the article had been published years earlier, Bosch was nevertheless startled by how young Mittel was in the photo. He looked at the story again and checked the man's age. Doing the arithmetic, he realized that currently Mittel was barely sixty years old.

Bosch pushed the newspaper clips aside and got up. For a long time he stood at the sliding glass door to the deck and stared at the lights across the pass. He began to consider what he knew about circumstances thirty-three years old. Conklin, according to Katherine Register, knew Marjorie Lowe. It was clear from the murder book that he had somehow reached into the investigation of her death for reasons unknown. His reach was then apparently covered up for reasons unknown. This had occurred only three months before he announced his candidacy for district attorney and less than a year before a key figure in the investigation, Johnny Fox, died while in his political employ.

Bosch thought that it was obvious that Fox would have been known to Mittel, the campaign manager. Therefore, he further concluded, whatever it was that Conklin did or knew, it was likely that Mittel, his front-man and the architect of his political run, had knowledge of it as well.

Bosch went back to the table and turned to the list of names in his notebook. Now he picked up the pen and circled Mittel's name as well. He felt like having another beer but he settled for a cigarette.

In the morning Bosch called the LAPD personnel office and asked them to check whether Eno and McKittrick were still current. He doubted they were still around but knew he had to make the check. It would be embarrassing if he went through a search for them only to find one or both still on the payroll. The clerk checked the roll and told him no such officers were currently on the force.

He decided he would have to put on his Harvey Pounds pose after that. He dialed the DMV in Sacramento, gave the lieutenant's name and asked for Ms. Sharp again. By the tone she inflected in the single word "Hello" after picking up the phone, Bosch had no doubt that she remembered him.

"Is this Ms. Sharp?"

"That's who you asked for, isn't it?"

"I did, indeed."

"Then it's Ms. Sharp. What can I do for you?"

"Well, I wanted to mend our fences, so to speak. I have a few more names I need driver's license addresses for and I thought that directly working with you would expedite the matter and perhaps repair our working relationship."

"Honey, we don't have a working relationship. Hold the line, please."

She punched the button before he could say anything. The line was dead for so long that he began to believe his scam to burn Pounds wasn't worth it. Finally, a different clerk picked up and said Ms. Sharp had instructed her to help. Bosch gave her Pounds's serial number and then the names Gordon Mittel, Arno Conklin, Claude Eno and Jake McKittrick. He said he needed the home addresses on their licenses.

He was put on hold again. During the time he waited he held the phone to his ear with his shoulder and fried an egg over easy in a pan on the stove. He made a sandwich out of it with two slices of white toast and cold salsa from a jar he kept in the refrigerator. He ate the dripping sandwich while leaning over the sink. He had just wiped his mouth and poured himself a second cup of coffee when the clerk finally picked back up.

"Sorry it took so long."

"No problem."

He then remembered he was Pounds and wished he hadn't said that.

The clerk explained that she had no addresses or license information on Eno or McKittrick, then gave him addresses for Conklin and Mittel. Goff had been right. Conklin lived in Park La Brea. Mittel lived above Hollywood on Hercules Drive in a development called Mount Olympus.

Bosch was too preoccupied at that point to continue the Pounds charade. He thanked the clerk without further confrontation and hung up. He thought about what his next move should be. Eno and McKittrick were either dead or out of state. He knew he could get their addresses through the department's personnel office but that might take all day. He picked up the phone again and called Robbery-Homicide, asking for Detective Leroy Ruben. Ruben had put nearly forty years in on the department, half of it in RHD. He might know something about Eno and McKittrick. He might also know Bosch was on stress leave.

"Ruben, can I help you?"

"Leroy, it's Harry Bosch. What do you know?"

"Not much, Harry. Enjoying the good life?"

Right away he was telling Bosch he knew of his situation. Bosch knew now that his only alternative was to be straight with him. To a point.

"It ain't bad. But I'm not sleeping late every day."

"No? What're you getting up for?"

"I'm kind've freelancing on an old case, Leroy. That's why I called. I want to try to track down a couple of old dicks. Thought maybe you'd know of them. They were out of Hollywood."

"Who are they?"

"Claude Eno and Jake McKittrick. Remember them?"

"Eno and McKittrick. No . . . I mean, yeah, I think I remember McKittrick. He checked out . . . it must've been ten, fifteen years ago. He went back to Florida, I think. Yeah, Florida. He was here in RHD for a year or so. At the end there. The other one, Eno, I don't remember any Eno."

"Well, it was worth a try. I'll see what I can find in Florida. Thanks, Leroy."

"Hey, Harry, what gives anyway?"

"It's just an old case I had in my desk. It's giving me something to do while I see what happens."

"Any word?"

"Not yet. They got me talking to the shrink. If I can talk my way past her, I'll get back to the table. We'll see."

"Okay, well, good luck. You know, me and some of the boys here, when we heard that story we laughed our asses off. We heard about that guy Pounds. He's an asshole. You done good, kid."

"Well, let's hope I didn't do so good that I lost my job."

"Ah, you'll be all right. They send you to Chinatown a few times, brush you off and send you back into the ring. You'll be okay."

"Thanks, Leroy."

After hanging up, Bosch got dressed for the day, putting on a fresh shirt and the same suit as the day before.

He headed downtown in his rented Mustang and spent the next two hours in a bureaucratic maze. He first went to the Personnel Office at Parker Center, told a clerk what he wanted and then waited half an hour for a supervisor to tell him all over again. The supervisor told him he had wasted his time and that the information he sought was at City Hall.

He walked across the street to the City Hall annex, took the stairs up and then crossed on the tramway over Main Street into the white obelisk

of City Hall. He took the elevator up to the Finance Department, on
nine, showed his ID card to another counter clerk and told her that, in
the interest of streamlining the process, maybe he should talk to a supervisor first.

He waited on a plastic chair in a hallway for twenty minutes before he
was ushered into a small office cramped with two desks, four file cabinets
and several boxes on the floor. An obese woman with pale skin and black
hair, sideburns and the slight hint of a mustache sat behind one of the
desks. On her calendar blotter Bosch noticed a food stain from some
prior mishap. There was also a reusable plastic quart soda container with
a screw-on top and straw on her desk. A plastic name plate on the desk
said Mona Tozzi.

"I'm Carla's supervisor. She said you are a police officer?"

"Detective."

He pulled the chair away from the empty desk and sat down in front
of the fat woman.

"Excuse me, but Cassidy is probably going to need her chair when she
gets back. That's her desk."

"When's she coming back?"

"Anytime. She went up for coffee."

"Well, maybe if we hurry we'll be done by then and I'll be out of
here."

She gave a short who-do-you-think-you-are laugh that sounded
more like a snort. She said nothing.

"I've spent the last hour and a half trying to get just a couple addresses from the city and all I get are a bunch of people who want to send
me to someone else or make me wait out in the hall. And what's funny
about that is that I work for the city myself and I'm trying to do a job for
the city and the city isn't giving me the time of day. And, you know, my
shrink tells me I've got this post-traumatic stress stuff and should take life
easier. But, Mona, I gotta tell you, I'm getting pretty fucking frustrated
with this."

She stared at him a moment, probably wondering if she could possibly make it out the door if he decided to go nuts on her. She then pursed
her lips, which served to change her mustache from a hint to an announcement, and took a hard pull on the straw of her soda container.

Bosch saw a liquid the color of blood go up through the straw into her mouth. She cleared her throat before talking in a comforting tone.

"Tell you what, Detective, why don't you tell me what it is you are trying to find?"

Bosch put on his hopeful face.

"Great. I knew there was somebody who cared. I need to get the addresses where pension checks for two different retired officers are sent each month."

Her eyebrows mated as she frowned.

"I'm sorry, but those addresses are strictly confidential. Even within the city. I couldn't give—"

"Mona, let me explain something. I'm a homicide investigator. Like you, I work for the city. I have leads on an old unsolved murder that I am following up on. I need to confer with the original case detectives. We're talking about a case more than thirty years old. A woman was killed, Mona. I can't find the two detectives that originally worked the case and the police personnel people sent me over here. I need the pension addresses. Are you going to help me?"

"Detective—is it Borsch?"

"Bosch."

"Detective Bosch, let me explain something to you. Just because you work for the city does not give you access to confidential files. I work for the city but I don't go over to Parker Center and say let me see this or let me see that. People have a right to privacy. Now, this is what I can do. And it is all I can do. If you give me the two names, I will send a letter to each person asking them to call you. That way, you get your information, I protect the files. Would that work for you? They'll go out in the mail today. I promise."

She smiled but it was the phoniest smile Bosch had seen in days.

"No, that wouldn't work at all, Mona. You know, I'm really disappointed."

"I can't help that."

"But you can, don't you see?"

"I have work to do, Detective. If you want me to send the letter, give me the names. If not, that's your decision."

He nodded that he understood and brought his briefcase up from the floor to his lap. He saw her jump when he angrily unsnapped the locks. He opened it and took out his phone. He flipped it open and dialed his home number, then waited for the machine to pick up.

Mona looked annoyed.

"What are you doing?"

He held his hand up for silence.

"Yes, can you transfer me to Whitey Springer?" he said to his tape.

He watched her reaction while acting like he wasn't. He could tell, she knew the name. Springer was the City Hall columnist for the *Times*. His specialty was writing about the small bureaucratic nightmares, the little guy against the system. Bureaucrats could largely create these nightmares with impunity, thanks to civil service protections, but politicians read Springer's column and they wielded tremendous power when it came to patronage jobs, transfers and demotions at City Hall. A bureaucrat vilified in print by Springer might be safe in his or her job but there likely would never be advancement, and there was nothing stopping a city council member from calling for an audit on an office or a council observer to sit in the corner. The word to the wise was to stay out of Springer's column. Everybody knew that, including Mona.

"Yeah, I can hold," Bosch said into the phone. Then to Mona, he said, "He's gonna love this one. He's got a guy trying to solve a murder, the victim's family waiting for thirty-three years to know who killed her, and some bureaucrat sitting in her office sucking on a quart of fruit punch isn't giving him the addresses he needs just to talk to the other cops who worked the case. I'm not a newspaper man but I think that's a column. He'll love it. What do you think?"

He smiled and watched her face flush almost as red as her fruit punch. He knew it was going to work.

"Okay, hang up the phone," she said.

"What? Why?"

"HANG UP! Hang up and I'll get the information."

Bosch flipped the phone closed.

"Give me the names."

He gave her the names and she got up angrily and silently to leave the room. She could barely fit around the desk but made the maneuver like a ballerina, the pattern instilled in her body's memory by repeated practice.

"How long will this take?" he asked.

"As long as it takes," she answered, regaining some of her bureaucratic bluster at the door.

"No, Mona, you got ten minutes. That's all. After that, you better not come back 'cause Whitey's gonna be sitting here waiting for you."

She stopped and looked at him. He winked.

After she left he got up and went around the side of the desk. He pushed it about two inches closer to the opposite wall, narrowing her path back to her chair.

She was back in seven minutes, carrying a piece of paper. But Bosch could see it was trouble. She had a triumphant look on her face. He thought of that woman who had been tried a while back for cutting off her husband's penis. Maybe it was the same face she had when she ran out the door with it.

"Well, Detective Borsch, you've got a little problem."

"What is it?"

She started around the desk and immediately rammed her thick thigh into its Formica-topped corner. It looked more embarrassing than painful. She had to flail her arms for balance and the impact of the collision shook the desk and knocked her container over. The red liquid began leaking out of the straw onto the blotter.

"Shit!"

She quickly moved the rest of the way around the desk and righted the container. Before sitting down she looked at the desk, suspicious that it had been moved.

"Are you all right?" Bosch asked. "What is the problem with the addresses?"

She ignored his first question, forgot her embarrassment and looked at Bosch and smiled. She sat down. She spoke as she opened a desk drawer and took out a wad of napkins stolen from the cafeteria.

"Well, the problem is you won't be talking to former detective Claude Eno anytime soon. At least, I don't think you will."

"He's dead."

She started wiping up the spill.

"Yes. The checks go to his widow."

"What about McKittrick?"

"Now McKittrick is a possibility. I have his address here. He's over in Venice."

"Venice? So what's the problem with that?"

"That's Venice, Florida."

She smiled, delighted with herself.

"Florida," Bosch repeated.

He had no idea there was a Venice in Florida.

"It's a state, over on the other side of the country."

"I know where it is."

"Oh, and one other thing. The address I have is only a P.O. box. Sorry about that."

"Yeah, I bet. What about a phone?"

She tossed the wet napkins into a trash can in the corner of the room.

"We have no phone number. Try information."

"I will. Does it say there when he retired?"

"You didn't ask me to get that."

"Then give me what you've got."

Bosch knew he could get more, that they'd have to have a phone number somewhere, but he was handicapped because this was an unauthorized investigation. If he pushed things too far, then he'd only succeed in having his activities discovered and then halted.

She floated the paper across the desk to him. He looked at it. It had two addresses on it, the P.O. box for McKittrick and the street address in Las Vegas for Eno's widow. Her name was Olive.

Bosch thought of something.

"When do the checks go out?"

"Funny you should ask."

"Why?"

"Because today's the last day of the month. They always go out the last day of the month."

That was a break and he felt like he deserved it, that he had worked for it. He picked up the paper she had given him and slipped it into his briefcase, then he stood up.

"Always a pleasure to do work with the public servants of the city."

"Likewise. And, uh, Detective? Could you return the chair to the place you found it? As I said, Cassidy will need it."

"Of course, Mona. Pardon my forgetfulness."

After the bout with bureaucratic claustrophobia, Bosch decided he needed some air to recover. He took the elevator down to the lobby and out the main doors to Spring Street. As he walked out, he was directed by a security officer to walk down the right side of the wide-staired entrance to the great building because there was a film location shoot taking place on the left side. Bosch watched what they were doing as he stepped down the stairs and then decided to take a break and have a smoke.

He sat down on one of the concrete sidings along the stairs and lit a cigarette. The film shoot involved a group of actors posing as reporters who rushed down the stairs of City Hall to meet and question two men getting out of a car at the curb. They rehearsed it twice and then shot it twice while Bosch sat there and smoked two cigarettes. Each time, the reporters all yelled the same thing at the two men.

"Mr. Barrs, Mr. Barrs, did you do it? Did you do it?"

The two men refused to answer and pushed through the pack and up the stairs with the reporters backtracking. On one of the takes one of the reporters stumbled as he moved backwards, fell on his back on the stairs and was partially trampled by the others. The director kept the scene going, perhaps thinking that the fall added a touch of realism to the scene.

Bosch figured that the filmmakers were using the steps and front facade of City Hall as a courthouse setting. The men coming from the car were the defendant and his high-priced lawyer. He knew that City Hall was frequently used for such shots because it actually looked more like a courthouse than any real courthouse in the city.

Bosch was bored after the second take, though he guessed there would be many more. He got up and walked down to First and then over to Los Angeles Street. He took that back to Parker Center. Along the way he was asked for spare change only four times, which he thought was a low count for downtown and possibly a sign of improving economic times. In the lobby of the police building he passed the bank of pay phones and on a whim stopped, picked one of the phones off the hook and dialed 305-555-1212. He had dealt with Metro-Dade Police in Miami several times over the years and 305 was the only Florida area code that readily came to mind. When the operator came on he asked for Venice and she informed him that 813 was the proper area code.

He then redialed and got information in Venice. First he asked the operator what the nearest large city to Venice was. She told him that was Sarasota and he asked what the nearest large city was to that. When she said St. Petersburg, he finally started getting his bearings. He knew where St. Petersburg was on a map—the west coast of Florida—because he knew the Dodgers occasionally played spring training games there and he had looked it up once.

He finally gave the operator McKittrick's name and promptly got a tape recording saying the number was unlisted at the customer's request. He wondered if any of the detectives he had dealt with by phone at Metro-Dade could get the number for him. He still had no idea exactly where Venice was or how far it was from Miami. Then he decided to leave it alone. McKittrick had taken steps to make it difficult to be contacted. He used a P.O. box and had an unlisted phone. Bosch didn't know why a retired cop would take such steps in a state three thousand miles away from where he had worked but he felt sure that the best approach to McKittrick was going to have to be in person. A telephone call, even if Bosch got the number, was easy to avoid. Someone standing right at your door was different. Besides, Bosch had caught a break; he knew McKittrick's pension check was in the mail to his P.O. box. He was sure he could use it to find the old cop.

He clipped his ID card to his suit and went up to the Scientific Investigation Division. He told the woman behind the counter that he had to talk to someone in Latent Prints and pushed through the half door and down the hall to the print lab like he always did, without waiting for her go-ahead.

The lab was a large room with two rows of work tables with overhead fluorescent lights. At the end of the room were two desks with AFIS computer terminals on them. Behind them was a glass-walled room with the mainframes inside. There was condensation on the glass because the mainframe room was kept cooler than the rest of the lab.

Because it was lunchtime there was only one technician in the lab and Bosch didn't know him. He was tempted to turn around and come back later when someone else might be there, but the tech looked up from one of the computer terminals and saw him. He was a tall, skinny man with glasses and a face that had been ravaged by acne when he was younger. The damage gave him a permanently sullen expression.

"Yes?"

"Yeah, hi, howya doin'?"

"I'm doing fine. What can I do for you?"

"Harry Bosch, Hollywood Division."

He put out his hand and the other man hesitated, then shook it tentatively.

"Brad Hirsch."

"Yeah, I think I've heard your name. We've never worked together but that probably won't last. I work homicide so it seems I basically get around to working with everybody in here eventually."

"Probably."

Bosch sat down on a chair to the side of the computer module and pulled his briefcase onto his lap. He noticed that Hirsch was looking into his blue computer screen. He seemed more comfortable looking there than at Bosch.

"Reason I'm here is, at the moment, it's kind of slow out in Tinseltown. And so I've been going through some old cases. I came across this one from nineteen sixty-one."

"Nineteen sixty-one?"

"Yeah, it's old. A female . . . . cause of death blunt force trauma, then he made it look like a strangulation, a sex crime. Anyway, nobody was ever popped for it. It never went anywhere. In fact, I don't think anyone's really looked at it since the due diligence in sixty-two. A long time. Anyway, the thing is, the reason I'm here, is that back then the cops on this pulled a decent set of prints at the crime scene. They got a bunch of partials and some full rounds. And I've got them here."

Bosch took the yellowed print card out of the briefcase and held it out to the man. Hirsch looked at it but didn't take it. He looked back at the computer screen and Bosch placed the print card down on the keyboard in front of him.

"And, well, as you know, that was before we had these fancy computers and all of this technology you got here. All they did with this back then was use it to compare these to a suspect's prints. They got no match, they let the guy go and then they just shoved these in an envelope. They've been sitting in the case file ever since. So what I was thinking was, we could—"

"You want to run them through AFIS."

"Yeah, right. You know, take a shot at it. Spin the dice, maybe we get lucky and pick up a hitchhiker on the information highway. It's happened before. Edgar and Burns out on the Hollywood table nailed an old one this week with an AFIS run. I was talking to Edgar and he said one of you guys down here—I think it was Donovan—said the computer has access to millions of prints from all across the country."

Hirsch nodded unenthusiastically.

"And that's not just criminal print files, right?" Bosch asked. "You've got military, law enforcement, civil service, everything. That right?"

"Yes, that's right. But, look, Detective Bosch, we—"

"Harry."

"Okay, Harry. This is a great tool that's getting better all the time. You're correct about that but there still are human and time elements here. The comparison prints have to be scanned and coded and then those codes have to be entered into the computer. And right now we have a backup that's running twelve days."

He pointed to the wall above the computer. There was a sign with changeable numbers on it. Like the signs in the union office that said X number of days since the last death in the line of duty.

AUTOMATED FINGERPRINT IDENTIFICATION SYSTEM
Search Requests Will Take 12 Days To Process
No Exception!

"So, you see, we can't take everybody who walks in here and put them at the front of the pack, okay? Now if you want to fill out a search request form, I can—"

"Look, I know there are exceptions. Especially in homicide cases. Somebody made that run for Burns and Edgar the other day. They didn't wait twelve days. They were put through right away and they cleared three homicides just like that."

Bosch snapped his fingers. Hirsch looked at him and then back to the computer.

"Yes, there are exceptions. But that comes from on high. If you want to talk to Captain LeValley, maybe she'll approve it. If you—"

"Burns and Edgar didn't talk to her. Somebody just did it for them."

"Well, then that was against the rules. They must have known somebody who did it for them."

"Well, I know you, Hirsch."

"Why don't you just fill out a request and I'll see what—"

"I mean, what's it take, ten minutes?"

"No. In your case much longer. This print card you have is an antique. It's obsolete. I'd have to run it through the Livescan machine, which would then assign codes to the prints. Then I'd have to hand-enter the codes it gives me. Then depending on the restrictions on the run you want, it could take—"

"I don't want any restrictions. I want it compared to all data bases."

"Then the computer time can run as long as thirty, forty minutes."

With a finger Hirsch punched his glasses back up his nose as if punctuating his resolve not to break the rules.

"Well, Brad," Bosch said, "the problem is I don't know how much time I've got on this. Certainly not twelve days. No way. I'm working on it now because I have the time, but the next time I get a fresh call that will be it, I'll be off it. That's the nature of homicide, you know? So, are you sure there isn't something we can do right now?"

Hirsch didn't move. He just stared at the blue screen. It reminded Bosch of the youth hall, when kids would literally shut down like a computer on standby when the bullies taunted them.

"What are you doing now, Hirsch? We could do it right now."

Hirsch looked at him for a long moment before talking.

"I'm busy. And look, Bosch, I know who you are, okay? That's an interesting story about pulling old cases but I know it's a lie. I know you're on a stress leave. The story's getting around. And you shouldn't even be here and I shouldn't be talking to you. So, could you please leave me alone? I don't want to get into trouble. I don't want people to get the wrong idea, you know?"

Bosch looked at him but Hirsch's eyes had moved back onto the computer screen.

"Okay, Hirsch, let me tell you a real story. One—"

"I really don't want any more stories, Bosch. Why don't you just—"

"I'm going to tell you this story, then I'm leaving, okay? Just this one story."

"Okay, Bosch, okay. You tell the story."

Bosch looked at him silently and waited for Hirsch to make eye contact but the latent print technician's eyes remained on the computer screen as if it were his security blanket. Bosch told the story anyway.

"One time, a long time ago, I was almost twelve and I'm swimming in this pool, you see, and I'm under the water but I've got my eyes open. And I look up and I see up through the water up to the edge of the pool. I see this dark figure. You know, it was hard to figure out what it was, all wavy and all. But I could tell it was a man and there wasn't supposed to be a man up there. So I came up for air at the side of the pool and I was right. It was a man. He was wearing this dark suit. And he reached down and grabbed me by the wrist. I was just a scrawny little runt. It was easy for him to do. He pulled me out and he gave me this towel to put on my shoulders and he led me over to a chair and he told me . . . he told me that my mother was dead. Murdered. He said they didn't know who did it, but whoever he was, he left his fingerprints. He said, 'Don't worry, son, we got the fingerprints and they're as good as gold. We'll get him.' I remember those words exactly. "We'll get him.' Only they never did. And now I'm going to. That's my story, Hirsch."

Hirsch's eyes dropped down to the yellowed print card on the keyboard.

"Look, man, it's a bad story, but I can't be doing this. I'm sorry."

Bosch stared at him a moment and then slowly stood up.

"Don't forget the card," Hirsch said.

He picked it up and held it up to Bosch.

"I'll leave it here. You're going to do the right thing, Hirsch. I can tell."

"No, don't. I can't do—."

"I'm leaving it here!"

The power of his voice shocked even Bosch and it seemed to have scared Hirsch. The print tech replaced the card on the keyboard. After a few seconds of silence Bosch leaned down and spoke quietly.

"Everybody wants the chance to do the right thing, Hirsch. It makes them feel good inside. Even if doing it doesn't exactly fit inside the rules, sometimes you have to rely on the voice inside that tells you what to do."

Bosch stood back up and took out his wallet and a pen. He pulled out a business card and wrote some numbers on it. He put it down on the keyboard next to the print card.

"That's got my portable and my home on it. Don't bother calling the office, you know I won't be there. I'll be waiting to hear from you, Hirsch."

He walked slowly out of the lab.

Waiting for the elevator, Bosch guessed that his effort to persuade Hirsch had fallen on deaf ears. Hirsch was the type of guy whose exterior scars masked deeper interior wounds. There were a lot in the department like him. Hirsch had grown up intimidated by his own face. He'd probably be the last person to dare go outside the bounds of his job or the rules. Another department automaton. For him, doing the right thing was ignoring Bosch. Or turning him in.

He punched at the elevator button with his finger again and contemplated what else he could do. The AFIS search was a long shot but he still wanted it done. It was a loose end and any thorough investigation took care of loose ends. He decided he would give Hirsch a day and then he'd make another run at him. If that didn't work, he'd try another tech. He'd try them all until he got the killer's prints into that machine.

The elevator finally opened and he squeezed on. That was one of the only things you could rely on inside Parker Center. Cops would come and go, chiefs, even political power structures, but the elevators would always move slowly and always be crowded when they got to you. Bosch pushed the unlighted button marked B as the doors slowly closed and the square room started to descend. While everyone stood and stared blankly at the lighted numbers over the door, Bosch looked down at his briefcase.

No one in the small space spoke. Until, as the car slowed to its next stop, Bosch heard his first name spoken from behind. He turned his head slightly, not sure if it had been someone speaking to him or the name had been directed toward someone else.

His eyes fell on Assistant Chief Irvin S. Irving standing in the rear of the elevator. They exchanged nods just as the doors opened on the first floor. Bosch wondered if Irving had seen him push the button for the basement. There was no reason for a man on involuntary stress leave to be going to the basement.

Bosch decided the car was too crowded for Irving to have seen what button he had pushed. He stepped off the elevator into the alcove off the main lobby and Irving followed him out and caught up with him.

"Chief."

"What brings you all the way in, Harry?"

It was said casually but the question signaled that there was more than passing interest from Irving. They started walking toward the exit, Bosch quickly putting a story together.

"I have to go over to Chinatown anyway, so I dropped by to go to payroll. I wanted to see about them sending my check to my house instead of out to Hollywood, since I'm not sure when I'll be back."

Irving nodded and Bosch was pretty sure he had bought it. He was about Bosch's size but had the stand-out feature of a completely shaved head. That feature and his reputation for intolerance for corrupt cops got him the nickname within the department of Mr. Clean.

"You're in Chinatown today? I thought you were Monday, Wednesday, Friday. That was the schedule I approved."

"Yes, that's the schedule. But she had an opening come up today and wanted me to come in."

"Well, I'm glad to hear you being so cooperative. What happened to your hand?"

"Oh, this?" Bosch held up his hand as if it were someone else's that he had just noticed at the end of his arm. "I've been using some of my free time to do some work around the house and I cut it on a piece of broken glass. I'm still doing clean-up from the quake."

"I see."

Bosch guessed that he didn't buy that one. But he didn't really care.

"I'm getting a quick lunch in the federal plaza," Irving said. "You want to come along?"

"Thanks just the same, Chief. I already ate."

"Okay, well, take care of yourself. I mean that."

"I will. Thanks."

Irving started off and then stopped.

"You know, we're handling this situation with you a little differently because I hope to get you back in there at Hollywood homicide without any change in grade or position. I'm waiting to hear from Dr. Hinojos but I understand it will be a few more weeks, at least."

"That's what she tells me."

"You know, if you're willing to do it, an apology in the form of a letter to Lieutenant Pounds could be beneficial. When push comes to shove, I'm going to have to sell him on letting you back in there. That will be the hard part. I think getting you a clean bill from the doctor won't be a problem. I can simply issue the order and Lieutenant Pounds will have to accept it, but that won't ease the pressure there. I would rather work it that he accepts your return and everybody's happy."

"Well, I heard he already's got a replacement for me."

"Pounds?"

"He paired my partner with somebody off autos. Doesn't sound to me like he's expecting or planning on me coming back, Chief."

"Well, that's news to me. I'll talk to him about that. What do you think about this letter? It could go a long way toward helping your situation."

Bosch hesitated before answering. He knew Irving wanted to help him. The two of them shared an unspoken bond. Once they had been complete enemies in the department. But contempt had eroded into a truce which now was more a line of wary mutual respect.

"I'll think about the letter, Chief," Bosch finally said. "I'll let you know."

"Very well. You know, Harry, pride gets in the way of a lot of the right decisions. Don't let that happen to you."

"I'll think about it."

Bosch watched him bound off around the fountain memorial to officers killed in the line of duty. He watched until Irving got to Temple and started to cross Los Angeles Street to the federal plaza, where there was an

array of fast-food emporiums. Then Bosch figured it was safe and turned
to go back inside.

He skipped waiting for the elevator again and went down the stairs to
the basement.

Most of the underground floor of Parker Center was taken up by the
Evidence Storage Division. There were a few other offices, like the Fugi-
tives Division, but it was generally a quiet floor. Bosch found no pedes-
trian traffic on the long yellow linoleum hallway and was able to get to
the steel double doors of ESD without running into anyone else he knew.

The police department held physical evidence on investigations that
had not yet gone to the district attorney or city attorney for filing. Once
that happened, the evidence usually stayed with the prosecutor's office.

Essentially, that made ESD the city's temple of failure. What was behind the steel doors Bosch opened was the physical evidence from thousands of unsolved crimes. Crimes that had never resulted in prosecution.
It even smelled of failure. Because it was in the basement of the building,
there was a damp odor here that Bosch always believed was the rank stink
of neglect and decay. Of hopelessness.

Bosch stepped into a small room that was essentially a wire-mesh
cage. There was another door on the other side but there was a sign on it
that said ESD STAFF ONLY. There were two windows cut in the mesh. One
was closed and a uniform officer sat behind the other working on a crossword puzzle. Between the two windows was another sign that said DO
NOT STORE LOADED FIREARMS. Bosch walked up to the open window and
leaned on the counter. The officer looked up after filling in a word on
the puzzle. Bosch saw the name tag on his uniform said Nelson. Nelson
read Bosch's ID card so Bosch didn't have to bother to introduce himself,
either. It worked out nicely.

"Her . . . on—how you say that?"

"Hieronymus. Rhymes with anonymous."

"Hieronymus. Isn't there a rock and roll band named that?"

"Maybe."

"What can I do for you, Hieronymus from Hollywood?"

"I got a question."

"Shoot."

Bosch put the pink evidence check slip on the counter.

"I want to pull the box on this case. It's pretty old. Would it still be around anywhere?"

The cop took the slip, looked at it and whistled when he saw the year. While writing the case number down on a request log, he said, "Should be here. Don't see why not. Nothing gets tossed, you know. You want to look at the Black Dahlia case, we got that. That's what, fifty-something years old. We got 'em going back even further. If it ain't solved, it's here."

He looked up at Bosch and winked.

"Be right back. Why don't you fill out the form."

Nelson pointed with his pen out the window to a counter on the back wall where the standard request forms were. He got up and disappeared from the window. Bosch heard him yell to someone else in the back.

"Charlie! Hey, Char-LEE!"

A voice from somewhere in the back yelled a response that was unintelligible.

"Take the window," Nelson called back. "I'm taking the time machine."

Bosch had heard about the time machine. It was a golf cart they used to get back to the deep recesses of the storage facility. The older the case, the farther back in time it went, the farther away it was from the front windows. The time machine got the window cops back there.

Bosch walked over to the counter and filled out a request form, then reached in the window and put it on the crossword puzzle. While he was waiting, he looked around and noticed another sign on the back wall. NARCOTICS EVIDENCE NOT RELEASED WITHOUT 492 FORM. Bosch had no idea what that form was. Somebody came through the steel doors then carrying a murder book. A detective, but Bosch didn't recognize him. He opened it on the counter, got a case number and then filled out a form. He then went to the window. There was no sign of Charlie. After a few minutes, the detective turned to Bosch.

"Anybody working back there?"

"Yeah, one guy went to get me a box. He told another guy to watch. I don't know where he is."

"Shit."

He rapped sharply with his knuckles on the counter. In a few minutes another uniform cop came to the window. He was an old horse, with white hair and a pear shape. Bosch guessed he'd been working in the basement for years. His skin was as white as a vampire's. He took the other detective's evidence request slip and was gone. Then both Bosch and the other detective were left waiting. Bosch could tell the other man had started looking at him but was acting like he wasn't.

"You're Bosch, right?" he finally asked. "From Hollywood?"

Bosch nodded. The other man put out his hand and smiled.

"Tom North, Pacific. We've never met."

"No."

Bosch shook his hand but didn't act enthusiastic about the introduction.

"We never met but listen, I worked Devonshire burglary for six years before I got my homicide gig in Pacific. Know who my CO was up there back then?"

Bosch shook his head. He didn't know and he didn't care but North didn't seem to realize that.

"Pounds. Lieutenant Harvey 'Ninety-eight' Pounds. The fuck. He was my CO. So, anyway, I heard through the network, you know, what you did to his ass. Put his face right through the fuckin' window. That's great, man, fuckin' great. More power to you. I laughed my ass off when I heard that."

"Well, I'm glad it entertained you."

"No, really, I know you're getting piped for it. I heard about that, too. But I just wanted to let you know you made my day and a lot of people are with you, man."

"Thanks."

"So what are you doing down here? I heard they had you on the Fifty-One-Fifty list."

It annoyed Bosch to realize that there were those in the department whom he didn't even know who knew what had happened to him and what his situation was. He tried to keep calm.

"Listen, I—"

"Bosch! You gotta box!"

It was the time traveler, Nelson. He was at the window, pushing a light blue box through the opening. It was about the size of a boot box and was held closed with red tape that was cracking with age. It looked like the box was powdered with dust. Bosch didn't bother finishing his sentence. He waved off North and went to the box.

"Sign here," Nelson said.

He put a yellow slip down on top of the box. It kicked up a small dust cloud, which he waved away with his hand. Bosch signed the paper and took the box in two hands. He turned and saw North looking at him. North just nodded once. He seemed to know it wasn't the right time to ask questions. Bosch nodded back and headed to the door.

"Uh, Bosch?" North said. "I didn't mean anything about what I said. About the list. No offense, okay?"

Bosch stared at him as he pushed through the door with his back. But he didn't say anything. He then proceeded down the hall carrying the box with two hands, as if it contained something precious.

Carmen Hinojos was in her waiting room when Bosch got there a few minutes late. She ushered him in and waved off his apology for lateness as if it was unnecessary. She wore a dark blue suit and as he passed her in the doorway he smelled a light soapy fragrance. He took the seat on the right side of the desk near the window again.

Hinojos smiled and Bosch wondered why. There were two chairs on the other side of the desk from her. So far, in three meetings, he had taken the same one each time. The one closest to the window. He wondered if she had taken note of this and what, if anything, it meant.

"Are you tired?" she asked. "You don't look like you got much sleep last night."

"I guess I didn't. But I'm fine."

"Have you changed your mind about anything we discussed yesterday?"

"No, not really."

"You are continuing this private investigation?"

"For now."

She nodded in a way that told him she expected his reply.

"I want to talk about your mother today."

"Why? It's got nothing to do with why I'm here, why I'm on leave."

"I think it's important. I think it will help us get to what is happening with you, what has made you take on this private investigation of yours. It might explain a lot about your recent actions."

"I doubt it. What do you want to know?"

"When you spoke yesterday, you made several references to her lifestyle, but you never really came out and said what she did, what she was. Thinking about it after the session, I was wondering if you have trouble accepting what she was. To the point of not being able to say she—"

"Was a prostitute? There, I said it. She was a prostitute. I'm a grown man, Doctor. I accept the truth. I accept the truth in anything as long as it's the truth. I think you're going far afield here."

"Perhaps. What do you feel about her now?"

"What do you mean?"

"Anger? Hatred? Love?"

"I don't think about it. Certainly not hate. I loved her at the time. After she was gone that didn't change."

"What about abandonment?"

"I'm too old for that."

"What about back then? Back when it happened."

Bosch thought a moment.

"I'm sure there was some of that. Her lifestyle, her line of work, got her killed. And I was left behind the fence. I guess I was mad about that and felt abandoned. I was also hurt. The hurt was the worst part. She loved me."

"What do you mean, left behind the fence?"

"I told you yesterday. I was in McClaren, the youth hall."

"Right. So her death prevented you from leaving there, correct?"

"For a while."

"How long?"

"I was there on and off until I was sixteen. I lived a few months two different times with some fosters but I always got sent back. Then, when I was sixteen, another couple took me. I was with them until I was seventeen. I found out later that they kept getting the DPSS checks for a year after I'd split."

"DPSS?"

"Department of Public Social Services. Now they call it the Division of Youth Services. Anyway, when you took a kid into your home as foster parents, you got a monthly support payment. A lot of people took kids in just for those checks. I'm not saying these people did, but they never told DPSS I wasn't in their home anymore after I left."

"I understand. Where were you?"

"Vietnam."

"Wait a minute, let's go back. You said that two different times before this you lived with foster parents but were then sent back. What happened? Why were you sent back?"

"I don't know. They didn't like me. They said it wasn't working out. I went back into the dorms behind the fence and waited. I think getting rid of a teenage boy was about as easy as selling a car with no wheels. The fosters always wanted the younger ones."

"Did you ever run away from the hall?"

"A couple times. I always got caught in Hollywood."

"If placing teenagers was so difficult, how did it happen to you the third time, when you were even older, sixteen?"

Bosch laughed falsely and shook his head.

"You'll get a kick out of this. I was chosen by this guy and his wife because I was left-handed."

"Left-handed? I don't follow."

"I was a lefty and I could throw a pretty good fastball."

"What do you mean?"

"Ah, Jesus, it was—see, Sandy Koufax was with the Dodgers then. He was a lefty and I guess they were paying him about a zillion bucks a year to pitch. This guy, the foster, his name was Earl Morse, he had played semipro baseball or something and never really made it. So, he wanted to *create* a left-handed major league prospect. Good left-handers were pretty rare back then, I guess. Or he thought that. Anyway, they were the hot commodity. Earl thought he'd grab some kid with some potential, slap him into shape and then be his manager or agent or something when it came to contract time. He saw it as his way back into the game. It was crazy. But I guess he'd seen his own big league dream crash and burn. So he came out to McClaren and took a bunch of us into the field for a catch. We had a team, we played other halls, sometimes the schools in the Valley let us play them. Anyway, Earl took us out to throw the ball around and it was a tryout but none of us knew it at the time. It didn't even enter my mind what was going on until later. Anyway, he glommed on to me when he saw I was a lefty and could throw. He forgot the others like they were last season's program."

Bosch shook his head again at the memory.

"What happened? You went with him?"

"Yeah. I went with him. There was a wife, too. She never said much to me or him. He used to make me throw a hundred balls a day at a tire hanging in the back yard. Then every night he'd have these coaching sessions. I put up with it for about a year and then I split."

"You ran away?"

"Sort of. I joined the Army. I had to get Earl to sign for me, though. At first he wouldn't do it. He had major league plans for me. But then I told him I was never going to pick up another baseball as long as I lived. He signed. Then he and the wife kept cashing those DPSS checks while I was overseas. I guess the extra money helped make up for losing the prospect."

She was quiet for a long time. It looked to Bosch like she was reading her notes but he had not seen her write anything during this session.

"You know," he said into the silence, "about ten years later, when I was still in patrol, I pulled over a drunk driver coming off the Hollywood Freeway onto Sunset. He was all over the place. When I finally got him over and got up there to the window, I bent over to look in and it was Earl. It was a Sunday. He was coming home from the Dodgers. I saw the program on the seat."

She looked at him but didn't say anything. He was looking at the memory still.

"I guess he'd never found that lefty he was looking for . . . Anyway, he was so drunk he didn't recognize me."

"What did you do?"

"Took his keys and called his wife . . . I guess it was the only break I ever gave the guy."

She looked back down at the pad while asking her next question.

"What about your real father?"

"What about him?"

"Did you ever know who he was? Did you have any relationship at all?"

"I met him once. I was never curious about it until I came back from overseas. Then I traced it down. Turned out he was my mother's lawyer.

He had a family and all of that. He was dying when I met him, looked like a skeleton . . . So I never really knew him."

"His name was Bosch?"

"No. My name was just something she came up with. The painter, you know. She thought L.A. was a lot like his paintings. All the paranoia, the fear. Once she gave me a book that had his paintings in it."

More silence followed as she thought about this one, too.

"These stories, Harry," she finally said, "these stories that you tell are heartbreaking in their own way. It makes me see the boy who became the man. It makes me see the depth of the hole left by your mother's death. You know, you would have a lot to blame her for and no one would blame you for doing it."

He looked at her pointedly while composing a response.

"I don't blame her for anything. I blame the man who took her from me. See, these are stories about me. Not her. You can't get the feel for her. You can't know her like I did. All I know is that she did all she could to get me out of there. She never stopped telling me that. She never stopped trying. She just ran out of time."

She nodded, accepting his answer. A few moments passed.

"Did there come a time when she told you what she did . . . for a living?"

"Not really."

"How did you know?"

"I can't remember. I think I really didn't know for sure what she did until she was gone and I was older. I was ten when they took me away. I didn't really know why."

"Did she have men stay with her while you were together?"

"No, that never happened."

"But you must have had some idea about this life she was leading, that you both were leading."

"She told me she was a waitress. She worked nights. She used to leave me with a lady who had a room at the hotel. Mrs. DeTorre. She watched four or five kids whose mothers were doing the same thing. None of us knew."

He finished there but she didn't say anything and he knew he was expected to continue.

"One night I snuck out when the old lady fell asleep and I walked down to the Boulevard to the coffee shop where she said she worked. She wasn't in there. I asked and they didn't know what I was talking about . . ."

"Did you ask your mother about it?"

"No . . . The next night I followed her. She left in her waitress uniform and I followed her. She went to her best friend's place upstairs. Meredith Roman. When they came out, they were both wearing dresses, makeup, the whole thing. Then they both left in a cab and I couldn't follow them."

"But you knew."

"I knew something. But I was like nine or something. How much could I know?"

"What about the charade she followed, dressing every night like a waitress, did that anger you?"

"No. The opposite. I thought that was . . . I don't know, there was something noble about her doing that for me. She was protecting me, in a way."

Hinojos nodded that she saw his point.

"Close your eyes."

"Close my eyes?"

"Yes, I want you to close your eyes and think back to when you were a boy. Go ahead."

"What is this?"

"Indulge me. Please."

Bosch shook his head as if annoyed but did as she asked. He felt stupid.

"Okay."

"Okay, I want you to tell me a story about your mother. Whatever image or episode with her that you have the clearest in your mind, I want you to tell it to me."

He thought hard. Images of her passed through and disappeared. Finally, he came to one that stayed.

"Okay."

"Okay, tell it."

"It was at McClaren. She had come to visit and we were out at the fence at the ballfield."

"Why do you remember this story?"

"I don't know. Because she was there and that always made me feel good, even though we always ended up crying. You should have seen that place on visiting day. Everybody crying . . . And I remember it, too, because it was near the end. It wasn't too long after that she was gone. Maybe a few months."

"Do you remember what you talked about?"

"A lot of stuff. Baseball, she was a Dodgers fan. I remember one of the older kids had taken my new sneakers that she had given me for my birthday. She noticed I didn't have 'em on and she got pretty mad about it."

"Why did the older boy take your sneakers?"

"She asked the same thing."

"What did you tell her?"

"I told her the kid took my shoes because he could. You see, they could call that place whatever they wanted but basically it was a prison for kids and it had the same societies as a prison has. Your dominant cliques, your submissives, everything."

"What were you?"

"I don't know. I pretty much kept to myself. But when some older, bigger kid took my shoes, I was a submissive. It was a way of surviving."

"Your mother was unhappy about this?"

"Well, yeah, but she didn't know the score. She wanted to go complain or something. She didn't know that if she did that it would only make it worse for me there. Then she suddenly did realize what the deal was. She started crying."

Bosch was silent, picturing the scene perfectly in his mind. He remembered the dampness in the air and the smell of the orange blossoms from the nearby groves.

Hinojos cleared her throat before breaking into his memory.

"What did you do when she started crying?"

"I probably started crying, too. I usually did. I didn't want her to feel bad but there was a comfort in knowing she knew what was happening to me. Only mothers can do that, you know? Make you feel good when you're sad . . ."

Bosch still had his eyes closed and was seeing only the memory.

"What did she tell you?"

"She . . . she just told me she was going to get me out. She said that her lawyer was going to go to court soon to appeal the custody ruling and the unfit mother finding. She said there were other things she could do, too. The point was, she was getting me out."

"That lawyer was your father?"

"Yes, but I didn't know it . . . Anyway, what I'm saying is that the courts were wrong about her. That's the thing that bothers me. She was good to me and they didn't see that . . . anyway, I remember she promised me that she would do what she had to do, but she would get me out."

"But she never did."

"No. Like I said, she ran out of time."

"I'm sorry."

Bosch opened his eyes and looked at her.

"So am I."

Bosch had parked in a public lot off Hill Street. It cost him twelve dollars for his car. He then got onto the 101 and headed north toward the hills. As he drove, he occasionally looked over at the blue box on the seat next to him. But he didn't open it. He knew that he had to but he would wait for home.

He turned the radio on and listened as the DJ introduced a song by Abbey Lincoln. Bosch had never heard it before but he immediately liked the words and the woman's smoky voice.

> Bird alone, flying high
> Flying through a clouded sky
> Sending mournful, soulful sounds
> Soaring over troubled grounds

After he got to Woodrow Wilson and followed his usual routine of parking a half block away from his home, Bosch brought the box inside and placed it on the dining room table. He lit a cigarette and paced the room, looking down occasionally at the box. He knew what was in it. He had the evidence list from the murder book. But he couldn't overcome a feeling that by opening the box he was invading some secret privacy, committing a sin that he didn't understand.

Finally, he took his keys out. There was a small pen knife on the ring and he used it to slice through the red tape that sealed the box. He put the knife down and without thinking about it any further lifted the top off the box.

The victim's clothes and other belongings were wrapped individually in plastic bags, which Bosch took out of the box one by one and placed on the table. The clear plastic was yellowed but he could see through it. He did not remove anything from the bags but instead just held each piece of evidence up and studied it in its sterile covering.

He opened the murder book to the evidence list and made sure nothing was missing. It was all there. He held the small bag containing the gold earrings up to the light. They were like frozen tear drops. He put the bag back down and at the bottom of the box he saw the blouse, folded neatly in plastic, the spot of blood exactly where the evidence sheet said it was, on the left breast, about two inches from the center button.

Bosch ran his finger over the plastic where the spot was. It was then that he realized something. There was no other blood. He knew that it was the thing that had bothered him as he read the murder book but he had been unable to get ahold of the thought then. Now he had it. The blood. No blood on the undergarments, the skirt or the stockings, or pumps. Only on the blouse.

Bosch also knew the autopsy had described a body with no lacerations. Then where had the blood come from? He wanted to look at the crime scene and autopsy photos but knew that he couldn't. There was no way he would open that envelope.

Bosch pulled the bag containing the blouse from the box and read the evidence tag and other markings. Nowhere did it mention or give any reference code for any analysis ever being done on the blood.

This invigorated him. There was a good chance that the blood spot came from the killer, not the victim. He had no idea whether blood that old could still be typed or even submitted for DNA analysis but he intended to find out. The problem, he knew, was comparison. It didn't matter if the blood could still be analyzed if there was nothing to compare it to. To get blood from Conklin or Mittel or anyone, for that matter, he would need a court order. And to get that, he needed evidence. Not just suspicions and hunches.

He had gathered the evidence bags together to replace in the box when he stopped to study one he had not considered closely before. It contained the belt that had been used to strangle the victim.

Bosch studied it a few moments as if it were a snake he was trying to identify before cautiously reaching into the box and picking it up. He could see the evidence tag tied through one of the belt holes. On the smooth silver sea shell buckle there was black powder. He could see that part of the ridge lines from a thumbprint were still there.

He held the belt up to the light. It pained him to look at it but he did. The belt was an inch in width, made of black leather. The sea shell buckle was the largest ornamentation but smaller silver shells were attached along its length. Looking at it brought back the memory. He hadn't really chosen it. Meredith Roman had taken him to the May Co. on Wilshire. She had seen the belt on a rack with many others and told him his mother would like it. She paid for it and allowed him to give it to his mother as a birthday present. Meredith had been right. His mother wore the belt often, including every time she visited him after the court took him away. And including the night she was murdered.

Bosch read the evidence tag but all it said was the case number and McKittrick's name. On the tongue he noticed that the second and fourth holes were imperfect circles, distended by the spoke of the buckle during wear. He guessed that maybe his mother wore it tighter at times, maybe to impress someone, or looser at times, over bulkier clothing. He now knew everything about the belt except who had used it last to kill her.

He realized then that whoever had held this belt, this weapon, before the police had been responsible for taking a life and indelibly changing his own. He carefully replaced it in the box and put the other clothing in on top of it. He then put the lid back on top.

Bosch couldn't stay in the house after that. He felt he had to get out. He didn't bother changing his clothes. He just got in the Mustang and started driving. It was dark now and he took Cahuenga down into Hollywood. He told himself he didn't know or care where he was going but that was a lie. He knew. When he got to Hollywood Boulevard he turned east.

The car took him to Vista, where he turned north and then cut into the first alley. The headlights sliced through the darkness and he saw a small homeless encampment. A man and woman huddled under a cardboard lean-to. Two other bodies, wrapped in blankets and newspapers, lay nearby. A small glow from dying flames came from the rim of a trash can. Bosch cruised by slowly, his eyes further down the alley, to the spot he knew from the crime scene drawing that was in the murder book.

The Hollywood souvenir store was now an adult book and video store. There was an alley entrance for shy customers and several cars were parked alongside the rear of the building. Bosch stopped near the door and killed the lights. He just sat in the car, feeling no need to get out. He had never been to the alley, to the spot, before. He just wanted to sit and watch and feel for a few moments.

He lit a cigarette and watched as a man carrying a bag walked quickly out the door of the adult shop to a car parked at the end of the alley.

Bosch thought about a time when he was a small boy and still with his mother. They'd had a small apartment on Camrose then and during the summer they'd sit in the back courtyard on the nights she wasn't working or on Sunday afternoons and listen to the music coming over the hill from the Hollywood Bowl. The sound was bad, attacked by traffic and the white noise of the city before it got to them, but the high notes were clear. What he liked about it wasn't the music but that she was there. It was their time together. She always told him that she would take him one day to the bowl to hear "Scheherazade." It was her favorite. They never got the chance. The court took him away from her and she was dead before she could get him back.

Bosch finally heard the philharmonic perform "Scheherazade" the year he spent with Sylvia. When she saw tears welling in the corners of his eyes, she thought it was because of the pure beauty of the music. He never got around to telling her it was something else.

A blur of motion caught his attention and someone banged a fist on the driver's side window. Bosch's left hand instinctively went under his jacket to his waist, but there was no gun there. He turned and looked into the face of an old woman whose years were etched like hash marks on her face. It looked like she was wearing three sets of clothes. When she was done knocking on the window, she opened her palm and held it out. Still startled, Bosch quickly reached into his pocket and pulled out a five.

He started the car so he could put the window down and handed the money out to her. She said nothing. She just took it and walked away. Bosch watched her go and wondered how had she ended up in this alley. How had he?

Bosch drove out of the alley and back out to Hollywood Boulevard. He started cruising again. At first aimlessly but soon he found his purpose. He wasn't yet ready to confront Conklin or Mittel but he knew where they were and he wanted to see their homes, their lives, the places they had ended up.

He stayed on the Boulevard until Alvarado and then took that down to Third, where he started west. The drive took him from the Third World poverty of the area known as Little Salvador past the faded mansions of Hancock Park and then to Park La Brea, a huge complex of apartments, condominiums and attendant rest homes.

Bosch found Ogden Drive and cruised slowly down it until he saw the Park La Brea Lifecare Center. There's another irony, he thought. Lifecare. The only thing the place probably cared about was when you were going to die, so your space could be sold to the next one.

It was a nondescript twelve-story building of concrete and glass. Through the glass facade of the lobby Bosch could see a security guard at a post. In this town, even the elderly and infirm weren't safe. He glanced up the front of the building and saw most of the windows were dark. Only nine o'clock and the place was already dead. Someone honked at him from behind and he sped up and away, thinking about Conklin and what his life might be like. He wondered if the old man in his room up there ever gave a thought to Marjorie Lowe after so many years.

Bosch's next stop was Mount Olympus, the gaudy outcropping of modern Roman-style homes above Hollywood. The look was supposed to be neoclassical but he had heard it referred to more than once as neo*crassical*. The huge, expensive homes were jammed side by side as close as teeth. There were ornate columns and statues but the only thing that seemed classic about most of the place was the kitsch. Bosch took Mount Olympus Drive off Laurel Canyon, turned on Electra and then went to Hercules. He was driving slowly, looking for addresses on curbs to match the one he had written in his notebook that morning.

When he found Mittel's house, he stopped on the street, stunned. It was a house that he knew. He had never been inside it, of course, but everyone knew it. It was a circular mansion that sat atop one of the most recognizable promontories in the Hollywood Hills. Bosch looked at the place with awe, imagining its interior size and its exterior ocean-to-mountain views. Its rounded walls lit from the outside with white lights, it looked like a spaceship that had alighted on a mountaintop and was poised to take to the air once again. Classic kitsch it wasn't. This was a home that bespoke its owner's power and influence.

An iron gate guarded a long driveway that went up a hill to the house. But tonight the gate was open and Bosch could see several cars and at least three limousines parked along one side of the drive. Other cars were parked in the circle at the top. It only dawned on Bosch that there was a party underway at the house when a red blur passed the car window and the door was suddenly sprung open. Bosch turned and looked into the face of a swarthy Latino man in a white shirt and red vest.

"Good evening, sir. We will take your car here. If you could walk up the drive on the left side, the greeters will find you."

Bosch stared at the man unmoving, thinking.

"Sir?"

Bosch tentatively stepped out of the Mustang and the man in the vest gave him a slip of paper with a number on it. He then slipped into the car and drove away. Bosch stood there, aware that he was about to let events control him, something he knew he should avoid. He hesitated and looked back at the tail lights of the Mustang gliding away. He let the temptation take him.

Bosch fastened his top button and pulled his tie back into place as he walked up the driveway. He passed a small army of men in red vests and as he came all the way up past the limousines, a startling view of the lighted city came into view. He stopped and just looked for a moment. He could see from the moonlit Pacific in one direction to the towers of downtown in the other. The view alone was worth the price of the house, no matter how many millions that was.

The sound of soft music, laughter and conversation came from his left. He followed it down a stone path that curved along the form of the house. The drop-off to the houses down the hill was steep and deadly. He finally came to a flat yard that was lighted and full of people milling about beneath a tent as white as the moon. Bosch guessed there were at least a hundred and fifty well-dressed people sipping cocktails and taking small hors d'oeuvres off trays carried by young women wearing short black dresses, sheer stockings and white aprons. He wondered where the red vests were putting all the cars.

Bosch immediately felt underdressed and was sure he would be identified in seconds as a gate-crasher. But there was something so otherworldly about the scene that he held his ground.

A surfer in a suit approached him. He was about twenty-five, with short, sun-bleached hair and a dark tan. He wore a custom-fitted suit that looked as if it had cost more than every piece of clothing Bosch owned combined. It was light brown but the wearer probably described it as cocoa. He smiled the way enemies smile.

"Yes, sir, how are we doing tonight?"

"I'm doing fine. I don't know about you, yet."

The surfer in a suit smiled a little more brightly at that.

"I'm Mr. Johnson and I'm providing security for the benefit tonight. Might I inquire if you brought your invitation with you?"

Bosch hesitated for only a moment.

"Oh, I'm sorry. I didn't realize I needed to bring that along. I didn't think Gordon would need security at a benefit like this."

He hoped dropping Mittel's first name would give the surfer pause before he did anything rash. The surfer frowned for only a moment.

"Then could I ask you just to sign in for me?"

"Of course."

Bosch was led to a table to the side of the entrance area. Taped across the front of it was a red, white and blue banner that said ROBERT SHEPHERD NOW! It told Bosch all he needed to know about the affair.

There was a guest registry on the table and a woman sat behind it in a black crushed-velvet cocktail dress that did little to camouflage her breasts. Mr. Johnson seemed more intent on these two items than on Bosch as he signed the name Harvey Pounds in the registry.

As he signed, Bosch noticed a stack of pledge cards and a champagne goblet filled with pencils on the table. He picked up an information sheet and started to read about the unannounced candidate. Johnson finally pulled his eyes away from the table hostess and checked the name Bosch had written.

"Thank you, Mr. Pounds. Enjoy yourself."

He disappeared into the crowd then, probably to check on whether a

Harvey Pounds was on the list of invitees. Bosch decided he'd stay a few minutes, see if he could spot Mittel and then leave before the surfer came looking for him.

He stepped away from the entrance and out from beneath the tent. After crossing a short lawn to a retainer wall, he tried to act like he was just enjoying the view. And it was a view; the only higher one would have been from a jet coming in to LAX. But on the jet you wouldn't have the breadth of vision, the cool breeze, or the sounds from the city below.

Bosch turned around and looked back at the crowd under the tent. He studied the faces but could not spot Gordon Mittel. There was no sign of him. There was a large knot of people beneath the center of the tent and Bosch realized that it was a grouping of people trying to reach their hands toward the unannounced candidate, or at least the man Bosch assumed was Shepherd. Harry noticed that while the crowd seemed to exhibit solidarity in terms of wealth, it cut across all age lines. He guessed that many were there to see Mittel as much as Shepherd.

One of the women in black-and-white came out from under the white canopy and toward him with a tray of champagne glasses. He took one, thanked her, and turned back to the view. He sipped at it and supposed that it was top quality, but he wouldn't be able to tell the difference. He decided he should gulp it and go when a voice from his left interrupted.

"Wonderful view, isn't it? Better than a movie. I could stand here for hours."

Bosch turned his head to acknowledge the speaker but didn't look at him. He didn't want to get involved.

"Yeah, it's nice. But I'll take the mountains I have."

"Really? Where is that?"

"The other side of the hill. On Woodrow Wilson."

"Oh, yes. There are some very nice properties there."

Not mine, Bosch thought. Unless you like neoearthquake classic.

"The San Gabriels are brilliant in the sun," the conversationalist said. "I looked there but then I bought here."

Bosch turned. He was looking at Gordon Mittel. The host put out his hand.

"Gordon Mittel."

Bosch hesitated but then figured Mittel was used to people losing a step or stuttering in his presence.

"Harvey Pounds," Bosch said, taking his hand.

Mittel was wearing a black tuxedo. He was as overdressed for the crowd as Bosch was underdressed. His gray hair was cropped short and he had a smooth machine tan. He was as trim and tight as a rubber band stretched around a stack of hundreds and looked at least five to ten years younger than he was.

"Glad to meet you, glad you could come," he said. "Did you meet Robert yet?"

"No, he's kind of in the middle of the pack there."

"Yes, that's true. Well, he'll be happy to meet you when he gets the chance."

"I guess he'll be happy to take my check as well."

"That, too." Mittel smiled. "Seriously, though, I hope you can help us out. He's a good man and we need people like him in office."

His smile seemed so phony that Harry wondered if Mittel had already pegged him as a crasher. Bosch smiled back and patted the right breast of his jacket.

"I've got the checkbook right here."

Doing that, Bosch remembered what he really had in his pocket and got an idea. The champagne, though only a single glass, had emboldened him. He suddenly realized he wanted to spook Mittel and maybe get a look at his real colors.

"Tell me," he said, "is Shepherd the one?"

"I don't quite follow."

"Is he going all the way to the White House someday? Is he the one that's going to take you?"

Mittel sloughed off a frown or maybe it was a glimmer of annoyance.

"I guess we shall see. We've got to get him into the Senate first. That's the important thing."

Bosch nodded and made a show of scanning the crowd.

"Well, it looks like you have the right people here. But, you know, I don't see Arno Conklin. Are you still tight with him? He was your first, wasn't he?"

Mittel's forehead creased with a deep furrow.

"Well . . ." Mittel seemed to be uncomfortable, but then it quickly passed. "To tell the truth, we haven't spoken in a long time. He's retired now, an old man in a wheelchair. Do you know Arno?"

"Never spoken to him in my life."

"Then tell me, what prompts a question about ancient history?"

Bosch hiked his shoulders.

"I guess I'm just a student of history, that's all."

"What do you do for a living, Mr. Pounds? Or are you a full-time student?"

"I'm in law."

"We have something in common then."

"I doubt it."

"I'm a Stanford man. How about you?"

Bosch thought a moment.

"Vietnam."

Mittel frowned again and Bosch saw the interest go out of his eyes like water down a drain.

"Well, I tell you, I ought to mingle a little more. Watch the champagne, and if you decide you don't want to drive, one of the boys on the driveway can get you home. Ask for Manuel."

"The one in the red vest?"

"Uh, yes. One of them."

Bosch held up his glass.

"Don't worry, this is only my third."

Mittel nodded and disappeared back into the crowd. Bosch watched him cross beneath the tent, stop to shake a few hands, but eventually make it to the house. He entered through a wall of French doors into what looked like a living room or some sort of viewing area. Mittel walked to a couch and bent down to speak quietly to a man in a suit. This man looked to be about the same age as Mittel but with a harder appearance. He had a sharp face and, though sitting, clearly had a much heavier body. As a younger man he had probably used his strength, not his brain. Mittel straightened up and the other man just nodded. Mittel then disappeared into the further recesses of his house.

Bosch finished his glass of champagne and started moving through the crowd under the tent toward the house. As he got near the French doors, one of the black-and-white women asked if he needed help finding something. He said he was looking for the bathroom and she directed him to another door to the left. He went where he was told and found the door was locked. He waited for a few moments and the door finally opened, emitting a man and a woman. They giggled when they saw Bosch waiting and headed back to the tent.

Inside the bathroom Bosch opened his jacket and took a folded piece of paper from the inside pocket on the left. It was the photocopy of the Johnny Fox story that Keisha Russell had given him. He unfolded it and took out a pen. He circled the names Johnny Fox, Arno Conklin and Gordon Mittel, then, under the story, wrote, "What prior work experience got Johnny the job?"

He refolded the page twice and ran his fingers tightly over the creases. Then, on the outside, he wrote, "For Gordon Mittel Only!"

Back under the tent, Bosch found a black-and-white woman and gave her the folded paper.

"You have to find Mr. Mittel right away," he told her. "Give him this note. He's waiting on it."

He watched her go and then made his way back out through the crowd to the sign-in table at the entry area. He quickly bent over the guest registry and wrote his mother's name down. The table hostess protested that he had already signed in.

"This is for somebody else," he said.

For an address, he wrote Hollywood and Vista. He left the line for a telephone number blank.

Bosch scanned the crowd again and saw neither Mittel nor the woman he had given the note to. Then he looked into the room beyond the French doors and Mittel appeared with the note in his hand. He walked slowly into the room, studying it. Bosch could tell by the direction of his eyes that he was studying the note scribbled on the bottom. Even with his phony tan, he seemed to Bosch to go pale.

Bosch took a step back into the entrance alcove and watched. He could feel his heart beating at a quicker pace. He felt like he was watching some secret play on a stage.

There was a look of perplexed anger on Mittel's face now. Bosch saw him hand the page to the rough man who still sat in the cushioned chair. Then Mittel turned to the glass panels and looked out at the people under the tent. He said something and Bosch thought he could read his lips.

"Son of a bitch."

Then he started talking more quickly, barking orders. The man on the chair rose and Bosch knew instinctively that it was his cue to leave. He walked quickly back out to the driveway and trotted down to the group of men in red vests. He handed his valet ticket and a ten-dollar bill to one of them and said in Spanish that he was in a great hurry.

Still, it seemed to take forever. As he waited nervously, Bosch kept his eyes on the house, waiting for the rough man to appear. He had watched which direction the valet had gone for his car and he was ready to bolt that way if necessary. He began to wish he had his gun. Whether he really needed it or not did not matter. In this moment he knew it gave him a sense of security that he felt naked without.

The surfer in a suit appeared at the top of the driveway and strode down toward Bosch. At the same time, Bosch saw his Mustang approaching. He walked out into the street, ready to take it. The surfer got to him first.

"Hey, buddy, hold on a sec—"

Bosch turned from his approaching car and hit him in the jaw, sending him backward onto the driveway. He moaned and rolled onto his side, both hands clutching his jaw. Bosch was sure the jaw was dislocated if not broken. He shook away the pain in his hand as the Mustang screeched to a stop.

The man in the red vest was slow in getting out. Bosch pulled him away from the open door and jumped in. As he settled in behind the wheel he looked up the driveway and saw the rough man was now coming. When he saw the surfer on the ground, he started running but his steps were unsteady on the downgrade of the driveway. Bosch saw his heavy thighs pressing the fabric of his pants and suddenly he slipped and fell. Two of the red vests went to help him up but he angrily shoved them away.

Bosch gunned the car and sped away. He worked his way up to Mulholland and turned east toward home. He could feel adrenaline surging through him. Not only had he gotten away, but it was clear he had struck a nerve with a hammer. Let Mittel think about that for a while, he thought. Let him sweat. Then he yelled out loud in the car, though no one could hear except himself.

"Spooked ya, didn't I, you fuck!"

He banged his palm triumphantly on the steering wheel.

He dreamed of the coyote again. The animal was on a mountain path where there were no homes, no cars, no people. It was moving very quickly through the dark as if it was trying to get away. But the path and place were his. He knew the land and knew he would escape. What it was he fled from was never clear, never seen. But it was there, behind him in the dark. And the coyote knew by instinct it must get away.

The phone woke Bosch, breaking into the dream like a knife stabbed through paper. Bosch pulled the pillow off his head, rolled to his right and his eyes were immediately assaulted by the light of dawn. He had forgotten to close the blinds. He reached for the phone on the floor.

"Hold on," he said.

He put the phone down on the bed, sat up and rubbed a hand across his face. He squinted at the clock. It was ten minutes after seven. He coughed and cleared his throat, then picked the phone back up.

"Yeah."

"Detective Bosch?"

"Yeah."

"It's Brad Hirsch. I'm sorry to call so early."

Bosch had to think a moment. Brad Hirsch? He had no idea who it was.

"Yeah, it's okay," he said while he continued to search his mind for the name.

A silence followed.

"I'm the one . . . In Latents? Remember, you—"

"Hirsch? Yeah, Hirsch. I remember. What's up?"

"I wanted to tell you I made the AFIS run you wanted. I came in early and ran it with another search I'm doing for Devonshire Homicide. I don't think anybody will know."

Bosch kicked his legs over the side of the bed, opened a drawer in the bed table and took out a pad and a pencil. He noticed that he had taken the pad from the Surf and Sand Hotel in Laguna Beach. He remembered he had spent a few days with Sylvia there the year before.

"Yeah, you made the run? What'd you get?"

"Well, that's the thing. I'm sorry but I got nothing."

Bosch threw the pad back into the open drawer and threw himself backward on the bed.

"No hits?"

"Well, the computer came up with two candidates. I then did a visual comparison and it was no good. No matches. I'm sorry. I know this case means . . ."

He didn't finish.

"You took it through all the data bases?"

"Every one on our network."

"Let me ask you something. All those data bases, do they include DA's employees and LAPD personnel?"

There was silence as Hirsch must have been mulling over what the question might mean.

"You there, Hirsch?"

"Yes. The answer is yes."

"How far back? You know what I mean? These bases have prints going how far back?"

"Well, each data base is different. The LAPD's is extensive. I'd say we have prints on everybody who's worked here since World War II."

Well, that clears Irving and the rest of the cops, Bosch thought. But that didn't bother him much. His sights were definitely somewhere else.

"What about people working for the DA?"

"The DA's office would be different," Hirsch said. "I don't think they started printing employees until the middle sixties."

Conklin had been there during that time, Bosch knew, but he would already have been elected DA. It would seem that he would not have submitted his own prints, especially if he knew there was a print card in a murder book somewhere that could possibly be matched to him.

He thought of Mittel. He would have been out of the DA's office by the time employees' prints were taken as a matter of course.

"What about the federal base?" he asked. "What if some guy worked for a president and got the kind of clearance you need to go visit the White House, would those prints be in that base?"

"Yes, they'd be in twice. In the federal employees base and in the FBI's. They keep prints on record of everyone they do background investigations on, if that's what you mean. But remember, just because somebody visits the president, it doesn't mean they get printed."

Well, Mittel isn't a scratch but it's close, Bosch thought.

"So what you're saying," Bosch said, "is that whether or not we have complete data files going back to 1961, whoever belongs to those prints I gave you hasn't been printed since then?"

"That's not one hundred percent but it's close. The person who left these prints probably hasn't been printed—at least by any contributor to the data banks. We can only reach so far with this. One way or another we can pull prints on one out of about every fifty or so people in the country. But I just didn't get anything this time. Sorry."

"That's okay, Hirsch, you tried."

"Well, I guess I'll be getting back to work now. What do you want me to do with the print card?"

Bosch thought a moment. He wondered if there was any other avenue to chase down.

"Tell you what, can you just hold on to it? I'll come by the lab and pick it up when I can. Probably be by later today."

"Okay, I'll put it in an envelope for you in case I'm not here. Good-bye."

"Hey, Hirsch?"

"Yeah?"

"It feels good, don't it?"

"What's that?"

"You did the right thing. You didn't get a match but you did the right thing."

"Yeah, I guess."

He was acting like he didn't understand because he was embarrassed, but he understood.

"Yeah, I'll see you, Hirsch."

After hanging up, Bosch sat on the side of the bed, lit a cigarette and thought about what he was going to do with the day. The news from Hirsch was not good but it wasn't daunting. It certainly didn't clear Arno Conklin. It might not even have cleared Gordon Mittel. Bosch wasn't sure whether Mittel's work for presidents and senators would have required a fingerprint check. He decided his investigation was still intact. He wasn't changing any plans.

He thought about the night before and the wild-ass chance he had taken confronting Mittel the way he had. He smiled at his own recklessness and thought about what Hinojos might make of it. He knew she'd say it was a symptom of his problem. She wouldn't see it as a tactful way of flushing the bird from the bush.

He got up and started the coffee and then showered, shaved and got ready for the day. He took his coffee and the box of cereal from the refrigerator out to the deck, leaving the sliding door open so he could hear the stereo. He had KFWB news on.

It was cool and crisp outside but he could tell it would get warmer later. Blue jays were swooping in and out of the arroyo below the deck and he could see black bees the size of quarters working in the yellow flowers of the primrose jasmine.

There was a story on the radio about a building contractor making a fourteen-million-dollar bonus for completing the rebuilding of the 10 freeway three months ahead of schedule. The officials who gathered to announce the engineering feat likened the fallen freeway to the city itself. Now that it was back upright, so, too, was the city. The city was on the move again. They had a lot to learn, Bosch thought.

Afterward, he went in and got out the yellow pages and started working the phone in the kitchen. He called the major airlines, shopped around and made arrangements to fly to Florida. But flying on one day's notice, the best deal he could get was still seven hundred dollars, a shocking amount to him. He put it on a credit card so that he could pay it off over time. He also reserved a rental car at Tampa International Airport.

When he had that finished he went back out to the deck and thought about the next project he had to tackle:

He needed a badge.

For a long time he sat on the deck chair and contemplated whether he needed it for his own sense of security or because it was a bona fide necessity to his mission. He knew how naked and vulnerable he had felt this week without the gun and the badge, extremities he had carried on his body for more than twenty years. But he had avoided the temptation to carry the back-up gun that he knew was in the closet next to the front door. That he could do, he knew. But the badge was different. More so than the gun, the badge was the symbol of what he was. It opened doors better than any key, it gave him more authority than any words, than any weapon. He decided the badge was a necessity. If he was going to Florida and was going to scam McKittrick, he had to look legit. He had to have a badge.

He knew his badge was probably in a desk drawer in Assistant Chief Irving S. Irving's office. There was no way he could get to it and not be discovered. But he knew where there was another one that would work just as well.

Bosch looked at his watch. Nine-fifteen. It was forty-five minutes until the daily command meeting at Hollywood Station. He had plenty of time.

Bosch pulled into the rear parking lot of the station at five minutes after ten. He was sure that Pounds, who was punctual about everything he did, would already have gone down the front hall to the captain's office with the overnight logs. The meeting was held every morning and included the station's CO, patrol captain, watch lieutenant and detective commander, who was Pounds. They were routine affairs and never lasted longer than twenty minutes. The members of the station's command staff simply drank coffee and went through the overnight reports and ongoing problems, complaints or investigations of particular note.

Bosch went in the back door by the drunk tank and then up the hallway to the detective bureau. It had been a busy morning. There were already four men handcuffed to benches in the hallway. One of them, a drug hype Bosch had seen in the station before and used as an unreliable informant on occasion, asked Bosch for a smoke. It was illegal to smoke in any city-owned building. Bosch lit a cigarette anyway and put it in the man's mouth because both his needle-scarred arms were cuffed behind his back.

"What is it this time, Harley?" Bosch asked.

"Shit, a guy leaves his g'rage open, he's asking me to come in. Isn't that right?"

"Tell that one to the judge."

As Bosch walked away one of the other lockdowns yelled at him from down the hallway.

"What about me, man? I need a smoke."

"I'm out," Bosch said.

"Fuck you, man."

"Yeah, that's what I thought."

He came into the detective bureau through the rear door. The first thing he did was confirm that Pounds's glass office was empty. He was at the command meeting. Then he checked the coatrack up at the front and saw he was in business. As he walked down the aisle formed by the separation of the investigation tables, he exchanged nods with a few of the other detectives.

Edgar was at the homicide table sitting across from his new partner, who was in Bosch's old chair. Edgar heard one of the "Hi, Harry" greetings and turned around.

"Harry, wassup?"

"Hey, man, just came in to get a couple things. Hang on a sec, it's hot outside."

Bosch walked to the front of the bureau, where old Henry of the Nod Squad sat at the desk behind the counter. He was working on a crossword puzzle and Bosch could see several erasure marks had turned the grid gray.

"Henry, howzit hanging? You getting anywhere with that?"

"Detective Bosch."

Bosch slipped his sport coat off and hung it on a hook on the rack next to a jacket with a gray cross-hatch pattern. It was on a hanger and Bosch knew it belonged to Pounds. As he put his coat on the hook with his back to Henry and the rest of the bureau, he snaked his left hand inside the other coat, felt for the interior pocket and then pulled out Pounds's badge wallet. He knew it would be there. Pounds was a creature of habit and Bosch had seen the badge wallet in the suit coat once before. He put the wallet into his pants pocket and turned around as Henry continued talking. Bosch had only a momentary tinge of hesitation at the seriousness of what he was doing. Taking another cop's badge was a crime, but Bosch looked at Pounds as being the reason he did not have his own badge. In the inventory of his morality, what Pounds had done to him was equally wrong.

"If you want to see the lieutenant, he's down the hall at a meeting," Henry said.

"No, I don't want to see the lieutenant, Henry. In fact, don't even tell him I was here. I don't want his blood pressure to go up, you know. I'm just going to get a few things and get out of here, okay?"

"That's a deal. I don't want him cranky, either."

Bosch didn't have to worry about anyone else in the bureau telling Pounds he had been in. He gave Henry a friendly clasp on the shoulder as he walked behind him, sealing the agreement. He went back to the homicide table and as he approached, Burns began to rise from Bosch's old spot.

"You need to get in here, Harry?" he asked.

Bosch thought he could detect nervous energy in the other man's voice. He understood his predicament and wasn't going to make it a difficult time for him.

"Yeah, if you don't mind," he said. "I figured I'd get my personal stuff out of there so you can move in the right way."

Bosch came around and opened the drawer at the table. There were two boxes of Junior Mints on top of old paperwork that had been shoved in long ago.

"Oh, those are mine, sorry," Burns said.

He reached in for the two boxes of candy and stood next to the table, holding them like a big kid in a suit while Bosch went through the paperwork.

It was all a show. Bosch took some of the paperwork and dumped it in a manila file and then pointed with his hand, signaling to Burns he could put his candy back.

"Be careful, Bob."

"It's Bill. Careful of what?"

"Ants."

Bosch went to the bank of file cabinets that ran along the wall to the side of the table and opened one of the drawers with his business card taped to it. It was three up from the bottom, waist-high, and it was one he knew was almost empty. With his back to the table again, he pulled the badge wallet out of his pocket and put it in the drawer. Then, with his hands in the drawer and out of sight, he opened the wallet and took out the gold badge. He then put it in one pocket and the wallet back in the other. For good measure, he pulled a file out of the drawer and closed it.

He turned around and looked at Jerry Edgar.

"Okay, that's it. Just some personal stuff I might need. Anything going on?"

"Nah, quiet."

Back at the coatrack, Bosch turned his back on the bureau again and used one hand to reach for his coat while using the other to take the badge wallet from his pocket and slip it back into Pounds's coat. He then put his coat on, said good-bye to Henry and went back to the homicide table.

"I'm outta here," he said to Edgar and Burns while picking up the two files he had pulled. "I don't want Ninety-eight to see me and throw a fit. Good luck, boys."

On the way out, Bosch stopped and gave the hype another cigarette. The lockdown who had complained before was no longer on the bench or Bosch would have given him one, too.

Back in the Mustang, he dumped the files on the backseat and took his empty badge wallet out of his briefcase. He slipped Pounds's badge into place next to his own ID card. It would work, he decided, as long as no one looked too closely at it. The badge said LIEUTENANT across it. Bosch's ID card identified him as a detective. It was a minor discrepancy and Bosch was happy with it. Best of all, he thought, there was a good chance Pounds would not notice that the badge was missing for some time. He rarely left the station to go to crime scenes and so rarely had to open the wallet or show his badge. There was a good chance its disappearance would go unnoticed. All he had to do was get it back into place when he was done with it.

Bosch ended up outside the door of Carmen Hinojos's office early for his afternoon session. He waited until exactly three-thirty and knocked. She smiled as he entered her office and he noticed that the late-afternoon sun came through the window and splashed light directly across her desk. He moved toward the chair he usually took but then stopped himself and sat on the chair to the left of the desk. She noticed this and frowned at him as if he were a schoolboy.

"If you think I care which chair you sit in, you are wrong."

"Am I? Okay."

He got up and moved to the other chair. He liked being near the window.

"I might not be here for Monday's session," he said after settling in.

She frowned again, this time more seriously.

"Why not?"

"I'm going away. I'll try to be back."

"Away? What happened to your investigation?"

"It's part of it. I'm going to Florida to track down one of the original investigators. One's dead, the other one's in Florida. So I've got to go to him."

"Couldn't you just call?"

"I don't want to call. I don't want to give him the chance to put me off."

She nodded.

"When do you leave?"

"Tonight. I'm taking a red-eye to Tampa."

"Harry, look at you. You practically look like the walking dead. Can't you get some sleep and take a plane in the morning?"

"No, I've gotta get out there before the mail arrives."

"What's that mean?"

"Nothing. It's a long story. Anyway, I wanted to ask you something. I need your help."

She contemplated this for several seconds, apparently weighing how far she wanted to go into the pool without knowing how deep it was.

"What is it you want?"

"Do you ever do any forensic work for the department?"

She narrowed her eyes, not seeing where this was going.

"A little. From time to time somebody will bring me something, or maybe ask me to do a little profiling of a suspect. But mostly the department uses outside contractors. Forensic psychiatrists who have experience with this."

"But you've been to crime scenes?"

"Actually, no. I've only looked at photos brought to me and worked from them."

"Perfect."

Bosch pulled his briefcase onto his lap and opened it. He took out the envelope of crime scene and autopsy photos that had been in the murder book and gently placed them on her desk.

"Those are from this case. I don't want to look at them. I can't look at them. But I need someone to do it and tell me what's there. There's probably nothing but I'd like another opinion. The investigation these two guys did on this case was . . . well, it was almost like there was no investigation."

"Oh, Harry." She shook her head. "I'm not sure this is wise. Why me?"

"Because you know what I'm doing. And because I trust you. I don't think I can trust anybody else."

"Would you trust me if there was no ethical constraint on me telling others about what we've talked about here?"

Bosch studied her face.

"I don't know," he finally said.

"I thought so."

She slid the envelope to the side of the desk.

"Let's put these aside for now and go on with the session. I really have to think about this."

"Okay, you can take them. But let me know, okay? I just want your feel for them. As a psychiatrist and as a woman."

"We'll see."

"What do you want to talk about?"

"What is happening with the investigation?"

"Is that a professional question, Dr. Hinojos? Or are you just curious about the case?"

"No, I'm curious about you. And I'm worried about you. I'm still not convinced that what you are doing is safe—either psychologically or physically. You're mucking around in the lives of powerful people. And I'm caught in the middle. I know what you're doing but am almost powerless to make you stop. I'm afraid you tricked me."

"Tricked you?"

"You pulled me into this. I bet you've wanted to show me these pictures since you told me what you're doing."

"You're right, I have. But there was no trick. I thought this was a place where I could talk about anything. Isn't that what you said?"

"Okay, I wasn't tricked, just led down the path. I should've seen it coming. Let's move on. I want to talk more about the emotional aspect of what you are doing. I want to know more about why finding this killer is so important to you after so many years."

"It should be obvious."

"Make it more obvious for me."

"I can't. I can't put it into words. All I know is that everything changed for me after she was gone. I don't know how things would have been if she hadn't been taken away but . . . everything changed."

"Do you understand what you're saying and what it means? You're looking at your life in two parts. The first part is with her, which you seem to have imbued with a happiness I'm sure was not always there. The second part is your life after, which you acknowledge has not met expectations or is in some way unsatisfactory. I think you've been unhappy for a long time, possibly all of that time. This recent relationship you had may have been a highlight but you were still and, I think, have always been, an unhappy man."

She rested a moment but Bosch didn't speak. He knew she wasn't done.

"Now, maybe the traumas of the last few years—both personally for you and for your community at large—have made you take stock of yourself. And I fear that you believe, whether subconsciously or not, that by going back and bringing some form of justice to what happened to your mother, you will be righting your life. And there's the problem. Whatever happens with this private investigation of yours, it's not going to change things. It just can't be done."

"You're saying that I can't blame what happened then for what I am now?"

"No, listen to me, Harry. All I'm saying is you are the sum of many parts, not the sum of one. It's like dominoes. Several different blocks must click together for you to arrive at the end, at the point you are at now. You don't jump from the first domino to the last."

"So I should just give it up? Just let it go?"

"I'm not saying that. But I am finding it hard to see the emotional benefit or healing you will get from this. In fact, I think there is the possibility that you may do yourself more damage than repair. Does that make any sense?"

Bosch stood up and went to the window. He stared out but didn't compute what he saw. He felt the warmth of the sun on him. He didn't look at her as he spoke.

"I don't know what makes sense. All I know is that on every level it seems to make sense that I do this. In fact, I feel . . . I don't know what the word is, maybe ashamed. I feel ashamed that I haven't done this long before now. A lot of years have gone by and I just let them go. I feel like I let her down somehow . . . that I let myself down."

"That's understa—"

"Remember what I told you the first day? Everybody counts or nobody counts. Well, for a long time she didn't count. Not with this department, this society, not even with me. I have to admit that, not even with me. Then I opened that file this week and I could see that her death was just put away. It was buried, just like I had buried it. Somebody put the fix in because she didn't count. They did it because they could. And then when I think about how long I've let it go . . . it makes me want to . . . I don't know, just hide my face or something."

He stopped, unable to put into words what he wanted to say. He looked down and noticed there were no ducks in the butcher shop window.

"You know," he said, "she might've been what she was but sometimes I feel like I didn't even deserve that . . . I guess I got what I deserved in life."

He stayed at the window, not looking at her. It was several moments before Hinojos spoke.

"I guess this is the point where I should tell you that you're being too hard on yourself, but I don't think that would help much."

"No, it wouldn't."

"Could you come back here and sit down? Please?"

Bosch did as he was asked. Finally, after he was seated, his eyes met hers. She spoke first.

"What I want to say is that you are mixing things up. Putting the cart before the horse. You can't take the blame because this case may have been covered up. First of all, you had nothing to do with that, and secondly, you didn't even realize that until you read through the file this week."

"But don't you see? Why didn't I look at it before? I'm not new here. I've been a cop twenty years. I should've been there before this. I mean, so what that I didn't know the details. I knew she was killed and nothing was ever done about it. That was enough."

"Look, Harry, think about this, okay? On the plane over tonight, just give it some thought. You've engaged yourself in a noble pursuit but you have to safeguard against damaging yourself further. The bottom line is that it is not worth that. It's not worth the toll you may have to pay."

"Not worth it? There's a killer out there. He thinks he made it away free. For years, he has thought that. Decades. And I'm going to change that."

"You're not understanding what I'm saying. I don't want any guilty person to get away, especially with murder. But what I am talking about here is you. You are my only concern here. There is a basic rule of nature. No living thing sacrifices itself or hurts itself needlessly. It's the will of survival and I fear the circumstances of your life may have blunted your own survival skills. You may be throwing it to the wind, not caring what happens to you emotionally, physically, in every way, in this pursuit. I don't want to see you hurt."

She took a breather. He said nothing.

"I have to say," she continued quietly, "I'm very nervous about this. I've never had this situation come up before and I've counseled a lot of cops in nine years here."

"Well, I got bad news for you." He smiled. "I went and crashed a party last night at Mittel's. I think I may have spooked him. At least, I spooked myself."

"Shit!"

"Is that some new psychiatric term? I'm not familiar with it."

"This isn't funny. Why'd you do that?"

Bosch thought a moment.

"I don't know. It was kind of a whim type of thing. I was just driving by his house and there was a party. It kind of . . . it just made me angry for some reason. Him having a party and my mother . . ."

"Did you speak to him about the case?"

"No. I didn't even tell him my name. We just kind've sparred around for a few minutes but then I left him something. Remember that newspaper clip I showed you Wednesday? I left that for him. I saw him read it. I think it struck a nerve."

She exhaled loudly.

"Now, step outside yourself and look as an uninvolved observer at what you did. If you can. Was that a smart thing to do, going there like that?"

"I already have thought about it. No, it wasn't smart. It was a mistake. He'll probably warn Conklin. They'll both know somebody's out there, coming for them. They'll close ranks."

"You see, you are proving my point for me. I want you to promise me you won't do anything foolish like that again."

"I can't."

"Well, then I have to tell you that a patient-doctor relationship can be broken if the therapist believes the patient is endangering himself or others. I told you I was almost powerless to stop you. Not completely."

"You'd go to Irving?"

"I will if I believe you are being reckless."

Bosch felt anger as he realized she had ultimate control over him and what he was doing. He swallowed the anger and held up his hands, surrendering.

"All right. I won't go crashing any parties again."

"No. I want more than that. I want you to stay away from these men that you think may have been involved."

"What I'll promise you is that I won't go to them until I have the whole thing in the bag."

"I mean it."

"So do I."

"I hope so."

They were silent for nearly a minute after that. It was a cooling-off period. She turned slightly in her chair, not looking at him, probably thinking what to say next.

"Let's move on," she finally said. "You understand that this whole thing, this pursuit of yours, has eclipsed what we're supposed to be doing here?"

"I know."

"So we're prolonging my evaluation."

"Well, that doesn't bother me as much anymore. I need the time off the job for this other thing."

"Well, as long as you are happy," she said sarcastically. "Okay, then I want to go back to the incident that brought you to me. The other day you were very general and very short in your description of what happened. I understand why. I think we were both feeling each other out at that point. But we are far past that now. I'd like a fuller story. You said the other day that Lieutenant Pounds set things into motion?"

"That's right."

"How?"

"First of all, he's a commander of detectives who has never been a detective himself. Oh, technically, he probably spent a few months on a table somewhere along the line so he'd have it on his résumé, but basically he's an administrator. He's what we call a Robocrat. A bureaucrat with a badge. He doesn't know the first thing about clearing cases. The only thing he knows about it is how to draw a line through the case on this little chart he keeps in his office. He doesn't know the first thing about the differences between an interview and an interrogation. And that's fine, the department is full of people like him. I say let them do their job and let me do mine. The problem is Pounds doesn't realize where he's good and where he's bad. It's led to problems before. Confrontations. It finally led to the incident, as you keep calling it."

"What did he do?"

"He touched my suspect."

"Explain what that means."

"When you've got a case and you bring someone in, he's all yours. Nobody goes near him, understand? The wrong word, the wrong question and it could spoil a case. That's a cardinal rule; don't touch somebody else's suspect. It doesn't matter if you're a lieutenant or the damn chief, you stay clear until you check first with the guys with the collar."

"So what happened?"

"Like I told you the other day, my partner Edgar and I brought in this suspect. A woman had been killed. One of these ones who puts ads in the sex tabs you can buy on the Boulevard. She gets called to one of those shithole motel rooms on Sunset, has sex with the guy and ends up stabbed to death. That's the short story. The stab wound's to the upper right chest. The john, he plays it cool, though. He calls the cops and says it was her knife and she tried to rob him with it. He says he turned her arm and put it into her. Self-defense. Okay, so that's when me and Edgar show up and right away we see some things don't fit with that story."

"Like what?"

"First of all, she's a lot smaller than he is. I don't see her coming at him with a knife. Then there's the knife itself. It's a serrated steak knife, 'bout eight inches long, and she had one of those little purses without a strap."

"A clutch."

"Yeah, I guess. Anyway, that knife wouldn't've fit in it, so how'd she bring it in? As they say on the street, her clothes fit tighter than the rubbers in her purse, so she wasn't hiding it on her, either. And there was more. If her purpose was to rip the guy off, why have sex first? Why not pull the knife, take his shit and go? But that didn't happen. His story was that they did it first, then she came at him, which explained why she was still naked. Which, of course, raised another question. Why rob the guy when you're naked? Where you going to run like that?"

"The guy was lying."

"Seemed obvious. Then we got something else. In her purse—the clutch—was a piece of paper on which she had written down the motel's name and the room number. It was consistent with a right-handed person. Like I said, the stab was to the upper right chest of the victim. So it doesn't add up. If she came at him, the chances are the knife would be in her right hand. If the john then turns it into her, it's likely the wound would be on the left side of the chest, not the right."

Bosch made a motion of pulling his right hand toward his chest, showing how awkward it would be for it to stab his right side.

"There was all kinds of stuff that wasn't right. It was a downward-grade wound, also inconsistent with it being in her hand. That would have been upward-grade."

Hinojos nodded that she understood.

"The problem was, we had no physical evidence contradicting his story. Nothing. Just our feeling that she wouldn't have done it the way he said. The wound stuff wasn't enough. And then, in his favor, was the knife. It was on the bed, we could see it had fingerprints in the blood. I had no doubt they'd be hers. That's not hard to do once she's dead. So while it didn't impress me, that didn't matter. It's what the DA would think and then what a jury would think after that. Reasonable doubt is a big black hole that swallows cases like this. We needed more."

"So what happened?"

"It's what we call a he-said-she-said. One person's word against the other, but only the other is dead in this case. Makes it even harder. We had nothing but his story. So what you do in a case like that is you sweat the guy. You turn him. And there's a lot of ways to do it. But, basically, you gotta break him down in the rooms. We—"

"The rooms?"

"The interrogation rooms. In the bureau. We took this guy into a room. As a witness. We didn't formally arrest him. We asked if he'd come down, said that we had to straighten a few things out about what she did, and he said sure. You know, Mr. Cooperative. Still cool. We stuck him in a room and then Edgar and I went down to the watch office to get some of the good coffee. They've got good coffee there, one of those big urns that was donated by some restaurant that got wrecked in the quake. Everybody goes in there to get coffee. Anyway, we're takin' our time, talkin' about how we're going to go at this guy, which one of us wanted him first, and so on. Meantime, fuckin' Pounds—excuse me—sees the guy in the room through the little window and goes in and informs him. And—"

"What do you mean, informs him?"

"Reads him his rights. This is our goddamn witness and Pounds, who doesn't know what the hell he's doing, thinks he's gotta go in there and give the guy the spiel. He thinks like we forgot or something."

Bosch looked at her with outrage on his face but immediately saw she didn't understand.

"Wasn't that the right thing to do?" she asked. "Aren't you required by law to inform people of their rights?"

Bosch struggled to contain his anger, reminding himself that Hinojos might work for the department, but she was an outsider. Her perceptions of police work were likely based more on the media than on the actual reality.

"Let me give you a quick lesson on what's the law and what's real. We—the cops—have the deck stacked against us. What *Miranda* and all the other rules and regs amount to is that we have to take some guy we know is, or at least think is, guilty and basically say, 'Hey, look, we think you did it and the Supreme Court and every lawyer on the planet would advise you not to talk to us, but, how about it, will you talk to us?' It just doesn't work. You gotta get around that. You gotta use guile and some bluffing and you gotta be sneaky. The rules of the courts are like a tightrope that you're walking on. You have to be very careful but there is a chance you can walk on it to get to the other side. So when some asshole who doesn't know shit walks in on your guy and informs him, it can pretty much ruin your whole day, not to mention the case."

He stopped and studied her. He still saw skepticism. He knew then that she was just another citizen who would be scared shitless if she ever got a dose of the way things really were on the street.

"When someone is informed, that's it," he said. "It's over. Me and Edgar came back in from coffee and the john sits there and says he thinks he wants his lawyer. I said, 'What lawyer, who's talking about lawyers? You're a witness, not a suspect,' and he tells us that the lieutenant just read him his rights. I don't know at that moment who I hated more, Pounds for blowing it or this guy for killing the girl."

"Well, tell me this, what would have happened if Pounds had not done what he did?"

"We would've made friendly with the guy, asked him to tell his story in as much detail as possible and hoped there would be inconsistencies when compared to what he'd told the uniforms. Then we would have said, 'The inconsistencies in your statements make you a suspect.' *Then* we would have informed him and hopefully clubbed the shit out of him with the inconsistencies and the problems we found with the scene. We would have tried, and maybe succeeded, in finessing a confession. Most of what we do is just get people to talk. It's not like the stuff on T,V. It's a hundred times harder and dirtier. But just like you, what we do is get people to talk . . . Anyway, that's my view. But we'll never know now what could've happened because of Pounds."

"Well, what did happen after you found out he'd been informed?"

"I left the room and walked straight into where Pounds was in his office. He knew something was wrong because he stood up. I remember that. I asked him if he'd informed my guy and when he said yes, we got into it. Both of us, screaming . . . then I don't really remember how it happened. I'm not trying to deny anything. I just don't remember the details. I must've grabbed him and pushed him. And his face went through the glass."

"What did you do when that happened?"

"Well, some of the guys came running in and pulled me out of there. The station commander sent me home. Pounds had to go to the hospital to fix his nose. IAD took a statement from him and I was suspended. And then Irving stepped in and changed it to ISL. Here I am."

"What happened with the case?"

"The john never talked. He got his lawyer and waited it out. Edgar went with what we had to the DA last Friday and they kicked it. They said they weren't going into court with a no-witness case with a few minor inconsistencies . . . Her prints were on the knife. Big surprise. What it came down to is that she didn't count. At least not enough for them to take the chance of losing."

Neither of them spoke for a few moments. Bosch guessed that she was thinking about the corollaries between this case and his mother's.

"So what we've got," he finally said, "is a murderer out there on the street and the guy who allowed him to go free is back behind his desk, the broken glass already replaced, business as usual. That's our system. I got mad about it and look what it got me. Stress leave and maybe the end of my job."

She cleared her throat before going into her appraisal of the story.

"As you have set down the circumstances of what happened, it is quite easy to see your rage. But not the ultimate action you took. Have you ever heard the phrase, 'a mad minute?'"

Bosch shook his head.

"It's a way of describing a violent outburst that has its roots in several pressures on an individual. It builds up and is released in a quick moment—usually violently, often against a target not wholly responsible for the pressure."

"If you need me to say Pounds was an innocent victim, I'm not going to say it."

"I don't need that. I just need you to look at this situation and how it could happen."

"I don't know. Shit just happens."

"When you physically attack someone, don't you feel that you lower yourself to the same level as the man who was set free?"

"Not by a long shot, Doctor. Let me tell you something, you can look at all parts of my life, you can throw in earthquakes, fires, floods, riots and even Vietnam, but when it came down to just me and Pounds in that glass room, none of that mattered. You can call it a mad minute or whatever you want. Sometimes, the moment is all that matters and in that moment I was doing the right thing. And if these sessions are designed to make me see I did something wrong, forget it. Irving buttonholed me the other day in the lobby and asked me to think about an apology. Fuck that. I did the right thing."

She nodded, adjusted herself in her seat and looked more uncomfortable than she had through his long diatribe. Finally, she looked at her watch and he looked at his. His time was up.

"So," he said, "I guess I've set the cause of psychotherapy back a century, huh?"

"No, not at all. The more you know of a person and the more you know of a story, the more you understand how things happen. It's why I enjoy my job."

"Same here."

"Have you spoken to Lieutenant Pounds since the incident?"

"I saw him when I dropped off the keys to my car. He had it taken away. I went into his office and he practically got hysterical. He's a very small man and I think he knows it."

"They usually do."

Bosch leaned forward, ready to get up and leave, when he noticed the envelope she had pushed to the side of her desk.

"What about the photos?"

"I knew you'd bring that up one more time."

She looked at the envelope and frowned.

"I need to think about it. On several levels. Can I keep them while you go to Florida? Or will you need them?"

"You can keep 'em."

At four-forty in the morning California time the air carrier landed at Tampa International Airport. Bosch leaned bleary-eyed against a window in the coach cabin, watching the sun rising in the Florida sky for the first time. As the plane taxied, he took off his watch and moved the hands ahead three hours. He was tempted to check into the nearest motel for some real sleep but knew he didn't have the time. From the AAA map he had brought with him, it looked like it was at least a two-hour drive down to Venice.

"It's nice to see a blue sky."

It was the woman next to him in the aisle seat. She was leaning over toward him, looking out the window herself. She was in her mid-forties with prematurely gray hair. It was almost white. They had talked a bit in the early part of the flight and Bosch knew she was heading back to Florida rather than visiting as he was. She had given L.A. five years but had had enough. She was going home. Bosch didn't ask who or what she was coming home to, but had wondered if her hair was white when she had first landed in L.A. five years before.

"Yeah," he replied. "These night flights take forever."

"No, I meant the smog. There is none."

Bosch looked at her and then out the window, studying the sky. "Not yet."

But she was right. The sky had a quality of blue he rarely saw in L.A. It was the color of swimming pools, with billowing white cumulus clouds floating like dreams in the upper atmosphere.

The plane cleared out slowly. Bosch waited until the end, got up and rolled his back to relieve the tension. The joints of his backbone cracked like dominoes going down. He got his overnighter out of the compartment above and headed out.

As soon as he stepped off the plane into the jetway, the humidity surrounded him like a wet towel with an incubating warmth. He made it into the air-conditioned terminal and decided to scratch his plan to rent a convertible.

A half hour later he was on the 275 freeway crossing Tampa Bay in another rented Mustang. He had the windows up and the air conditioning on but he was sweating as his body still had not acclimated to the humidity.

What struck him most about Florida on this first drive was its flatness. For forty-five minutes not a hillrise came in sight until he reached the concrete-and-steel mountain called the Skyway Bridge. Bosch knew that the steeply graded bridge over the mouth of the bay was a replacement for one that had fallen but he drove across it fearlessly and above the speed limit. After all, he came from postquake Los Angeles, where the unofficial speed limit *under* bridges and overpasses was on the far right side of the speedometer.

After the skyway the freeway merged with the 75 and he reached Venice two hours after landing. Cruising along the Tamiami Trail, he found the small pastel-painted motels inviting as he struggled with fatigue, but he drove on and looked for a gift shop and a pay phone.

He found both in the Coral Reef Shopping Plaza. The Tacky's Gifts and Cards store wasn't due to open until ten and Bosch had five minutes to waste. He went to a pay phone on the outside wall of the sand-colored plaza and looked up the post office in the book. There were two in town so Bosch took out his notebook and checked Jake McKittrick's zip code. He called one of the post offices listed in the book and learned that the other one catered to the zip code Bosch had. He thanked the clerk who had provided the information and hung up.

When the gift shop opened, Bosch went to the cards aisle and found a birthday card that came with a bright red envelope. He took it to the counter without even reading the inside or the outside of the card. He picked a local street map out of a display next to the cash register and put that on the counter as well.

"That's a nice card," said the old woman who rang up the sale. "I'm sure she'll just love it."

She moved as if she were underwater and Bosch wanted to reach over the counter and punch in the numbers himself, just to get it going.

In the Mustang, Bosch put the card in the envelope without signing it, sealed it and wrote McKittrick's name and post office box number on the front. He then started the car and got back on the road.

It took him fifteen minutes working with the map to find the post office on West Venice Avenue. When he got inside, he found it largely deserted. An old man was standing at a table slowly writing an address on an envelope. Two elderly women were in line for counter service. Bosch stood behind them and realized that he was seeing a lot of senior citizens in Florida and he'd only been here a few hours. It was just like he had always heard.

Bosch looked around and saw the video camera on the wall behind the counter. He could tell by its positioning it was there more for recording customers and possible robbers than for surveilling the clerks, though their workstations were probably fully in view as well. He was undeterred. He took a ten-dollar bill out of his pocket, folded it cleanly and held it with the red envelope. He then checked his loose change and came up with the right amount. It seemed like an excruciatingly long time as the one clerk waited on the women.

"Next in line."

It was Bosch. He walked up to the counter where the clerk waited. He was about sixty and had a perfect white beard. He was overweight and his skin seemed too red to Bosch. As if he was mad or something.

"I need a stamp for this."

Bosch put down the change and the envelope. The ten-dollar bill was folded on top of it. The postman acted like he didn't see it.

"I was wondering, did they put the mail out yet in the boxes?"

"They're back there doin' it now."

He handed Bosch a stamp and swiped the change off the counter. He didn't touch the ten or the red envelope.

"Oh, really?"

Bosch picked up the envelope, licked the stamp and put it on. He then put the envelope back down on top of the ten. He was sure the postman had observed this.

"Well, jeez, I really wanted to get this to my Uncle Jake. It's his birthday today. Any way somebody could run it back there? That way he'd get it when he came in today. I'd deliver it in person but I've got to get back to work."

Bosch slid the envelope with the ten underneath it across the counter, closer to white beard.

"Well," he said, "I'll see what I can do."

The postman shifted his body to the left and turned slightly, shielding the transaction from the video camera. In one fluid motion he took the envelope and the ten off the counter. He quickly transferred the ten to his other hand and it dove for cover in his pocket.

"Be right back," he called to the people still in line.

Out in the lobby, Bosch found Box 313 and looked through the tiny pane of glass inside. The red envelope was there along with two white letters. One of the white envelopes was upside down and its return address was partially visible.

City of
Departm
P.O. Bo
Los Ang
90021-3

Bosch felt reasonably sure the envelope carried McKittrick's pension check. He had beaten the mail to him. He walked out of the post office, bought two cups of coffee and a box of doughnuts in the convenience store next door and then returned to the Mustang to wait in the day's growing heat. It wasn't even May yet. He couldn't imagine what a summer must be like here.

Bored with watching the post office door after an hour, Bosch turned on the radio and found it tuned to a channel featuring a southern evangelical ranter. It took several seconds before Harry realized that the

speaker's subject was the Los Angeles earthquake. He decided not to
change the station.

"And ah ask, is it a coincidence that this cata-clysmic calamity was
centered in the very heart of the ind'stry that poe-loots this entarh na-
tion with the smut of pone-ography? I think not! I believe the Lahd
struck a mighty blow to the infidels engaged in this vile and mul-tie-
billyon-dollah trade when he cracked the uth asundah. It is a sign, mah
frens, a sign of things that ah to come. A sign that all is not right in—"

Bosch turned it off. A woman had just come out of the post office
holding a red envelope among other pieces of mail. Bosch watched her
cross the parking lot to a silver Lincoln Town Car. Bosch instinctively
jotted the plate number down, though he had no law enforcement contact in this part of the state who would run it for him. The woman was
in her mid-sixties, Bosch guessed. He had been waiting for a man, but her
age made her fit. He started the Mustang and waited for her to pull out.

She drove north on the main highway toward Sarasota. Traffic moved
slowly. After about fifteen minutes and maybe two miles, the Town Car
took a left on Vamo Road and then almost immediately took a right on
a private road camouflaged by tall trees and green growth. Bosch was
only ten seconds behind her. As he came up to the drive, he slowed but
didn't turn in. He saw a sign set back in the trees.

Welcome To
PELICAN COVE
Condominium Homes, Dockage

The Town Car passed by a guard shack with a red-and-white-striped
gate arm coming down behind it.

"Shit!"

Bosch hadn't anticipated anything like a gated community. He assumed that such things were rare outside of Los Angeles. He looked at
the sign again, then turned around and headed out to the main road. He
remembered seeing another shopping plaza right before he had turned
on to Vamo.

There were eight homes in Pelican Cove listed in the For Sale section
of the *Sarasota Herald-Tribune*, but only three were for sale by owner.

Bosch went to a pay phone in the plaza and called the first one. He got a tape. On the second call the woman who answered said her husband was golfing for the day and she felt uncomfortable showing the property without him. On the third call, the woman who answered invited Bosch to come over right away and even said she'd have fresh lemonade prepared when he got there.

Bosch felt a momentary pang of guilt about taking advantage of a stranger who was just trying to sell her home. But it passed quickly as he considered that the woman would never know she had been used in such a way, and he had no other alternative for getting to McKittrick.

After he was cleared at the gate and got directions to the lemonade lady's unit, Bosch drove through the densely wooded complex, looking for the silver Town Car. It didn't take him long to see that the complex was mostly a retirement community. He passed several elderly people in cars or on walks, almost all of them with white hair and skin browned by the sun. He quickly found the Town Car, checked his location against the map given to him at the guard shack and was about to make a cursory visit to the lemonade lady to avoid suspicion. But then he saw another silver Town Car. It was a popular car with the older set, he guessed. He took out his notebook and checked the plate number he had written down. Neither car had been the one he had followed earlier.

He drove on and finally found the right Town Car in a secluded spot in the far reaches of the complex. It was parked in front of a two-story building of dark wood siding surrounded by oak and paper trees. It looked to Bosch as if there were six units in the building. Easy enough, he thought. He consulted the map and got back on course to the lemonade lady. She was on the second floor of a building on the other side of the complex.

"You're young," she said when she answered the door.

Bosch wanted to say the same thing back to her but held his tongue. She looked like she was in her mid- to late thirties, which put her three decades behind anyone Bosch had seen around the complex so far. She had an attractive and evenly tanned face framed in brown shoulder-length hair. She wore blue jeans, a blue oxford shirt and a black vest with a colorful pattern in the front. She didn't bother with much makeup, which Bosch liked. She had serious green eyes, which he also didn't disagree with.

"I'm Jasmine. Are you Mr. Bosch?"

"Yes. Harry. I just called."

"That was quick."

"I was nearby."

She invited him in and started the rundown.

"It's three bedrooms, like the paper said. Master suite has a private bath. Second bath off the main hall. The view is what makes the place, though."

She pointed Bosch toward a wall of sliding glass doors that looked out on a wide expanse of water dotted with mangrove islands. Hundreds of birds perched in the branches of these otherwise untouched islands. She was right, the view was beautiful.

"What is that?" Bosch asked. "The water."

"That's—you're not from around here, are you? That's Little Sarasota Bay."

Bosch nodded while computing the mistake he had made by blurting out the question.

"No, I'm not from around here. I'm thinking of moving here though."

"Where from?"

"Los Angeles."

"Oh, yes, I've heard. A lot of people are bailing out. Because the ground won't stop shaking."

"Something like that."

She led him down a hallway to what must have been the master suite. Bosch was immediately struck by how the room didn't seem to fit this woman. It was all dark and old and heavy. A mahogany bureau that looked like it weighed a ton, matching bedside tables with ornate lamps and brocaded shades. The place smelled old. It couldn't be where she slept.

He turned and noticed on the wall next to the door an oil painting that was a portrait of the woman standing next to him. It was a younger likeness of her, the face much gaunter, more severe. Bosch was wondering what kind of person hangs a painting of herself in her bedroom when he noticed that the painting was signed. The artist's name was Jazz.

"Jazz. Is that you?"

"Yes. My father insisted on hanging that in here. I actually should have taken it down."

She went to the wall and began to lift the painting off.

"Your father?"

He moved to the other side of the painting to help her.

"Yes. I gave this to him a long time ago. At the time I was thankful he didn't hang it out in the living room where his friends would see it but even here is a little too much."

She turned the painting so the back faced outward and leaned it against the wall. Bosch put together what she had been saying.

"This is your father's place."

"Oh, yes. I've just been staying here while the ad ran in the paper. You want to check out the master bath? It has a Jacuzzi tub. That wasn't mentioned in the ad."

Bosch moved closely by her to the bathroom door. He looked down at her hands, a natural instinct, and saw no rings on any of her fingers. He could smell her as he passed and the scent he picked up was the same as her name: Jasmine. He was beginning to feel some kind of attraction to her but wasn't sure if it was the titillation of being there under false pretenses or an honest pull. He was exhausted, he knew, and decided that was it. His defenses were down. He gave the bathroom a quick once-over and stepped out.

"Nice. Did he live here alone?"

"My father? Yes, alone. My mother died when I was little. My father passed away over Christmas."

"I'm sorry."

"Thank you. What else can I tell you?"

"Nothing. I was just curious about who had been living here."

"No. I mean, what else can I tell you about the condo?"

"Oh, I . . . nothing. It's very nice. I'm still in the looking-around stage, I guess, not sure what I'm going to do. I—"

"What are you really doing?"

"Excuse me?"

"What are you doing here, Mr. Bosch? You're not looking to buy a condo in here. You're not even looking at the place."

There was no anger in her voice. It was a voice full of the confidence she had in reading people. Bosch felt himself turning red. He had been found out.

"I'm just . . . I'm just here to look at places."

It was a terribly weak comeback and he knew it. But it was all he could think of to say. She sensed his predicament and let him off the hook.

"Well, I'm sorry if I embarrassed you. Do you want to see the rest of the place?"

"Yes—uh, well, did you say it was three bedrooms? That's really too big for what I'm looking for."

"Yes, three. But it said that in the newspaper ad, too."

Luckily, Bosch knew he probably couldn't get any redder than he already was.

"Oh," he said. "I must've missed that. Uh, thanks for the tour, though. It's a very nice place."

He moved quickly through the living room toward the door. As he opened it he looked back at her. She spoke before he could say anything.

"Something tells me it's a good story."

"What's that?"

"Whatever it is you're doing. If you ever feel like telling it, the number's in the paper. But you already know that."

Bosch nodded. He was speechless. He stepped through the door and closed it behind him.

By the time he drove back to where he had seen the Town Car, his face had returned to its normal color but he still felt embarrassed about being cornered by the woman. He tried to dismiss it and concentrate on the task at hand. He parked and went to the first-floor door that was nearest the Town Car and knocked. Eventually, an old woman opened the door and stared at him with frightened eyes. One hand clasped the handle of a small two-wheeled cart that carried an oxygen bottle. Two clear plastic tubes snaked over her ears and across both cheeks to her nose.

"I'm sorry to disturb you," he said quickly. "I was looking for the McKittricks."

She raised a frail hand, formed a fist with the thumb out and jerked it up toward the ceiling. Her eyes went up that way, too.

"Upstairs?"

She nodded. He thanked her and headed for the stairs.

The woman who had picked up the red envelope answered the next door he knocked on and Bosch exhaled as if he had spent a lifetime looking for her. It almost felt that way.

"Mrs. McKittrick?"

"Yes?"

Bosch pulled out his badge case and flipped it open. He held the wal-

let so that his first two fingers crossed most of the badge, obscuring the
LIEUTENANT.

"My name's Harry Bosch. I'm a detective with the LAPD. I was
wondering if your husband was here. I'd like to talk to him."

An immediate concern clouded her face.

"LAPD? He hasn't been out there in twenty years."

"It's about an old case. I was sent out to ask him about it."

"Well, you could've called."

"We didn't have a number. Is he here?"

"No, he's down with the boat. He's going fishing."

"Where's that? Maybe I can catch him."

"Well, he doesn't like surprises."

"I guess it will be a surprise whether you tell him or I tell him.
Doesn't make any difference to me. I just have to talk to him, Mrs.
McKittrick."

Maybe she was used to the no-debate tone that cops can put into their
voice. She gave in.

"You walk around the building here and go straight back past the next
three buildings. Go left, you'll see the docks after that."

"Where's his boat?"

"It's slip six. It says *Trophy* in big letters on the side. You can't miss it.
He hasn't left yet because I'm supposed to bring his lunch down."

"Thanks."

He had started away from the door to the side of the building when
she called after him.

"Detective Bosch? Are you going to be a while? Should I make you a
sandwich, too?"

"I don't know how long I'll be but that would be nice of you."

As he headed toward the docks, he realized that the woman named
Jasmine had never offered him the lemonade she had promised.

It took Bosch fifteen minutes to find the little inlet where the docks were. After that, McKittrick was easy enough to spot. There were maybe forty boats in slips but only one of them was occupied. A man with a deep tan set off by his white hair stood in the stern bending over the outboard engine. Bosch studied him as he got closer but saw nothing recognizable about the man. He did not fit with the image Bosch had in his mind's eye of the man who had pulled him from the pool so long ago.

The cover was off the boat engine and the man was doing something with a screwdriver. He wore khaki shorts and a white golf shirt that was too old and stained for golf but was fine for boating. The boat was about twenty feet long, Bosch guessed, and had a small cabin near the bow, where the helm was. There were fishing rods erected in holders along the sides of the boat, two rods per side.

Bosch stopped on the dock at the bow of the boat on purpose. He wanted to be at a distance from McKittrick when he showed the badge. He smiled.

"Never thought I'd see somebody from the Hollywood homicide table so far away from home," he said.

McKittrick looked up but showed no surprise. He showed nothing.

"Nope, you're wrong. This is home. When I was over there, that's when I was far away."

Bosch gave a that's-fair-enough nod and showed the badge. He held it the same way as when he'd showed it to McKittrick's wife.

"I'm Harry Bosch, from Hollywood homicide."

"Yeah, that's what I heard."

Bosch was the one who showed surprise. He could not think of who in L.A. would have tipped McKittrick to his arrival. No one knew. He had only told Hinojos and he could not fathom that she would betray him.

McKittrick relieved him by gesturing to the portable phone on the dashboard of the boat.

"The wife called."

"Oh."

"So what's this all about, Detective Bosch? When I used to work there, we did things in pairs. It was safer that way. You folks that under-staffed, you're going singleton?"

"Not really. My partner's chasing down another old case. These are such long shots, they're not wasting money sending two."

"I assume you're going to explain that."

"Yeah. As a matter of fact, I am. Mind if I come down there?"

"Suit yourself. I'm fixing to shove off as soon as the wife comes with the food."

Bosch began walking along the finger dock to the side of McKittrick's boat. He then stepped down into the craft. It wobbled on the water with the added weight but then steadied. McKittrick lifted the engine cover and began snapping it back in place. Bosch felt grossly out of place. He wore street shoes with black jeans, an Army green T-shirt and a black light-weight sport jacket. And he was still hot. He took the jacket off and folded it over one of the two chairs in the cockpit.

"What are you going for?"

"Whatever's biting. What are you going for?"

He looked directly at Bosch when he asked this and Harry saw that his eyes were brown like beer-bottle glass.

"Well, you heard about the earthquake, didn't you?"

"Sure, who didn't? You know, I've been through quakes and 'canes and you can keep the quakes. At least with a hurricane, you see it com-ing. You take Andrew, he left a lot of devastation, but think how much it woulda been if nobody knew he was about to hit. That's what you get with your earthquakes."

It took Bosch a few moments to place Andrew, the hurricane that had slammed the South Florida coast a couple of years earlier. It was hard to keep track of all the disasters in the world. There were enough just in L.A. He looked out across the inlet. He saw a fish jump and its reentry create a stampede of jumping among the others in the school. He looked at McKittrick and was about to tell him when he realized it was probably something McKittrick saw every day of his life.

"When'd you leave L.A.?"

"Twenty-one years ago. I got my twenty in and *pffft*, I was gone. You can have L.A., Bosch. Shit, I was out there for the Sylmar quake in seventy-one. Knocked down a hospital and a couple freeways. At the time we were living in Tujunga, a few miles from the epicenter. I'll always remember that one. It was like God and the devil meetin' in the room and you were there with 'em playin' referee. Goddamn . . . So what's the quake got to do with you being here?"

"Well, it's kind of a strange phenomenon but the murder rate's fallen off. People are being more civil, I guess. We—"

"Maybe there's nothing left there worth killing for."

"Maybe. Anyway, we're usually running seventy, eighty murders a year in the division, I don't know what it was like when you—"

"We'd do less than half that. Easy."

"Well, we're running way below the average this year. It's given us time to go back through some of the old ones. Everybody on the table's taken a share. One of the ones I've got has your name on it. I guess you know your partner from back then passed away and—"

"Eno's dead? Goddamn, I didn't know that. I thought I would've heard about that. Not that it would've mattered a whole hell of a lot."

"Yeah, he's dead. His wife gets the pension checks. Sorry, you hadn't heard."

"That's okay. Eno and me . . . well, we were partners. That's about it."

"Anyway, I'm here because you're alive and he isn't."

"What's the case?"

"Marjorie Lowe." He waited a moment for a reaction from McKittrick's face and got none. "You remember it? She was found in the trash in an alley off—"

"Vista. Behind Hollywood Boulevard between Vista and Gower. I remember them all, Bosch. Cleared or not, I remember every goddamn one of them."

But you don't remember me, Bosch thought but didn't say.

"Yeah, that's the one. Between Vista and Gower."

"What about it?"

"It was never cleared."

"I know that," McKittrick said, his voice rising. "I worked sixty-three cases during seven years on the homicide table. I worked Hollywood, Wilshire, then RHD. Cleared fifty-six. I'll put that up against anybody. Today they're lucky if they clear half of 'em. I'll put it up against you blind."

"And you'd win. That's a good record. This isn't about you, Jake. It's about the case."

"Don't call me Jake. I don't know you. Never seen you before in my life. I—wait a minute."

Bosch stared at him, astonished that he might actually remember the pool. But then he realized that McKittrick had stopped because of his wife's approach along the dock. She was carrying a plastic cooler. McKittrick waited silently for her to put it down on the dock near the boat and he hoisted it aboard.

"Oh, Detective Bosch, you'll be way too hot in that," Mrs. McKittrick said. "Do you want to come back up and borrow a pair of Jake's shorts and a white T-shirt?"

Bosch looked at McKittrick, then up at her.

"No, thanks, ma'am, I'm fine."

"You are going fishing, aren't you?"

"Well, I haven't exactly been invited and I—"

"Oh, Jake, invite him fishing. You're always looking for somebody to go out with you. Besides, you can catch up on all that blood-and-guts stuff you used to love in Hollywood."

McKittrick looked up at her and Bosch could see the horses fighting against the restraints. He was able to get it under control.

"Mary, thanks for the sandwiches," he said calmly. "Now, could you go back up to the house and leave us be?"

She threw him a frown and shook her head as if he were a spoiled boy. She went back the way she had come without another word. The two of them left on the boat let some time go by before Bosch finally spoke and tried to recover the situation.

"Look, I'm not here for any reason other than to ask you a few questions about this case. I'm not trying to suggest there was anything wrong with the way it was handled. I'm just taking another look at it. That's all."

"You left something out."

"What's that?"

"That you're full of shit."

Bosch could feel the horses rearing up in himself. He was angry at this man's questioning his motives, even though he was right to do so. He was on the verge of shedding the nice-guy skin and going at him. But he knew better. He knew that for McKittrick to act this way, there must be a reason. Something about the old case was like a pebble in his shoe. He had worked it over to the side where it didn't hurt when he walked. But it was still in there. Bosch had to make him want to take it out. He swallowed his own anger and tried to stay level.

"Why am I full of shit?" he said.

McKittrick's back was to him. The former cop was reaching down under the steering console. Bosch couldn't see what he was trying to do, except he guessed he was maybe looking for a hidden set of boat keys.

"Why are you full of shit?" McKittrick answered as he turned around. "I'll tell you why. Because you come here flashing that bullshit badge around when we both know you don't have a badge."

McKittrick was pointing a Beretta twenty-two at Bosch. It was small but it would do the job at this distance, and Bosch had to believe that McKittrick knew how to use it.

"Jesus, man, what's the problem with you?"

"I had no problem until you showed up."

Bosch held his hands chest-high in a nonthreatening pose.

"Just take it easy."

"You take it easy. Put your fucking hands down. I want to see that badge again. Take it out and toss it over here. Slowly."

Bosch complied, all the while trying to look around the docks without turning his head more than a few inches. He didn't see anyone. He was alone. And unarmed. He threw the badge wallet down on the deck near McKittrick's feet.

"Now I want you to walk around the bridge to the bow up there. Stand against the bow rail where I can see you. I knew somebody would try to fuck with me someday. Well, you picked the wrong guy and the wrong day."

Bosch did as instructed and went up to the bow. He grabbed the railing for support and turned around to face his captor. Without taking his eyes off Bosch, McKittrick bent and picked up the wallet. Then he moved into the cockpit and put the gun down on top of the console. Bosch knew if he tried for it McKittrick would get there first. McKittrick reached down and turned something and the engine kicked over.

"What are you doing, McKittrick?"

"Oh, now it's McKittrick. What happened to the friendly 'Jake'? Well, what's doing is, we're going fishing. You wanted to fish, that's what we'll do. You try to jump and I'll shoot you in the water. I don't care."

"I'm not going anywhere. Just take it easy."

"Now, reach down to that cleat and unhook that line. Throw it up on the dock."

When Bosch had finished completing the order, McKittrick picked up the gun and stepped back three paces into the stern. He untied the other line and pushed off from a pylon. He returned to the helm and gently put the boat in reverse. It glided out of the slip. McKittrick then put it in forward and they started moving through the inlet toward the mouth of the canal. Bosch could feel the warm salt breezes drying the sweat on his skin. He decided he would jump as soon as they got to some open water, or where there were other boats with people on them.

"Kind of surprised you're not carrying. What kind of guy says he's a cop, then doesn't carry a piece?"

"I am a cop, McKittrick. Let me explain."

"You don't have to, boy, I already know. Know all about you."

McKittrick flipped open the badge wallet and Bosch watched him study the ID card and the gold lieutenant's badge. He threw it on the console.

"What do you know about me, McKittrick?"

"Don't worry, I still have a few teeth left, Bosch, and I still have a few friends in the department. After the wife called, I made a call. One of my friends. He knew all about you. You're on leave, Bosch. Involuntary. So I don't know about this bullshit story about earthquakes you were spinning. Makes me think maybe you picked up a little freelance work while you're off the job."

"You got it wrong."

"Yeah, well, we'll see. Once we get out into some open water, you're gonna tell me who sent you or you're gonna be fish food. Makes no difference to me."

"Nobody sent me. I sent myself."

McKittrick slapped his palm against the red ball on the throttle lever and the boat surged forward. Its bow rose and Bosch grabbed the railing to hold on.

"Bullshit!" McKittrick yelled above the engine noise. "You're a liar. You lied before, you're lying now."

"Listen to me," Bosch yelled. "You said you remember every case."

"I do, goddamnit! I can't forget them."

"Cut it back!"

McKittrick pulled the throttle back and the boat evened off and the noise reduced.

"On the Marjorie Lowe case you pulled the dirty work. You remember that? Remember what we call the dirty work? You had to tell the next of kin. You had to tell her kid. Out at McClaren."

"That was in the reports, Bosch. So—"

He stopped and stared at Bosch for a long moment. Then he flipped open the badge case and read the name. He looked back at Bosch.

"I remember that name. The swimming pool. You're the kid."

"I'm the kid."

McKittrick let the boat drift in the shallows of Little Sarasota Bay while Bosch told the story. He asked no questions. He simply listened. At a moment where Bosch paused, he opened the cooler his wife had packed and took out two beers, handing one to Bosch. The can felt ice-cold in Bosch's hand.

Bosch didn't pull the tab on his beer until he finished the story. He had told everything he knew to McKittrick, even the nonessential part about his run-in with Pounds. He had a hunch, based on McKittrick's anger and bizarre behavior, that he had been wrong about the old cop. He had flown out to Florida believing he was coming to see either a corrupt or a stupid cop and he wasn't sure which he would dislike more. But now he believed that McKittrick was a man who was haunted by memories and the demons of choices made badly many years ago. Bosch thought that the pebble still had to come out of the shoe and that his own honesty was the best way to get to it.

"So that's my story," he said at the end. "I hope she packed more than two of these."

He popped the beer and drank nearly a third of it. It tasted delicious going down his throat in the afternoon sun.

"Oh, there's plenty more where that came from," McKittrick replied. "You want a sandwich?"

"Not yet."

"No, what you want is my story now."

"That's what I came for."

"Well, let's get out there to the fish."

He restarted the engine and they followed a trail of channel markers south through the bay. Bosch finally remembered he had sunglasses in the pocket of his sport coat and put them on.

It seemed like the wind was cutting in on him from all directions and on occasion its warmth would be traded for a cool breeze that would come up off the surface of the water. It was a long time since Bosch had been on a boat or had even been fishing. For a man who had had a gun pointed at him twenty minutes earlier, he realized he felt pretty good.

As the bay tapered off into a canal, McKittrick pulled back on the throttle and cut their wake. He waved to a man on the bridge of a giant yacht tied up outside a waterside restaurant. Bosch couldn't tell if he knew the man or was just being neighborly.

"Take it on a line even with the lantern on the bridge," McKittrick said.

"What?"

"Take it."

McKittrick stepped away from the wheel and into the stern of the boat. Bosch quickly stepped behind the wheel, sighted the red lantern hanging at center point beneath the span of a drawbridge a half mile ahead and adjusted the wheel to bring the boat into line. He looked back and saw McKittrick pull a plastic bag of small dead fish out of a compartment in the deck.

"Let's see who we've got here today," he said.

He went to the side of the boat and leaned well over the gunwale. Bosch saw him start slapping an open palm on the side of the boat. McKittrick then stood up, surveyed the water for about ten seconds and repeated the banging.

"What's going on?" Bosch asked.

Just as he said it, a dolphin crested the water off the port stern and reentered no more than five feet from where McKittrick was standing. It was a slippery gray blur and Bosch wasn't exactly sure at first what had happened. But the dolphin quickly resurfaced next to the boat, its snout out of the water and chattering. It sounded like it was laughing. McKittrick dropped two of the fish into its open mouth.

"That's Sergeant, see the scars?"

Bosch took a quick look back at the bridge to make sure they were still reasonably on line and then stepped back to the stern. The dolphin was still there. McKittrick pointed down into the water beneath its dorsal fin. Bosch could see three white stripes slashed across its smooth gray back.

"He got too close to a prop one time and it cut him up. The people up at Mote Marine took care of him. But he was left with those sergeant's stripes."

Bosch nodded as McKittrick fed the dolphin again. Without looking up to see if they were off course, McKittrick said, "You better get the wheel."

Bosch turned and saw that they had drifted far off line. He went back to the wheel and corrected the course. He stayed there while McKittrick remained in the back, throwing fish to the dolphin, until they passed under the bridge. Bosch decided he could wait him out. Whether it was while they were going out or coming in didn't matter. He was going to get McKittrick's story. He was not going to leave without it.

Ten minutes after the bridge they came to a channel that took them out to the Gulf of Mexico. McKittrick dropped lures from two of the poles into the water and put out about a hundred yards of line on each one. He took the wheel back from Bosch then, yelling into the wind and engine noise.

"I want to take it out to the reefs. We'll troll until we're there and then we'll do some drift fishing in the shallows. We'll talk then."

"Sounds like a plan," Bosch yelled back.

Nothing hit either of the lures, and about two miles from the shore McKittrick killed the engines and told Bosch to bring in one line while he handled the other. It took Bosch, who was left handed, a few moments to get himself coordinated on the right-handed reel but then he started smiling.

"I don't think I've done this since I was a kid. At McClaren every now and then they'd put us on a bus and take us out to the Malibu Pier."

"Jesus, that pier still there?"

"Yeah."

"Must be like fishing in a cesspool by now."

"I guess."

McKittrick laughed and shook his head.

"Why do you stay there, Bosch? Doesn't sound like they particularly want you."

Bosch thought a moment before answering. The comment was on point but he wondered if it was on point from McKittrick or whoever the source was he had called.

"Who'd you call back there about me?"

"I'm not telling you. That's why he talked to me, because he knew I wouldn't tell you."

Bosch nodded, signaling he'd let it go.

"Well, you're right," he said. "I don't think they particularly want me back there. But I don't know. It's kind've like the more they push one way, the more I push the other. I feel like if they'd stop asking or trying to make me leave, then I'd probably want to do it."

"I guess I know what you mean."

McKittrick stowed the two rods they had used and set to work outfitting the other two with hooks and buckshot weights.

"We're going to use mullet."

Bosch nodded. He didn't know the first thing about it. But he watched McKittrick closely. He thought it might be a good time to start.

"So you punched out after your twenty in L.A. What'd you do after that?"

"You're looking at it. I moved back here—I'm from Palmetto, up the coast, originally. I bought a boat and became a fishing guide. Did that another twenty, retired and now I fish for my own damned self."

Bosch smiled.

"Palmetto? Isn't that the name of those big cockroaches?"

"No. Well, yeah, but it's also the name of a scrub palm. That's what the town's named for, not the bug."

Bosch nodded and watched as McKittrick opened a bag of mullet strips and hooked pieces on each line. After opening fresh beers, they cast on separate sides of the boat and then sat on the gunwales, waiting.

"Then how'd you end up in L.A.?" Bosch asked.

"What was that somebody said about going west young man? Well, after Japan surrendered I passed through L.A. on my way back home and

I saw those mountains going all the way up from the sea to the sky . . . Damn, I ate dinner at the Derby my first night in town. I was going to blow my whole wallet and you know who saw me there in uniform and picked up the tab? Goddamn Clark Gable. I'm not kidding you. I fuckin' fell in love with that place and it took me almost thirty years to see the light . . . Mary's from L.A., you know. Born and raised. She likes it out here fine."

He nodded to reassure himself. Bosch waited a few moments and McKittrick was still looking off at distant memories.

"He was a nice guy."

"Who's that?"

"Clark Gable."

Bosch crunched the empty beer can in his hand and got another.

"So tell me about the case," he said after popping it. "What happened?"

"You know what happened if you read the book. It was all in there. It got dumped. One day we had an investigation, the next we were writing 'No leads at this time.' It was a joke. That's why I remember the case so well. They shouldn't've done what they did."

"Who's they?"

"You know, the big shots."

"What did they do?"

"They took it away from us. And Eno let them. He cut some deal with them himself. Shit."

He shook his head bitterly.

"Jake," Bosch tried. He got no protest this time over using the first name. "Why don't you start at the beginning. I need to know everything I can from you."

McKittrick was quiet while he reeled in. His bait hadn't been touched. He recast it, put the rod in one of the gunwale pipes and got another beer. From beneath the console he grabbed a Tampa Bay Lightning cap and put it on. He leaned on the gunwale with his beer and looked at Bosch.

"Okay, kid, listen, I got nothin' against your mother. I'm just gonna tell you this the way it fell, okay?"

"That's all I want."

"You want a hat? You're gonna get burned."

"I'm fine."

McKittrick nodded and finally started.

"Okay, so we got the call out from home. It was a Saturday morning. One of the footbeat guys had found her. She hadn't been killed in that alley. That much was clear. She'd been dropped off. By the time I got down there from Tujunga, the crime scene investigation was already underway. My partner was there, too. Eno. He was the senior man, he was there first. He took charge of it."

Bosch put his rod in a pipe and went to his jacket.

"You mind if I take notes?"

"No, I don't mind. I guess I've been waiting for somebody to care about this one since I walked away from it."

"Go ahead. Eno was in charge."

"Yeah, he was the man. You've got to understand something. We'd been a team maybe three, four months at that time. We weren't tight. After this one, we'd never be tight. I switched off after about a year. I went in for the transfer. They moved me to Wilshire dicks, homicide table. Never had much to do with him after that. He never had much to do with me."

"Okay, what happened with the investigation?"

"Well, it was like anything else that you'd expect. We were going through the routine. We had a list of her KAs—got it mostly from the vice guys—and were working our way through it."

"The known associates, did they include clients? There was no list in the murder book."

"I think there were a few clients. And the list didn't go into the book because Eno said so. Remember, he was the lead."

"Okay. Johnny Fox was on the list?"

"Yeah, he was at the top of it. He was her . . . uh, manager and—"

"Her pimp, you mean."

McKittrick looked at him.

"Yeah. That's what he was. I wasn't sure what you, uh—"

"Forget it. Go on."

"Yeah, Johnny Fox was on the list. We talked to about everybody who knew her and this guy was described by everybody as one mean guy. He had a history."

Bosch thought of Meredith Roman's report that he had beaten her.

"We'd heard that she was trying to get away from him. I don't know, either to go out on her own or maybe go straight. Who knows? We heard—"

"She wanted to be a straight citizen," Bosch interrupted. "That way she could get me out of the hall."

He felt foolish for saying it, knowing his saying it was not convincing.

"Yeah, whatever," McKittrick said. "Point is, Fox was none too happy about that. That put him at the top of our list."

"But you couldn't find him. The chrono says you watched his place."

"Yeah. He was our man. We had prints we had taken off the belt—the murder weapon—but we had no comparisons from him. Johnny had been pulled in a few times in the past but never booked. Never printed. So we really needed to bring him in."

"What did it tell you, that he'd been picked up but never booked?"

McKittrick finished his beer, crunched it in his hand and walked the empty over to a large bucket in the corner of the deck and dropped it.

"To be honest, at the time it didn't hit me. Now, of course, it's obvious. He had an angel watching over him."

"Who?"

"Well, on one of the days we were watching Fox's place, waiting for him to show up, we got a message on the radio to call Arno Conklin. He wanted to talk about the case. ASAP. Now this was a holy shit kind of call. For two reasons. One, Arno was going great guns then. He was running the city's moral commandos at the time and had a lock on the DA's office, which was coming open in a year. The other reason was that we'd only had the case a few days and hadn't come near the DA's office with anything. So now all of a sudden the most powerful guy in the agency wants to see us. I'm thinking . . . I don't really know what I was thinking. I just knew it—hey, you got one!"

Bosch looked at his pole and saw it bend from a violent jerk on the line. The reel started spinning as the fish pulled against the drag. Bosch grabbed the pole out of the pipe and jerked it back. The hook was set well. He started reeling but the fish had a lot of fight and was pulling out more line than he was reeling in. McKittrick came over and tightened the drag dial, which immediately put a more pronounced bend in the pole.

"Keep the pole up, keep the pole up," McKittrick counseled.

Bosch did as he was told and spent five minutes battling the fish. His arms started to ache. He felt a strain on his lower back. McKittrick put on gloves and when the fish finally surrendered and Bosch had it alongside the boat, he bent over and hooked his fingers into the gills and brought it on board. Bosch saw a shiny blue-black fish that looked beautiful in the sunlight.

"Wahoo," McKittrick said.

"What?"

McKittrick held the fish up horizontally.

"Wahoo. Over there in your fancy L.A. restaurants I think they call it Ono. Here, we just call it wahoo. Meat cooks up white as halibut, you wanna keep it?"

"No, put it back. It's beautiful."

McKittrick roughly pulled the hook from the gulping mouth of the fish and then held the catch out to Bosch.

"You want to hold it? Must be twelve, thirteen pounds."

"Nah, I don't need to hold it."

Bosch stepped closer and ran his finger along the slick skin of the fish. He could almost see himself in the reflection of its scales. He nodded to McKittrick and the fish was thrown back into the water. For several seconds it remained motionless, about two feet below the surface. Post-traumatic stress syndrome, Bosch thought. Finally, the fish seemed to come out of it and darted down into the depths. Bosch put the hook through one of the eyelets on his pole and put the pole back in its pipe. He was done fishing. He got another beer out of the cooler.

"Hey, you want a sandwich, go ahead," McKittrick said.

"No. I'm fine."

Bosch wished the fish hadn't interrupted them.

"You were saying that you guys got the call from Conklin."

"Yeah, Arno. Only I had it wrong. The request for a meeting was only for Claude. Not me. Eno went alone."

"Why only Eno?"

"I never knew and he acted like he didn't know, either. I just assumed it was because he and Arno had a prior relationship of some kind."

"But you don't know what."

"No. Claude Eno was about ten years older than me. He'd been around."

"So what happened?"

"Well, I can't tell you what happened. I can only tell you what my partner said happened. Understand?"

He was telling Bosch that he didn't trust his own partner. Bosch had known that feeling himself at times and nodded that he understood.

"Go ahead."

"He came back from the meeting saying Conklin asked him to lay off Fox because Fox was clear on this case and Fox was working as an informant on one of the commando investigations. He said Fox was important to him and he didn't want him compromised or roughed up, especially over a crime he didn't commit."

"How was Conklin so sure?"

"I don't know. But Eno told me that he told Conklin that assistant DA's, no matter who they are, didn't decide whether someone was clear or not for the police, and that we weren't backing off until we talked to Fox for ourselves. Faced with that, Conklin said he could deliver Fox to be interviewed and fingerprinted. But only if we did it on Conklin's turf."

"Which was . . . ?"

"His office in the old courthouse. That's gone now. They built that big square thing right before I left. Horrible-looking thing."

"What happened in the office? Were you there for that?"

"Yeah, I was there but nothing happened. We interviewed him. Fox was there with Conklin, so was the Nazi."

"The Nazi?"

"Conklin's enforcer, Gordon Mittel."

"He was there?"

"Yup. I guess he was sort of watching out for Conklin while Conklin was watching out for Fox."

Bosch showed no surprise.

"Okay, so what did Fox tell you?"

"Like I said, not much. At least, that's how I remember it. He gave us an alibi and the names of the people who could verify it. I took his prints."

"What'd he say about the victim?"

"He said pretty much what we'd already heard from her girlfriend."

"Meredith Roman?"

"Yeah, I think that's it. He said she went to a party, was hired as kind of a decoration to be on some guy's arm. He said it was in Hancock Park. He didn't have the address. He said he had nothing to do with setting it up. That didn't make sense to us. You know, a pimp not knowing where . . . not knowing where one of his girls was. It was the one thing we had and when we started leaning on him about it, Conklin stepped in like a referee."

"He didn't want you leaning on him."

"Craziest thing I ever saw. Here was the next DA—everybody knew he was going to run. Here he was taking this bastard's side against us . . . Sorry about that bastard comment."

"Forget it."

"Conklin was trying to make it seem like we were out of line, while all the time this big-piece-of-shit Fox was sitting there smiling with a toothpick in the side of his mouth. It's what, thirty-somethin' years ago and I can still remember that toothpick. Galled the Jesus out of me. So to make a long story short, we never did get to brace him on having set up the date she went on."

The boat rocked on a high wake and Bosch looked around and didn't see any other boat. It was weird. He looked out across the water and for the first time realized how different it was from the Pacific. The Pacific was a cold and forbidding blue, the Gulf a warm green that invited you.

"We left," McKittrick continued. "I figured we'd have another shot at him. So we left and started to work on his alibi. It turned out to be good. And I don't mean it was good because his own witnesses said it was. We did the work. We found some independent people. People that didn't know him. As I remember it, it was rock solid."

"You remember where he was?"

"Spent part of the night in a bar over there on Ivar, place a lot of the pimps hung around. Can't remember the name of it. Then later he drove out to Ventura, spent most of the rest of the night in a card room until he got a phone call, then he split. The other thing about this was that it didn't smack of an alibi set up for this particular night. This was his routine. He was well known in all of these places."

"What was the phone call?"

"We never knew. We didn't know about it until we started checking his alibi and somebody mentioned it. We never got to ask Fox about it. But to be honest, we didn't care too much at that point. Like I said, his alibi was solid and he didn't get the call until later in the morning. Four, five o'clock. The vic—your mother had been dead a good long while by then. TOD was midnight. The call didn't matter."

Bosch nodded but it was the kind of detail he would not have left open if it had been his investigation. It was too curious a detail. Who calls a poker room that early in the morning? What kind of call would make Fox up and leave the game?

"What about the prints?"

"I had 'em checked anyway and they didn't match those on the belt. He was clean. The dirtbag was clear."

Bosch thought of something.

"You did check the prints on the belt against the victim's, right?"

"Hey, Bosch, I know you highfalutin' guys think you're the cat's ass now but we were known for having a brain or two back in those days."

"Sorry."

"There were a few prints on the buckle that were the victim's. That's it. The rest were definitely the killer's because of their location. We got good direct lifts and partials on two other spots where it was clear the belt had been grasped by the full hand. You don't hold a belt that way when you're putting it on. You hold it that way when you're putting it around someone's neck."

They were both silent after that. Bosch couldn't figure out what McKittrick was telling him. He felt deflated. He had thought that if he got McKittrick to open up, the old cop would point the finger at Fox or Conklin or somebody. But he was doing none of that. He really wasn't giving Bosch anything.

"How come you remember so many details, Jake? It's been a long time."

"I've had a long time to think about it. When you finish up, Bosch, you'll see, there'll always be one. One case that stays with you. This is the one that stayed with me."

"So what was your final take on it?"

"My final take? Well, I never got over that meeting at Conklin's office. I guess you had to be there but it just . . . it just seemed that the one that was in charge of that meeting was Fox. It was like he was calling the shots."

Bosch nodded. He could see that McKittrick was struggling for an explanation of his feelings.

"You ever interview a suspect with his lawyer there jumpin' in and out of the conversation?" McKittrick asked. "You know, 'Don't answer this, don't answer that.' Shit like that."

"All the time."

"Well, it was like that. It was like Conklin, the next DA for Chrissake, was this shitheel's lawyer, objecting all the time to our questions. What it came down to was that if you didn't know who he was or where we were, you'd've sworn he was working for Fox. Both of them, Mittel, too. So, I felt pretty sure Fox had his hooks into Arno. Somehow he did. And I was right. It was all confirmed later."

"You mean when Fox died?"

"Yeah. He got killed in a hit and run while working for the Conklin campaign. I remember the newspaper story on it didn't say nothin' about his background as a pimp, as a Hollywood Boulevard hoodlum. No, he was just this guy who got run down. Joe Innocent. I tell ya, that story must've cost Arno a few dollars and made a reporter a little richer."

Bosch could tell there was more so he said nothing.

"I was in Wilshire dicks by then," McKittrick continued. "But I got curious when I heard about it. So I called over to Hollywood to see who was on it. It was Eno. Big surprise. And he never made a case on anybody. So that about confirmed what I was thinking about him, too."

McKittrick stared off across the water to where the sun was getting low in the sky. He threw his empty beer can at the bucket. It missed and bounced over the side into the water.

"Fuck it," he said. "I guess we should head in."

He started reeling in his line.

"What do you think Eno got out of all of this?"

"I don't know exactly. He might've just been trading favors, something like that. I'm not saying he got rich, but I think he got something out of the deal. He wouldn't do it for nothing. I just don't know what it was."

McKittrick started taking the rods out of the pipes and stowing them on hooks along the sides of the stern.

"In 1972 you checked the murder book out of archives, how come?"

McKittrick looked at him curiously.

"I signed the same checkout slip a few days ago," Bosch explained. "Your name was still on it."

McKittrick nodded.

"Yeah, that was right after I put in my papers. I was leaving, going through my files and stuff. I'd hung on to the prints we took off the belt. Kept the card. Also hung on to the belt."

"Why?"

"You know why. I didn't think it would be safe in that file or in the evidence room. Not with Conklin as DA, not with Eno doing him favors. So I kept the stuff. Then a bunch of years went by and it was there when I was cleaning shit out and going to Florida. So right before I decided to punch out, I put the print card back in the murder book and went down and put the belt back in the evidence box. Eno was already in Vegas, retired. Conklin had crashed and burned, was out of politics. The case was long forgotten. I put the stuff back. I guess maybe I hoped someday somebody like you would take a look at it."

"What about you? Did you look at the book when you put the card back?"

"Yeah, and I saw I had done the right thing. Somebody had gone through it, stripped it. They pulled the Fox interview out of it. Probably was Eno."

"As the second man on the case you had to do the paper, right?"

"Right. The paperwork was mine. Most of it."

"What did you put on the Fox interview summary that would have made Eno need to pull it?"

"I don't remember anything specific, just that I thought the guy was lying and that Conklin was out of line. Something like that."

"Anything else you remember that was missing?"

"Nah, nothing important, just that. I think he just wanted to get Conklin's name out of it."

"Yeah, well, he missed something. You'd noted his first call on the Chronological Record. That's how I knew."

"Did I? Well, good for me. And here you are."

"Yeah."

"All right, we're heading in. Too bad they weren't really biting today."

"I'm not complaining. I got my fish."

McKittrick stepped behind the wheel and was about to start the engine when he thought of something.

"Oh, you know what?" He moved to the cooler and opened it. "I don't want Mary to be disappointed."

He pulled out the plastic bags that contained the sandwiches his wife had made.

"You hungry?"

"Not really."

"Me neither."

He opened the bags and dumped the sandwiches over the side. Bosch watched him.

"Jake, when you pulled out that gun, who'd you think I was?"

McKittrick didn't say anything as he neatly folded the plastic bags and put them back in the cooler. When he straightened up, he looked at Bosch.

"I didn't know. All I knew was that I thought I might have to take you out here and dump you like those sandwiches. Seems like I've been hiding out here all my life, waiting for them to send somebody."

"You think they'd go that far over time and distance?"

"I don't have any idea. The more time that goes by, the more I doubt it. But old habits die hard. I always keep a gun nearby. Doesn't matter that most times I don't even remember why."

They rode in from the Gulf with the engine roaring and the soft spray of the sea in their faces. They didn't talk. That was done with. Occasionally, Bosch glanced over at McKittrick. His old face fell under the shadow of his cap brim. But Bosch could see his eyes in there, looking at something that had happened a long time before and no longer could be changed.

After the boat trip Bosch felt the onset of a headache from the combination of too much beer and too much sun. He begged off an invitation to dinner from McKittrick, saying he was tired. Once in his car, he took a couple of Tylenol caplets out of his overnighter, downed them without any liquid chaser and hoped they would do the job. He took out his notebook and reviewed some of the things he had written about McKittrick's story.

He had come to like the old cop by the end of the fishing trip. Maybe he saw some of himself in the older man. McKittrick was haunted because he had let the case go. He had not done the right thing. And Bosch knew he was guilty of the same during all the years he had ignored the case that he knew was there waiting for him. He was making up for that now, and so was McKittrick by talking to him. But both of them knew it might be too little too late.

Bosch wasn't sure what he would do next when he got back to Los Angeles. It seemed to him that his only move was to confront Conklin. He was reluctant to do this because he knew he would go into such a confrontation soft, with only his suspicions and no hard evidence. Conklin would have the upper hand.

A wave of desperation came over him. He did not want the case to come to this. Conklin hadn't flinched in almost thirty-five years. He wouldn't with Bosch in his face now. Harry knew he needed something else. But he had nothing.

He started the car but left it in Park. He turned the air conditioner on high and added what McKittrick had told him into the stew of what he already knew. He began formulating a theory. For Bosch, this was one of the most important components of homicide investigation. Take the facts and shake them down into hypothesis. The key was not to become beholden to any one theory. Theories changed and you had to change with them.

It seemed clear from McKittrick's information that Fox had a hold on Conklin. What was it? Well, Bosch thought, Fox dealt in women. The theory that emerged was that Fox had gotten a hook into Conklin through a woman, or women. The news clips at the time reported Conklin was a bachelor. The morals of the time would have dictated then as now that as a public servant and soon-to-be candidate for top prosecutor, Conklin needed not necessarily to be celibate but, at least, not to have succumbed privately to the very vices he was publicly attacking. If he had done that and was exposed, he could kiss his political career goodbye, let alone his position as commander of the DA commandos. So, Bosch concluded, if this was Conklin's flaw and it was through Fox that such dalliances were arranged, then Fox would hold an almost unbeatable hand when it came to having juice with Conklin. It would explain the unusual circumstances of the interview McKittrick and Eno conducted with Fox.

The same theory, Bosch knew, would work to an even greater degree if Conklin had done more than succumb to the vice of sex but had gone further: if he had killed a woman Fox had sent to him, Marjorie Lowe. For one thing, it would explain how Conklin knew for sure that Fox was in the clear on the murder—because he was the killer himself. For another, it would explain how Fox got Conklin to run interference for him and why he was later hired as a Conklin campaign worker. The bottom line was, if Conklin was the killer, Fox's hook would be set even deeper and it would be set for good. Conklin would be like that wahoo at the end of the line, a pretty fish unable to get away.

Unless, Bosch knew, the man at the other end of the line and holding the rod were to go away somehow. He thought about Fox's death and saw how it fit. Conklin let some time separate one death from the other. He played like a hooked fish, even agreeing to Fox's demand for a straight job with the campaign, and then, when all seemed clear, Fox was run down in the street. Maybe a payoff to a reporter kept the victim's background quiet—if the reporter even knew it—and a few months later Conklin was crowned district attorney.

Bosch considered where Mittel would fit into the theory. He felt it was unlikely that all of this had transpired in a vacuum. It was Bosch's guess that Mittel, as Conklin's right-hand man and enforcer, would know what Conklin knew.

Bosch liked his theory but it angered him, largely because that was all it was, theory. He shook his head as he realized he was back to ground zero. All talk, no evidence of anything.

He grew weary thinking about it and decided to put the thoughts aside for a while. He turned the air down because it was too cool against his sunburned skin and put the car in gear. As he slowly cruised through Pelican Cove toward the gatehouse, his thoughts drifted to the woman who was trying to sell her dead father's condo. She had signed the name Jazz on the self-portrait. He liked that.

He turned the car around and drove toward her unit. It was still daylight and no lights shone from behind the building's windows when he got there. He couldn't tell if she was there or not. Bosch parked nearby and watched for a few minutes, debating what he should do, if anything at all.

Fifteen minutes later, when it seemed that indecisiveness had paralyzed him, she stepped out the front door. He was parked nearly twenty yards away, between two other cars. His paralytic affliction eased enough for him to slide down in his seat to avoid detection. She walked out into the parking lot and behind the row of cars which included Bosch's rental. He didn't move or turn to follow her movement. He listened. He waited for the sound of a car starting. Then what, he wondered. Follow her? What are you doing?

He jerked upright at the sound of sharp rapping on the window next to him. It was her. Bosch was flustered but managed to turn the key so he could lower the window.

"Yes?"

"Mr. Bosch, what are you doing?"

"What do you mean?"

"You've been sitting out here. I saw you."

"I . . ."

He was too humiliated to finish.

"I don't know whether to call security or not."

"No, don't do that. I, uh, I was just—I was going to go to your door. To apologize."

"Apologize? Apologize for what?"

"For today. For earlier, when I was inside. I—you were right, I wasn't looking to buy anything."

"Then what were you doing?"

Bosch opened the car door and stepped out. He felt disadvantaged with her looking down at him in the car.

"I'm a cop," he said. "I needed to get in here to see someone. I used you and I'm sorry. I am. I didn't know about your father and all of that."

· She smiled and shook her head.

"That's the dumbest story I've ever heard. What about L.A., was that part of the story?"

"No. I'm from L.A. I'm a cop there."

"I don't know if I'd go around admitting that if I were you. You guys've got some bad PR problems."

"Yeah, I know. So . . ." He felt his courage rising. He told himself he was flying out in the morning and it didn't matter what happened because he'd never see her or this state again. "You said something before about lemonade but I never got any. I was thinking, maybe I could tell you the story, apologize and have some lemonade or something."

He looked over toward the door of the condo.

"You L.A. cops are pushy," she said but she was smiling. "One glass and the story better be good. After that, we both gotta go. I'm driving up to Tampa tonight."

They started walking toward the door and Bosch realized he had a smile on his face.

"What's in Tampa?"

"It's where I live and I miss it. I've been down here more than up there since I put the condo on the market. I want to spend a Sunday at my own place and in my own studio."

"That's right, a painter."

"I try to be."

She opened the door for him and allowed him in first.

"Well, that's okay by me. I have to get to Tampa sometime tonight. I fly out in the morning."

While nursing a tall glass of lemonade, Bosch explained his scam of using her to get into the complex to see another resident and she didn't seem upset. In fact, he could tell she admired the ingenuity of it. Bosch didn't tell her how it had backfired anyway when McKittrick had pulled a gun on him. He gave her a vague outline of the case, never mentioning its personal connection to himself, and she seemed intrigued by the whole idea of solving a murder that happened thirty-three years earlier.

The one glass of lemonade turned into four and the last two were spiked nicely with vodka. They took care of what was left of Bosch's headache and put a nice bloom on everything. Between the third and the fourth she asked if he would mind if she smoked and he lit cigarettes for both of them. And as the sky darkened over the mangroves outside, he finally turned the conversation toward her. Bosch had sensed a loneliness about her, a mystery of some sort. Behind the pretty face there were scars. The kind that couldn't be seen.

Her name was Jasmine Corian but she said that friends called her Jazz. She spoke of growing up in the Florida sun, of never wanting to leave it. She had married once but it was a long time ago. There was nobody in her life now and she was used to it. She said she concentrated most of her life on her art and, in a way, Bosch understood what she meant. His own art, though few would call it that, took most of his life as well.

"What do you paint?"

"Portraits mostly."

"Who are they?"

"Just someone I know. Maybe I'll paint you, Bosch. Someday."

He didn't know what to say to that so he made a clumsy transition to safer ground.

"Why don't you give this place to a realtor to sell? That way you could stay in Tampa and paint."

"Because I wanted the diversion. I also didn't want to give a realtor the five percent. This is a nice complex. These units sell pretty well without realtors. A lot of Canadian investment. I think I'll sell it. This was only the first week I've run the ad."

Bosch just nodded and wished he had kept the conversation on her painting instead of realtors. The clumsy change seemed to have clogged things up a bit.

"I was thinking, you want to have dinner?"

She looked at him solemnly, as if the request and her answer had far deeper implications. They probably did. At least, he thought they did.

"Where would we go?"

That was a stall but he played along.

"I don't know. It's not my town. Not my state. You could pick a place. Around here or on the way up to Tampa. I don't care. I'd like your company, though, Jazz. If you want to."

"How long has it been since you were with a woman? I mean on a date."

"On a date? I don't know. A few months, I guess. But, look, I'm not a hard-luck case. I'm just in town and alone and thought maybe you'd—"

"It's okay, Harry. Let's go."

"To eat?"

"Yes, to eat. I know a place on the way up. It's above Longboat. You'll have to follow me."

He smiled and nodded.

She drove a Volkswagen Beetle convertible that was powder blue with one red fender. He couldn't lose her in a hailstorm let alone the slow-moving Florida highways.

Bosch counted two drawbridges that they had to stop for before they got to Longboat Key. From there they headed north for the length of the island, crossed a bridge onto Anna Maria Island and finally stopped at a place called the Sandbar. They walked through the bar and sat on a deck overlooking the Gulf. It was cool and they ate crabs and oysters chased with Mexican beer. Bosch loved it.

They didn't talk much but didn't need to. It was always in the silences that Bosch felt most comfortable with the women who had moved through his life. He felt the vodka and beer working on him, warming him toward her, sanding off any sharp edges to the evening. He felt a desire for her growing and tugging at him. McKittrick and the case had somehow been pushed into the darkness at the back of his mind.

"This is good," he said when he was finally nearing his capacity for food and drink. "It's great."

"Yeah, they do it right. Can I tell you something, Bosch?"

"Go ahead."

"I was only kidding about what I was saying about L.A. cops before. But I have known some cops before . . . and you seem different. I don't know what it is but it's like you've got too much of yourself left, you know?"

"I guess." He nodded. "Thanks. I think."

They both laughed and then in a hesitant move, she leaned over and kissed him quickly on the lips. It was nice and he smiled. He could taste garlic.

"I'm glad you're already sunburned or you'd be turning red again."

"No, I wouldn't. I mean, that was a nice thing to say."

"You want to come home with me, Bosch?"

Now he hesitated. Not because there was any deliberation in his answer. But he wanted her to have the chance to withdraw it in case she had spoken too quickly. After a moment of silence from her he smiled and nodded.

"Yes, I would like that."

They left then and cut inland to the freeway. Bosch wondered as he tailed the Volkswagen if she would change her mind as she drove alone. He got his answer at the Skyway bridge. As he pulled up to the tollbooth with his dollar already in hand, the tolltaker shook his head and waved off the money.

"Nope. That lady in the bug got ya covered."

"Yeah?"

"Yeah. You know her?"

"Not yet."

"I think you're goin' to. Good luck."

"Thanks."

Now Bosch couldn't lose her in a blizzard. As the drive grew longer, he found himself in a growing sense of an almost adolescent euphoria of anticipation. He was captured by the directness of this woman and he was wondering how and what that would translate to when they were making love.

She led him north to Tampa and then into an area called Hyde Park. Overlooking the bay, the neighborhood consisted of old Victorian and Craftsman-style houses with sweeping front porches. Her home was an apartment above the three-car garage set behind a gray Victorian with green trim.

As they got to the top of the steps and she was putting the key into the knob, Bosch thought of something and didn't know what to do. She opened the door and looked at him. She read him.

"What's wrong?"

"Nothing. But I was thinking, maybe I should go find a drugstore or something and then come back."

"Don't worry, I've got what you'll need. But can you stand out here for a second? I just want to make a mad dash inside and clean up a few things."

He looked at her.

"I don't care about that."

"Please?"

"Okay. Take your time."

He waited for about three minutes and then she opened the door and pulled him in. If she had cleaned up, she had done it in the dark. The only light came from what Bosch could see was the kitchen. She took his hand and led him away from the light to a darkened hallway that gave way to her bedroom. Here she turned on the light, revealing a sparely furnished room. A wrought-iron bed with a canopy was the centerpiece. There was a night table of unfinished wood next to it, a matching unfinished bureau and an antique Singer sewing machine table on which stood a blue vase with dead flowers in it. There was nothing hung on any of the walls, though Bosch saw a nail protruding from the plaster above the vase. Jasmine noticed the flowers and quickly took the vase off the table and headed out the door.

"I have to go dump this. I haven't been here in a week and forgot to change them."

Moving the flowers raised a slightly acrid smell in the room. While she was gone Bosch looked at the nail again and thought he could see the delineation of a rectangle on the wall. Something had hung there, he decided. She hadn't come in to clean up. If she had, she would have gotten rid of the flowers. She'd come in to take down a painting.

When she came back into the room, she put the empty vase back on the table.

"Would you like another beer? I have some wine, too."

Bosch moved toward her, intrigued even more by her mysteries.

"No, I'm fine."

Without further word they embraced. He could taste beer and garlic and cigarette smoke as he kissed her but didn't care. He knew she was getting the same from him. He pressed his cheek against hers and with his nose he came across the spot on her neck where she had dabbed perfume. Night-blooming jasmine.

They moved onto the bed, each taking pieces of clothing off between hard kisses. Her body was beautiful, the tan lines distinct. He kissed her lovely small breasts and gently pushed her back on the bed. She told him to wait and she rolled to the side and from the drawer of the bed table extracted a strip of three condom packages and handed it to him.

"Is this wishful thinking?" he asked.

They both burst out laughing and it seemed to make things all the better.

"I don't know," she said. "We'll see."

For Bosch, sexual encounters had always been a question of timing. The desires of two individuals rose and subsided on their own courses. There were emotional needs separate from physical needs. And sometimes all of those things clicked together in a person and then clicked in tandem with those of the other person. Bosch's encounter with Jasmine Corian was one of those times. The sex created a world without intrusion. One so vital that it could have lasted an hour or maybe only a few minutes and he wouldn't have known the difference. At the end, he was above her, looking into her open eyes, and she clutched his upper arms as if she were holding on for her life. Both of their bodies shuddered in unison and then he lay still on top of her, catching his breath from the hollow between her neck and shoulder. He felt so good he had the urge to laugh out loud but he didn't think she'd understand. He stifled it and made it sound like a muffled cough.

"Are you okay?" she asked softly.

"I've never felt better."

Eventually, he moved off her, backing down over her body. He kissed both of her breasts, then sat up with her legs on either side of him. He removed the condom while using his body to shield her view of the process.

He got up and walked to the door he hoped was the bathroom and found it was a closet. The next door he tried was the bathroom and he flushed the condom down the toilet. He absentmindedly wondered if it would end up somewhere in Tampa Bay.

When he came back from the bathroom she was sitting up with the sheet bunched around her waist. He found his sport coat on the floor and got out his cigarettes. He gave her one and lit it. Then he bent over and kissed her breasts again. Her laugh was infectious and it made him smile.

"You know, I like it that you didn't come equipped."

"Equipped? What are you talking about?"

"You know, that you offered to go to the drugstore. It shows what kind of man you are."

"What do you mean?"

"If you had come over here from L.A. with a condom in your wallet, that would've been so . . . I don't know, premeditated. Like some guy just on the make. The whole thing would have had no spontaneity. I'm glad you weren't like that, Harry Bosch, that's all."

He nodded, trying to follow her line of thought. He wasn't sure he understood. And he wondered what he should think of the fact that she *was* equipped. He decided to drop it and lit his cigarette.

"How'd you hurt your hand like that?"

She had noticed the marks on his fingers. Bosch had taken the Band-Aids off while flying over. The burns had healed to the point that they looked like red welts on two of his fingers.

"Cigarette. I fell asleep."

He felt he could tell her the truth about everything about himself.

"God, that's scary."

"Yeah. I don't think it will happen again."

"Do you want to stay with me tonight?"

He moved closer to her and kissed her on the neck.

"Yes," he whispered.

She reached over and touched the zipper scar on his left shoulder. The women he was with in bed always seemed to do this. It was an ugly mark and he never understood why they were drawn to touch it.

"You got shot?"

"Yeah."

"That's even scarier."

He hiked his shoulders. It was history and he never really thought about it anymore.

"You know, what I was trying to say before is that you're not like most cops I've known. You've got too much of your humanity left. How'd that happen?"

He shook his shoulders again like he didn't know.

"Are you okay, Bosch?"

He stubbed out his cigarette.

"Yeah, I'm fine. Why?"

"I don't know. You know what that guy Marvin Gaye sang about, don't you? Before he got killed by his own dad? He sang about sexual healing. Said it's good for the soul. Something like that. Anyway, I believe it, do you?"

"I suppose."

"I think you need healing in your life, Bosch. That's the vibe I'm getting."

"You want to go to sleep now?"

She lay down again and pulled the sheet up. He walked around the room naked, turning out the lights. When he was under the sheet in the dark, she turned on her side so her back was to him and told him to put his arm around her. He moved up close behind her and did. He loved her smell.

"How come people call you Jazz?"

"I don't know. They just do. Because it goes with the name."

After a few moments she asked him why he had asked that.

"Because. You smell like both your names. Like the flower and the music."

"What does jazz smell like?"

"It smells dark and smoky."

They were silent for a long while after that and eventually Bosch thought she was asleep. But he still could not make it down. He lay with his eyes open, looking at the shadows of the room. Then she spoke softly to him.

"Bosch, what's the worst thing you've ever done to yourself?"

"What do you mean?"

"You know what I mean. What's the worst thing? What's the thing that keeps you awake at night if you think about it too hard?"

He thought for a few moments before answering.

"I don't know." He forced an uneasy and short laugh. "I guess I've done a lot of bad things. I suppose a lot of them are to myself. At least I think about them a lot . . ."

"What's one of them? You can tell me."

And he knew that he could. He thought he could tell her almost anything and not be judged harshly.

"When I was a kid—I grew up mostly in a youth hall, like an orphanage. When I was new there, one of the older kids took my shoes, my sneakers. They didn't fit him or anything but he did it because he knew he could do it. He was one of the rulers of the roost and he took 'em. I didn't do anything about it and it hurt."

"But you didn't do it. That's not what I—"

"No, I'm not done. I just told you that because you had to know that part. See, when I got older and I was one of the big shots in the place, I did the same thing. I took this new kid's shoes. He was smaller, I couldn't even put 'em on. I just took them and I . . . I don't know, I threw them out or something. But I took them because I could. I did the same thing that was done to me . . . And sometimes, even now, I think about it and I feel bad."

She squeezed his hand in a way he thought was meant to be comforting but said nothing.

"Is that the kind of story you wanted?"

She just squeezed his hand again. After a while he spoke.

"I think the one thing I did that I regret the most, though, was maybe letting a woman go."

"You mean like a criminal?"

"No. I mean like we lived—we were lovers and when she wanted to go, I didn't really . . . do anything. I didn't put up a fight, you know. And when I think about it, sometimes I think that maybe if I had, I could've changed her mind . . . I don't know."

"Did she say why she was leaving?"

"She just got to know me too well. I don't blame her for anything. I've got baggage. I guess maybe I can be hard to take. I've lived alone most of my life."

Silence filled the room again and he waited. He sensed that there was something more she wanted to say or be asked. But when she spoke he wasn't sure if she was talking about him or herself.

"They say when a cat is ornery and scratches and hisses at everybody, even somebody who wants to comfort it and love it, it's because it wasn't held enough when it was a kitten."

"I never heard that before."

"I think it's true."

He was quiet a moment and moved his hand up so that it was touching her breasts.

"Is that what your story is?" he asked. "You weren't held enough."

"Who knows."

"What was the worst thing you ever did to yourself, Jasmine? I think you want to tell me."

He knew she wanted him to ask it. It was true confessions time and he began to believe that the whole night had been directed by her to arrive at this one question.

"You didn't try to hold on to someone you should have," she said. "I held on to someone I shouldn't have. I held on too long. Thing is, I knew what it was leading to, deep down I knew. It was like standing on the tracks and seeing the train coming at you but being too mesmerized by the bright light to move, to save yourself."

He had his eyes open in the dark still. He could barely see the outline of her shoulder and cheek. He pulled himself closer to her, kissed her neck and in her ear whispered, "But you got out. That's what's important."

"Yeah, I got out," she said wistfully. "I got out."

She was silent for a while and then reached up under the covers and touched his hand. It was cupped over one of her breasts. She held her hand on top of it.

"Good night, Harry."

He waited a while, until he heard the measured breathing of her sleep, and then he was finally able to drift off. There was no dream this time. Just warmth and darkness.

In the morning Bosch awoke first. He took a shower and borrowed Jasmine's toothbrush without asking. Then he dressed in the clothes he'd worn the day before and went out to his car to retrieve his overnight bag. Once he was dressed in fresh clothes he ventured into the kitchen to see about coffee. All he found was a box of tea bags.

Leaving the idea behind, he walked around the apartment, his steps creaking on the old pine floors. The living room was as spare as the bedroom. A sofa with an off-white blanket spread on it, a coffee table, an old stereo with a cassette but no CD player. No television. Again, nothing on the walls but the telltale indication that there had been. He found two nails in the plaster. They weren't rusted or painted over. They hadn't been there very long.

Through a set of French doors the living room opened up to a porch enclosed in windows. There was rattan furniture out here and several potted plants, including a dwarf orange tree with fruit on it. The entire porch was redolent with its smell. Bosch stepped close to the windows and by looking south down the alley behind the property, he could see the bay. The morning sun's reflection on it was pure white light.

He walked back across the living room to another door on the wall opposite the French doors. Immediately upon opening this door, he could smell the sharp tang of oils and turpentine. This was where she painted. He hesitated but only for a moment, then walked in.

The first thing he noticed was that the room had a window that gave a direct view of the bay across the backyards and garages of three or four houses down the alley. It was beautiful and he knew why she chose this room for her art. At center on a paint-dappled drop cloth was an easel but no stool. She painted standing. He saw no overhead lamp or artificial light source anywhere else in the room. She painted only by true light.

He walked around the easel and found the canvas on it had been untouched by the painter. Along one of the side walls was a high work counter with various tubes of paint scattered about. There were palette boards and coffee cans with brushes stacked in them. At the end of the counter was a large laundry sink for washing up.

Bosch noticed more canvases leaning against the wall under the counter. They were faced inward and appeared to be unused pieces like the one on the easel, waiting for the artist's hand. But Bosch suspected otherwise. Not with the exposed nails in the walls in the other rooms of the apartment. He reached under the counter and slid a few of the canvases out. As he did this he almost felt as if he was on some case, solving some mystery.

The three portraits he pulled out were painted in dark hues. None were signed though it was obvious all were the work of one hand. And that hand was Jasmine's. Bosch recognized the style from the painting he had seen at her father's house. Sharp lines, dark colors. The first one he looked at was of a nude woman with her face turned away from the painter and into the shadows. The sense Bosch felt was that the darkness was taking the woman, rather than her turning to the darkness. Her mouth was completely in shadow. It was as if she was mute. The woman, Bosch knew, was Jasmine.

The second painting seemed to be part of the same study as the first. It was the same nude in shadow, though she was now facing the viewer. Bosch noted that in the portrait Jasmine had given herself fuller breasts than in reality and he wondered if this was done on purpose and had some meaning, or was perhaps a subliminal improvement made by the painter. He noticed that beneath the veneer of gray shadow over the painting there were red highlights on the woman. Bosch knew little about the art, but he knew this was a dark portrait.

Bosch looked at the third painting he had pulled out and found this to be unattached to the first two, save for the fact that again it was a nude portrait of Jasmine. But this piece he clearly recognized as a reinterpretation of "The Scream" by Edvard Munch, a painting that had always fascinated Bosch but that he had only seen in books. In the piece before him, the figure of the frightened person was Jasmine. The location had been transferred from Munch's horrific, swirling dreamscape to the Skyway bridge. Bosch clearly recognized the bright yellow vertical piping of the bridge's support span.

"What are you doing?"

He jumped as if stabbed in the back. It was Jasmine, at the door of the studio. She wore a silk bathrobe she held closed with her arms. Her eyes were puffy. She had just woken up.

"I'm looking at your work, is that okay?"

"This door was locked."

"No, it wasn't."

She reached to the doorknob and turned it, as if that could disprove his claim.

"It wasn't locked, Jazz. I'm sorry. I didn't know you didn't want me in here."

"Could you put those back under there, please?"

"Sure. But why'd you take them off the walls?"

"I didn't."

"Was it because they're nudes, or is it because of what they mean?"

"Please don't ask me about this. Put them back."

She left the doorway and he put the paintings back where he found them. He left the room and found her in the kitchen filling a tea kettle with water from the sink. Her back was to him and he walked in and lightly put a hand on her back. Even so, she started slightly at his touch.

"Jazz, look, I'm sorry. I'm a cop. I get curious."

"It's okay."

"Are you sure?"

"Yes, I'm sure. You want some tea?"

She had stopped filling the kettle but did not turn around or make a move to put it on the stove.

"No. I was thinking maybe I could take you out for breakfast."

"When do you leave? I thought you said the plane's this morning."

"That was the other thing I was thinking about. I could stay another day, leave tomorrow, if you want me to. I mean, if you'll have me. I'd like to stay."

She turned around and looked at him.

"I want you to stay, too."

They embraced and kissed but she quickly pulled back.

"It's not fair, you brushed your teeth. I have monster breath."

"Yeah, but I used your toothbrush, so it evens out."

"Gross. Now I have to get a new one."

"That's right."

They smiled and she gave him a tight hug around the neck, his trespass in her studio seemingly forgotten.

"You call the airline and I'll get ready. I know where we can go."

When she pulled away he held her in front of him. He wanted to bring it up again. He couldn't help it.

"I want to ask you something."

"What?"

"How come those paintings aren't signed?"

"They're not ready to be signed."

"The one at your father's was signed."

"That was for him, so I signed it. Those others are for me."

"The one on the bridge. Is she going to jump?"

She looked at him a long time before answering.

"I don't know. Sometimes when I look at it, I think she is. I think the thought is there, but you never know."

"It can't happen, Jazz."

"Why not?"

"Because it can't."

"I'll get ready."

She broke away from him then and left the kitchen.

He went to the wall phone next to the refrigerator and dialed the airline. While making the arrangements to fly out Monday morning, he decided on a whim to ask the airline agent if it was possible to route his new flight back to Los Angeles through Las Vegas. She said not without a three-hour-and-fourteen-minute layover. He said he'd take it. He had to pay fifty dollars on top of the seven hundred they already had from him in order to make the needed changes. He put it on his credit card.

He thought about Vegas as he hung up. Claude Eno might be dead .

but his wife was still cashing his checks. She might be worth the fifty-dollar layover.

"Ready?"

It was Jasmine calling from the living room. Bosch stepped out of the kitchen and she was waiting for him in cut-off jeans and a tank top beneath a white shirt she left open and tied above her waist. She already had on sunglasses.

She took him to a place where they poured honey on top of the biscuits and served the eggs with grits and butter. Bosch hadn't had grits since basic training at Benning. The meal was delicious. Neither of them spoke much. The paintings and the conversation they had before falling asleep the night before were not mentioned. It seemed that what they had said was better left for the dark shadows of night, and maybe her paintings, too.

When they were done with their coffee, she insisted on picking up the check. He got the tip. They spent the afternoon cruising in her Volkswagen with the top down. She took him all over the place, from Ybor City to St. Petersburg Beach, burning up a tank of gas and two packs of cigarettes. By late in the afternoon they were at a place called Indian Rocks Beach to look at the sunset over the Gulf.

"I've been a lot of places," Jasmine told him. "I like the light here the best."

"Ever been out to California?"

"No, not yet."

"Sometimes the sunset looks like lava pouring down on the city."

"That must be beautiful."

"It makes you forgive a lot, forget a lot . . . That's the thing about Los Angeles. It's got a lot of broken pieces to it. But the ones that still work, really do work."

"I think I know what you mean."

"I'm curious about something."

"Here we go again. What?"

"If you don't show your paintings to anybody, how do you make a living?"

It was from out of left field but he had been thinking about it all day.

"I have money from my father. Even before he died. It's not a lot but I don't need a lot. It's enough. If I don't feel the need to sell my work when it is finished, then as I am doing it, it won't be compromised. It will be pure."

It sounded to Bosch like a convenient way of explaining away the fear of exposing oneself. But he let it go. She didn't.

"Are you always a cop? Always asking questions?"

"No. Only when I care about someone."

She kissed him quickly and walked back to the car.

After stopping by her place to change, they had dinner in a Tampa steak house where the wine list was actually a book so thick it came on its own pedestal. The restaurant itself seemed to be the work of a slightly delusional Italian decorator, a dark blend of gilded rococo, garish red velvet and classical statues and paintings. It was the kind of place he would expect her to suggest. She mentioned that this meateater's palace was actually owned by a vegetarian.

"Sounds like somebody from California."

She smiled and was quiet for a while after that. Bosch's mind wandered to the case. He had spent the entire day without giving it a thought. Now a pang of guilt thrummed in his mind. It was almost as if he felt he was shunting his mother aside to pursue the selfish pleasure of Jasmine's company. Jasmine seemed to read him and to know he was privately debating something.

"Can you stay another day, Harry?"

He smiled but shook his head.

"I can't. I gotta go. But I'll be back. As soon as I can."

Bosch paid for dinner with a credit card he guessed was reaching its limit and they headed back to her apartment. Knowing their time together was drawing to a close, they went right to the bed and made love.

The feel of her body, its taste and its scent seemed perfect to Bosch. He didn't want the moment to end. He'd had immediate attractions to women before in his life and had even acted on them. But never one that felt so fully engaging and complete. He guessed that it was because of all he did not know about her. That was the hook. She was a mystery. Physically, he could not get any closer than he was to her during these moments, yet there was so much of her hidden, unexplored. They made love in gentle rhythm and held each other in a deep, long kiss at the end.

Later, he lay on his side, next to her, his arm across the flatness of her belly. One of her hands traced circles in his hair. The true confessions began.

"Harry, you know, I haven't been with a lot of men in my life."

He didn't respond because he didn't know what the proper response could be. He was well past caring about a woman's sexual history for anything other than health reasons.

"What about you?" she asked.

He couldn't resist.

"I haven't been with a lot of men, either. In fact, none, as far as I know."

She punched him on the shoulder.

"You know what I mean."

"The answer is no. I haven't been with a lot of women in my life. Not enough, at least."

"I don't know, the men that I've been with, most of them, it's like they wanted something from me I didn't have. I don't know what it was but I just didn't have it to give. Then I either left too soon or stayed too long."

He propped himself up on one elbow and looked at her.

"Sometimes I think that I know strangers better than I know anybody else, even myself. I learn so much about people in my job. Sometimes I think I don't even have a life. I only have their life . . . I don't know what I'm talking about."

"I think you do. I understand. Maybe everybody's like this."

"I don't know. I don't think so."

They were quiet for a while after that. Bosch leaned down and kissed her breasts, holding a nipple between his lips for a long moment. She brought her hands up and held his head to her chest. He could smell the jasmine.

"Harry, have you ever had to use your gun?"

He pulled his head up. The question seemed out of place. But through the darkness he could see her eyes on him, watching and waiting for an answer.

"Yes."

"You killed someone."

It wasn't a question.

"Yes."

She said nothing else.

"What is it, Jazz?"

"Nothing. I was just wondering how that would be. How you would go on."

"Well, all I can tell you is that it hurts. Even when there was no choice and they had to go down, it hurts. You just have to go on."

She was silent. Whatever she had needed to hear from him he hoped she had gotten. Bosch was confused. He didn't know why she had asked such questions and wondered if she was testing him in some way. He lay back on his pillow and waited for sleep but confusion kept it away from him. After a while she turned on the bed and put her arm over him.

"I think you are a good man," she whispered close to his ear.

"Am I?" he whispered back.

"And you will come back, won't you?"

"Yes. I'll come back."

Bosch went to every rental counter in McCarran International Airport in Las Vegas but none had a car left. He silently chastised himself for not making a reservation and walked outside the terminal into the dry crisp air to catch a cab. The driver was a woman and when Bosch gave the address, on Lone Mountain Drive, he could clearly see her disappointment in the rearview mirror. The destination wasn't a hotel, so she wouldn't be picking up a return fare.

"Don't worry," Bosch said, understanding her problem. "If you wait for me, you can take me back to the airport."

"How long you gonna be? I mean, Lone Mountain, that's way out there in the sand pits."

"I might be five minutes, I might be less. Maybe a half hour. I'd say no longer than a half hour."

"You waiting on the meter?"

"On the meter or you. Whatever you want to do."

She thought about it a moment and put the car in drive.

"Where are all the rental cars, anyway?"

"Big convention in town. Electronics or something."

It was a thirty-minute ride out into the desert northwest of the strip. The neon-and-glass buildings retreated and the cab passed through residential neighborhoods until these, too, became sparse. The land was a ragged brown out here and dotted unevenly with scrub brush. Bosch knew the roots of every bush spread wide and sucked up what little moisture was in the earth. It made for a terrain that seemed dying and desolate.

The houses, too, were few and far between, each one an outpost in a no-man's-land. The streets had been gridded and paved long ago but the boomtown of Las Vegas hadn't quite caught up yet. It was coming, though. The city was spreading like a patch of weeds.

The road began to rise toward a mountain the color of cocoa mix. The cab shook as a procession of eighteen-wheel dump trucks thundered by with loads of sand from the excavation pits the driver had mentioned. And soon the paved roadway gave way to gravel and the cab sent up a tail of dust in its wake. Bosch was beginning to think the address the smarmy supervising clerk at City Hall had given him was a phony. But then they were there.

The address to which Claude Eno's pension checks were mailed each month was a sprawling ranch-style house of pink stucco and dusty white tile roof. Looking past it, Bosch could see where even the gravel road ended just past it. It was the end of the line. Nobody had lived farther away than Claude Eno.

"I don't know about this," the driver said. "You want me to wait? This is like the goddamn moon out here."

She had pulled into the driveway behind a late 1970s-model Olds Cutlass. There was a carport where another car was parked hidden beneath a tarp that was blue in the further recesses of the carport but bleached nearly white along the surfaces sacrificed to the sun.

Bosch took out his fold of money and paid the driver thirty-five dollars for the ride out. Then he took two twenties, ripped them in half and handed one side of each over the seat to her.

"You wait, you get the other half of those."

"Plus the fare back to the airport."

"Plus that."

Bosch got out, realizing it would probably be the quickest forty bucks ever lost in Las Vegas if nobody answered the door. But he was in luck. A woman who looked to be in her late sixties opened the door before he could knock. And why not, he thought. In this house, you could see visitors coming for a mile.

Bosch felt the blast of air-conditioning escaping through the open door.

"Mrs. Eno?"

"No."

Bosch pulled out his notebook and checked the address against the black numbers tacked on the front wall next to the door. They matched.

"Olive Eno doesn't live here?"

"You didn't ask that. I'm not Mrs. Eno."

"Can I please speak with Mrs. Eno then?" Annoyed with the woman's preciseness, Bosch showed the badge he had gotten back from McKittrick after the boat ride. "It's police business."

"Well, you can try. She hasn't spoken to anybody, at least anybody outside her imagination, in three years."

She motioned Bosch in and he stepped into the cool house.

"I'm her sister. I take care of her. She's in the kitchen. We were in the middle of lunch when I saw the dust come up on the road and heard you arrive."

Bosch followed her down a tiled hallway toward the kitchen. The house smelled like old age, like dust and mold and urine. In the kitchen a gnome-like woman with white hair sat in a wheelchair, barely taking up half of the space it gave for an occupant. There was a slide-on tray in front of it and the woman's gnarled pearl-white hands were folded together on top of it. There were milky blue cataracts on both eyes and they seemed dead to the world outside the body. Bosch noticed a bowl of applesauce on the nearby table. It only took him a few seconds to size up the situation.

"She'll be ninety in August," said the sister. "If she makes it."

"How long has she been like this?"

"Long time. I've been taking care of her for three years now." She then bent into the gnome's face and loudly added, "Isn't that right, Olive?"

The loudness of the question seemed to kick a switch and Olive Eno's jaw started working but no sound that was intelligible issued. She stopped the effort after a while and the sister straightened up.

"Don't worry about it, Olive. I know you love me."

She wasn't as loud with that sentence. Maybe she feared Olive might actually muster a denial.

"What's your name?" Bosch asked.

"Elizabeth Shivone. What's this about? I saw that badge of yours says Los Angeles, not Las Vegas. Aren't you off the beat here a bit?"

"Not really. It's about her husband. One of his old cases."

"Claude's been dead going on five years now."

"How did he die?"

"Just died. His pump went out. Died right there on the floor, about where you're standing."

They both looked down at the floor as if maybe his body was still there.

"I came to look through his things," Bosch said.

"What things?"

"I don't know. I was thinking maybe he kept files from his time with the police."

"You better tell me what you're doing here. This doesn't sound right to me."

"I'm investigating a case he worked back in 1961. It's still open. Parts of the file are missing. I thought maybe he'd taken it. I thought maybe there might be something important that he kept. I don't know what. Anything. I just thought it was worth a try."

He could see that her mind was working and her eyes suddenly froze for a second when her memory snagged on something.

"There is something, isn't there?" he said.

"No. I think you should go."

"It's a big house. Did he have a home office?"

"Claude left the police thirty years ago. He built this house in the middle of nowhere just to be away from all of that."

"What did he do when he moved out here?"

"He worked casino security. A few years at the Sands, then twenty at the Flamingo. He was getting two pensions and took good care of Olive."

"Speaking of which, who's signing those pension checks these days?"

Bosch looked at Olive Eno to make his point. The other woman was silent a long moment, then went on the offense.

"Look, I could get power of attorney. Look at her. It wouldn't be a problem. I take care of her, mister."

"Yeah, you feed her applesauce."

"I have nothing to hide."

"You want somebody to make sure or do you want to let it end right here? I don't really care what you're doing, lady. I don't really care if you're even her sister or not. If I was betting, I'd say you're not. But I don't really care right now. I'm busy. I just want to look through Eno's things."

He stopped there and let her think about it. He looked at his watch.

"No warrant then, right?"

"I don't have a warrant. I've got a cab waiting. You make me get a warrant and I'm going to stop being such a nice guy."

Her eyes went up and down his body as if to measure how nice and how not nice he could be.

"The office is this way."

She said the words as if they were bites out of wood planks. She swiftly led him down the hall again and then off to the left into a study. There was an old steel desk as the room's centerpiece, a couple of four-drawer file cabinets, an extra chair and not much else.

"After he died, Olive and I moved everything into those file cabinets and haven't looked at it since."

"They're all full?"

"All eight. Have at it."

Bosch reached his hand into his pocket and took out another twenty-dollar bill. He tore it in half and gave one side to Shivone.

"Take that out to the cab driver. Tell her I'm going to be a little longer than I thought."

She exhaled loudly, snatched the half and left the room. After she was gone Bosch went to the desk and opened each of the drawers. The first two he tried were empty. The next contained stationery and office supplies. The fourth drawer contained a checkbook that he quickly leafed through and saw it was an account covering household expenses. There was also a file containing recent receipts and other records. The last drawer in the desk was locked.

He started with the bottom file drawers and worked his way up.

Nothing in the first few seemed even remotely connected with what Bosch was working on. There were files labeled with the names of different casinos and gaming organizations. The files in another drawer were labeled by people's names. Bosch looked through a few of these and determined they were files on known casino cheats. Eno had built a library of home intelligence files. By this time, Shivone had come back from her errand and had taken the seat opposite the desk. She was watching Bosch and he threw a few idle questions at her while he looked.

"So what did Claude do for the casinos?"

"He was a bird dog."

"What's that?"

"Kind've an undercover thing. He mingled in the casinos, gambled with house chips, watched people. He was good at picking out the cheats and how they did it."

"Guess it takes one to know one, right?"

"What's that crack supposed to mean? He did a good job."

"I'm sure he did. Is that how he met you?"

"I'm not answering any of your questions."

"Okay by me."

He had only the two top drawers left. He opened one and found it contained no files at all. Just an old, dust-covered Rolodex and other items that had probably sat on the top of the desk at one point. There was an ashtray, a clock and a pen holder made of carved wood that had Eno's name carved on it. Bosch took the Rolodex out and put it on top of the cabinet. He blew the dust off it and then began turning it until he came to the C's. He looked through the cards but found no listing for Arno Conklin. He met with similar failure when he tried to find a listing for Gordon Mittel.

"You're not going to look through that whole thing, are you?" Shivone asked in exasperation.

"No, I'm just going to take it with me."

"Oh, no you don't. You can't just come in here and—"

"I'm taking it. If you want to make a complaint about it, be my guest. Then I'll make a complaint about you."

She went quiet after that. Bosch went on to the next drawer and found it contained about twelve files on old LAPD cases from the 1950s and early 1960s. Again, he didn't have the time to study them, but he checked all the labels and none was marked Marjorie Lowe. By randomly pulling out a few of the files it became clear to him that Eno had made copies of files on some of his cases to take with him when he left the department. Of the random selections, all were murders, including two of prostitutes. Only one of the cases was closed.

"Go get me a box or a bag or something for these files," Bosch said over his shoulder. When he sensed the woman in the room had not moved, he barked, "Do it!"

She got up and left. Bosch stood gazing at the files and thinking. He had no idea if these were important or not. He had no idea what they meant. He only knew he should take them in case they turned out to be important. But what bothered him more than what the files that were in the drawer could mean was the feeling that something was certainly missing. This was based on his belief in McKittrick. The retired detective was sure his former partner, Eno, had some kind of hold on Conklin, or at the very least, some kind of deal with him. But there was nothing here about that. And it seemed to Bosch that if Eno was holding something on Conklin, it would still be here. If he kept old LAPD files, then he kept whatever he had on Conklin. In fact, he would have kept it in a safe place. Where?

The woman came back and dropped a cardboard box on the floor. It was the kind a case of beer had come in. Bosch put a foot-thick stack of files in it along with the Rolodex.

"You want a receipt?" he asked.

"No, I don't want anything from you."

"Well, there is still something I need from you."

"This doesn't end, does it?"

"I hope it does."

"What do you want?"

"When Eno died, did you help the old lady—uh, your sister, that is—did you help her clear out his safe deposit box?"

"How'd—"

She stopped herself but not soon enough.

"How'd I know? Because it's obvious. What I'm looking for, he would have kept in a safe place. What did you do with it?"

"We threw everything away. It was meaningless. Just some old files and bank statements. He didn't know what he was doing. He was old himself."

Bosch looked at his watch. He was running out of time if he was going to make his plane.

"Get me the key for this desk drawer."

She didn't move.

"Hurry up, I don't have a lot of time. You open it or I'll open it. But if I do it, that drawer isn't going to be much use to you anymore."

She reached into the pocket of her house dress and pulled out the house keys. She reached down and unlocked the desk drawer, pulled it open and then stepped away.

"We didn't know what any of it was, or what it meant."

"That's fine."

Bosch moved to the drawer and looked in. There were two thin manila files and two packs of envelopes with rubber bands holding them together. The first file he looked through contained Eno's birth certificate, passport, marriage license and other personal records. He put it back in the drawer. The next file contained LAPD forms and Bosch quickly recognized them as the pages and reports that had been removed from the Marjorie Lowe murder book. He knew he had no time to read them at the moment and put the file in the beer box with the other files.

The rubber band on the first package of envelopes snapped when he tried to remove it and he was reminded of the band that had been around the blue binder that contained the case files. Everything about this case was old and ready to snap, he thought.

The envelopes were all from a Wells Fargo Bank branch in Sherman Oaks and each one contained a statement for a savings account in the name of McCage Inc. The address of the corporation was a post office box, also in Sherman Oaks. Bosch randomly took envelopes from different spots in the pack and studied three of them. Though separated by years in the late 1960s, each statement was basically the same. A deposit of one thousand dollars was made in the account on the tenth of each month and on the fifteenth a transfer of an equal amount was made to an account with a Nevada Savings and Loan branch in Las Vegas.

Without looking further, Bosch concluded that the bank statements might be the records of some kind of payoff account Eno kept. He quickly looked through the envelopes at the postmarks looking for the most recent one. He found none more recent than the late 1980s.

"What about these envelopes? When did he stop getting them?"

"What you see is what you get. I have no idea what they mean and Olive didn't know either back when they drilled his box."

"Drilled his box?"

"Yeah, after he died. Olive wasn't on the safe deposit box. Only him. We couldn't find his key. So we had to have it drilled."

"There was money, too, wasn't there?"

She waited a moment, probably wondering if he was going to demand that, too.

"Some. But you're too late, it's already spent."

"I'm not worried about that. How much was there?"

She pinched her lips and acted like she was trying to remember. It was a bad act.

"C'mon. I'm not here for the money and I'm not from the IRS."

"It was about eighteen thousand."

Bosch heard a horn honk from outside. The cabdriver was getting restless. Bosch looked at his watch. He had to go. He tossed the envelope packs into the beer box.

"What about his account at Nevada Savings and Loan? How much was in it?"

It was a scam question based on his guess that the account that the money from Sherman Oaks was transferred to was Eno's. Shivone hesitated again. A delay punctuated by another horn blast.

"It was about fifty. But most of that's gone, too. Taking care of Olive, you know?"

"Yeah, I bet. Between that and the pensions, it's gotta be rough," Bosch said with all the sarcasm he could put into it. "I bet your accounts aren't too thin, though."

"Look, mister, I don't know who you think you are but I'm the only one in the world that she has and who cares about her. That's worth something."

"Too bad she doesn't get to decide what it's worth instead of you. Answer one question for me and then I'm out of here and you can go back to taking whatever you can off her . . . Who are you? You're not her sister. Who are you?"

"It's none of your business."

"That's right. But I could make it my business."

She put on a look that showed Bosch what an affront he was to her delicate sensibilities but then seemed to gain a measure of self-esteem. Whoever she was, she was proud of it.

"You want to know who I am? I was the best woman he ever had. I was with him for a long time. She had his wedding band but I had his heart. Near the end, when they were both old and it didn't matter, we dropped the pretension and he brought me in here. To live with them. Take care of them. So don't you dare tell me I don't deserve something out of it."

Bosch just nodded. Somehow, as sordid as the story seemed, he found a measure of respect for her for just having told the truth. And he felt sure it was.

"When did you meet?"

"You said one question."

"When did you meet?"

"When he was at the Flamingo. We both were. I was a dealer. Like I said, he was a bird dog."

"He ever talk about L.A., about any cases, any people from back there?"

"No, never. He always said that was a closed chapter."

Bosch pointed to the envelope stacks in the box.

"Does the name McCage mean anything?"

"Not to me."

"What about these account statements?"

"I never saw any of those things until the day we opened that box. Didn't know he even had an account over at Nevada Savings. Claude had secrets. He even kept secrets from me."

At the airport Bosch paid off the cab driver and struggled into the main terminal with his overnighter and the beer box full of files and other things. In one of the stores along the main terminal mall he bought a cheap canvas satchel and transferred the items he had taken from Eno's office into it. It was small enough so he didn't have to check it. Printed on the side of the bag was LAS VEGAS—LAND OF SUN AND FUN! There was a logo depicting the sun setting behind a pair of dice.

At his gate he had a half hour before they loaded the plane, so he found a section of open seats as far away as possible from the cacophony of the rows of slot machines set in the center of the circular terminal.

He began going through the files in the satchel. The one he was most interested in was the one containing records stolen from the Marjorie Lowe murder book. He looked through the documents and found nothing unusual or unexpected.

The summary of the McKittrick-Eno interview of Johnny Fox with Arno Conklin and Gordon Mittel present was here and Bosch could sense the contained outrage at the situation in McKittrick's writing. In the last paragraph it was no longer contained.

Interview with suspect was regarded by the undersigned as fruitless because of the intrusive behavior of A. Conklin and G. Mittel. Both "prosecutors" refused to allow "their" witness to answer questions fully or in the undersign's opinion with the whole truth. J. Fox remains suspect at this time until verification of his alibi and fingerprint analysis.

Nothing else in the documents was of note and Bosch realized that they were probably removed from the file by Eno solely because they mentioned Conklin's involvement in the case. Eno was covering up for Conklin. When Bosch asked himself why Eno was doing this, he immediately thought of the bank statements that had been in the safe deposit box with the stolen documents. They were records of the deal.

Bosch took out the envelopes and, going by the postmarks, began putting them in chronological order. The earliest one he could find was mailed to the McCage Inc. postal drop in November 1962. That was one year after the death of Marjorie Lowe and two months after the death of Johnny Fox. Eno had been on the Lowe case and then, according to McKittrick, he had investigated the Fox killing.

Bosch felt in his gut that he was right. Eno had squeezed Conklin. And maybe Mittel. He somehow knew what McKittrick didn't, that Conklin had been involved with Marjorie Lowe. Maybe he even knew Conklin had killed her. He had enough to put Conklin on the line for a thousand bucks a month for life. It wasn't a lot. Eno wasn't greedy, though a thousand a month in the early sixties probably more than matched what he was making on the job. But the amount didn't matter to Bosch. The payment did. It was an admission. If it could be traced to Conklin, it was hard evidence. Bosch felt himself getting excited. The records hoarded by a corrupt cop dead five years now might be all he needed to go head to head with Conklin.

He thought of something and looked around for the usual bank of phones. He checked his watch and looked over at the gate. People were milling about, ready to board and getting anxious. Bosch put the file and envelopes back into the satchel and carried his things to the phone.

Using his AT&T card, he dialed information in Sacramento and then dialed the state offices and asked for the corporate records unit. In three minutes he knew that McCage Inc. was not a California corporation and never was, at least in records going back to 1971. He hung up and went through the same process again, this time calling the Nevada state offices in Carson City.

The phone clerk told him the incorporation of McCage Inc. was defunct and asked if he was still interested in what information the state had. He excitedly said yes and was told by the clerk that she had to switch to microfiche and it would take a few minutes. While he waited, Bosch got out a notebook and got ready to take notes. He saw the gate door had been opened and people were just starting to board the plane. He didn't care, he'd miss it if he had to. He was too juiced to do anything but hang on to the phone.

Bosch studied the rows of slot machines in the center of the terminal. They were crowded with people trying their last chance at luck before leaving or their first chance after stepping off planes from all over the country and the world. Gambling against the machines had never appealed much to Bosch. He didn't understand it.

As he watched those milling about, it was easy to pick who was winning and who wasn't. It didn't take a detective to study the faces and know. He saw one woman with a stuffed teddy bear clamped under her arm. She was working two machines at once and Bosch could see that all she was doing was doubling her losses. To her left was a man in a black cowboy hat who was filling the machine with coins and pulling the arm back as quickly as he could. Bosch could see he was playing a dollar machine and was going to the five-dollar max on every roll. Bosch figured that, in the few minutes he watched, the man had spent sixty dollars with no return. At least he wasn't carrying a stuffed animal.

Bosch turned back to check the gate. The line of boarders had thinned to a few stragglers. Bosch knew he was going to miss it. But that was okay. He hung on and stayed calm.

Suddenly there was a shout and Bosch looked over and saw the man with the cowboy hat waving it as his machine was paying off a jackpot. The woman with the stuffed animal stepped back from her machines and solemnly watched the payoff. Each metallic *ching* of the dollars dropping in the tray must have been like a hammer pounding in her skull. A steady reminder that she was losing.

"Take a look at me now, baby!" the cowboy whooped.

It didn't appear that the exclamation was directed at anyone in particular. He stooped down and started scooping the coins into his hat. The woman with the teddy bear went back to work on her machines.

Just as the gate door was being closed, the clerk came back on the phone. She told Bosch the immediately available records showed McCage was incorporated in November 1962 and was dissolved by the state twenty-eight years later when a year went by without renewal fees or taxes being paid to keep the incorporation current. Bosch knew this had occurred because Eno had died.

"Do you want the officers?" the clerk asked.

"Yes, I do."

"Okay, president and chief executive officer is Claude Eno. That's E-N-O. Vice president is Gordon Mittel with two T's. And the treasurer is listed as Arno Conklin. That first name's spelled—"

"I got it. Thanks."

Bosch hung up the phone, grabbed his overnighter and the satchel and ran to the gate.

"Just in time," the attendant said with a tone of annoyance. "Couldn't leave those one-armed bandits alone, huh?"

"Yeah," Bosch said, not caring.

She opened the door and he went down the hallway and onto the plane. It was only half filled. He ignored his seat assignment and found an empty row. While he was pushing his luggage into the overhead storage bin, he thought of something. Once in his seat he took out his notebook and opened it to the page where he had just written the notes of his conversation with the incorporation clerk. He looked at the abbreviated notations.

Prez., CEO—C.E.

VP—G.M.

Treas.—A.C.

He then wrote only the initials in a line.

CE GM AC

He looked at the line for a moment and then smiled. He saw the anagram and wrote it on the next line.

MC CAGE

Bosch felt the blood jangling through his body. It was the feeling of knowing he was close. He was on a roll those people out there at the slot machines and all the casinos in the desert could never understand. It was a high they would never feel, no matter how many sevens came up on the dice or how many black jacks they were dealt. Bosch was getting close to a killer and that made him as juiced as any jackpot winner on the planet.

Driving the Mustang out of LAX an hour later, Bosch rolled the windows down and bathed his face in the cool, dry air. The sound of the breeze through the grove of eucalyptus trees at the airport gateway was always there like a welcome home. Somehow, he always found it reassuring when he came back from his trips. It was one of the things he loved about the city and he was glad it always greeted him.

He caught the light at Sepulveda and used the time to change the time on his watch. It was five minutes after two. He decided that he would have just enough time to get home, change into fresh clothes and grab something to eat before heading to Parker Center and his appointment with Carmen Hinojos.

He drove quickly under the 405 overpass and then took the curving on-ramp up onto the crowded freeway. As he turned the wheel to negotiate the turn, he realized that his upper arms ached deep in the biceps and he wasn't sure if it was from his fight with the fish on Saturday or from the way Jasmine had gripped his arms while they made love. He thought about her for a few more minutes and decided he would call her at the house before heading downtown. Their parting that morning already seemed long ago to him. They had made promises to meet again as soon as possible and Bosch hoped the promises would be kept. She was a mystery to him, one in which he knew he had not yet even begun to scratch the surface.

The 10 wasn't set to reopen until the following day, so Bosch bypassed the exit and stayed on the 405 until it rose over the Santa Monica Mountains and dropped into the Valley. He took the long way because he bet it would be faster, and because he had a mail drop in Studio City that he had been using since the post office refused to deliver mail to a redtagged structure.

He transferred onto the 101 and promptly hit a wall of traffic inching its way along the six lanes. He stayed with it until impatience got the better of him. He exited Coldwater Canyon Boulevard and started taking surface streets. On Moorpark Road he passed several apartment buildings that still hadn't been demolished or repaired, the red tags and yellow tape bleached near-white by the months in the sun. Many of the condemned buildings still had signs like $500 MOVES YOU IN! and NEWLY REMODELED. On one red-tagged structure with the telltale crisscross stress fractures running along its entire length, someone had spray-painted a slogan that many took as the epitaph of the city in the months since the earthquake.

THE FAT LADY HAS SUNG

Somedays it was hard not to believe it. But Bosch tried to keep the faith. Somebody had to. The newspaper said more people were leaving than coming. But no matter, Bosch thought, I'm staying.

He cut over to Ventura and stopped at the private mailbox office. There was nothing but bills and junk mail in his box. He stopped at a deli next door and ordered the special, turkey on whole wheat with avocado and bean sprouts, to go. After that, he stayed on Ventura until it became Cahuenga and then took the turn off to Woodrow Wilson Drive and the climb up the hill to home. On the first curve he had to slow on the narrow road to squeeze by an LAPD squad car. He waved but he knew they wouldn't know him. They would be out of North Hollywood Division. They didn't wave back.

He followed his usual practice of parking a half block away from his house and then walking back. He decided to leave the satchel in the trunk because he might need the files downtown. He headed down the street to his house with his overnighter in one hand and the sandwich bag in the other.

As he got to the carport, he noticed a patrol car coming up the road. He watched it and noticed it was the same two patrolmen he had just passed. They had turned around for some reason. He waited at the curb to see if they would stop to ask him for directions or maybe an explanation of his wave, and because he didn't want them to see him enter the condemned house. But the car drove by with neither of the patrolmen even looking at him. The driver had his eyes on the road and the passenger was talking into the radio microphone. It must be a call, Bosch thought. He waited until the car had gone around the next curve and then headed into the carport.

After opening the kitchen door, Bosch stepped in and immediately felt that something was amiss. He took two steps in before placing it. There was a foreign odor in the house, or at least the kitchen. It was the scent of perfume, he realized. No, he corrected, it was cologne. A man wearing cologne had either recently been in the house or was still there.

Bosch quietly placed his overnighter and the sandwich bag on the kitchen floor and reached to his waist. Old habits died hard. He still had no gun and he knew his backup was on the shelf in the closet near the front door. For a moment he thought about running out to the street in hopes of catching the patrol car but he knew it was long gone.

Instead, he opened a drawer and quietly withdrew a small paring knife. There were longer blades in there but the small knife would be easier to handle. He stepped toward the archway that led from the kitchen to the house's front entry. At the threshold, still hidden from whoever might be out there, he stopped, tilted his head forward and listened. He could hear the low hiss of the freeway down the hill behind the house, but nothing from within. Nearly a minute of silence passed. He was about to step out of the kitchen when he heard a sound. It was the slight whisper of cloth moving. Maybe the crossing or uncrossing of legs. He knew someone was in the living room. And he knew by now that they would know that he knew.

"Detective Bosch," a voice said from the silence of the house. "It is safe for you. You can come out."

Bosch knew the voice but was operating at such an acute level of intensity, he couldn't immediately compute it and place it. All he knew was that he had heard it before.

"It's Assistant Chief Irving, Detective Bosch," the voice said. "Could you please step out? That way you don't get hurt and we don't get hurt."

Yes, that was the voice. Bosch relaxed, put the knife down on the counter, the sandwich bag in the refrigerator and stepped out of the kitchen. Irving was there, sitting in the living room chair. Two men in suits whom Bosch didn't recognize sat on the couch. Looking around, Bosch could see his box of letters and cards from the closet sitting on the coffee table. He saw the murder book that he had left on the dining room table was sitting on the lap of one of the strangers. They had been searching his house, going through his things.

Bosch suddenly realized what had happened outside.

"I saw your lookout. Anybody want to tell me what's going on?"

"Where've you been, Bosch?" one of the suits asked.

Bosch looked at him. Not a single glimmer of recognition hit him.

"Who the fuck are you?"

He bent down and picked the box of cards and letters up off the coffee table, where it had been in front of the man.

"Detective," Irving said, "This is Lieutenant Angel Brockman and this is Earl Sizemore."

Bosch nodded. He recognized one of the names.

"I've heard of you," he said, looking at Brockman. "You're the one who sent Bill Connors to the closet. That must've been good for IAD man of the month. Quite an honor."

The sarcasm in Bosch's voice was unmistakable, as he intended it to be. The closet was where most cops kept their guns while off duty; going to the closet was department slang for a cop killing himself. Connors was an old beat cop in Hollywood Division who had killed himself the year before while he was under IAD investigation for trading dime bags of heroin to runaway girls for sex. After he was dead, the runaways had admitted making up the complaints because Connors was always hassling them to move off his beat. He had been a good man but saw everything stacked against him and decided to go to the closet.

"That was his choice, Bosch. And now you've got yours. You want to tell us where you've been the last twenty-four?"

"You want to tell me what this is about?"

He heard a clunking sound coming from the bedroom.

"What the hell?" He walked to the door and saw another suit in his bedroom, standing over the open drawer of the night table. "Hey, fuckhead, get out of there. Get out now!"

Bosch stepped in and kicked the drawer closed. The man stepped back, raised his hands like a prisoner and walked out to the living room.

"And this is Jerry Toliver," Irving added. "He's with Lieutenant Brockman, IAD. Detective Sizemore has joined us here from RHD."

"Fantastic," Bosch said. "So everybody knows everybody. What's going on?"

He looked at Irving as he said this, believing if he was going to get a straight answer from anyone here, it would be him. Irving was generally a straight shooter when it came to his dealings with Bosch.

"De—Harry, we have got to ask you some questions," Irving said. "It would be best if we explain things later."

Bosch could tell this one was serious.

"You got a warrant to be in here?"

"We'll show it to you later," Brockman said. "Let's go."

"Where are we going?"

"Downtown."

Bosch had had enough run-ins with the Internal Affairs Division to know things were being handled differently here. Just the fact that Irving, the second-highest-ranking officer in the department, was with them was an indication of the gravity of the situation. He guessed it was more than their simply finding out about his private investigation. If it was just that, Irving wouldn't have been here. There was something terribly wrong.

"All right," Bosch said, "who's dead?"

All four looked at him with faces of stone, confirming that in fact someone was dead. Bosch felt his chest tighten and for the first time he began to be scared. The names and faces of people he had involved flashed through his mind. Meredith Roman, Jake McKittrick, Keisha Russell, the two women in Las Vegas. Who else? Jazz? Could he have possibly put her in some kind of danger? Then it hit him. Keisha Russell. The reporter had probably done what he told her not to. She had gone to Conklin or Mittel and asked questions about the old clip she had pulled for Bosch. She had walked in blindly and was now dead because of her mistake.

"Keisha Russell?" he asked.

He got no reply. Irving stood up and the others followed. Sizemore kept the murder book in his hand. He was going to take it. Brockman went into the kitchen, picked up the overnighter and carried it to the door.

"Harry, why don't you ride with Earl and I?" Irving said.

"How 'bout I meet you guys down there."

"You ride with me."

It was said sternly. It invited no further debate. Bosch raised his hands, acknowledging he had no choice, and moved toward the door.

Bosch sat in the back of Sizemore's LTD, directly behind Irving. He looked out the window as they went down the hill. He kept thinking of the young reporter's face. Her eagerness had killed her but Bosch couldn't help but share the blame. He had planted the seed of mystery in her mind and it had grown until she couldn't resist it.

"Where'd they find her?" he asked.

He was met only with silence. He couldn't understand why they said nothing, especially Irving. The assistant chief had led him to believe in the past that they had an understanding, if not a liking, between each other.

"I told her not to do anything," he said. "I told her to sit on it a few days."

Irving turned his body so that he could partially see Bosch behind him.

"Detective, I don't know who or what you're talking about."

"Keisha Russell."

"Don't know her."

He turned back around. Bosch was puzzled. The names and faces went through his mind again. He added Jasmine but then subtracted her. She knew nothing about the case.

"McKittrick?"

"Detective," Irving said and again struggled to turn around to look at Bosch. "We are involved in the investigation of the homicide of Lieutenant Harvey Pounds. These other names are not involved. If you think they are people that should be contacted, please let me know."

Bosch was too stunned to answer. Harvey Pounds? That made no sense. He had nothing to do with the case, didn't even know about it. Pounds never left the office, how could he have gotten into danger?

Then it came to him, washing over him like a wave of water that brought with it a chill. He understood. It made sense. And in the moment that he saw that it did, he also saw his own responsibility as well as his own predicament.

"Am I . . . ?"

He couldn't finish.

"Yes," Irving said. "You are currently considered a suspect. Now maybe you will be quiet until we can set up a formal interview."

Bosch leaned his head against the window glass and closed his eyes.

"Ah, Jesus . . ."

And in that moment he realized he was no better than Brockman was for having sent a man to the closet. For Bosch knew in the dark part of his heart that he was responsible. He didn't know how or when it had happened but he knew.

He had killed Harvey Pounds. And he carried Pounds's badge in his pocket.

Bosch was numb to most of what was going on around him. After they reached Parker Center he was escorted up to Irving's office on the sixth floor and then placed in a chair in the adjoining conference room. He was in there alone for a half hour before Brockman and Toliver came in. Brockman sat directly across from Bosch, Toliver to Harry's right. It was obvious to Bosch by their being in Irving's conference room instead of an IAD interview room that Irving wanted to keep a tight control on this one. If it turned out to be a cop-killed-cop case, he'd need all the control he could muster to contain it. It could be a publicity debacle to rival those of the Rodney King days.

Through his daze and the jarring images of Pounds being dead, a pressing thought finally got Bosch's attention: he was in serious trouble himself. He told himself he couldn't retreat into a shell. He must be alert. The man sitting across from him would like nothing better than to hang a killing on Bosch and he was willing to go to any extreme to do it. It wasn't good enough that Bosch knew in his own mind that he had not, at least physically, killed Pounds. He had to defend himself. And so he resolved that he would show Brockman nothing. He would be just as tough as anybody in the room. He cleared his throat and began before Brockman got the chance.

"When did it happen?"

"I'm asking the questions."

"I can save you time, Brockman. Tell me when it happened and I'll tell you where I was. We'll get this over with. I understand why I'm a suspect. I won't hold it against you but you're wasting your time."

"Bosch, don't you feel anything at all? A man is dead. You worked with him."

Bosch stared at him a long moment before answering in an even voice.

"What I feel doesn't matter. Nobody deserves to be killed, but I'm not going to miss him and I certainly won't miss working for him."

"Jesus." Brockman shook his head. "The man had a wife, a kid in college."

"Maybe they won't miss him, either. You never know. The guy was a prick at work. No reason to expect him to be anything else at home. What's your wife think about you, Brockman?"

"Save it, Bosch. I'm not falling for any of your—"

"Do you believe in God, Brickman?"

Bosch used Brockman's nickname in the department, awarded to him for his methodical way of building cases against other cops, like the late Bill Connors.

"This isn't about me or what I believe in, Bosch. We're talking about you."

"That's right, we're talking about me. So, I'll tell you what I think. I'm not sure what I believe. My life's more than half over and I still haven't figured it out. But the theory I'm leaning toward is that everybody on this planet has some kind of energy that makes them what they are. It's all about energy. And when you die, it just goes somewhere else. And Pounds? He was bad energy and now it's gone somewhere else. So I don't feel too bad about him dying, to answer your question. But I'd like to know where that bad energy went. Hope you didn't get any, Brickman. You already have a lot."

He winked at Brockman and saw the momentary confusion in the IAD detective's face as he tried to interpret what the jibe had meant. He seemed to shake it off and go on.

"Enough of the bullshit. Why did you confront Lieutenant Pounds in his office on Thursday? You know that was off limits while you are on leave."

"Well, it was kind've like one of those Catch-22 situations. I think that's what they call 'em. It was off limits to go there but then Pounds, my commanding officer, called me up and told me I had to turn in my car. See, it was that bad energy working. I was already on involuntary leave but he couldn't leave well enough alone. He had to take my car, too. So I brought him in the keys. He was my supervisor and it was an order. So going there broke one of the rules but not going would have broken one, too."

"Why'd you threaten him?"

"I didn't."

"He filed an addendum to the assault complaint of two weeks earlier."

"I don't care what he filed. There was no threat. The guy was a coward. He probably felt threatened. But there was no threat. There is a difference."

Bosch looked over at the other suit. Toliver. It looked as if he was going to be silent the whole time. That was his role. He just stared at Bosch as if he were a TV screen.

Bosch looked around the rest of the room and for the first time noticed the phone on the banquette to the left of the table. The green light signaled a conference call was on. The interview was being piped out of the room. Probably to a tape recorder. Probably to Irving in his office next door.

"There is a witness," Brockman said.

"To what?"

"The threat."

"I'll tell you what, Lieutenant, why don't you tell me exactly what the threat was so I know what we're talking about. After all, if you believe I made it, what's wrong with me knowing what it was I said?"

Brockman gave it some thought before answering.

"Very simple, as most are, you told him if he ever, quote, fucked with you again, you'd kill him. Not too original."

"But damning as hell, right? Well, fuck you, Brockman, I never said that. I don't doubt that that asshole wrote up an addendum, that was just his style, but whoever this wit is you got, they're full of shit."

"You know Henry Korchmar?"

"Henry Korchmar?"

Bosch had no idea whom he was talking about. Then he realized Brockman meant old Henry of the Nod Squad. Bosch had never known his last name and so hearing it in this context had confused him.

"The old guy? He wasn't in the room. He's no witness. I told him to get out and he did. Whatever he told you, he probably backed Pounds because he was scared. But he wasn't there. You go ahead with it, Brockman. I'll be able to pull twelve people out of that squadroom who watched the whole thing through the glass. And they'll say Henry wasn't in there, they'll say Pounds was a liar and everybody knew it, and then where's your threat?"

Brockman said nothing into the silence so Bosch continued.

"See, you didn't do your work. My guess is that you know everybody who works in that squadroom thinks people like you are the bottom feeders of this department. They've got more respect for the people they put in jail. And you know that, Brickman, so you were too intimidated to go to them. Instead, you rely on some old man's word and he probably didn't even know Pounds was dead when you talked to him."

Bosch could tell by the way Brockman's eyes darted away that he had nailed him. Empowered with the victory, he stood up and headed toward the door.

"Where are you going?"

"To get some water."

"Jerry, go with him."

Bosch paused at the door and looked back.

"What, do you think I'm going to run, Brockman? You think that and you don't know the first thing about me. You think that and you haven't prepared for this interview. Why don't you come over to Hollywood one day and I'll teach you how to interview murder suspects. Free of charge."

Bosch walked out, Toliver following. At the water fountain down the hall, he took a long drink of water and then wiped his mouth with his hand. He felt nervous, frayed. He didn't know how long it would be before Brockman could see through the front he was putting up.

As he walked back to the conference room, Toliver stayed a silent three paces behind him.

"You're still young," Bosch said over his shoulder. "There might be a chance for you, Toliver."

Bosch stepped back into the conference room just as Brockman stepped through a door from the other side of the room. Bosch knew it was a direct entrance to Irving's office. He had once worked an investigation of a serial killer out of this room and under Irving's thumb.

Both men sat down across from each other again.

"Now, then," Brockman started. "I'm going to read you your rights, Detective Bosch."

He took a small card from his wallet and proceeded to read to Bosch the Miranda warning. Bosch knew for sure the phone line was going to a tape recorder. This was something they would want on tape.

"Now," Brockman said when he was finished. "Do you agree to waive those rights and talk to us about this situation?"

"It's a situation now, huh? I thought it was a murder. Yeah, I'll waive."

"Jerry, go get a waiver, I don't have one here."

Jerry got up and left through the hallway door. Bosch could hear his feet moving quickly on the linoleum, then a door open. He was taking the stairs down to IAD on the fifth.

"Uh, let's start by—"

"Don't you want to wait until you have your witness back? Or is this being secretly recorded without my knowledge?"

This immediately flustered Brockman.

"Yes, Bosch it's being sec—it's being recorded. But not secretly. We told you before we started that we'd be taping."

"Good cover-up, Lieutenant. That last line, that was a good one. I'll have to remember that one."

"Now, let's start with—"

The door opened and Toliver came in with a sheet of paper. He handed it to Brockman, who studied it a moment, made sure it was the correct form and slid it across the table to Bosch. Harry grabbed it and quickly scribbled a signature on the appropriate line. He was familiar with the form. He slid it back and Brockman put it off to the side of the table without looking at it. So he didn't notice the signature Bosch had written was "Fuck You."

"All right, let's get this going. Bosch, give us your whereabouts over the last seventy-two hours."

"You don't want to search me first, do you? How 'bout you, Jerry?"

Bosch stood up, opening his jacket so they could see he was not armed. He thought by taunting them like this they would do the exact opposite and not search him. Carrying Pounds's badge was a piece of evidence that would probably put him in the ground if they discovered it.

"Siddown, Bosch!" Brockman barked. "We're not going to search you. We're trying to give you every benefit of the doubt but you make it damn hard."

Bosch sat back down, relieved for the time being.

"Now, just give us your whereabouts. We don't have all day."

Bosch thought about this. He was surprised by the window of time they wanted. Seventy-two hours. He wondered what had happened to Pounds and why they hadn't narrowed time of death to a shorter span.

"Seventy-two hours ago. Well, about seventy-two hours ago it was Friday afternoon and I was in Chinatown at the Fifty-One-Fifty building. Which reminds me, I'm due over there in ten minutes. So, boys, if you'll excuse me . . ."

He stood up.

"Siddown, Bosch. That's been taken care of. Sit down."

Bosch sat down and said nothing. He realized, though, that he actually felt disappointed he would miss the session with Carmen Hinojos.

"Come on, Bosch, let's hear it. What happened after that?"

"I don't remember all the details. But I ate over at the Red Wind that night, also stopped at the Epicentre for a few drinks. Then I got to the airport about ten. I took a red-eye to Florida, to Tampa, spent the weekend there and got back about an hour and a half before I found you people illegally inside my home."

"It's not illegal. We had a warrant."

"I've been shown no warrant."

"Never mind that, what do you mean you were in Florida?"

"I guess I mean I was in Florida. What do you think it means?"

"You can prove this?"

Bosch reached into his pocket, took out his airline folder with the ticket receipt and slid it across the table.

"For starters there's the ticket receipt. I think there's one in there for a rental car, too."

Brockman quickly opened the ticket folder and started reading.

"What were you doing there?" he asked without looking up.

"Dr. Hinojos, that's the company shrink, said I should try to get away.

And I thought, how 'bout Florida? I'd never been there and all my life I've liked orange juice. I thought, what the hell? Florida."

Brockman was flustered again. He wasn't expecting something like this. Bosch could tell. Most cops never realized how important the initial interview with a suspect or witness was to an investigation. It informed all other interviews and even court testimony that followed. You had to be prepared. Like lawyers, you had to know most of the answers before you asked the questions. The IAD relied so much on its presence as an intimidating factor that most of the detectives assigned to the division never really had to prepare for interviews. And when they hit a wall like this, they didn't know what to do.

"Okay, Bosch, uh, what did you do in Florida?"

"You ever heard that song Marvin Gaye sang? Before he got killed? It's called—"

"What are you talking about?"

"—'Sexual Healing.' It says it's good for the soul."

"I've heard it," Toliver said.

Both Brockman and Bosch looked at him.

"Sorry," he offered.

"Again, Bosch," Brockman said. "What are you talking about?"

"I'm talking about that I spent most of the time with a woman I know there. Most of the other time I spent with a fishing guide on a boat in the Gulf of Mexico. What I'm talking about, asshole, is that I was with people almost every minute. And the times I wasn't weren't long enough for me to fly back here and kill Pounds. I don't even know when he was killed but I'll tell you right now you don't have a case, Brockman, because there is no case. You're looking in the wrong direction."

Bosch had chosen his words carefully. He was unsure what, if anything, they knew about his private investigation and he wasn't going to give them anything if he could help it. They had the murder book and the evidence box but he thought that he might be able to explain all of that away. They also had his notebook because he had stuffed it into his overnighter at the airport. In it were the names, numbers and addresses of Jasmine and McKittrick, the address of the Eno house in Vegas, and other notes about the case. But they might not be able to put together what it all meant. Not if he was lucky.

Brockman pulled a notebook and pen from the inside pocket of his jacket.

"Okay, Bosch, give me the name of the woman and this fishing guide. I need their numbers, everything."

"I don't think so."

Brockman's eyes widened.

"I don't care what you think, give me the names."

Bosch said nothing, just stared down at the table in front of him.

"Bosch, you've told us your whereabouts, now we need to confirm them."

"I know where I was at, that's all I need."

"If you're in the clear, as you claim, let us check it out, clear you and move on to other things, other possibilities."

"You've got the airlines and the car rental right there. Start with that. I'm not dragging people into this who don't need to be. They're good people and unlike you, they like me. I'm not going to let you spoil that by having you come in with your concrete block feet and step all over the relationships."

"You don't have a choice, Bosch."

"Oh, yes, I do. Right now, I do. You want to try to make a case against me, do it. If it gets to that point, I'll bring these people out and they'll blow your shit away, Brockman. You think at the moment you've got PR problems in the department over sending Bill Connors to the closet? You'll end this case with worse PR than Nixon had. I'm not giving you the names. If you want to write something down there in your notebook, just write that I said 'Fuck you.' That ought to cover it."

Brockman's face got kind of blotchy with pinks and whites. He was quiet a moment before speaking.

"Know what I think? I still think you did it. I think you hired somebody to do it and you went waltzing off to Florida so you'd be nowhere near here. A fishing guide. If that doesn't sound like a conjured-up piece of shit I don't know what does. And the woman? Who was she, some hooker you picked up in a bar? What was she, a fifty-dollar alibi? Or did you go a hundred?"

In one explosive move, Bosch shoved the table toward Brockman, catching him completely by surprise. It slid under his arms and crashed into his chest. His chair tipped back against the wall behind him. Bosch kept the pressure on his end and pinned Brockman against the wall. Bosch pushed back on his own chair until it was against the wall behind him. He raised his left leg and put his foot against the table to keep the pressure on it. He saw the blotches of color on Brockman's face become more pronounced as he went without air. His eyes bugged. But he had no leverage and couldn't move the table off himself.

Toliver was slow to react. Stunned, he seemed to look at Brockman for a long moment as if awaiting orders before jumping up and moving toward Bosch. Bosch was able to fend off his first effort, shoving the younger man back into a potted palm tree that was in the corner of the room. While Bosch did this, he saw in his peripheral vision a figure enter the room through the other door. Then his chair was abruptly knocked over and he was on the ground with a heavy weight on top of him. By turning his head slightly he could see it was Irving.

"Don't move, Bosch!" Irving yelled in his ear. "Settle down right now!"

Bosch went limp to signify his compliance and Irving got off him. Bosch stayed still for a few moments and then put a hand up on the table to pull himself up. As he got up, he saw Brockman hacking and trying to get air into his lungs while holding both hands against his chest. Irving held one hand out to Bosch's chest as a calming gesture and a means of stopping him from taking another run at Brockman. With his other hand, he pointed at Toliver, who was trying to right the potted palm. It had become uprooted and wouldn't stand up. He finally just leaned it against the wall.

"You," Irving snapped at him. "Out."

"But, sir, the—"

"Get out!"

Toliver quickly left through the hallway door as Brockman was finally finding his voice.

"Buh . . . Bosch, you sonova bitch, you . . . you're going to jail. You—"

"Nobody's going to jail," Irving said sternly. "Nobody's going to jail."

Irving stopped to gulp down some air. Bosch noticed that the assistant chief seemed just as winded as anybody in the room.

"There will be no charges on this," Irving finally continued. "Lieutenant, you baited him and got what you got."

Irving's tone invited no debate. Brockman, his chest still heaving, put his elbows on the table and began running his fingers through his hair, trying to look as if he still had some composure but all he had was defeat. Irving turned to Bosch, anger bunching the muscles of his jaw into hard surfaces.

"And you. Bosch, I don't know how to help you. You're always the loose cannon. You knew what he was doing, you've done it yourself. But you couldn't sit there and take it. What kind of man are you?"

Bosch didn't say anything and he doubted Irving wanted a spoken answer. Brockman started coughing and Irving looked back at him.

"Are you all right?"

"I think."

"Go across the street, have one of the paramedics check you out."

"No, I'm all right."

"Good, then go down to your office, take a break. I have someone else I want to have talk to Bosch."

"I want to continue the inter—"

"The interview is over, Lieutenant. You blew it." Then, looking at Bosch, he added, "You both did."

Irving left Bosch alone in the conference room and in a few moments Carmen Hinojos walked in. She took the same seat that Brockman had sat in. She looked at Bosch with eyes that seemed filled with equal parts anger and disappointment. But Bosch didn't flinch under her gaze.

"Harry, I can't believe—"

He held a finger up to his mouth, silencing her.

"What is it?"

"Are our sessions still supposed to be private?"

"Of course."

"Even in here?"

"Yes. What is it?"

Bosch got up and walked to the phone on the counter. He pushed the button that disconnected the conference call. He returned to his seat.

"I hope that was left on unintentionally. I'm going to speak to Chief Irving about that."

"You're probably speaking to him right now. The phone was too obvious. He's probably got the room wired."

"C'mon, Harry, this isn't the CIA."

"No, it's not. Sometimes it's even worse. All I'm saying is Irving, the IAD, they still might be listening somehow. Be careful what you say."

Carmen Hinojos looked exasperated.

"I'm not paranoid, Doctor. I've been through this before."

"All right, never mind. I really don't care who's listening or not. I can't believe what you just did. It makes me very sad and disappointed. What have our meetings been about? Nothing? I'm sitting in there hearing you resort to the same type of violence that brought you to me in the first place. Harry, this isn't some joke. This is real life. And I have to make a decision that could very well decide your future. This makes it all the more difficult to do."

He waited until he was sure she was done.

"You were in there with Irving the whole time?"

"Yes, he called and explained the situation and asked me to come over and sit in. I have to say—"

"Wait a minute. Before we go any further. Did you talk to him? Did you tell him about our sessions?"

"No, of course not."

"Okay, for the record, I just want to reiterate that I do not give up any of my protections under the patient-doctor relationship. We okay on that?"

For the first time she looked away from him. He could see her face turning dark with anger.

"Do you know what an insult that is for you to tell me that? What, do you think I'd tell him about our sessions just because he may have ordered me to?"

"Did he?"

"You don't trust me at all, do you?"

"Did he?"

"No, he didn't."

"That's good."

"It's not just me. You don't trust anyone."

Bosch realized that he had been out of line. He could see, though, that there was more hurt than anger in her face.

"I'm sorry, you're right, I shouldn't have said that. I'm just . . . I don't know, I've got my back to the corner here, Doctor. When that happens, sometimes you forget who's on your side and who isn't."

"Yes, and as a matter of course you respond with violence against those who you perceive are not on your side. This is not good to see. It's very, very disappointing."

He looked away from her and over to the potted palm in the corner. Before leaving the room, Irving had replanted it, getting his hands dirty with black soil. Bosch noticed it was still slightly tilted to the left.

"So what are you doing up here?" he asked. "What does Irving want?"

"He wanted me to sit in his office and listen to your interview on the conference line. He said he was interested in my evaluation of your answers as to whether I believed you could have been responsible for the death of Lieutenant Pounds. Thanks to you and your attack on your interviewer, he didn't need any evaluation from me. It's clear at this point you are prone to and quite capable of violence against fellow police officers."

"That's bullshit and you know it. Damn it, what I did in here to that guy masquerading as a cop was a lot different than what they think I did. You're talking about things that are worlds apart and if you don't see that, you're making your living in the wrong business."

"I'm not so sure."

"Have you ever killed anyone, Doctor?"

Saying the question reminded him of his true confessions conversation with Jasmine.

"Of course not."

"Well, I have. And believe me it's a lot different than roughing up some pompous ass in a suit with a shine on its ass. A lot different. If you or they think that doing one means you can do the other, you all have a lot to learn."

They were both quiet for a long while, letting their anger ebb away.

"All right," he finally said. "So what happens now?"

"I don't know. Chief Irving just asked me to sit in with you, to calm you. I guess he's figuring out what to do next. I guess I'm not doing a very good job of calming you."

"What did he say when he first asked you to come up here and listen?"

"He just called me and explained what happened and said he wanted my take on the interview. You have to understand something, despite your problems with authority, he is one person who I think is in your court on this. I don't think he honestly believes you're involved in the death of your lieutenant—at least directly. But he realizes that you are a viable suspect who needs to be questioned. I think if you had held your temper during the interview this all might've been over for you soon. They would've checked your story in Florida and that would have been the end of it. I even told them that you told me you were going to Florida."

"I don't want them checking my story. I don't want them involved."

"Well, it's too late. He knows you're up to something."

"How?"

"When he called to ask me to come over he mentioned the file on your mother's case. The murder book. He said it was found at your house. He also said they found the stored evidence from the case there . . ."

"And?"

"And he asked if I knew what you were doing with all of it."

"So he did ask you to reveal what we've talked about in our sessions."

"In an indirect way."

"Sounds pretty direct to me. Did he say specifically that it was my mother's case?"

"Yes, he did."

"What did you tell him?"

"I told him that I was not at liberty to discuss anything that was talked about in our sessions. It didn't satisfy him."

"I'm not surprised."

Another wave of silence washed between them. Her eyes wandered the room. His stayed on hers.

"Listen, what do you know about what happened to Pounds?"

"Very little."

"Irving must have told you something. You must've asked."

"He said Pounds was found in the trunk of his car Sunday evening. I guess he had been there a while. A day maybe. The chief said he . . . the body showed signs of torture. Particularly sadistic mutilation, he said. He didn't go into detail. It had happened before Pounds was dead. They do know that. He said that he'd been in a lot of pain. He wanted to know if you were the type of man who could've done that."

Bosch said nothing. He was imagining the crime scene in his mind.

His guilt came crushing back down on him and for a moment he thought he might even get nauseous.

"For what it's worth, I said no."

"What?"

"I told him you weren't the type of man who could've done that."

Bosch nodded. But his thoughts were already a great distance away again. What had happened to Pounds was becoming clear and Bosch carried the guilt of having set things in motion. Though legally innocent, he knew he was morally culpable. Pounds was a man he despised, had less respect for than some of the murderers he had known. But the weight of the guilt was bearing down on him. He ran his hands hard over his face and through his hair. He felt a shudder move through his body.

"Are you all right?" Hinojos asked.

"I'm fine."

Bosch took out his cigarettes and started to light one with his Bic.

"Harry, you better not. This isn't my office."

"I don't care. Where was he found?"

"What?"

"Pounds! Where was he found?"

"I don't know. You mean where was the car? I don't know. I didn't ask."

She studied him and he noticed the hand that held his cigarette was shaking.

"All right, Harry, that's it. What's the matter? What is going on?"

Bosch looked at her for a long moment and nodded.

"Okay, you want to know? I did it. I killed him."

Her face immediately reacted as if perhaps she had seen the killing firsthand, so close that she had been spattered with blood. It was a horrible face. Repulsed. And she moved back in her chair as if even a few more inches of separation from him were needed.

"You . . . you mean this story about Florida was—"

"No. I don't mean I killed him. Not with my hands. I mean what I've done, what I've been doing. It got him killed. I got him killed."

"How do you know? You can't know for sure that—"

"I know. Believe me, I know."

He looked away from her to a painting on the wall over the banquette. It was a generic depiction of a beach scene. He looked back at Hinojos.

"It's funny . . . ," he said but didn't finish. He just shook his head.

"What is?"

He got up and reached to the potted palm and stubbed the cigarette out in the dark soil.

"What is funny, Harry?"

He sat back down and looked at her.

"The civilized people in the world, the ones who hide behind culture and art and politics . . . and even the law, they're the ones to watch out for. They've got that perfect disguise goin' for them, you know? But they're the most vicious. They're the most dangerous people on earth."

It seemed to Bosch that the day would never end, that he would never get out of the conference room. After Hinojos left, it was Irving's turn. He came in silently, took the Brockman seat and folded his hands on the table and said nothing. He looked irritated. Bosch thought maybe he smelled the smoke. Bosch didn't care about that but he found the silence discomforting.

"What about Brockman?"

"He's gone. You heard me tell him, he blew it. So did you."

"How's that?"

"You could've talked your way out of it. Could've let him check your story and be done with it. But you had to make another enemy. You had to be Harry Bosch."

"That's where you and I differ, Chief. You oughta get out of the office and come out on the street again sometime. I didn't make Brockman an enemy. He was my enemy before I even met him. They all are. And, you know, I'm really getting tired of everybody analyzing me and sticking their noses up my ass. It's getting real old."

"Somebody's got to do it. You don't."

"You don't know a thing about it."

Irving waved Bosch's pale defense away like cigarette smoke.

"So what now?" Bosch continued. "Why are you here? You going to try to break my alibi now? Is that it? Brockman's out and you're in?"

"I don't need to break your alibi. It's been checked and it looks like it holds. Brockman and his people have already been instructed to follow other avenues of investigation."

"What do you mean, it's been checked?"

"Give us some credit here, Bosch. The names were in your notebook."

He reached into his coat and pulled out the notebook. He tossed it across the table to Bosch.

"This woman that you spent some time with over there, she told me enough to the point that I believed it. You might want to call her yourself, though. She certainly seemed confused by my call. I was rather circumspect in my explanation."

"I appreciate that. So, then, I guess I'm free to split?"

Bosch stood up.

"In a technical sense."

"And the other senses?"

"Sit down for a minute, Detective."

Bosch held his hands up. He'd gone this far. He decided he might as well go all the way and hear it all. He sat back down in his chair with a meager protest.

"My butt's getting sore from all this sitting."

"I knew Jake McKittrick," Irving said. "Knew him well. We worked Hollywood together many years ago. But you know that already. As nice as it is to touch base with an old colleague, I can't say I enjoyed anything about the conversation I had with my old friend Jake."

"You called him, too."

"While you were in here with the doctor."

"So then what do you want from me? You got the story from him, what's left?"

Irving drummed his fingers on the tabletop.

"What do I want? What I want is for you to tell me that what you are doing, what you have been doing, is in no way connected to what has happened to Lieutenant Pounds."

"I can't, Chief. I don't know what happened to him, other than that he's dead."

Irving studied Bosch for a long moment, contemplating something, deciding whether to treat him as an equal and tell him the story.

"I guess I expected an immediate denial. Your answer already suggests that you think there might be a correlation. I can't tell you how much that bothers me."

"Anything is possible, Chief. Let me ask you this. You said Brockman and his crew were out chasing other leads—I guess avenues is what you said. Are any of these avenues viable? I mean, did Pounds have a secret life or are they just out there chasing their tails?"

"There's nothing that stands out. I'm afraid you were the best lead. Brockman still thinks so. He wants to pursue the theory that you hired a hitman of some sort and then flew to Florida to establish an alibi."

"Yeah, that's a good one."

"I think it stretches credibility some. I told him to drop it. For the moment. And I'm telling you to drop what you are doing. This woman in Florida sounds like the kind of person you could spend some time with. I want you to get on a plane and go back to her. Stay a couple weeks. When you come back, we'll talk about going back on the homicide table at Hollywood."

Bosch was unsure whether there was a threat in all that Irving had just said. If not a threat, then maybe a bribe.

"And if I don't?"

"If you don't, then you are stupid. And you deserve whatever happens to you."

"What is it that you think I'm doing, Chief?"

"I don't *think*, I *know* what you're doing. It's easy. You pulled the book on your mother's homicide. Why at this particular point in time you've done this, I don't know. But you're out running a freelance investigation and that's a problem for us. You have to stop it, Harry, or I'll stop you. I'll shut you down. Permanently."

"Who are you protecting?"

Bosch saw the anger move into Irving's face as his skin turned from pink to an intense red. His eyes seemed to grow smaller and darker with fury.

"Don't you ever suggest such a thing. I've dedicated my life to this depart—"

"It's yourself, isn't it? You knew her. You found her. You're afraid of being dragged into this if I put something together on it. I bet you already knew everything McKittrick told you on the phone."

"That's ridiculous, I—"

"Is it? Is it? I don't think so. I've already talked to one witness who remembers you from those days on the Boulevard beat."

"What witness?"

"She said she knew you. She knows my mother knew you, too."

"The only person I am protecting is you, Bosch. Can't you see that? I'm *ordering* you to stop this investigation."

"You can't. I don't work for you anymore. I'm on leave, remember? Involuntary leave. That makes me a citizen now, and I can do whatever I goddamn want to do as long as it's legal."

"I could charge you with possession of stolen documents—the murder book."

"It wasn't stolen. Besides, what if you bullshit a case, what's that, a misdemeanor? They'll laugh you out of the city attorney's office on your ass with that."

"But you'd lose your job. That would be it."

"You're a little late with that one, Chief. A week ago that would've been a valid threat. I'd have to consider it. But it doesn't matter anymore. I'm free of all of that bullshit now and this is all that matters to me and I don't care what I have to do, I'm doing it."

Irving was silent and Bosch guessed that the assistant chief was realizing that Bosch had moved beyond his reach. Irving's hold over Bosch's job and future had been his leverage before. But Bosch had finally broken free. Bosch began again in a low, calm voice.

"If you were me, Chief, could you just walk away? What does doing what I do for the department matter if I can't do this for her . . . and for me?"

He stood up and put the notebook into his jacket pocket.

"I'm going. Where's the rest of my stuff?"

"No."

Bosch hesitated. Irving looked up at him and Bosch saw the anger was gone now.

"I did nothing wrong," Irving said quietly.

"Sure you did," Bosch said just as quietly. He leaned over the table until he was only a few feet away. "We all did, Chief. We let it go. That was our crime. But not anymore. At least, not with me. If you want to help, you know how to reach me."

He headed toward the door.

"What do you want?"

Bosch looked back at him.

"Tell me about Pounds. I need to know what happened. It's the only way I'll know if it's connected."

"Then sit down."

Bosch took the chair by the door and sat down. They both took some time to calm down before Irving finally spoke.

"We started looking for him Saturday night. We found his car Sunday noon in Griffith Park. One of the tunnels closed after the quake. It was like they knew we'd be looking from the air, so they put the car in a tunnel."

"Why'd you start looking before you knew he was dead?"

"The wife. She started calling Saturday morning. She said he'd gotten a call Friday night at home, she didn't know who. But whoever it was managed to convince Pounds to leave the house and meet him. Pounds didn't tell his wife what it was about. He said he'd be back in an hour or two. He left and never came back. In the morning she called us."

"Pounds is unlisted, I assume."

"Yes. That gives rise to the probability it was someone in the department."

Bosch thought about this.

"Not necessarily. It just had to be someone with connections to people in the city. People that could get his number with a phone call. You ought to put out the word. Grant amnesty to anyone who comes forward and says they gave up the number. Say you'll go light in exchange for the name of the person they gave it to. That's who you want. Chances are whoever gave out the number didn't know what was going to happen."

Irving nodded.

"That's an idea. Within the department there are hundreds who could get his number. There may be no other way to go."

"Tell me more about Pounds."

"We went to work right there in the tunnel. By Sunday the media had wind that we were looking for him, so the tunnel worked to our advantage. No helicopters flying over, bothering us. We just set up lights in the tunnel."

"He was in the car?"

Bosch was acting like he knew nothing. He knew that if he expected Hinojos to respect his confidences, he must in turn respect hers.

"Yes, he was in the trunk. And, my God, was it bad. He . . . He'd been stripped of his clothes. He'd been beaten. Then then there was the evidence of torture . . ."

Bosch waited but Irving had stopped.

"What? What did they do to him?"

"They burned him. The genitals, nipples, fingers . . . My God."

Irving ran his hand over his shaven scalp and closed his eyes while he did it. Bosch could see that he could not get the images out of his mind. Bosch was having trouble with it, too. His guilt was like a palpable object in his chest.

"It was like they wanted something from him," Irving said. "But he couldn't give it. He didn't have it and . . . and they kept at him."

Suddenly, Bosch felt the slight tremor of an earthquake and reached for the table to steady himself. He looked at Irving for confirmation and realized there was no tremor. It was himself, shaking again.

"Wait a minute."

The room tilted slightly then righted itself.

"What is it?"

"Wait a minute."

Without another word Bosch stood up and went out the door. He quickly went down the hall to the men's room by the water fountain. There was someone in front of one of the sinks shaving but Bosch didn't take the time to look at him. He pushed through one of the stall doors and vomited into the toilet, barely making it in time.

He flushed the toilet but the spasm came again and then again until he was empty, until he had nothing left inside but the image of Pounds naked and dead, tortured.

"You okay in there, buddy?" a voice said from outside the stall.

"Just leave me alone."

"Sorry, just asking."

Bosch stayed in the stall a few more minutes, leaning against the wall. Eventually, he wiped his mouth with toilet paper and then flushed it down. He stepped out of the stall unsteadily and went to the sink. The other man was still there. Now he was putting on a tie. Bosch glanced at him in the mirror but didn't recognize him. He bent over the sink and rinsed his face and mouth out with cold water. He then used paper towels to dry off. He never looked at himself once in the mirror.

"Thanks for asking," he said as he left.

Irving looked as if he hadn't moved while Bosch was gone.

"Are you all right?"

Bosch sat down and took out his cigarettes.

"Sorry, but I'm gonna smoke."

"You already have been."

Bosch lit up and took a deep drag. He stood up and walked to the trash can in the corner. There was an old coffee cup in it and he took it to use as an ashtray.

"Just one," he said. "Then you can open the door and air the place out."

"It's a bad habit."

"In this town so is breathing. How did he die? What was the fatal injury?"

"The autopsy was this morning. Heart failure. The strain on him was too much, his heart gave way."

Bosch paused a moment. He felt the beginning of his strength coming back.

"Why don't you tell me the rest of it?"

"There is no rest of it. That's it. There was nothing there. No evidence on the body. No evidence in the car. It had been wiped clean. There was nothing to go on."

"What about his clothes?"

"They were there in the trunk. No help. The killer kept one thing, though."

"What?"

"His shield. The bastard took his badge."

Bosch just nodded and averted his eyes. They were both silent for a long time. Bosch couldn't get the images out of his mind and he guessed Irving was having the same problem.

"So," Bosch finally said, "looking at what had been done to him, the torture and everything, you immediately thought of me. That's a real vote of confidence."

"Look, Detective, you had put the man's face through a window two weeks earlier. We had gotten an added report from him that you had threatened him. What—"

"There was no threat. He—"

"I don't care if there was or wasn't. He made the report. That's the point. True or false, he made the report, therefore, he felt threatened by you. What were we supposed to do, ignore it? Just say, 'Harry Bosch? Oh, no, there's no way our own Harry Bosch could do this,' and go on? Don't be ridiculous."

"All right, you're right. Forget it. He didn't say anything at all to his wife before leaving?"

"Only that someone called and he had to go out for an hour to a meeting with a very important person. No name was mentioned. The call came in about nine Friday night."

"Is that exactly how she said he said it?"

"I believe so. Why?"

"Because if he said it in that way, then it sounds like two people may be involved."

"How so?"

"It just sounds as though one person called him to set up a meeting with a second person, this very important person. If that person had made the call, then he would have told the wife that so and so, the big important guy, just called and I have to go meet him. See what I mean?"

"I do. But whoever called could have also used the name of an important person as bait to draw Pounds out. That actual person may not have been involved at all."

"That's also true. But I think that whatever was said, it would have to have been convincing to get Pounds out at night, by himself."

"Maybe it was someone he already knew."

"Maybe. But then he probably would have told his wife the name."

"True."

"Did he take anything with him? A briefcase, files, anything?"

"Not that we know of. The wife was in the TV room. She didn't see him actually go out the door. We've been over all of this with her, we've been all over the house. There's nothing. His briefcase was in his office at the station. He didn't even take it home with him. There's nothing to go on. To be honest, you were the best candidate and you're clear now. It brings me back to my question. Could what you've been doing have had anything to do with this?"

Bosch could not bring himself to tell Irving what he thought, what he knew in his gut had happened to Pounds. It wasn't the guilt that stopped him, though. It was the desire to keep his mission to himself. In that moment he realized that vengeance was a singular thing, a solo mission, something never to be spoken of out loud.

"I don't know the answer," he said. "I told Pounds nothing. But he wanted me to go down. You know that. The guy's dead but he was an asshole and he wanted me to go down. So he'd have had his ear to the ground for anything about me. A couple people have seen me around in the last week. Word could've gotten back to him and he could've blundered into something. He wasn't much of an investigator. He could've made a mistake. I don't know."

Irving looked at him through dead eyes. Bosch knew he was trying to determine how much was true and how much was bullshit. Bosch spoke first.

"He said he was going to meet someone important."

"Yes."

"Look, Chief, I don't know what McKittrick told you about the conversation I had out there with him, but you know there were important people involved back . . . you know, with my mother. You were there."

"Yes, I was there, but I wasn't part of the investigation, not after the first day."

"Did McKittrick tell you about Arno Conklin?"

"Not today. But back then. I remember once when I asked him what was happening with the case, he told me to ask Arno. He said Arno was running interference for someone on it."

"Well, Arno Conklin was an important person."

"But now? He's an old man if he's even still alive."

"He's alive, Chief. And you have to remember something. Important men surround themselves with important men. They're never alone. Conklin may be old but there could be someone else who isn't."

"What are you telling me, Bosch?"

"I'm telling you to leave me alone. I have to do this. I'm the only one who can. I'm telling you to keep Brockman and everybody else away from me."

Irving stared at him a long moment and Bosch could tell he didn't know which way to go with this. Bosch stood up.

"I'll keep in touch."

"You're not telling me everything."

"It's better that way."

He stepped through the door into the hallway, remembered something and then stepped back into the room with Irving.

"How am I going to get home? You brought me here."

Irving reached over to the phone.

Bosch went through the fifth-floor door to the Internal Affairs Division and found no one behind the counter. He waited a few moments for Toliver to show up since Irving had just ordered him to drive Bosch home, but the young IAD detective never showed. Bosch figured it was just one more mind game they were trying to play with him. He didn't want to walk around the counter and have to find Toliver so he just yelled his name out. Behind the counter was a door that was slightly ajar and he was reasonably sure Toliver heard the call.

But the person who stepped through the door was Brockman. He stared at Bosch for a long moment without saying anything.

"Look, Brockman, Toliver is supposed to run me home," Bosch said to him. "I don't want anything else to do with you."

"Yeah, well, that's too bad."

"Just get Toliver."

"You better watch out for me, Bosch."

"Yeah, I know. I'll be watching."

"Yeah, and you won't see me coming."

Bosch nodded and looked past him to the door where he expected Toliver to step out any moment. He just wanted to diffuse the situation and get his ride home. He considered walking out and catching a cab, but he knew in rush hour it would probably cost him fifty bucks. He didn't have it on him. Plus, he liked the idea of having an IAD shine chauffeur him home.

"Hey, killer?"

Bosch looked back at Brockman. He was getting tired of this.

"What's it like to fuck another killer? Must really be something, to go all the way to Florida for it."

Bosch tried to stay cool but he felt his face betray himself. For he suddenly knew who and what Brockman was talking about.

"What are you talking about?"

Brockman's face lit up with a bully's delight as he read Bosch's surprised look.

"Oooh, baby! She didn't even bother telling you, did she?"

"Tell me what?"

Bosch wanted to reach over the counter and drag Brockman across it but at least outwardly he maintained his cool.

"Tell you what? I'll tell you what. I think your whole story stinks and I'm going to bust it open. Then Mr. Clean upstairs isn't going to be able to protect you."

"He said you were told to leave me alone, that I was clear."

"Fuck him and fuck you. When I come in with your alibi in a bag, he's not going to have a choice but to cut you loose."

Toliver stepped through the doorway behind the counter. He was holding a set of car keys in his hands. He stood silently behind Brockman with his eyes down.

"First thing I did was run her on the computer," Brockman said. "She's got a record, Bosch. You didn't know that? She's a killer, just like you. Takes one to know one, I guess. Nice couple."

Bosch wanted to ask a thousand questions but he wouldn't ask any of this man. He felt a deep void opening inside as he began jettisoning his feelings for Jazz. He realized that she had left all the signs out for him but he hadn't read them. Even so, the feeling that descended on him with the strongest grip was one of betrayal.

Bosch pointedly ignored Brockman and looked at Toliver.

"Hey, kid, you going to give me a ride or what?"

Toliver moved around the counter without answering.

"Bosch, I already got you on an association beef," Brockman said. "But I'm not satisfied."

Bosch went to the hallway door and opened it. It was against LAPD regulations to associate with known criminals. Whether Brockman could make a charge like that stick was the least of Bosch's worries. He headed out the door with Toliver following. Before it closed Brockman yelled after them.

"Give her a kiss for me, killer."

At first, Bosch sat silently next to Jerry Toliver on the ride back to his house. He had a waterfall of thoughts dropping through his mind and decided to simply ignore the young IAD detective. Toliver left the police scanner on and the sporadic chatter was the only thing resembling conversation in the car. They had caught the crest of the evening commute out of downtown and were moving at an excruciatingly slow pace toward the Cahuenga pass.

Bosch's guts ached from the wracking convulsions of nausea of an hour earlier and he kept his arms crossed in front of him as if he were cradling a baby. He knew he had to compartmentalize his thoughts. As much as he was confused and curious about what Brockman had alluded to in regard to Jasmine, he knew he had to put it aside. At the moment, Pounds and what had happened to him were more important.

He tried to piece together the chain of events and the conclusion he drew was obvious. His stumbling into the party at Mittel's and delivery of the photocopy of the *Times* clip had set off a reaction that ended with the murder of Harvey Pounds, the man whose name he had used. Though he had given Mittel only the name at the party, it was somehow traced back to the real Pounds, who was then tortured and killed.

Bosch guessed that it was the DMV calls that had doomed Pounds.

Fresh from receiving the threatening news clip at the fund-raiser from a man who had introduced himself as Harvey Pounds, Mittel likely would have put his lengthy arm out to find out who this man was and what his purpose was. Mittel had connections from L.A. to Sacramento to Washington, D.C. He could have quickly found out that Harvey Pounds was a cop. Mittel's campaign financing work had put a good number of legislators in seats in Sacramento. He would certainly have the connections in the capital city to find out if anyone was running traces on his name. And if he had that done, then he would have learned that Harvey Pounds, an LAPD lieutenant, had inquired not only about him but about four other men who would be of vital interest to him as well. Arno Conklin, Johnny Fox, Jake McKittrick and Claude Eno.

True, all the names were involved in a case and conspiracy almost thirty-five years old. But Mittel was at the center of that conspiracy and the snooping around by Pounds would be more than enough, Bosch believed, for someone of his position to take some kind of action to find out what Pounds was doing.

Because of the approach the man he thought was Pounds had made at the party, Mittel had probably concluded he was being set upon by a chiseler, an extortionist. And he knew how to eliminate the problem. Like Johnny Fox had been eliminated.

That was the reason Pounds had been tortured, Bosch knew. For Mittel to make sure the problem went no further than Pounds, he had to know who else knew what Pounds knew. The problem was that Pounds didn't know anything himself. He had nothing to give. He was tormented until his heart could take it no longer.

A question that remained unanswered in Bosch's mind was what Arno Conklin knew of all this. He had not yet been contacted by Bosch. Did he know of the man who approached Mittel? Did he order the hit on Pounds or was it solely Mittel's reaction?

Then Bosch saw a bump in his theory that needed refining. Mittel had come face to face with him posing as Harvey Pounds at the fund-raiser. The fact that Pounds was tortured before he died indicated that Mittel was not present at the time, or he would have seen that they were brutalizing the wrong man. Bosch wondered now if they understood that they had, in fact, killed the wrong man, and if they would be looking for the right one.

He mulled over the point that Mittel could not have been there and decided that it fit. Mittel was not the type to get involved in the blood work. He'd have no problem calling the shots, he just wouldn't want to see them fired. Bosch realized the surfer in a suit had also seen him at the party and, therefore, could not have been directly involved in the killing of Harvey Pounds, either. That left the man Bosch had seen through the French doors at the house. The man with the wide body and thick neck whom he had seen Mittel show the newspaper clip to. The man who had slipped and fallen while coming down the driveway for Bosch.

Bosch realized that he didn't know how close he had come to being where Pounds was now. He reached into his jacket pocket for his cigarettes and started to light one.

"Do you mind not smoking?" Toliver asked, his first words of the thirty-minute journey.

"Yeah, I do mind."

Bosch finished lighting the smoke and put his Bic away. He lowered the window.

"There. You happy? The exhaust fumes are worse than the smoke."

"It's a nonsmoking vehicle."

Toliver tapped his finger on a plastic magnet that was on the dashboard ashtray cover. It was one of the little doodads that were distributed when the city passed a widespread antismoking law that forbade the practice in all city buildings and allowed for half of the department's fleet to be declared nonsmoking vehicles. The magnet showed a cigarette in the middle of a red circle with a slash through it. Beneath the circle it said THANK YOU FOR NOT SMOKING. Bosch reached over, peeled the magnet off and threw it out the open window. He saw it bounce once on the pavement and stick on the door of a car one lane over.

"Now it's not. Now it's a smoking car."

"Bosch, you're really fucked, you know that?"

"Write me up, kid. Add it to the association beef your boss is working on. I don't care."

They were silent for a few moments and the car crept further away from Hollywood.

"He's bluffing you, Bosch. I thought you knew that."

"How so?"

He was surprised that Toliver was turning.

"He's just bluffing, that's all. He's still hot about what you did with that table. But he knows it won't stick. It's an old case. Voluntary manslaughter. A domestic violence case. She walked on five years probation. All you have to do is say you didn't know and it gets shitcanned."

Bosch could almost guess what the case was about. She had practically told him during true confessions. She stayed too long with someone. That was what she had said. He thought of the painting he had seen in her studio. The gray portrait with the highlights red like blood. He tried to pull his mind away from it.

"Why're you telling me this, Toliver? Why are you going against your own?"

"Because they're not my own. Because I want to know what you meant by what you said to me in the hallway."

Bosch couldn't even remember what he said.

"You told me it wasn't too late. Too late for what?"

"Too late to get out," Bosch said, recalling the words he had thrown as a taunt. "You're still a young guy. You better get yourself out of IAD before it's too late. You stay too long and you'll never get out. Is that what you want, spend your career busting cops for trading hookers dime bags?"

"Look, I want to work out of Parker and I don't want to wait ten years like everybody else. It's the easiest and fastest way for a white guy to get in there."

"It's not worth it, is what I'm telling you. Anybody stays in IAD more than two, three years, they're there for life because nobody else wants 'em, nobody else trusts 'em. They're lepers. You better think about it. Parker Center isn't the only place in the world to work."

A few moments of silence passed as Toliver tried to muster a defense.

"Somebody's got to police the police. A lot of people don't seem to understand that."

"That's right. But in this department nobody polices the police who police the police. Think about that."

The conversation was interrupted by the sharp tone he recognized as his mobile phone. On the back seat of the car were the items the searchers had taken from his apartment. Irving had ordered it all returned. Among them was his briefcase and inside it he heard his phone. He reached back, flipped the briefcase open and grabbed the phone.

"Yeah. It's Bosch."

"Bosch, it's Russell."

"Hey, I got nothing to tell you yet, Keisha. I'm still working on it."

"No, I have something to tell you. Where are you?"

"I'm in the soup. The 101 coming up to Barham, my exit."

"Well, I have to talk to you, Bosch. I'm writing a story for tomorrow. You will want to comment, I think, if only in your defense."

"My defense?"

A dull thud went through him and he felt like saying, What now? But he held himself in check.

"What are you talking about?"

"Did you read my story today?"

"No, I haven't had the time. What—"

"It's about the death of Harvey Pounds. Today I have a follow . . . It concerns you, Bosch."

Jesus, he thought. But he tried to keep calm. He knew that if she detected any panic in his voice she would gain confidence in whatever it was she was about to write. He had to convince her she had bad information. He had to undermine that confidence. Then he realized Toliver was sitting next to him and would hear everything he said.

"I have a problem talking now. When is your deadline?"

"Now. We have to talk now."

Bosch looked at his watch. It was twenty-five minutes until six.

"You can go to six, right?"

He'd worked with reporters before and knew that was the deadline for the *Times*'s first edition.

"No, I can't go to six. If you want to say something, say it now."

"I can't. Give me fifteen minutes and then call back. I can't talk now."

There was a pause and then she said, "Bosch, I can't push it far past then. You better be able to talk then."

They were at the Barham exit now and they'd be up to his house in ten minutes.

"Don't worry about it. In the meantime, you go warn your editor that you might be pulling the story."

"I will not."

"Look, Keisha, I know what you're going to ask me about. It's a plant and it's wrong. You have to trust me. I'll explain in fifteen minutes."

"How do you know it's a plant?"

"I know. It came from Angel Brockman."

He flipped the phone closed and looked over at Toliver.

"See, Toliver? Is that what you want to do with your job? With your life?"

Toliver said nothing.

"When you get back, you can tell your boss that he can shove tomorrow's *Times* up his ass. There isn't going to be any story. See, even the reporters don't trust IAD guys. All I had to do was mention Brockman. She'll start backpedaling when I tell her I know what's going on. Nobody trusts you guys, Jerry. Get out of it."

"Oh, and like *everybody* trusts you, Bosch."

"Not everybody. But I can sleep at night and I've been on the job twenty years. Think you'll be able to? What have you got in, five, six years? I'll give you ten, Jerry. That's all for you. Ten and out. But you'll look like one of these guys who puts in thirty."

His prediction was met with a stony silence from Toliver. Bosch didn't know why he even cared. Toliver was part of the team trying to put him in the dirt. But something about the young cop's fresh face gave him the benefit of the doubt.

They made the last curve on Woodrow Wilson and Bosch could see his house. He could also see a white car with a yellow plate parked in front of it and a man wearing a yellow construction helmet standing in front holding a toolbox. It was the city building inspector. Gowdy.

"Shit," Bosch said. "This one of IAD's tricks, too?"

"I don't—if it is, I don't know anything about it."

"Yeah, sure."

Without a further word Toliver stopped in front of the house and Bosch got out with his returned property. Gowdy recognized him and immediately came over as Toliver pulled away from the curb.

"Listen, you're not living in this place, are ya?" Gowdy asked. "It's been red-tagged. We gotta call said somebody bootlegged the electric."

"I gotta call, too. See anybody? I was just going to check it out."

"Don't bullshit me, Mr. Bosch. I can see you've made some repairs. You gotta know something, you can't repair this place, you can't even go in. You gotta demolition order and it's overdue. I'm gonna put in a work order and have a city contractor do it. You'll get the bill. No use waitin' any longer. Now, you might as well get out of here because I'm going to pull the electric and padlock it."

He bent down to put the toolbox on the ground and proceeded to open it up and retrieve a set of stainless steel hinges and hasp locks he would apply to the doors.

"Look, I've got a lawyer," Bosch said. "He's trying to work it out with you people."

"There's nothing to work out. I'm sorry. Now if you go in there again, you're subject to arrest. If I find these locks have been tampered with, you're also subject to arrest. I'll call North Hollywood Division. I'm not fooling with you anymore."

For the first time it occurred to Bosch that it might be a show, that the man might want money. He probably didn't even know Bosch was a cop. Most cops couldn't afford to live up here and wouldn't want to if they could. The only reason Bosch could afford it was he had bought the property with a chunk of money he had made years earlier on a TV movie deal based on a case he had solved.

"Look, Gowdy," he said, "just spell it out, okay? I'm slow about these things. Tell me what you want and you've got it. I want to save the house. That's all I care about."

Gowdy looked at him for a long moment and Bosch realized he had been wrong. He could see the indignation in Gowdy's eyes.

"You keep talking like that and you could go to jail, son. I'll tell you what I'm going to do. I'm going to forget what you just said. I—"

"Look, I'm sorry . . ." Bosch looked back at the house. "It's just like, I don't know, the house is the only thing I've got."

"You've got more than that. You just haven't thought about it. Now, I'm going to cut you a break here. I'll give you five minutes to go inside and get what you need. After that, I'm putting the locks on it. I'm sorry. But that's the way it is. If that house goes down the hill on the next one, maybe you'll thank me."

Bosch nodded.

"Go on. Five minutes."

Bosch went inside and grabbed a suitcase from the top shelf of the hallway closet. First he put his second gun in it, then he dumped in as much of the clothing from the bedroom closet as he could. He walked the overstuffed suitcase out to the carport, then came back inside for another load. He opened the drawers of his bureau and dumped them on the bed, then wrapped everything in the bedclothes and carried that out as well.

He went past the five-minute mark but Gowdy didn't come in after him. Bosch could hear him working with a hammer on the front door.

After ten minutes he had a large stack of belongings gathered in the carport. Included there was the box in which he kept his keepsakes and photos, a fireproof box containing his financial and personal records, a stack of unopened mail and unpaid bills, the stereo and two boxes containing his collection of jazz and blues LPs and CDs. Looking at the pile of belongings, he felt forlorn. It was a lot to fit into a Mustang, but he knew it wasn't much to show for almost forty-five years on the planet.

"That it?"

Bosch turned around. It was Gowdy. He was holding a hammer in one hand and a steel latch in the other. Bosch saw a keyed lock was hooked through one of the belt loops on his pants.

"Yeah," Bosch said. "Do it."

He stepped back and let the inspector go to work. The hammering had just begun when his phone rang. He had forgotten about Keisha Russell.

He had the phone in his jacket pocket instead of his briefcase now. He took it out and flipped it open.

"Yeah, it's Bosch."

"Detective, it's Dr. Hinojos."

"Oh . . . Hi."

"Something wrong?"

"No, uh, yeah, I was expecting somebody else. I've got to keep this line open for a few minutes. I've got a call coming in. Can I call you back?"

Bosch looked at his watch. It was five minutes until six.

"Yes," Hinojos said. "I'll be at the office until six-thirty. I want to talk to you about something, and to see how you fared on the sixth floor after I left."

"I'm fine, but I'll call you back."

As soon as he flipped the phone closed, it rang again in his hand.

"Bosch."

"Bosch, I'm up against it and don't have time for bullshit." It was Russell. She also didn't have time to identify herself. "The story is that the investigation into the killing of Harvey Pounds has turned inward and detectives spent several hours with you today. They searched your home and they believe you are the prime suspect."

"Prime suspect? We don't even use those words, Keisha. Now I *know* you're talking to one of those squints in IAD. They wouldn't know how to run a homicide investigation if the doer came up and bit them on their shiny ass."

"Don't try to deflect what we're talking about here. It's really simple. Do you or don't you have a comment on the story for tomorrow's paper? If you want to say something, I have just enough time to get it in the first run."

"On the record, I have no comment."

"And off?"

"Off the record, not for attribution or any use at all, I can tell you that you're full of shit, Keisha. Your story is wrong. Flat-out wrong. If you run it as you have just summarized it for me, you will have to write another one tomorrow correcting it. It will say I am not a suspect at all. Then, after that, you'll have to find another beat to cover."

"And why is that?" she asked haughtily.

"Because this is a smear orchestrated by Internal Affairs. It's a plant. And when it is read tomorrow by everybody else in the department they'll know it is and they'll know you fell for it. They won't trust you. They'll think you're just a front for people like Brockman. No one that it is important for you to have a source relationship with will want to have that relationship with you. Including me. You'll be left covering the police commission and rewriting the press releases out of media relations. And then, of course, whenever Brockman wants to cream somebody else, he'll pick up the phone and call."

There was silence on the line. Bosch looked up at the sky and saw it turning pink with the start of sunset. He looked at his watch. It was one minute until her deadline.

"You there, Keisha?"

"Bosch, you're scaring me."

"You should be scared. You got about a minute to make a big decision."

"Let me ask you this. Did you attack Pounds two weeks ago and throw him through a window?"

"On or off the record?"

"It doesn't matter. I just need an answer. Quick!"

"Off the record, that's more or less accurate."

"Well, that would seem to make you a suspect in his death. I don't see—"

"Keisha, I've been out of the state for three days. I got back today. Brockman brought me in and talked to me for less than an hour. My story checked and I was kicked free. I'm not a suspect. I'm talking to you from the front of my house. You hear that hammering? That's my house. I've got a carpenter here. Are prime suspects allowed to go home at night?"

"How can I confirm all of this?"

"Today? You can't. You've got to pick. Brockman or me. Tomorrow, you can call Assistant Chief Irving and he'll confirm—if he is willing to talk to you."

"Shit! Bosch, I can't believe this. If I go to my editor at deadline and tell him a story that they had budgeted for the front page since the three o'clock meeting is not a story . . . I might be looking for a new beat and a new paper to cover it for."

"There's other news in the world, Keisha. They can find something for the front page. This will pay off for you in the long run, anyway. I'll spread the word about you."

There was a brief silence while she made her decision.

"I can't talk. I have to get in there and grab him. Good-bye, Bosch. I hope I'm still working here the next time we talk."

She was gone before he could say good-bye.

He walked up the street to the Mustang and drove it down to the house. Gowdy had finished with the latches and both doors now had locks on them. The inspector was out at his car using the front hood as a desk. He was writing on a clipboard and Bosch guessed he was moving slowly so as to make sure Bosch left the property. Bosch started loading his pile of belongings into the Mustang. He didn't know where he was going to take himself.

He put the thought of his homelessness aside and began thinking about Keisha Russell. He wondered if she would be able to stop the story so late in the game. It had probably taken on a life of its own. Like a monster in the newspaper's computer. And she, its Dr. Frankenstein, would likely have little power over stopping it.

When he had everything in the Mustang, he waved a salute to Gowdy, got in and drove down the hill. Down at Cahuenga he didn't know which way to turn because he still didn't know where he should go. To the right was Hollywood. To the left was the Valley. Then he remembered the Mark Twain. In Hollywood, only a few blocks from the station on Wilcox, the Mark Twain was an old residence hotel with efficiencies that were generally clean and neat—a lot more so than the surrounding neighborhood. Bosch knew this because he had stashed witnesses there on occasion. He also knew that there were a couple of units that were two-room efficiencies with private baths. He decided he would go for one of them and turned right. The phone rang almost as soon as he had made the decision. It was Keisha Russell.

"You owe me big time, Bosch. I killed it."

He felt relief and annoyance at the same time. It was typical thinking for a reporter.

"What are you talking about?" he countered. "You owe me big time for saving your ass."

"Well, we'll see about that. I'm still going to check this out tomorrow. If it falls the way you said, I'm going to Irving to complain about Brockman. I'll burn him."

"You just did."

Realizing she had just confirmed Brockman as the source, she laughed uneasily.

"What did your editor say?"

"He thinks I'm an idiot. But I told him there's other news in the world."

"Good line."

"Yeah, I'm going to keep that one in my computer. So what's going on? And what's happening with those clips I got you?"

"The clips are still percolating. I can't really talk about anything yet."

"Figures. I don't know why I keep helping you, Bosch, but here goes.

Remember you asked about Monte Kim, the guy who wrote that first clip I gave you?"

"Yeah. Monte Kim."

"I asked about him around here and one of the old rewrite guys told me he's still alive. Turns out that after he left the *Times* he worked for the DA's office for a while. I don't know what he's doing now but I got his number and his address. He's in the Valley."

"Can you give it to me?"

"I guess so, since it was in the phonebook."

"Damn, I never thought of that."

"You might be a good detective, Bosch, but you wouldn't make much of a reporter."

She gave him the number and address, said she'd be in touch and hung up. Bosch put the phone down on the seat and thought about this latest piece of information as he drove into Hollywood. Monte Kim had worked for the district attorney. Bosch had a pretty good idea which one that would be.

The man behind the front desk at the Mark Twain didn't seem to recognize Bosch, though Harry was reasonably sure he was the same man he had dealt with before while renting rooms for witnesses. The counterman was tall and thin and had the hunched-over shoulders of someone carrying a heavy burden. He looked like he'd been behind the desk since Eisenhower.

"You remember me? From down the street?"

"Yeah, I remember. I didn't say anything 'cause I didn't know if this was an undercover job or not."

"No. No undercover. I wanted to know if you have one of the big rooms in the back open. One with a phone."

"You want one?"

"That's why I'm asking."

"Who you going to put in there this time? I don't want no gangbangers again. Last time, they—"

"No, no gangbangers. Only me. I want the room."

"You want the room?"

"That's right. And I won't paint on the walls. How much?"

The desk man seemed nonplussed by the fact that Bosch wanted to stay there himself. He finally recovered and told Bosch he had his choice:

thirty dollars a day, two hundred a week or five hundred a month. All in advance. Bosch paid for a week with his credit card and waited anxiously while the man checked to make sure the charge would clear.

"Now, how much for the parking space in the loading zone out front?"

"You can't rent that."

"I want to park out front, make it harder for one of your other tenants to rip my car off."

Bosch took out his money and slid fifty dollars across the counter.

"If parking enforcement comes by, tell them it's cool."

"Yeah."

"You the manager?"

"And owner. Twenty-seven years."

"Sorry."

Bosch went out to get his things. It took him three trips to bring everything up to room 214. The room was in the back and its two windows looked across an alley to the back of a one-story building that housed two bars and an adult film and novelties store. But Bosch had known all along it would be no garden spot. It wasn't the kind of place where he would find a terry cloth robe in the closet and mints on the pillow at night. It was just a couple of notches up from the places where you slid your money to the clerk through a slot in the bulletproof glass.

One room had a bureau and a bed, which had only two cigarette burns in the bedspread, and a television mounted in a steel frame that was bolted to the wall. There was no cable, no remote and no courtesy *TV Guide*. The other room had a worn green couch, a small table for two and a kitchenette that had a half refrigerator, a bolted-down microwave and a two-coil electric range. The bathroom was off the hallway that connected the two rooms and came complete with white tile that had yellowed like old men's teeth.

Despite the drab circumstances and his hopes that his stay would be temporary, Bosch tried his best to transform the hotel room into a home. He hung some clothes in the closet, put his toothbrush and shaving kit in the bathroom and set the answering machine up on the phone, though nobody knew his number. He decided that in the morning he'd call the telephone company and have a forwarding tape put on his old line.

Next he set up the stereo on the bureau. For the time being he just placed the speakers on the floor on either side of the bureau. He then rummaged through his box of CDs and came across a Tom Waits recording called "Blue Valentine." He hadn't listened to it in years so he put it on.

He sat down on the bed near the phone and listened and thought for a few minutes about calling Jazz in Florida. But he wasn't sure what he could say or ask. He decided it might be better to just let it go for now. He lit a cigarette and went to the window. There was nothing happening in the alley. Across the tops of the buildings he could see the ornate tower of the nearby Hollywood Athletic Club. It was a beautiful building. One of the last in Hollywood.

He closed the musty curtains, turned around and studied his new home. After a while he yanked the spread off the bed along with the other covers and then remade it with his own sheets and blanket. He knew it was a small gesture of continuity but it made him feel less lonely. It also made him feel a little bit as though he knew what he was doing with his life at that point and it made him forget for a few more moments about Harvey Pounds.

Bosch sat on the newly made bed and leaned back on the pillows propped against the headboard. He lit another cigarette. He studied the wounds on his two fingers and saw that the scabs had been replaced with hard pink skin. They were healing nicely. He hoped the rest of him would, too. But he doubted it. He knew he was responsible. And he knew he had to pay. Somehow.

He absentmindedly pulled the phone off the bed table and placed it on his chest. It was an old one with a rotary dial. Bosch lifted the receiver and looked at the dial. Who was he going to call? What was he going to say? He replaced the receiver and sat up. He decided he had to get out.

Monte Kim lived on Willis Avenue in Sherman Oaks in the midst of a ghost town of apartment buildings red-tagged after the quake. Kim's apartment building was a gray-and-white Cape Cod affair that sat between two empties. At least they were supposed to be empty. As Bosch pulled up he saw lights go out in one of the buildings. Squatters, he guessed. Like Bosch had been, always on alert for the building inspector.

Kim's building looked as though it had been either completely spared by the quake or already completely repaired. Bosch doubted it was the latter. He believed the building was more a testament to the serendipitous violence of nature, and maybe a builder who didn't cut corners. The Cape Cod had stood up while the buildings around it cracked and slid.

It was a common, rectangular building with apartment entrances running down each side of it. But to get to one of the doors, you had to be buzzed through a six-foot-tall electronic gate. The cops called them "feel good" gates because they made the dwellers inside feel safer, but they were worthless. All they did was put up a barrier for legitimate visitors to the building. Others could simply climb over, and they did, all over the city. Feel good gates were everywhere.

He said only that it was the police when Kim's voice sounded on the intercom and he was buzzed in. He took the badge wallet out of his pocket as he walked down to apartment eight. When Kim opened up, Bosch shoved the open badge wallet through the door and about six inches from his face. He held it so his finger was across the badge and obscured the marking that said LIEUTENANT. He then pulled the wallet back quickly and put it away.

"I'm sorry, I didn't catch the name on there," Kim said, still blocking the way.

"Hieronymus Bosch. But people call me Harry."

"You're named for the painter."

"Sometimes I feel old enough that I think he was named for me. Tonight's one of those nights. Can I come in? This shouldn't take long."

Kim led him into the living room with a confused look on his face. It was a decent-sized and neat room with a couch and two chairs and a gas fireplace next to the TV. Kim took one of the chairs and Bosch sat on the end of the couch. He noticed a white poodle sleeping on the carpet next to Kim's chair. Kim was an overweight man with a wide, florid face. He wore glasses that pinched his temples and what was left of his hair was dyed brown. He wore a red cardigan sweater over a white shirt and old khakis. Bosch guessed Kim wasn't quite sixty. He had been expecting an older man.

"I guess this is where I ask, 'What's this all about?'"

"Yeah, and I guess this is where I tell you. Problem is I'm not sure how to begin. I'm investigating a couple of homicides. You can probably help. But I wonder if you'd indulge me and let me ask you some questions going a while back? Then, when we're done, I'll explain why."

"Seems unusual but . . ."

Kim raised his hands and waved off any problems. He made a movement in his chair as if to get more comfortable. He checked the dog and then squinted his eyes as if that might better help him understand and answer the questions. Bosch could see a film of sweat developing in the defoliated landscape that had once been his scalp.

"You were a reporter for the *Times*. How long did that last?"

"Oh, boy, that was just a few years in the early sixties. How do you know that?"

"Mr. Kim, let me ask these questions first. What kind of reporting did you do?"

"Back then they called us cub reporters. I was on the crime beat."

"What do you do now?"

"Currently, I work out of my home. I'm in public relations. I have an office upstairs in the second bedroom. I had an office in Reseda but the building was condemned. You could see daylight through the cracks."

He was like most people in L.A. He didn't have to preface his remarks by saying he was talking about earthquake damage. It was understood.

"I have several small accounts," he continued. "I was a local spokesman for the GM plant in Van Nuys until they closed it down. Then I went out on my own."

"What made you quit the *Times* back in the sixties?"

"I got—Am I a suspect in something?"

"Not at all, Mr. Kim. I'm just trying to get to know you. Indulge me. I'll get to the point. You were saying why you quit the *Times.*"

"Yes, well, I got a better job. I was offered the position of press spokesman for the district attorney at the time, Arno Conklin. I took it. Better pay, more interesting than the cop beat and a brighter future."

"What do you mean, brighter future?"

"Well, actually I was wrong about that. When I took the job I thought the sky would be the limit with Arno. He was a good man. I figured I'd eventually—you know, if I stayed with him—ride with him to the governor's mansion, maybe the Senate in Washington. But things didn't turn out. I ended up with an office in Reseda with a crack in the wall I could feel the wind come through. I don't see why the police would be interested in all—"

"What happened with Conklin? Why didn't things turn out?"

"Well, I'm not the expert on this. All I know is that in sixty-eight he was planning on running for attorney general and the office was practically his for the taking. Then he just . . . dropped out. He quit politics and went back to practice law. And it wasn't to harvest the big corporate bucks that sit out there when these guys go into private practice. He opened a one-man law firm. I admired him. As far as I heard, sixty percent or better of his practice was pro bono. He was working for free most of the time."

"Like he was serving a penance or something?"

"I don't know. I guess."

"Why'd he drop out?"

"I don't know."

"Weren't you part of the inner circle?"

"No. He didn't have a circle. He had one man."

"Gordon Mittel."

"Right. You want to know why he didn't run, ask Gordon." Then it clicked in Kim's brain that Bosch had introduced the name Gordon Mittel to the conversation. "Is this about Gordon Mittel?"

"Let me ask the questions first. Why do you think Conklin didn't run? You must have some idea."

"He wasn't officially in the race in the first place, so he didn't have to make any public statement about dropping out. He just didn't run. There were a lot of rumors, though."

"Like what?"

"Oh, lots of stuff. Like he was gay. There were others. Financial trouble. Supposedly there was a threat from the mob that if he won, they'd kill him. Just stuff like that. None of it was ever more than backroom talk amongst the town politicos."

"He was never married?"

"Not as far as I know. But as far as him being gay, I never saw anything like that."

Bosch noted that the top of Kim's head was slick now with sweat. It was already warm in the room but he kept the cardigan on. Bosch made a quick change of tracks.

"Okay, tell me about the death of Johnny Fox."

Bosch saw the quick glimmer of recognition pass behind the glasses but then it disappeared. But it was enough.

"Johnny Fox, who's that?"

"C'mon, Monte, it's old news. Nobody cares what you did. I just need to know the story behind the story. That's why I'm here."

"You're talking about when I was a reporter? I wrote a lot of stories. That was thirty-five years ago. I was a kid. I can't remember everything."

"But you remember Johnny Fox. He was your ticket to that brighter future. The one that didn't happen."

"Look, what are you doing here? You're not a cop. Did Gordon send you? After all these years, you people think I . . ."

He stopped.

"I am a cop, Monte. And you're lucky I got here before Gordon did.

Something's coming undone. The ghosts are coming back. You read in the paper today about that cop found in his trunk in Griffith Park?"

"I saw it on the news. He was a lieutenant."

"Yeah. He was my lieutenant. He was looking into a couple old cases. Johnny Fox was one of them. Then he ended up in his trunk. So you'll have to excuse me if I'm a little nervous and pushy, but I need to know about Johnny Fox. And you wrote the story. You wrote the story after he got killed that made him out to be an angel. Then you end up on Conklin's team. I don't care what you did, I just want to know what you did."

"Am I in danger?"

Bosch hiked his shoulders in his best who-knows-and-who-cares gesture.

"If you are, then we can protect you. You don't help us, we can't help you. You know how it goes."

"Oh my God! I knew this—What other cases?"

"One of Johnny's girls who got killed about a year before him. Her name was Marjorie Lowe."

Kim shook his head. He didn't recognize the name. He ran his hand over his scalp, using it like a squeegee to move the sweat into the thicker hair. Bosch could tell he had perfectly primed the fat man to answer the questions.

"So what about Fox?" Bosch asked. "I don't have all night."

"Look, I don't know anything. All I did was a favor for a favor."

"Tell me about it."

He composed himself for a long moment before speaking.

"Look, you know who Jack Ruby was?"

"In Dallas?"

"Yeah, the guy who killed Oswald. Well, Johnny Fox was the Jack Ruby of L.A., okay? Same era, same kind of guy. Fox ran women, was a gambler, knew which cops could be greased and greased them when he needed to. It kept him out of jail. He was a classic Hollywood bottom feeder. When he ended up dead on the Hollywood Division blotter, I saw it but was going to pass. He was trash and we didn't write about trash. Then a source I had in the cop shop told me Johnny had been on Conklin's payroll."

"That made it a story."

"Yeah. So I called up Mittel, Conklin's campaign manager, and ran it by him. I wanted a response. I don't know how much you know about that time, but Conklin had this squeaky-clean image. He was the guy attacking every vice in the city and here he had a vice hoodlum on the payroll. It was a great story. Though Fox didn't have a record, I don't think, there were intel files on him and I had access to them. The story was going to do damage and Mittel knew it."

He stopped there at the edge of the story. He knew the rest but to speak of it out loud he had to be pushed over the edge.

"Mittel knew it," Bosch said. "So he offered you a deal. He'd make you Conklin's flak if you cleaned up the story."

"Not exactly."

"Then what? What was the deal?"

"I'm sure any kind of statute has passed . . ."

"Don't worry about it. Just tell me and only me, you and your dog will ever know it."

Kim took a deep breath and continued.

"This was mid-campaign so Conklin already had a spokesman. Mittel offered me a job as deputy spokesman after the election. I'd work out of the office in the Van Nuys Courthouse, handle the Valley stuff."

"If Conklin won."

"Yeah, but that was a given. Unless this Fox story caused a problem. But I held out, used some leverage. I told Mittel I wanted to be the main spokesman after Arno's election or forget it. He got back to me later and agreed."

"After he talked to Conklin."

"I guess. Anyway, I wrote a story that left out the details of Fox's past."

"I read it."

"That's all I did. I got the job. It was never mentioned again."

Bosch sized Kim up for a moment. He was weak. He didn't see that being a reporter was a calling just the same as being a cop. You took an oath to yourself. Kim had seemingly had no difficulty breaking it. Bosch could not imagine someone like Keisha Russell acting the same way under the same circumstances. He tried to cover his distaste and move on.

"Think back now. This is important. When you first called up Mittel and told him about Fox's background, did you get the impression that he already knew the background?"

"Yes, he knew. I don't know if the cops had told him that day or he had known all along. But he knew Fox was dead and he knew who he was. I think he was a little surprised that I knew and he became eager to make a deal to keep it out of the paper . . . It was the first time I ever did anything like that. I wish I hadn't done it."

Kim looked down at the dog and then to the beige rug and Bosch knew it was a screen on which he saw how his life diverged sharply the moment he took the deal. It went from where it was going to where it eventually was.

"Your story didn't name any cops," Bosch said. "Do you remember who handled it?"

"Not really. It was so long ago. It would have been a couple guys from the Hollywood homicide table. Back then, they handled fatal accidents. Now there's a division for that."

"Claude Eno?"

"Eno? I remember him. It might've been. I think I remember that it . . . Yes, it was. Now I remember. He was on it alone. His partner had transferred or retired or something and he was working alone, waiting for his next partner to transfer in. So they gave him the traffic cases. They were usually pretty light, as far as any investigation went."

"How do you remember so much of this?"

Kim pursed his lips and struggled for an answer.

"I guess . . . Like I said, I wish I never did what I did. So, I guess, I think about it a lot. I remember it."

Bosch nodded. He had no more questions and was already thinking of the implications of how Kim's information fit with his own. Eno had worked both cases, Lowe and Fox, and later retired, leaving behind a mail-drop corporation with Conklin's and Mittel's name on it that collected a thousand dollars a month for twenty-five years. He realized that compared to Eno, Kim had settled for too little. He was about to get up when he thought of something.

"You said that Mittel never mentioned the deal you made or Fox again."

"That's right."

"Did Conklin ever say anything about either one?"

"No, he never mentioned a thing, either."

"What was your relationship like? Didn't he treat you as a chiseler?"

"No, because I wasn't a chiseler," Kim protested but the indignation in his voice was hollow. "I did a job for him and I did it well. He was always very nice to me."

"He was in your story on Fox. I don't have it here but in it he said he had never met Fox."

"Yeah, that was a lie. I made that up."

Bosch was confused.

"What do you mean? You mean, you made up the lie?"

"In case they went back on the deal. I put Conklin in the story saying he didn't know the guy because I had evidence he did. They knew I had it. That way, if after the election they reneged on the deal, I could dredge up the story again and show Conklin said he didn't know Fox but he did. I could then make the inference that he also knew Fox's background when he hired him. It wouldn't have done much good because he'd have already been elected, but it would do some PR damage. It was my little insurance policy. Understand?"

Bosch nodded.

"What was the evidence you had that Conklin knew Fox?"

"I had photos."

"What photos?"

"They were taken by the society photographer for the *Times* at the Hollywood Masonic Lodge's St. Patrick's Day dance a couple of years before the election. There's two of them. Conklin and Fox are at a table. They were scratches but one day I was—"

"What do you mean, scratches?"

"Photos never published. Outtakes. But, see, I used to look at the society stuff in the photo lab, so I could learn who the big shots in the city were and who they were out with and so on. It was useful information. One day I saw these photos of Conklin and some guy that I recognized but wasn't sure from where. It was because of the social background. This wasn't Fox's turf so at the time I didn't recognize him. Then, when Fox got killed and I was told he worked for Conklin, I remembered the photos and who the other man was. Fox. I went back to the scratch files and pulled them out."

"They were just sitting there together at this dance?"

"In the photos? Yeah. And they were smiling. You could tell they knew each other. These weren't posed shots. In fact, that's why each was a scratch. They weren't good photos, not for the society page."

"Anybody else with them?"

"A couple women, that was it."

"Go get the photos."

"Oh, I don't have them anymore. I tossed them after I didn't need them anymore."

"Kim, don't bullshit me, okay? There was never a time you didn't need them. Those photos are probably why you are alive today. Now go get them or I'll take you downtown for withholding evidence, then I'll come back with a warrant and tear this place apart."

"All right! Jesus! Wait here. I have one of them."

He got up and went up the stairs. Bosch just stared at the dog. It was wearing a sweater that matched Kim's. He heard a closet door being moved on rollers, then a heavy thud. He guessed a box had been taken off the shelf and dropped to the floor. In a few more moments, Kim's heavy steps were coming down the stairs. As he passed the couch, he handed Bosch a black-and-white eight-by-ten that was yellowed around the edges. Bosch stared at it for a long time.

"I have the other in a safe deposit box," Kim said. "It's a clearer shot of the two of them. You can tell it's Fox."

Bosch didn't say anything. He was still looking at the photo. It was a flashbulb shot. Everybody's face was lit up white as snow. Conklin sat across a table from the man Bosch assumed was Fox. There were a half dozen drink glasses on the table. Conklin was smiling and heavy-lidded—that was probably why the photo was a scratch—and Fox was turned slightly away from the camera, his features indistinguishable. Bosch guessed you would have had to know him to recognize him. Neither of them seemed aware of the photographer's presence. Flashbulbs were probably going off all over the place.

But more so than the men, Bosch studied the two women in the photo. Standing next to Fox and bending over to whisper in his ear was a woman in a dark one-piece dress that was tight around the middle. Her hair was swirled on top of her head. It was Meredith Roman. And sitting across the table and next to Conklin, mostly obscured by him, was Marjorie Lowe. Bosch guessed that if you didn't already know her, she wouldn't have been recognizable. Conklin was smoking and had his hand up to his face. His arm blocked off half of Bosch's mother's face. It almost looked as if she was peeking around a corner at the camera.

Bosch turned the photo over and there was a stamp on the back that said *TIMES* PHOTO BY BORIS LUGAVERE. It was dated March 17, 1961, seven months before his mother's death.

"Did you ever show this to Conklin or Mittel?" Bosch finally asked.

"Yeah. When I made my case for head spokesman. I gave Gordon a copy. He saw that it was proof the candidate knew Fox."

Mittel must also have seen that it was proof that the candidate knew a murder victim, Bosch realized. Kim didn't know what he had. But no wonder he got the head spokesman's job. You're lucky you're alive, he thought but didn't say.

"Did Mittel know it was only a copy?"

"Oh yeah, I made that clear. I wasn't stupid."

"Did Conklin ever mention it to you?"

"Not to me. But I assume Mittel told him about it. Remember, I said he had to get back to me about the job I wanted. Who would he have to clear it with, he was campaign manager? So he must've talked to Conklin."

"I'm going to keep this."

Bosch held up the photo.

"I've got the other."

"Have you stayed in touch with Arno Conklin over the years?"

"No. I haven't spoken to him in, I don't know, twenty years."

"I want you to call him now and I—"

"I don't even know where he is."

"I do. I want you to call him and tell him you want to see him tonight. Tell him it has to be tonight. Tell him it's about Johnny Fox and Marjorie Lowe. Tell him not to tell anyone you are coming."

"I can't do that."

"Sure you can. Where's your phone? I'll help you."

"No, I mean, I can't go see him tonight. You can't make—"

"You're not going to see him tonight, Monte. I'm going to be you. Now where's your phone?"

At Park La Brea Lifecare, Bosch parked in a visitor's space in the front lot and got out of the Mustang. The place looked dark; few windows in the upper stories had lights on behind them. He checked his watch—it was only nine-fifty—and moved toward the glass doors of the lobby.

He felt a slight pull in his throat as he made the walk. Deep down he had known as soon as he finished reading the murder book that his sights were set on Conklin and that it would come to this. He was about to confront the man he believed had killed his mother and then used his position and the people he surrounded himself with to walk away from it. To Bosch, Conklin was the symbol of all that he never had in his life. Power, home, contentment. It didn't matter how many people had told him on the trail that Conklin was a good man. Bosch knew the secret behind the good man. His rage grew with each step he took.

Inside the door a uniformed guard sat behind a desk working on a crossword puzzle torn from the *Times Sunday Magazine*. Maybe he had been working on it since then. He looked up at Bosch as if he was expecting him.

"Monte Kim," Bosch said. "One of the residents is expecting me. Arno Conklin."

"Yeah, he called down." The guard consulted a clipboard, then turned it around and handed the pen to Bosch. "Been a long time since he's had any visitors. Sign here, please. He's up in nine-oh-seven."

Bosch signed and dropped the pen on the clipboard.

"It's kind of late," the guard said. "Visitation is usually over by nine."

"What's that mean? You want me to leave? Fine." He held his brief-case up. "Mr. Conklin can just roll his wheelchair down to my office to-morrow to pick this stuff up. I'm the one making a special trip here, buddy. For him. Let me up or not, I don't care. He cares."

"Whoah, whoah, whoah, hold on there, partner. I was just saying it was late and you didn't let me finish. I'm going to let you go up. No problem. Mr. Conklin specifically requested it and this ain't no prison. I'm just saying all the visitors are gone, okay? People are sleeping. Just keep it down, is all. No reason to blow a gasket."

"Nine-oh-seven, you said?"

"That's right. I'll call him and tell him you're on your way up."

"Thanks."

Bosch moved past the guard toward the elevators without apology. He was forgotten as soon as he was out of Bosch's sight. Only one thing, one person, occupied his mind now.

The elevator moved about as quickly as the building's inhabitants. When he finally got to the ninth floor, Bosch walked past a nurses' sta-tion but it was empty, the night nurse apparently tending to a resident's needs. Bosch headed the wrong way down the hall, then corrected him-self and headed back the other way. The paint and linoleum in the hall-way were fresh but even top-dollar places like this couldn't completely eliminate the lingering smell of urine, disinfectant and the sense of closed lives behind the closed doors. He found the door to nine-oh-seven and knocked once. He heard a faint voice telling him to enter. It was more like a whimper than a whisper.

Bosch was unprepared for what he saw when he opened the door. There was a single light on in the room, a small reading lamp to the side of the bed. It left most of the room in shadow. An old man sat on the bed propped against three pillows, a book in his frail hands, bifocals on the bridge of his nose. What Bosch found so eerie about the tableau before him was that the bedcovers were bunched around the old man's waist but were flat on the remainder of the bed. The bed was flat. There were no legs. Compounding this shock was the wheelchair to the right of the bed. A plaid blanket had been thrown over the seat. But two legs in black pants and loafers extended from beneath it and down to the chair's footrests. It looked as if half the man was in his bed but he had left his other half in the chair. Bosch's face must have shown his confusion.

"Prosthesis," said the raspy voice from the bed. "Lost my legs . . . diabetes. Almost nothing of me left. Except an old man's vanity. I had the legs made for public appearances."

Bosch stepped closer to the light. The man's skin was like the back of peeled wallpaper. Yellowish, pale. His eyes were deep in the shadows of his skeletal face, his hair just a whisper around his ears. His thin hands were ribbed with blue veins the size of earthworms under his spotted skin. He was death, Bosch knew. Death certainly had a better grip on him than life did.

Conklin put the book on the table near the lamp. It seemed to be a labor for him to make the reach. Bosch saw the title. *The Neon Rain*.

"A mystery," Conklin said, a small cackle following. "I indulge myself with mysteries. I've learned to appreciate the writing. I never did before. Never took the time. Come in, Monte, no need to be afraid of me. I'm a harmless old man."

Bosch stepped closer until the light was on his face. He saw Conklin's watery eyes study him and conclude that he was not Monte Kim. It had been a long time but Conklin seemed to be able to tell.

"I came in Monte's place," he whispered.

Conklin turned his head slightly and Bosch saw his eyes fall on the emergency call button on the bed table. He must have figured he had no chance and no strength for another reach. He turned back to Bosch.

"Who are you, then?"

"I'm working on a mystery, too."

"A detective?"

"Yes. My name's Harry Bosch and I want to ask you about . . ."

He stopped. There was a change in Conklin's face. Bosch could not tell if it was fear or maybe recognition but something had changed. Conklin brought his eyes up to Bosch's and Bosch realized the old man was smiling.

"Hieronymus Bosch," he whispered. "Like the painter."

Bosch nodded slowly. He now realized he was as shocked as the old man.

"How do you know that?"

"Because I know of you."

"How?"

"Through your mother. She told me about you and your special name. I loved your mother."

It was like getting hit in the chest with a sandbag. Bosch felt the air go out of him and he put a hand down on the bed to hold himself steady.

"Sit. Please. Sit."

Conklin held out a shaky hand, motioning Bosch onto the bed. He nodded when Bosch did as he had been told.

"No!" Bosch said loudly as he rose off the bed almost as soon as he had sat down on it. "You used her and you killed her. Then you paid off people to bury it with her. That's why I'm here. I came for the truth. I want to hear you tell it and I don't want to hear any bullshit about loving her. You're a liar."

Conklin had a pleading look in his eyes, then he turned them away, toward the dark side of the room.

"I don't know the truth," he said, his voice like dried leaves blown along the sidewalk. "I take responsibility and therefore, yes, it could be said I killed her. The only truth I know is that I loved her. You can call me a liar but that is the truth. You could make an old man whole again if you believed that."

Bosch couldn't fathom what was happening, what was being said.

"She was with you that night. In Hancock Park."

"Yes."

"What happened? What did you do?"

"I killed her . . . with my words, my actions. It took me many years to realize that."

Bosch moved closer until he was hovering over the old man. He wanted to grab him and shake some sense out of him. But Arno Conklin was so frail that he might shatter.

"What are you talking about? Look at me. What are you talking about?"

Conklin turned his head on a neck no wider than a glass of milk. He looked at Bosch and nodded solemnly.

"You see, we made plans that night. Marjorie and I. I had fallen for her against all better judgment and advice. My own and others. We were going to get married. We'd decided. We were going to get you out of that youth hall. We had many plans. That was the night we made them. We were both so happy that we cried. The next day was Saturday. I wanted to go to Las Vegas. Take the car and drive through the night before we could change our minds or have them changed for us. She agreed and went home to pick up her things . . . She never came back."

"That's your story? You expect me—"

"You see, after she had left, I made one call. But that was enough. I called my best friend to tell him the good news and to ask him to stand with me as my best man. I wanted him to go with us to Las Vegas. Do you know what he said? He declined the honor of being my best man. He said that if I married that . . . that woman, I'd be finished. He said he wouldn't let me do that. He said he had great plans for me."

"Gordon Mittel."

Conklin nodded sadly.

"So what are you saying, Mittel killed her? You didn't know?"

"I didn't know."

He looked down at his feeble hands and balled them into tiny fists on the blanket. They looked completely powerless. Bosch only watched.

"I did not realize it for many years. It was beyond the pale to consider that he had done it. And then, of course, I must admit I was thinking of myself at the time. I was a coward, thinking only of my escape."

Bosch was not tracking what he was saying. But it didn't seem that Conklin was talking to him, anyway. The old man was really telling himself the story. He suddenly looked up from his reverie at Bosch.

"You know, I knew someday you would come."

"How?"

"Because I knew you would care. Maybe no one else. But I knew you would. You had to care. You were her son."

"Tell me about what happened that night. Everything."

"I need you to get me some water. For my throat. There's a glass there on the bureau, a fountain in the hallway. Don't let it run too long. It gets too cold and hurts my teeth."

Bosch looked at the glass on the bureau and then back at Conklin. He was seized with a fear that if he left the room for even a minute the old man might die and take the story with him. Bosch would never hear it.

"Go. I'll be fine. I certainly can't go anywhere."

Bosch glanced at the call button. Again, Conklin knew his thoughts.

"I am closer to hell than heaven for what I've done. For my silence. I need to tell my story. I think you'd be a better confessor than any priest could be."

As Bosch stepped into the hallway with the glass, he saw a figure of a man turn the corner at the end of the hall and disappear. He thought the man was wearing a suit. It wasn't the guard. He saw the fountain and filled the glass. Conklin smiled weakly as he took the glass and murmured a thanks before drinking. Bosch then took the glass back and put it on the night table.

"Okay," Bosch said. "You said she left that night and never came back. How did you find out what happened?"

"By the next day, I was afraid something had happened. I finally called my office and made a routine check to see what had come in on the overnight reports. Among the things they told me was that there had been a homicide in Hollywood. They had the victim's name. It was her. It was the most horrible day of my life."

"What happened next?"

Conklin rubbed a hand on his forehead and continued.

"I learned that she had been found that morning. She—I was in shock. I couldn't believe this could have happened. I had Mittel make some inquiries but there was nothing useful coming out. Then the man who had . . . introduced me to Marjorie called."

"Johnny Fox."

"Yes. He called and he said he had heard the police were looking for him. He said he was innocent. He threatened me. He said if I did not protect him, he would reveal to the police that Marjorie was with me that last night. It would be the end of my career."

"So you protected him."

"I turned it over to Gordon. He investigated Fox's claim and confirmed his alibi. I cannot remember it now but it was confirmed. He had been in a card game or somewhere where there had been many witnesses. Since I was confident that Fox was not involved, I called the detectives assigned to the case and arranged for him to be interviewed. In order to protect Fox and thereby protect myself, Gordon and I concocted a story in which we told the detectives that Fox was a key witness in a grand jury investigation. The plan was successful. The detectives turned their attention elsewhere. At one point I spoke to one of them and he told me he believed that Marjorie was the victim of some sort of a sex killer. You see, they were quite rare back then. The detective said the outlook on the case was not good. I'm afraid that I never suspected . . . Gordon. Such a horrible thing to do to an innocent person. It was right there in front of my face but I didn't see it for so long. I was a fool. A puppet."

"You're saying that it wasn't you and that it wasn't Fox. You're saying that Mittel killed her to eliminate a threat to your political career. But that he didn't tell you. It was all his idea and he just went out and did it."

"Yes, I say that. I told him, I told him that night when I called, I said that she meant more to me than all of the plans he had for me, that I had for myself. He said it would mean the end of my career and I accepted it. I accepted it as long as I started the next part of my life with her. I believe those minutes were the most peaceful of my life. I was in love and I had made a stand."

He softly pounded a fist onto the bed, an impotent gesture.

"I told Mittel I didn't care what he thought the damage to my career would be. I told him we were going to move away. I didn't know where. La Jolla, San Diego, I threw a few places out. I didn't know where we were going to go but I was defiant. I was mad at him for not sharing the joy of our decision. And in doing so I provoked him, I know now, and I hastened your mother's death."

Bosch studied him a long moment. His agony seemed sincere. Conklin's eyes looked as haunted as the portholes on a sunken ship. There was only blackness behind them.

"Did Mittel ever admit this to you?"

"No, but I knew. I guess it was a subconscious knowledge but then something he said years later brought it out. It confirmed it in my mind. And that was the end of our relationship."

"What did he say? When?"

"Many years later. It was at the time I was preparing for a run for attorney general. Do you believe such a charade occurred? Me the liar, the coward, the conspirator being groomed for the office of the state's top law enforcement officer. Mittel came to me one day and said that I needed to take a wife before the election year. He was that blunt about it. He said there were rumors about me that could cost me votes. I said that was preposterous and that I wouldn't take a wife just to assuage some rednecks out in Palmdale or the desert somewhere. Then he made a comment, just a flippant, offhand comment as he was leaving my office."

He broke off to reach for the glass of water. Bosch helped him and he slowly drank. Bosch noticed the medicinal smell about him. It was horrible. It reminded him of dead people and the morgue. Bosch took the glass when Conklin was done and put it back.

"What was the comment?"

"As he was leaving my office, he said, and I remember it word for word, he said, 'Sometimes I wish I hadn't saved you from that whore scandal. Maybe if I hadn't, we wouldn't have this problem now. People would know you aren't queer.' Those were his words."

Bosch just stared at him for a moment.

"It might've been just a figure of speech. He could have just meant that he had saved you from the scandal of knowing her by taking the steps to keep you out of it. It's not evidence that he killed her or had her killed. You were a prosecutor, you know that's not enough. It wasn't direct evidence of anything. Didn't you ever directly confront him?"

"No. Never. I was too intimidated by him. Gordon was becoming a powerful man. More powerful than I. So I said nothing to him. I simply dismantled my campaign and folded my tent. I left the public life and haven't spoken to Gordon Mittel since that time. More than twenty-five years."

"You went into private practice."

"Yes. I took up pro bono work as my self-imposed penance for what I was responsible for. I wish I could say it helped suture the wounds of my soul but it did not. I'm a helpless man, Hieronymus. So tell me, did you come here to kill me? Don't let my story dissuade you from believing I deserve it."

The question at first startled Bosch into silence. Finally, he shook his head and spoke.

"What about Johnny Fox? He had his hooks into you after that night."

"Yes, he did. He was very capable as extortionists go."

"What happened with him?"

"I was forced to hire him as a campaign employee, paying him five hundred dollars a week for practically nothing. You see what a farce my life had become? He was killed in a hit and run before picking up his first paycheck."

"Mittel?"

"I would assume that he was responsible, though I must admit he's a rather convenient scapegoat for all the bad deeds I've been involved in."

"You didn't think that it was just a little too coincidental that he got killed?"

"Things are so much clearer in hindsight." He shook his head sadly. "At the time I remember being thrilled with my luck. The one thorn in my side had been removed by serendipity. You have to remember, at the time I had no inkling that Marjorie's death was in any way connected to me. I simply saw Fox as being a man on the make. When he was removed through the luck of an automobile mishap, I was pleased. A deal was made with a reporter to keep Fox's background on the QT and everything was fine . . . But, of course, it wasn't. It never was. Gordon, genius that he was, didn't plan on me not being able to get over Marjorie. And I'm still not."

"What about McCage?"

"Who?"

"McCage Incorporated. Your payoffs to the cop. Claude Eno."

Conklin was quiet a moment while he composed an answer.

"Of course, I knew Claude Eno. I didn't care for him. And I never paid him a dime."

"McCage was incorporated in Nevada. It was Eno's company. You and Mittel are both listed as corporate officers. It was a payoff scam. Eno was getting a grand a month from somewhere. You and Mittel."

"No!" Conklin said as forcefully as he could. The word came out as little more than a cough. "I don't know about McCage. Gordon could have set it up, even signed for me or made me sign unwittingly. As district attorney he took care of things for me. I signed when he told me to sign."

He said it while looking directly at Bosch and Harry believed him. Conklin had admitted to far worse deeds. Why would he lie about paying off Eno?

"What did Mittel do when you folded your tent, when you told him you were through?"

"By then he was already quite powerful. Politically. His law firm represented the city's upper tier and his political work was branching out, growing. Still, I was the centerpiece. The plan was to take the attorney general's office and then the governor's mansion. Who knows what after that. So Gordon . . . he was unhappy. I refused to see him but we talked on the phone. When he could not convince me to change my mind, he threatened me."

"How?"

"He told me that if I ever attempted to assault his reputation, he would see to it that I was indicted for Marjorie's death. And I had no doubt that he could have done it."

"From best man to greatest enemy. How'd you ever get hooked up with him?"

"I guess he slipped in the door while I wasn't looking. I never saw the real face until it was too late . . . I don't think in my life I've come across any one as cunningly focused as Gordon. He was—is—a dangerous man. I'm sorry I ever brought your mother into his path."

Bosch nodded. He had no more questions and didn't know what else to say. After a few moments during which Conklin seemed to be lost in thought, the old man spoke up.

"I think, young man, that you only run into a person that is a perfect fit once in your life. When you find the one that you think fits, then grab on for dear life. And it's no matter what she's done in the past. None of that matters. Only the holding on matters."

Bosch nodded again. It was all he could think of to do.

"Where did you meet her?"

"Oh . . . I met her at a dance. She was introduced and, of course, she was younger than me so I didn't think there would be any interest from her. But I was wrong . . . We danced. We dated. And I fell in love."

"You didn't know about her past?"

"At the time, no. But she told me eventually. By then I didn't care."

"What about Fox?"

"Yes, he was the liaison. He introduced us. I didn't know who he was, either. He said he was a business man. You see, for him, it was a business move. Introduce the girl to the prosecutor, sit back and see what happens.

I never paid her and she never asked me for money. All the while we fell in love, Fox must have been weighing his options."

Bosch wondered if he should take the photo from Monte Kim out of his case and show it to Conklin, but he decided not to tempt the old man's memory with the reality of a photo. Conklin spoke while Bosch was still thinking about it.

"I'm very tired now and you never answered my question."

"What question?"

"Did you come here to kill me?"

Bosch looked at his face and his useless hands and realized he felt the stirring of sympathy.

"I didn't know what I was going to do. I just knew I was coming."

"You want to know about her?"

"My mother?"

"Yes."

Bosch thought about the question. His own memories of his mother were dim and fading farther all the time. And he had few recollections about her that came from others.

"What was she like?" he said.

Conklin thought for a moment.

"She is hard for me to describe. I felt a great attraction to her . . . that crooked smile . . . I knew she had secrets. I suppose all people do. But hers ran deep. And despite all of that, she was full of life. And, you see, I didn't think I was at the time we met. That's what she gave to me."

He drank from the glass of water again, emptying it. Bosch offered to get more but Conklin waved off the offer.

"I had been with other women and they wanted to show me off like a trophy," he said. "Your mother wasn't like that. She'd rather stay at home or take a picnic basket to Griffith Park than go to the clubs on the Sunset Strip."

"How did you find out about . . . what she did?"

"She told me. The night she told me about you. She said she needed to tell me the truth because she needed my help. I have to admit . . . the shock was . . . I initially thought of myself. You know, protecting myself. But I admired her courage in telling me and I was in love by then. I couldn't turn away."

"How did Mittel know?"

"I told him. I regret it to this day."

"If she . . . If she was as you described her, why did she do what she did? I've never . . . understood."

"I haven't, either. As I told you, she had her secrets. She didn't tell me them all."

Bosch looked away from him and out the window. The view was to the north. He could see the lights of the Hollywood Hills glimmering in the mist from the canyons.

"She used to tell me that you were a tough little egg," Conklin said from behind him. His voice was almost hoarse now. It was probably more talking than he had done in months. "She once told me that she knew it didn't matter what happened to her because you were tough enough to make it through."

Bosch said nothing. He just looked through the window.

"Was she right?" the old man asked.

Bosch's eyes followed the crestline of the hills directly north. Somewhere up there the lights glowed from Mittel's spaceship. He was up there somewhere waiting for Bosch. He looked back at Conklin, who was still waiting for an answer.

"I think maybe the jury's still out."

Bosch leaned against the stainless steel wall of the elevator as it descended. He realized how different his feelings were from those that he held while the elevator had been carrying him up. He had ridden up with hatred pounding in his chest like a cat in a burlap bag. He didn't even know the man he carried it for. Now he looked upon that man as a pitiful character, a half of a man who lay with his frail hands folded on the blanket, waiting, maybe hoping, for death to come and end his private misery.

Bosch believed Conklin. There was something about his story and his pain that seemed too genuine to be dismissed as an act. Conklin was far beyond posing. He was facing his grave. He had called himself a coward and a puppet and Bosch could think of nothing much harsher that a man could put on his own tombstone.

In realizing that Conklin spoke the truth, Bosch knew that he had already met the real enemy face to face. Gordon Mittel. The strategist. The fixer. The killer. The man who held the strings to the puppet. Now they would meet again. But this time, Bosch planned to make it on his terms.

He pushed the L button again as if that might coax the elevator to descend faster. He knew it was a useless gesture but he did it again.

When the elevator finally opened, the lobby seemed empty and sterile. The guard was there, behind his desk, working on his word puzzle. There wasn't even the sound of a far-off TV. Only the silence of old people's lives. He asked the guard if he needed him to sign out and he was waved off.

"Look, sorry I was an asshole before," Bosch offered.

"Don't worry about it, partner," the guard replied. "It gets to the best of us."

Bosch wondered what the "it" was he was talking about but said nothing. He nodded solemnly, as if he got most of his life lessons from security guards. He pushed through the glass doors and headed down the steps into the parking lot. It was getting cool and he turned up the collar of his jacket. He saw the sky was clear and the moon as sharp as a sickle. As he approached the Mustang he noticed the trunk of the car next to it was open and a man was bent over, attaching a jack to the rear bumper. Bosch picked up his pace and hoped he wouldn't be asked to help out. It was too cold and he was tired of talking to strangers.

He passed the crouched man and then, not used to the rental car keys, he fumbled as he tried to get the proper key into the Mustang's door lock. Just as he got the key in the slot, he heard a shoe scuff along the pavement behind him and a voice said, "Excuse me, fella."

Bosch turned, trying to quickly think of an excuse for why he couldn't help the man. But all he saw was the blur of the other man's arm coming down. Then he saw an explosion of red the color of blood.

Then all he saw was black.

Bosch followed the coyote again. But this time the animal did not take him on the path through the mountain brush. The coyote was out of his element. He led Bosch up a steep incline of pavement. Bosch looked around and realized he was on a tall bridge over a wide expanse of water that his eyes followed to the horizon. Bosch became panicked as the coyote got too far ahead of him. He chased the animal but it crested the rise of the bridge and disappeared. The bridge was now empty, except for Bosch. He struggled to the top and looked around. The sky was blood red and seemed to be pulsing with the sound of a heartbeat.

Bosch looked in all directions but the coyote was gone. He was alone.

But suddenly he wasn't alone. The hands of someone unseen grabbed him from behind and pushed him toward the railing. Bosch struggled. He swung his elbows wildly and dug his heels in and tried to stop his movement to the edge. He tried to speak, to yell for help, but nothing came from his throat. He saw the water shimmering like the scales of a fish below him.

Then, as quickly as they had taken hold of him, the hands were gone and he was alone. He spun around and no one was there. From behind he heard a door close sharply. He turned again and there was no one. And there was no door.

Bosch woke up in darkness and pain to the sound of muffled shouting. He was lying on a hard surface and at first it was a struggle just to move. Eventually, he slid his hand across the ground and determined it was carpet. He knew he was inside somewhere, lying on a floor. Across the expanse of darkness he saw a small line of dim light. He stared at it for some time, using it as a focal point, before realizing that it was the crack of light emitted at the bottom edge of a door.

He pulled himself up into a sitting position and the movement made his interior world slide and melt like a Dalí painting. A feeling of nausea came over him and he closed his eyes and waited for several seconds until equilibrium returned. He raised his hand to the side of his head where the pain came from and found the hair matted with a stickiness he knew by smell was blood. His fingers carefully traced the matted hair to a two-inch-long gash in his scalp. He touched it gingerly and determined that the blood had clotted for now. The wound was no longer bleeding.

He didn't think he could stand so he crawled toward the light. The dream of the coyote broke into his mind and then disappeared in a flash of red pain.

He found the door knob was locked. That didn't surprise him. But the effort exhausted him. He leaned back against the wall and closed his eyes. Inside, his instinct to seek a means of escape and his desire to lay up and mend fought for his attention. The battle was interrupted only by the start of the voices again. Bosch could tell they did not come from the room on the other side of the door. They were farther away, yet near enough to be understood.

"Stupid fuck!"

"Look, I tol' you, you didn't say anything about any briefcase. You—"

"There had to have been one. Use your common sense."

"You said bring the man. I brang the man. You want, I go back to the car and look for a briefcase. But you dint say nothin' about—"

"You can't go back, you fool! The place will be crawling with cops. They probably have his car and the briefcase already."

"I didn't see any briefcase. Maybe he didn't have one."

"And maybe I should have depended on someone else."

Bosch realized that they were talking about him. He also recognized the angry voice as belonging to Gordon Mittel. It had the crisp delivery and haughtiness of the man Bosch had met at the fund-raiser. The other voice Bosch didn't recognize, though he had a good idea who it was. Though defensive and submissive, it was a gruff voice full of the timbre of violence. Bosch guessed it was the man who had hit him. And he imagined that to be the man he had seen Mittel with inside the house during the fund-raiser.

It took Bosch several minutes to consider the content of what they were arguing about. A briefcase. His briefcase. It wasn't in the car, he knew. Then he realized he must have forgotten it, left it in Conklin's room. He had brought it up with him so he could take out the photo Monte Kim had given him and the bank statements from Eno's safe deposit box and confront the old man with his lies. But the old man hadn't lied. He hadn't denied Bosch's mother. And so the photo and statements weren't necessary. The briefcase lay at the foot of the bed, forgotten.

He thought about the last exchange he had heard. Mittel told the other man he could not go back, that the police would be there. This made no sense to him. Unless someone had witnessed the attack on him. Maybe the security guard. It gave him hope, then he dashed it himself when he thought of another possibility. Mittel was taking care of all the loose ends and Conklin had to be one of them. Bosch slumped against the wall. He knew he was now the last loose end. He sat there in silence until he heard Mittel's voice once more.

"Go get him. Bring him outside."

As quickly as he could, not yet formulating a plan, Bosch crawled back toward the spot where he thought he had been when he woke up. He rammed into something heavy, put his hands on it and determined it was a pool table. He quickly found the corner and reached into the pocket. His hand closed on a billiard ball. He pulled it out, quickly trying to think of a way to conceal it. Finally, he shoved it inside his sport coat so that it rolled down the inside of the left sleeve to the crook in his elbow. There was more than enough room. Bosch liked large jackets because they gave him room to grab his gun. That made the sleeves baggy. He believed that by cocking his arm he could conceal the heavy ball in the folds of the sleeve.

As he heard a key hit the doorknob, he moved to his right and sprawled on the carpet, closed his eyes and waited. He hoped he was in or close to the spot on the carpet where he had been dropped by his captors. In moments, he heard the door open and then light burned through his eyelids. There was nothing after that. No sound or movement. He waited.

"Forget it, Bosch," the voice said. "That only works in movies."

Bosch didn't move.

"Look, your blood is all over the carpet. It's on the doorknob here."

Bosch realized he must have left a trail to the door and back. His half-hatched plan to surprise his captor and overtake him had no chance now. He opened his eyes. There was a light on the ceiling directly overhead.

"All right," he said. "What do you want?"

"Get up. Let's go."

Bosch slowly got up. It was an actual struggle but he added to it, ad libbing a bit. And when he was all the way up, he saw blood on the green felt bumper of the pool table. He quickly stumbled and grabbed the spot for support. He hoped the man in the room had not seen the blood was already there.

"Get away from there, goddamnit. That's a five-thousand-dollar table. Look at the blood . . . shit."

"Sorry. I'll pay for it."

"Not where you're going. Let's go."

Bosch recognized him. It was the man he guessed it would be. Mittel's man from the party. And his face matched his voice. Gruff, strong, he had broken a few boards with it. He had a ruddy complexion set off by two small brown eyes that never seemed to blink.

He wore no suit this time. At least that Bosch could see. He was dressed in a bulky blue jumpsuit that looked brand-new. It was a splatter suit. Bosch knew that professional killers often used them. It was easier to clean up after a job and you didn't mess up your suit. Just zip off the splatter suit, dump it, and you're on your way.

Bosch stood on his own and took a step but immediately bent over and folded his arms across his stomach. He thought this was the best way to conceal the weapon he had.

"You really hit me, man. My balance is shot. I think I might get sick or something."

"You get sick and I'll make you clean it up with your tongue. Like a fuckin' cat."

"I guess I won't get sick then."

"You're a funny guy. Let's go."

The man backed away from the door and into the room. He then signaled Bosch out. For the first time Bosch saw that he carried a gun. It looked like a Beretta twenty-two and was held down low at his side.

"I know what you're thinking," he said. "Only a twenty-two. You think you could take maybe two, three shots and still get to me. Wrong. I got hollow points in here. I'll put you down with one shot. Tear a hole the size of a soup bowl outta your back. Remember that. Walk ahead a'me."

He was playing it smart, Bosch noticed, not coming closer than five or six feet even though he had the gun. Once Bosch was through the door, the man issued directions. They walked down a hallway, through what looked like a living room and then through another room that Bosch thought would also qualify as a living room. This one Bosch recognized by the French doors and windows. It was the room off the party lawn at Mittel's mansion on Mount Olympus.

"Go out the door. He's waiting for you out there."

"What did you hit me with, man?"

"Tire iron. Hope it put a splinter in your skull, but it don't matter if it did or didn't."

"Well, I think it did anyway. Congratulations."

Bosch stopped at one of the French doors as if he expected it to be opened for him. Outside the party tent was gone. And out near the edge of the overhang he saw Mittel standing with his back turned to the house. He was silhouetted by the lights of the city extending out into infinity from below.

"Open it."

"Sorry, I thought . . . never mind."

"Yeah, never mind. Just get out there. We don't have all night."

Out on the lawn, Mittel turned around. Bosch could see he was holding the badge wallet with his ID in one hand and the lieutenant's badge in the other. The gunman stopped Bosch with a hand on his shoulder, then moved back to his six-foot distance.

"So, then, Bosch is the real name?"

Bosch looked at Mittel. The former prosecutor turned political backdoor man smiled.

"Yes. That's the real name."

"Well, then, how do you do, Mr. Bosch?"

"It's Detective, actually."

"Detective, actually. You know, I was wondering about that. Because that's what this ID card says but then this badge says something completely different. It says lieutenant. And that's curious. Wasn't that a lieutenant I read about in the papers? The one who was found dead and without his badge? Yes, I'm sure it was. And wasn't his name, Harvey Pounds, the same name that you used when you were parading around here the other night? Again, I think so, but correct me if I am wrong, Detective Bosch."

"It's a long story, Mittel, but I am a cop. LAPD. If you want to save yourself a few years in prison, you'll get this old fuck with the gun away from me and call me an ambulance. I've got a concussion, at least. It might be worse."

Before speaking, Mittel put the badge in one of the pockets of his jacket and the ID wallet in the other.

"No, I don't think we'll be making any calls on your behalf. I think things have gone a little too far for humanitarian gestures like that. Speaking of the human existence, it's a shame that your play here the other night cost an innocent man his life."

"No. It's a fucking crime *you* killed an innocent man."

"Well, I was thinking more along the lines that it was you who killed him. I mean, of course, you are ultimately responsible."

"Just like a lawyer, passing the buck. Should've stayed out of politics, Gordie. Stuck to the law. You'd probably have your own TV commercials by now."

Mittel smiled.

"And what? Given up all of this?"

He spread his arms to take in the house and the magnificent view. Bosch followed the arc of his arm to look at the house but he was really trying to get a bead on the other man, the one with the gun. He spotted him standing five feet directly behind him, the gun at his side. He was still too far away for Bosch to risk making a move. Especially in his condition. He moved his arm slightly and felt the billiard ball nesting in the crook of his elbow. It was reassuring to him. It was all he had.

"The law is for fools, Detective Bosch. But I must correct you. I don't really consider myself to be in politics. I consider myself to be just a fixer. A solver of problems of any kind for anyone. Political problems just happen to be my forte. But now, you see, I have to fix a problem that is neither political nor someone else's. This one is my own."

He raised his eyebrows as though he could hardly believe it himself.

"And that's why I have invited you here. Why I asked Jonathan to bring you along. You see, I had an idea that if we watched Arno Conklin, our mystery party crasher of the other night would eventually show up. And I wasn't disappointed."

"You're a clever man, Mittel."

Bosch turned his head slightly so that he could see Jonathan in his peripheral vision. He was still out of reach. Bosch knew he had to draw him closer.

"Hold your ground, Jonathan," Mittel said. "Mr. Bosch is not one to get excited about. Just a minor inconvenience."

Bosch looked back at Mittel.

"Just like Marjorie Lowe, right? She was just a minor inconvenience. Just a nobody who didn't count."

"Now, that's an interesting name to bring up. Is that what this is about, Detective Bosch?"

Bosch stared at him, too angry to speak.

"Well, the only thing I can admit to is that I did use her death to my advantage. I saw it as an opportunity, you could say."

"I know all about it, Mittel. You used her to get control of Conklin. But eventually even he saw through your lies. It's over now. It doesn't matter what you do to me here, my people will be coming. You can count on it."

"The old give-up-the-place-is-surrounded-ploy. I don't think so. This badge business . . . something tells me that you've exceeded your bounds on this one. I think maybe this is what they call an unofficial investigation and the fact that you used a false name before and were carrying a dead man's badge tend to bear me out . . . I don't think anyone is coming. Are they?"

Bosch's mind raced but he drew a blank and remained silent.

"I think you're just a small-time extortionist who stumbled onto something somehow and wants a payoff to go away. Well, we're going to give you a payoff, Detective Bosch."

"There are people who know what I know, Mittel," Bosch blurted. "What are you going to do, go out and kill them all?"

"I'll take that suggestion under advisement."

"What about Conklin? He knows the whole story. Anything happens to me, I guarantee he'll go right to the cops."

"As a matter of fact, you could say Arno Conklin is with the police right now. But I don't think he's saying much."

Bosch dropped his head and slumped a little. He had guessed that Conklin was dead but had hoped he was wrong. He felt the billiard ball move in his sleeve and he folded his arms again to cover up.

"Yes. Apparently, the former district attorney threw himself from his window after your visit."

Mittel stepped aside and pointed out into the lights below. Far off Bosch could see the cluster of lighted buildings that were Park La Brea. And he could see blue and red lights flashing at the base of one of the buildings. It was Conklin's building.

"Must have been a truly traumatic moment," Mittel continued. "He chose death rather than give in to extortion. A principled man to the end."

"He was an old man!" Bosch yelled angrily. "Goddamnit, why?"

"Detective Bosch, keep your voice down or Jonathan will have to lower it for you."

"You're not getting away this time," Bosch said in a lower, tighter, controlled voice.

"As far as Conklin goes, I assume the final declaration will be suicide. He was very sick, you know."

"Right, a guy with no legs walks over to the window and decides to throw himself out."

"Well, if the authorities don't believe that, then maybe they will come up with an alternate scenario when they find your fingerprints in the room. I'm sure you obliged us by leaving a few."

"Along with my briefcase."

That hit Mittel like a slap across the face.

"That's right. I left it there. And there's enough in it to bring them up this mountain to see you, Mittel. They'll come for you!"

Bosch yelled the last line at him as a test.

"Jon!" Mittel barked.

Almost before the word was out of Mittel's mouth, Bosch was clubbed from behind. The impact came on the right side of the neck and he went down to his knees, careful to keep his arm bent and the heavy ball in place. He slowly, more slowly than was needed, got up. Since the impact had been on the right, he assumed that Jonathan had hit him with his gun hand.

"By providing me with the location of the briefcase, you have answered the most important question I had," Mittel said. "The other, of course, was what was in the briefcase and how it would concern me. Now, the problem I have is that without the briefcase or the ability to get it I have no way of checking the veracity of what you tell me here."

"So I guess you're fucked."

"No, Detective, I think that would more accurately describe your situation. However, I have one other question before you go off. Why, Detective Bosch? Why were you bothering with something so old and so meaningless?"

Bosch looked at him for a long time before answering.

"Because everybody counts, Mittel. Everybody."

Bosch saw Mittel nod in the direction of Jonathan. The meeting was over. He had to make his play.

"Help!"

Bosch yelled it as loudly as he could. And he knew the gunman would make his move toward him immediately. Anticipating the same swing of the gun to the right side of the neck, Bosch spun to his right. As he moved he straightened his left arm and used the centrifugal force of the move to let the billiard ball roll down his sleeve into his hand. In continuing the move, he swung his arm up and out. And as he turned his face he saw Jonathan inches behind him, swinging his own hand down, the fingers laced around the Beretta. He also saw the surprise on Jonathan's face as he realized his swing would surely miss and that his momentum prevented him from correcting the course.

After Jonathan's arm went by harmlessly and he was vulnerable, Bosch's arm arced downward. Jonathan made a last-second lunge to his left but the billiard ball in Bosch's fist still caught him with a glancing blow to the right side of his head. It made a sound like a lightbulb popping and Jonathan's body followed the momentum of his falling arm. He fell face first on the grass, his body on top of the gun.

Almost immediately, the man tried to get up and Bosch delivered a vicious kick to his ribs. Jonathan rolled off the gun and Bosch came down on his body with his knees, swinging his fist into the back of his head and neck two more times before realizing that he still gripped the billiard ball and that he had hurt the man enough.

Breathing as if he had just come up for air, Bosch glanced around and saw the gun. He quickly grabbed it up and looked for Mittel. But he was gone.

The slight sound of running on grass caught his attention and he looked to the far northern line of the lawn. He caught a glimpse of Mittel then, just as he disappeared into the darkness at the spot where the flat, manicured grass gave way to the rugged brush of the hilltop.

"Mittel!"

Bosch jumped up and followed. At the point where he had last seen Mittel, he found a path worn into the brush. He realized it was an old coyote trail that had been widened over time by human feet. He raced down it, the yawning drop-off to the city below no more than two feet on his right.

He saw no sign of Mittel and followed the trail along the edge of the drop-off until the house was no longer in sight behind him. Finally he stopped after coming across nothing that indicated Mittel was even near or had taken this path.

Breathing heavily, his head pounding where he was wounded, Bosch came upon a steep bluff rising off the side of the trail and saw that it was ringed with old beer bottles and other debris. The bluff was a popular lookout spot. He put the gun in his waistband and then used his hands for balance and purchase as he climbed ten feet to its top. He did a slow three-sixty-degree turn while on top of the bluff but saw nothing. He listened but the hiss of the city's traffic precluded any chance of his hearing Mittel moving in the brush. He decided to give it up, to get back to the house and call out an air unit before Mittel could get away. They'd find him with a spotlight if the chopper could get out here quickly enough.

As he gingerly slid back down the bluff, Mittel suddenly came at him from the darkness to the right. He had been hiding behind a thick growth of brush and Spanish sword plants. He dove into Bosch's midsection, knocking him down onto the trail, his weight on top of him. Bosch felt the man's hands going for the gun still in his waistband. But Bosch was younger and stronger. The surprise attack was Mittel's last card. Bosch closed his arms around him and rolled to his left. Suddenly, the weight was off and Mittel was gone.

Bosch sat up and looked about, then pulled himself over to the edge. He pulled the gun out of his waistband and then leaned over and looked down. There was only darkness when he looked directly down the side of the rugged hill. He could see the rectangular roofs of houses about a hundred and fifty yards down. He knew they were built along the twisting roads that fed off Hollywood Boulevard and Fairfax Avenue. He did another complete turn and then looked down again. He didn't see Mittel anywhere.

Bosch surveyed the scene beneath him in its entirety until his eyes caught the backyard lights flicking on behind one of the houses directly below. He watched as a man came out of the house carrying what looked like a rifle. The man slowly approached a round backyard spa platform, the rifle pointed ahead of him. The man stopped at the edge of the spa and reached to what must have been the outdoor electrical box.

The tub light came on, silhouetting the body of a man floating in a circle of blue. Even from on top of the hill Bosch could see the swirls of blood seeping from Mittel's body. Then the voice of the man with the rifle came up the hillside intact.

"Linda, don't come out! Just call the police. Tell them we got a body in our hot tub."

Then the man looked up the hillside and Bosch moved back away from the edge. Immediately, he wondered why he'd had the instinctive reaction to hide.

He got up and slowly made his way back to Mittel's house along the path. As he walked, he looked out across the city at the lights shimmering in the night and thought it was beautiful. He thought about Conklin and Pounds and then pushed the guilt out of his mind with thoughts about Mittel, about how his death finally closed the circle begun so long ago. He thought of the image of his mother in Monte Kim's photo. Her looking timidly around the edge of Conklin's arm. He waited for the feeling of satisfaction and triumph that he knew was supposed to come with vengeance accomplished. But none of it ever came to him. He only felt hollow and tired.

When he got back to the perfect lawn behind the perfect mansion, the man called Jonathan was gone.

Assistant Chief Irvin S. Irving stood in the open doorway of the examination suite. Bosch was sitting on the side of the padded table holding an ice pack to his head. The doctor had given it to him after putting in the stitches. He noticed Irving when he adjusted the bag in his hand.

"How do you feel?"

"I'll live, I guess. That's what they tell me, at least."

"Well, that's better than you can say for Mittel. He took the high dive."

"Yeah. What about the other one?"

"Nothing on him. We got his name, though. You told the uniforms Mittel called him Jonathan. So that means he's probably Jonathan Vaughn. He's worked for Mittel for a long time. They're working on it, checking the hospitals. Sounds like you might've hurt him enough that he'd come in."

"Vaughn."

"We're trying to do a background on him. So far, not much. He's got no record."

"How long was he with Mittel?"

"That we're not sure of. We've talked to Mittel's people at the law firm. Not what you'd call cooperative. But they say Vaughn has been around forever. He was described by most people as Mittel's personal valet."

Bosch nodded and put the information away.

"There's also a driver. We picked him up but he isn't saying much. A little surfer punk. He couldn't talk if he wanted to anyway."

"What do you mean?"

"His jaw is broken. Wired shut. He won't talk about that, either."

Bosch just nodded again and looked at him. There didn't seem to be anything hidden in what he had said.

"The doctor said you have a severe concussion but the skull is not fractured. Minor laceration."

"Could've fooled me. My head feels like the Goodyear blimp with a hole in it."

"How many stitches?"

"I think he said eighteen."

"He said you'll probably have headaches and keep the knot up there and the eye hemorrhages for a few days. It'll look worse than it is."

"Well, nice to know he's telling somebody what's going on. I haven't heard anything from him. Just the nurses."

"He'll be in in a minute. He was probably waiting for you to come out of it a little more."

"Come out of what?"

"You were a little dazed when we got up there to you, Harry. You sure you want to talk about this now? It can wait. You're hurt and need to take it—"

"I'm okay. I want to talk. You been by the scene at Park La Brea?"

"Yes, I was there. I was there when we got the call from Mount Olympus. I've got your briefcase in the car, by the way. You left it there, didn't you? With Conklin?"

He started to nod but stopped because it made things swirl.

"Good," he said. "There's something there I want to keep."

"The photo?"

"You looked through it?"

"Bosch! You must be groggy. It was found at the scene of a crime."

"Yeah, I know, sorry."

He waved off his objection. He was tired of fighting.

"So, the crew working the scene up on the hill already told me what happened. At least, the early version based on the physicals. What I'm not clear about is what got you up there. You know, how all of this figures. You want to run it down for me or wait until maybe tomorrow?"

Bosch nodded once and waited a moment for his mind to clear. He hadn't tried to collect the story into one cohesive thought yet. He thought about it some more and finally gave it a shot.

"I'm ready."

"Okay, I want to read you your rights first."

"What, again?"

"It's just a procedure so it doesn't look like we're cutting any slack to one of our own. You've got to remember, you were at two places tonight and at both somebody took a big fall. It doesn't look good."

"I didn't kill Conklin."

"I know that and we have the security guard's statement. He says you left before Conklin took the dive. So you're gonna be okay. You're clear but I have to follow procedure. Now, you still want to talk?"

"I waive my rights."

Irving read them to him from a card anyway and Bosch waived them again.

"Okay, then, I don't have a waive form. You'll have to sign that later."

"You want me to tell the story?"

"Yes, I want you to tell the story."

"Okay, here we go."

But then he stopped as he tried to put it into words.

"Harry?"

"Okay, here it is. In 1961 Arno Conklin met Marjorie Lowe. He was introduced by local scumbucket Johnny Fox, who made his living off making such introductions and arrangements. Usually for money. This initial meeting between Arno and Marjorie was at the St. Pat's party at the Masonic Lodge on Cahuenga."

"That's the photo in the briefcase, right?"

"Right. Now, at that first meeting, according to Arno's story, which I believe, he didn't know that Marjorie was a pro and Fox was a pimp. Fox arranged the introduction because he probably saw the opportunity and had one eye on the future. See, if Conklin knew it was a pay-to-play sort of thing, he would have walked away. He was the top county vice commando. He would have walked away."

"So he didn't know who Fox was either?" Irving asked.

"That's what he said. He just said he was innocent. If you find that hard to take, the alternative is harder; that this prosecutor would openly consort with these types of people. So, I'm going with Arno's story. He didn't know."

"Okay, he didn't know he was being compromised. So what was in it for Fox and . . . your mother?"

"Fox is easy. Once Conklin went with her, Fox had a nice hook into him and he could reel him in whenever he wanted. Marjorie is something else and I've been thinking about it but it still isn't clear. But you can say this, most women in that situation are looking for a way out. She could have played along with Fox's plan because she had her own plan. She was looking for a way out of the life."

Irving nodded and added to the hypothesis.

"She had a boy in the youth hall and wanted to get him out. Being with Arno could only help."

"That's right. The thing of it was, Arno and Marjorie did something none of the three of them expected. They fell in love. Or at least Conklin did. And he believed she did, too."

Irving took a chair in the corner, crossed his legs and stared thoughtfully at Bosch. He said nothing. Nothing about his demeanor indicated he was anything else but totally interested and believing in Bosch's story. Bosch's arm was getting tired of holding the ice pack up and he wished he could lie down. But there was only the table in the examination suite. He continued the story.

"So they fall in love and their relationship continues and somewhere along the line she tells him. Or maybe Mittel did some checking and told him. It doesn't matter. What matters is that at some point Conklin knew the score. And again, he surprises everybody."

"How?"

"On October twenty-seven, nineteen sixty-one, he proposes marriage to Marj—"

"He told you this? Arno told you this?"

"He told me tonight. He wanted to marry her. She wanted to marry him. On that night back then, he finally decided to chuck it all, to risk losing everything he had to gain the one thing he wanted most."

Bosch reached into his jacket on the table and took out his cigarettes. Irving spoke up.

"I don't think this is a—nothing, never mind."

Bosch lit a smoke with his lighter.

"It was the bravest act of his life. You realize that? That took balls to be willing to risk everything like that . . . But he made a mistake."

"What?"

"He called his friend Gordon Mittel to ask him to go with them to Vegas to be best man. Mittel refused. He knew it would be the end of a promising political career for Conklin, maybe even his own career, and he wanted no part of it. But then he went further than just refusing to be best man. See, he saw Conklin as the white horse on which he would be able to ride into the castle. He had big plans for himself and Conklin and he wasn't going to sit back and let some . . . some Hollywood whore ruin it. He knew from Conklin's call that she had gone home to pack. So Mittel went there and intercepted her somehow. Maybe told her that Conklin had sent him. I don't know."

"He killed her."

Bosch nodded and this time he didn't go dizzy.

"I don't know where, maybe in his car. He made it look like a sex crime by tying the belt around her neck and tearing up her clothes. The semen . . . it was already there because she had been with Conklin . . . After she was dead, Mittel took the body to the alley near the Boulevard and put her in the trash. The whole thing stayed a secret for a lot of years after that."

"Until you came along."

Bosch didn't answer. He was savoring his cigarette and the relief of the end of the case.

"What about Fox?" Irving asked.

"Like I said, Fox knew about Marjorie and Arno. And he knew they were together the night before Marjorie was found dead in that alley. That knowledge gave Fox a powerful piece of leverage over an important man, even if the man was innocent. Fox used it. In who knows how many ways. Within a year he was on Arno's campaign payroll. He was hooked on him like a bloodsucking leech. So Mittel, the fixer, finally stepped in. Fox died in a hit and run while supposedly handing out Conklin campaign fliers. Would've been easy to set up, make it look like it was an accident and the driver just fled. But that's no surprise. The same guy who worked the Marjorie Lowe case worked the hit and run. Same result. Nobody ever arrested."

"McKittrick?"

"No. Claude Eno. He's dead now. Took his secrets with him. But Mittel was paying him off for twenty-five years."

"The bank statements?"

"Yeah, in the briefcase. You look, you'll probably find records somewhere linking Mittel to the payments. Conklin said he didn't know about them and I believe him . . . You know, somebody ought to check all the elections Mittel worked on over the years. They'll probably find out he was a rat fucker that could've held his own in the Nixon White House."

Bosch ground his cigarette out on the side of a trash can next to the table and dropped the butt in. He started to feel very cold and put his jacket back on. It was smudged with dirt and dried blood.

"You look like a mess in that, Harry," Irving said. "Why don't you—"

"I'm cold."

"Okay."

"You know, he didn't even scream."

"What?"

"Mittel. He didn't even scream when he went down that hill. I can't figure that out."

"You don't have to. It's just one of those—"

"And I didn't push him. He jumped me in the brush and when we rolled, he went over. He didn't even scream."

"I understand. No one is saying—"

"All I did was start to ask questions about her and people started dying."

Bosch was staring at an eye chart on the far wall of the room. He could not figure out why they would have such a thing in an emergency room examination suite.

"Christ . . . Pounds . . . I—"

"Yes, I know what happened," Irving interrupted.

Bosch looked over at him.

"You do?"

"We interviewed everyone in the squad. Edgar told me that he made a computer run for you on Fox. My only conclusion is that Pounds either overheard or somehow got wind of it. I think he was monitoring what your close associates were doing after you went on ISL. Then he must've taken it a step further and stumbled into Mittel and Vaughn. He ran DMV traces on the parties involved. I think it got back to Mittel. He had the connections that would have warned him."

Bosch was silent. He wondered if Irving really believed that scenario or if he was signaling to Bosch that he knew what had really happened and was letting it go by. It didn't matter. Whether or not Irving blamed him or took departmental action against him, Bosch's own conscience would be the hardest thing to live with.

"Christ," he said again. "He got killed instead of me."

His body started shuddering then. As if saying the words out loud had started some kind of exorcism. He threw the ice pack into the trash can and wrapped his arms around himself. But the shuddering wouldn't stop. It seemed to him that he would never be warm again, that his shaking was not a temporary affliction but a permanent part of him now. He had the warm salty taste of tears in his mouth and he realized then that he was crying. He turned his face away from Irving and tried to tell him to leave but he couldn't say anything. His jaw was locked as tight as a fist.

"Harry?" he heard Irving say. "Harry, you okay?"

Bosch managed to nod, not understanding how Irving could not see his body shaking. He moved his hands into the pockets of his jacket and pulled it closed around him. He felt something in his left pocket and started absentmindedly pulling it out.

"Look," Irving was saying, "the doctor said you could get emotional. This knock on the head . . . they do weird things to you. Don't wor— Harry, are you sure you're okay? You're turning blue, son. I'm gonna— I'll go get the doctor. I'll—"

He stopped as Bosch managed to remove the object from his jacket. He held his palm upright. Clasped in his shaking hand was a black eight ball. Much of it was smeared with blood. Irving took it from him, having to practically pry his fingers off it.

"I'll go get somebody," was all he said.

Then Bosch was alone in the room, waiting for someone to come and the demon to leave.

Because of the concussion, Bosch's pupils were dilated unevenly and purple hemorrhages bulged below them. He had a hell of a headache and a one-hundred-degree temperature. As a precaution, the emergency room physician ordered that he be admitted and monitored, not allowed to sleep until four in the morning. He tried to pass the time by reading the newspaper and watching the talk shows but they only seemed to worsen the pain. Finally, he just stared at the walls until a nurse came in, checked on him and told him he could sleep. After that, nurses kept coming into his room and waking him at two-hour intervals. They checked his eyes and temperature and asked if he was okay. They never gave him anything for the headache. They told him to go back to sleep. If he dreamed of the coyote during the short sleep cycles, or anything else, he didn't remember it.

Finally, at noon, he got up for good. He was unsteady on his feet at first but equilibrium quickly came back to him. He made his way into the bathroom and studied his image in the mirror. He burst out laughing at what he saw, though it was not that funny. It was just that he seemed to be about to laugh or cry or do both at any given moment.

He had a small shaved spot on his skull where there was an L-shaped seam of stitches. It hurt when he touched the wound but he laughed about that, too. He managed to comb hair over it with his hand, fairly well camouflaging the injury.

The eyes were another matter. Still dilated unevenly and now cracked with red veins, they looked like the bad end of a two-week bender. Below them, deep purple triangles pointed to the corners of the eyes. A double shiner. Bosch didn't think he'd ever had one before.

Stepping back into the room he saw that his briefcase had been left by Irving next to the bed table. He bent to pick it up and almost lost his balance, grabbing on to the table at the last moment. He got back into bed with the briefcase and began examining its contents. He had no purpose in mind, he just wanted to be doing something.

He leafed through his notebook, finding it hard to concentrate on the words. He then re-read the five-year-old Christmas card from Meredith Roman, now Katherine Register. He realized he needed to call her, that he wanted to tell her what happened before she read about it in the paper or heard it on the news. He found her number in his notebook and dialed on the room's phone. He got her answering machine and left a message.

"Meredith, uh, Katherine . . . this is Harry Bosch. I need to talk to you today when you get a minute. Some things have happened and I think you'll, uh, feel better about things when you hear from me. So, give me a call."

Bosch left a variety of numbers on the tape, including his mobile, the Mark Twain and the hospital room and then hung up.

He opened the accordion pocket in the lid of the briefcase and slipped out the photo Monte Kim had given him. He studied his mother's face for a long time. The thought that eventually poked through was a question. Bosch had no doubt from what Conklin had said that he had loved her. But he wondered if she really loved Conklin back. Bosch remembered a time when she had visited him at McClaren. She had promised to get him out. At the time, the legal effort was going slowly and he knew that she had no faith in courts. When she made the promise, he knew she wasn't thinking about the law, only ways to get around it, to manipulate it. And he believed she would have found a way to do it if her time hadn't been taken away.

He realized, looking at the photo, that Conklin might simply have been part of the promise, part of the manipulation. Their marriage plan was her way of getting Harry out. From unwed mother with an arrest record to wife of an important man. Conklin would be able to get Harry out, to win back Marjorie Lowe's custody of her son. Bosch considered that love may have had nothing to do with it on her part, that it was only opportunity. In all the visits to McClaren, she had never spoken of Conklin or any man in particular. If she had truly been in love, wouldn't she have told him?

And in considering that question, Bosch realized that his mother's effort to save him was what might ultimately have led to her death.

"Mr. Bosch, are you okay?"

The nurse moved quickly into the room and put the food tray down on the table with a rattle. Bosch didn't answer her. He barely noticed her. She took the napkin off the tray and used it to wipe the tears off his cheeks.

"It's okay," she soothed. "It's okay."

"Is it?"

"It's the injury. Nothing to be embarrassed about. Head injuries jumble the emotions. One minute you're crying, the next you're laughing. Let me open these curtains. Maybe that will cheer you up."

"I think I just want to be left alone."

She ignored him and opened the curtains and Bosch had a view of another building twenty yards away. It did cheer him up, though. The view was so bad it made him laugh. It also reminded him he was in Cedars. He recognized the other medical tower.

The nurse then closed his briefcase so she could roll the table over the bed. On the tray was a plate containing Salisbury steak, carrots and potatoes. There was a roll that looked as hard as the eight ball he had found in his pocket the night before and some kind of red dessert wrapped in plastic. The tray and its smell made him feel the onset of nausea.

"I'm not going to eat this. Is there any Frosted Flakes?"

"You have to eat a full meal."

"I just woke up. You people kept me up all night. I can't eat this. It's making me sick."

She quickly picked up the tray and headed to the door.

"I'll see what I can do. About the Frosted Flakes."

She looked back at him and smiled before heading out the door.

"Cheer up."

"Yeah, that's the prescription."

Bosch didn't know what to do with himself but wait for time to pass. He started thinking about his encounter with Mittel, about what was said and what was meant. There was something about it that bothered him.

He was interrupted by a beeping sound coming from the side panel of the bed. He looked down and found it was the phone.

"Hello?"

"Harry?"

"Yes."

"It's Jazz. Are you okay?"

There was a long silence. Bosch didn't know if he was ready for this yet, but now it was unavoidable.

"Harry?"

"I'm fine. How'd you find me?"

"The man who called me yesterday. Irving something. He—"

"Chief Irving."

"Yes. He called and told me you were hurt. He gave me the number."

That annoyed Bosch but he tried not to show it.

"Well, I'm fine, but I can't really talk."

"Well, what happened?"

"It's just a long story. I don't want to go through it now."

Now she was quiet. It was one of those moments when both people try to read the silence, pick up each other's meanings in what they weren't saying.

"You know, don't you?"

"Why didn't you tell me, Jasmine?"

"I . . ."

More silence.

"Do you want me to tell you now?"

"I don't know . . ."

"What did he tell you?"

"Who?"

"Irving."

"It wasn't from him. He doesn't know. It was somebody else. Somebody trying to hurt me."

"It was a long time ago, Harry. I want to tell you what happened . . . but not on the phone."

He closed his eyes and thought for a minute. Just hearing her voice had renewed his sense of connection to her. But he had to question whether he wanted to get into this.

"I don't know, Jazz. I've got to think about—"

"Look, what was I supposed to do? Wear a sign or something to warn you away from the start? You tell me, when was a good time for me to tell you? Was it right after that first lemonade? Should I have said, 'Oh, by the way, six years ago I killed the man I was living with when he tried to rape me for the second time in the same night?' Would that have been proper?"

"Jazz, don't . . ."

"Don't what? Look, the cops didn't believe my story here, what should I expect from you?"

He could tell she was crying now, not so that he was supposed to hear. But he could tell it in her voice, full of loneliness and pain.

"You said things to me," she said. "I thought . . ."

"Jazz, we spent a weekend together. You're putting too much—"

"Don't you dare! Don't you tell me it didn't mean anything."

"You're right. I'm sorry . . . Look, this isn't the right time. I've got too much going on. I gotta call you back"

She didn't say anything.

"Okay?"

"Okay, Harry, you call me."

"Okay, goodbye, Jazz."

He hung up and kept his eyes closed for a while. He felt the numbness of disappointment that comes from broken hopes and wondered if he would ever talk to her again. In analyzing his thoughts he realized how much they seemed to be the same. And so his fear was not of what she had done, whatever the details were. His fear was that he would indeed call her and that he would become entwined with someone with more baggage than himself.

He opened his eyes and tried to put the thoughts aside. But he came back to her. He found himself marveling at the randomness of their meeting. A newspaper want ad. It might as well have said Single White Killer Seeks Same. He laughed out loud but it wasn't funny.

He turned the television on as a distraction. There was a talk show on and the host was interviewing women who stole their best friend's men. The best friends were also on and every question devolved into a verbal cat fight. Bosch turned the sound down and watched for ten minutes in silence, studying the contortions of the women's angry faces.

After a while he turned it off and rang the nurses' station on the intercom to inquire about his cereal. The nurse he spoke to knew nothing about his request for breakfast at lunch time. He tried Meredith Roman's number again but hung up when he got the tape.

Just as Bosch was getting hungry enough to be tempted to call for the return of the Salisbury steak, a nurse finally came back in with another food tray. This one contained a banana, a small glass of orange juice, a plastic bowl with a little box of Frosted Flakes in it and a pint-size carton of milk. He thanked her and began eating the cereal out of the box. The other stuff he didn't want.

He picked up the phone and dialed the main number at Parker Center and asked for Assistant Chief Irving's office. The secretary who eventually answered said Irving was in conference with the police chief and could not be disturbed. Bosch left his number.

Next he dialed Keisha Russell's number at the paper.

"It's Bosch."

"Bosch, where have you been? You turn your phone off?"

Bosch reached into his briefcase and took the phone out. He checked the battery.

"Sorry, it's dead."

"Great. That doesn't help me any, does it? The two biggest names in that clip I gave you end up dead last night and you don't even call. Some deal we made."

"Hey, this is me on the phone, right?"

"So what've you got for me?"

"What've you got already? What are they saying about it?"

"They're not saying jack. I've been waiting on you, man."

"But what are they really saying?"

"I mean it, nothing. They're saying both deaths are being investigated and that there is no clear connection. They're trying to pass it off as a big coincidence."

"What about the other man? Did they find Vaughn?"

"Who's Vaughn?"

Bosch couldn't figure out what was happening, why there was a cover-up. He knew he should wait to hear from Irving but the anger was growing in his throat.

"Bosch? You there? What other man?"

"What are they saying about me?"

"You? They're not saying anything."

"The other man's name is Jonathan Vaughn. He was there, too. Up at Mittel's last night."

"How do you know?"

"I was there, too."

"Bosch, you were there?"

Bosch closed his eyes but his mind couldn't penetrate the shroud being thrown over the case by the department. He didn't get it.

"Harry, we had a deal. Tell me the story."

He noted that it was the only time she had ever used his first name. He continued to say nothing while he tried to figure out what was happening and weighed the consequences of talking to her.

"Bosch?"

Back to normal.

"All right. You got your pencil? I'm going to give you enough to get started. You'll have to go to Irving to get the rest."

"I've been calling him. He won't even take my calls."

"He will when he knows you have the story. He'll have to."

By the time he was done telling her the story he was fatigued and his head was hurting again. He was ready to go to sleep, if it would have him. He wanted to forget everything and just sleep.

"That's an incredible story, Bosch," she said when he was done. "I'm sorry, you know, about your mother."

"Thanks."

"What about Pounds?"

"What about him?"

"Is it connected? Irving was honchoing that investigation. Now he's doing this one."

"You'll have to ask him."

"If I can get him on the line."

"When you call over there, tell the adjutant to tell Irving you're call-ing on behalf of Marjorie Lowe. He'll call you back when he gets the message. I guarantee it."

"Okay, Bosch, last thing. We didn't talk about this at the start like we should have. Can I use your name as a source?"

Bosch thought about it but only for a few moments.

"Yeah, you can use it. I don't know what my name's worth anymore but you can use it."

"Thanks. I'll see you. You're a pal."

"Yeah, I'm a pal."

He hung up and closed his eyes. He dozed off but wasn't sure for how long. He was interrupted by the phone. It was Irving and he was angry.

"What did you do?"

"What do you mean?"

"I just got a message from a reporter. She says she's calling because of Marjorie Lowe. Have you talked to reporters about this?"

"I talked to one."

"What did you tell her?"

"I told her enough so that you won't be able to let this one blow away."

"Bosch . . ."

He didn't finish. There was a long silence and then Bosch spoke first.

"You were going to cover it all up, weren't you? Shove it in the trash with her. You see, after everything that's happened, she still doesn't count, does she?"

"You don't know what you're talking about."

Bosch sat up. Now he was angry. Immediately, he was hit with ver-tigo. He closed his eyes until it passed.

"Well, then why don't you tell me what I don't know? Okay, Chief? You're the one who doesn't know what you're talking about. I heard what you people put out. That there may be no connection between Conklin and Mittel. What kind of—you think I'm going to sit here for that? And Vaughn. Not even a mention of him. A fucking mechanic in a splatter suit, he throws Conklin out the window and is ready to put me in the dirt. He's the one who did Pounds and he doesn't even rate a mention by you people. So, Chief, why don't you tell me what the fuck I don't know, okay?"

"Bosch, listen to me. *Listen* to me. Who did Mittel work for?"

"I don't know and I don't care."

"He was employed by very powerful people. Some of the most powerful in this state, some of the most powerful in the country. And—"

"I don't give a shit!"

"—a majority of the city council."

"So? What are you telling me? The council and the governor and the senators and all of those people, what, are they all involved now, too? You covering their asses, too?"

"Bosch, would you calm down and make sense? Listen to yourself. Of course, I'm not saying that. What I am trying to explain to you is that if you taint Mittel with this, then you taint many very powerful people who associated with him or who used his services. That could come back to haunt this department as well as you and me in immeasurable ways."

That was it, Bosch saw. Irving the pragmatist had made a choice, probably along with the police chief, to put the department and themselves ahead of the truth. The whole deal stunk like rotting garbage. Bosch felt exhaustion roll over him like a wave. He was drowning in it. He'd had enough of this.

"And by covering it up, you are helping them in immeasurable ways, right? And I'm sure you and the chief have been on the phone all morning letting each of those powerful people know just that. They'll all owe you, they'll all owe the department a big one. That's great, Chief. That's a great deal. I guess it doesn't matter that the truth is nowhere to be found in it."

"Bosch, I want you to call her back. Call that reporter and tell her that you took this knock on the head and you—"

"No! I'm not calling anybody back. It's too late. I told the story."

"But not the whole story. The whole story is just as damaging to you, isn't it?"

There it was. Irving knew. He either outright knew or had made a pretty good guess that Bosch had used Pounds's name and was ultimately responsible for his death. That knowledge was now his weapon against Bosch.

"If I can't contain this," Irving added, "I may have to take action against you."

"I don't care," Bosch said quietly. "You can do whatever you want to me, but the story is coming out, Chief. The truth."

"But is it the truth? The whole truth? I doubt it and deep in inside I know you doubt it, too. We'll never know the whole truth."

A silence followed. Bosch waited for him to say more and when there was only more silence, he hung up. He then disconnected the phone and finally went to sleep.

Bosch awoke at six the next morning with dim memories of his sleep having been interrupted by a horrible dinner and the visits of nurses through the night. His head felt thick. He gently touched the wound and found it not as tender as the day before. He got up and walked around the room a bit. His balance seemed back to normal. In the bathroom mirror his eyes were still a colorful mess but the dilation of the pupils had evened out. It was time to go, he knew. He got dressed and left the room, briefcase in hand and carrying his ruined jacket over his arm.

At the nurses' station he pushed the elevator button and waited. He noticed one of the nurses behind the counter eyeing him. She apparently didn't readily recognize him, especially with his street clothes on.

"Excuse me, can I help you?"

"No, I'm fine."

"Are you a patient?"

"I was. I'm leaving. Room four-nineteen. Bosch."

"Wait a moment, sir. What are you doing?"

"I'm leaving. Going home."

"What?"

"Just send me the bill."

The elevator doors opened and he stepped in.

"You can't do that," the nurse called. "Let me get the doctor."

Bosch raised his hand and waved good-bye.

"Wait!"

The doors closed.

He bought a newspaper in the lobby and caught a cab outside. He told the driver to take him to Park La Brea. Along the way, he read Keisha Russell's story. It was on the front page and it was pretty much an abbreviated account of what he had told her the day before. Everything was qualified with the caveat that it was still under investigation, but it was a good read.

Bosch was mentioned throughout by name as a source and main player in the story. Irving was also a named source. Bosch figured the assistant chief must have decided in the end to throw in with the truth, or a close approximation of it, once Bosch had already let it out. It was the pragmatic thing to do. This way it seemed like he had a handle on things. He was the voice of conservative reason in the story. Bosch's statements were usually followed by those from Irving cautioning that the investigation was still in its infancy and no final conclusions had been made.

The part Bosch liked best about the story were the statements from several statesmen, including most of the city council, expressing shock both at the deaths of Mittel and Conklin and at their involvement in and/or cover-up of murders. The story also mentioned that Mittel's employee, Jonathan Vaughn, was being sought by police as a murder suspect.

The story was most tenuous in regard to Pounds. It contained no mention that Bosch was suspected or known to have used the lieutenant's name or that his using it had led to Pounds's death. The story simply quoted Irving as saying the connection between Pounds and the case was still under investigation but that it appeared that Pounds might have stumbled onto the same trail Bosch had been following.

Irving had held back when he talked to Russell even after threatening Bosch. Harry could only believe it was the assistant chief's desire not to see the department's dirty laundry in print. The truth would hurt Bosch but could damage the department as well. If Irving was going to make a move against him, Bosch knew it would be inside the department. It would remain private.

Bosch's rented Mustang was still in the La Brea Lifecare parking lot.

He had been lucky; the keys were in the door lock where he had left them a moment before being attacked by Vaughn. He paid the driver and went to the Mustang.

Bosch decided to take a cruise up Mount Olympus before going to the Mark Twain. He plugged his phone into the cigarette lighter so it would recharge and headed up Laurel Canyon Boulevard.

On Hercules Drive, he slowed outside the gate in front of Mittel's grounded spaceship. The gate was closed and there was yellow police-line tape still hanging from it. Bosch saw no cars in the driveway. It was quiet and peaceful. And soon he knew that a FOR SALE sign would be erected and the next genius would move in and think he was master of all he surveyed.

Bosch drove on. Mittel's place wasn't what he really wanted to see, anyway.

Fifteen minutes later Bosch came around the familiar turn on Woodrow Wilson but immediately found things unfamiliar. His house was gone, its disappearance as glaring in the landscape as a tooth missing from a smile.

At the curb in front of his address were two huge construction waste bins filled with splintered wood, mangled metal and shattered glass, the debris of his home. A mobile storage container had also been placed at the curb and Bosch assumed—hoped—it contained the salvageable property removed before the house was razed.

He parked and walked over to the flagstone path that formerly had led to his front door. He looked down and all that was left were the six pylons that poked out of the hillside like tombstones. He could rebuild upon these. If he wanted.

Movement in the acacia trees near the footings of the pylons caught his eye. He saw a flash of brown and then the head of a coyote moving slowly through the brush. It never heard Bosch or looked up. Soon it was gone. Harry lost sight of it in the brush.

He spent another ten minutes there, smoking a cigarette and waiting, but he saw nothing else. He then said a silent good-bye to the place. He had the feeling he wouldn't be back.

When Bosch got to the Mark Twain, the city's morning was just starting. From his room he heard a garbage truck making its way down the alley, taking away another week's debris. It made him think of his house again, fitted nicely into two dumpsters.

Thankfully, the sound of a siren distracted him. He could identify it as a squad car as opposed to a fire engine. He knew he'd get a lot of that with the police station just down the street. He moved about his two rooms and felt restless and out of it, as if life was passing by while he was stuck here. He made coffee with the machine he had brought from home and it only served to make him more jittery.

He tried the paper again but there was nothing of real interest to him except the story he had already read on the front page. He paged through the thin Metro section anyway and saw a report that the county commission chambers were being outfitted with bulletproof desk blotters that the commissioners could hold up in front of them in the event a maniac came in spraying bullets. He threw the section aside and picked up the front section again.

Bosch reread the story about his investigation and couldn't escape a growing feeling that something was wrong, that something was left out or incomplete. Keisha Russell's reporting had been fine. That wasn't the problem. The problem was in seeing the story in words, in print. It didn't seem as convincing to him as it had been when he recounted it for her or for Irving or even for himself.

He put the newspaper aside, leaned back on the bed and closed his eyes. He went over the sequence of events once more and in doing so finally realized the problem that gnawed at him was not in the paper but in what Mittel had said to him. Bosch tried to recall the words exchanged between them on the manicured lawn behind the rich man's house. What had really been said there? What had Mittel admitted to?

Bosch knew that at that moment on the lawn, Mittel was in a position of seeming invulnerability. He had Bosch captured, wounded and doomed before him. His attack dog, Vaughn, stood ready with a gun to Bosch's back. In that situation, Bosch believed there would be no reason for a man of Mittel's ego to hold back. And, in fact, he had not held back. He had boasted of his scheme to control Conklin and others. He had freely, though indirectly, admitted that he had caused the deaths of Conklin and Pounds. But despite those admissions, he had not done the same when it came to the killing of Marjorie Lowe.

Through the fragmented images of that night, Bosch tried to recall the exact words said and couldn't quite get to them. His visual recollection was good. He had Mittel standing in front of the blanket of lights. But the words weren't there. Mittel's mouth moved but Bosch couldn't get the words. Then, finally, after working at it for a while, it came to him. He had it. Opportunity. Mittel had called her death an opportunity. Was that an acknowledgement of culpability? Was he saying he killed her or had her killed? Or was he simply admitting that her death presented an opportunity for him to take advantage of?

Bosch didn't know and not knowing felt like a heavy weight in his chest. He tried to put it out of his mind and eventually started drifting off toward sleep. The sounds of the city outside, even the sirens, were comforting. He was at the threshold of unconsciousness, almost there, when he suddenly opened his eyes.

"The prints," he said out loud.

Thirty minutes later he was shaved, showered and in fresh clothes heading downtown. He had his sunglasses on and he checked himself in the mirror. His battered eyes were hidden. He licked his fingers and pressed his curly hair down to better cover the shaved spot and the stitches in his scalp.

At County-USC Medical Center, he drove through the back lot to the parking slots nearest the rear garage bays of the Los Angeles County medical examiner's office. He walked in through one of the open garage doors and waved to the security guard, who knew him by sight and nodded back. Investigators weren't supposed to go in the back way but Bosch had been doing it for years. He wasn't going to stop until someone made a federal case out of it. The minimum-wage guard was an unlikely candidate to do that.

He went up to the investigators' lounge on the second floor, hoping not only that there would be someone there he knew but, more important, someone Bosch hadn't alienated over the years.

He swung the door open and immediately was hit with the smell of fresh coffee. But the room was bad news. Only Larry Sakai was in the room, sitting at a table with newspapers spread across it. He was a coroner's investigator Bosch had never really liked and the feeling was mutual.

"Harry Bosch," Sakai said after looking up from the newspaper he held in his hands. "Speak of the devil, I'm reading about you here. Says here you're in the hospital."

"Nah, I'm here, Sakai. See me? Where's Hounchell and Lynch? Either of them around?"

Hounchell and Lynch were two investigators who Bosch knew would do him a favor without having to think about it too long. They were good people.

"Nah, they're out baggin' and taggin'. Busy morning. Guess things are picking up again."

Bosch had heard a rumor through the grapevine that while removing victims from one of the collapsed apartment buildings after the earthquake, Sakai had gone in with his own camera and taken photos of people dead in their beds—the ceilings crushed down on top of them. He then sold the prints to the tabloid newspapers under a false name. That was the kind of guy he was.

"Anybody else around?"

"No, Bosch, jus' me. Whaddaya want?"

"Nothing."

Bosch turned back to the door, then hesitated. He needed to make the print comparison and didn't want to wait. He looked back at Sakai.

"Look, Sakai, I need a favor. You want to help me out? I'll owe you one."

Sakai leaned forward in his chair. Bosch could see just the point of a toothpick poking out between his lips.

"I don't know, Bosch, having you owe me one is like having the old whore with AIDS say she'll give me a free one if I pay for the first."

Sakai laughed at the comparison he had created.

"Okay, fine."

Bosch turned and pushed through the door, keeping his anger in check. He was two steps down the hall when he heard Sakai call him back. Just as he had hoped. He took a deep breath and went back into the lounge.

"Bosch, c'mon, I didn't say I wouldn't help you out. Look, I read your story here and I feel for what you're going through, okay?"

Yeah, right, Bosch thought but didn't say.

"Okay," he said.

"What do you need?"

"I need to get a set of prints off one of the customers in the cooler."

"Which one?"

"Mittel."

Sakai nodded toward the paper, which he had thrown back onto the table.

"That Mittel, huh?"

"Only one I know of."

Sakai was quiet while he considered the request.

"You know, we make prints available to investigating officers assigned to homicides."

"Cut the crap, Sakai. You know I know that and you know, if you read the paper, that I'm not the IO. But I still need the prints. You going to get them for me or am I just wasting my time here?"

Sakai stood up. Bosch knew that Sakai knew that if he backed down now after making the overture, then Bosch would gain a superior position in the netherworld of male interaction and in all their dealings that would follow. If Sakai followed through and got the prints, then the advantage would obviously go to him.

"Cool your jets, Bosch. I'm gonna get the prints. Why don't you get yourself a cup of coffee and sit down? Just put a quarter in the box."

Bosch hated the idea of being beholden to Sakai for anything but he knew this was worth it. The prints were the one way he knew to end the case. Or tear it open again.

Bosch had a cup of coffee and in fifteen minutes the coroner's investigator was back. He was still waving the card so the ink would dry. He handed it to Bosch and went to the counter to get another cup of coffee.

"This is from Gordon Mittel, right?"

"Right. That's what it said on the toe tag. And, man, he got busted up pretty good in that fall."

"Glad to hear it."

"You know, it sounds to me like that story in the newspaper ain't as solid as you LAPD guys claim if you're sneaking around here gettin' the guy's prints."

"It's solid, Sakai, don't worry about it. And I better not get any calls from any reporters about me picking up prints. Or I'll be back."

"Don't give yourself a hernia, Bosch. Just take the prints and leave. Never met anybody who tried so hard to make the person doin' him a favor feel bad."

Bosch dumped his coffee cup in a trash can and started out. At the door he stopped.

"Thanks."

It burned him to say it. The guy was an asshole.

"Just remember, Bosch, you owe me."

Bosch looked back at him. He was stirring cream into his cup. Bosch walked back, sticking his hand in his pocket. When he got to the counter he pulled out a quarter and dropped it into the slotted tin box that was the coffee fund.

"There, that's for you," Bosch said. "Now we're even."

He walked out and in the hallway he heard Sakai call him an asshole. To Bosch that was a sign that all might be right in the world. His world, at least.

When Bosch got to Parker Center fifteen minutes later, he realized he had a problem. Irving had not returned his ID tag because it was part of the evidence recovered from Mittel's jacket in the hot tub. So Bosch loitered around the front of the building until he saw a group of detectives and administrative types walking toward the building from the City Hall annex. When the group moved inside and around the entry counter, Bosch stepped up behind them and got by the duty officer without notice.

Bosch found Hirsch at his computer in the Latent Fingerprint Unit and asked him if he still had the Lifescan from the prints off the belt buckle.

"Yeah, I've been waiting for you to pick them up."

"Well, I got a set I want you to check against them first."

Hirsch looked at him but hesitated only a second.

"Let's see 'em."

Bosch got the print card Sakai had made out of his briefcase and handed it over. Hirsch looked at it a moment, turning the card so it reflected the overhead light better.

"These are pretty clean. You don't need the machine, right? You just want to compare these to the prints you brought in before."

"That's right."

"Okay, I can eyeball it right now if you want to wait."

"I want to wait."

Hirsch got the Lifescan card out of his desk and took it and the coroner's card to the work counter, where he looked at them through a magnifying lamp. Bosch watched his eyes going back and forth between the prints as if he were watching a tennis ball go back and forth across a net.

Bosch realized as he watched Hirsch work that more than anything else in the world he wanted the print man to look up at him and say that the prints from the two cards in front of him matched. Bosch wanted this to be over. He wanted to put it away.

After five minutes of silence, the tennis match was over and Hirsch looked up at him and gave him the score.

When Carmen Hinojos opened her waiting room door she seemed pleasantly surprised to see Bosch sitting on the couch.

"Harry! Are you all right? I didn't expect to see you here today."

"Why not? It's my time, isn't it?"

"Yes, but I read in the paper you were at Cedars."

"I checked out."

"Are you sure you should have done that? You look . . ."

"Awful?"

"I didn't want to say that. Come in."

She ushered him in and they took their usual places.

"I actually look better than I feel right now."

"Why? What is it?"

"Because it was all for nothing."

His statement put a confused look on her face.

"What do you mean? I read the story today. You solved the murders, including your mother's. I thought you'd be quite different than this."

"Well, don't believe everything you read, Doctor. Let me clarify things for you. What I did on my so-called mission was cause two men to be murdered and another to die by my own hands. I solved, let's see, I solved one, two, three murders, so that's good. But I didn't solve the murder I set out to solve. In other words, I've been running around in circles causing people to die. So, how did you expect me to be during our session?"

"Have you been drinking?"

"I had a couple beers with lunch but it was a long lunch and I think that a minimum of two beers is required considering what I just told you. But I am not drunk, if that is what you want to know. And I'm not working, so what's the difference?"

"I thought we agreed to cut back on—"

"Oh, fuck that. This is the real world here. Isn't that what you called it? The real world? Between now and the last time we talked, I've killed someone, Doc. And you want to talk about cutting back on booze. Like it means anything anymore."

Bosch took out his cigarettes and lit one. He kept the pack and the Bic on the arm of the chair. Carmen Hinojos watched him for a long time before speaking again.

"You're right. I'm sorry. Let's go to what I think is the heart of the problem. You said you didn't solve the murder you set out to solve. That, of course, is your mother's death. I am only going by what I read, but to-day's *Times* attributes her killing to Gordon Mittel. Are you telling me that you now know that to be incontrovertibly wrong?"

"Yes. I now know that to be incontrovertibly wrong."

"How?"

"Simple. Fingerprints. I went down to the morgue, got Mittel's prints and had them compared to those on the murder weapon, the belt. No match. He didn't do it. Wasn't there. Now, I don't want you to get the wrong idea. I'm not sitting here with a guilty conscience over Mittel. He was a man who decided to kill people and then had them killed. Just like that. At least two times I'm sure of, then he was going to have me killed, too. So I say fuck him. He got what he had coming. But I'll carry Pounds and Conklin around with me for a long time. Maybe forever. And one way or another, I'll pay for it. It's just that it would make that weight eas-ier to carry if there had been a reason. Any good reason. Know what I mean? But there isn't a reason. Not anymore."

"I understand. I don't—I'm not sure how to proceed with this. Do you want to talk some about your feelings in regard to Pounds and Conklin?"

"Not really. I've thought about it enough already. Neither man was innocent. They did things. But they didn't have to die like they did. Especially Pounds. Jesus. I can't talk about it. I can't even think about it."

"Then how will you go on?"

"I don't know. Like I said, I have to pay."

"What is the department going to do, any idea?"

"I don't know. I don't care. It's bigger than the department to decide. I have to decide my penance."

"Harry, what does that mean? That concerns me."

"Don't worry, I'm not going to the closet. I'm not that type."

"The closet?"

"I'm not going to stick a gun in my mouth."

"Through what you've said here today, it is already clear you have accepted responsibility for what happened to these two men. You're facing it. In effect, you are denying denial. That is a foundation you can build on. I am concerned about this talk about penance. You have to go on, Harry. No matter what you do to yourself, it doesn't bring them back. So the best you can do is go on."

He didn't say anything. He suddenly grew tired of all the advice, of her intervention in his life. He was feeling resentful and frustrated.

"Do you mind if we cut the session short today?" he asked. "I'm not feeling so hot."

"I understand. It's no problem. But I want you to promise me something. Promise me we will talk again before you make any decisions."

"You mean about my penance?"

"Yes, Harry."

"Okay, we'll talk."

He stood up and attempted a smile but it came out more like a frown. Then he remembered something.

"By the way, I apologize for not getting back to you the other night when you called. I was waiting on a call and couldn't talk and then I just kind of forgot. I hope you were just checking on me and it wasn't too important."

"Don't worry about it. I forgot myself. I was just calling to see how you made it through the rest of the afternoon with Chief Irving. I also wanted to see if you wanted to talk about the photos. It doesn't matter now."

"You looked at them?"

"Yes. I had a couple of comments but—"

"Let's hear them."

Bosch sat back down. She looked at him, weighing his suggestion, and decided to go ahead.

"I have them here."

She bent down to get the envelope out of one of the lower drawers of the desk. She almost disappeared from Bosch's view. Then she was up and placed the envelope on the desk.

"I guess you should take these back."

"Irving took the murder book and the evidence box. He's got it all now except for those."

"You sound like you're unhappy about that, or that you don't trust him with it. That's a change."

"Aren't you the one who said I don't trust anyone?"

"Why don't you trust him?"

"I don't know. I just lost my suspect. Gordon Mittel's clear and I'm starting from ground zero. I was just thinking about the percentages . . ."

"And?"

"Well, I don't know the numbers but a significant number of homicides are reported by the actual doer. You know, the husband who calls up crying, saying his wife is missing. More often than not, he's just a bad actor. He killed her and thinks calling the cops helps convince everybody he's clean. Look at the Menendez brothers. One of 'em calls up boohooing about mom and dad being dead. Turns out he and the brother were the ones who shotgunned them. There was a case up in the hills a few years back. This little girl was missing. It was Laurel Canyon. It made the papers, TV. So the people up there organized search parties and all of that and a few days later one of the searchers, a teen-aged boy who was one of the girl's neighbors, found her body under a log near Lookout Mountain. It turned out he was the killer. I got him to confess in fifteen minutes. The whole time of the search I was just waiting for the one who would find the body. It was percentages. He was a suspect before I even knew who it was."

"Irving found your mother's body."

"Yes. And he knew her before that. He told me once."

"It seems like a stretch to me."

"Yeah. Most people probably thought that about Mittel, too. Right up until they fished him out of the hot tub."

"Isn't there an alternative scenario? Isn't it possible that maybe the original detectives were correct in their assumption back then that there was a sex killer out there and that tracking him was hopeless?"

"There's always alternative scenarios."

"But you always seem drawn toward finding someone of power, a person of the establishment, to blame. Maybe that's not the case here. Maybe it's a symptom of your larger desire to blame society for what happened to your mother . . . and to you."

Bosch shook his head. He didn't want to hear this.

"You know, all this psychobabble . . . I don't . . . Can we just talk about the photos?"

"I'm sorry."

She looked down at the envelope as if she was seeing right through it to the photos inside it.

"Well, it was very difficult for me to look at them. As far as their forensic value goes, there wasn't a lot there. The photos show what I would call a statement homicide. The fact that the ligature, the belt, was still wrapped around her neck seems to indicate that the killer wanted police to know exactly what he did, that he had been deliberate, that he had had control over this victim. I also think the choice of placement is significant as well. The trash bin had no top. It was open. That suggests that placing the body there may not have been an effort to hide it. It was also a—"

"He was saying she was trash."

"Right. Again, a statement. If he was just getting rid of a body, he could've put it anywhere in that alley, but he chose the open dumpster. Subconsciously or not, he was making a statement about her. So to make a statement such as that about a person, he would have to have known her to some degree. Known about her. Known she was a prostitute. Known enough to judge her."

Irving came to Bosch's mind again but he said nothing.

"Well," he said instead, "couldn't it have been a statement about all women? Could it be some sick fuck who—excuse me—some nut who hated all women and thought all women were trash? That way he wouldn't have to have known her. Maybe somebody who simply wanted to kill a prostitute, any prostitute, to make a statement about them."

"Yes, that's a possibility, but like you I'm going with the percentages.

The kind of sick fuck you are talking about—which, incidentally, in psychobabble we call a sociopath—is much rarer than the one who keys on specific targets, specific women."

Bosch shook his head dismissively and looked out the window.

"What is it?"

"It's just frustrating, that's all. There wasn't much in the murder book about them taking a hard look at anybody in her circle, any of the neighbors, nothing like that. To do it now is impossible. It makes me feel like it's hopeless."

He thought of Meredith Roman. He could go to her to ask about his mother's acquaintances and customers, but he didn't know if he had the right to reawaken that part of her life.

"You have to remember," Hinojos said, "in 1961 a case like this would probably have seemed impossible to solve. They wouldn't even have known how to start. It just didn't happen as often as today."

"They're almost impossible to solve today, too."

They sat in silence for a few moments. Bosch thought about the possibility that the killer was some hit-and-run nut. A serial killer who was long gone into the darkness of time. If that was the case, then his private investigation was over. It was a failure.

"Do you have anything else on the photos?"

"That's really all I had—no, wait. There was one thing. And you may already have this."

She picked the envelope up and opened it. She reached in and began sliding out a photo.

"I don't want to look at that," Bosch said quickly.

"It's not a photo of her. Actually, it's her clothing, laid out on a table. Is that okay to look at?"

She paused, her hand holding the photo half in and half out of the envelope. Bosch waved his hand, telling her to go ahead.

"I've already seen the clothes."

"Then you've probably already considered this."

She slid the photo to the edge of the desk and Bosch leaned forward to study it. It was a color photo that had yellowed with age, even inside the envelope. The same items of clothing he had found in the evidence box were spread out on a table in a formation that outlined a body, in the way a woman might put them out on a bed before dressing. It reminded

Bosch of cutouts for paper dolls. Even the belt with the sea shell buckle was there, but it was between the blouse and the black skirt, not at the imaginary neck.

"Okay," she said. "What I found odd here was the belt."

"The murder weapon."

"Yes. Look, it has the large silver shell as the buckle and there are smaller silver shells as ornamentation. It's rather showy."

"Right."

"But the buttons on the blouse are gold. Also, the photos of the body, they show she was wearing gold teardrop earrings and a gold neck chain. Also a bracelet."

"Right, I know that. They were in the evidence box, too."

Bosch didn't understand what she was getting at.

"Harry, this is not a universal rule or anything, that's why I hesitate to bring it up. But usually people—women—don't mix and match gold and silver. And it appears to me your mother was well dressed on this evening. That she had jewelry on that matched the buttons of her blouse. She was coordinated and she had style. What I am saying is that I don't think she would have worn this belt with those other items. It was silver and it was showy."

Bosch said nothing. Something was poking its way into his mind and its point was sharp.

"And lastly, this skirt buttons on the hip. It's a style that is still around and I even have something similar to it myself. What's so functional about it is that because of the wide waistband it can be worn with or without a belt. There are no loops."

Bosch stared at the photo.

"No loops."

"Right."

"So what you're saying is . . ."

"This might not have been her belt. It might have—"

"But it was. I remember it. The sea shell belt. I gave it to her for her birthday. I identified it for the cops, for McKittrick the day he came to tell me."

"Well . . . then that shoots down everything I was going to say. I guess maybe when she came into the apartment the killer was already waiting with it."

"No, it didn't happen in her apartment. They never found the crime scene. Listen, never mind whether it was her belt or not, what were you going to say?"

"Oh, I don't know, just a theory about it possibly being the property of another woman who may have been the motivating factor behind the killer's action. It's called aggression transference. It doesn't make sense now with this evidence but there are examples of what I was going to suggest. A man takes his ex-girlfriend's stockings and strangles another woman with them. In his mind, he's strangling the girlfriend. Something like that. I was going to suggest it could have happened in this case with the belt."

But Bosch was no longer listening. He turned and looked out the window but wasn't seeing anything either. In his mind, he was seeing the pieces falling together. The silver and gold, the belt with two of the punch holes worn, two friends as close as sisters. One for both and both for one.

But then one was leaving the life. She'd found a white knight.

And one was staying behind.

"Harry, are you okay?"

He looked over at Hinojos.

"You just did it. I think."

"Did what?"

He reached for his briefcase and from it withdrew the photo taken at the St. Patrick's Day dance more than three decades before. He knew it was a long shot but he needed to check. This time he didn't look at his mother. He looked at Meredith Roman, standing behind the sitting Johnny Fox. And for the first time he saw that she wore the belt with the silver sea shell buckle. She had borrowed it.

It dawned on him then. She had helped Harry pick the belt out for his mother. She had coached him and she chose it not because his mother would like it but because she liked it and knew she would get to use it. Two friends who shared everything.

Bosch shoved the photo back into the briefcase and shut it. He stood up.

"I gotta go."

Bosch used the same ruse he had earlier to get back into Parker Center. Coming out of the elevator on the fourth floor, he practically ran into Hirsch, who was waiting to go down. He grabbed hold of the young print tech's arm and held him in the hallway as the elevator doors closed.

"You going home?"

"I was trying to."

"I need one more favor. I'll buy you lunch, I'll buy you dinner, I'll buy you whatever you want if you do it for me. It's important and it won't take long."

Hirsch looked at him. Bosch could see he was beginning to wish he'd never gotten involved.

"What's that saying, Hirsch? 'In for a penny, in for a pound.' Whaddaya say?"

"I've never heard it."

"Well, I have."

"I'm having dinner with my girlfriend tonight and I—"

"That's great. This won't take that long. You'll make it to your dinner."

"All right. What is it you need?"

"Hirsch, you're my goddamn hero, you know that?"

Bosch doubted he even had a girlfriend. They went back to the lab. It was deserted, since it was almost five on a slow day. Bosch put his brief-case on one of the abandoned desks and opened it. He found the Christ-mas card and took it out by holding a corner between two fingernails. He held it up for Hirsch to see.

"This came in the mail five years ago. You think you can pull a print off it? A print from the sender? My prints are going to be on there, too, I'm sure."

Hirsch furrowed his brow and studied the card. His lower lip jutted outward as he contemplated the challenge.

"All I can do is try. Prints on paper are usually pretty stable. The oils last long and sometimes leave ridge patterns in the paper even when they evaporate. Has it been in its envelope?"

"Yeah, for five years, until last week."

"That helps."

Hirsch carefully took the card from Bosch and walked over to the work counter, where he opened the card and clipped it to a board.

"I'm going to try the inside. It's always better. Less chance of you having touched it inside. And the writer always touches the inside. Is it all right if this gets kind of ruined?"

"Do what you have to do."

Hirsch studied the card with a magnifying glass, then lightly blew over the surface. He reached to a rack of spray bottles over the work table and took down one marked NINHYDRIN. He sprayed a light mist over the surface of the card and in a few minutes it began to turn purple around the edges. Then light shapes began to bloom like flowers on the card. Fingerprints.

"I've got to bring this out some," Hirsch said, more to himself than Bosch.

Hirsch looked up at the rack and his eyes followed the row of chem-ical reagents until he found what he was looking for. A spray bottle marked ZINC CHLORIDE. He sprayed it on the card.

"This should bring the storm clouds in."

The prints turned the deep purple shade of heavy rain clouds. Hirsch then took down a bottle labeled PD, which Bosch knew meant physical developer. After the card was misted with PD, the prints turned a grayish black and were more defined. Hirsch looked them over with his magnifying lamp.

"I think this is good enough. We won't need the laser. Now, look at these here, Detective."

Hirsch pointed to a print that appeared to have been left by a thumb on the left side of Meredith Roman's signature and two smaller finger marks above it.

"These look like marks left by someone trying to hold the card steady while it was being written on. Any chance that you might've touched it this way?"

Hirsch held his fingers in place an inch over the card in the same position that the hand that left the prints would have been in. Bosch shook his head.

"All I ever did was open it and read it. I think those are the prints we want."

"Okay. Now what?"

Bosch went to his briefcase and pulled out the print cards Hirsch had returned to him earlier in the day. He found the card containing the lifts from the belt with the sea shell buckle.

"Here," he said. "Compare this to what you got on the Christmas card."

"You got it."

Hirsch pulled the magnifying glass with the ringed light attachment in front of him and once again began his tennis match eye movement as he compared the prints.

Bosch tried to envision what had happened. Marjorie Lowe was going to Las Vegas to get married to Arno Conklin. The very thought of it must have been absurdly wonderful to her. She had to go home and pack. The plan was to drive through the night. If Arno was planning to bring along a best man, perhaps Marjorie was to bring a maid of honor. Maybe she would have gone upstairs to ask Meredith to come. Or maybe she would have gone to her to borrow back the belt that her son had given her. Maybe she would have gone to say good-bye.

But something happened when she got there. And on her happiest night Meredith killed her.

Bosch thought about the interview reports that had been in the murder book. Meredith told Eno and McKittrick that Marjorie's date on the night she died had been arranged by Johnny Fox. But she didn't go to the party herself because she said Fox had beaten her the night before and she was not presentable. The detectives noted in the report that she had a bruise on her face and a split lip.

Why didn't they see it then, Bosch wondered. Meredith had sustained those injuries while killing Marjorie. The drop of blood on Marjorie's blouse had come from Meredith.

But Bosch knew why they hadn't seen it. He knew the investigators dismissed any thought in that direction, if they ever even had any, because she was a woman. And because Fox backed her story. He admitted he beat her.

Bosch now saw what he believed was the truth. Meredith killed Marjorie and then hours later called Fox at his card game to give him the news. She asked him to help her get rid of the body and hide her involvement.

Fox must have readily agreed, even to the point of his willingness to say he beat her, because he saw the larger picture. He lost a source of income when Marjorie was killed but that would have been tempered by the increased leverage the murder would give him over Conklin and Mittel. Keeping it unsolved would make it even better. He'd always be a threat to them. He could walk into the police station at any time to tell what he knew and lay it on Conklin.

What Fox didn't realize was that Mittel could be as cunning and vicious as he was. He learned that a year later on La Brea Boulevard.

Fox's motivation was clear. Bosch still wasn't sure about Meredith's. Could she have done it for the reasons Bosch had set out in his mind? Would the abandonment of a friend have led to the rage of murder? He began to believe there was still something left out. He still didn't know it all. The last secret was with Meredith Roman and he would have to go get it.

An odd thought pushed through these questions to Bosch. The time of death of Marjorie Lowe was about midnight. Fox didn't get his call and leave his card game until roughly four hours later. Bosch now assumed that the murder scene was Meredith's apartment. Now he wondered, what did she do in that place for four hours with the body of her best friend lying there?

"Detective?"

Bosch looked away from his thoughts to Hirsch, who was sitting at the desk nodding his head.

"You got something?"

"Bingo."

Bosch just nodded.

It was confirmation of more than just the match of fingerprints. He knew it was a confirmation that all the things he had accepted as the truths of his life could be as false as Meredith Roman.

The sky was the color of a ninhydrin bloom on white paper. It was cloudless and growing dark purple with the aging of dusk. Bosch thought of the sunsets he had told Jazz about and realized that even that was a lie. Everything was a lie.

He stopped the Mustang at the curb in front of Katherine Register's home. There was another lie. The woman who lived here was Meredith Roman. Changing her name didn't change what she had done, didn't change her from guilty to innocent.

There were no lights on that he could see from the street, no sign of life. He was prepared to wait but didn't want to deal with the thoughts that would intrude as he sat alone in the car. He got out, crossed the lawn to the front porch and knocked on the door.

While he waited, he got out a cigarette and was lighting it when he suddenly stopped. He realized that what he was doing was his reflex of smoking at death scenes where the bodies were old. His instincts had reacted before he had consciously registered the odor from the house. Outside the door it was barely noticeable, but it was there. He looked back out to the street and saw no one. He looked back at the door and tried the knob. It turned. As he opened it, he felt a rush of cool air and the odor came out to meet him.

The house was still, the only sound the hum of the air conditioner in the window of her bedroom. That was where he found her. He could tell right away that Meredith Roman had been dead for several days. Her body was in the bed, the covers pulled up to her head on the pillow. Only her face, what was left of it, was visible. Bosch's eyes did not linger on the image. The deterioration had been extensive and he guessed that maybe she had been dead since the day he had visited.

On the table next to the bed were two empty glasses, a half-gone fifth of vodka and an empty bottle of prescription pills. Bosch bent down to read the label and saw the prescription was for Katherine Register, one each night before bed. Sleeping pills.

Meredith had faced her past and administered her own penance. She had taken the blue canoe. Suicide. Bosch knew it wasn't for him to decide but it looked that way. He turned to the bureau because he remembered the Kleenex box and he wanted to use a tissue to cover his tracks. But there on the top, near the photos in gilded frames, was an envelope that had his name on it.

He picked it up, took some tissues and left the room. In the living room, a bit farther away from the source of the horrible odor but not far enough, he turned the envelope over to open it and noticed the flap was torn. The envelope had been opened already. He guessed maybe Meredith had reopened it to read again what she had written. Maybe she'd had second thoughts about what she was doing. He dismissed the question and took the note out. It was dated a week earlier. Wednesday. She had written it the day after his visit.

Dear Harry,

If you are reading this then my fears that you would learn the truth were well founded. If you are reading this then the decision I have made tonight was the correct one and I have no regrets as I make it. You see, I would rather face the judgment of afterlife than have you look at me while knowing the truth.

I know what I have taken from you. I have known all my life. It does no good to say I am sorry or to try to explain. But it still amazes me how one's life can change forever in a few moments of uncontrolled rage. I was angry at Marjorie when she came to me that night so full of hope and happiness. She was leaving me. For a life with you. With him. For a life we had only dreamed was possible.

What is jealousy but a reflection of your own failures? I was jealous and angry and I struck at her. I then made a feeble effort to cover what I had done. I am sorry, Harry, but I took her from you and with that took any chance you ever had. I've carried the guilt every day since then and I take it with me now. I should have paid for my sin a long time ago but someone convinced me otherwise and helped me get away. There is no one left to convince me now.

I don't ask for your forgiveness, Harry. That would be an insult. I guess all I want is for you to know my regrets and to know that sometimes people who get away don't really get away. I didn't. Not then, not now. Good-bye.

Meredith

Bosch reread the note and then stood there thinking about it for a long time. Finally, he folded it and put it back in its envelope. He walked over to the fireplace, lit the envelope on fire with his Bic and then tossed it onto the grate. He watched the paper bend and burn until it bloomed like a black rose and went out.

He went to the kitchen and lifted the receiver off the phone after wrapping his hand in tissue. He put it on the counter and dialed nine-one-one. As he walked toward the front door, he could hear the tiny voice of the Santa Monica police operator asking who was there and what the problem was.

He left the door unlocked and wiped the exterior knob with the tissue after stepping out onto the porch. He heard a voice from behind him.

"She writes a good letter, don't she?"

Bosch turned around. Vaughn was sitting on the rattan love seat on the porch. He was holding a new twenty-two in his hand. It looked like another Beretta. He looked none the worse for wear. He didn't have the black eyes that Bosch had, or the stitches.

"Vaughn."

Bosch couldn't think of anything else to say. He couldn't imagine how he had been found by him. Could Vaughn have been daring enough to hang around Parker Center and follow Bosch from there? Bosch

looked out into the street and wondered how long it would take the police operator to dispatch a car to the address the computer gave her for
the 911 call. Even though Bosch had said nothing on the line, he knew
they would eventually send a car to check it out. He had wanted them to
find Meredith. If they took their time about it, they would probably find
him as well. He had to stall Vaughn for as long as possible.

"Yeah, nice note," the man with the gun said. "But she left something
out, don't you think?"

"What's left out?"

Vaughn seemed not to have heard him.

"It's funny," he said. "I knew your mother had a kid. But I never met
you, never even saw you. She kept you away from me. I wasn't good
enough, I guess."

Bosch continued to stare as things began to fall together.

"Johnny Fox."

"In the flesh."

"I don't understand. Mittel . . ."

"Mittel had me killed? No, not really. I killed myself, I guess you
could say. I read that story you people put in the paper today. But you had
it wrong. Most of it, at least."

Bosch nodded. He knew now.

"Meredith killed your mother, kid. Sorry about that. I just helped her
take care of it after the fact."

"And then you used her death to get to Conklin."

Bosch didn't need any confirmation from Fox. He was just trying to
chew up time.

"Yeah, that was the plan, to get to Conklin. Worked pretty good, too.
Got me out of the sewer. Only I found out pretty fast that the real power
was Mittel. I could tell. Between the two of them, Mittel could go the
distance. So I threw in with him, you could say. He wanted a better hold
on the golden boy. He wanted an ace up his own sleeve. So I helped."

"By killing yourself? I don't get it."

"Mittel told me that supreme power over someone is the power they
don't know you have until you need to use it. You see, Bosch, Mittel always suspected that Conklin was really the one who did your mother."

Bosch nodded. He saw where the story was going.

"And you never told Mittel that Conklin wasn't the killer."

"That's right. I never told him about Meredith. So knowing that, look at it from his side. Mittel figured that if Conklin was the doer and he believed I was dead, then he'd think he was home free. See, I was the only loose end, the one who could tie him in. Mittel wanted him to think he was clear. He wanted it because he wanted Conklin at ease. He didn't want him to lose his drive, his ambition. Conklin was going places and Mittel didn't want him to even hesitate. But he also wanted to keep an ace up his sleeve, something that he could always pull out if Conklin tried to step out of line. That was me. I was the ace. So we arranged that little hit and run, me and Mittel. Thing is, Mittel never had to play the ace with Conklin. Conklin gave Mittel a lot of good years after that. By the time he backed out on that attorney general thing, Mittel was well diversified. By then he had a congressman, a senator, a quarter of the local pols on his client list. You could say by then he had already climbed on Conklin's shoulders to the higher ground. He didn't need Arno anymore."

Bosch nodded again and thought a moment about the scenario. All those years. Conklin believed it had been Mittel who killed her and Mittel believed it had been Conklin. It was neither.

"So who was the one you ran over?"

"Oh, just somebody. It doesn't matter. He was just a volunteer, you could say. I picked him up on Mission Street. He thought he was handing out Conklin fliers. I planted my ID in the bottom of the satchel I gave him. He never knew what hit him or why."

"How'd you get away with it?" Bosch asked, though he thought he already knew the answer to that as well.

"Mittel had Eno on the line. We set it up so that it happened when he was next up on call. He took care of everything and Mittel took care of him."

Bosch could see that the setup also gave Fox a share of power over Mittel. And he'd ridden along with him ever since. A little plastic surgery, a nicer set of clothes, and he was Jonathan Vaughn, aid to the wunderkind political strategist and rainmaker.

"So how'd you know I'd show up here?"

"I'd kept tabs on her over the years. I knew she was here. Alone. After our little run-in on the hill the other night, I came here to hide, to sleep. You gave me a headache—what the hell you hit me with?"

"The eight ball."

"I guess I should have thought of that when I put you in there. Anyway, I found her like that in the bed. I read the note and knew who you were. I figured you'd be back. Especially after you left that message on the phone yesterday."

"You've been here all this time with . . ."

"You get used to it. I put the air on high, closed the door. You get used to it."

Bosch tried to imagine it. Sometimes he believed that he was used to the smell, but he knew he wasn't.

"What did she leave out of the note, Fox?"

"That was the part about her wanting Conklin for herself. See, I tried her with Conklin first. But it didn't take. Then I set him up with Marjorie and got the fireworks. Nobody expected that he'd want to end up marrying her, though. Least of all Meredith. There was only room on the horse with the white knight for one rider. That was Marjorie. Meredith couldn't handle that. Must've been a hell of a cat fight."

Bosch said nothing. But the truth stung his face like a sunburn. That's what it had all come down to, a cat fight between whores.

"Let's go to your car now," Fox said.

"Why?"

"We need to go to your place now."

"For what?"

Fox never answered. A Santa Monica squad car stopped in front of the house just as Bosch asked his question. Two officers started getting out.

"Be cool, Bosch," Fox said quietly. "Be cool if you want to live a little longer."

Bosch saw Fox turn the aim of his gun toward the approaching officers. They could not see it because of the thick bougainvillea running along the front of the porch. One of them started to speak.

"Did someone here call nine—"

Bosch took two steps and launched himself over the railing to the lawn. As he did it, he yelled a warning.

"He's got a gun! He's got a gun!"

On the ground, Bosch heard Fox start running on the wood decking of the porch. He guessed he was going for the door. Then came the first shot. He was sure it came from behind him, from Fox. Then the two cops opened up like the Fourth of July. Bosch couldn't count all the shots. He stayed on the grass with his arms spread wide and his hands up, just hoping they wouldn't send one his way.

It was over in no more than eight seconds. When the echoes died and silence returned, Bosch yelled again.

"I'm unarmed! I'm a police officer! I am no threat to you! I am an unarmed police officer!"

He felt the end of a hot gun barrel pressed against his neck.

"Where's the ID?"

"Right inside coat pocket."

Then he remembered he still didn't have it. The cop's hands grasped him by the shoulders.

"I'm going to roll you over."

"Wait a minute. I don't have it."

"What is this? Roll over."

Bosch complied.

"I don't have it with me. I've got other ID though. Left inside pocket."

The cop started going through his jacket. Bosch was scared.

"I'm not going to do anything wrong here."

"Just be quiet."

The cop got Bosch's wallet out and looked at the driver's license that was behind a clear plastic window.

"Whaddaya got, Jimmy?" the other cop yelled. Bosch couldn't see him. "He legit?"

"Says he's a cop, got no badge. Got a DL here."

Then he hunched back down over Bosch and patted the rest of his body in a search for weapons.

"I'm clean."

"All right, turn back over."

Bosch did so and his hands were cuffed behind his back. He then heard the man above him call in for backup and an ambulance on his radio.

"All right, get up."

Bosch did as he was told. For the first time he could see the porch. The other cop stood with his handgun pointing down at Fox's crumpled body at the front door. Bosch was led up the steps to the porch. He could see Fox was still alive. His chest was heaving, he had wounds in both legs and the stomach and it looked like one slug had gone through both cheeks. His jaw hung open. But his eyes seemed even wider as he stared at death coming for him.

"I knew you'd fire, you fuck," Bosch said to him. "Just die now."

"Shut up," the one called Jimmy ordered. "Right now."

The other cop pulled him away from the front door. Out in the street, Bosch could see neighbors joining together in little knots or watching from their own porches. Nothing like gunshots in suburbia for getting people together, he thought. The smell of spent gunpowder in the air does it better than a barbecue any day.

The young cop got right up in Bosch's face. Harry could see that his name plate identified him as D. Sparks.

"Okay, what the fuck's going on here? If you're a cop, tell us what's going on."

"You two are a couple of heroes, that's what's going on."

"Tell the story, man. I don't have time for bullshit."

Bosch could hear approaching sirens now.

"My name's Bosch. I'm with LAPD. This man you shot is the suspect in the killing of Arno Conklin, the former district attorney of this county, and LAPD Lieutenant Harvey Pounds. I'm sure you've heard about these cases."

"Jim, you hear that?" He turned back to Bosch. "Where's your badge?"

"Stolen. I can give you a number to call. Assistant Chief Irvin Irving. He'll tell you about me."

"Never mind that. What's he doing here?"

He pointed to Fox.

"He told me he was hiding out. Earlier today I got a call to come to this address and he was here waiting to ambush me. See, I could identify him. He had to take me out."

The cop looked down at Fox wondering if he should believe such an incredible story.

"You got here right in time," Bosch said. "He was going to kill me."

D. Sparks nodded. He was beginning to like the sound of this story. Then concern creased his brow.

"Who called 911?" he asked.

"I did," Bosch said. "I came here, found the door open and went in. I was calling 911 when he got the jump on me. I just dropped the phone because I knew you people would come."

"Why call 911 if he hadn't grabbed you yet?"

"Because of what's in the back bedroom."

"What?"

"There's a woman in the bed. She looks like she's been dead about a week."

"Who is she?"

Bosch looked at the young cop's face.

"I don't know."

Why didn't you reveal that you knew she was your mother's killer? Why did you lie?"

"I don't know. I haven't figured it out. It's just that there was something about what she wrote and what she did at the end that . . . I don't know, I just felt like that was enough. I just wanted to let it go."

Carmen Hinojos nodded her head as if she understood but Bosch wasn't sure he did himself.

"I think that's a good decision, Harry."

"You do? I don't think anybody else would think it was a good decision."

"I'm not talking about on a procedural or criminal justice level. I'm just talking about on a human level. I think you did the right thing. For yourself."

"I guess . . ."

"Do you feel good about it?"

"Not really . . . You were right, you know."

"I was? About what?"

"About what you said about me finding out who did it. You warned me. Said it might do me more harm than good. Well, that was an understatement . . . Some mission I gave myself, right?"

"I'm sorry if I was right. But as I said in the last session, the deaths of those men can't be—"

"I'm not talking about them anymore. I'm talking about something else. You see, I know now that my mother was trying to save me from that place I was at. Like she had promised me that day out by the fence that I told you about. I think that whether she loved Conklin or not, she was thinking of me. She had to get me out and he was the way to do it. So, ultimately, you see, it was because of me that she died."

"Oh, please, don't tell yourself that, Harry. That's ridiculous."

Bosch knew that the anger in her voice was real.

"If you are going to take that form of logic," she continued, "you can come up with any reason why she was killed, you can argue that your own birth set circumstances in motion that led to her death. You see how silly that is?"

"Not really."

"It's the same argument you made the other day about people not taking responsibility. Well, the inverse of that is people who take too much responsibility. And you are becoming one of them. Let that go, Harry. Let it go. Let someone else take some responsibility for some things. Even if that someone else is dead. Being dead does not absolve them of everything."

He was cowed by the forcefulness of her admonition. He just looked at her for a long moment. He could tell her outburst would signal a natural break in the session. The discussion of his guilt was done. She had ended it and he had his instructions.

"I'm sorry to have raised my voice."

"No problem."

"Harry, what do you hear from the department?"

"Nothing. I'm waiting on Irving."

"What do you mean?"

"He kept my . . . culpability out of the paper. Now it's his move. He's either going to come at me with IAD—if he can make a case against me impersonating Pounds—or he's going to let it go. I'm betting he's going to let it go."

"Why?"

"The one thing about the LAPD is that it is not into self-flagellation. Know what I mean? This case is very public and if they do something to me, they know there's always the danger it will get out and it will be one more black eye for the department. Irving sees himself as the protector of the department's image. He'll put that ahead of taking me down. Besides, he'll have leverage on me now. I mean, he thinks he will."

"You seem to know Irving and the department well."

"Why?"

"Chief Irving called me this morning and asked me to forward a positive RTD evaluation to his office as soon as possible."

"He said that? He wants a positive return-to-duty report?"

"Yes, those were his words. Do you think you are ready for that?"

He thought a few moments but didn't answer the question.

"Has he done that before? Told you how to evaluate somebody?"

"No. It's a first time and I'm very concerned about it. It undermines my position here if I simply accede to his wishes. It's quite a dilemma because I don't want you caught in the middle."

"What if he didn't tell you which way to go, what would your evaluation be? Positive or negative?"

She played with a pencil on the desktop for a few moments while considering the question.

"It's very close, Harry, but I think you need more time."

"Then don't do it. Don't give in to him."

"That's quite a change. Only a week ago all you could talk about was getting back to the job."

"That was a week ago."

There was a palpable sadness in his voice.

"Stop beating yourself to death with it," she said. "The past is like a club and you can only hit yourself in the head with it so many times before there is serious and permanent damage. I think you're at your limit. For what it's worth, I think you are a good and clean and ultimately kind man. Don't do this to yourself. Don't ruin what you have, what you are, with this kind of thinking."

He nodded as if he understood but he had dismissed her words as soon as he heard them.

"I've been doing a lot of thinking the last couple of days."

"About what?"

"Everything."

"Any decisions on anything?"

"Almost. I think I'm going to pull the pin, leave the department."

She leaned forward and folded her arms on the desk. A serious look creased her brow.

"Harry, what are you talking about? This is not like you. Your job and your life are the same. I think it's good to have some distance but not total separation. I—" She stopped when she seemed to come upon an idea. "Is this your idea of penance, of making up for what happened?"

"I don't know . . . I just . . . For what I did, something has to be paid. That's all. Irving's not going to do anything. I will."

"Harry, you made a mistake. A serious mistake, yes. But for that you are giving up your career, the one thing that even you readily admit you do well? You're going to throw it all away?"

He nodded.

"Did you pull the papers yet?"

"Not yet."

"Don't do it."

"Why not? I can't do this anymore. It's like I'm walking around handcuffed to a chain of ghosts."

He shook his head. They were having the same debate that he had been having in his mind for the last two days, since the night at Meredith Roman's house.

"Give it some time," Hinojos said. "All I'm saying is, think about it. You're on paid leave now. Use it. Use the time. I'll tell Irving he's not getting an RTD from me yet. Meantime, you just give it some time and think hard on it. Go away somewhere, sit on the beach. But think about it before you turn in your papers."

Bosch raised his hands in surrender.

"Please, Harry. I want to hear you say it."

"All right. I'll do some more thinking."

"Thank you."

She let some silence underline his agreement.

"Remember what you said about seeing the coyote on the street last week?" she asked quietly. "About it being the last coyote?"

"I remember."

"I think I know how you felt. I'd hate to think that I was seeing the coyote for the last time, too."

From the airport Bosch took the freeway to the Armenia exit and then south to Swann. He found that he didn't even need the rent-a-car map. He went east on Swann into Hyde Park and then down South Boulevard to her place. He could see the bay shimmering in the sun at the end of the street.

At the top of the stairs the door was open but the screen door was closed. Bosch knocked.

"Come in. It's open."

It was her. Bosch pushed through the screen into the living room. She wasn't there but the first thing he noticed was a painting on the wall where before there had been only the nail. It was a portrait of a man in shadows. He was sitting at a table alone. The figure's elbow was on the table and the hand was up against his cheek, obscuring the face and making the deep set of the eyes the focal point of the painting. Bosch stared at it a moment until she called again.

"Hello? I'm in here."

He saw the door to her studio was open a half foot. He stepped over and pushed it open. She was there, standing in front of the easel, dark earth-tone oils on the palette in her hand. There was a single errant slash of ocher on her right cheek. She immediately smiled.

"Harry."

"Hello, Jasmine."

He moved in closer to her and stepped around the side of the easel. The portrait had only just been started. But she had begun with the eyes. The same eyes in the portrait that hung on the wall in the other room. The same eyes he saw in the mirror.

She hesitantly came closer to him. There was not a glimmer of embarrassment or unease in her face.

"I thought that if I painted you, you would come back."

She dropped her brush into an old coffee can bolted to the easel and came even closer. She embraced him and they kissed silently. At first it was a gentle reunion, then he put his hand against her back and pulled her tightly against his chest as if she were a bandage that could stop his bleeding. After a while she pulled back, brought her arms up and held his face in her hands.

"Let me see if I got the eyes right."

She reached up and took off his sunglasses. He smiled. He knew the purple below his eyes was almost gone but they were still red-rimmed and shot with swollen capillaries.

"Jesus, you took the red-eye."

"It's a long story. I'll tell you later."

"God, put these back on."

She hooked the glasses back on and laughed.

"It's not that funny. It hurt."

"Not that. I got paint on your face."

"Well, then I'm not alone."

He traced the slash on her face. They embraced again. Bosch knew they could talk later. For now he just held her and smelled her and looked over her shoulder to the brilliant blue of the bay. He thought of something the old man in the bed had told him. When you find the one that you think fits, then grab on for dear life. Bosch didn't know if she was the one, but for the moment he held on with everything he had left.

TRUNK MUSIC

This is for my editor, Michael Pietsch

TRUNK MUSIC

I

As he drove along Mulholland Drive toward the Cahuenga Pass, Bosch began to hear the music. It came to him in fragments of strings and errant horn sequences, echoing off the brown summer-dried hills and blurred by the white noise of traffic carrying up from the Hollywood Freeway. Nothing he could identify. All he knew was that he was heading toward its source.

He slowed when he saw the cars parked off to the side of a gravel turn-off road. Two detective sedans and a patrol car. Bosch pulled his Caprice in behind them and got out. A single officer in uniform leaned against the fender of the patrol car. Yellow plastic crime-scene tape—the stuff used by the mile in Los Angeles—was strung from the patrol car's sideview mirror across the gravel road to the sign posted on the other side. The sign said, in black-on-white letters that were almost indistinguishable behind the graffiti that covered the sign:

L.A.F.D. FIRE CONTROL
MOUNTAIN FIRE DISTRICT ROAD
NO PUBLIC ADMITTANCE—NO SMOKING!

The patrol cop, a large man with sun-reddened skin and blond bristly hair, straightened up as Bosch approached. The first thing Bosch noted about him other than his size was the baton. It was holstered in a ring on his belt and the business end of the club was marred, the black acrylic paint scratched away to reveal the aluminum beneath. Street fighters wore their battle-scarred sticks proudly, as a sign, a not so subtle warning. This cop was a headbanger. No doubt about it. The plate above the cop's breast pocket said his name was Powers. He looked down at Bosch through Ray-Bans, though it was well into dusk and a sky of burnt orange clouds was reflected in his mirrored lenses. It was one of those sundowns that reminded Bosch of the glow the fires of the riots had put in the sky a few years back.

"Harry Bosch," Powers said with a touch of surprise. "When did you get back on the table?"

Bosch looked at him a moment before answering. He didn't know Powers but that didn't mean anything. Bosch's story was probably known by every cop in Hollywood Division.

"Just did," Bosch said.

He didn't make any move to shake hands. You didn't do that at crime scenes.

"First case back in the saddle, huh?"

Bosch took out a cigarette and lit it. It was a direct violation of department policy but it wasn't something he was worried about.

"Something like that." He changed the subject. "Who's down there?"

"Edgar and the new one from Pacific, his soul sister."

"Rider."

"Whatever."

Bosch said nothing further about that. He knew what was behind the contempt in the uniform cop's voice. It didn't matter that he knew Kizmin Rider had the gift and was a top-notch investigator. That would mean nothing to Powers, even if Bosch told him it was so. Powers probably saw only one reason why he was still wearing a blue uniform instead of carrying a detective's gold badge: that he was a white man in an era of female and minority hiring and promotion. It was the kind of festering sore better left undisturbed.

Powers apparently registered Bosch's nonresponse as disagreement and went on.

"Anyway, they told me to let Emmy and Sid drive on down when they get here. I guess they're done with the search. So you can drive down instead of walking, I guess."

It took a second for Bosch to register that Powers was referring to the medical examiner and the Scientific Investigation Division tech. He'd said the names as if they were a couple invited to a picnic.

Bosch stepped out to the pavement, dropped the half cigarette and made sure he put it out with his shoe. It wouldn't be good to start a brush fire on his first job back with the homicide table.

"I'll walk it," he said. "What about Lieutenant Billets?"

"Not here yet."

Bosch went back to his car and reached in through the open window for his briefcase. He then walked back to Powers.

"You the one who found it?"

"That was me."

Powers was proud of himself.

"How'd you open it?"

"Keep a slim jim in the car. Opened the door, then popped the trunk."

"Why?"

"The smell. It was obvious."

"Wear gloves?"

"Nope. Didn't have any."

"What did you touch?"

Powers had to think about it for a moment.

"Door handle, the trunk pull. That'd be about it."

"Did Edgar or Rider take a statement? You write something up?"

"Nothing yet."

Bosch nodded.

"Listen, Powers, I know you're all proud of yourself, but next time don't open the car, okay? We all want to be detectives but not all of us are. That's how crime scenes get fucked up. And I think you know that."

Bosch watched the cop's face turn a dark shade of crimson and the skin go tight around his jaw.

"Listen, Bosch," he said. "What I know is that if I just called this in as a suspicious vehicle that *smells* like there's a stiff in the trunk, then you people would've said, 'What the fuck does Powers know?' and left it there to rot in the sun until there was nothing left of your goddamn crime scene."

"That might be true but, see, then that would be our fuckup to make. Instead, we've got you fucking us up before we start."

Powers remained angry but mute. Bosch waited a beat, ready to continue the debate, before dismissing it.

"Can you lift the tape now, please?"

Powers stepped back to the tape. He was about thirty-five, Bosch guessed, and had the long-practiced swagger of a street veteran. In L.A. that swagger came to you quickly, as it had in Vietnam. Powers held the yellow tape up and Bosch walked under. As he passed, the cop said, "Don't get lost."

"Good one, Powers. You got me there."

The fire road was one lane and overgrown at its sides with brush that came as high as Bosch's waist. There was trash and broken glass strewn along the gravel, the trespasser's answer to the sign at the gate. Bosch knew the road was probably a favorite midnight haunt for teenagers from the city below.

The music grew louder as he went farther in. But he still could not identify it. About a quarter mile in, he came to a gravel-bedded clearing that he guessed was a staging point for fire-fighting apparatus in the event that a brush fire broke out in the surrounding hills. Today it would serve as a crime scene. On the far side of the clearing Bosch saw a white Rolls-Royce Silver Cloud. Standing near it were his two partners, Rider and Edgar. Rider was sketching the crime scene on a clipboard while Edgar worked with a tape measure and called out measurements. Edgar saw Bosch and gave an acknowledging wave with a latex-gloved hand. He let the tape measure snap back into its case.

"Harry, where you been?"

"Painting," Bosch said as he walked up. "I had to get cleaned up and changed, put stuff away."

As Bosch stepped closer to the edge of the clearing, the view opened below him. They were on a bluff rising above the rear of the Hollywood Bowl. The rounded music shell was down to the left, no more than a quarter mile. And the shell was the source of the music. The L.A. Philharmonic's end-of-the-season Labor Day weekend show. Bosch was looking down at eighteen thousand people in concert seats stretching up the opposite side of the canyon. They were enjoying one of the last Sunday evenings of the summer.

"Jesus," he said out loud, thinking of the problem.

Edgar and Rider walked over.

"What've we got?" Bosch asked.

Rider answered.

"One in the trunk. White male. Gunshots. We haven't checked him out much further than that. We've been keeping the lid closed. We've got everybody rolling, though."

Bosch started walking toward the Rolls, going around the charred remnants of an old campfire that had burned in the center of the clearing. The other two followed.

"This okay?" Bosch asked as he got close to the Rolls.

"Yeah, we did the search," Edgar said. "Nothing much. Got some leakage underneath the car. That's about it, though. Cleanest scene I've been at in a while."

Jerry Edgar, called in from home like everybody else on the team, was wearing blue jeans and a white T-shirt. On the left breast of the shirt was a drawing of a badge and the words LAPD Homicide. As he walked past Bosch, Harry saw that the back of the shirt said Our Day Begins When Your Day Ends. The tight-fitting shirt contrasted sharply with Edgar's dark skin and displayed his heavily muscled upper body as he moved with an athletic grace toward the Rolls. Bosch had worked with him on and off for six years but they had never become close outside of the job. This was the first time it had dawned on Bosch that Edgar actually was an athlete, that he must regularly work out.

It was unusual for Edgar not to be in one of his crisp Nordstrom's suits. But Bosch thought he knew why. His informal dress practically guaranteed he would avoid having to do the dirty work, next-of-kin notification.

They slowed their steps when they got close to the Rolls, as if perhaps whatever was wrong here might be contagious. The car was parked with its rear end facing south and visible to the spectators in the upper levels of the Bowl across the way. Bosch considered their situation again.

"So you want to pull this guy out of there with all those people with their wine and box lunches from the Grill watching?" he asked. "How do you think that's going to play on the TV tonight?"

"Well," Edgar replied, "we thought we'd kind of leave that decision to you, Harry. You being the three."

Edgar smiled and winked.

"Yeah, right," Bosch said sarcastically. "I'm the three."

Bosch was still getting used to the idea of being a so-called team leader. It had been almost eighteen months since he had officially investigated a homicide, let alone headed up a team of three investigators. He had been assigned to the Hollywood Division burglary table when he returned to work from his involuntary stress leave in January. The detective bureau commander, Lieutenant Grace Billets, had explained that his assignment was a way of gradually easing him back into detective work. He knew that explanation was a lie and that she had been told where to put him, but he took the demotion without complaint. He knew they would come for him eventually.

After eight months of pushing papers and making the occasional burglary arrest, Bosch was called into the CO's office and Billets told him she was making changes. The division's homicide clearance rate had dipped to its lowest point ever. Fewer than half of the killings were cleared. She had taken over command of the bureau nearly a year earlier, and the sharpest decline, she struggled to admit, had come under her own watch. Bosch could have told her that the decline was due in part to her not following the same statistical deceptions practiced by her predecessor, Harvey Pounds, who had always found ways of pumping up the clearance rate, but he kept that to himself. Instead, he sat quietly while Billets laid out her plan.

The first part of the plan was to move Bosch back to the homicide table as of the start of September. A detective named Selby, who barely pulled his weight, would go from homicide to Bosch's slot on the burglary table. Billets was also adding a young and smart detective transfer she had previously worked with in the Pacific Division detective bureau, Kizmin Rider. Next, and this was the radical part, Billets was changing the traditional pairing of detectives. Instead, the nine homicide detectives assigned to Hollywood would be grouped into three teams of three. Each of the three teams would have a detective third grade in charge. Bosch was a three. He was named team leader of squad one.

The reasoning behind the change was sound—at least on paper. Most homicides are solved in the first forty-eight hours after discovery or they aren't solved at all. Billets wanted more solved so she was going to put more detectives on each one. The part that didn't look so good on paper, especially to the nine detectives, was that previously there had been four pairs of partners working homicide cases. The new changes meant each detective would be working every third case that came up instead of every fourth. It meant more cases, more work, more court time, more overtime, and more stress. Only the overtime was considered a positive. But Billets was tough and didn't care much for the complaints of the detectives. And her new plan quickly won her the obvious nickname.

"Anybody talk to Bullets yet?" Bosch asked.

"I called," Rider said. "She was up in Santa Barbara for the weekend. Left a number with the desk. She's coming down early but she's still at least an hour and a half from us. She said she was going to have to drop the hubby off first and would probably just roll to the bureau."

Bosch nodded and stepped to the rear of the Rolls. He picked up the smell right away. It was faint but it was there, unmistakable. Like no other. He nodded to no one in particular again. He placed his briefcase on the ground, opened it and took a pair of latex gloves from the cardboard box inside. He then closed the case and placed it a few feet behind him and out of the way.

"Okay, let's take a look," he said while stretching the gloves over his hands. He hated how they felt. "Let's stand close, we don't want to give the people in the Bowl more of a show than they paid for."

"It ain't pretty," Edgar said as he stepped forward.

The three of them stood together at the back end of the Rolls to shield the view from the concertgoers. But Bosch knew that anybody with a decent pair of field glasses would know what was going on. This was L.A.

Before opening the trunk, he noticed the car's personalized license plate. It said TNA. Before he could speak, Edgar answered his unasked question.

"Comes back to TNA Productions. On Melrose."

"T and A?"

"No, the letters, T-N-A, just like on the plate."

"Where on Melrose?"

Edgar took a notebook out of his pocket and looked through the pages. The address he gave was familiar to Bosch but he couldn't place it. He knew it was down near Paramount, the sprawling studio that took up

the entire north side of the fifty-five-hundred block. The big studio was
surrounded by smaller production houses and mini-studios. They were
like sucker fish that swam around the mouth of the big shark, hoping for
the scraps that didn't get sucked in.

"Okay, let's do it."

He turned his attention back to the trunk. He could see that the lid
had been lightly placed down so it would not lock closed. Using one
rubber-coated finger, he gently lifted it.

As the trunk was opened, it expelled a sickeningly fetid breath of
death. Bosch immediately wished he had a cigarette but those days were
through. He knew what a defense lawyer could do with one ash from a
cop's smoke at a crime scene. Reasonable doubts were built on less.

He leaned in under the lid to get a close look, careful not to touch the
bumper with his pants. The body of a man was in the trunk. His skin was
a grayish white and he was expensively dressed in linen pants sharply
pressed and cuffed at the bottom, a pale blue shirt with a flowery pattern
and a leather sport coat. His feet were bare.

The dead man was on his right side in the fetal position except his
wrists were behind him instead of folded against his chest. It appeared to
Bosch that his hands had been tied behind him and the bindings then removed, most likely after he was dead. Bosch looked closely and could see
a small abrasion on the left wrist, probably caused by the struggle against
the bindings. The man's eyes were closed tightly and there was a whitish,
almost translucent material dried in the corners of the sockets.

"Kiz, I want you taking notes on appearance."

"Right."

Bosch bent farther into the trunk. He saw a froth of purged blood
had dried in the dead man's mouth and nose. His hair was caked with
blood which had spread over the shoulders and to the trunk mat, coating
it with a coagulated pool. He could see the hole in the floor of the trunk
through which blood had drained to the gravel below. It was a foot from
the victim's head and appeared to be evenly cut in the metal underlining
in a spot where the floor mat was folded over. It was not a bullet hole. It
was probably a drain or a hole left by a bolt that had vibrated loose and
fallen out.

In the mess that was the back of the man's head, Bosch could see two
distinct jagged-edged penetrations to the lower rear skull—the occipital

protuberance—the scientific name popping easily into his mind. Too many autopsies, he thought. The hair close to the wounds was charred by the gasses that explode out of the barrel of a gun. The scalp showed stippling from gunpowder. Point-blank shots. No exit wounds that he could see. Probably twenty-twos, he guessed. They bounce around inside like marbles dropped into an empty jelly jar.

Bosch looked up and saw a small spray of blood splattered on the inside of the trunk lid. He studied the spots for a long moment and then stepped back and straightened up. He appraised the entire view of the trunk now, his mind checking off an imaginary list. Because no blood drips had been found on the access road into the clearing, he had no doubts that the man had been killed here in the trunk. Still, there were other unknowns. Why here? Why no shoes and socks? Why were the bindings taken off the wrists? He put these questions aside for the time being.

"You check for the wallet?" he asked without looking at the two others.

"Not yet," Edgar replied. "Recognize him?"

For the first time Bosch looked at the face as a face. There was still fear etched on it. The man had closed his eyes. He had known what was coming. Bosch wondered if the whitish material in the eyes was dried tears.

"No, do you?"

"Nope. It's too messy, anyway."

Bosch gingerly lifted the back of the leather coat and saw no wallet in the back pockets of the dead man's pants. He then opened the jacket and saw the wallet was there in an inside pocket that carried a Fred Haber men's shop label on it. Bosch could also see a paper folder for an airline ticket in the pocket. With his other hand he reached into the jacket and removed the two items.

"Get the lid," he said as he backed away.

Edgar closed it over as gently as an undertaker closing a coffin. Bosch then walked over to his briefcase, squatted down and put the two items down on it.

He opened the wallet first. There was a full complement of credit cards in slots on the left side and a driver's license behind a plastic window on the right. The name on the license said Anthony N. Aliso.

"Anthony N. Aliso," Edgar said. "Tony for short. TNA. TNA Productions."

The address was in Hidden Highlands, a tiny enclave off Mulholland in the Hollywood Hills. It was the kind of place that was surrounded by walls and had a guard shack manned twenty-four hours a day, mostly by off-duty or retired LAPD cops. The address went well with the Rolls-Royce.

Bosch opened the billfold section and found a sheaf of currency. Without taking the money out, he counted two one-hundred-dollar bills and nine twenties. He called the amount out so that Rider could make a note of it. Next he opened the airline folder. Inside was the receipt for a one-way ticket on an American Airlines flight departing Las Vegas for LAX at 10:05 Friday night. The name on the ticket matched the driver's license. Bosch checked the back flap of the ticket folder, but there was no sticker or staple indicating that a bag had been checked by the ticket holder. Curious, Bosch left the wallet and the ticket on the case and went to look into the car through the windows.

"No luggage?"

"None," Rider said.

Bosch went back to the trunk and raised the lid again. Looking in at the body, he hooked a finger up the left sleeve of the jacket and pulled it up. There was a gold Rolex watch on the wrist. The face was encircled with a ring of tiny diamonds.

"Shit."

Bosch turned around. It was Edgar.

"What?"

"You want me to call OCID?"

"Why?"

"Wop name, no robbery, two in the back of the head. It's a whack job, Harry. We oughta call OCID."

"Not yet."

"I'll tell you right now that's what Bullets is gonna wanna do."

"We'll see."

Bosch appraised the body again, looking closely at the contorted, bloodied face. Then he closed the lid.

Bosch stepped away from the car and to the edge of the clearing. The spot offered a brilliant view of the city. Looking east across the sprawl of Hollywood, he could easily pick up the spires of downtown in the light haze. He saw the lights of Dodger Stadium were on for the twilight game. The Dodgers were dead even with Colorado with a month to go and Nomo due to pitch the game. Bosch had a ticket in his inside coat pocket. But he knew that bringing it along had been wishful thinking. He wouldn't get anywhere near the stadium tonight. He also knew Edgar was right. The killing had all the aspects of a mob hit. The Organized Crime Intelligence Division should be notified—if not to take over the investigation entirely, then at least to offer advice. But Bosch was delaying that notification. It had been a long time since he'd had a case. He didn't want to give it up yet.

He looked back down at the Bowl. It looked like a sellout to him, the crowd seated in an elliptical formation going up the opposite hill. The seating sections farthest away from the music shell were the highest up the hill and at an almost even level with the clearing where the Rolls was parked. Bosch wondered how many of the people were watching him at that moment. Again he thought of the dilemma he faced. He had to get the investigation going. But he knew that if he pulled the body out of the trunk with such an audience watching, there likely would be hell to pay for the bad public relations such a move would cause the city and the department.

Once again Edgar seemed to know his thoughts.

"Hell, Harry, they won't care. At the jazz festival a few years back, there was a couple up on this spot doing the nasty for half an hour. When they were done, they got a standing ovation. Guy stands up buck naked and takes a little bow."

Bosch looked back at him to see if he was serious.

"I read it in the *Times*. The 'Only in L.A.' column."

"Well, Jerry, this is the Philharmonic. It's a different crowd, know what I mean? And I don't want this to end up in 'Only in L.A.,' okay?"

"Okay, Harry."

Bosch looked at Rider. She hadn't said much of anything yet.

"What do you think, Kiz?"

"I don't know. You're the three."

Rider was small, five feet and no more than a hundred pounds with her gun on. She would never have made it before the department relaxed the physical requirements to attract more women. She had light brown skin. Her hair was straightened and kept short. She wore jeans and a pink oxford shirt beneath a black blazer. On her small body, the jacket did not do much to disguise a 9mm Glock 17 holstered on her right hip.

Billets had told him that she had worked with Rider in Pacific. Rider had worked robbery and fraud cases but was called out on occasion to work homicides in which there were overlying financial aspects. Billets had said Rider could break a crime scene down as well as most veteran homicide detectives. She had pulled strings to get Rider's transfer approved but was already resigned to the fact that she wouldn't stay long in the division. Rider was marked for travel. Her double minority status coupled with the facts that she was good at what she did and had a guardian angel—Billets wasn't sure who—at Parker Center practically guaranteed her stay in Hollywood would be short. It was a bit of final seasoning before she headed downtown to the Glass House.

"What about the OPG?" Bosch asked.

"Held up on that," Rider said. "Thought we'd be here a while before we moved the car."

Bosch nodded. It was what he expected her to say. The official police garage was usually last on the call-out list. He was just stalling, trying to make a decision while asking questions he already knew the answers to.

Finally he made his decision on what to do.

"Okay, go ahead and call," he said. "Tell them to come now. And tell them to bring a flatbed. Okay? Even if they've got a hook in the neighborhood, make 'em turn around. Tell 'em it's gotta be a flat. There's a phone in my briefcase."

"Got it," Rider said.

"Why the flatbed, Harry?" Edgar asked.

Bosch didn't answer.

"We're moving the whole show," Rider said.

"What?" Edgar asked.

Rider went to the briefcase without answering. Bosch held back a smile. She knew what he was doing, and he began to see some of the promise Billets had talked about. He got out a cigarette and lit it. He put the burnt match into the cellophane around the pack and replaced it in the pocket of his coat.

He noticed as he smoked that the sound at the edge of the clearing, where he could look directly down into the Bowl, was much better. After a few moments he was even able to identify the piece being played.

"*Sheherazade,*" he said.

"What's that, Harry?" Edgar asked.

"The music. It's called *Sheherazade*. Ever heard it?"

"I'm not sure I'm hearing it now. All the echoes, man."

Bosch snapped his fingers. Out of the blue a thought had pushed through. In his mind he saw the studio's arched gate, the replica of the Arc de Triomphe in Paris.

"That address on Melrose," Bosch said. "That's near Paramount. One of those feeder-fish studios right nearby. I think it's Archway."

"Yeah? I think you're right."

Rider walked up then.

"We've got a flat on the way," she said. "ETA is fifteen. I checked on SID and ME. Also on the way. SID has somebody just wrapped up a home invasion in Nichols Canyon, so they should be right over."

"Good," Bosch said. "Either of you go over the story with the swinging stick, yet?"

"Not since the preliminary," Edgar said. "Not our type. Thought we'd leave him for the three."

The unspoken meaning of this was that Edgar had sensed the racist animosity Powers radiated toward himself and Rider.

"Okay, I'll take him," Bosch said. "I want you two to finish the charting, then do another sweep of the immediate area. Take different areas this time."

He realized he had just told them things he didn't need to tell them.

"Sorry. You know what to do. All I'm saying is let's take this one by the numbers. I've got a feeling it's going eight by ten on us."

"What about OCID?" Edgar asked.

"I told you, not yet."

"Eight by ten?" Rider said, a confused expression on her face.

"Eight by ten case," Edgar told her. "Celebrity case. Studio case. If that's a hotshot from the industry in that trunk, somebody from Archway, we're going to get some media on this. More than some. A dead guy in the trunk of his Rolls is news. A dead industry guy in the trunk of his Rolls is bigger news."

"Archway?"

Bosch left them there as Edgar filled her in on the facts of life when it came to murder, the media and the movie business in Hollywood.

. . .

Bosch licked his fingers to put the cigarette out and then put it with the used match in the cellophane wrapper. He slowly began walking the quarter mile back to Mulholland, once again searching the gravel road in a back-and-forth manner. But there was so much debris on the gravel and in the nearby brush that it was impossible to know if anything—a cigarette butt, a beer bottle, a used condom—was related to the Rolls or not. The one thing he looked closest for was blood. If there was blood on the road that could be linked to the victim, it could indicate that he was killed elsewhere and left in the clearing. No blood probably meant the killing had taken place right there.

He realized as he made the fruitless search that he was feeling relaxed, maybe even happy. He was back on the beat and following his mission once again. Mindful that the man in the trunk had to have perished for him to feel this way, Bosch quickly wrote that guilt off. The man would have ended up in the trunk whether Bosch had ever made it back to the homicide table or not.

When Bosch got to Mulholland he saw the fire trucks. There were two of them and a battalion of firefighters standing around them, seemingly waiting for something. He lit another cigarette and looked at Powers.

"You've got a problem," the uniform cop said.

"What?"

Before Powers answered, one of the firefighters stepped up. He wore the white helmet of a battalion chief.

"You in charge?" he asked.

"That's me."

"Chief Jon Friedman," he said. "We've got a problem."

"That's what I hear."

"The show down in the Bowl is supposed to end in ninety minutes. After that we've got the fireworks. Problem is this fellow says you got yourself a dead body up there and a crime scene. That's the problem. If we can't get up there to set up a safety position for the fireworks, there isn't going to be any fireworks. We can't allow it. If we're not in position, we could see the whole down slope of these hills go up with one errant missile. Know what I mean?"

Bosch noticed Powers smirking at his dilemma. Bosch ignored him and returned his attention to Friedman.

"Chief, how long do you need to set up?"

"Ten minutes max. We just got to be there before the first one goes up."

"Ninety minutes?"

"About eighty-five now. There's gonna be a lot of angry people down there if they don't get their fireworks."

Bosch realized he wasn't as much making decisions as having them made for him.

"Chief, hold here. We'll be out in an hour and fifteen. Don't cancel the show."

"You sure about that?"

"Count on it."

"Detective?"

"What, Chief?"

"You're breaking the law with that cigarette."

He nodded toward the graffiti-covered sign.

"Sorry, Chief."

Bosch walked out to the road to stamp out the smoke while Friedman headed back to his people to radio in that the show would go on. Bosch realized the danger and caught up to him.

"Chief, you can say the show will go on, but don't put anything out on the air about the body. We don't need the media out here, helicopters swooping over."

"I gotcha."

Bosch thanked him and turned his attention to Powers.

"You can't clear a scene in an hour and fifteen," Powers said. "The ME isn't even here."

"Let me worry about that, Powers. You write something up yet?"

"Not yet. Been dealing with these guys. Would've helped if one of you folks had a two-way with you up there."

"Then why don't you run it down for me from the start?"

"What about them?" Powers asked, nodding in the direction of the clearing. "Why isn't one of them talking to me? Edgar and Rider?"

"Because they're busy. You want to run it down for me or not?"

"I already told you."

"From the start, Powers. You told me what you did once you checked the car out. What made you check it?"

"There's nothin' much to tell. I usually make a pass by here each watch, chase away the dirtbags."

He pointed across Mulholland and up to the crest of the hill. There was a line of houses, most on cantilevers, clinging to the crestline. They looked like mobile homes suspended in air.

"People up there call the station all the time, say they got campfires going down here, beer parties, devil worship, who knows what. Guess it ruins their view. And they don't want nothin' to spoil that million-dollar view. So I come up and sweep out the trash. Mostly bored little pissants from the Valley. Fire Department used to have a lock on the gate here, but a deuce plowed through it. That was six months ago. Takes the city at least a year to repair anything 'round here. Shit, I requisitioned batteries for my Mag three weeks ago and I'm still waiting for them. If I didn't buy them myself, I'd be working the fuckin' night watch without a flashlight. City doesn't care. This ci—"

"So what about the Rolls, Powers? Let's stay on the subject."

"Yeah, well, I usually make it by after dark, but because of the show in the Bowl I swung by early today. Saw the Rolls then."

"You came on your own? No complaint from up the hill?"

"No. Today I just cruised it on my own. On account of the show. I figured there might be some trespassers."

"Were there?"

"A few—people waiting to hear the music. Not the usual crowd, though. That's refined music, I guess you'd call it. I chased 'em out anyway, and when they were gone, the Rolls was what was left. But there was no driver for it."

"So you checked it out."

"Yeah, and I know the smell, man. Popped it with the slim and there he was. The stiff. Then I backed out and called the pros."

There was a note of sarcasm in the way he said the last word. Bosch ignored it.

"The people you chased, you get any names?"

"No, like I told you, I chased them, then noticed that nobody got in and drove away in the Rolls. It was too late by then."

"What about last night?"

"What about it?"

"Did you make it by here?"

"I was off. I'm on Tuesday-Saturday but I switched with a buddy last night 'cause he had something to do tonight."

"So then what about Friday night?"

He shook his head.

"Three watch is always busy Friday. I had no time for free cruising and we didn't get a complaint as far as I know . . . so I never made it by."

"Just chasin' the radio?"

"I had calls backed up on me all night. I didn't even get a ten-seven."

"No dinner break, that's dedication, Powers."

"What's that supposed to mean?"

Bosch saw he had made a mistake. Powers was consumed by job frustrations and he had pushed him too far. Powers turned crimson again and slowly took off his Ray-Bans before speaking.

"Let me tell you something, big shot. You got in while the getting was good. The rest of us? We get shit. We—I've been trying for so many years I can't count to get a gold shield and I've got about as much chance of getting one as whoever's in the trunk of that Rolls-Royce. But I'm not laying down. I'm still out here five nights a week chasin' the radio. Says 'Protect and Serve' on the car door and I'm doin' it, man. So don't give me any shit about dedication."

Bosch hesitated until he was sure Powers was done.

"Look, Powers, I didn't mean to give you shit. Okay? You want a cigarette?"

"I don't smoke."

"Okay, let's try this again." He waited a beat while Powers put the mirrors back on his eyes and seemed to calm down. "You always work alone?"

"I'm the Z car."

Bosch nodded. Zebra unit. An officer of many stripes, meaning he handled a variety of calls, usually trash calls, while cars with two officers aboard handled the hotshots—the prime, possibly dangerous, calls. Zebras worked patrol alone and often had free rein of the entire division. They were in the supervisory level between the sergeants and the grunts who were assigned to patrol geographic slices of the division known as basic car areas.

"How often you chase people outta here?"

"Once or twice a month. Can't say what happens on the other shifts or with the basic cars. But shit calls like this usually go to the Z car."

"You got any shakes?"

Shakes were three-by-five cards formally called field interview, or FI, cards. Cops filled them out when they stopped suspicious people but did not have enough evidence to arrest them, or when making such an arrest—in this case, for trespassing—would be a waste of time. The American Civil Liberties Union called such stops shakedowns and an abuse of police powers. The name stuck, even with the cops.

"I've got some, yeah, at the station."

"Good. We'd like to have a look if you could dig them out. Also, think you could ask the cops in the basic car if they've noticed the Rolls here the last few days?"

"Is this where I'm supposed to thank you for letting me have a part in the big bad investigation and ask you to put in a good word for me with the deputy chief of dicks?"

Bosch stared at him a few moments before answering.

"No, this is where I tell you to have the cards ready for us by nine tonight or I'll put in a word about that with the patrol skipper. And never mind the basic car people. We'll go ahead and talk to them ourselves. Don't want you to miss your ten-seven two shifts in a row, Powers."

Bosch started back toward the crime scene, moving slowly again and checking the other side of the gravel road. Twice he had to step off the gravel and into the brush to let the official police garage truck pass and then the Scientific Investigation Division van.

By the time he got to the clearing, he again had come up with nothing during his search and was sure the victim had been murdered in the trunk while the Rolls was parked in the clearing. He saw Art Donovan, the SID tech, and Roland Quatro, the photographer who came with him, starting their work. Bosch walked up to Rider.

"Anything?" she asked.

"No. You?"

"Nothing. I think the Rolls must've been driven in with our guy in the trunk. Then the doer gets out, opens the lid and pops him twice. He closes the trunk and walks out. Somebody picks him up out on Mulholland. Clean scene back here."

Bosch nodded.

"Him?"

"Well, I'm going with the percentages for now."

Bosch walked over to Donovan, who was bagging the wallet and airline ticket in a clear plastic evidence envelope.

"Art, we've got a problem."

"You're telling me. I was just thinking I can rig some tarps over light tripods, but I don't think you'll be able to block the view for everybody in the Bowl. Some of them are going to get a show all right. I guess it will make up for canceling the fireworks. That is, unless you're just planning to sit tight with it until after the show."

"Nah, we do that and some defense lawyer will tear us new assholes in court for delaying things. Every lawyer went to school on O. J., Art. You know that."

"So then what do we do?"

"Just do what you've got to do here with some speed and then we'll take the whole thing to the print shed. You know if anybody's in there right now?"

"No, it should be free," Donovan said slowly. "You mean you're talking about the whole thing? The body, too?"

Bosch nodded.

"Besides, you can do a better job with it in the shed, right?"

"Absolutely. But what about the ME? They've got to sign off on something like this, Harry."

"I'll deal with that. Before we put it on the flatbed, though, make sure you guys have got stills and video in case things shift during transit. Also, run a print card off the guy and give it to me."

"You got it."

While Donovan went to Quatro to explain the drill, Bosch huddled with Edgar and Rider.

"Okay, for now we're going to run with this one. If you had plans for the rest of the night, make your calls. It's going to be a long one. This is how I want to break it up."

He pointed up to the homes on the crestline.

"First, Kiz, I want you to go up there and do a house-to-house. You know the routine. See if anybody remembers seeing the Rolls or knows how long it's been here. Maybe somebody heard the shots. They might've echoed up the side of the hill. We want to try to pin down the time this happened. After that, I—you got a phone?"

"No. I have a rover in the car."

"No. I want to keep everything about this off the air."

"I can use a phone in somebody's house."

"Okay, call me when you're done or I'll page you when I'm done. Depending on how things shake out, you and I will either do next of kin or his office after that."

She nodded. Bosch turned to Edgar.

"Jerry, you go in and work from the station. You've got the paper on this one."

"She's the rookie."

"Well, then, next time don't show up in a T-shirt. You can't go knocking on doors dressed like that."

"I got a shirt in the car. I'll change."

"Next time. You're on the paper on this one. But before you start, I want you to put Aliso through the box and see what you get on him. He's got a DL issued last year, so they've got his thumbprint on file through DMV. See if you can get somebody from prints to compare it to the print card Art's getting for you right now. I want the ID confirmed as soon as possible."

"There ain't going to be anybody in prints t'night. Art's the guy on call. He should do this."

"Art's going to be tied up. See if you can shake somebody at home loose. We need the ID."

"I'll try but I can't prom—"

"Good. After that, I want you to call everybody who works a basic car in this area and see if anyone's seen the Rolls. Powers—the guy up at the road—is going to pull shake cards on the kids who hang out here. I want you to start running them down, too. After that you can start the paper going."

"Shit, with all this, I'll be lucky if I start typing before *next* Monday."

Bosch ignored his whining and appraised both his partners.

"I'll stay with the body. If I get tied up, Kiz, you go on to check out the office address and I'll handle next of kin. Okay, everybody know what's what?"

Rider and Edgar nodded. Bosch could tell Edgar was still annoyed about something.

"Kiz, you head out now."

She walked away and Bosch waited until she was out of earshot before speaking.

"Okay, Jerry, what's the problem?"

"I just want to know if that's how it's going to be on this team. Am I going to get the shit work while the princess skates?"

"No, Jerry, it's not going to be like that, and I think you know me well enough not to ask. What's the real problem?"

"I don't like your choices on this, Harry. We should be on the phone with Organized Crime right now. If anything looks like an OC case, this is it. I think you should call 'em, but I think 'cause you're fresh back on the table and been waiting for a case so long, you're not making the call. That's the problem."

Edgar held his hands out as if to indicate how obvious this was.

"You know, you've got nothing to prove here, Harry. And there's never going to be a shortage of bodies to come along. This is Hollywood, remember? I think we should just turn this one over and wait for the next one."

Bosch nodded.

"You may be right," he said. "You probably are. About all of it. But I'm the three. So we do it my way for now. I'm going to call Bullets and tell her what we've got, then I'm going to call OCID. But even if they roll out, we're going to keep a part of this. You know that. So let's do it good. Okay?"

Edgar nodded reluctantly.

"Look," Bosch said, "your objection is noted for the record, okay?"

"Sure, Harry."

Bosch saw the blue ME's van pull into the clearing then. The tech behind the wheel was Richard Matthews. It was a break. Matthews wasn't as territorial as some of the others, and Bosch figured he could convince him to go along with the plan to move the whole package to the print shed. Matthews would understand that it was the only choice.

"Stay in touch," Bosch said as Edgar walked off.

Edgar sullenly waved without looking back.

For the next few moments Bosch stood alone in the midst of the activities of the crime scene. He realized he truly reveled in his role. The start of a case always seemed to jazz him this way, and he knew how much he had missed it and craved it during the last year and a half.

Finally, he put his thoughts aside and walked toward the ME's van to talk to Matthews. There was a burst of applause from the Bowl as *Sheherazade* ended.

The print shed was a World War II Quonset hut that sat in the City Services equipment yard behind the police headquarters at Parker Center. It had no windows and a double-wide garage door. The interior was painted black and every crack or crevice where light might come in was taped over. There were thick black curtains that could be pulled closed after the garage door was shut. When they were pulled, the interior was as black as a loan shark's heart. The techs who worked there even referred to the place as "the cave."

While the Rolls was being unloaded from the OPG truck, Bosch took his briefcase to a workbench inside the shed and got the phone out. The Organized Crime Investigation Division was a secret society within the greater closed society of the department. Bosch knew very little about OCID and was acquainted with few detectives assigned to the unit. The OCID was a mysterious force, even to those within the department. Not many knew exactly what it did. And this, of course, bred suspicions and jealousies.

Most OCID detectives were known in Detective Services as bigfooters. They swooped down to take investigations away from detectives like Bosch, but they didn't often make cases in return. Bosch had seen many investigations disappear under their door with not many prosecutions of OC wise guys resulting. They were the only division in the department with a black budget—approved in closed session by the chief and a police commission that largely followed his lead. From there, the money disappeared into the dark, to pay for informants, investigations and high-tech equipment. Many of their cases disappeared in that netherworld as well.

Bosch asked the communications operator to connect his call to the OCID supervisor on call for the weekend. As he waited for the patch through, he thought again about the body in the trunk. Anthony Aliso—if that was who it was—had seen it coming and closed his eyes.

Bosch hoped it wouldn't be that way for himself. He didn't want to know.

"Hello," a voice said.

"Yes, this is Harry Bosch. I'm the D-three on a homicide call out in Hollywood. Who am I speaking with?"

"Dom Carbone. I've got the weekend call out. You going to spoil it?"

"Maybe." Bosch tried to think. The name was vaguely familiar but he could not place it. He was sure they had never worked together. "That's why I'm calling. You might want to take a look at this."

"Run it down for me."

"Sure. White male found in the trunk of his Silver Cloud with two in the back of the head. Probably twenty-twos."

"What else?"

"Car was on a fire road off Mulholland. Doesn't look like a straight robbery. At least, not a personal robbery. I got cards and cash in the wallet and a Presidential on his wrist. Diamonds at every hour on the hour."

"You're not telling me who the stiff is. Who's the stiff?"

"Nothing confirmed yet but—"

"Just give it to me."

Bosch had trouble not being able to put a face with the voice over the phone.

"It looks like the ID is going to be Anthony N. Aliso, forty-eight years old. Lives up in the hills. Looks like he has some kind of company with an office at one of the studios down on Melrose near Paramount. TNA Productions is the name of his outfit. I think it's over at Archway Studios. We'll know more in a little while."

He only got silence in return.

"Mean anything?"

"Anthony Aliso."

"Yeah, right."

"Anthony Aliso."

Carbone repeated the name slowly, as if it were a fine wine he was tasting before deciding whether to accept the bottle or spit it out. He was then quiet for another long moment.

"Nothing hits me right away, Bosch," he finally said. "I can make a couple calls. Where you going to be?"

"The print shed. He's here with us and I'll be here a while."

"What do you mean, you got the guy's body there in the shed?"

"It's a long story. When do you think you can get back to me?"

"As soon as I make the calls. You been over to his office?"

"Not yet. We'll get there sometime tonight."

Bosch gave him the number of his cellular phone, then closed it and put it in his coat pocket. For a moment he thought about Carbone's reaction to the victim's name. He finally decided he could not read anything into it.

After the Cloud was rolled into place in the shed and the doors shut, Donovan pulled the curtains closed. There was fluorescent lighting overhead which he left on while he got his equipment ready. Matthews, the coroner's tech, and his two assistants—the body movers—huddled over a workbench getting the tools they would need out of a case.

"Harry, I'm going to take my time with this, okay? First I'll laser the trunk with the guy in it. Then we take him out. Then we glue it and laser it again. Then we worry about the rest of it."

"Your show, man. Whatever time you need."

"I'll need your help with the wand when I shoot pictures. Roland had to go to shoot another scene."

Bosch nodded and watched as the SID tech screwed an orange filter onto a Nikon camera. He put the camera strap over his head and turned on the laser. It was a box about the size of a VCR with a cable attachment that led to a foot-long wand with a hand grip on it. From the end of the wand a strong orange beam was emitted.

Donovan opened a cabinet and took out several pairs of orange-tinted safety glasses which he handed to Bosch and the others. He put the last pair on himself. He gave Bosch a pair of latex gloves to put on as well.

"I'll do a quick run around the outside of the trunk and then open her up," Donovan said.

Just as Donovan moved to the switch box to cut off the overheads, the phone in Bosch's pocket buzzed. Donovan waited while Bosch answered. It was Carbone.

"Bosch, we're taking a pass."

Harry didn't say anything for a moment and neither did Carbone. Donovan hit the light switch and the room plunged into complete blackness.

"You're saying you don't have this guy," Bosch finally spoke into the dark.

"I checked around, made some calls. Nobody seems to know this guy. Nobody's working him. . . . Clean, as far as we know. . . . You said he was put in his trunk and capped twice, huh? . . . Bosch, you there?"

"Yeah, I'm here. Yeah, capped twice in the trunk."

"Trunk music."

"What?"

"It's a wise guy saying outta Chicago. You know, when they whack some poor slob they say, 'Oh, Tony? Don't worry about Tony. He's trunk music now. You won't see him no more.' But the thing is, Bosch, this doesn't seem to fit. We don't know this guy. People I talked to, they think maybe somebody's trying to make you think it's OC connected, know what I mean?"

Bosch watched as the laser beam cut through the blackness and bombarded the rear of the trunk with searing light. With the glasses on, the orange was filtered out and the light was a bright, intense white. Bosch was ten feet away from the Rolls, but he could see glowing patterns on the trunk lid and the bumper. This always reminded him of those National Geographic shows in which a submersible camera moved through the ocean's black depths, putting its light on sunken ships or aircraft. It was somehow eerie.

"Look, Carbone," he said, "you aren't even interested in coming out to take a look?"

"Not at this time. Of course, give me a call back if you come across anything, you know, that shows different than what I told you. And I'll do some more checking tomorrow. I got your number."

Bosch was secretly pleased that he wasn't going to get bigfooted by the OCID, but he was also surprised at the brush-off. The quickness with which Carbone had dismissed the case seemed unusual.

"Any other details you want to give me, Bosch?"

"We're just starting. But let me ask you, you ever hear of a hitter takes the vic's shoes with him? Also, he unties the body afterward."

"Takes his shoes . . . unties him. Uh, not offhand, no. Nobody specific. But like I said, I'll ask around in the morning and I'll put it on our box. Anything else cute about this one?"

Bosch didn't like what was happening. Carbone seemed too interested while saying he wasn't. He said Tony Aliso wasn't connected, yet he still wanted the details. Was he just trying to be helpful or was there something more to it?

"That's about all we got at the moment," Bosch said, deciding not to give up anything else for free. "Like I said, we're just getting going here."

"Okay, then, give me the morning and I'll do some more checking. I'll call if I come up with anything, okay?"

"Right."

"Check you later. But you know what I think you have there, Bosch? You've got a guy, he was probably making sandwiches with somebody's wife. Lotta times things look like pro hits that aren't, you know what I mean?"

"Yeah, I know what you mean. I'll talk to you later."

Bosch walked to the rear of the Rolls. Up close he could see the pattern swirls he had noticed in the laser light before appeared to be swipe marks made with a cloth. It looked like the whole car had been wiped down.

But when Donovan moved the wand over the bumper, the laser picked up a partial shoe print on the chrome.

"Did anybody—"

"No," Bosch said. "Nobody put their foot there."

"Okay, then. Hold the wand on the print."

Bosch did so while Donovan bent over and took several photos, bracketing the exposure settings to make sure he had at least one clear shot. It was the forward half of the foot. There was a circle pattern at the ball of the foot with lines extending from it like the rays of a sun. There was a cross-cut pattern through the arch and then the print was cut off by the edge of the bumper.

"Tennis shoe," Donovan said. "Maybe a work shoe."

After he photographed it, he moved the wand around the trunk again, but there was nothing but wipe marks.

"Okay," Donovan said. "Open it."

Using a penlight to guide his way, Bosch made it to the driver's door and bent in to pull the trunk release. Shortly afterward, the smell of death flooded the shed.

It looked to Bosch as though the body had not shifted during the

transport. But the victim took on a ghoulish look under the harsh examination of the laser, his face almost skeletal, like the monsters painted
in Day-Glo in fun-house hallways. The blood seemed blacker and the
bone chips in the jagged wound were luminescent in bright counter-
point.

On his clothes, small strands of hair and tiny threads glowed. Bosch
moved in with a pair of tweezers and a plastic vial like the kind made to
hold a stack of silver half dollars. He carefully picked these pieces of potential evidence off the clothing and collected them in the vial. It was
painstaking work and there was nothing much there. He knew this kind
of material could be found on anybody at anytime. It was common.

When he was done he said to Donovan, "The tail of the jacket. I
flipped it up to check for a wallet."

"Okay, pull it back down."

Bosch did so, and there on Aliso's hip was another footprint. It
matched the footprint on the bumper but was more complete. On the
heel was another circle pattern with off-shooting lines. In the lower arch
was what looked like a brand name but it was unreadable.

Regardless of whether they could identify the shoe, Bosch knew it
was a good find. It meant that a careful killer had made a mistake. At least
one. If nothing else, it gave rise to the hope that there might be other
mistakes, that they might eventually lead him to the killer.

"Take the wand."

Bosch did so and Donovan did his thing with the camera again.

"I'm just shooting this to document it, but we'll take the jacket off
before the body goes," he said.

Next Donovan moved the laser up around the inside of the trunk lid.
Here the laser illuminated numerous fingerprints, mostly thumbprints,
where a hand would have been placed to prop the lid open while loading
things in or out. Many of the prints overlapped each other, a sign that
they were old, and Bosch knew right away they probably belonged to the
victim himself.

"I'll shoot these, but don't count on anything," Donovan said.

"I know."

When he was done, Donovan put the wand and the camera on top of
the laser box and said, "Okay, why don't we take this fellow out of there,
lay 'im out and scan 'im real quick before he's outta here?"

Without waiting for an answer, he flipped the fluorescents back on and everybody put their hands to their eyes as the harsh light blinded them. A few moments later the body movers and Matthews went to the trunk and started transferring the corpse to a black plastic body bag they had unfolded on a gurney.

"This guy is loose," Matthews said as they put the corpse down.

"Yeah," Bosch said. "What do you think?"

"Forty-two to forty-eight. But let me do some stuff and see what we've got."

But first Donovan put out the lights again and moved the wand over the body, from the head down. The tear pools in the eye sockets glowed white in the light. There were a few hairs and fibers on the dead man's face and Bosch dutifully collected them. There was also a slight abrasion high on the right cheekbone, which had been hidden when the body was lying on its right side in the trunk.

"He could've been hit or it mighta been from being shoved into the trunk," Donovan said.

As the beam moved down over the chest, Donovan got excited.

"Well lookee here."

Glowing in the laser light were what looked like a complete hand-print on the right shoulder of the leather jacket and two smudged thumbprints, one on each of the lapels. Donovan bent down very close to look.

"This is treated leather, it doesn't absorb the acids in the prints. We caught a major break here, Harry. This guy wears anything else and for-get it. The hand is excellent. These thumbs didn't take . . . I think we can raise them up with some glue. Harry, bend one of the lapels over."

Bosch reached for the left lapel and carefully turned the cloth over. There on the inside of the crease were four more fingerprints. He turned the right lapel and saw four more there. It appeared that someone had grabbed Tony Aliso by the lapels.

Donovan whistled.

"This looks like two different people. Look at the size of the thumbs on the lapel and the hand on the shoulder. I'd say the hand is smaller, Harry. Maybe a woman. I don't know. But the hands that grabbed this guy by the lapels were big."

Donovan got scissors from a nearby toolbox and carefully cut the sport coat off the body. Bosch then held it as Donovan went over it with the laser wand. Nothing else came up besides the shoe print and the fingerprints they had already sighted. Bosch carefully hung the jacket over a chair at the counter and came back to the body. Donovan was moving the laser over the lower extremities.

"What else?" Donovan said to no one except maybe the body. "Come on now, tell us a story."

There were more fibers and some old stains on the pants. Nothing that stood out as possibly significant until they reached the cuffs. Bosch pulled open the cuff on the right leg and in the crease was a large buildup of dust and fibers. Also, five tiny pieces of gold glitter glowed in the laser beam. Bosch carefully tweezered these into a separate plastic vial. From the left cuff, he recovered two more similar pieces.

"What is it?" he asked.

"Got me. Looks like glitter or something."

Donovan moved the wand over the bare feet. They were clean, which indicated to Bosch that the victim's shoes had probably been removed after he was forced into the trunk of the Rolls.

"Okay, that's it," Donovan said.

The lights came back on and Matthews went to work with the corpse, rotating joints, opening the shirt to look at the lividity level of the blood, opening the eyes and swiveling the head. Donovan paced around, waiting for the coroner's tech to finish so he could continue the laser show. He walked over to Bosch.

"Harry, you want the swag on this?"

"Swag?"

"Scientific wild ass guess."

"Yeah," Bosch said, amused. "Give me the swag."

"Well, I think somebody gets the drop on this guy. Ties him up, dumps him in the trunk and drives him to that fire road. He's still alive, okay? Then our doer gets out, opens the trunk, puts his foot on the bumper ready to do the job but can't get all the way in there to put the muzzle against the bone, you know? That was important to him. To do the job right. So he sticks his big foot on this poor guy's hip, leans further in and bam, bam, out go the headlights. What do you think?"

Bosch nodded.

"I think you are on to something."

He had already been thinking along the same lines but was past those deductions to the problem.

"Then how does he get back?" he asked.

"Back to where?"

"If this guy was in the trunk the whole time, then the doer drove the Rolls. If he drove there in the Rolls, then how's he get back to wherever he intercepted Tony?"

"The other one," Donovan said. "We've got two different prints on the jacket. Somebody could've followed behind the Rolls. The woman. The one who put her hand on the vic's shoulder."

Bosch nodded. He had already been puzzling with this but didn't like something about the scenario Donovan had woven. He wasn't sure what it was.

"Okay, Bosch," Matthews interrupted. "You want to hear this tonight or you want to wait for the report?"

"T'night," Bosch said.

"Okay then, listen up. Lividity was fixed and unchanged. The body was never moved once the heart stopped pumping." He referred to a clipboard. "Let's see, what else? We've got ninety percent rigor mortis resolution, cornea clouding and we've got skin slippage. I think you take all of that and it's forty-eight hours, maybe a couple hours less. Let us know if you come up with any markers and we might do better."

"Will do," Bosch said.

By markers he knew Matthews meant that if he traced the victim's last day and found out what he had eaten last and when, the ME could get a better fix on time of death by studying the digestion of food in the stomach.

"He's all yours," Bosch said to Matthews. "Any idea on the post?"

"You caught the tail end of a holiday weekend. That's bad luck for you. Last I heard, we've run on twenty-seven homicides in the county so far. We probably won't cut this one until Wednesday, if you're lucky. Don't call us, we'll call you."

"Yeah, I've heard that one before."

But the delay didn't really bother Bosch this time. In cases like this, the autopsy usually held few surprises. It was pretty clear how the victim died. The mystery was why and by whom.

Matthews and his assistants wheeled the corpse out, leaving Bosch and Donovan alone with the Rolls. Donovan stared at the car silently, contemplating it the way a matador looks at the bull he is going to fight.

"We're going to get her secrets, Harry."

Bosch's phone buzzed then and he fumbled getting it out of his jacket and open. It was Edgar.

"We got the ID, Harry. It is Aliso."

"You got this off the prints?"

"Yeah. Mossler's got a fax at home. I sent him everything and he eyeballed it."

Mossler was one of the SID's latent-print men.

"This is with the DL thumbprint?"

"Right. Also, I pulled a full set of Tony's prints from an old pop for soliciting. Mossler had those to look at, too. It's Aliso."

"Okay, good work. What else you got?"

"Like I said, I ran this guy. He's pretty clean. Just the soliciting arrest back in seventy-five. Few other things, though. His name comes up as a victim on a burglary up at his house in March. And on the civil indexes I've got a few civil actions against the guy. Breach-of-contract stuff, it looks like. A trail of broken promises and pissed-off people, Harry, good motive stuff."

"What were the cases about?"

"That's all I've got for now, just the abstracts in the civil index. I'll have to pull the actual cases when I can get into the courthouse."

"Okay. Did you check Missing Persons?"

"Yeah, I did. He was never reported. You got anything there?"

"Maybe. We might've gotten lucky. Looks like we are going to get some prints off the body. Two sets."

"Off the body? That's very cool."

"Off the leather jacket."

Bosch could tell Edgar was excited. Both detectives knew that if the prints were not those of a suspect, then they would surely be fresh

enough to belong to people who had seen the victim in the time shortly
before his death.

"You call OCID?"

Bosch was waiting for him to ask.

"Yeah. They're taking a pass."

"What?"

"That's what they said. At least for now. Until we find something they
might be interested in."

Bosch wondered if Edgar even believed he had made the call.

"That doesn't figure, Harry."

"Yeah, well, all we can do is our job. You hear from Kiz?"

"Not yet. Who'd you talk to over at Organized Crime?"

"Guy named Carbone. He was on call."

"Never heard of him."

"Well, neither had I. I gotta go, Jerry. Let me know what you know."

As soon as Bosch hung up, the door to the shed opened and in stepped
Lieutenant Grace Billets. She quickly scanned the room and saw Donovan working in the car. She asked Bosch to step outside and that was
when he knew she was unhappy.

She closed the door after he stepped out. She was in her forties and
had as many years on the job as Bosch, give or take a couple, but they had
never worked together before her assignment as his commanding officer.
She was of medium build, with reddish-brown hair she kept short. She
wore no makeup. She was dressed entirely in black—jeans, T-shirt and
blazer. She also wore black cowboy boots. Her only concession to femi-
ninity was the pair of thin gold hoop earrings. Her manner was no concession to anything.

"What's going on, Harry? You moved the body *in* the car?"

"Had to. It was either that or dump it out of the car with about ten
thousand people watching us instead of the fireworks they were supposed
to see."

Bosch explained the situation in detail and Billets listened silently.
When he was done, she nodded.

"I'm sorry," she said. "I didn't know the details. It looks like it was
your only choice."

Bosch liked that about her. She wasn't always right and she was willing to admit it.

"Thanks, Lieutenant."

"So what do we have?"

When Bosch and Billets stepped back into the shed, Donovan was at one of the worktables working with the leather jacket. He had hung it on a wire inside an empty one-hundred-gallon aquarium and then dropped in a Hard Evidence packet. The packet, when broken open, emitted cyano-acrylate fumes which would attach to the amino acids and oils of finger-prints and crystallize, thereby raising the ridges and whorls and making them more visible and photo-ready.

"How's it look?" Bosch asked.

"Real good. We're going to get something off this. Howdy, Lieu-tenant."

"Hello there," Billets said.

Bosch could tell she didn't remember Donovan's name.

"Listen, Art," he said, "when you get those together, get them over to the print lab and then call me or Edgar and tell us. We'll get somebody over there to do them code three."

Code three was a patrol response code meaning lights and siren au-thorized. Bosch needed the prints to be handled quickly. So far, they were the best lead.

"Will do, Harry."

"What about the Rolls? Can I get in it yet?"

"Well, I'm not quite through with it. You can go in. Just be careful."

Bosch began searching the interior of the car, checking the door and seat pockets first and finding nothing. He checked the ashtray and found it empty, not even an ash. He made a mental note that the victim appar-ently didn't smoke.

Billets stood nearby, watching but not helping. She had risen to detective bureau commander primarily on the success of her skills as an administrator, not as an investigator. She knew when to watch and not get in the way.

Bosch checked under the seats and found nothing of interest. He opened the glove compartment last and a small square piece of paper fell out. It was a receipt for an airport valet company. Holding it by the cor-ner, Bosch walked it over to the workbench and told Donovan to check it for prints when he got the chance.

He went back to the glove compartment and found the lease agreement and registration of the car, its service records and a small tool kit with a flashlight. There was also a half-used tube of Preparation H, a hemorrhoid medication. It seemed like an odd place to keep it, but Bosch guessed that maybe Aliso kept the tube handy for long drives.

He bagged all of the items from the compartment separately and while doing so noticed an extra battery in the tool kit. It struck him as odd because the flashlight obviously took two batteries. Having one extra would not do much good.

He pressed the flashlight's on/off switch. It was dead. He unscrewed the cap and one battery slid out. Looking into the barrel, Bosch saw a plastic bag. He used a pen to reach in and pull the bag out. It contained about two dozen brown capsules.

Billets stepped closer.

"Poppers," Bosch said. "Amyl nitrate. Supposed to help you get it up and keep it there. You know, improve your orgasm."

He suddenly felt the need to explain his knowledge was not based on personal experience.

"It's come up in other cases before."

She nodded. Donovan walked over with the valet ticket in a clear plastic envelope.

"A couple smudges. Nothing we can work with."

Bosch took it back. He then carried the various plastic evidence bags he had to the counter.

"Art, I'm taking the receipt, the poppers and the car's service records, okay?"

"You got it."

"I'll leave you the plane ticket and the wallet. You are also going to put some speed on the prints from the jacket and what else? Oh yeah, those sparkles. What do you think?"

"Hopefully tomorrow. The rest of the fiber stuff I'll take a look at, but it's probably going to be exclusionary."

That meant most of the material they had collected would sit in storage after a quick examination by Donovan, and come into play only if a suspect was identified. It would then be used either to tie that suspect to the crime scene or to exclude him.

Bosch took a large envelope off a shelf over the counter, put all the pieces of evidence he was taking into it, then put it in his briefcase and snapped it closed. He headed for the curtain with Billets.

"Good to see you again, Art," she said.

"Likewise, Lieutenant."

"You want me to call OPG to come get the car?" Bosch asked.

"Nah, I'm going to be here a while," Donovan said. "Gotta use the vac and I might think of something else to do. I'll take care of it, Harry."

"Okay, man, later."

Bosch and Billets stepped through the curtain and then through the door. Outside he lit a cigarette and looked up at the dark, starless sky. Billets lit one of her own.

"Where to?" she asked.

"Next of kin. You want to come? It's always a fun thing."

She smiled at his sarcasm.

"No, I think I'll pass on that. But before you leave, what's your gut on this, Harry? I mean, OCID passing without taking a look, that kind of bothers me."

"Me, too." He took a long drag and exhaled. "My gut is that this one's going to be tough. Unless something good comes out of those prints. That's our only real break so far."

"Well, tell your people that I want everybody in at eight for a round-table on what we've got so far."

"Let's make it nine, Lieutenant. I think by then we should have something back from Donovan on the prints."

"Okay, nine then. I'll see you then, Harry. And from now on, when we're talking like this, you know, informally, call me Grace."

"Sure, Grace. Have a nice night."

She expelled her smoke in a short burst that sounded like the start of a laugh.

"You mean, what's left of it."

On the way up to Mulholland Drive and Hidden Highlands Bosch paged Rider and she called back from one of the houses she was visiting. She said it was the last of the houses overlooking the clearing where the Rolls was parked. She told him the best she could come up with was a resident who remembered seeing the white Rolls-Royce from the back deck of his home on Saturday morning about ten. The same resident also believed the car was not there on Friday evening when he was out on the deck to watch the sunset.

"That fits with the time frame the ME's looking at and the plane ticket. I think we're zeroing in on Friday night, sometime after he got in from Vegas. Probably on his way home from the airport. Nobody heard any shots?"

"Not that I've found. There's two houses where I got no answer. I was going to go back and try them now."

"Maybe you can catch them tomorrow. I'm heading up to Hidden Highlands. I think you should go with me."

They made arrangements to meet outside the entrance to the development where Aliso had lived, and Bosch closed the phone. He wanted Kiz along when he told Aliso's next of kin he was dead because it would be good for her to learn the grim routine and because the percentages called for whoever that next of kin was to be considered a possible suspect. It was always good to have a witness with you when you first spoke to the person who later could become your quarry.

Bosch looked at his watch. It was nearly ten. Taking care of the notification meant they probably wouldn't be getting to the victim's office until midnight. He called the communications center and gave the operator the address on Melrose and had her look it up in the cross directory. It came back to Archway Pictures, as Bosch had guessed. He knew they had caught a bit of a break. Archway was a midsize studio that largely rented offices and production facilities to independent filmmakers. As far as Bosch knew, it hadn't made its own films since the 1960s. The break was that he knew someone in security over there. Chuckie Meachum was a former Robbery-Homicide bull who had retired a few years earlier and taken a job as assistant director of security at Archway. He would be useful in smoothing their way in. Bosch considered calling ahead and arranging for Chuckie Meachum to meet them at the studio but decided against it. He decided he didn't want anyone to know he was coming until he got there.

He got to Hidden Highlands fifteen minutes later. Rider's car was parked on the shoulder off Mulholland. Bosch pulled up and she got in his car. Then he pulled into the entrance lane next to the gatehouse. It was a small brick structure with a single guard inside. Hidden Highlands was maybe a little richer but not that different from many of the other small, wealthy and scared enclaves nestled in the hills and valleys around Los Angeles. Walls and gates, guardhouses and private security forces were the secret ingredients of the so-called melting pot of southern California.

A guard in a blue uniform stepped out of the gatehouse carrying a clipboard and Bosch had his badge wallet out and open. The guard was a tall, thin man with a worn, gray face. Bosch didn't recognize him, though he had heard in the station that most of the guards working here were off-duty uniforms from Hollywood Division. In the past he had seen postings for part-time jobs on the bulletin board outside the roll call room.

The guard gave Bosch a once-over in a laconic manner, avoiding a look at the badge on purpose.

"Kenahepyou?" he finally said.

"I need to go to the home of Anthony Aliso."

He gave the address on Hillcrest that had been on the victim's driver's license.

"Your names?"

"Detective Harry Bosch, LAPD. Says it right here. This is Detective Kizmin Rider."

He proffered the badge wallet, but it was still ignored. The guard was writing on his clipboard. Bosch saw his name tag said Nash. He also saw that the tin badge said CAPTAIN across it.

"They expecting you at the Aliso place?"

"I don't think so. It's police business."

"Okay, but I've got to call ahead. It's the development's rules, you know."

"I prefer you didn't do that, Captain Nash."

Bosch hoped his use of the security guard's title would win him over. Nash thought a moment.

"Tell you what," he said. "You go on ahead and I'll come up with a reason for delaying making the call a few minutes. I'll just say I'm up here by myself t'night and I got kind of busy, if there's a complaint."

He stepped back and reached in the open door of the gatehouse. He pressed a button on the inside wall and the crossguard went up.

"Thanks, Captain. You work out of Hollywood?"

Bosch knew he didn't. He could tell Nash wasn't even a cop. He didn't have the cold eyes of a cop. But Bosch was playing to him, just in case he became a useful source of information later on.

"Nah," Nash said. "I'm full-time. That's why they made me captain of the watch. Everybody else is part-time out of Hollywood or West Hollywood sheriffs. I run the schedule."

"Then how'd you get stuck on the night shift on Sunday night?"

"Everybody can use some OT now and then."

Bosch nodded.

"You're right about that. Hillcrest, where's that?"

"Oh, yeah, forgot. Take your second left. That's Hillcrest. The Aliso place is about the sixth house on the right. Nice view of the city from the pool."

"Did you know him?" Rider asked, leaning down so she could see Nash through Bosch's window.

"Aliso?" Nash said, bending farther to look in at her. He thought a moment. "Not really. Just like I know people when they come through here. I'm just the same to them as the pool man, I guess. I notice you asked *did* I know him. Am I not going to get the chance?"

"Smart man, Mr. Nash," Rider said.

She straightened up, finished with the conversation. Bosch nodded his thanks and drove through the gate to Hillcrest. As he passed the broad, manicured lawns surrounding houses the size of apartment buildings, he filled Rider in on what he had learned at the print shed and from Edgar. He also admired the properties they were passing. Many of them were surrounded by walls or tall hedges that looked as though they were trimmed into sharp edges every morning. Walls within walls, Bosch thought. He wondered what the owners did with all of their space besides fearfully guard it.

It took them five minutes to find the Aliso house on a cul-de-sac at the top of the hill. He passed through the open gates of an estate with a Tudor-style mansion set behind a circular driveway made of gray paver stones. Bosch got out with his briefcase and looked up at the place. It was intimidating in its size, but its style was not much to speak of. He wouldn't want it, even if he had the money.

After getting to the door and pushing the doorbell button, he looked at Rider.

"You ever done this before?"

"No. But I grew up in South L.A. A lot of drive-bys. I was around when people got the news."

Bosch nodded.

"Not to belittle that experience, but this is different. What is important is not what you hear said, it's what you observe."

Bosch pushed the lighted button again. He could hear the bell sound from inside the house. He looked at Rider and could tell she was about to ask a question, when the door was opened by a woman.

"Mrs. Aliso?" Bosch asked.

"Yes?"

"Mrs. Aliso, I'm Detective Harry Bosch with the LAPD. This is my partner, Detective Kizmin Rider. We need to speak with you concerning your husband."

He held out his badge wallet and she took it from his hand. Usually, they didn't do that. Usually, they recoiled from it or looked at it like it was some strange and fascinating object not to be touched.

"I don't under—"

She stopped when the sound of a phone ringing began somewhere behind her in the big house.

"Would you excuse me a moment? I have to—"

"That's probably Nash at the gate. He said he had to call ahead, but there was a lineup of cars behind us. I guess we beat him here. We need to come in to talk to you, ma'am."

She stepped back in and opened the door wide for him. She looked about five to ten years younger than her husband had been. She was maybe forty, attractive, with dark straight hair and a trim build. She wore a lot of makeup on a face Bosch guessed had been sculpted at times by the surgeon's knife. Still, through the makeup she looked tired, worn. He could see her face was flushed pink, as though she might have been drinking. She wore a light blue dress that showed off her legs. They were tan and the muscles still taut. Bosch could see she had been considered very beautiful at one time but was sliding into that stage when a woman believes her beauty may be leaving—even if it isn't. Maybe that was why she had all the makeup on, Bosch guessed. Or maybe it was because she was still expecting her husband to show up.

Bosch closed the door after they entered and they followed the woman into a large living room with an incongruous mix of modern prints on the walls and French antiques on the thick white carpet. The phone was still ringing. She told Bosch and Rider to sit down and then walked through the living room into another hallway, which she crossed to what looked like a den. He heard her answer the phone, tell Nash that the delay was all right and hang up.

She came back into the living room then and sat on a couch with a muted flower print. Bosch and Rider took nearby chairs with a matching pattern. Bosch took a quick look around and saw no photographs in frames. Only the artwork. It was always one of the first things he looked for when he had to quickly judge a relationship.

"I'm sorry," he said. "I didn't get your name."

"Veronica Aliso. What about my husband, Detective? Is he hurt?"

Bosch leaned forward in his chair. No matter how many times he did this, he never got used to it and he was never sure he was doing it the right way.

"Mrs. Aliso . . . I am very sorry, but your husband is dead. He was the victim of a homicide. I am sorry to have to tell you this."

He watched her closely and she said nothing at first. She instinctively crossed her arms in front of her and brought her face down in a pained grimace. There were no tears. Not yet. In his experience, Bosch had seen them come either right away—as soon as they opened the door and saw him and knew—or much later, when it sank in that the nightmare was reality.

"I don't . . . How did this happen?" she asked, her eyes staring down at the floor.

"He was found in his car. He'd been shot."

"In Las Vegas?"

"No. Here. Not far. It looks like he was coming home from the airport when . . . when he was somehow stopped by somebody. We're not sure yet. His car was found off Mulholland Drive. Down by the Bowl."

He watched her a little more. She still had not looked up. Bosch felt a sense of guilt pass over him. Guilt because he was not watching this woman with sympathy. He had been in this place too many times for that. Instead, he watched her with an eye for false mannerisms. In these situations his suspicion outweighed his compassion. It had to.

"Can I get you anything, Mrs. Aliso?" Rider asked. "Water? Do you have coffee? Do you want something stronger?"

"No. I'm fine. Thank you. It's just a terrible shock."

"Do you have any children in the house?" Rider asked.

"No, we . . . no children. Do you know what happened? Was he robbed?"

"That's what we're trying to find out," Bosch said.

"Of course. . . . Can you tell me, was there much pain?"

"No, there was no pain," Bosch said.

He thought of the tears welled in Tony Aliso's eyes. He decided not to tell her about that.

"It must be hard, your job," she said. "Telling people this sort of thing."

He nodded and looked away. For a moment he thought of the old squad room joke about the easiest way to do next-of-kin notification. When Mrs. Brown opens the door, you say, "Are you the widow Brown?"

He looked back at the widow Aliso.

"Why did you ask if it happened in Las Vegas?"

"Because that was where he was."

"How long was he supposed to be there?"

"I don't know. He never scheduled it with a return. He always bought open-ended tickets so he could come back when he wanted to. He always said he'd be back when his luck changed. For the worse."

"We have reason to believe he came back to Los Angeles on Friday night. His car wasn't found until this evening. That's two days, Mrs. Aliso. Did you try to call him in Las Vegas during that time?"

"No. We usually didn't speak when he was over there."

"And how often was it that he went?"

"Once or twice a month."

"For how long each time?"

"Anywhere from two days to once he spent a week. Like I said, it all depended on how he was doing."

"And you never called him there?" Rider asked.

"Rarely. Not at all this time."

"Was it business or pleasure that took him there?" Bosch asked.

"He always told me it was both. He said he had investors to see. But it was an addiction. That's what I believed. He loved to gamble and could afford to do it. So he went."

Bosch nodded but didn't know why.

"This last time, when did he go?"

"He went Thursday. After leaving the studio."

"You saw him last then . . . ?"

"Thursday morning. Before he went to the studio. He left for the airport from there. It's closer."

"And you had no idea when to expect him back."

He said it as a statement. It was out there for her to challenge if she wanted to.

"To be honest, I was just beginning to wonder tonight. It usually doesn't take long for that place to separate a man from his money. I thought it was a little long, yes. But I didn't try to track him down. And then you came."

"What did he like to play over there?"

"Everything. But poker the most. It was the only game where you weren't playing against the house. The house took a cut, but you were playing against the other players. That's how he explained it to me once. Only he called the other players schmucks from Iowa."

"Was he always alone over there, Mrs. Aliso?"

Bosch looked down at his notebook and acted as if he was writing something important and that her answer wasn't. He knew it was cowardly.

"I wouldn't know."

"Did you ever go with him at all?"

"I don't like to gamble. I don't like that city. That city is a horrible place. They can dress it up all they want, it's still a city of vices and whores. Not just the sexual kind."

Bosch studied the cool anger in her dark eyes.

"You didn't answer the question, Mrs. Aliso," Rider said.

"What question?"

"Did you ever go to Las Vegas with him?"

"At first, yes. But I found it boring. I haven't been in years."

"Was your husband in any kind of serious debt?" Bosch asked.

"I don't know. If he was, he didn't tell me. You can call me Veronica."

"You never asked if he was getting into trouble?" Rider asked.

"I just assumed that he would tell me if he was."

She turned the hard dark eyes on Rider now, and Bosch felt a weight lift off him. Veronica Aliso was challenging them to disagree.

"I know this probably makes me some kind of a suspect, but I don't care," she said. "You have your job to do. It must be obvious to you that my husband and I . . . let's just say we coexisted here. So as to your questions about Nevada, I couldn't tell you whether he was a million up or a million down. Who knows, he could've beaten the odds. But I think he would have bragged about it if he had."

Bosch nodded and thought about the body in the trunk. It didn't seem like that of a man who had beaten any odds.

"Where did he stay in Las Vegas, Mrs. Aliso?"

"Always at the Mirage. I do know that. You see, not all of the casinos have poker tables. The Mirage has a classy one. He always said that if I needed to call, call there. Ask for the poker pit if there is no answer in the room."

Bosch took a few moments to write this down. He found that often silence was the best way to get people to talk and reveal themselves. He hoped Rider realized that he was leaving holes of silence in the interview on purpose.

"You asked if he went there alone."

"Yes?"

"Detectives, in the course of your investigation I believe you will undoubtedly learn that my husband was a philanderer. I ask only one thing of you, please do your best to keep that information from me. I simply don't want to know."

Bosch nodded and was silent a moment while he composed his thoughts. What kind of woman wouldn't want to know? he wondered. Maybe one who already did. He looked back at her and their eyes connected again.

"Aside from gambling, was your husband in any other kind of trouble as far as you know?" he asked. "Work-related, financial?"

"As far as I know he wasn't. But he kept the finances. I could not tell you what our situation is at the moment. When I needed money I asked him, and he always said cash a check and tell him the amount. I have a separate account for household expenses."

Without looking up from the notebook, Bosch said, "Just a few more and we'll leave you alone for now. Did your husband have any enemies that you know of? Anybody who would want to harm him?"

"He worked in Hollywood. Backstabbing is considered an art form there. Anthony was as skilled at it as anyone else who has been in the industry twenty-five years. Obviously that means there could always be people who were unhappy with him. But who would do this, I don't know."

"The car . . . the Rolls-Royce is leased to a production company over at Archway Studios. How long had he worked there?"

"His office was there, but he didn't work for Archway per se. TNA Productions is his . . . was his own company. He simply rented an office and a parking spot on the Archway lot. But he had about as much to do with Archway as you do."

"Tell us about his production company," Rider said. "Did he make films?"

"In a manner of speaking. You could say he started big and ended small. About twenty years ago he produced his first film. *The Art of the Cape*. If you saw it, you were one of the few. Bullfight movies are not popular. But it was critically acclaimed, played the film festival circuit and then the art houses and it was a good start for him."

She said that Aliso had managed to make a couple more films for general release. But after that his production and moral values steadily declined, until he was producing a procession of exploitative dreck.

"These films, if you want to call them that, are notable only for the number of exposed breasts in them," she said. "In the business, it's called straight-to-video stock. In addition to that Tony was quite successful in literary arbitrage."

"What is that?"

"He was a speculator. Mostly scripts, but he did manuscripts, books on occasion."

"And how would he speculate on them?"

"He'd buy them. Wrap up the rights. Then when they became valuable or the author became hot, he'd go to market with them. Do you know who Michael St. John is?"

The name sounded familiar but Bosch could not place it. He shook his head. Rider did the same.

"He's one of the screenwriters of the moment. He'll be directing studio features within a year or so. He's the flavor-of-the-month, so to speak."

"Okay."

"Well, eight years ago when he was in the USC film school and was hungry and was trying to find an agent and trying to catch the attention of the studios, my husband was one of the vultures who circled overhead. You see, my husband's films were so low-budget that he'd get students to shoot them, direct them, write them. So he knew the schools and he knew talent. Michael St. John was one he knew had talent. Once when he was desperate, he sold Anthony the rights to three of his student screenplays for two thousand dollars. Now, anything with St. John's name on it goes for at least six figures."

"What about these writers, how do they take this?"

"Not well. St. John was trying to buy his scripts back."

"You think he could have harmed your husband?"

"No. You asked me what he did and I told you. If you are asking who would kill him, I don't know."

Bosch jotted a couple of notes down.

"You mentioned that he said that he saw investors when he went to Las Vegas," Rider said.

"Yes."

"Can you tell us who they were?"

"Schmucks from Iowa, I would assume. People he would meet and persuade to invest in a movie. You'd be surprised how many people jump at a chance to be part of a Hollywood movie. And Tony was a good salesman. He could make a two-million budget flick sound like the sequel to *Gone with the Wind*. He convinced me."

"How so?"

"He talked me into being in one of his movies once. That's how I met him. Made it sound like I was going to be the new Jane Fonda. You know, sexy but smart. It was a studio picture. Only the director was a coke addict and the writer couldn't write and the movie was so bad it was never released. That was it for my career and Tony never made a studio picture again. He spent the rest of his life making video garbage."

Looking around the tall-ceilinged room at the paintings and furniture, Bosch said, "Doesn't look like he did too badly at it."

"No, he didn't," she responded. "I guess we have those people from Iowa to thank for that."

Her bitterness was stifling. Bosch looked down at his notebook just so he could avert his eyes from her.

"All this talk," she said then. "I need some water. Do either of you want something?"

"Water would be fine," Bosch said. "We're not going to be much longer."

"Detective Rider?"

"I'm fine, thank you."

"I'll be right back."

While she was gone Bosch stood up and looked around the living room in a manner that suggested he wasn't really interested. He said nothing to Rider. He was standing near a side table looking at a carved glass figurine of a nude woman when Veronica Aliso came back in with two glasses of ice water.

"I just want to ask you a few more questions about this past week," Bosch said.

"Fine."

He sipped from his glass and remained standing.

"What would your husband have taken with him to Las Vegas as far as luggage went?"

"Just his overnighter."

"What did it look like?"

"It was a hanging bag that, you know, folded over. It was green with brown leather trim and straps. He had a name tag on it."

"Did he take a briefcase or any work with him?"

"Yes, his briefcase. It was one of those aluminum shell kind. You know, they are lightweight but impossible to break into or something. Is the luggage missing?"

"We're not sure. Do you know where he kept the key to the briefcase?"

"On his key chain. With the car keys."

There had been no car keys in the Rolls or on Aliso's body. Bosch realized that the reason they might have been taken was to open the briefcase. He put the glass down next to the figurine and looked at it again.

He then began writing the descriptions of the briefcase and hanging bag in his notebook.

"Did your husband wear a wedding ring?"

"No. He did wear quite an expensive watch, though. It was a Rolex. I gave it to him."

"The watch was not taken."

"Oh."

Bosch looked up from his notebook.

"Do you remember what your husband was wearing on Thursday morning? When you last saw him?"

"Um, just clothes . . . uh, he had on his white pants and a blue shirt and his sport coat."

"His black leather sport coat?"

"Yes."

"Mrs. Aliso, do you remember if you hugged him or kissed him good-bye?"

This seemed to fluster her, and Bosch immediately regretted the way he had phrased the question.

"I'm sorry. What I meant was that we found some fingerprints on the jacket. On the shoulder. And if you might have touched him there on the day he left, it could explain this piece of evidence."

She was quiet a moment and Bosch thought that she was finally going to begin to cry. But instead, she said, "I might have but I don't remember. . . . I don't think I did."

Bosch opened his briefcase and looked for a print screen. He found one in one of the pockets. It looked like a photo slide but the center was a double-sided screen with ink between the screens. A thumb could be pressed on the A side and a fingerprint would be imprinted on a card held against the B side.

"I want to take your thumbprint so we can compare it to the print taken off the jacket. If you did not touch him there, then it might be a good lead for us."

She stepped over to him and he pressed her right thumb down on the print screen. When he was done she looked at her thumb.

"No ink."

"Yes, that's nice. No mess. We just started using these a few years ago."

"The print on the jacket, did it belong to a woman?"

He looked at her and held her eyes for a moment.

"We won't know for sure until we get a match."

As he put the card and the print screen back in the briefcase, he noticed the evidence bag containing the poppers. He took it out and held it up for her to look at.

"Do you know what these are?"

She narrowed her eyes and shook her head no.

"Amyl nitrate poppers. Some people use them to enhance sexual performance and satisfaction. Do you know if your husband ever used these?"

"You found them with him?"

"Mrs. Aliso, I'd rather that you'd just answer my questions. I know this is difficult, but there are some things I can't tell you yet. I will when I can. I promise."

"No, he didn't use them . . . with me."

"I'm sorry that I have to be so personal, but we want to catch the person who did this. We both want that. Now, your husband was about ten or twelve years older than you." He was being charitable here. "Did he have problems performing sexually? Is there any chance he might have been using poppers without your knowledge?"

She turned to go back to her chair. When she was seated again she said, "I wouldn't know."

Now Bosch narrowed his eyes. What was she trying to say? His silence worked. She answered before he had to ask, but as she spoke she looked directly at Rider, the unspoken message being that as a woman Rider might sympathize.

"Detective, I haven't had . . . I guess, sexual relations is the way it is said in these matters. My husband and I . . . not in almost two years."

Bosch nodded and looked down at his notebook. The page was blank but he couldn't bring himself to write this latest piece of information down with her watching them. He folded the notebook closed and put it away.

"You want to ask me why, don't you?"

He just looked at her and she answered with a measure of defiance in her face and voice.

"He had lost interest."

"Are you sure?"

"He told me that to my face."

Bosch nodded.

"Mrs. Aliso, I'm sorry for the loss of your husband. I'm also sorry for the intrusion and the personal questions. I'm afraid, though, that there will be more as the investigation progresses."

"I understand."

"There is one other thing I'd like to cover."

"Yes, what is it?"

"Did your husband have a home office?"

"Yes."

"Could we take a quick look at it?"

She stood up and they followed her down the second hallway to the office. They both stepped into the room and Bosch looked around. It was a small room with a desk and two file cabinets. There was a TV on a cart in front of a wall of shelves. Half were filled with books and the rest stacked with scripts, the titles written with Magic Markers on the edges of the pages. There was a golf bag leaning in the corner.

Bosch walked over and studied the desk. It was spotless. He came around and saw that the desk contained two file drawers. He opened these and found one empty and one containing several files. He quickly looked through the file tabs and saw that they apparently were files containing personal finance records and tax documents. He closed the drawers, deciding that a search of the office could probably keep.

"It's late," he said. "This is not the time. I want you to understand, though, that investigations like this often shoot off into many directions. But we have to follow up on everything. We're going to need to come in here tomorrow and go through your husband's things. We'll probably take a lot with us. We'll have a warrant so everything will be perfectly legal."

"Yes. Of course. But can't I just give you permission to take what you need?"

"You could, but it would be better this way. I'm talking about check books, savings account records, credit card statements, insurance, everything. We'll probably need the records on your household account, too."

"I understand. What time?"

"I don't know yet. I'll call first. Or someone will. Do you know, did your husband leave a will?"

"Yes. Both of us made wills. They're with our attorney."

"How long ago was that?"

"The will? Oh, a long time. Years."

"In the morning, I'd like you to call the attorney and tell him we'll need a copy of it. Are you up to doing that?"

"Of course."

"What about insurance?"

"Yes, we have policies. The attorney, Neil Denton in Century City, will have them also."

"Okay, we'll worry about that tomorrow. I need to seal this room now."

They stepped back into the hallway and Bosch closed the door. From his briefcase he took a sticker that said

CRIME SCENE
DO NOT ENTER PREMISES
CALL LAPD 214 485-4321

Bosch pressed the sticker across the door jamb. If anyone entered the room now, they would have to cut the sticker or peel it off. Bosch would know.

"Detective?" Veronica Aliso said quietly from behind him.

Bosch turned around.

"I am the suspect, aren't I?"

Bosch put the two papers he had peeled off the back of the sticker in his pocket.

"I suppose everyone and no one is a suspect at this point. We're looking at everything. But, yes, Mrs. Aliso, we're going to be looking at you."

"I guess I shouldn't have been so candid before, then."

Rider said, "If you've got nothing to hide, the truth shouldn't hurt you."

Bosch knew from long experience never to say such a thing. He knew the words were false before they were out of her mouth. Judging by the small, thin smile on Veronica Aliso's face, she knew it as well.

"Are you new at this, Detective Rider?" she asked while looking at Bosch with that smile.

"No, ma'am, I've been a detective for six years."

"Oh. And I guess I don't have to ask Detective Bosch."

"Mrs. Aliso?" Bosch asked.

"Veronica."

"There is one last thing you could clear up for us tonight. We do not know yet exactly when your husband was killed. But it would help us concentrate on other matters if we could quickly eliminate routine avenues of—"

"You want to know if I have an alibi, is that it?"

"We just want to know where you were the last few days and nights. It's a routine question, nothing else."

"Well, I hate to bore you with my life's details, because I'm afraid that's what they are, boring. But other than a trip to the mall and supermarket Saturday afternoon, I haven't left the house since I had dinner with my husband Wednesday night."

"You've been here alone?"

"Yes . . . but I think you can verify this with Captain Nash at the gate. They keep records of who comes in as well as out of Hidden Highlands. Even the residents. Also, on Friday our pool man was here in the afternoon. I gave him his check. I can get you his name and number."

"That won't be necessary right now. Thank you. And again, I'm sorry for your loss. Is there anything we can do for you right now?"

She seemed to be withdrawing into herself. He was not sure she had heard his question.

"I'm fine," she finally said.

He picked up his briefcase and headed down the hallway with Rider. It ran behind the living room and took them directly to the front door. All the way along the hallway there were no photographs on the wall. It didn't seem right to him, but he guessed nothing had been right in this house for a while. Bosch studied dead people's rooms the way scholars studied dead people's paintings at the Getty. He looked for the hidden meanings, the secrets of lives and deaths.

At the door Rider went out first. Bosch then stepped out and looked back down the hall. Veronica Aliso was framed at the other end in the light. He hesitated for a beat. He nodded and walked out.

They drove in silence, digesting the conversation, until they got to the gatehouse and Nash came out.

"How'd it go?"

"It went."

"He's dead, isn't he? Mr. Aliso."

"Yeah."

Nash whistled quietly.

"Captain Nash, you keep records here of when cars come in and out?" Rider asked.

"Yes. But this is private property. You'd need a—"

"Search warrant," Bosch said. "Yes, we know. But before we go to all that trouble, tell me something. Say I come back with a warrant, are your gate records going to tell me when exactly Mrs. Aliso came in and out of here the last few days?"

"Nope. It'll only tell you when her car did."

"Gotcha."

Bosch dropped off Rider at her car and they drove separately down out of the hills to the Hollywood Division station on Wilcox. On the way Bosch thought about Veronica Aliso and the fury she seemed to hold in her eyes for her dead husband. He didn't know how it fit or if it even fit at all. But he knew they would be coming back to her.

Rider and Bosch stopped briefly in the station to update Edgar and pick up cups of coffee. Bosch then called Archway and arranged for the security office to call in Chuckie Meachum from home. Bosch did not tell the duty officer who took the call what it was about or what office inside the studio they would be going to. He just told the officer to get Meachum there.

At midnight they went out the rear door of the station house, past the fenced windows of the drunk tank and to Bosch's car.

"So what did you think of her?" Bosch finally asked as he pulled out of the station lot.

"The embittered widow? I think there wasn't much to their marriage. At least at the end. Whether that makes her a killer or not, I don't know."

"No pictures."

"On the walls? Yeah, I noticed that."

Bosch lit a cigarette and Rider didn't say anything about it, although it was a violation of department policy to smoke in the detective car.

"What do you think?" Rider asked.

"I'm not sure yet. There's what you said. The bitterness you could almost put in a glass if you ever ran out of ice. Couple other things I'm still thinking about."

"Like what?"

"Like all the makeup she had on and the way she took my badge out of my hand. Nobody's ever done that before. It's like . . . I don't know, like maybe she was waiting for us."

When they got to the entrance of Archway Pictures, Meachum was standing under the half-size replica of the Arc de Triomphe smoking a cigarette and waiting. He was wearing a sport coat over a golf shirt and had a bemused smile on his face when he recognized Bosch pulling up. Bosch had spent time with Meachum in the Robbery-Homicide Division ten years before. Never partnered, but they worked a few of the same task forces. Meachum had gotten out when the getting out was good. He pulled the pin a month after the Rodney King tape hit the news. He knew. He told everybody it was the beginning of the end. Archway hired him as the assistant director of security. Nice job, nice pay, plus he was pulling in the twenty-year pension of half pay. He was the one they talked about when they talked about smart moves. Now, with all the baggage the LAPD carried—the King beating, the riots, the Christopher Commission, O.J. Simpson and Mark Fuhrman—a retiring dick would be lucky if a place like Archway hired him to work the front gate.

"Harry Bosch," Meachum said, leaning down to look in. "What it is, what it is?"

The first thing Bosch had noticed was that Meachum had gotten his teeth capped since he'd last seen him.

"Chuckie. Long time. This is my partner, Kiz Rider."

Rider nodded and Meachum nodded and studied her a moment. Black female detectives were a rarity in his day, even though he hadn't been off the job more than five years.

"So what's shaking, Detectives? Why'd you want to go and pull me out of the hot tub?"

He smiled, showing off the teeth. Bosch guessed he knew that they had been noticed.

"We got a case. We want to take a look at the vic's office."

"It's here? Who's the stiff?"

"Anthony N. Aliso. TNA Productions."

Meachum crinkled his eyes. He had the deep tan of a golfer who never misses his Saturday morning start and usually gets away for at least nine once or twice during the week.

"Doesn't do anything for me, Harry. You sure he—"

"Look it up, Chuck. He's here. Was."

"All right, tell you what, park the car over in the main lot and we'll go back to my office, grab a cup and look this guy up."

He pointed toward a lot directly through the gate and Bosch did as instructed. The lot was almost empty and was next to a huge soundstage with an outside wall painted powder blue with puffs of white clouds. It was used for shooting exteriors when the real sky was too brown with smog.

They followed Meachum on foot to the studio security offices. Entering the suite, they passed by a glass-walled office in which a man in a brown Archway Security outfit sat at a desk surrounded by banks of video monitors. He was reading the *Times* sports page, which he quickly dropped into a trash can next to the desk when he saw Meachum.

Bosch saw that Meachum didn't seem to notice because he had been holding the door open for them. When he turned, he casually saluted the man in the glass office and led Bosch and Rider back to his office.

Meachum slid in behind his desk and turned to his computer. The monitor screen depicted an intergalactic battle among assorted space ships. Meachum hit one key and the screen saver disappeared. He asked Bosch to spell Aliso's name and he punched it into the computer. He then tilted the monitor so Bosch and Rider couldn't see the screen. Bosch was annoyed by this but he didn't say anything. After a few moments, Meachum did.

"You're right. He was here. Tyrone Power Building. Had one of the little cubbyholes they rent to nonplayers. Three-office suite. Three losers. They share a secretary who comes with the rent."

"How long's he been here? That say?"

"Yeah. Almost seven years."

"What else you got there?"

Meachum looked at the screen.

"Not much. No record of problems. He complained once about somebody dinging his car in the parking lot. Says here he drove a Rolls-

Royce. Probably the last guy in Hollywood who hadn't traded in his Rolls on a Range Rover. That's tacky, Bosch."

"Let's go take a look."

"Well, I'll tell you what, why don't you and Detective Riley go out there and grab a cup of joe while I make a call about that? I'm not sure what our procedure is for this."

"First of all, Chuck, it's Rider, not Riley. And second, we're running a homicide investigation here. Whatever your procedures are, we are expecting you to allow us access."

"You're on private property here, buddy. You've got to keep that in mind."

"I will." Bosch stood up. "And when you make your call, the thing you should keep in mind is that so far the media haven't gotten wind of any of this. I didn't think it would be good to pull Archway into this sort of thing, especially since we don't know for sure what's involved here. You can tell whoever you're calling that I'll try to keep it that way."

Meachum smirked and shook his head.

"Still the same old Bosch. Your way or the highway."

"Something like that."

While waiting, Bosch had time to gulp down a cup of lukewarm coffee from a pot that had been on a warmer in the outer office for the better part of the night. It was bitter, but he knew the cup he'd had at the station would not take him through the night. Rider passed on the coffee, instead drinking water from a dispenser in the hallway.

After nearly ten minutes Meachum came out of his office.

"Okay, you got it. But I'll tell you right now that me or one of my people gotta be in there the whole time as observers. That going to be a problem for you, Bosch?"

"No problem."

"Okay, let's go. We'll take a cart."

On the way out he opened the door to the glass room and stuck his head in.

"Peters, who's roving?"

"Uh, Serrurier and Fogel."

"Okay, get on the air and tell Serrurier to meet us at Tyrone Power. He's got keys, right?"

"Right."

"Okay, do it." Meachum made a motion to close the door but stopped. "And Peters? Leave the sports page in the trash can."

They took a golf cart to the Tyrone Power Building because it was on the other side of the lot from the security offices. Along the way Meachum waved to a man dressed entirely in black who was coming out of one of the buildings they passed.

"We've got a shoot on New York Street tonight, otherwise I'd take you through there. You'd swear you were in Brooklyn."

"Never been," Bosch said.

"Me neither," Rider added.

"Then it doesn't matter, unless you wanted to see them shooting."

"The Tyrone Power Building will be just fine."

"Fine."

When they got there, another uniformed man was waiting. Serrurier. At Meachum's instructions he first unlocked a door to a reception area that served the three separate offices of the suite, then the door to the office Aliso had used. Meachum then told him to go back out on roving patrol of the studio.

Meachum's calling it a closet was not too far off. Aliso's office was barely large enough for Bosch, Rider and Meachum to stand in together without having to smell each other's breath. It contained a desk with a chair behind it and two more close in front of it. Against the wall behind the desk was a four-drawer file cabinet. The left wall was hung with framed one-sheets advertising two classic films: *Chinatown* and *The Godfather*, both of which had been made down the street at Paramount. Aliso had countered these on the right wall with framed posters of his own efforts, *The Art of the Cape* and *Casualty of Desire*. There were also smaller frames of photos depicting Aliso with various celebrities, many of the shots taken in the same office with Aliso and the celebrity of the moment standing behind the desk smiling.

Bosch first studied the two posters. Each one carried the imprimatur along the top *Anthony Aliso Presents*. But it was the second poster, for *Casualty of Desire*, that caught his attention. The artwork beneath the title of the film showed a man in a white suit carrying a gun down at his side, a desperate look on his face. In larger scale, a woman with flowing dark hair that framed the image looked down on him with sultry eyes. The poster was a rip-off of the scene depicted in the *Chinatown* poster on the other wall. But there was something entrancing about it. The woman, of course, was Veronica Aliso, and Bosch knew that was one reason why.

"Nice-looking woman," Meachum said from behind him.

"His wife."

"I see that. Second billing. Only I never heard of her."

Bosch nodded at the poster.

"I think this was her shot."

"Well, like I said, nice-looking gal. I doubt she looks like that anymore."

Bosch studied the eyes again and remembered the woman he had seen just an hour ago. The eyes were still as dark and gleaming, a little cross of light at the center of each.

Bosch looked away and began to study the framed photos. He immediately noticed that one of them was of Dan Lacey, the actor who had portrayed Bosch eight years earlier in a mini-series about the search for a serial killer. The studio that had produced it had paid Bosch and his then partner a lot of money to use their names and technical advice. His partner took the money and ran, retired to Mexico. Bosch bought a house in the hills. He couldn't run. He knew the job was his life.

He turned and took in the rest of the small office. There were shelves against the wall near the door and these were piled with scripts and videotapes, no books save for a couple of directories of actors and directors.

"Okay," Bosch said. "Chuckie, you stand back by the door and observe like you said. Kiz, why don't you start with the desk and I'll start with the files."

The files were locked and it took Bosch ten minutes to open them with the picks he got out of his briefcase. It then took an hour just to make a cursory study of the files. The drawers were stocked with notes and financial records regarding the development of several films that Bosch had never heard of. This did not seem curious to him after what Veronica Aliso had said and because he knew little about the film business anyway. But it seemed from his understanding of the files he was quickly scanning that large sums of money had been paid to various film services companies during the production of the films. And what struck Bosch the most was that Aliso seemed to have financed a hell of a nice lifestyle from this little office.

After he was finished going through the fourth and bottom drawer, Bosch stood and straightened his back, his vertebrae popping like dominoes clicking together. He looked at Rider, who was still going through the drawers of the desk.

"Anything?"

"A few things of interest but no smoking gun, if that's what you mean. Aliso's got a flag here from the IRS. His corporation was going to be audited next month. Other than that, there is some correspondence between Tony Aliso and St. John, the flavor-of-the-month Mrs. Aliso mentioned. Heated words but nothing overtly threatening. I've still got one drawer to go."

"There's a lot in the files. Financial stuff. We're going to have to go through it all. I'd like you to be the one. You going to be up for it?"

"No problem. What I'm seeing so far is a lot of routine, if not sloppy, business records. It just happens to be the movie business here."

"I'm going outside to catch a smoke. When you're done there, why don't we switch and you take the files, I'll take the desk."

"Sounds like a plan."

Before going out he ran his eyes along the shelves by the door and read the titles of the videotapes. He stopped when he came to the one he was looking for. *Casualty of Desire.* He reached up and took it down. The cover carried the same artwork as the movie poster.

He stepped back and put it on the desk so it would be gathered with things they would be taking. Rider asked what it was.

"It's her movie," he said. "I want to watch it."

"Oh, me too."

Outside, Bosch stood in the small courtyard by a bronze statue of a man he guessed was Tyrone Power and lit a cigarette. It was a cool night and the smoke in his chest warmed him. The studio grounds were very quiet now.

He walked over to a trash can next to a bench in the courtyard and used it to tip his ashes. He noticed a broken coffee mug at the bottom of the can. There were several pens and pencils scattered in the can as well. He recognized the Archway insignia, the Arc de Triomphe with the sun rising in the middle of the arch, on one of the fragments. He was about to reach into the trash can to pick out what looked like a gold Cross pen when he heard Meachum's voice and turned around.

"She's going places, isn't she? I can tell."

He was lighting his own cigarette.

"Yeah, that's what I hear. It's our first case together. I don't really know her, and from what I hear I shouldn't try. She's going to the Glass House as soon as the time is right."

Meachum nodded and flicked his ashes onto the pavement. Bosch watched him glance up toward the roofline above the second floor and give another one of his casual salutes. Bosch looked up and saw the camera moored to the underside of the roof eave.

"Don't worry about it," Bosch said. "He can't see you. He's reading about the Dodgers last night."

"S'pose you're right. Can't get good people these days, Harry. I get guys who like driving around in the carts all day, hoping they're going to be discovered like Clint Eastwood or something. Had a guy run into a wall the other day 'cause he was so intent on talking with a couple creative execs walking by. There's one of them oxymorons for you. Creative executive . . ."

Bosch was silent. He didn't care about anything that Meachum had just said.

"You ought to come work here, Harry. You've gotta have your twenty in by now. You should pull the pin and then come work for me. Your lifestyle will rise a couple of notches. I guarantee it."

"No thanks, Chuck. Somehow I just don't see myself tooling around in one of your golf carts."

"Well, the offer's there. Anytime, buddy. Anytime."

Bosch put his cigarette out on the side of the trash can and dropped the dead butt inside. He decided that he didn't want to go picking through the can with Meachum watching. He told Meachum he was heading back in.

"Bosch, I gotta tell you something."

Bosch looked back at him and Meachum raised his hands.

"We're going to have a problem if you want to take anything out of that office without a warrant. I mean, I heard what you said about that tape and now she's in there stacking stuff on the desk to go. But I can't let you take anything."

"Then you are going to be here all night, Chuck. There are a lot of files in there and a lot of work to do. It'd be a lot easier for us to haul it all back to the bureau now."

"I know that. I've been there. But this is the position I've been instructed to take. We need the warrant."

Bosch used the phone on the receptionist's desk to call Edgar, who was still in the detective bureau just beginning the paperwork the case would generate. Bosch told him to drop that work for the moment and start drawing up search warrants for all financial records in Aliso's home and the Archway offices and any being held by his attorney.

"You want me to call the duty judge tonight?" Edgar asked. "It's almost two in the morning."

"Do it," Bosch said. "When you have 'em signed, bring them out here to Archway. And bring some boxes."

Edgar groaned. He was getting all the shit work. Nobody liked waking up a judge in the middle of the night.

"I know, I know, Jerry. But it's got to be done. Anything else going on?"

"No. I called the Mirage, talked to a guy in security. The room Aliso used was rebooked over the weekend. It's open now and he's got a hold on it, but it's spoiled."

"Probably. . . . Okay, man, next time you'll eat the bear. Get on those warrants."

In Aliso's office, Rider was already looking through the files. Bosch told her Edgar was working on a warrant and that they would have to draw up an inventory for Meachum. He also told her to take a break if she wanted but she declined.

Bosch sat down behind the desk. It had the usual clutter. There was a phone with a speaker attachment, a Rolodex, a blotter, a magnetic block that held paper clips to it and a wood carving that said TNA Productions in script. There was also a tray stacked with paperwork.

Bosch looked at the phone and noticed the redial button. He lifted the handset and pushed the button. He could tell by the quick procession of tones that the last call made on the phone had been long distance. After two rings it was answered by a female voice. There was loud music in the background.

"Hello?" she said.

"Yes, hello, who's this?"

She giggled.

"I don't know, who's this?"

"I might have the wrong number. Is this Tony's?"

"No, it's Dolly's."

"Oh, Dolly's. Okay, uh, then where are you located?"

She giggled again.

"On Madison, where do you think? How do you think we got the name?"

"Where's Madison?"

"We're in North Las Vegas. Where are you coming from?"

"The Mirage."

"Okay, just follow the boulevard out front to the north. You go all the way past downtown and past a bunch of cruddy areas and into North Las Vegas. Madison is your third light after you go under the overpass. Take a left and we're a block down on the left. What's your name again?"

"It's Harry."

"Well, Harry, I'm Rhonda. As in . . ."

Bosch said nothing.

"Come on, Harry, you're supposed to say, 'Help me, Rhonda, help, help me, Rhonda.'"

She sang the line from the old Beach Boys song.

"Actually, Rhonda, there *is* something you can help me with," Bosch said. "I'm looking for a buddy of mine. Tony Aliso. He been in there lately?"

"Haven't seen him this week. Haven't seen him since Thursday or Friday. I was wondering how you got the dressing room number."

"Yeah, from Tony."

"Well, Layla isn't here tonight, so Tony wouldn't be coming in anyway, I don't think. But you can come on out. He don't have to be here for you to have a good time."

"Okay, Rhonda, I'll try to swing by."

Bosch hung up. He took a notebook out of his pocket and wrote down the name of the business he had just called, the directions to it and the names Rhonda and Layla. He drew a line under the second name.

"What was that?" Rider asked.

"A lead in Vegas."

He recounted the call and the inference made about the person named Layla. Rider agreed that it was something to pursue, then went back to the files. Bosch went back to the desk. He studied the things on top of it before going to the things in it.

"Hey, Chuckie?" he asked.

Meachum, leaning against the door with his arms folded in front of him, raised his eyebrows by way of response.

"He's got no 'phone tape. What about when the receptionist isn't out there? Do phone calls go to the operator or some kind of a phone service?"

"Uh, no, the whole lot's on voice mail now."

"So Aliso had voice mail? How do I get into it?"

"Well, you've got to have his code. It's a three-digit code. You call the voice mail computer, punch in the code and you pick up your messages."

"How do I get his code?"

"You don't. He programmed it himself."

"There's no master code I can break in with?"

"Nope. It's not that sophisticated a system, Bosch. I mean, what do you want, it's phone messages."

Bosch took out his notebook again and checked the notes for Aliso's birthday.

"What's the voice mail number?" he asked.

Meachum gave him the number and Bosch called the computer. After a beep he punched in 721 but the number was rejected. Bosch drummed his fingers on the desk, thinking. He tried 862, the numbers corresponding with TNA, and a computer voice told him he had four messages.

"Kiz, listen to this," he said.

He put the phone on speaker and hung up. As the messages were played back Bosch took a few notes, but the first three messages were from men reporting on technical aspects of a planned film shoot, equipment rental and costs. Each call was followed by the electronic voice which reported when on Friday the call had come in.

The fourth message made Bosch lean forward and listen closely. The voice belonged to a young woman and it sounded like she was crying.

"Hey, Tone, it's me. Call me as soon as you get this. I almost feel like

calling your house. I need you. That bastard Lucky says I'm fired. And
for no reason. He just wants to get his dick into Modesty. I'm so . . . I
don't want to have to work at the Palomino or any of those other places.
The Garden. Forget it. I want to come out there to L.A. Be with you.
Call me."

The electronic voice said the call had come in at 4 A.M. on Sunday—
long after Tony Aliso was dead. The caller had not given her name. It was
therefore obviously someone Aliso would have known. Bosch wondered
if it was the woman Rhonda had mentioned, Layla. He looked at Rider
and she just shook her shoulders. They knew too little to judge the significance of the call.

Bosch sat in the desk chair contemplating things a few moments. He
opened a drawer but didn't start through it. His eyes traveled up the wall
to the right of the desk and roamed across the photos of the smiling Tony
Aliso posed with celebrities. Some of them had written notes on the
photos but they were hard to read. Bosch studied the photo of his cellu-
loid alter ego, Dan Lacey, but couldn't read the small note scrawled across
the bottom of the photo. Then he looked past the ink and realized what
he was looking at. On Aliso's desk in the photo was an Archway mug
crammed with pens and pencils.

Bosch took the photo off the wall and called Meachum's name.
Meachum came over.

"Somebody was in here," Bosch told him.

"What are you talking about?"

"When was the trash can emptied outside?"

"How the hell would I know? What are—"

"The surveillance camera out there on the roof, how long you keep
the tapes?"

Meachum hesitated a second but then answered.

"We roll 'em over every week. We'd have seven days off that camera.
It's all stop action, ten frames a minute."

"Let's go take a look."

Bosch didn't get home until four. That left him only three hours to sleep
before an agreed-upon breakfast meeting with Edgar and Rider at seven-

thirty, but he was too strung out on coffee and adrenaline to even think about shutting his eyes.

The house had the sour tang of a fresh-paint smell and he opened the sliders onto the back deck to let in the cool night air. He checked out the Cahuenga Pass below and watched the cars on the Hollywood Freeway cutting through. He was always amazed at how there were always cars on the freeway, no matter what the hour. In L.A. they never stopped.

He thought about putting on a CD, some saxophone music, but instead just sat down on the couch in the dark and lit a cigarette. He thought about the different currents running through the case. Going by the preliminary take on the victim, Anthony Aliso had been a financially successful man. That kind of success usually brought with it a thick insulation from violence and murder. The rich were seldom murdered. But something had gone wrong for Tony Aliso.

Bosch remembered the tape and went to his briefcase, which he had left on the dining room table. Inside it there were two video cassettes, the Archway surveillance tape and the copy of *Casualty of Desire*. He turned on the TV and put the movie in the video player. He began watching in the dark.

After viewing the tape it was obvious to Bosch that the movie deserved the fate it had received. It was badly lit and in some frames the end of a boom microphone hovered above the players. This was particularly jarring in scenes shot in the open desert where there should have been nothing above but blue sky. It was basic filmmaking gone wrong. And added to the amateurish look of the film were the poor performances of the players. The male lead, an actor Bosch had never seen before, was woodenly ineffective in portraying a man desperate to hold on to his young wife, who used sexual frustration and taunting to coerce him into committing crimes, eventually including murder, all for her morbid satisfaction. Veronica Aliso played the wife and was not much better an actor than the male lead.

When lighted well, she was stunningly beautiful. There were four scenes in which she appeared partially nude and Bosch watched these with a voyeuristic fascination. But overall it was not a good role for her, and Bosch also understood why her career, like her husband's, had not moved forward. She might blame her husband and harbor resentment toward him, but the bottom line was that she was like thousands of beautiful women who came to Hollywood every year. Her looks could put a pause in your heart, but she could not act to save her life.

In the climactic scene of the film, in which the husband was apprehended and the wife cut him loose with the cops, she delivered her lines with the conviction and weight of a blank page of typing paper.

"It was him. He's crazy. I couldn't stop him until it was too late. Then I couldn't tell anyone because it . . . it would look like I was the one who wanted them all dead."

Bosch watched all the way through the credits and then rewound the tape by using the remote. He never got off the couch. He then turned the TV off and put his feet up on the couch. Looking through the open sliders he could see the light of dawn etching the ridgeline across the Pass. He still wasn't tired. He kept thinking about the choices people make with their lives. He wondered what would have happened if the performances had been at least passable and the film had found a distributor. He wondered if that would have changed things now, if it would have kept Tony Aliso out of that trunk.

The meeting at the station with Billets didn't start until nine-thirty. Though the squad room was deserted because of the holiday, they all rolled chairs into the lieutenant's office and closed the door. Billets started things off by saying that members of the local media, apparently having picked up on the case by checking the coroner's overnight log, were already beginning to take a more than routine interest in the Aliso murder. Also, she said, the department weight all the way up the line was questioning whether the investigation should be turned over to the elite Robbery-Homicide Division. This, of course, grated on Bosch. Earlier in his career he had been assigned to RHD. But then a questionable on-duty shooting resulted in his demotion to Hollywood. And so it was particularly upsetting to him to think of turning over the case to the big shots downtown. If OCID had been interested, that would have been easier to accept. But Bosch told Billets that he could not accept turning the case over to RHD after his team had spent almost an entire night without sleep on it and had produced some viable leads. Rider jumped in and agreed with him. Edgar, still riding his sulk over being put on the paperwork, remained silent.

"Your point is well taken," Billets said. "But when we're done here, I have to call Captain LeValley at home and convince her we've got a handle on this. So let's go over what we have. You convince me, I'll convince her. She'll then let them know how we feel about it downtown."

Bosch spent the next thirty minutes talking for the team and carefully recounting the night's investigation. The detective squad's only television/VCR was kept in the lieutenant's office because it wasn't safe to leave it unlocked, even in a police station. He put in the tape Meachum had dubbed off the Archway surveillance tape and queued up the part that included the intruder.

"The surveillance camera this was shot from turns a frame every six seconds, so it's pretty quick and jerky but we've got the guy on it," Bosch said.

He hit the play button and the screen depicted a grainy black and white view of the courtyard and front of the Tyrone Power Building. The lighting made it appear to be late dusk. The time counter on the bottom of the screen showed the time and date to be eight-thirteen the evening before.

Bosch put the machine on slow motion, but still the sequence he wanted to show Billets was over very quickly. In six quick frames they showed a man go to the door of the building, hunch over the knob and then disappear inside.

"Actual time at the door was about thirty to thirty-five seconds," Rider said. "It may look from the tape like he had a key, but that's too long to open a door with a key. The lock was picked. Somebody good and fast."

"Okay, here he comes back out," Bosch said.

When the time counter hit eight-seventeen, the man was captured on the video emerging from the doorway. The video jumped and the man was in the courtyard heading toward the trash can, then it jumped and the man was walking away from the trash can. Then he was gone. Bosch backed the tape up and froze it on the last image of the man as he walked from the trash can. It was the best image. It was dark and the man's face was blurred but still possibly recognizable if they ever found someone to compare it to. He was white, with dark hair and a stocky, powerful build. He wore a golf shirt with short sleeves, and the watch on his right wrist, visible just above one of the black gloves he wore, had a chrome band that glinted with the reflection of the courtyard light. Above the wrist was the dark blur of a tattoo on the man's forearm. Bosch pointed these things out to Billets and added that he would be taking the tape to SID to see if this last frame, the best of those showing the intruder, could be sharpened in any way by computer enhancement.

"Good," Billets said. "Now, what do you think he was doing in there?"

"Retrieving something," Bosch said. "From the time he goes in until he comes out, we've got less than four minutes. Not a lot of time. Plus he had to pick the interior door to Aliso's office. Whatever he is doing in there, he knocks an Archway mug off the desk and it breaks on the floor. He does what he was there to do, then gathers up the broken mug and the pens and dumps them in the trash can on his way out. We found the broken mug and the pens in the can last night."

"Any prints?" Billets asked.

"Once we figured there was a break-in, we backed out and had Donovan come on out when he was done with the Rolls. He got prints but nothing we can use. He got Aliso's and mine and Kiz's. As you can see on the video, the guy wore gloves."

"Okay."

Bosch involuntarily yawned and Edgar and Rider followed suit. He drank from the cup of stale coffee he had brought into the office with him. He had long had the caffeine jitters but knew if he stopped feeding the beast now he would quickly crash.

"And the theory on what this intruder was retrieving?" Billets asked.

"The broken mug puts him at the desk rather than the files," Rider said. "Nothing in the desk seemed disturbed. No empty files, nothing like that. We think it was a bug. Somebody put a bug in Aliso's phone and couldn't afford to let us find it. The phone was right next to the mug in the pictures on Aliso's walls. The intruder somehow knocked it over. Funny thing is, we never checked the phone for a bug. If whoever this guy was had left well enough alone, we probably would have never tumbled to it."

"I've been to Archway," Billets said. "It's got a wall around it. It's got its own private security force. How's this guy get in? Or are you suggesting an inside job?"

"Two things," Bosch said. "There was a film shooting in progress at the studio on the New York Street set. That meant a lot of people in and out of the front gate. Maybe this guy was able to slip through with part of the shooting crew. The direction in which he walks off in the video is to the north. That's where New York Street is. The gate is to the south. Also, the north side of the studio butts up against the Hollywood Cemetery. You're right, there is a wall. But at night, after the cemetery is closed, it's dark and secluded. Our guy could've climbed the wall there. Whatever way he did it, he had practice."

"What do you mean?"

"If he was taking a bug out of Tony Aliso's phone, it had to have been planted there in the first place."

Billet nodded.

"Who do you think he was?" she asked quietly.

Bosch looked at Rider to see if she wanted to answer. When she didn't speak, he did.

"Hard to say. The timing is the catch. Aliso's probably been dead since Friday night, his body's not found till about six last night. Then this break-in comes at eight-thirteen. That's after Aliso's been found and after people start finding out about it."

"But eight-thirteen, that's before you talked to the wife?"

"Right. So that kind of threw a wrench into it. I mean, I was all set to say let's go full speed on the wife and see what we get. Now, I'm not so sure. See, if she's involved, this break-in doesn't make sense."

"Explain."

"Well, first you've got to figure out why he was being bugged. And what's the most likely answer? The wife put a PI or somebody on Tony to see if he was screwing around. Okay?"

"Okay."

"Now, saying that's the case, if the wife was involved in putting her husband down into that trunk, why would she or her PI or whoever wait until last night—this is after the body's been found—to pull the bug out of there? It doesn't make sense. It only makes sense if the two things were not related, if the killing and the bug are separate. Understand?"

"I think so."

"And that's why I'm not ready to chunk everything and just look at the wife. Personally, I think she might be good for this. But there's too much we don't know right now. It doesn't feel right to me. There's something else running through all of this, and we don't know what yet."

Billets nodded and looked at all the investigators.

"This is good. I know there isn't a lot that is solid yet, but it's still good work. Anything else? What about the prints Art Donovan pulled off the victim's jacket last night?"

"For now we've struck out. He put them on AFIS, NCIC, the whole works, and got blanked."

"Damn."

"They're still valuable. We come up with a suspect, the prints could be a clincher."

"Anything else from the car?"

"No," Bosch said.

"Yes," Rider said.

Billets raised her eyebrows at the contradiction.

"One of the prints Donovan found on the inside lip of the trunk lid," Rider said. "It came back to Ray Powers. He's the P-3 who found the body. He overstepped when he popped the trunk. He obviously left his print when he opened it. We caught it and no harm, no foul, but it was sloppy work and he should have never opened the trunk in the first place. He should've called us."

Billets glanced at Bosch and he guessed she was wondering why he hadn't brought this to her attention. He looked down at her desk.

"Okay, I'll take care of it," Billets said. "I know Powers. He's been around and he should certainly know procedure."

Bosch could have defended Powers with the explanation the cop had given the day before but he let it go. Powers wasn't worth it. Billets went on.

"So where do we go from here?"

"Well, we've got a lot of ground to cover," Bosch said. "I once heard this story about a sculptor and somebody asked him how he turned a block of granite into a beautiful statue of a woman. And he said that he just chips away everything that isn't the woman. That's what we have to do now. We've got this big block of information and evidence. We've got to chip away everything that doesn't count, that doesn't fit."

Billets smiled and Bosch suddenly felt embarrassed about the analogy, though he believed it was accurate.

"What about Las Vegas?" she asked. "Is that part of the statue or the part we need to chip away?"

Now Rider and Edgar were smiling.

"Well, we've got to go there, for one thing," Bosch said, hoping he didn't sound defensive. "Right now all we know is that this victim went there and was dead pretty soon after he came back. We don't know what he did there, whether he won, lost, whether somebody tailed him back here from there. For all we know, he could've hit a jackpot there and was followed back here and ripped off. We've got a lot of questions about Las Vegas."

"Plus, there's the woman," Rider said.

"What woman?" Billets asked.

"Right," Bosch said. "The last call made on Tony Aliso's office line was to a club in North Las Vegas. I called it and got the name of a woman I think he was seeing over there. Layla. There was—"

"Layla? Like that song?"

"I guess. There also was a message from an unnamed woman on his office line. I think it might have been this Layla. We've got to talk to her."

Billets nodded, made sure Bosch was done and then laid down the battle plan.

"All right," Billets said. "First off, all media inquiries are to be directed to me. The best way to control information on this is to have it come from one mouth. For the moment, we'll tell the reporters it is obviously under investigation and we are leaning toward a possible carjacking or robbery scenario. It's innocuous enough and will probably appease them. Everyone okay with that?"

The three detectives nodded.

"Okay, I'm going to make a case with the captain to keep the case here with us. It looks to me like we have three or four avenues which need to be pursued vigorously. Granite that we have to chip away at, as Harry would say.

"Anyway, it will also help me with the captain if we are already scrambling on these things. So, Harry, I want you to get on a plane as soon as possible and get to Vegas. I want you on that end of it. But if there's nothing there, I want you to get in and get out. We'll need you back here. Okay?"

Bosch nodded. It would have been his choice if he were the one making the decisions, but he felt a pang of discomfort that she was doing it.

"Kiz, you stick with the financial trail. I want to be in a position of knowing everything about this guy Anthony Aliso by tomorrow morning. You're also going to have to go up to the house with the search warrant, so while you are there, take another shot at the wife, see what else you can get about the marriage when you're picking up the records. I don't know, if you get a chance, sit down with her, try to get a heart-to-heart."

"I don't know," Rider said. "I think we're past the heart-to-heart. She's a smart woman, smart enough to already know we're taking a look at her. I almost think that to be safe we've got to advise her next time any of us talk to her. It was pretty close last night."

"Use your judgment on that," Billets said. "But if you advise, she's probably going to call her lawyer."

"I'll see what I can do."

"And Jerry, you—"

"I know, I know, I've got the paper."

It was the first time he had spoken in fifteen minutes. Bosch thought he was carrying his sulk to the limit.

"Yes, you have the paper. But I also want you on the civil cases and this screenwriter guy who was having the dispute with Aliso. It sounds to me to be the longest shot, but we've got to cover everything. Get that cleared up and it will help narrow our focus."

Edgar mock-saluted her.

"Also," she said, "while Harry's putting together the trail in Vegas, I want you to put it together from the airport here. We've got his parking stub. I think you should start there. When I talk to the media I'll also give a detailed description of the car—can't be that many white Clouds around—and say we're looking for anyone who might've seen it Friday night. I'll say we're trying to re-create the victim's ride from the airport. Maybe we'll get lucky and get some help from the John Qs out there."

"Maybe," Edgar said.

"Okay then, let's do it," Billets said.

The three of them stood up while Billets stayed seated. Bosch took his time taking the tape out of the VCR so that the other two were out of the office when he was done, and he was alone with Billets.

"I'd heard that you didn't have any actual time on a homicide table while you were coming up," he said to her.

"That's true. My only job as an actual detective was working sexual crimes in Valley Bureau."

"Well, for what it's worth, I would have assigned things just the way you just did."

"But did it annoy you that I did it instead of you?"

Bosch thought a moment.

"I'll get over it."

"Thank you."

"No problem. Listen, that thing about Powers leaving his print, I probably would have told you about it, but I didn't think this meeting was the right time. I chewed him out for opening the car yesterday. He said if he hadn't opened it and waited for us to check it out, the car would probably still be sitting out there. He is an asshole but he makes a point."

"I understand."

"You pissed at me for not telling you?"

Billets thought a moment.

"I'll get over it."

II

Bosch fell asleep a few minutes after belting himself into a window seat on the Southwest shuttle from Burbank to Las Vegas. It was a deep, dreamless sleep and he didn't wake until the clunk of the landing gear hitting the tarmac jolted him forward. As the plane taxied to its gate he came out of the fog and felt himself re-energized by the hour-long rest.

It was high noon and 104 degrees when he walked out of the terminal. As he headed toward the garage where his rental car was waiting, he felt his newfound energy being leached away by the heat. After finding his car in its assigned parking stall, he put the air-conditioning on high and headed toward the Mirage.

Bosch had never liked Las Vegas, though he came often on cases. It shared a kinship with Los Angeles; both were places desperate people ran to. Often, when they ran from Los Angeles, they came here. It was the only place left. Beneath the veneer of glitz and money and energy and sex beat a dark heart. No matter how much they tried to dress her up with neon and family entertainment, she was still a whore.

But if any place could sway him from that opinion it was the Mirage. It was the symbol of the new Las Vegas, clean, opulent, legit. The windows of its tower glinted gold in the sun. And inside no money had been spared in its rich casino design. As Bosch walked through the lobby he

was first mesmerized by the white tigers in a huge glassed-in environment that any zookeeper in the world would salivate over. Next, as he
waited in line to check in, he eyed the huge aquarium behind the front
desk. Sharks lazily turned and moved back and forth behind the glass. Just
like the white tigers.

When it was Bosch's turn to check in, the desk clerk noticed a flag on
his reservation and called security. A day-shift supervisor named Hank
Meyer appeared and introduced himself. He said that Bosch would have
the complete cooperation of the hotel and casino.

"Tony Aliso was a good and valued customer," he said. "We want to
do what we can to help. But it's highly unlikely that his death had anything to do with his stay here. We run the cleanest ship in the desert."

"I know that, Hank," Bosch said. "And I know it is a reputation you
don't want blemished. I'm not expecting to find anything inside the Mirage, but I need to go through the motions. So do you, right?"

"Right."

"Did you know him?"

"No, I didn't. I've been on day shift the entire three years I've been
here. From what I understand, Mr. Aliso primarily gambled at night."

Meyer was about thirty and had the clean-cut image that the Mirage,
and now all of Las Vegas, wanted to present to the world. He went on to
explain that the room Aliso had last stayed in at the hotel was sealed and
was being held that way for Bosch's inspection. He gave Bosch the key
and asked that he return it as soon as he was finished with the room. He
also said the poker pit dealers and sports book clerks who worked the
night shift would be made available for interviews. All of them knew Aliso because of his regular visits.

"You have an eye in the sky over the poker tables?"

"Uh, yes, we do."

"You have video from Thursday going into Friday? I'd like to see it if
you do."

"That won't be a problem."

Bosch made arrangements to meet Meyer at the second-floor security
office at four. That was when the casino shifts changed and the dealers
who knew Aliso would report for work. He could look at the surveillance tape from the poker pit's overhead camera then as well.

A few minutes later, alone in his room, Bosch sat on the bed and looked around. The room was smaller than he had expected but it was very nice, by far the most comfortably appointed room he had ever seen in Las Vegas. He pulled the phone off the side table onto his lap and called the Hollywood Division to check in. Edgar picked up the line.

"It's Bosch."

"Well, the Michelangelo of murder, the Rodin of homicide."

"Funny. So what's going on over there?"

"Well, for one thing, Bullets won the battle," Edgar said. "Nobody from RHD has come around to snatch the case."

"That's good. What about you? You making any progress?"

"I almost have the murder book up to speed. I have to put it aside now, though. The screenwriter is coming in at one-thirty for a sit-down. Says he doesn't need a lawyer."

"Okay, I'll leave you to it. Tell the lieutenant I checked in."

"Yeah, and by the way, she wants another confab on how things are going at six. You should call in and we'll put you on the speaker."

"Will do."

Bosch sat on the bed a few moments wishing he could lie back on it and sleep. But he knew he couldn't. He had to drive the case forward.

He got up and unpacked his overnighter, hanging his two shirts and one pair of pants in the closet. He put his extra underwear and socks on the closet shelf, then left the room and took an elevator to the top floor. The room Aliso had used was at the end of the corridor. The card key Meyer had given him worked without a problem and he stepped into a room about twice the size of his own. It was a combination bedroom and sitting room and had an oval Jacuzzi next to the windows that looked out across the expanse of the desert and the smooth cocoa-colored mountain chain to the northwest of the city. Directly below was a view of the pool and the hotel's porpoise-habitat attraction. Looking down, he could see one of the gray fish moving beneath the shimmering water. It looked as out of place as Bosch felt in the suite he stood in.

"Dolphins in the desert," he said out loud.

The room was plush by any standards in any city and obviously was kept for high rollers. Bosch stood by the bed for a few moments and just looked around. There was nothing that seemed out of place and the thick carpet had the uniformed waves left by a recent vacuuming. He guessed that if there had been anything of evidentiary value in the room it was gone now. But still he went through the motions. He looked under the bed and in the drawers. Behind the bureau he found a matchbook from a local Mexican restaurant called Las Fuentes, but there was no telling how long it had been there.

The bathroom was tiled in pink marble floor to ceiling. The fixtures were polished brass. Bosch looked around for a moment but saw nothing of interest. He opened the glass door to the shower stall and looked in and also found nothing. But as he was closing the door his eyes caught on something on the drain. He reopened the door and looked down, then pressed his finger on the tiny speck of gold caught in the rubber sealant around the drain fitting. He raised his finger and found the tiny piece of glitter stuck to his finger. He guessed that it was a match to the pieces of glitter found in the cuffs of Tony Aliso's pants. Now all he needed was to figure out where they were and where they had come from.

The Metro Police Department was on Stewart Street in downtown. Bosch stopped at the front desk and explained he was an out-of-town investigator wanting to make a courtesy check-in with the homicide squad. He was directed to the third-floor detective bureau, where a desk man escorted him through a deserted squad room to the commander's office. Captain John Felton was a thick-necked, deeply tanned man of about fifty. Bosch figured he had probably given the welcome speech to at least a hundred cops from all over the country in the last month alone. Las Vegas was that kind of place. Felton asked Bosch to sit down and he gave him the standard spiel.

"Detective Bosch, welcome to Las Vegas. Lucky for you I decided to come in on the holiday to take care of some of this paperwork that haunts me. Otherwise, there'd be nobody here. Anyway, I hope you find your stay enjoyable and productive. If there is anything you need, don't hesitate to call. I can promise you nothing, but if you request something that is within my power to provide, I will be more than happy to provide it. So, that out of the way, why don't you tell me what brings you here?"

Bosch gave him a quick rundown on the case. Felton wrote down the name Tony Aliso and the last days he was known to have stayed in Las Vegas and where.

"I'm just trying to run down his activities on the days he was here."

"You think he was followed from here and then taken off in L.A.?"

"I don't think anything at the moment. We don't have evidence of that."

"And I hope you won't find any. That's not the kind of press we want to get in L.A. What else you got?"

Bosch pulled his briefcase onto his lap and opened it.

"I've got two sets of prints taken off the body. We—"

"The body?"

"He was wearing a treated leather jacket. We got the prints with the laser. Anyway, we ran them on AFIS, NCIC, California DOJ, the works, but got nothing. I thought maybe you'd run them through your own computer, see what happens."

While the Automated Fingerprint Identification System used by the LAPD was a computer network of dozens of fingerprint databases across the country, it didn't connect them all. And most big-city police departments had their own private databases. In Vegas they would be prints taken from people who applied for jobs for the city or the casinos. They were also prints taken from people on the sly, prints the department shouldn't legally have because their owners had simply fallen under the suspicion of the department but had never been arrested. It was against this database that Bosch was hopeful Felton would check the sets from the Aliso case.

"Well, let me see what you have," Felton said. "I can't promise anything. We've probably gotta few that the national nets don't, but it's a long shot."

Bosch handed over print cards Art Donovan had prepared for him.

"So you are starting at the Mirage?" the captain asked after he put the cards to the side of his desk.

"Yeah. I'll show his picture around, go through the motions, see what I can come up with."

"You're telling me everything you know, right?"

"Right," Bosch lied.

"Okay." Felton opened a desk drawer and took out a business card and handed it over to Bosch. "That's got my office and pager on it. Call me if anything comes up. I've got the pager with me at all times. Meantime, I'll get back to you about the prints, one way or the other, by tomorrow morning."

Bosch thanked him and left. In the lobby of the police station he called the SID office at LAPD and asked Donovan if he'd had time to check out the tiny pieces of glitter they had found in the cuffs of Tony Aliso's pants.

"Yeah, but you aren't going to like it," Donovan said. "It's just glitter. Tinted aluminum. You know, like they use in costuming and in celebrations. Your guy probably went to a party or something, they were throwing this stuff around, maybe popping it out of party favors or something, and some of it got on him. He could brush off what he could see, but he didn't see the particles that fell into the cuffs of his pants. They stayed."

"Okay. Anything else?"

"Uh, no. Not on the evidence at least."

"Then on what?"

"Well, Harry, you know the guy from OCID that you were talking on the phone with last night while we were in the shed?"

"Carbone?"

"Yeah, Dominic Carbone. Well, he dropped by the lab today. He was asking questions about what we found last night."

Bosch's vision darkened. He said nothing and Donovan continued.

"He said he was here on something else and was just acting curious. But, Harry, I don't know. It seemed more than just a passing interest, if you know what I mean."

"Yeah, I know what you mean. How much did you tell him?"

"Well, before I caught on and started wondering what was going on, I sort of let slip we pulled prints off the jacket. Sorry, Harry, but I was proud. It's rare that we pull righteous prints off a dead guy's jacket, and I guess I was sort of braggin' about it."

"It's okay. You tell him we didn't get anything with them?"

"Yeah, I said they came back clean. But then . . . then he asked for a copy of the set, said he might be able to do something with them, whatever that means."

"What did you do?"

"What do you think? I gave him a set."

"You what?"

"Just kidding, Harry. I told him to call you if he wanted a set."

"Good. What else you tell him?"

"That's it, Harry."

"Okay, Art, it's cool. I'll check you later."

"See you, Harry. Hey, where are you, anyway?"

"Vegas."

"Really? Hey, put down a five for me on seven on the roulette wheel. Do it one time. I'll pay you when you get back. Unless I win. Then you pay me."

Bosch got back to his room forty-five minutes before his appointment with Hank Meyer. He used the time to shower, shave and change into one of his fresh shirts. He felt refreshed, ready to go back into the desert heat.

Meyer had arranged to have the sports book clerks and dealers who worked the poker pit on the previous Thursday and Friday evening shifts to be interviewed one at a time in his office. There were six men and three women. Eight were dealers and one was the clerk Aliso always placed his sports bets with. During any shift, the poker dealers rotated around the casino's six poker tables every twenty minutes. This meant that all eight had dealt cards to Aliso during his last visit to Las Vegas, and by virtue of his regular trips to the casino, they readily recognized him and knew him.

With Meyer sitting by watching, Bosch quickly moved through the interviews with the poker dealers in an hour. He was able to establish that Aliso usually played the five-to-ten table. This meant each hand started with a five-dollar ante and each deal carried a minimum bet of five dollars and a maximum of ten. Three raises were allowed per deal. Since the game was seven card stud, that meant there were five deals per hand. Bosch quickly realized that if a table was full with eight players, each hand could easily result in several hundred dollars being at stake in the pot. Aliso was playing in a league far removed from the Friday night poker games Bosch had participated in with the dicks from the detective bureau.

According to the dealers, Aliso had played for about three hours on Thursday night and had come out about even. He played another two hours early Friday evening, and it was estimated that he left the tables a couple thousand short. None of them recalled Aliso ever being a big winner or loser during previous visits. He always came out a few thousand light or heavy. He seemed to know when to quit.

The dealers also noted that Aliso was always quick with the gratuity. His standard tip was ten dollars in chips for every win, a twenty-five chip on particularly big pots. It was that practice more than anything else that endeared him to their memories. He always played alone, drank gin and tonic and small-talked with the other players. In recent months, the dealers said, Aliso had been in the company of a young blond woman, barely into her twenties. She never played but would work the slots nearby and come back to Tony when she needed more money. Tony never introduced her to anybody and none of the dealers ever overheard her name. In his notebook, where Bosch jotted this down, he wrote "Layla?" after this entry.

After the dealers came Aliso's favorite sports book clerk. She was a mousy-looking bottle-blonde named Irma Chantry. She lit a cigarette as soon as she sat down and talked in a voice that indicated she had never gone long without a smoke. She said that on both of the last two nights Aliso had been in town he had bet on the Dodgers.

"He had a system," she said. "He always doubled up until he won."

"How do you mean?"

"Well, that first night he put a grand down on the Dodgers to win. They lost. So the next day he comes in and puts down two big ones on them again. They won. So after you take out the casino vig, he was almost a grand up for the trip. Except he never picked it up."

"He didn't collect?"

"Nope. But that's not unusual. His chit was good as long as he kept it. He could come in anytime, and we'd stick it in the computer. It'd happened before. He'd win but he wouldn't collect until the next time he was in town."

"How do you know he didn't take it to another clerk?"

"Tony wouldn't do that. He always cashed out with me, that way he could tip me. He always said I was his lucky charm."

Bosch thought a moment. He knew the Dodgers had played at home Friday night, and Aliso's plane left Las Vegas at ten. Therefore, it was a pretty safe bet that Aliso had to be at McCarran International or already on his plane heading back to L.A. before the game was over. But there was no betting receipt found in his wallet or on his person. Harry considered the missing briefcase again. Would it have been in there? Could a betting slip worth four thousand dollars minus the vig be motive for his murder? It seemed unlikely, but still, it was something to pursue. He looked at Irma, who was drawing so hard on her cigarette that he could see the outline of her teeth on her cheeks.

"What if somebody else cashed the bet? With another clerk. Is there any way to tell that?"

Irma hesitated and Meyer broke in.

"There's a good chance," he said. "Each receipt is coded with a clerk number and time the bet was placed."

He looked at Irma.

"Irma, you remember taking very many two-thousand-dollar bets on the Dodgers on Friday?"

"Nope, not a one, other than Tony's."

"We'll get on it," Meyer said to Bosch. "We'll start going through the cashed receipts going back to Friday night. If Mr. Aliso's bet was cashed, then we'll know when it was cashed and we'll have video of who cashed it."

Bosch looked at Irma again. She was the only one of the casino employees he had talked to who had referred to Aliso by his first name. He wanted to ask her if there was something more than a gambling relationship between them. But he knew that it was likely that employees were forbidden by the casino to date or fraternize with the guests. He couldn't ask her in front of Meyer and expect a straight reply. He made a mental note to track Irma down later and then excused her from the interview.

Bosch looked at his watch and saw he had forty minutes until the conference call with Billets and the others. He asked Meyer if he'd had a chance to get the surveillance tapes from the eye in the sky over the poker pit for Thursday and Friday.

"I just want to see the guy gambling," he said. "I want to get a feel for him in life."

"I understand and, yes, the tapes are ready for viewing. I told you we wanted to cooperate completely."

They left the office and walked down a corridor to a tech room. The room was dimly lit and very quiet except for the thrum of an air conditioner. There were six consoles arranged in two lines where men in gray blazers sat and watched banks of six video monitors per console. On the video screens Bosch could see various overhead views of gambling tables. Each console had an electronic control board that allowed the operator to change focus or magnification of a particular camera view.

"If they wanted to," Meyer whispered, "they could tell you what cards a player is holding at any black jack table in the house. It's amazing."

Meyer led Bosch to a supervisor's office off the tech room. There was more video equipment as well as a bank of tape storage units. There was a small desk and another man in a gray blazer sat behind it. Meyer introduced him as Cal Smoltz, the supervisor.

"Cal, are we set up?"

"This screen here," Smoltz said, pointing to one of the fifteen-inch monitors. "We'll start with Thursday. I had one of the dealers come in and ID your guy. He shows up at eight-twenty on Thursday and plays until eleven."

He started the tape. It was grainy black and white, similar to the quality of the Archway surveillance tape, but this one was filmed in real time. No jerking movements. It began with the man Bosch recognized as Aliso being led to an open chair at a table by a pit boss. The pit boss carried a rack of chips which he put down on the table in front of Aliso's spot. Aliso nodded and exchanged smiles with the dealer, a woman Bosch had interviewed earlier, and began to play.

"How much in the rack?" Bosch asked.

"Five hundred," Smoltz said. "I've already gone through this on fast speed. He never buys another rack and at the end when he cashes out, he looks like he's just shy of a full rack. You want it on real time or fast speed?"

"Speed it up."

Bosch watched closely as the tape sped through the hours. He saw Aliso take four gin and tonics, fold early on most of the deals, win five big pots and lose six others. It was pretty uneventful. Smoltz slowed the tape down when the time counter neared eleven, and Bosch watched as Aliso called for the pit boss, cashed out and left the frame of the camera.

"Okay," Smoltz said. "On Friday, we have two tapes."

"How come?" Bosch asked.

"He played at two tables. When he first showed up, there wasn't a seat open at the five-and-dime table. We only have one because there aren't that many customers who want to play for those stakes. So he played on a one-to-five until something came open. This tape is the one-to-five, the cheaper table."

Another video began and Bosch watched as Aliso went through the same motions as in the other tape. This time, Bosch noticed, Aliso was wearing the leather sports jacket. He also noticed that while Aliso exchanged the routine nod and smile with the dealer, he thought he saw Aliso nod at a player across the table. It was a woman and she nodded back. But the angle of the camera was bad and Bosch could not see her face. He told Smoltz to keep it on real-time play and he watched the tape for a few minutes, waiting to see if any other acknowledgment would pass between the two players.

It appeared that no further communication was occurring between the two. But five minutes into the tape a dealer rotation occurred, and when the new dealer sat down, also a woman Bosch had interviewed an hour earlier, she acknowledged both Aliso and the woman across the table from him.

"Can you freeze it there?" Bosch asked.

Without answering, Smoltz froze the image on the screen.

"Okay," Bosch said. "Which dealer is that?"

"That's Amy Rohrback. You talked to her."

"Right. Hank, could you bring her back up here?"

"Uh, sure. Can I ask why?"

"This player," Bosch said, pointing on the screen to the woman across from Aliso. "She acknowledged Aliso when he sat down. Amy Rohrback just acknowledged her. She must be a regular. She knew Aliso and Rohrback. I might want to talk to her and your dealer might know her name."

"Okay, I'll go get her, but if she's in the middle of a dealing rotation I'll have to wait."

"That's fine."

While Meyer went down to the casino, Bosch and Smoltz continued to review the tapes on fast speed. Aliso played for twenty-five minutes at the one-to-five table before the pit boss came around, picked up his rack of chips and moved him to the more expensive five-to-ten table. Smoltz put in the tape for that table and Aliso played there, losing miserably, for two more hours. Three times he bought five-hundred-dollar racks of chips and each time he quickly lost them. Finally, he put the few remaining chips he had left down as a tip for the dealer and got up and left the table.

The tape was finished and Meyer still hadn't returned with Rohrback. Smoltz said he would spool up the tape with the mystery woman on it so it would be ready. When it was, Bosch told him to fast-forward it to see if there was ever a moment when her face was visible. Smoltz did so and after five minutes of straining to watch the quick movements of the people on the tape, Bosch saw the mystery woman look up at the camera.

"There! Back it up and slow it down."

Smoltz did so and Bosch watched the screen as the woman took out a cigarette, lit it and leaned her head back, her face toward the ceiling camera, and exhaled. The discharged smoke blurred her image. But before it had done so, Bosch thought he had recognized her. He was frozen to silence. Smoltz backed the tape up to the moment her face was most clearly visible and froze the image on the screen. Bosch just stared silently.

Smoltz was saying something about the image being the best they could hope for when the door opened and Meyer came back in. He was alone.

"Uh, Amy had just started a deal set, so it's going to be another ten minutes or so. I gave her the message to come back up."

"You can call down there and tell her never mind," Bosch said, his eyes still on the screen.

"Really? How come?"

"I know who she is."

"Who is she?"

Bosch was silent a moment. He didn't know if it was seeing her light the cigarette or some pang of deeper anxiety, but he dearly wanted a cigarette.

"Just somebody. I knew her a long time ago."

Bosch sat on the bed with the phone on his lap, waiting for the conference call. But his mind was far off. He was remembering a woman he had long believed was out of his life. What had it been now, four, five years? His mind was such a rush of thoughts and emotions, he couldn't remember for sure. It had been long enough, he realized. It should be no surprise to him that she was out of prison by now.

"Eleanor Wish," he said out loud.

He thought of the jacaranda trees outside her townhouse in Santa Monica. He thought of them making love and the small crescent scar barely visible on her jawline. He remembered the question she had asked him so long ago, when they were making love. "Do you believe you can be alone and not be lonely?"

The phone rang. Bosch jerked out of his reverie and answered. It was Billets.

"Okay, Harry, we're all here. Can you hear me all right?"

"It's not good but it probably won't get any better."

"Right, city equipment. Okay, let's start by everybody kind of reporting on the day's events. Harry, you want to go first?"

"All right. There's not a lot to tell."

He went over the details of what he had done so far, stressing the missing betting receipt as something to watch for. He told of his review of the surveillance tapes but left out mention of his recognizing Eleanor Wish. He had decided that there was no definitive sign of a connection between her and Aliso and that for the time being he would keep it to himself. He ended his summary by telling the others of his plans to check out Dolly's, the place Aliso had last called from his office line at Archway, and the woman named Layla who was mentioned when Bosch called there.

Next it was Edgar's turn. He announced the flavor-of-the-month screenwriter had been cleared through alibi and Edgar's own gut instinct that the young man might have rightfully hated Aliso but was not of the personality type that would act on that hate with a twenty-two.

Edgar said he had also interviewed the employees at the garage where Aliso had his car washed and waxed while he went to Las Vegas. Part of the service was airport pickup, and Edgar said the man who picked Aliso up said that Tony was alone, relaxed and in no hurry.

"It was a routine pickup," Edgar said. "Aliso took his car and went home. Gave the guy a twenty-buck tip. So whoever put him down, they intercepted him on the way home. My guess is it was somewhere up there on Mulholland. Lot of deserted curves. You could stop a guy if you did it quick. Probably two people."

"What did the valet say about luggage?" Bosch asked.

"Oh, yeah," Edgar said. "He said that as near as he could remember, Tony had the two bags the wife described, a silver briefcase and one of those hanging bags. He hadn't checked either one for the flight."

Bosch nodded, though he was alone.

"What about the media?" Bosch said. "We put anything out yet?"

"It's being handled," Billets said. "Media relations is putting out a release first thing tomorrow. It will have a picture of the Rolls. They'll also make the car available at the OPG for video. And I'll be available for sound bites. I'm hoping the stations will pick it up. Anything else, Jerry?"

Edgar concluded by saying he had the murder book up to speed and that he was halfway through the list of plaintiffs from the various lawsuits against Aliso. He said he would be setting up interviews for the next day with others who had allegedly been wronged by Aliso. Lastly, he said he had called the coroner's office and the autopsy on Aliso had not yet been scheduled.

"Okay," Billets said. "Kiz, what do you have?"

Rider broke her report into two parts. The first was on her interview with Veronica Aliso, which she covered quickly, saying the woman had been extremely closemouthed during their morning interview in comparison to the night before when Bosch and Rider brought her the news of her husband's death. The morning session consisted mostly of yes and no answers and a few added details. The couple had been married seventeen years. They had no children. Veronica Aliso had been in two of her husband's films and never worked again.

"You think she talked to a lawyer about talking to us?" Bosch asked.

"She didn't say so, but I think that's exactly what's going on," Rider said. "Just getting what I got was like pulling teeth."

"Okay, what else?" Billets said, trying to keep the discussion moving.

Rider went on to the second part of her day's investigation, which was the focus on the financial records of Anthony Aliso. Even listening on the poor conference line connection, Bosch could tell Kiz was excited about what she had learned so far.

"Basically, this guy's financial portfolio shows an extremely comfortable standard of living. He's got high-five-figure sums in his personal bank accounts, zeroed-out credit cards, that house that has a seven-hundred-thousand mortgage against a value of a million one. That's it, though, as far as what I could find. The Rolls is leased, his wife's Lincoln is leased, and the office we know is leased."

She paused a moment before going on.

"Incidentally, Harry, if you have the time, here's something you might want to check out over there. Both the cars are leased to his company, TNA Productions, through a dealership over there in Vegas. You might want to check it out if there's time. It's called Ridealong—one word—Incorporated. The address is two thousand and two Industrial Drive, suite three-thirty."

Bosch's jacket, with his notebook inside it, was on a chair on the other side of the room. He wrote the name and address down on a little pad that was on the night table.

"Okay," Rider said, "so now we go on to his business, and this is where it gets pretty interesting. I'm really only halfway through the records we pulled out of his office, but so far it looks like this guy was into a class A scam. And I'm not talking about ripping off some schmuck's student screenplays. I think that was just his side hobby. I'm talking about him running a laundry. I think he was a front for somebody."

She waited a beat before going on. Bosch moved to the edge of the bed, excitement tickling the back of his neck.

"We've got tax returns, production orders, equipment rentals, pays and owes from the making of several films—more than a dozen. All of it straight-to-video stuff. Like Veronica said, it's just this side of porno. I looked at some of the tapes he had in his office and it was all pretty awful stuff. Not much in the way of narrative unless you count the buildup of tension waiting for the female lead to get naked.

"The only problem is that the ledgers don't match what's on the film and most of the big checks paid by TNA Productions went to mail drops and companies that I'm finding out don't exist anywhere but on paper."

"How do you mean?" Billets asked.

"I'm saying his business records show a million to a million five going into each of these so-called movies, and you look at the tapes and, I'm telling you, there can't be more than a hundred, maybe two hundred thousand involved. My brother works in the business as an editor, and I know enough to know that the kind of money Aliso's books show being spent on these movies is not being spent on these movies. I think that what he was doing was using these flicks to launder money, lots of money."

"Run it down, Kiz," Billets said. "Just how would he do it?"

"Okay, start with his source. We'll call him Mr. X for now. Mr. X has a million bucks he shouldn't have. Whether it's from drugs or whatever, he needs to clean it up, legitimize it so he can put it in the bank and spend it without drawing attention. He gives it to Tony Aliso—invests it in Tony's production company. Aliso then makes a cheap movie with it, spending less than a tenth of it.

"But when it comes to keeping the books, he makes it look like he's used all of the money for production costs. He's got checks going out almost weekly to various production companies, prop companies, movie equipment companies. All the checks are in the eight- to nine-thousand range, just under the government reporting limit."

Bosch listened carefully as she spoke. He had his eyes closed and concentrated. He admired Rider's ability to cull all of this out of the records.

"Okay, then at the end of production, Tony probably dubs a few thousand copies of the flick, sells them or tries to sell them to independent video stores and distributors—because the chains wouldn't touch this crap—and that's that, end of show. But what he has done is turned around and given back to Mr. X, his original investor, about eighty cents on the dollar in the form of payments to these dummy companies. It's a shell game. Whoever is behind these companies is being paid with his own money for services *not* rendered. But now the money's legit. It's clean and he can walk into any bank in America and deposit it, pay taxes on it, then spend it. Meantime, Tony Aliso takes a nice production fee for his end of it and goes on to the next flick. It looks like he was handling two or three of these productions a year and clearing half a million in fees himself."

They were all silent for a few moments before Rider spoke again.

"There's only one problem," Rider said.

"He's got the IRS on him," Bosch said.

"Riiiiiight," she responded, and he could visualize the smile on her face. "It's a nice scam but it was about to go down the toilet. The IRS was going to take a look at Tony's books later this month, and there is a good chance that if I could come up with this in just one day, the feds would pick up on it in an hour."

"That would make Tony a danger to Mr. X," Edgar said.

"Especially if he was going to cooperate with the audit," Rider added.

Someone on the other end of the line whistled, but Bosch couldn't tell who it was. He guessed it was Edgar.

"So what's next, find Mr. X?" Bosch asked.

"For starters," Rider replied. "I'm working up a request I'll fax to the state department of corporations tomorrow morning. It's got all the dummy companies on it. Maybe, whoever he is, he was foolish enough to put a real name or address on the incorporation forms. I'm also working on another search warrant. I have the canceled checks from Tony's company. I want the records of the accounts the checks were deposited to, maybe find out where the money went after Tony cleaned it up."

"What about the IRS?" Bosch asked. "Have you talked to them?"

"They're closed for the holiday. But according to the notice Aliso got in the mail, there is a criminal prefix on the audit number. That makes me think this wasn't a random audit. They were tipped somehow. There's an agent assigned to it and I'll be on the phone to him first thing in the morning."

"You know," Edgar said, "this whole thing about OCID taking a pass is beginning to stink. Whether Tony was hooked up with the Eye-talians or not, this shit is as organized as organized crime can get. And I'd bet my last button that they'd heard somewhere along the line, whether it was from the IRS or not, about our guy here."

"I think you're right," Billets said.

"I forgot to mention something," Bosch threw in. "Today I was talking with Art Donovan. He said the guy I talked to at OCID last night, a supe named Carbone, well he just happens to show up over at SID today and starts asking Art about the case. Art says the guy's acting like he's not interested, but he's very interested, you know what I mean?"

Nobody said anything for a long moment.

"So what do we do?" Edgar asked.

Bosch closed his eyes again and waited. Whatever Billets said would determine the course of the case as well as affect his regard for her. Bosch knew what her predecessor would have done. He would have made sure the case was dumped on OCID.

"We don't do anything," Billets finally said. "It's our case, we work it. But be careful. If OCID is sniffing around after taking a pass, then there is something going on here we don't know about yet."

Another silence passed and Bosch opened his eyes. He was liking Billets better all the time.

"Okay," Billets said. "I think we should be focusing on Tony's company as a priority. I want to shift most of our attention there. Harry, can you wrap up Vegas quickly and get back here?"

"Unless I find something, I should be out of here before lunch tomorrow. But remember this, last night Mrs. Aliso told us that Tony always told her he came to Vegas to see investors. Maybe our Mr. X is right here."

"Could be," Billets said. "Okay then, again, people, it's been good work. Let's stay on it."

They said their good-byes and Bosch put the phone back on the side table. He felt invigorated by the advances of the investigation. He just sat there a moment and reveled in the feeling of the adrenaline jazzing through his body. It had been a long time coming. He squeezed his hands into fists and banged them together.

Bosch stepped out of the elevator and began moving through the casino. It was quieter than most casinos he had been in—there wasn't any yelling or whooping from the craps table, no begging of the dice to come up seven. The people who gambled here were different, Bosch thought. They came with money and they'd leave with money no matter how much they lost. The smell of desperation wasn't here. This was the casino for the well-heeled and thick-walleted.

He passed by a crowded roulette wheel and remembered Donovan's bet. He squeezed between two smoking Asian women, put down a five and asked for a chip but was told it was a twenty-five-dollar-minimum table. One of the Asians pointed with her cigarette across the casino to another roulette table.

"They'll take your five over there," she said with distaste.

Bosch thanked her and headed over to the cheap table. He put a five chip down on the seven and watched the wheel turn, the little metal ball bouncing over the numbers. It did nothing for him. He knew that true-blue gamblers said it wasn't the winning and losing, it was the anticipation. Whether it was the next card, the fall of the dice or the number the little ball stopped on, it was those few seconds of waiting and hoping and wishing that charged them, that addicted them. But it did nothing for Bosch.

The ball stopped on five and Donovan owed Bosch five. Bosch turned and started looking for the poker pit. He saw a sign and headed that way. It was early, not yet eight, and there were several chairs open at the tables. He checked the faces and did not see Eleanor Wish, though he wasn't really expecting to. Bosch recognized many of the dealers he had interviewed earlier, including Amy Rohrback. He was tempted to take one of the empty chairs at her table and ask how she had recognized Eleanor Wish but figured it wouldn't be cool to question her while she worked.

While he considered what to do, the pit boss stepped up to him and asked if he was waiting to play. Bosch recognized him as the one from the video who had led Tony Aliso to his place at the tables.

"No, I'm just watching," Bosch said. "You got a minute while it's slow?"

"A minute for what?"

"I'm the cop who's been interviewing your people."

"Oh, yeah. Little Hank told me about that."

He introduced himself as Frank King and Bosch shook his hand.

"Sorry, I couldn't come up. But I don't work on rotation. I had to be here. This is about Tony A., right?"

"Yeah, you knew him, right?"

"Sure, we all knew him. Good guy. Too bad about what happened."

"How do you know what happened?"

Bosch had specifically not told any of the dealers about Aliso's demise during the interviews.

"Little Hank," King said. "He said he got shot up or something in L.A. What do you want, I mean you live in L.A. you take your chances."

"I guess. How long have you known him?"

"We go back years, me and Tony. I used to be at the Flamingo before the Mirage opened. Tony stayed there back then. He's been coming out here a long time."

"You ever socialize with him? Outside the casino?"

"Once or twice. But that was usually by accident. I'd be some place and Tony'd just happen to come in or something. We'd have a drink, be cordial, but that was about it. I mean, he was a guest of the hotel and I'm an employee. We weren't buddies, if you know what I mean."

"I get it. What places did you run into him?"

"Oh, Jesus, I don't know. You're talking—hold on a sec."

King cashed out a player who was leaving Amy Rohrback's table. Bosch had no idea how much the man had started with, but he was leaving with forty dollars and a frown. King sent him away with a better-luck-next-time salute and then came back to Bosch.

"Like I was saying, I saw him in a couple bars. You're talking a long time ago. One was the round bar at the Stardust. One of my buddies was the barkeep and I used to drop by there after work time to time. I saw Tony there and he sent over a drink. This was probably three years ago, at least. I don't know what good it does you."

"Was he alone?"

"No, he was with some broad. Young piece of fluff. Nobody I recognized."

"All right, what about the other time, when was that?"

"That was maybe last year sometime. I was with a bachelor party—it was for Marty, who runs the craps here—and we all went to get straightened out at Dolly's. It's a strip club on the north side. And Tony was in there, too. He was by hisself and he came over and had a drink. In fact, he bought the whole table a drink. Must've been eight of us. He was a nice guy. That was it."

Bosch nodded. So Aliso had been a regular at Dolly's going back at least a year. Bosch was planning to go there, to get a line on the woman named Layla. She was probably a dancer, Bosch guessed, and Layla was more than probably not her real name.

"You seen him more recently with anybody?"

"You mean a broad?"

"Yeah, some of the dealers said there was a blonde recently."

"Yeah, I think I saw him a couple, three times with the blonde. He was giving her the dough to play the machines while he played cards. I don't know who it was, if that's what you mean."

Bosch nodded.

"That it?" King asked.

"One more thing. Eleanor Wish, you know her? She was playing the cheap table on Friday night. Tony played for a while at the same table. It looked like they knew each other."

"I know a player named Eleanor. I never knew her last name. She the looker, brown hair, brown eyes, still in nice shape despite, as they say, the encroachment of time?"

King smiled at his clever use of words. Bosch didn't.

"That sounds like her. She a regular?"

"Yeah, I see her in here maybe once a week, maybe less. She's a local, as far as I know. The local players run a circuit. Not all the casinos have live poker, see. It doesn't earn a lot for the house. We have it as a courtesy to our customers, but we hope they play a little poker and a lot of black jack. Anyway, the locals run a circuit so they don't play against the same faces all the time. So they maybe play here one night, over to Harrah's the next, then it's the Flamingo, then maybe they work the downtown casinos a few nights. You know, like that."

"You mean she's a pro?"

"No, I mean she's a local and she plays a lot. Whether she's got a day job or lives off poker I don't know. I don't think I ever cashed her out for more than two bills. That's not a lot. The other thing is I heard she tips the dealers too well. The pros don't do that."

Bosch asked King to list all the casinos in the city that he knew offered live poker, then thanked him.

"You know, I doubt you're going to find anything other than Tony knowin' her to say hello to, that's all."

"Why's that?"

"Too old. She's a nice lookin' gal, but she was too old for Tony. He liked 'em young."

Bosch nodded and let him go. He then wandered through the casino in a quandary. He didn't know what to do about Eleanor Wish. He was intrigued by what she was doing and King's explanation about her being

a once-a-week regular seemed to make her recognition of Aliso innocent
enough. But while she most likely had nothing to do with the case,
Bosch felt the desire to talk to her. To tell her he was sorry for the way
things had turned out, for the way he had made them turn out.

He saw a bank of pay phones near the front desk and used one to call
information. He asked for a listing for Eleanor Wish and got a recording
saying the phone number was unlisted at the customer's request. Bosch
thought a moment and then dug through the pocket of his jacket. He
found the card that Felton, the Metro detectives captain, had given him
and paged him. He waited with his hand on the phone so no one else
could use it for four minutes before it rang.

"Felton?"

"Yeah, who's this?"

"Bosch. From earlier today?"

"Right. L.A. I still haven't gotten the prints back. I'm expecting to
hear something first thing."

"No, I'm not calling about that. I was wondering if you or any of
your people have enough juice with the phone company to get me a listing, number and address."

"It's unlisted?"

Bosch felt like telling him that he wouldn't be calling if the account
was listed but let it go.

"Yeah, unlisted."

"Who is it?"

"A local. Somebody who was playing poker with Tony Aliso on Friday night."

"So?"

"So, Captain, they knew each other and I want to talk to her. If you
can't help me, fine. I'll find her some other way. I was calling because you
told me to call if I needed something. This is what I need. Can you do it
or not?"

There was silence for a few moments before Felton came back.

"Okay, give it to me. I'll see what I can get. Where you going to be?"

"I'm mobile. Can I ring you back?"

Felton gave him his home number and told him to call back in a
half hour.

Bosch used the time to walk across the Strip to Harrah's to check out the poker room. Eleanor Wish wasn't there. He then went back out onto the Strip and headed down to the Flamingo. He took his jacket off because it was still very warm out. It would be dark soon and he hoped it would cool off then.

In the Flamingo casino he found her. She was playing at a one-to-four table with five men. The seat on her left was open but Bosch didn't take it. Instead, he hung back with the crowd around a roulette table and watched her.

Eleanor Wish's face showed total concentration on the cards as she played. Bosch watched as the men she was playing against stole looks at her, and it gave Bosch a weird thrill to know they secretly coveted her. In the ten minutes he watched, she won one hand—he was too far away to see what she won with—and bailed out early on five others. It looked as though she was well ahead. She had a full rack in front of her and six stacks of chips on the blue felt.

After he watched her win a second hand—this time a massive pot—and the dealer began to push the pile of blue chips to her spot, Bosch looked around for a pay phone. He called Felton at home and got Wish's home phone and address. The captain told him that the address, on Sands Avenue, was not far off the strip in an area of apartment buildings mostly inhabited by casino employees. Bosch didn't tell him that he had already found her. Instead, he thanked him and hung up.

When Bosch got back to the poker room she was gone. The five men were still there, but there was a new dealer and no Eleanor Wish. Her chips were gone. She had cashed out and he had lost her. Bosch cursed to himself.

"You looking for someone?"

Bosch turned around. It was Eleanor. There was no smile on her face, just a slight look of irritation or maybe defiance. His eyes fell to the small white scar on her jawline.

"I, uh . . . Eleanor . . . yeah, I was looking for you."

"You were always so obvious. I picked you out one minute after you were there. I would've gotten up then but I was bringing that guy from Kansas along. He thought he knew when I was bluffing. He didn't know shit. Just like you."

Bosch was tongue-tied. This was not how he had envisioned this happening and he didn't know how to proceed.

"Look, Eleanor, I, uh, just wanted to see how you were doing. I don't know, I just . . ."

"Right. So you just flew out to Vegas to look me up? What's going on, Bosch?"

Bosch looked around. They were standing in a crowded section of the casino. Players passing on both sides of them, the cacophony of the slot machine din and whoops of success and failure created a blur of sight and sound around him.

"I'll tell you. Do you want to get a drink or something, maybe something to eat?"

"One drink."

"You know a place that's quiet?"

"Not here. Follow me."

They left through the front doors of the casino and walked out into the dry heat of the night. The sun was all the way down now and it was neon that lit the sky.

"There's a bar in Caesar's that's quiet. It doesn't have any machines."

She led him across the street and onto the people mover that delivered them to the front door of Caesar's Palace. They walked past the front desk and into a circular bar where there were only three other customers. Eleanor had been right. It was an oasis with no poker or slot machines. Just the bar. He ordered a beer and she ordered scotch and water. She lit a cigarette.

"You didn't used to smoke before," he said. "In fact, I remember you were—"

"That was a long time ago. Why are you here?"

"I'm on a case."

During the walk over he'd had time to compose himself and put his thoughts in order.

"What case and what does it have to do with me?"

"It's got nothing to do with you, but you knew the guy. You played poker with him on Friday at the Mirage."

Curiosity and confusion creased her brow. Bosch remembered how she used to do that and remembered how attractive he'd found it. He wanted to reach over and touch her but he didn't. He had to remind himself that she was different now.

"Anthony Aliso," he said.

He watched the surprise play on her face and believed instantly that it was real. He wasn't a poker player from Kansas who couldn't read a bluff. He had known this woman and believed from the look on her face she clearly did not know Aliso was dead until he told her.

"Tony A . . . ," she said and then let it trail off.

"Did you know him well or just to play against?"

She had a distant look in her dark eyes.

"Just when I'd see him there. At the Mirage. I've been playing there on Fridays. A lot of fresh money and faces come in. I'd see him there a couple times a month. For a while I thought he was a local, too."

"How'd you find out he wasn't?"

"He told me. We had a drink together a couple months ago. There were no seats at the tables. We put our names in and told Frank, he's the night man, to come get us at the bar when there was an opening. So we had a drink and that's when he told me he was from L.A. He said he was in the movie business."

"That's it, nothing else?"

"Well, yeah, he said other things. We talked. Nothing that stands out, though. We were passing the time until one of our names came up."

"You didn't see him again outside of playing?"

"No, and what's it to you? Are you saying I'm a suspect because I had a drink with the guy?"

"No, I'm not saying that, Eleanor. Not at all."

Bosch got out his own cigarettes and lit one. The waitress in a white-and-gold toga brought their drinks, and they settled into a silence for a long moment. Bosch had lost his momentum. He was back to not knowing what to say.

"Looked like you were doing pretty good tonight," he tried.

"Better than most nights. I got my quota and I got out."

"Quota?"

"Whenever I get two hundred up I cash out. I'm not greedy and I know luck doesn't last for long on any given night. I never lose more than a hundred, and if I'm lucky enough to get two hundred ahead, then I'm done for the night. I got there early tonight."

"How'd you—"

He stopped himself. He knew the answer.

"How'd I learn to play poker well enough to live off it? You spend three and a half years inside and you learn to smoke and play poker and other things."

She looked directly at him as if daring him to say anything about it. After another long moment she broke away and got out another cigarette. Bosch lit it for her.

"So there's no day job? Just the poker?"

"That's right. I've been doing this almost a year now. Kind of hard to find a straight job, Bosch. You tell 'em you're a former FBI agent and their eyes light up. Then you tell them you just got out of federal prison and they go dead."

"I'm sorry, Eleanor."

"Don't be. I'm not complaining. I make more than enough to get by, every now and then I meet interesting people like your guy Tony A., and there's no state income tax here. What do I have to complain about, except maybe that it gets to be over a hundred degrees in the shade about ninety times a year too many?"

The bitterness was not lost on him.

"I mean I'm sorry about everything. I know it doesn't do you any good now, but I wish I had it to do all over again. I've learned things since then, and I would've played it all differently. That's all I wanted to tell you. I saw you on the surveillance tape playing with Tony Aliso and I wanted to find you to tell you that. That's all I wanted."

She stubbed her half-finished smoke out in the glass ashtray and took a strong pull on her glass of scotch.

"I guess I should be going, then," she said.

She stood up.

"Do you need a ride anywhere?"

"No, I actually have a car, thank you."

She started out of the bar in the direction of the front doors but after a few yards stopped and came back to the table.

"You're right, you know."

"About what?"

"About it not doing me any good now."

With that she left. Bosch watched her push through the revolving doors and disappear into the night.

. . .

Following the directions he had written down when he spoke with Rhonda over the phone in Tony Aliso's office, Bosch found Dolly's on Madison in North Las Vegas. It was strictly an upper-crust club: twenty-dollar cover, two-drink minimum and you were escorted to your seat by a large man in a tuxedo with a starched collar that cut into his neck like a garrote. The dancers were upper-crust, too. Young and beautiful, they probably were just shy of having enough coordination and talent to work the big room shows on the Strip.

Bosch was led by the tuxedo to a table the size of a dinner plate about eight feet from the main stage, which was empty at the moment.

"A new dancer will be on stage in a couple minutes," the man in the tuxedo told Bosch. "Enjoy the show."

Bosch didn't know if he was supposed to tip the guy for seating him at such a close-up location as well as putting up with the tuxedo, but he let it go and the man didn't hang around with his hand out. Bosch had barely gotten his cigarettes out when a waitress in a red silk negligee, high heels and black fishnet stockings floated over and reminded him of the two-drink minimum. Bosch ordered beer.

While he waited for his two beers, Bosch took a look around. Business seemed slow, it being the Monday night tail-end of a holiday weekend. There were maybe twenty men in the place. Most of them were sitting by themselves and not looking at each other while they waited for the next nude woman to entertain them.

There were full-length mirrors on the side and rear walls. A bar ran along the left side of the room, and cut into the wall in the back was an arched entrance above which a red neon sign that glowed in the darkness announced PRIVATE DANCERS. The front wall was largely taken up by a shimmering curtain and the stage. A runway projected from the stage through the center of the room. The runway was the focus of several bright lights attached to a metal gridwork on the ceiling. Their brightness made the runway almost glow in contrast to the dark and smoky atmosphere of the seating area.

A disk jockey in a sound booth at the left side of the stage announced the next dancer would be Randy. An old Eddie Money song, "Two Tickets to Paradise," started blaring over the sound system as a tall brunette wearing blue jeans cut off to expose the lower half of her bottom and a neon pink bikini top charged through the shimmering curtain and started moving to the beat of the music.

Bosch was immediately mesmerized. The woman was beautiful and the first thought he had was to question why she was doing this. He had always believed that beauty helped women get away from many of the hardships of life. This woman, this girl, was beautiful and yet here she was. Maybe that was the real draw for these men, he thought. Not the glimpse of a naked woman, but the knowledge of submission, the thrill of knowing another one had been broken. Bosch began to think he had been wrong about beautiful women.

The waitress put down two beers on the little table and told Bosch he owed fifteen dollars. He almost asked her to repeat the price but then figured it came with the territory. He handed her a twenty, and when she started digging through the stack of bills on her tray for his change he waved it off.

She clutched his shoulder and bent down to his ear, making sure that she was at an angle that afforded him a look at her full cleavage.

"Thank you, darlin'. I 'preciate that. Let me know if you need anything else."

"There is one thing. Is Layla here tonight?"

"No, she's not here."

Bosch nodded. And the waitress straightened up.

"How about Rhonda then?" Bosch asked.

"That's Randy up there."

She pointed to the stage and Bosch shook his head and signaled her to come closer.

"No, Rhonda, like help, help me Rhonda. She working tonight? She was here last night."

"Oh, that Rhonda. Yeah, she's around. You just missed her set. She's probably in the back changing."

Bosch reached into his pocket for his money and put a five on her bar tray.

"Will you go back and tell her the friend of Tony's she talked to last night wants to buy her a drink?"

"Sure."

She squeezed his shoulder again and went off. Bosch's attention was drawn to the stage, where Randy's first song had just ended. The next song was "Lawyers, Guns and Money" by Warren Zevon. Bosch hadn't heard it in a while and he remembered how it had been an anthem among the uniforms back when he had worked patrol.

The dancer named Randy soon slipped out of her outfit and was nude except for a garter stretched tightly around her left thigh. Many of the men got up and met her as she danced her way slowly down the runway. They slid dollar bills under the garter. And when a man put a five under the strap, Randy bent down over him, using his shoulder to steady herself, and did an extra wiggle and kissed his ear.

Bosch watched this and was thinking that he now had a pretty good idea how Tony Aliso ended up with the small handprint on his shoulder, when a petite blond woman slid into the seat next to him.

"Hi. I'm Rhonda. You missed my show!"

"I heard that. I'm sorry."

"Well, I go back on in a half hour and do it all over again. I hope you'll stay. Yvonne said you wanted to buy me a drink?"

As if on cue Bosch saw the waitress heading their way. Bosch leaned over to Rhonda.

"Listen, Rhonda, I'd rather take care of you than give my money to the bar. So do me a favor and don't go exorbitant on me."

"Exorbitant . . . ?"

She crinkled her face up in a question.

"Don't go ordering champagne."

"Oh, I gotcha."

She ordered a martini and Yvonne floated back into the darkness.

"So, I didn't catch your name."

"Harry."

"And you're a friend of Tony's from L.A. You make movies, too?"

"No, not really."

"How do you know Tony?"

"I just met him recently. Listen, I'm trying to find Layla to get a message to her. Yvonne tells me she's not on tonight. You know where I can find her?"

Bosch noticed her stiffen. She knew something wasn't right.

"First of all, Layla doesn't work here anymore. I didn't know that when I talked to you last night, but she's gone and won't be back. And secondly, if you're a friend of Tony's, then how come you're asking me how to find her?"

She wasn't as dumb as Bosch had thought. He decided to go direct.

"Because Tony got himself killed, so I can't ask him. I want to find Layla to tell her and maybe warn her."

"*What?*" she shrieked.

Her voice cut through the loud music like a bullet through a slice of bread. Everybody in the place, including the naked Randy on the stage, looked in their direction. Bosch had no doubt that everyone in the place must think he had just propositioned her, offering an insulting fee for an equally insulting act.

"Keep it down, Randy," he quickly said.

"It's Rhonda."

"Rhonda then."

"What happened to him? He was just here."

"Somebody shot him in L.A. when he got back. Now, do you know where Layla is or not? You tell me and I'll take care of you."

"Well, what are you? Are you really his friend or not?"

"In a way I'm his only friend right now. I'm a cop. My name's Harry Bosch and I'm trying to find out who did it."

Her face took on a look that seemed even more horrified than when he told her Aliso was dead. Sometimes telling people you were a cop did that.

"Save your money," she said. "I can't talk to you."

She got up then and moved quickly away toward the door next to the stage. Bosch threw her name out after her but it was crushed by the sound of the music. He casually took a look around and noticed behind him that the tuxedo man was eyeing him through the darkness. Bosch decided he wasn't going to stick around for Rhonda's second show. He took one more gulp of beer—he hadn't even touched his second glass— and got up.

As he neared the exit the tuxedo leaned back and knocked on the mirror behind him. It was then that Bosch realized there was a door cut into the glass. It opened and the tuxedo stepped to the side to block Bosch's exit.

"Sir, could you step into the office, please?"

"What for?"

"Just step in. The manager would like a word with you."

Bosch hesitated but through the door he could see a lighted office where a man in a suit sat behind a desk. He stepped in and the tuxedo came in behind him and shut the door.

Bosch looked at the man behind the desk. Blond and beefy. Bosch wouldn't know whom to bet on if a fight broke out between the tuxedoed bouncer and the so-called manager. They were both brutes.

"I just got off the phone with Randy in the dressing room, she says you were asking about Tony Aliso."

"It was Rhonda."

"Rhonda, whatever, never-the-fuck-mind. She said you said he was dead."

He spoke with a midwestern accent. Sounded like southside Chicago, Bosch guessed.

"Was and still is."

The blond nodded to the tuxedo and his arm came up in a split second and hit Bosch with a backhand in the mouth. Bosch went back against the wall, banging the back of his head. Before his mind cleared, the tuxedo twirled him around until he was face-against-the-wall and leaned his weight against him. He felt the man's hands begin patting him down.

"Enough of the wiseass act," the blond said. "What are you doing talking to the girls about Tony?"

Before Bosch could say anything the hands running over his body found his gun.

"He's strapped," the tuxedo said.

Bosch felt the gun being jerked out of his shoulder holster. He also tasted blood in his mouth and felt rage building in his throat. The hands then found his wallet and his cuffs. Tuxedo threw them on the desk in front of the blond and held Bosch pinned against the wall with one hand. By straining to turn his head Bosch could watch the blond open the wallet.

"He's a cop, let him go."

The hand came off his neck and Bosch gruffly pulled away from the tuxedo.

"An L.A. cop," the blond said. "Hieronymus Bosch. Like that painter, huh? He did some weird stuff."

Bosch just looked at him and he handed the gun and cuffs and wallet back.

"Why'd you have him hit me?"

"That was a mistake. See, most cops what come in here, they announce themselves, they tell us their business and we help 'em if we can. You were sneaking around, Anonymous Hieronymus. We have a business to protect here."

He opened a drawer and pulled out a box of tissues and proffered it to Bosch.

"Your lip's bleeding."

Bosch took the whole box.

"So this is true what she says you told her. Tony's dead."

"That's what I said. How well did you know him?"

"See, that's good. You assume I knew him and put that assumption in your question. That's good."

"So then answer it."

"He was a regular in here. He was always trying to pick off girls. Told 'em he'd put 'em in the movies. Same old stuff. But, hell, they keep falling for it. Last two years he cost me three of my best girls. They're in L.A. now. He left 'em high and dry once he got them there and did what he wanted with 'em. They never learn."

"Why'd you let him keep coming in if he was picking off your girls?"

"He spent a lot of bread in here. Besides, there's no shortage of quiff here in Vegas. No shortage at all."

Bosch headed in another direction.

"What about Friday? Was he here?"

"No, I don't—yes, yes he was. He stopped by for a short while. I saw him out there."

With his hand he indicated a panel of video monitors showing every angle of the club and front entrance. It was equally as impressive as the setup Hank Meyer had shown Bosch at the Mirage.

"You remember seeing him, Gussie?" the blond asked the tuxedo.

"Yeah, he was here."

"There you go. He was here."

"No problems? He just came and went?"

"Right, no problems."

"Then why'd you fire Layla?"

The blond pinched his lips tight for a moment.

"Now I get it," he said. "You're one of those guys what likes to weave a web with words, get somebody caught in it."

"Maybe."

"Well, nobody's caught anywhere. Layla was Tony's latest fuck, that's true, but she's gone now. She won't be back."

"Yeah, and what happened to her?"

"Like you heard, I fired her. Saturday night."

"For what?"

"For any number of infractions of the rules. But it doesn't really matter because it's none of your business, now is it?"

"What did you say your name is?"

"I didn't."

"Then how 'bout if I just call you asshole, how would that be?"

"People 'round here call me Lucky. Can we get on with this, please?"

"Sure, we can get on with it. Just tell me what happened to Layla."

"Sure, sure. But I thought you were here to talk about Tony, least that's what Randy said."

"Rhonda."

"Rhonda, right."

Bosch was losing his patience but managed to just stare at him and wait him out.

"Layla, right. Well, Saturday night she got into a beef with one of the other girls. It got a little nasty and I had to make a choice. Modesty is one of my best girls, best producers. She gave me an ultimatum: either Layla goes or she goes. I had to let Layla go. Modesty, man, she sells ten, twelve splits of champagne a night to those suckers out there. I had to back her over Layla. I mean, Layla's good and she's a looker but she ain't no Modesty. Modesty's our top girl."

Bosch just nodded. So far his story jibed with the phone message Layla had left for Aliso. By drawing it out of the blond man, Bosch was getting a sense of how much he could be believed.

"What was the trouble between Layla and the other girl about?" he asked.

"I don't know and don't really care. Just your typical catfight. They didn't like each other since day one. See, Bosch, every club has its top girl. And here, it's Modesty. Layla was trying to move in on that and Modesty didn't want to be moved in on. But I have to say, Layla was trouble since she came here. None of the girls liked her act. She stole songs from the other girls, wouldn't stop with the pussy dust even when I told her, we just had a lot of trouble with her. I'm glad she's gone. I gotta business to run here. I can't be babysitting a bunch of spoiled cunts."

"Pussy dust?"

"Yeah, you know, she put that sparkly stuff on her snatch, made it sparkle in the dark and twinkle in the lights. Only problem is those sparkles come off and get on the suckers. She does a lap dance on you and *you* end up with a crotch that glitters. Then you go home and the wife figures it out and raises holy hell. I lose customers. I can't have that shit, Bosch. If it hadn't been Modesty, it would have been something else. I got rid of Layla when I got the chance."

Bosch thought about the story for a few moments.

"Okay," he said. "Just give me her address and I'll be on my way."

"I would but I can't."

"Don't start that shit now. I thought we were having a conversation. Let me see your payroll records. There's got to be an address."

The man called Lucky smiled and shook his head.

"Payroll? We don't pay these broads a dime. They ought to pay us. Comin' in here, it's a license to make money."

"You must have a phone number or an address. You want your man Gussie here to go down to Metro on an assaulting-a-police-officer clip?"

"We don't have her address, Bosch, what can I tell you? Or her phone number."

He held his hands out, palms up.

"I mean, I don't have addresses on any of the girls. I set a schedule and they come in and they dance. They don't show, they aren't allowed back. See, it's nice and simple, streamlined, that way. It's the way we do it. And as far as the assault thing goes with Gussie, if you want to do that dance we'll do it. But remember you're the guy what came in here by hisself, never said who you were or what you wanted to nobody, had four beers in less than an hour and insulted one of the dancers before we asked you to leave. We can have affidavits to that effect in an hour."

He raised his arms again, this time in a hands-off manner as if to say it was Bosch's call. Bosch had no doubt that Yvonne and Rhonda would tell the story they were told to tell. He decided to cut his losses. He smiled glibly.

"Have a good night," he said and turned to the door.

"You, too, Officer," Lucky said to his back. "Come back when you have time and can enjoy the show."

The door opened by some unseen electronic means apparently controlled from the desk. Gussie allowed Bosch to leave first. He then followed behind as Bosch went through the main door to the valet stand. Bosch gave a Mexican man with a face like a crumpled paper lunch bag his parking stub. He and Gussie then waited in silence for the car to be brought up.

"No hard feelings, right?" Gussie finally said as the car was approaching. "I didn't know you was a cop."

Bosch turned to face him.

"No, you just thought I was a customer."

"Yeah, right. And I had to do what the boss told me to do."

He put his hand out. In his peripheral vision Bosch could see his car still coming. He took Gussie's hand and in a sharp move pulled the big man toward him at the same time he raised his knee and drove it into his groin. Gussie let out an *oomph* and doubled over. Bosch let go of his hand and quickly jerked the tail of the man's jacket up over his head, pinning his arms in the tangle. Finally, he brought his knee up into the jacket and felt it connect solidly with Gussie's face. The big man fell backward onto the hood of a black Corvette parked near the door just as the valet jumped out of Bosch's rental car and came scrambling around to defend his boss. The man was older and smaller than Bosch. This one wouldn't even be close and Bosch wasn't interested in any innocent bystanders. He held his finger up to stop the man.

"Don't," he said.

The man considered his situation while Gussie groaned through his tuxedo jacket. Finally, the valet raised his hands and stepped back, allowing Bosch a path to the car door.

"At least somebody around here makes the right choices," Bosch said as he slid in.

He looked through the windshield and saw Gussie's body slide down the slope of the Corvette's hood and fall to the pavement. The valet ran to his side.

As Bosch pulled out onto Madison, he checked the rearview mirror. The valet was pulling the jacket back over Gussie's head. Bosch could see blood on the bouncer's white shirt.

Bosch was too keyed up to go back to the hotel to sleep. He also had a bad mix of emotions weighing on him. Seeing the naked woman dancing still bothered him. He didn't even know her but thought he had invaded some private world of hers. He also felt angry at himself for lashing out at the brute, Gussie. But most of all, what bothered him was that he had played the whole scene wrong. He had gone to the strip club to try to get a line on Layla and he got nothing. At best, all he had come up with was the probable explanation for what the specks of glitter found in the cuffs of Tony Aliso's pants and the shower drain were and where they came from. It wasn't enough. He had to go back to L.A. in the morning and he had nothing.

When he got to a traffic light at the beginning of the Strip, he lit a cigarette, then took out his notebook and opened it to the page on which he had written down the address Felton had given him earlier in the night.

At Sands Boulevard he turned east and within a mile he came to the apartment complex where Eleanor Wish lived. It was a sprawling development with numbered buildings. It took him a while until he found hers and then figured out which unit was hers. He sat in his car and smoked and watched her lighted windows for a while. He wasn't sure what he was doing or what he wanted.

Five years earlier Eleanor Wish had done the worst and the best to him. She had betrayed him, put him in danger and she had also saved his life. She had made love to him. And then it all went bad. Still, he had often thought about her, the old what-might-have-been blues. She had a hold on him through time. She had been cold to him this night but he thought for sure the hold went both ways. She was his reflection, he had always been sure of that.

He got out of the car, dropped his dead cigarette and went to her door. She answered his knock quickly, almost as if she was expecting him. Or someone.

"How'd you find me? Did you follow me?"

"No. I made a call, that's all."

"What happened to your lip?"

"It's nothing. Are you going to ask me in?"

She backed up to allow him to enter. It was a small place with spare furnishings. It looked as though she was adding things over time, as she could afford them. He first noticed the print of Hopper's *Nighthawks* on the wall over the couch. It was a painting that always struck a chord with him. He had once had the same print on his own wall. It had been a gift from her five years before. A good-bye gift.

He looked from the painting to her. Their eyes met and he knew everything she had said earlier had been a front. He stepped closer to her and touched her, put his hand on her neck and ran a thumb along her cheek. He looked closely at her face. It was resolute, determined.

"This time it's been a long time for me," she whispered.

And he remembered that he had told her the same on the night they'd first made love. That was a lifetime ago, Bosch thought. What am I doing now? Can you pick up after so long and so many changes?

He pulled her close and they held each other and kissed for a long moment and then she wordlessly led him to the bedroom, where she quickly unbuttoned her blouse and dropped her jeans to the floor. She pressed herself to him again and they kissed while she worked her hands up his shirt, opening it and pressing her skin to his. Her hair smelled of smoke from the tables, but there was an underlying scent of perfume that reminded him of a night five years before. He remembered the jacaranda trees outside her window and how they put a violet snow on the ground.

They made love with an intensity that Bosch had forgotten that he had. It was a bruising, huffing physical act devoid of love, invigorated and driven solely, it seemed, by lust and maybe a memory. When he was done she pulled him toward her, into her, in rhythmic thrusts until she, too, reached her moment and subsided. Then, with the clarity of thought that always comes after, they became embarrassed about their nakedness, about how they had coupled with the ferocity of animals and now looked at each other as human beings.

"I forgot to ask," she said. "You're not married now, are you?"

She giggled. He reached to the floor to where his jacket had been thrown and pulled out the cigarettes.

"No," he said. "I'm alone."

"I should've known. Harry Bosch, the loner. I should've known."

She was smiling at him in the darkness. He saw it when the match flared. He lit the cigarette and then offered it to her. She shook her head no.

"How many women have there been since me? Tell me."

"I don't know, just a few. There was one, we were together about a year. That was the most serious one."

"What happened to her?"

"She went to Italy."

"For good?"

"Who knows?"

"Well, if you don't know, then she isn't coming back. At least to you."

"Yeah, I know. That one's been over a while."

He was silent for a moment and then she asked him who else there had been.

"There was a painter I met in Florida on a case. That didn't last long. After that, there's you again."

"What happened to the painter?"

Bosch shook his head as if to dismiss the inquiry. He didn't really enjoy reviewing his ill-fated romantic record.

"Distance, I guess," he said. "It just didn't work. I couldn't leave L.A., she couldn't leave where she was."

She moved closer to him and kissed him on the chin. He knew he needed a shave.

"What about you, Eleanor? Are you alone?"

"Yes. . . . The last man to make love to me was a cop. He was gentle but very strong. I don't mean in a physical way. In a life way. It was a long time ago. At the time we both needed healing. We gave it to each other. . . ."

They looked at each other in the darkness for a long moment and then she came closer. Just before their mouths met she whispered, "A lot of time gone past."

He thought about those words as she kissed him and then pushed him back on the pillows. She straddled him and started a gentle rocking motion with her hips. Her hair hung down around his face until he was in a perfect darkness. He ran his hands along her warm skin from her hips to her shoulders and then underneath to touch her breasts. He could feel her wetness on him but it was too soon for him.

"What's the matter, Harry?" she whispered. "You want to rest a while?"

"I don't know."

He kept thinking of those words. A lot of time gone past. Maybe too much time. She kept rocking.

"I don't know what I want," he said. "What do you want, Eleanor?"

"All I want is the moment. We've fucked everything else up, it's all we've got left."

After a while he was ready and they made love again. She was very silent, her movements steady and gentle. She stayed on top of him, her face above him, breathing in short rhythmic clips. Near the end, when he was just trying to hang on, waiting for her, he felt a teardrop hit his cheek. He reached up and smeared the tears on her face with his thumbs.

"It's all right, Eleanor, it's all right."

She put one of her hands on his face, feeling it in the dark as if she were a blind woman. In a short while they met at the moment when nothing in the world can intrude. Not words or even memories. It was just them together. They had the moment.

He slept on and off in her bed until nearly dawn. She slept soundly with her head on his shoulder but when he was lucky enough to doze off, it never lasted long. For the most part he lay there staring into the gray darkness, smelling their sweat and sex, wondering what road he was on now.

At six he extricated himself from her unconscious embrace and got dressed. When he was ready he kissed her awake and told her he must go.

"I go back to L.A. today but I want to come back to you as soon as I can."

She nodded sleepily.

"Okay, Bosch, I'll be waiting."

It was finally cool outside. He lit his first smoke of the day as he walked to his car. When he pulled onto Sands to head up to the Strip, he saw the sun was throwing a golden light on the mountains west of town.

The Strip was still lit by a million neon lights, though the crowds on the sidewalk had greatly decreased by this hour. Still, Bosch was awed by the spectacle of light. In every imaginable color and configuration, it was a megawatt funnel of enticement to greed that burned twenty-four hours a day. Bosch felt the same attraction that all the other grinders felt tug at them. Las Vegas was like one of the hookers on Sunset Boulevard in Hollywood. Even happily married men at least glanced their way, if only for a second, just to get an idea what was out there, maybe give them something to think about. Las Vegas was like that. There was a visceral attraction here. The bold promise of money and sex. But the first was a broken promise, a mirage, and the second was fraught with danger, expense, physical and mental risk. It was, where the real gambling took place in this town.

When he got to his room, he noticed the message light was blinking. He called the operator and was told that someone named Captain Felton had called at one and then again at two and then someone named Layla at four. There were no messages or numbers left by either of the callers. Bosch put the phone down and frowned. He figured it was too early to call Felton. But it was the call from Layla that most interested him. If it had been the real Layla who had called, then how did she know where to reach him?

He decided that it had probably been through Rhonda. The night before when he had called from Tony Aliso's office in Hollywood, he had asked Rhonda for directions from the Mirage. She could have passed that on to Layla. He wondered why she had called. Maybe she hadn't heard about Tony until Rhonda had told her.

Still, he decided to put Layla on a back burner for the moment. With the financial probe Kizmin Rider had opened up in L.A., the focus of the case seemed to be shifting. It was important for them to talk to Layla but his priority was to get back to L.A. He picked the phone back up and called Southwest and booked a 10:30 flight to L.A. He figured that would give him time to check in with Felton, then check out the dealership where Rider said Tony Aliso had leased his cars and still make it back to the Hollywood Division by lunchtime.

Bosch stripped off his clothes and took a long hot shower, washing the sweat of the night away. When he was done he wrapped a towel around himself and used another to wipe the fog off the mirror so he could shave. He noticed that his lower lip had swollen on one side to the size of a marble and his mustache did little to hide it. His eyes were red-rimmed and bloodshot. He wondered as he got the bottle of Visine drops out of his shaving bag if Eleanor had found a single thing about him attractive.

When he stepped back into the room to get dressed, he was greeted by a man he had never seen before sitting in the chair by the window. He was holding a newspaper, which he put down when he noticed Bosch step into the room clad only in the towel.

"It's Bosch, right?"

Bosch looked to the bureau and saw his gun was still sitting there. It was closer to the man in the chair but Bosch thought he might be able to get to it first.

"Easy now," the man said. "We're in this together. I'm a cop. With Metro. Felton sent me."

"What the fuck you doing in my room?"

"I came up, got no answer. I could hear the shower. I had a friend from downstairs slip me in. I didn't want to wait around in the hall. Go ahead, get dressed. Then I'll tell you what we got."

"Let me see some ID."

The man got up and approached Bosch, pulling a wallet from his inside coat pocket and putting a bored look on his face. He opened the wallet, flashing the badge and ID card.

"Iverson. From Metro. Captain Felton sent me."

"What's so important that Felton had to send somebody to break into my room?"

"Look, I didn't break in, okay? We've been calling all night and got no answer. We first of all wanted to make sure you were all right. And, secondly, the captain wants you to be in on the arrest, so he sent me over to try to find you. We gotta get going. Why don't you get dressed?"

"What arrest?"

"That's what I'm trying to tell you if you'd get dressed and we could get going. You hit the jackpot with those prints you flew in here with."

Bosch looked at him for a moment and then went to the closet to grab a pair of pants and some underwear. He then went into the bathroom to put them on. When he came back out, he said one word to Iverson.

"Talk."

Bosch quickly finished dressing as Iverson began.

"You know the name Joey Marks?"

Bosch thought a moment and then said it sounded familiar but he couldn't place it.

"Joseph Marconi. They call him Joey Marks. Used to, before he tried to put on legitimate airs. Now, it's Joseph Marconi. Anyway, he got the name Joey Marks 'cause that's what he did, he left marks on anybody who crossed him, got in his way."

"Who is he?"

"He's the Outfit's guy in Vegas. You know what the Outfit is, right?"

"The Chicago Mafia family. They control or have the say, at least, on everything west of the Mississippi. That includes Vegas and L.A."

"Hey, you took some geography, didn't you? I probably won't have to school you too much then on what's what out here. You already've got a score card."

"You're saying the prints on my vic's jacket came from Joey Marks?"

"In your dreams. But they did come back to one of his top guys and, Bosch, that's like manna from heaven. We're taking this guy down today, pulling him right the fuck out of bed. We're going to turn him, Bosch, make him our boy and through him we'll finally get Joey Marks. He's been a thorn in our side going on near a decade now."

"Aren't you forgetting something?"

"No, I don't think—oh, yeah, of course you and the LAPD have our undivided thanks for this."

"No, you're forgetting it's my case. It's not your case. What the fuck you people think you're doing taking this guy down without even talking to me?"

"We tried to call. I told you that."

Iverson sounded hurt.

"So? You don't get me and you just go ahead with the plan?"

Iverson didn't answer. Bosch finished tying his shoes and stood up ready to go.

"Let's go. Take me to Felton. I can't believe you guys."

On the elevator down Iverson said that while Bosch's exception to the plan was noted, it was too late to stop anything. They were heading out to a command post in the desert and from there they would move in on the suspect's house, which was out near the mountains.

"Where's Felton?"

"He's out there at the CP."

"Good."

Iverson was silent during most of the ride out, which was good because it allowed Bosch to think about this latest development. He realized suddenly that Tony Aliso might have been washing money for Joey Marks. Marks was Rider's Mr. X, he guessed. But something went wrong. The IRS audit was endangering the scheme and thereby endangering Joey Marks. Marks had responded by eliminating the washer.

The story felt good to Bosch, but there were still things that didn't jibe. The break-in at Aliso's office two days after he was dead. Why did whoever that was wait until then, and why didn't they take all the financial records? The records—if connections between the dummy corporations and Joey Marks could be made—might be just as dangerous to Marks as Aliso was. Bosch found himself wondering if the hitter and the B&E man were the same person. It didn't seem so.

"What's this guy's name, the one the prints matched?"

"Luke Goshen. We only had his prints on file because he had to give 'em to get the entertainment license for one of Joey's strip clubs. The license is in Goshen's name. It keeps Joey out of it. Nice and clean. Only not anymore. The prints tie Goshen to a murder and that means Joey isn't far behind."

"Wait a minute, what's the name of the club?"

"Dolly's. It's in—"

"North Las Vegas. Son of a bitch."

"What, I say something?"

"This Goshen guy, do they call him Lucky?"

"Probably not after today. His luck's about to run out. Sounds like you know of him."

"I met the prick last night."

"You're shitting me."

"At Dolly's. The last phone call from Aliso's office in L.A. was to Dolly's. I found out he was coming out here and spending time with one of the dancers at that place. I went to check it out last night and fucked up. Goshen had one of his guys give me this."

Bosch touched the bump on his lip.

"I was wondering where you got that. Which one give you that?"

"Gussie."

"Fucking Big John Flanagan. We'll be bringing his lard ass in today, too."

"John Flanagan? How they get Gussie out of that?"

"It's on account he's the best-dressed bouncer in the county. You know, the tuxedo. He gets all gussied up to go to work. That's how he got that one. I hope you didn't let him get away with puttin' that knot on your lip."

"We had a little discussion in the parking lot before I left."

Iverson laughed.

"I like you, Bosch. You're a tough nut."

"I'm not sure I like you yet, Iverson. I'm still not happy about you people trying to take over my case."

"It'll work out for all of us. You're going to clear your case and we're going to take a couple of major douche bags out of the picture. City fathers are going to be smiling all around."

"We'll see."

"There's one other thing," Iverson said. "We were already working a tip on Lucky when you showed up."

"What are you talking about?"

"We got a tip. It was anonymous. Came in Sunday to the bureau. Guy won't give his name but says he was in a strip club the night before and hears a couple of big guys talking about a hit. He heard one call the other Lucky."

"What else?"

"Just something about the guy being put in the trunk and then getting capped."

"Felton know this when I talked to him yesterday?"

"No, it hadn't filtered up to him. It came up last night after he found out the prints you brought matched Goshen. One of the guys in the bureau had taken the tip and was going to check it out. Put out a flier on it. It would've eventually gotten over there to L.A. and you woulda come calling. You're just here sooner rather than later."

They had completely left the urban sprawl of the city and the chocolate-brown mountain chain rose in front of them. There were sporadic patches of neighborhoods. Homes that were built way out and were waiting for the city to catch up. Bosch had been out this way once before on an investigation, going to a retired cop's house. It had reminded him of no-man's-land then and it still did now.

"Tell me about Joey Marks," Bosch said. "You said he's trying to go legitimate?"

"No, I said he's trying to give the appearance of legitimacy. That's two different things. Guy like that, he'll never be legitimate. He can clean up his act, but he's always going to be a grease spot on the road."

"What's he into? If you believe the media, the mob was run out of town to make way for all the All-American family."

"Yeah, I know the tune. It's true, though. Vegas has changed in ten years. When I first made it to the bureau, you could practically take your pick of the casinos and go to work. They all had connections. If it wasn't the front office, then it was the suppliers, the unions, whatever. Now it's cleaned up. It's gone from sin city to fuckin' Disneyland. We got more water slides than whorehouses now. I think I liked it the old way. Had more of an edge, know what I mean?"

"Yeah, I know what you mean."

"Anyway, the important thing is we ninety-nine percent have the mob out of the casinos. That's the good thing. But there's still a lot of what we call ancillary action around. That's where Joey fits in. He runs a string of high-rent strip bars, mostly in North Vegas because nudity and alcohol are allowed there and the money is in alcohol. Very hard to watch, that money. We figure he's siphoning a couple mil a year off the top on the clubs alone. We've had the IRS go after his books but he does too good a job.

"Let's see, we think he also has a piece of some of the brothels up north. Then he's got the usual, your standard loan-sharking and fencing operations. He runs a book and has the street tax on almost anything that moves in town. You know, the escort services, peep shows, all of that. He's the king. He can't go in any of the casinos 'cause he's in the commission's black book but it doesn't matter. He's the king."

"How does he have a betting book in a town where you can walk into any casino and bet on any game, any race, anywhere?"

"You gotta have money to do that. Not with Joey. He'll take your bet. And if you are unlucky enough to lose, then you better come up with the money quick or you're one sorry motherfucker. Remember how he got his name. Well, suffice it to say his employees carry on the tradition. See, that's how he gets his hooks into people. He gets them to owe him and then they have to give him a piece of what they have, whether it's a company that makes paint in Dayton or something else."

"Maybe a guy who makes cheap movies in L.A."

"Yeah, like that. That's how it works. They open up to him or they get two broken knees or worse. People still disappear in Vegas, Bosch. It might look like it's all volcanoes and pyramids and pirate ships on the outside, but on the inside it's still dark enough for people to disappear in."

Bosch reached over and turned the air up a notch. The sun was already all the way up and the desert was beginning to bake.

"This is nothing," Iverson said. "Wait till about noon. If we're out here then, forget about it. We'll be over one-ten easy."

"What about Joey's air of legitimacy?"

"Yeah, well, like I said, he's got holdings all over the country. Pieces of the legitimate world he got through these various scams. He also reinvests. He cleans up all the cash he's pulling out of his various enterprises and then puts it into legit stuff, even charities. He's got car dealerships, a country club on the east side, a goddamn wing of a hospital named after one of his kids who died in a swimming pool. His picture gets in the paper at ribbon cuttings, Bosch. I tell you, we've either got to fucking take the guy down or give him the key to the city and I don't know which would be more appropriate."

Iverson shook his head.

After a few minutes of silence they were there. Iverson pulled into a county fire station and drove around back, where there were several more detective cars and several men standing around them holding paper cups of coffee. One of them was Captain Felton.

Bosch had forgotten to take a bulletproof vest with him from Los Angeles and had to borrow one from Iverson. He was also given a plastic raid jacket that said LVPD in bright yellow letters across the chest when it was zipped closed.

They were standing around Felton's Taurus, going over the plan and waiting for the uniform backup. Execution of the warrant was going to be done by Vegas rules, the captain said. That meant at least one uniform team had to be there when they kicked the door.

By this time Bosch had already had his "friendly" exchange with Felton. The two had gone into the fire station to get Bosch some coffee, and Bosch had given the police captain an earful for the way he had handled the discovery that the prints Bosch had brought with him belonged to Lucky Luke Goshen. Felton feigned contrition and told Bosch he'd be involved in calling the shots from that moment on. Bosch had to back down after that. He'd gotten what he wanted, at least in the captain's words. Now he just had to watch that Felton walked the talk.

Besides Felton and Bosch, there were four others standing around the car. They were all from Metro's Organized Crime Unit. It was Iverson and his partner, Cicarelli, and then another pair, Baxter and Parmelee. The OCU was part of Felton's domain in the department, but it was Baxter who was running the show. He was a black man who was balding, with gray hair lightly powdered around the sides of his head. He was heavily muscled and had a countenance that said I want no hassles. He seemed to Bosch to be a man accustomed to both the violent and violence. There was a difference.

Luke Goshen's home was known to them. From their banter Bosch figured that they had watched the place before. It was about a mile farther west from the station, and Baxter had already made a drive-by and determined that Goshen's black Corvette was in the carport.

"What about a warrant?" Bosch asked.

He could just envision the whole thing getting kicked out of court because of a warrantless entry into the suspect's house.

"The prints were more than enough for a warrant to search the premises and arrest your man," Felton said. "We took it to a judge first thing this morning. We also had our own information, which I think Iverson told you about."

"Look, his prints were on the guy but it doesn't mean he did it. It doesn't make a case. We're acting too quickly here. My guy was put down in L.A. I've got nothing putting Luke Goshen there. And your own information? That's a joke. You've got an anonymous call, that's it. It doesn't mean shit."

They all looked at Bosch as if he had just belched at the debutante ball.

"Harry, let's get another cup," Felton said.

"I'm fine."

"Let's get one anyway."

He put his arm on Bosch's shoulder and led him back toward the sta-

tion. Inside at the kitchen counter, where there was a coffee urn, Felton
poured himself another cup before speaking.

"Look, Harry, you gotta go with this. This is a major opportunity for
us and for you."

"I know that. I just don't want to blow it. Can't we hold off on this
until we're sure of what we've got? It's my case, Captain, and you're still
running the show."

"I thought we had that all straightened out."

"I thought we did, too, but I might as well be pissing in the wind."

"Look, Detective, we're going to go up the road and take this guy
down, search his place and put him in a little room. I guarantee that if he
isn't your man, he's going to give him to you. And he's going to give us
Joey Marks along the way. Now, come on, get with the program and get
happy."

He cuffed Bosch on the shoulder and headed back out to the lot.
Bosch followed in a few moments. He knew that he was whining over
nothing. You find somebody's prints on a body, you bring him in. That's a
given. You sweat the details later. But Bosch didn't like being a bystander.
That was the real rub and he knew it. He wanted to run the show. Only
out here in the desert, he was a fish out of water, flopping on the sand. He
knew he should call Billets, but it was too late for her to do anything and
he didn't like the idea of telling her he had let this one get away from him.

The patrol car with the two uniforms was there when Bosch stepped
out of the fire station and back into the oven.

"All right," Felton said. "We're all here. Mount up and let's go get
this fucker."

They were there in five minutes. Goshen lived in a house that rose out
of the scrubland on Desert View Avenue. It was a large house but not one
that looked particularly ostentatious. The one thing that looked out of
the ordinary was the concrete-block wall and gate that surrounded the
half-acre property. The house was in the middle of nowhere but its owner needed to put a security wall around it.

They all stopped their cars on the shoulder of the road and got out.
Baxter had come prepared. From the trunk of his Caprice he pulled out
two stepladders that they would use to scale the wall next to the driveway
gate. Iverson was the first to go over. When he got to the top of the wall,

he put the other ladder in place on the other side but hesitated before climbing down into the front yard.

"Anybody see any dogs?"

"No dogs," Baxter said. "I checked this morning."

Iverson went down and the others followed him over. While he waited for his turn, Bosch looked around and could just see the neon demarcation of the Strip several miles to the east. Above this the sun was a neon red ball. The air had gone from warm to hot and was as dry and rough as sandpaper. Bosch thought of the cherry-flavored Chap Stick in his pocket that he had bought at the hotel gift shop. But he didn't want to use it in front of the local boys.

After Bosch had scaled the wall and was approaching the house behind the others, he looked at his watch. It was now almost nine but the house seemed dead. No movement, no sound, no lights, nothing. Curtains were closed across every window.

"You sure he's here?" Bosch whispered to Baxter.

"He's here," Baxter replied without lowering his voice. "I jumped the wall about six and touched the hood of the Vette. It was warm. He hadn't been home long. He's in there asleep, I guarantee it. Nine o'clock to this guy is like four in the morning for normal people."

Bosch looked over at the Corvette. He remembered it from the night before. As he looked around further, he realized the confines within the walls of the compound were carpeted in lush, green grass. It must have cost a fortune to plant and another one to keep it watered. The property sat in the desert like a towel on the beach. Bosch was drawn from his wonder by the sound of Iverson hitting the front door with his foot.

With weapons drawn, Bosch and the others followed Iverson into the dark opening to the house. They went in screaming the usual identifiers—*Police!* and *Don't Move!*—and quickly moved down a hallway to the left. Bosch followed the sharp slashes of light from their flashlights. Almost immediately he heard female screams and then a light came on in a room at the end of the hall.

By the time he got in there, he saw Iverson kneeling on a king-size bed, holding his Smith & Wesson short barrel six inches from the face of Luke Goshen. The big man Bosch had encountered the night before was wrapped in the bed's black silk sheets and looked as calm about the situation as Magic Johnson used to look while shooting free throws with the game on the line. He even took the time to glance up at the ceiling to view the reflection of the scene in the mirror.

It was the women who weren't calm. Two of them, both nude, stood on either side of the bed, oblivious to their nakedness but fully in the latter stages of fright. Finally, Baxter quieted them with a loud shout of "Shut up!"

It took a few moments for the silence to sink in. Nobody moved. Bosch never took his eyes off Goshen. He was the only danger in the room. He sensed that the other cops, who had branched off to search the house, had now moved into the room behind him along with the two uniform cops.

"On your face, Luke," Iverson finally ordered. "You girls get some clothes on. Now!"

One of the women said, "You can't just—"

"Shut up!" Iverson cut her off. "Or you go in to town like that. Your choice."

"I'm not go—"

"Randy!" Goshen boomed with a voice as deep as a barrel. "Shut the fuck up and get dressed. They're not taking you anywhere. You, too, Harm."

All the men but Goshen instinctively looked at the woman he had called Harm. She looked like she weighed about ninety pounds. She had soft blond hair, breasts she could hide in a child's tea cups and a gold hoop piercing one of the folds of her vagina. There was a look of fright etched on her face that had completely crowded out any hint of beauty.

"Harmony," she whispered, understanding their dilemma.

"Well, get dressed, Harmony," Felton said. "Both of you. Turn to the wall and get dressed."

"Just get 'em their clothes and get 'em out of here," Iverson said.

Harmony was stepping into a pair of jeans when she stopped and looked at the men giving conflicting orders.

"Well, which is it?" Randy asked in an irritated voice. "You people got your shit together or what?"

Bosch recognized her as the woman who had been dancing in Dolly's the night before.

"Get 'em out of here!" Iverson yelled. "Now."

The uniforms moved in to usher the naked women out.

"We're going," Randy yelped. "Don't touch me."

Iverson yanked the sheets off Goshen and began cuffing his hands behind his back. Goshen's blond hair ran in a thin and tightly braided ponytail down his back. Bosch hadn't noticed that the night before.

"Whatsa matter, Iverson?" he said, his face against the mattress. "You got a problem with a little poon hangin' around? You a little punk or something?"

"Goshen, do yourself a favor, shut your fuckin' hole."

Goshen laughed off the threat. He was a deeply tanned man who seemed even larger than Bosch recalled from the night before. He was completely buffed, his arms the size of hams. For a short moment, Bosch thought he understood Goshen's desire to sleep with two women. And why they willingly went with him in twos.

Goshen faked a yawn to make sure everyone knew he wasn't the least bit threatened by what was happening. He wore only black bikini underwear that matched the sheets. There were tattoos on his back. A one percent sign on the left shoulder blade, a Harley Davidson insignia on the right. On the upper left arm there was another tattoo. The number eighty-eight.

"What's this, your IQ?" Iverson said as he sharply slapped the arm.

"Fuck you, Iverson, and the phony fuckin' warrant you rode in on."

Bosch knew what the tattoo meant. He had seen it enough in L.A. The eighth letter of the alphabet was H. Eight-eight meant HH, short for Heil Hitler. It meant Goshen had spent some time with white supremacists. But most of the assholes Bosch came across with similar tattoos had gotten them in prison. It was amazing to him that Goshen apparently had no criminal record and had spent no time in stir. If he had, his name would have come up when the prints from Tony Aliso's jacket had been run through the AFIS computer. He put thoughts of this contradiction aside when Goshen managed to turn his head so that he was looking at Bosch.

"You," he said. "You're the one they should be arresting. After what you did to Gussie."

Bosch bent over the bed to reply.

"This ain't about last night. This is about Tony Aliso."

Iverson roughly turned Goshen over on the bed.

"What the fuck are you talking about?" Goshen asked angrily. "I'm clean on that, man. What are you—"

He tried to pull himself up into a sitting position but Iverson pushed him back down hard.

"Just sit tight," Iverson said. "We'll hear your sorry side of things. But we're going to have a look around first."

He took the warrant out of his pocket and dropped it on Goshen's chest.

"There's your warrant."

"I can't read it."

"Not my fault you didn't stay in school."

"Just hold it up for me."

Iverson ignored him and looked at the others.

"Okay, let's split up and see what we've got here. Harry, you take this room, okay, keep our friend here company?"

"Right."

Iverson then addressed the two uniforms.

"I want one of you guys in here. Just stand out of the way and keep your eyes on douche bag here."

One of the uniforms nodded and the others left the room. Bosch and Goshen looked at each other.

"I can't read this thing," Goshen said.

"I know," Bosch said. "You said that."

"This is bullshit. It's just a roust. You couldn't possibly have anything on me because I didn't do it."

"Then who'd you have do it? Gussie?"

"No, man, nobody. There's no way you'll be able to pin this on me. No fucking way. I want my lawyer."

"As soon as you're booked."

"Booked for what?"

"For murder, Lucky."

Goshen continued his denials and demands for a lawyer while Bosch ignored him and started looking around the room, checking the drawers of the dresser. He glanced back at Goshen every few seconds. It was like walking around a lion's cage. He knew he was safe but that didn't stop him from checking. He could tell Goshen was watching him in the mirror over the bed. When the big man finally quieted, Bosch waited a few moments and then started asking questions. He did it casually while he continued the search, as if he didn't really care about the answers.

"So where were you Friday night?"

"Fuckin' your mother."

"She's dead."

"I know it. It wasn't all that good."

Bosch stopped what he was doing and looked at him. Goshen wanted him to hit him. He wanted the violence. It was the playing field he understood.

"Where were you, Goshen? Friday night."

"Talk to my lawyer."

"We will. But you can talk, too."

"I was working the club. I have a fucking job, you know."

"Yeah, I know. When did you work till?"

"I don't know. Four. I go home after that."

"Yeah, right."

"It's the truth."

"Where were you, in that office?"

"That's right."

"Anybody see you? You ever come out before four?"

"I don't know. Talk to my lawyer."

"Don't worry. We will."

Bosch went back to the search and opened the closet door. It was a walk-in but it was only a third lined with clothes. Goshen lived light.

"Fuckin' A it's right," Goshen called from the bed. "You go check. Check it out."

The first thing Bosch did was to turn over the two pairs of shoes and the Nikes that were lined on the floor. He studied the sole patterns and none of them appeared even remotely like the pattern found on the bumper of the Rolls and Tony Aliso's hip. He glanced back out at Goshen to make sure the big man wasn't moving. He wasn't. Bosch next reached to the shelf above the clothes rod. He took a box down and found it full of photos. They were eight by ten publicity shots of dancers. They weren't nudes. Each young woman was posed provocatively in a skimpy costume. Each one's name was printed in the white border below the photo, accompanied by the name and number of Models A Million, which Bosch guessed was a local agency that provided dancers to clubs. He looked through the box until he found a photo with the name Layla on it.

He studied the photo of the woman he had been looking for the previous night. She had long flowing brown hair with blond highlights, a full figure, dark eyes and bee sting lips. In the photo they were parted just enough to show a hint of white teeth. She was a beautiful woman and there was something familiar about her but he couldn't place it. He decided that maybe the familiarity was the sexual malice that all the women in the photos and those whom he had seen the night before in the club seemed to convey.

Bosch took the box out of the closet and dropped it on the bureau. He held the picture of Layla out of it.

"What's with the pictures, Lucky?"

"They're all the girls I've been with. How 'bout you, cop? You had that many? I bet the ugliest one in there is better than the best one you've ever had."

"So what do you want to do, compare pricks, too? I'm glad you've had your fill of women, Lucky, 'cause there aren't going to be any more. I mean, sure, you'll be able to fuck or be fucked. It just won't be with women is all I'm saying."

Goshen was quiet while he contemplated this. Bosch put the photo of Layla on the bureau next to the box.

"Look, Bosch, just tell me what you guys've got and I'll tell you what I know so we can get this straightened out. You're wrong on this. I didn't do anything, so let's get this over with, stop wasting each other's time."

Bosch didn't answer. He went back into the closet and hiked up on his toes to see if there was anything else on the shelf. There was. A small cloth folded like a handkerchief. He took it down and unfolded it. It was soiled with oil. He smelled it and recognized it.

Bosch came out of the closet, tossed the rag so it hit Goshen in the face and fell onto the bed.

"What's this?"

"I don't know. What is it?"

"It's a rag with gun oil on it. Where's the gun?"

"I don't have a gun and that isn't mine, either. Never saw it before."

"Okay."

"What do you mean, okay? I never fuckin' saw it before."

"I mean, okay, Goshen. That's all. Don't get nervous."

"It's hard with you people sticking your nose up my ass."

Bosch bent over the night table. He opened the top drawer, found an empty cigarette box, a set of pearl earrings and an unopened box of condoms. Bosch threw the box at Goshen. It bounced off his huge chest and fell to the floor.

"You know, Goshen, just buying them ain't safe sex. You gotta put 'em on."

He opened the bottom drawer. It was empty.

"How long you lived here, Goshen?"

"Moved in right after I kicked your sister out on her ass. Put her on the street. Last I seen, she was selling it over on Fremont outside the Cortez."

Bosch straightened up and looked at him. Goshen was smiling. He wanted to provoke something. He wanted to control things, even handcuffed on the bed. Even if it cost him some blood.

"My mother, now my sister, who's next, my wife?"

"Yeah, I got something planned for her. I'll—"

"Shut up, would you? It's not working, understand? You're not getting to me. You can't get to me. So save your strength."

"Everybody can be gotten to, Bosch. Remember that."

Bosch looked at him and then stepped into the master bathroom. It was a large room with a separate shower and tub, almost in the same configuration as the room Tony Aliso had used at the Mirage. The toilet was in a small closet-size room behind a door with a slatted grill. Bosch started there. He quickly lifted the top of the water tank and found nothing unusual. Before putting the porcelain top back in place he leaned over the toilet and looked down the wall behind the tank. What he saw made him immediately call for the uniform in the bedroom.

"Yes, sir?" the cop said.

He looked like he wasn't yet twenty-five. His black skin had almost a bluish tint to it. He kept his hands on his equipment belt in a relaxed mode, his right just a few inches from his gun. It was the standard pose. Bosch saw that the nameplate above his breast pocket said Fontenot.

"Fontenot, take a look down here behind the tank."

The cop did as he was asked without even taking his hands off his belt.

"What is it?" he asked.

"I think it's a gun. Why don't you step back and let me pull it out?"

Bosch flattened his hand and reached it down into the two-inch space between the wall and the tank. His fingers closed on a plastic bag attached to the back of the tank with gray duct tape. He managed to pull it free and get the bag out. He held it up for Fontenot to see. The bag contained a blue metal pistol equipped with a three-inch screw-on silencer.

"A twenty-two?" Fontenot asked.

"Oh, yeah," Bosch said. "Go get Felton and Iverson, would you?"

"Right away."

Bosch followed Fontenot out of the bathroom. He was holding the bag containing the gun the way a fisherman holds a fish by its tail. When he stepped into the bedroom he couldn't help but smile at Goshen, whose eyes noticeably widened.

"That ain't mine," Goshen immediately protested. "That's a plant, you fuck! I don't be—Get me my goddamned lawyer, you son of a bitch!"

Bosch let the words go by but studied the look. He saw something flash in Goshen's eyes. It was there for only a second and then he covered up. It wasn't fear. He didn't think that was something Goshen would let slip into his eyes. Bosch believed he had seen something else. But what? He looked at Goshen and waited a moment for the look to return. Was it confusion? Disappointment? Goshen's eyes showed nothing now. But Bosch believed he knew the look. What he had seen had been surprise.

Iverson, Baxter and Felton then filed into the room. They saw the gun and Iverson yelped in triumph.

"Sayonara, *bay-bee!*"

His glee showed on his face. Bosch explained how and where he had found the weapon.

"These fuckhead gangsters," Iverson said, looking at Goshen. "Think the cops never saw *The Godfather*? Who'd you put it there for, Goshen? Michael Corleone?"

"I said get me my fucking lawyer!" Goshen yelled.

"You'll get your lawyer," Iverson said. "Now get up, you piece of shit. You gotta get dressed for the ride in."

Bosch held him at gunpoint while Iverson took one of the cuffs off. Then they both pointed guns at him while he got dressed in black jeans, boots and T-shirt—the shirt manufactured for a much smaller man.

"You guys are always tough in numbers," Goshen said as he went about putting the clothes on. "You ever come up against me alone, then it's going to be wet ass time."

"Come on, Goshen, we don't have all day," Iverson said.

When he was done, they cuffed him and stuffed him into the back of Iverson's car. Iverson locked the gun in the trunk, then they went back inside the house. In a short meeting inside the front hallway it was decided that Baxter and two of the other detectives would stay behind to finish the search of the house.

"What about the women?" Bosch asked.

"The uniforms will watch them until these boys are done," Iverson said.

"Yeah, but as soon as they leave they'll be on the phone. We'll have Goshen's lawyer down our throat before we even get started."

"I'll take care of that. Goshen's got one car here, right? Where's the keys?"

"Kitchen counter," one of the other detectives said.

"Okay," Iverson said. "We're out of here."

Bosch followed him through the kitchen, watching him pocket the keys that were on the counter, and then out into the carport by the Corvette. There was a little workroom here with tools hanging on a peg board. Iverson selected a shovel and then stepped out of the carport and around to the back yard.

Bosch followed and watched as Iverson found the spot where the telephone line came in from a pole at the street and connected to the house. He swung the shovel up and with one strike disconnected the line.

"Amazing how strong the wind can get out here in the open desert," he said.

He looked around behind the house.

"Those girls have no car and no phone," he said. "Nearest house is a half mile, city's about five. My guess is they'll stay put a while. That'll give us time. All we need."

Iverson took a baseball swing with the shovel and launched it out over the property wall and into the scrub brush. He started walking toward the front of the house and his car.

"What do you think?" Bosch asked.

"I think the bigger they are, the harder they fall. Goshen's ours, Harry. Yours."

"No. I mean about the gun."

"What about it?"

"I don't know. . . . It seems too easy."

"Nobody said criminals gotta be smart. Goshen's not smart. He's just been lucky. But not anymore."

Bosch nodded but he still didn't like it. It wasn't really a question of being smart or not. Criminals followed routines, instincts. This didn't make sense.

"I saw something in his eyes when he saw the gun. Like he was just as surprised to see it as we were."

"Maybe. Maybe he's just a good actor. And maybe it's not even the right gun. You'll have to take it back with you to run tests. Find out if it's the gun, Harry, then worry about if it's too easy."

Bosch nodded. He took out a cigarette and lit it.

"I don't know. I feel like I'm missing something."

"Look, Harry, you want to make a case or not?"

"I want a case."

"Then let's take him in and put him in a room, see what he has to say."

They were at the car. Bosch realized he had left the photo of Layla inside. He told Iverson to start the car and he'd be right back. When he came back with the photo and got in, he checked Goshen in the back and saw a trickle of blood running down from the corner of his mouth. Bosch looked at Iverson, who was smiling.

"I don't know, he must've bumped his face getting in. Either that or he did it on purpose to make it look like I did it."

Goshen said nothing and Bosch just turned around. Iverson pulled the car out onto the road and they headed back toward the city. The temperature was climbing rapidly and Bosch could already feel the sweat sticking his shirt to his back. The air conditioner labored to overcome the heat that had built up in the car while they were inside the house. The air was as dry as old bones. Bosch finally took out the Chap Stick and rolled it across his sore lips. He didn't care what Iverson or Goshen thought about it.

They took Goshen up to the detective bureau in a back elevator in which Goshen audibly farted. Then Bosch and Iverson walked him down a hallway off the squad room and into an interview room barely larger than a rest-room stall. They handcuffed him to a steel ring bolted to the center of the table and locked him in. Then they left him there. As Iverson closed the door, Goshen called after him that he wanted to make his phone call.

Bosch noticed that the squad room was almost deserted as they walked back toward Felton's office.

"Somebody die?" Bosch asked. "Where is everybody?"

"They're out picking up the others."

"What others?"

"The captain wanted to bring in your pal, Gussie, throw a scare at him. They're bringing in the girl, too."

"Layla? They found her?"

"No, not her. The one you had us run last night. The one that played with your victim at the Mirage. Turns out she's got a jacket."

Bosch reached over and yanked Iverson's arm to stop him.

"Eleanor Wish? You're bringing in Eleanor Wish?"

He didn't wait for Iverson's reply. He broke away from the man and charged into Felton's office. The captain was on the phone and Bosch paced anxiously in front of the desk waiting for him to hang up. Felton pointed at the door but Bosch shook his head. He could see Felton's eyes start to smolder as he told whoever was on the other end of the line he had to go.

"I can't talk right now," he said. "You don't have to worry, it's under control. I'll talk to you."

He hung up and looked at Bosch.

"What is it now?"

"Call your people. Tell them to leave Eleanor Wish alone."

"What are you talking about?"

"She had nothing to do with this. I checked her out last night."

Felton leaned forward and clasped his hands together as he thought.

"When you say you checked her out, what does that mean?"

"I interviewed her. She had a passing acquaintance with the victim, that's it. She's clean."

"Do you know who she is, Bosch? I mean, do you know her history?"

"She was an FBI agent assigned to the L.A. bank robbery squad. She went to prison five years ago on a conspiracy charge stemming from a series of burglaries involving bank safe deposit vaults. It doesn't matter, Captain, she's clean on this."

"I think it might be good to sweat her a little bit and take another go at her with one of my guys. Just to be sure."

"I'm already sure. Look, I—"

Bosch looked back at the office door and saw Iverson hanging around, trying to listen in. Bosch walked over and closed the door, then pulled a chair away from the wall and sat right in front of Felton's desk and leaned across to him.

"Look, Captain, I knew Eleanor Wish in L.A. I worked that case with the bank vaults. I . . . we were more than just partners on it. Then it all turned to shit and she went away. I hadn't seen her in five years until I saw her on the surveillance tape at the Mirage. That's why I called you last night. I wanted to talk to her but not because of the case. She's clean. She did her time and she's clean. Now call your people."

Felton was quiet. Bosch could see the wheels turning.

"I've been up most of the night working on this. I called your room a half dozen times to bring you in on it but you weren't there. I don't suppose you want to tell me where you were?"

"No, I don't."

Felton thought some more and then shook his head.

"I can't do it. I can't cut her loose yet."

"Why not?"

"Because there is something about her you apparently don't know."

Bosch closed his eyes for a moment like a boy expecting to get slapped by an angry mother but steadying himself to take it.

"What don't I know?"

"She might've only had a passing acquaintance with your victim, but she's got more than that with Joey Marks and his group."

It was worse than he expected.

"What are you talking about?"

"I put her name up for discussion with some of my people last night after you called. We've got her in a file. On numerous occasions she has been seen in the company of a man named Terrence Quillen who works for Goshen who works for Marks. Numerous times, Detective Bosch. In fact, I've got a team out looking for Quillen now. See what he has to say."

"In the company of, what does that mean?"

"Looked like strictly business, according to the reports."

Bosch felt like he'd been punched. This was impossible. He had spent the night with the woman. The sense of betrayal was building in him but a deeper gut sense told him she was true, that this was all some huge mix-up.

There was a knock on the door and Iverson poked his head in.

"FYI, the others are back, boss. They're puttin' them in the interview rooms."

"Okay."

"You need anything?"

"No, we're fine. Close the door."

After Iverson left, Bosch looked at the captain.

"Is she arrested?"

"No, we asked her to come in voluntarily."

"Let me talk to her first."

"I don't think that would be wise."

"I don't care if it's wise. Let me go talk to her. If she'll tell anybody, she'll tell me."

Felton thought a moment and then finally nodded his head.

"Okay, go ahead. You get fifteen minutes."

Bosch should have thanked him but didn't. He just got up quickly and went to the door.

"Detective Bosch?" Felton said.

Harry looked back from the door.

"I'll do what I can for you on this. But this cuts us in in a big way, you understand that?"

Bosch stepped out without answering. Felton had no finesse. It was understood without being said that Bosch was now beholden to him. But Felton had to say it anyway.

In the hallway, Bosch passed the first interview room, where they had placed Goshen, and opened the door to the second. Sitting there handcuffed to the table was Gussie Flanagan. His nose was misshapen and looked like a new potato. He had cotton jammed into the nostrils. He looked at Bosch with bloodshot eyes and recognition showed on his face. Bosch backed out and closed the door without saying a word.

Eleanor Wish was behind door number three. She was disheveled, obviously dragged from sleep by the Metro cops. But her eyes had the alert and wild quality of a cornered animal and that cut Bosch to the bone.

"Harry! What are they doing?"

He closed the door and moved quickly into the tiny room, touching her shoulder in a consoling manner and taking the seat across from her.

"Eleanor, I'm sorry."

"What? What did you do?"

"Yesterday when I saw you on the tape at the Mirage I asked Felton, he's the captain here, to get me your number and address because you were unlisted. He did. But then without my knowledge he ran your name and pulled up your package. Then on his own he had his people get you this morning. It's all part of this Tony Aliso thing."

"I told you. I didn't know him. I had one drink with him once. Just because I happened by chance to be at the same table with him they bring me in?"

She shook her head and looked away, the distress written on her face. This was the way it would always be, she now knew. The criminal record she carried would guarantee it.

"I've got to ask you something. I want to get this cleared up and get you out of here."

"What?"

"Tell me about this man Terrence Quillen."

He saw the shock in her eyes.

"Quillen? What does he—is he the suspect?"

"Eleanor, you know how this works. I can't tell you things. You tell me. Just answer the question. Do you know Terrence Quillen?"

"Yes."

"How do you know him?"

"He came up to me about six months ago when I was leaving the Flamingo. I had been out here four or five months. I was settling in, playing six nights a week by then. He came up to me and in his words told me what's what. He somehow knew about me. Who I was, that I'd just gotten out. He said there was a street tax. He said I had to pay it, that all the locals paid it, and that if I didn't there'd be trouble. He said that if I did pay it, he'd watch out for me. Be there if I ever got in a jam. You know how it goes, extortion plain and simple."

She broke then and started to cry. It took all of Bosch's will not to get up and try to hold her and comfort her in some way.

"I was alone," she said. "Scared. I paid. I pay him every week. What was I supposed to do? I had nothing and nowhere to go."

"Fuck it," Bosch said under his breath.

He got up and squeezed around the end of the table and grabbed hold of her. He pulled her to his chest and kissed the top of her head.

"Nothing's going to happen," he whispered. "I promise you that, Eleanor."

He held her there in silence for a few moments, listening to her quiet crying, until the door opened and Iverson stood there. He had a tooth-pick in his mouth.

"Get the fuck out of here, Iverson."

The detective slowly closed the door.

"I'm sorry," Eleanor said. "I'm getting you in trouble."

"No, you're not. It's all on me. Everything is on me."

A few minutes later he walked back into Felton's office. The captain looked up at him wordlessly.

"She was paying off Quillen to leave her alone. Two hundred a week. That was all it was. The street tax. She doesn't know anything about any-thing. She happened by chance to be at the same table as Aliso for about an hour Friday. She's clean. Now kick her loose. Tell your people."

Felton leaned back and started tapping his lower lip with the end of a pen. He was showing Bosch his deep-thinking pose.

"I don't know," he said.

"Okay, this is the deal. You let her go and I make a call to my people."

"And what'll you tell 'em?"

"I'll tell them I've gotten excellent cooperation from Metro out here and that we ought to run this as a joint operation. I'll say we're going to put the squeeze on Goshen here and go for the two-for-one sale. We're going to go for Goshen and Joey Marks because Marks was the one who would've ultimately pushed the button on Tony Aliso. I'll say it's highly recommended that Metro take the lead out here because they know the turf and they know Marks. Do we have a deal?"

Felton tapped out another code message on his lip, then reached over and turned the phone on his desk so Bosch could have access to it.

"Make the call now," he said. "After you talk to your CO, put me on the line. I want to talk to him."

"It's a her."

"Whatever."

A half hour later Bosch was driving a borrowed unmarked Metro car with Eleanor Wish sitting crumpled in the passenger seat. The call to Lieutenant Billets had gone over well enough for Felton to keep his end of the deal. Eleanor was kicked loose, though the damage was pretty much done. She had been able to eke out a new start and a new existence, but the underpinnings of confidence and pride and security had all been kicked out from beneath her. It was all because of Bosch and he knew it. He drove in silence, unable to even fathom what to say or how to make it better. And it cut him deeply because he truly wanted to. Before the previous night he had not seen her in five years, but she had never been far from his deepest thoughts, even when he had been with other women. There had always been a voice back there that whispered to him that Eleanor Wish was the one. She was the match.

"They're always going to come for me," she said in a small voice.

"What?"

"You remember that Bogart movie where the cop says, 'Round up the usual suspects,' and they go out and do it? Well, that's me now. They are going to mean me. I guess I never realized that until now. I'm one of the usual suspects. I guess I should thank you for slapping me in the face with reality."

Bosch said nothing. He didn't know how to respond because her words were true.

In a few minutes they were at her apartment and Bosch walked her in and sat her on the couch.

"You okay?"

"Fine."

"When you get a chance, look around and make sure they didn't take anything."

"I didn't have anything to take."

Bosch looked at the *Nighthawks* print on the wall above her. It was a painting of a lonely coffee shop on a dark night. A man and a woman sitting together, another man by himself. Bosch used to think he was the man alone. Now he stared at the couple and wondered.

"Eleanor," he said, "I have to go back. I'll come back here as soon as I can."

"Okay, Harry, thanks for getting me out."

"You going to be okay?"

"Sure."

"Promise?"

"Promise."

Back at Metro, Iverson was waiting for Bosch before they took their first shot at Goshen. Felton had acceded to leaving Goshen for Bosch. It was still his case.

In the hallway outside the interview room, Iverson tapped Bosch on the arm to stop him before going in.

"Listen, Bosch, I just want to say I don't know what you got going on with that woman and I guess it's nobody's business anymore since the captain let her go, but since we're going to be working together on Lucky here, I thought I'd clear the air. I didn't appreciate the way you spoke to me, telling me to get the fuck out and all."

Bosch looked at him a minute. The detective still had a toothpick in his mouth and Bosch wondered if it was the same one from before.

"You know, Iverson, I don't even know your first name."

"It's John, but people call me Ivy."

"Well, Iverson, I didn't appreciate the way you were sneaking around the captain's office or the interview room. In L.A. we've got a name for cops who sneak around and eavesdrop and are assholes on general principle. We call 'em squints. And I don't really care if you're offended by me or not. You're a squint. And you make any trouble for me from here on out and I'll go right to Felton and make trouble for you. I'll tell him about finding you in my room today. And if that's not enough, I'll tell 'im that I won six hundred bucks on the wheel in the casino last night but the money disappeared off the bureau after you were there. Now, you want to do this interview or not?"

Iverson grabbed Bosch by the collar and shoved him against the wall.

"Don't you fuck with me, Bosch."

"Don't you fuck with me, *Ivy*."

A smile slowly cracked across Iverson's face and he released his grip and stepped back. Bosch straightened his tie and shirt.

"Then let's do it, cowboy," Iverson said.

When they squeezed into the interview room, Goshen was waiting for them with his eyes closed, his legs up on the table and his hands laced behind his head. Bosch watched Iverson look down at the torn metal where the cuff ring had been attached to the table. Red flares of anger burst on his cheeks.

"Okay, asshole, get up," Iverson ordered.

Goshen stood up and brought his cuffed hands up. Iverson got out his keys and took the cuff off one wrist.

"Let's try this again. Sit down."

When Goshen was back down, Iverson cuffed his wrists behind his back, looping the chain through one of the steel slats of the chair back. Iverson then kicked out a chair and sat to the side of the gangster. Bosch sat across from him.

"Okay, Houdini, you also've got destroying public property on your list now," Iverson said.

"Wow, that's bold, Iverson. Really bold. That's like the time you came into the club and took Cinda into the fantasy booth. I think you called it interrogation. She called it something else. What's this going to be?"

Iverson's face now glowed with anger. Goshen puffed his chest up proudly and smirked at the detective's embarrassment.

Bosch shoved the table into Goshen's midsection and the big man doubled over it as his breath burst out. Bosch was up quickly and around the table. As he went, he pulled his keychain from his pocket. Then, using his elbow to keep Goshen's chest down on the table, he flicked open the blade of his pocket knife and sawed off the big man's ponytail. He went back to his seat and when Goshen lifted up, threw the six-inch length of hair on the table in front of him.

"Ponytails went out of style at least three years ago, Goshen. You probably didn't hear about it."

Iverson burst out in uproarious laughter. Goshen looked at Bosch with pale blue eyes that seemed as soulless as buttons on a machine. He didn't say a word. He was showing Bosch he could take it. He was stand-up. But Bosch knew even he couldn't stand up forever. Nobody can.

"You've got a problem, Lucky," Iverson said. "Big problems. You—"

"Wait a minute, wait a minute. I don't want to talk to you, Iverson. I don't want you to talk to me. You're a runt. I've got no respect for you. Understand? Anybody talks, let him talk."

Goshen nodded to Bosch. There was a silence during which Bosch looked from him to Iverson and then back.

"Go get a cup," Bosch said, without looking at Iverson. "We'll be fine in here."

"No, you—"

"Go get a cup."

"You sure?"

Iverson looked as if he were being kicked out of the college fraternity because the boys didn't think he fit in.

"Yeah, I'm sure. You got a rights form on you?"

Iverson got up. He took a folded piece of paper out of his coat pocket and tossed it on the table.

"I'll be right outside the door."

When Goshen and Bosch were alone they studied each other for a moment before Bosch spoke.

"You want a smoke?"

"Don't play the good guy with me. Just tell me what's what."

Bosch shrugged off the rebuke and got up. He moved behind Goshen and took his keys out again. This time he unlocked one of the cuffs. Goshen brought his hands up and began rubbing the wrists to get circulation going. He noticed the length of hair on the table and slapped it onto the floor.

"Let me tell you something, Mr. L.A. I've been to a place where it doesn't matter what they do to you, where nothing can hurt you. I've been there and back."

"Everybody's been to Disneyland, so what?"

"I'm not talking about fuckin' Disneyland, asshole. I spent three years in the penta down in Chihuahua. They didn't break me then, you aren't going to do it now."

"Let me tell you something then. In my life I've killed a lot of people. Just wanted you to know that up front. Time comes again, there won't be any hesitation. None. This isn't about good guy cops and bad guy cops, Goshen. That's the movies. The movies where the bad guys have ponytails, I guess. But this is real life. You are nothing to me but meat. And I'm gonna put you down. That's a given. It's just up to you how hard and how far you want to go down."

Goshen thought a moment.

"All right, so now we know each other. Talk to me. And I'll take that smoke now."

Bosch put his cigarettes and matches on the table. Goshen got one out and lit it. Bosch waited until he was done.

"I gotta advise you first. You know the routine."

Bosch opened the piece of paper Iverson had left and read Goshen his rights. He then had the man sign his name on it.

"This is being taped, isn't it?"

"Not yet."

"Okay then, what've you got?"

"Your fingerprints were on Tony Aliso's body. The gun we found behind the toilet will be going back to L.A. today. The prints are good to have, real good. But if the bullets they pick out of Tony's gourd match that gun, then it's all over. I don't care what kind of alibi you line up or what your explanation will be or if your lawyer's Johnny fucking Cochran, you won't just be meat, you'll be one hundred percent grade A dead meat."

"That gun ain't mine. It's a plant, goddamn it. You know it and I know it. And it's not going to fly, Bosch."

Bosch looked at him a moment and felt his face getting hot.

"You're saying I put that there?"

"I'm saying I watched the O.J. show. Cops out here are no different. I'm saying I don't know if it was you or Iverson or whoever, but that gun's a fuckin' plant, goddammit. That's what I'm saying."

Bosch traced a finger along the top of the table, waiting for the anger to dissipate to the point where he could control his voice.

"You hang on to that bullshit story, Goshen, and you'll go far with it. You'll go about ten years and then they'll strap you down and stick a needle in your arm. At least it's not the gas chamber anymore. They make it easy on you guys now."

Bosch leaned back but there wasn't a lot of room. The back of the chair hit the wall. He took out the Chap Stick and reapplied it.

"We own you now, Goshen. All you have left is one small window of opportunity. Call it a little piece of destiny still in your grasp."

"And what window's that?"

"You know what window, you know what I'm talking about. Guy like you doesn't move an inch without the okay. Give us the guy you worked the hit with and the guy who told you to put Tony in the trunk. You don't make a deal and there's no light at the end of the tunnel."

Goshen let out his breath and shook his head.

"Look, I did not do this. I did not!"

Bosch didn't expect him to say anything different. It wasn't that easy. He had to wear him down. He leaned across the table conspiratorially.

"Listen, I'm going to tell you something so that you know that I'm not bullshitting you. Maybe save some time, so you can decide where to go from here."

"Go ahead, but it's not going to change anything."

"Anthony Aliso was wearing a black leather jacket Friday night. Remember that? One with the two-inch lapels. It—"

"You're wasting your—"

"You grabbed him there, Goshen. Just like this."

Bosch reached across the table and demonstrated, using both hands to grab an imaginary set of lapels on a jacket Goshen wasn't wearing.

"Remember that? Tell me I'm wasting my time now. Remember, Goshen? You did it, you grabbed him like that. Now who is bullshitting who?"

Goshen shook his head but Bosch knew he had scored. The pale blues were looking inward at the memory.

"Kind of a freaky thing. Processed leather like that holds the amino acids from the prints. That's what the tech tells me. We got some nice ones. Enough to take to the DA or the grand jury. Enough for me to come out here. Enough for us to come right into your fucking house and hook you up."

He hesitated a moment until Goshen was looking at him.

"And now this gun turns up in your house. I guess we'll just have to wait on the ballistics if you don't want to talk anymore. But I've got a hunch about it. I like my chances."

Goshen slammed two open palms down on the steel table. It made a sound like a shot and echo.

"This is a setup. You people put—"

Iverson burst through the door, his gun out and aimed at Goshen. He jerked the weapon up like a TV cop.

"You okay?"

"Yeah," Bosch said. "Lucky here is just a little mad, is all. Give us a few more minutes."

Iverson went back out without a word.

"Nice play, but that's all it was," Goshen said. "Where's my phone call?"

Bosch leaned back across the table.

"You can make the call now. But you make the call and it's over right here. Because that won't be your lawyer. That will be Joey's lawyer. He'll be here to represent you, but we both know the one he'll be watching out for is Joey Marks."

Bosch stood up.

"I guess then we'll just have to settle for you. We'll go the distance on you."

"Yeah, but you don't have me, you prick. Fingerprints? You need more than that. That gun's a plant and everybody's going to know it."

"Yeah, you keep saying it. I'll know what I need to know from ballistics by tomorrow morning."

It was hard for Bosch to tell if that had registered because Goshen didn't give it much time to.

"I've got a fuckin' alibi! You can't pin this on me, man!"

"Yeah? What's your fuckin' alibi? How do you even know when he got hit?"

"You asked me about Friday night, right? That's the night."

"I didn't say that."

Goshen sat silent and motionless for a half minute. Bosch could see the eyes going to work. Goshen knew he had crossed one line with what he had said. Bosch guessed he was considering how far he should cross. Bosch pulled the chair out and sat back down.

"I got an alibi, so I'm in the clear."

"You're not in the clear till we say you are. What's your story?"

"No. I'm gonna tell my lawyer what it is."

"You're hurting yourself, Goshen. You've got nothing to lose telling me."

"Except my freedom, right?"

"I could go out, verify your story. Maybe then I'd start listening to your story about the gun being planted."

"Yeah, right, that's like puttin' the inmates in charge of the prison. Talk to my lawyer, Bosch. Now get me a fucking phone."

Bosch stood up and signaled for him to put his arms behind his back. He did so and Bosch cuffed him again, then left the room.

After Bosch filled them in on how Goshen had won round one, Felton told Iverson to take a phone into the interview room and allow the suspect to call his lawyer.

"I guess we'll let him stew," Felton said when he and Bosch were alone. "See how he likes his first taste of incarceration."

"He told me he did three years down in Mexico."

"He tells that to a lot of people he's trying to impress. Like the tattoos. When we were backgrounding him after he showed up a couple years ago, we never found anything about a Mexican prison and as far as we know, he's never ridden a Harley, let alone with any motorcycle gang. I think a night in county might soften him up. Maybe by round two we'll have the ballistics back."

Bosch said he had to use a phone to call his CO to check on what the plan was for the gun.

"Just pick an empty desk out there," Felton said. "Make yourself at home. Listen, I'll tell you how this most likely will go and you can tell your Lieutenant Billets. The lawyer he calls is most likely going to be Mickey Torrino. He's Joey Marks's top guy. He's going to object to extradition and meantime try to get bail. Any bail will do. All they want to do is get him out of our hands and into their hands and then they can make their decision."

"What decision?"

"Whether or not to whack him. If Joey thinks Lucky might flip, he'll just take him out to the desert somewhere and we'll never see him again. Nobody will."

Bosch nodded.

"So you go make your call and I'll call over to the prosecutor's office, see if we can't get an X hearing scheduled. I think the sooner the better. If you can get Lucky to L.A., he's going to be even more likely to start thinking about cutting a deal. That is, if we don't break him first."

"It'd be nice to have the ballistics before the extradition hearing. If we get a ballistics match, it will seal it. But things don't move so quickly in L.A., if you know what I mean. I doubt there's even been an autopsy."

"Well, make your call and then we'll reconnoiter."

Bosch used an empty desk next to Iverson's to make his call. He got Billets at her desk and he could tell she was eating. He quickly updated her on his failed effort to scam Goshen into talking and the plans to have the prosecutor's office in Las Vegas handle the extradition hearing.

"What do you want to do about the gun?" he asked when he was done.

"I want it back here as soon as possible. Edgar talked somebody over at the coroner's office into doing the cut this afternoon. We should have the bullets by tonight. If we have the gun, we can take the whole thing over to ballistics tomorrow morning. Today's Tuesday. I doubt there'd be an extradition hearing before Thursday. We'd have an answer from ballistics by then."

"Okay, I'll grab a plane."

"Good."

Bosch sensed something off about her tone. She was preoccupied by something other than ballistics and what she was eating.

"Lieutenant," he said. "What's up? Is there something I don't know about?"

She hesitated a moment and Bosch waited her out.

"Actually, something's come up."

Bosch's face flashed warm. He guessed that Felton had screwed him and told Billets about the Eleanor Wish situation.

"What is it?"

"I've made an ID on the guy who was in Tony Aliso's office."

"That's great," Bosch said, relieved but confused by her somber tone. "Who?"

"No, it's not great. It was Dominic Carbone from OCID."

Bosch was stunned into silence for a long moment.

"Carbone? What the . . . ?"

"I don't know. I've got some feelers out. I'd like you back here until we figure out what to do with this. Goshen will keep until the extradition hearing. He's not going to be talking to anyone but his lawyer. If you can get back, I'd like us all to get together and hash this around. I haven't talked to Kiz and Jerry yet today. They're still working the financial trail."

"How'd you make the ID on Carbone?"

"Pure luck. Things were kind of slow after I talked to you and the captain out there this morning. I took a drive downtown and stopped by Central. I've got a friend, she's a lieutenant, too, up in OC. Lucinda Barnes, you know her?"

"No."

"Anyway, I went up to see her. I wanted to kind of feel around, maybe get an idea why they took the pass on this one. And, lo and behold, we're sitting there talking and this guy walks through the squad and I think I recognize him but I'm not sure from where. I ask who he is and she tells me that's Carbone. And that's when I remembered. He's the guy on the tape. He had his suit jacket off and his sleeves rolled up. I even saw the tattoo. It's him."

"You tell all this to your friend?"

"Hell no. I just acted natural and got the hell out of there. I tell you, Harry, I don't like this inside stuff. I don't know what to do."

"We'll figure something. Look, I'm going to go. I'll be there as soon as I can. What you might want to do in the meantime, Lieutenant, is try to use some juice with ballistics. Tell them we'll be coming in with a code three in the morning."

Billets said she would do what she could on that.

After making arrangements to fly back to L.A., Bosch barely had time to take a cab back to the Mirage and check out and still make it by Eleanor's apartment to say good-bye. But his knock on her door went unanswered. He didn't know what kind of car she had, so it was impossible for him to check the lot to make sure she was gone. He went back to his rental and sat inside and waited as long as he could, until he was at risk of missing his flight. He then scribbled a message on a page from his notebook saying he would call her and went back to the door. He folded the page up tight and stuck it in the crack of the door jamb so that it would fall and be noticed the next time she opened the door.

He wanted to wait around longer and talk to her in person but he couldn't. Twenty minutes later he was leaving the security office of the airport. The gun from Goshen's house was wrapped in an evidence bag and safely in his briefcase. Five minutes later he was aboard a jet headed for the city of angels.

III

Billets had a weighted and worried look on her face when Bosch stepped into her office.

"Harry."

"Lieutenant. I dropped the gun at ballistics. They're waiting on the bullets. Whoever it was you talked to over there, they snapped to."

"Good."

"Where is everybody?"

"They're both over at Archway. Kiz spent the morning at the IRS and then went over to help Jerry with the interviews with Aliso's associates. I also borrowed a couple of people from Major Fraud to help with the books. They're tracing down these dummy corporations. They're going to go after the bank accounts. Search and seizure. When we freeze the money, then maybe some real live people will come out of the woodwork and claim it. My theory is that this Joey Marks was not the only one Aliso was washing money for. There's too much involved—if Kiz's numbers are right. Aliso was probably working for every mob combine west of Chicago."

Bosch nodded.

"Oh, by the way," she continued, "I told Jerry that you'd take the autopsy so he can stay at Archway. Then I want everybody back here at six to talk about what we have."

"Okay, when's the autopsy?"

"Three-thirty. That going to be a problem?"

"No. Can I ask you something, why'd you call Major Fraud in instead of OCID?"

"For obvious reasons. I don't know what to do about Carbone and OCID. I don't know whether to bring in Internal Affairs, look the other way or what."

"Well, we can't look the other way. They have something we need. And if you call in IAD, then forget it. That will freeze everything up down there and that will be that."

"What do they have that we need?"

"It stands to reason that if Carbone was pulling a bug out of that office, then—"

"There's tapes. Jesus, I forgot about that."

They dropped into silence for a few moments. Bosch pulled the chair out across from her desk and finally sat down.

"Let me take a run at Carbone, see if I can figure out what they were doing and get the tapes," he said. "We've got the leverage."

"This may have something to do with the chief and Fitzgerald, you know."

"Maybe."

She was referring to the intradepartmental skirmish between Deputy Chief Leon Fitzgerald, commander of OCID for more than a decade, and the man who was supposed to be his boss, the chief of police. In the time Fitzgerald had run the OCID, he had taken on an aura akin to J. Edgar Hoover's at the FBI, a keeper of secrets who would use them to protect his position, his division and his budget. It was believed by many that Fitzgerald had his minions investigate and keep tabs on more honest citizens, cops and elected officials of the city than the mobsters his division was charged with rooting out. And it was no secret within the department that there was an ongoing power struggle between Fitzgerald and the police chief. The chief wanted to rein in OCID and its deputy chief but Fitzgerald didn't want to be reined in. In fact, he wanted his domain to broaden. He wanted to be police chief. The struggle was largely at a name-calling standstill. The chief could not fire Fitzgerald outright because of civil service protections; and he could not get backing to simply gut and overhaul OCID from the police commission, mayor or city council members because it was believed that Fitzgerald had thick files on all of them, including the chief. These elected and appointed officials did not know what was in those files but they had to assume that the worst things they had ever done were duly recorded. And therefore they would not back the chief's move against Fitzgerald unless they and the chief were in a guaranteed no-lose position.

Most of this was department legend or rumor, but Bosch knew even legend and rumor usually have some basis in reality. He was reluctant to step behind this curtain and possibly into this fight, as Billets clearly was, but offered to do so because he saw no alternative. He had to know what OCID had been doing and what it was that Carbone was trying to protect by breaking into the Archway office.

"Okay," Billets said after some long thought. "But be careful."

"Where's the video from Archway?"

She pointed to the safe on the floor behind her desk. It was used to secure evidence.

"It will be safe," she said.

"It better be. It will probably be the only thing that keeps them off me."

She nodded. She knew the score.

The OCID offices were on the third floor of Central Division in downtown. The division was located away from police headquarters at Parker Center because the work of the OCID involved many undercover operations and it would not be wise to have so many undercovers going in and out of a place as public as the so-called Glass House, Parker Center. But it was that separation that helped foster the deepening gulf between Leon Fitzgerald and the police chief.

On the drive over from Hollywood, Bosch thought about a plan and knew just how he was going to play it by the time he got to the guard shack and flipped his ID to the rookie assigned parking lot duty. He read the name off the tag above the cop's breast pocket and drove into the lot and over toward the back doors of the station, then put the car in park and got out his phone. He called the OCID's main number and a secretary answered.

"Yeah, this is Trindle down on the parking lot," Bosch said. "Is Carbone there?"

"Yes, he is. If you hold a—"

"Just tell him to come down. Somebody busted into his car."

Bosch hung up and waited. In three minutes one of the doors at the rear of the station house opened and a man hurried out. Bosch recognized him from the Archway surveillance tape. Billets had been right on. Bosch put the car in drive and followed along behind the man. Eventually, he pulled up alongside him and lowered the window.

"Carbone."

"Yeah, what?"

He kept walking, barely giving Bosch a glance.

"Slow down. Your car's all right."

Carbone stopped and now looked closely at Bosch.

"What? What are you talking about?"

"I made the call. I just wanted to get you out here."

"Who the fuck are you?"

"I'm Bosch. We talked the other night."

"Oh, yeah. The Aliso caper."

Then it dawned on him that Bosch could have just taken the elevator up to the third floor if he wanted to see him.

"What is this, Bosch? What's going on?"

"Why don't you get in? I want to take a little ride."

"I don't know, man. I don't like the way you're doing this."

"Get in, Carbone. I think you better."

Bosch said it in a tone and with an accompanying stare that invited no choice but compliance. Carbone, who was about forty with a stocky build, hesitated a moment, then walked around the front of the car. He was wearing a nice dark blue suit like most mob cops liked to wear and he filled the car with the smell of a brisk cologne. Right away Bosch didn't like him.

They drove out of the parking lot and Bosch went north toward Broadway. There was a lot of traffic and pedestrians and they moved slowly. Bosch said nothing, waiting for Carbone.

"Okay, so what's so important you have to kidnap me away from the station?" he finally asked.

Bosch drove another block without answering. He wanted Carbone to sweat a little.

"You've got problems, Carbone," he finally said. "I just thought I should tell you. See, I want to be your friend, Carbone."

Carbone looked at Bosch with caution.

"I know I got problems," he said. "I'm paying two different women child support, my house still has cracks in the walls from the earthquake and the union ain't going to get us a raise again this year. So fuckin' what?"

"Those aren't problems, man. Those are inconveniences. I'm talking about real problems. About the break-in you did the other night over at Archway."

Carbone was silent for a long moment and Bosch wasn't sure but he thought the man was holding his breath.

"I don't know what you're talking about. Take me back."

"No, Carbone, see, that's the wrong answer. I'm here to help you, not hurt you. I'm your friend. And that goes for your boss, Fitzgerald, too."

"I still don't know what you're talking about."

"Okay, then I'll tell you what I'm talking about. I called you Sunday night and asked you about my stiff named Aliso. You call me back and tell me not only is OCID taking a pass, but you never heard of the guy. But as soon as you hang up the phone, you get over to Archway, break into the guy's office and pop the bug you people planted in his phone. That's what I'm talking about."

Bosch looked over at him for the first time and he saw the face of a man whose mind is racing to find a way out. Bosch knew he had him now.

"Bullshit, that's what you're talking about."

"Yeah, you dumb fuck? Next time you decide to do a little breaking and entering, look up. Check for cameras. Rodney King Rule Number One, don't get caught on tape."

He waited a moment to let that sink in and then put the final nails in the coffin.

"You knocked the mug off the desk and broke it. You then dumped it outside hoping nobody would notice anything. And one last thing about the rules. If you're going to do a B&E in short sleeves, then you ought to get yourself a Band-Aid or somethin' and cover up that tattoo on your arm, know what I mean? That's a slam-bang identifier when you got it on tape. And, Carbone, you're on tape, lots of tape."

Carbone wiped a hand across his face. Bosch turned on Third and they went into the tunnel that runs under Bunker Hill. In the darkness that shrouded the car, Carbone finally spoke.

"Who knows about this?"

"For the moment, just me. But don't get any ideas. Anything happens to me and the tape will get known by a lot of people. But for the moment, I can probably contain it."

"What do you want?"

"I want to know what was going on and I want all the tapes you took off his phone."

"Impossible. Can't do it. I don't have those tapes. It wasn't even my file. I just did what . . ."

"What Fitz told you to do. Yeah, I know. But I don't care about that. You go to Fitz or whoever's file it was and get it. I'll go with you if you want or I'll wait out in the car. But we're going back now to get them."

"I can't do it."

What Bosch knew he meant was that he couldn't get the tapes without going to Fitzgerald and telling him how he had so badly messed up the break-in.

"You're going to have to, Carbone. I don't give a shit about you. You lied to me and fucked with my case. You either get me the tapes and an explanation or this is what I do. I dub off three copies of the surveillance tape. One goes to the chief's office in the Glass House, one goes to Jim Newton at the *Times* and the last goes over to Stan Chambers at Channel 5. Stan's a good man, he'll know what to do with it. Do you know he's the one who got the Rodney King tape first?"

"Jesus, Bosch, you're killing me!"

"You've got your choice."

The autopsy was being conducted by a deputy coroner named Salazar. He had already started by the time Bosch got to the coroner's office at County-USC Medical Center. They said their perfunctory hellos and Bosch, garbed in the protective paper body suit and plastic mask, leaned back against one of the stainless counters and just watched. He wasn't expecting much from the autopsy. He had really only come for the bullets and his hope was that one of them would be usable for comparison purposes. It was well known that one reason hitters preferred to use twenty-twos on the job was that the soft bullets often became so misshapen after bouncing around in the brain case that they were worthless for ballistic comparison.

Salazar kept his long black hair in a ponytail that he then wrapped in a larger paper cap. Because he was in a wheelchair, he worked at an autopsy table that was lowered to accommodate him. This gave Bosch an unusually clear vantage point in viewing what was happening to the body.

In years past, Bosch would have maintained an ongoing banter with Salazar while the autopsy proceeded. But since his motorcycle accident, his nine-month medical leave and his return in a wheelchair, Salazar was no longer a cheerful man and rarely engaged in small talk.

Bosch watched as Salazar used a dulled scalpel to scrape a sample of the whitish material from the corners of Aliso's eyes. He placed the material in a paper bindle and put it in a petri dish. He placed the dish on a tray that held a small stand containing the test tubes filled with blood, urine and other samples of body materials to be scanned and tested.

"Think it was tears?" Bosch asked.

"I don't think so. Too thick. He had something in his eyes or on his skin. We'll find out what."

Bosch nodded and Salazar proceeded to open the skullcap and examine the brain.

"The bullets mushed this puppy," he said.

After a few minutes he used a pair of long tweezers to pick out two bullet fragments and drop them in a dish. Bosch stepped over and looked at them and frowned. At least one of the bullets had fragmented upon impact. The pieces were probably worthless for comparison purposes.

Then Salazar pulled out a complete bullet and dropped it in the tray.

"You might be able to work with this one," he said.

Bosch took a look. The bullet had mushroomed on impact but about half the shaft was still intact, and he could see the tiny scratches made when it was fired through the barrel of a gun. He felt a twinge of encouragement.

"This might work," he said.

The autopsy wrapped up in about ten more minutes. Overall, Aliso had gotten fifty minutes of Salazar's time. It was more than most. Bosch checked a clipboard that was on the counter and saw that it was the eleventh autopsy of the day for Salazar.

Salazar cleaned the bullets and put them in an evidence envelope. As he handed it to Bosch, he told the detective that he would be informed of the results of the analysis of the samples retrieved from the body as soon as it was completed. The only other thing that he thought was worth mentioning was that the bruise on Aliso's cheek was antemortem by four or five hours. This Bosch found to be very curious. He didn't know how it fit in. It would mean that someone had roughed Aliso up while he was in Las Vegas, yet he had been killed here in L.A. He thanked Salazar, calling him Sally as many people did, and headed out. He was in the hallway before he remembered something and went back to the door of the autopsy suite. When he stuck his head in, he saw Salazar tying the sheet around the body, making sure the toe tag hung free and could be read.

"Hey, Sally, the guy had hemorrhoids, right?"

Salazar looked back at him with a quizzical look on his face.

"Hemorrhoids? No. Why do you ask?"

"I found a tube of Preparation H in his car. In the glove box. It was half used."

"Hmmm . . . well, no hemorrhoids. Not on this one."

Bosch wanted to ask him if he was sure but knew that would be insulting. He let it go for the moment and left.

Details fueled any investigation. They were important and not to be misplaced or forgotten. As he headed toward the glass exit doors of the coroner's office, Bosch found himself bothered by the detail of the tube of Preparation H found in the glove box of the Silver Cloud. If Tony Aliso hadn't suffered from hemorrhoids, then whom did the tube belong to and why was it in his car? He could dismiss it as probably being unimportant, but that wasn't his way. Everything had its place in an investigation, Bosch believed. Everything.

His deep concentration on this problem caused Bosch to go through the glass doors and down the stairs to the parking lot before he saw Carbone standing there smoking a cigarette and waiting. When Bosch had dropped him off earlier, the OCID detective had begged for a couple of hours to get the tapes together. Bosch had agreed but hadn't told him that he was heading to an autopsy. So he now assumed that Carbone had called the bureau in Hollywood and been told by Billets or someone else that he was at the coroner's office. Bosch wouldn't check this with Carbone because he didn't want to show any kind of concern that the OCID detective had so easily found him.

"Bosch."

"Yeah."

"Somebody wants to talk."

"Who? When? I want the tapes, Carbone."

"Cool your jets for a couple minutes. Over here in the car."

He led Bosch to the second parking row, where there was a car with its engine running and its dark-tinted windows all the way up.

"Hop in the back," Carbone said.

Bosch nonchalantly walked to the door, still showing no concern. He opened it and ducked in. Leon Fitzgerald was sitting in the back. He was a tall man—more than six and a half feet—and his knees were pressed hard against the back of the driver's seat. He wore a beautiful suit of blue silk and held the stub of a cigar between his fingers. He was almost sixty and his hair was a jet-black dye job. His eyes, behind steel-rimmed glasses, were pale gray. His skin was pasty white. He was a night man.

"Chief," Bosch said, nodding.

He had never met Fitzgerald before but had seen him often enough at cop funerals and on television news reports. He was the embodiment of the OCID. No one else from the secretive division ever went on camera.

"Detective Bosch," Fitzgerald said. "I know of you. Know of your exploits. Over the years you have been suggested to me more than once as a candidate for our unit."

"Why didn't you call?"

Carbone had come around and gotten in the driver's seat. He started moving the car slowly through the lot.

"Because like I said, I know of you," Fitzgerald was saying. "And I know you would not leave homicide. Homicide is your calling. Am I correct?"

"Pretty much."

"Which brings us to the current homicide case you are pursuing. Dom?"

With one hand, Carbone passed a shoebox over the seat. Fitzgerald took it and put it on Bosch's lap. Bosch opened it and found it full of audiocassette tapes with dates written on tape stuck to the cases.

"From Aliso's phone?" he asked.

"Obviously."

"How long were you on it?"

"We'd only been listening for nine days. It hadn't been productive, but the tapes are yours."

"And what do you want in return, Chief?"

"What do I want?"

Fitzgerald looked out the window, down at the railroad switching yard in the valley below the parking lot.

"What do I want?" he asked again. "I want the killer, of course. But I also want you to be careful. The department's been through a lot these past few years. No need to hang our dirty laundry in public once again."

"You want me to bury Carbone's extracurricular activities."

Neither Fitzgerald nor Carbone said anything but they didn't have to. Everybody in the car knew that Carbone did what he did on orders. Probably orders from Fitzgerald himself.

"Then you've got to answer some questions."

"Of course."

"Why was there a bug on Tony Aliso's phone?"

"Same reason there's a bug on anyone's phone. We heard things about the man and set about finding out if they were true."

"What did you hear?"

"That he was dirty, that he was a scumbag, that he was a launderer for the mob in three states. We opened a file. We had just begun when he was killed."

"Then when I called, why did you pass on it?"

Fitzgerald took a long pull on his cigar and the car filled with its smell.

"There's a complicated answer to that question, Detective. Suffice it to say that we thought it best if we remained uninvolved."

"The tap was illegal, wasn't it?"

"It is extremely difficult under state law to gather the required information needed for a wiretap. The feds, they can get it done on a whim. We can't and we don't want to work with the feds all the time."

"It still doesn't explain why you passed. You could've taken the case from us and then controlled it, buried it, done whatever you wanted with it. No one would have known about illegal wiretaps or anything else."

"Perhaps. Perhaps it was a wrong choice."

Bosch realized they had underestimated him and his crew. Fitzgerald had believed the break-in would go unnoticed and therefore his unit's involvement would not be discovered. Bosch understood the tremendous leverage he held over Fitzgerald. Word about the illegal wiretap would be all the police chief would need to rid himself of Fitzgerald.

"So what else do you have on Aliso?" he asked. "I want everything. If I hear at any point you held something back, then your little black-bag job is going to get known. You know what I mean? It will get known."

Fitzgerald turned from the window and looked at him.

"I know exactly what you mean. But you are making a mistake if you are going to smugly sit there and believe you have all the high cards in this game."

"Then put whatever cards you have on the table."

"Detective, I am about to fully cooperate with you, but know this. If you seek to hurt me or anyone in my division with the information you get here, I will hurt you more. For example, there's this matter of your keeping company last night with a convicted felon."

He let that hang in the air with his cigar smoke. Bosch was stunned and angry but managed to swallow down his urge to throttle Fitzgerald.

"There is a department prohibition against any officer knowingly associating with criminals. I'm sure you know that, Detective, and understand the need for such a safeguard. If this were to become known about you, then your job could be in jeopardy. Then where would you and your mission be?"

Bosch didn't answer. He looked straight ahead, over the seat and out the front window. Fitzgerald leaned over so that he was almost whispering in his ear.

"This is what we know about you in just one hour," he said. "What if we spend a day? A week? And it's not just you, my friend. You can tell your lieutenant that there is a glass ceiling in the department for lesbians, especially if something like that should get out. Now her girlfriend, she could go further, her being black. But the lieutenant, she'd have to get used to Hollywood, you ask me."

He leaned back to his spot and returned his voice to normal modula-
tion.

"Do we have an understanding here, Detective Bosch?"

Bosch turned and finally looked at him.

"We have an understanding."

After dropping the bullets retrieved from Tony Aliso's head at the ballistics lab in Boyle Heights, Bosch made it back to the Hollywood Division
just as the investigators were gathering in Billets's office for the six
o'clock meeting. Bosch was introduced to Russell and Kuhlken, the two
fraud investigators, and everybody sat down. Also sitting in was a deputy
district attorney. Matthew Gregson was from Special Prosecutions, a unit
that handled organized crime cases as well as the prosecution of police
officers and other delicate matters. Bosch had never met him.

Bosch gave his report first and concisely brought the others up to date
on the occurrences in Las Vegas as well as the autopsy and his swing by the
department's gun shop. He said he'd been promised that the ballistics comparison would be done by ten the following morning. But Bosch made no
mention of his meetings with Carbone and Fitzgerald. Not because of the
threat Fitzgerald had made—or so Bosch told himself—but because the
information he had gleaned from those meetings was best not discussed
with such a large group in general and a prosecutor in particular. Apparently feeling the same way, Billets asked him no questions in this regard.

When Bosch was finished, Rider went next. She said she had talked
to the IRS auditor assigned to the TNA Productions case and gotten
very little information.

"Basically, they have a whistle-blowing program," she said. "You blow
the whistle on a tax scofflaw and you get a share of whatever taxes the
IRS finds it's been cheated out of. That's how this started. Only problem
is, according to Hirschfield, he's the IRS guy, this tip came in anony-
mously. Whoever blew the whistle didn't want a share. He said they got
a three-page letter outlining Tony Aliso's money-washing scam. He
would not show it to me because he claimed, anonymous or not, the
guidelines of the program call for strict confidence and the specific language of the letter could lead to identification of the author. He—"

"That's bullshit," Gregson said.

"Probably," Rider said. "But there was nothing I could do about it."

"Afterwards, give me the guy's name and I'll see what I can do."

"Sure. Anyway, they got this letter, did some preliminary looking at TNA's corporate filings over the years and decided the letter had merit. They sent the audit letter to Tony on August 1 and were going to do him at the end of this month. That was it with him—oh, the one thing he would tell me about the letter was that it was mailed from Las Vegas. It was on the postmark."

Bosch almost nodded involuntarily because that last bit of information fit with something Fitzgerald had told him.

"Okay, now for Tony Aliso's associates. Jerry and I spent the better part of the day interviewing the core group of people he used when making this trash he called film. He basically raided the local film schools, low-rent acting schools and strip bars for the so-called artistic talent for these shoots, but there were five men that he repeatedly worked with to get them off the ground. We took them all one by one and it appears they were not privy to financing of the movies or the books Tony kept. We think they were in the dark. Jerry?"

"That's right," Edgar said. "I personally think Tony picked these guys because they were stupid and didn't ask questions about that sort of stuff. He just sent them out, you know, over to USC or UCLA to grab some kid who'd want to direct or write one of these things. They'd go over to the Star Strip on La Cienega and talk girls into taking the bimbo parts. On and on, you know how it goes. Our conclusion is that this little money washing scam was Tony's. Only he and his customers knew."

"Which leads us to you guys," Billets said, looking at Russell and Kuhlken. "You got anything to tell us, yet?"

Kuhlken said they were still waist-deep in the financial records but they had so far traced money from TNA Productions to dummy corporations in California, Nevada and Arizona. The money went into the corporation bank accounts and was then invested in other, seemingly legitimate, corporations. He said when the trail was fully documented they would be in a position to use the IRS and federal statutes to seize the money as the illegal funds of a racketeering enterprise. Unfortunately, Russell said, the documentation period was long and difficult. It would be another week before they could move.

"Keep at it and take the time you need," Billets said, then she looked at Gregson. "So then, how are we doing? What should we be doing?"

Gregson thought a moment.

"I think we are doing fine. First thing tomorrow I'll call Vegas and find out who's handling the extradition hearing. I'm thinking that I possibly should go out there to babysit that. I'm not that comfortable at the moment with all of us here and Goshen over there with them. If we are lucky enough to pull a match out of ballistics, I think you and I, Harry, should go over there and not leave until we have Goshen with us."

Bosch nodded his agreement.

"After hearing all of these reports, I really have just one question," Gregson continued. "Why isn't there someone from OCID sitting in this room right now?"

Billets looked at Bosch and almost imperceptibly nodded. The question was being passed to him.

"Initially," Bosch said, "OCID was informed of the murder and the victim's ID and they passed. They said they didn't know Tony Aliso. As recently as two hours ago I had a conversation with Leon Fitzgerald and told him what it looked like we had. He offered whatever expertise his people had but felt we were too far along now to have fresh people come in. He wished us best of luck with it."

Gregson stared at him a long moment and then nodded. The prosecutor was in his mid-forties with short-cropped hair already completely gray. Bosch had never worked with him but he'd heard the name. Gregson had been around—long enough to know there was more to what Bosch had said. But he had also been around long enough to let it go for the time being. Billets didn't give him a lot of time to make something of it anyway.

"Okay, so why don't we brainstorm a little bit before we call it a night?" she said. "What do we think happened to this man? We're gathering a lot of information, a lot of evidence, but do we know what happened to him?"

She looked at the faces gathered in the room. Finally, Rider spoke up.

"My guess is that the IRS audit brought it all about," she said. "He got the notice in the mail and he made a fatal mistake. He told this guy in Vegas, Joey Marks, that the government was going to look at his books and his cheap movies and the scam was likely going to come out. Joey Marks responded the way you expect these guys to respond. He whacked him. He had his man Goshen follow Tony back home from Vegas so it would happen far away from him and Goshen puts him in the trunk."

The others nodded their heads in agreement. This included Bosch. The information he'd received from Fitzgerald fit with this scenario as well.

"It was a good plan," Edgar said. "Only mistake was the fingerprints Artie Donovan got off the jacket. That was pure luck and if we didn't have that, we probably wouldn't have any of this. That was the only mistake."

"Maybe not," Bosch said. "The prints on the jacket just hurried things along, but Metro in Vegas was already working a tip from an informant who overheard Lucky Goshen talking about hitting somebody and putting them in a trunk. It would've gotten back to us. Eventually."

"Well, I'd rather be already on it than waiting for eventually," Billets said. "Any alternative theories we should also be chasing? Are we clear on the wife, the angry screenwriter, his other associates?"

"Nothing that sticks out," Rider said. "There definitely was no love lost between the victim and the wife but she seems clean so far. I pulled the gatehouse log up there with a warrant and her car never left Hidden Highlands on Friday night. She seems clean."

"What about the letter to the IRS?" Gregson asked. "Who sent it? Obviously, someone with pretty good knowledge of what this man was doing, but who would that be?"

"This could all be part of a power play within the Joey Marks group," Bosch said. "Like I said before, something about the look on Goshen's face when he saw that gun and his claims later that it was a plant . . . I don't know, maybe somebody tipped the IRS knowing it would get Tony whacked and that they could then possibly lay it off on Goshen. With Goshen gone, this person moves up."

"You're saying Goshen didn't do it?" Gregson asked, his eyebrows arched.

"No. I think Goshen is probably good for it. But I don't think he was counting on that gun showing up behind the toilet. It doesn't make sense, anyway, to keep it around. So say he whacks out Tony Aliso on orders from Joey Marks. He gives the gun to somebody in his crew to get rid of.

Only that person goes and plants it at the house—this is the same person who sent the letter to the IRS in the first place to get the whole thing going. Now we come along and wrap Goshen up in a bow. The guy who stashed the gun and sent the letter, he's in a position to move up."

Bosch looked at their faces as they tried to follow the logic.

"Maybe Goshen isn't the intended target," Rider said.

Everyone looked at her.

"Maybe there's one more play. Maybe it's someone who wants Goshen and Joey Marks out of the way so he can move in."

"How will they get Marks now?" Edgar asked.

"Through Goshen," she said.

"If those ballistics come back a match," Bosch said, "then you can stick a fork in Goshen because he'll be done. He'll be looking at the needle or life without possibility. Or a reduced sentence if he gives us something."

"Joey Marks," Gregson and Edgar said at the same time.

"So who is the letter writer?" Billets asked.

"Who knows?" Bosch answered. "I don't know enough about the organization over there. But there's a lawyer who was mentioned by the cops there. A guy who handles everything for Marks. He'd know about Aliso's scam. He could pull this off. There's probably a handful of people close to Marks capable of doing it."

They all were silent for a long moment, each one thinking the story through and seeing that it could work. It was a natural conclusion to the meeting and Billets stood up to end it.

"Let's keep up the good work," she said. "Matthew, thanks for coming out. You'll be the first one I call when we get the ballistics in the morning."

Everyone else started standing up.

"Kiz and Jerry, flip a coin," Billets said. "One of you will have to go to Vegas to work the extradition escort with Harry. It's regulations. Oh, and Harry, could you wait a minute? There's something I need to discuss with you about another case."

After the others left, Billets told Bosch to close the door. He did so and then sat down in one of the chairs in front of her desk.

"So what happened?" she asked. "Did you really talk to Fitzgerald?"

"Well, I guess it was more that he talked to me, but, yeah, I met with him and Carbone."

"What's the deal?"

"Basically, the deal is that they didn't know Tony Aliso from a hole in the ground until they, too, got a letter, probably the same one that went to the IRS. I've got a copy of it. It has details. It was from somebody with knowledge, just like Kiz said. The letter OCID got also was postmarked in Las Vegas and it was addressed specifically to Fitzgerald."

"So their response was to bug his office phone."

"Right, illegal bug. They had just started—I have nine days' worth of tapes to listen to—when I call up and say Tony got whacked. They panicked. You know his situation with the chief. If it came out that first of all they illegally put the bug on Tony and second of all might have somehow been the cause of his death because Joey Marks found out, then the chief would pretty much have all he'd need to move Fitzgerald out and reestablish controls on OCID."

"So Fitzgerald sends Carbone in to get the bug and they play dumb about Tony."

"Right. Carbone didn't see the camera or we wouldn't know any of this."

"That prick. When this is over, the first thing I'm going to do is give it all to the chief."

"Uh . . ."

Bosch wasn't sure how to say it.

"What is it?"

"Fitzgerald could see that coming. I cut a deal with him."

"*What?*"

"I cut a deal. He gave me everything, the tapes, the letter. But their activities go no further than you and me. The chief never knows."

"Harry, how could you? You had no—"

"He's got something on me, Lieutenant. He's got something on you, too . . . and Kiz."

A long silence followed and Bosch watched the anger flush her cheeks.

"That arrogant bastard," she said.

Bosch told her what it was Fitzgerald had come up with. Since Bosch now was privy to her secret, he thought it was only fair that he tell her about Eleanor. Billets just nodded. She was clearly thinking more about her own secret and the consequences of Fitzgerald having knowledge of it.

"Do you think he actually put people on me? A tail?"

"Who knows? He's the kind of guy who sees opportunities and acts on them. He keeps information like money in a bank. In case of a rainy day. This was a rainy day for him and he pulled it out. I made the deal. Let's forget about it and move on with the case."

She was silent a moment and Bosch watched her for any sign of embarrassment. There was none. She looked directly at Bosch, her eyes searching him for any sign of judgment. There was none. She nodded.

"What else did they do after the letter came?"

"Not much. They put Aliso on a loose surveillance. I have the logs. But they weren't watching him Friday night. They knew he'd gone to Las Vegas, so they were planning to pick him up again after the holiday if he was back. They were really just getting started when it all went down."

She nodded again. Her mind wasn't on the subject. Bosch stood up.

"I'll listen to the tapes tonight. There's about seven hours but Fitzgerald said it's mostly Aliso talking to his girlfriend in Vegas. Nothing much else. But I'll listen anyway. You need anything else, Lieutenant?"

"No. Let's talk in the morning. I want to know about the ballistics as soon as you know."

"You got it."

Bosch headed to the door but she stopped him.

"It's weird, isn't it, when sometimes you can't tell the good guys from the bad."

He looked back at her.

"Yeah, it's weird."

The house still smelled of fresh paint when Bosch finally got home. He looked at the wall he had started to paint three days before and it seemed long ago. He didn't know when he'd finish now. The house had been a ground-up rebuilding job after the earthquake. He'd only been back a few weeks after more than a year of living in a residence hotel near the station. The earthquake, too, seemed long ago. Things happened fast in this city. Everything but the moment seemed like ancient history.

He got out the number Felton had given him for Eleanor Wish and called it but there was no answer, not even a machine picking up. He hung up and wondered if she had gotten the note he left for her. His hope was that they would somehow be together after this case was over. But if it came to that, he realized, he wasn't sure how he'd deal with the department's prohibition against associating with a convicted felon.

His thoughts about this spun into the question of how Fitzgerald had found out about her and the night they had spent together in her apartment. It seemed to him it was likely that Fitzgerald would maintain contacts with Metro, and he guessed that maybe Felton or Iverson had informed the deputy chief about Eleanor Wish.

Bosch made two sandwiches of lunch meat from the refrigerator and then took them, two bottles of beer and the box of tapes Fitzgerald had given him over to the chair next to his stereo. As he ate, he arranged the tapes in chronological order and then started playing them. There was a photocopy of a log and pen register with entries showing what time of day Aliso either received or made the calls and what number he had called.

More than half the calls were between Aliso and Layla, either placed to the club—Bosch could tell because of the background music and noise—or a number he assumed was her apartment. She never identified herself on any of the calls, but on the occasions Tony called her at the club he asked for her by her stage name, Layla. Other than that, he never used her name. Most of their conversations were about the minutia of daily life. He called her most often at home in the midafternoon. In one call to her home, Layla was angry at Aliso for waking her up. He complained that it was already noon and she reminded him that she had worked until four at the club. Like a chastened boy, he apologized and offered to call back. He did, at two.

In addition to the conversations with Layla there were calls to other women involving the timing of a scene that needed to be reshot for one of Tony's movies and various other film-related business calls. There were two calls placed by Aliso to his home but both of his conversations with his wife were quick and to the point. One time he said he was coming home and the other time he said he was going to be held up and wouldn't be home for dinner.

When Bosch was done it was after midnight and he had counted only one of the conversations as being of even marginal interest. It was a call placed to the dressing room at the club on the Tuesday before Aliso was murdered. In the midst of their rather boring, innocuous conversation, Layla asked him when he was coming out next.

"Comin' out Thursday, baby," Aliso replied. "Why, you miss me already?"

"No—I mean, yeah, sure, I miss you and all, Tone. But Lucky was asking if you were coming. That's why I asked."

Layla had a soft, little-girl voice that seemed unpracticed or fake.

"Well, tell him I'll be in Thursday night. You working then?"

"Yeah, I'm working."

Bosch turned off the stereo and thought about the one call that mattered. It meant Goshen knew, through Layla, that Aliso was coming out. It wasn't much, but it could probably be used by a prosecutor as part of an argument for premeditation. The problem was that it was tainted evidence. In legal terms, it did not exist.

He looked at his watch. It was late but he decided to call. He took the number off the log where Layla's number had been recorded by a pen register which read the tones that sounded when a number was punched into a phone. After four rings it was answered by a woman with a slow voice laced with practiced sexual intent.

"Layla?"

"No, this is Pandora."

Bosch almost laughed but he was too tired.

"Where's Layla?"

"She isn't here."

"This is a friend of hers. Harry. She tried to call me the other night. You know where she is or where I could reach her?"

"No. She hasn't been around for a couple days. I don't know where she is. Is this about Tony?"

"Yeah."

"Well, she's pretty upset. I guess if she wants to talk to you, she'll call you again. You in town?"

"Not right now. Where d'you guys live?"

"Uh, I don't think I'm going to tell you that."

"Pandora, is Layla scared of something?"

"Of course she is. Her old man gets killed. She thinks people might think she knows something, but she doesn't. She's just scared."

Bosch gave Pandora his home number and told her to have Layla call if she checked in.

After he hung up he looked at his watch and took out the little phone book he kept in his jacket. He called Billets's number and a man answered. Her husband. Bosch apologized for the late call, asked for the lieutenant and wondered while he waited what the husband knew about his wife and Kizmin Rider. When Billets picked up, Bosch told her about his review of the tapes and how little value they had.

"The one call establishes Goshen's knowledge of Aliso's trip to Vegas, as well as his interest in it. But that's about it. I think it's kind of marginal and we'll be okay without it. When we find Layla, we should be able to get the same information from her. Legally."

"Well, that makes me feel better."

Bosch heard her exhale. Her unspoken worry had obviously been that if the tapes contained any vital information, they would have to have been brought forward to prosecutors, thereby alienating Fitzgerald and ending her own career.

"Sorry for the late call," Bosch said, "but I thought you might want to know as soon as I knew."

"Thanks, Harry. I'll see you in the morning."

After he hung up he tried Eleanor Wish's line once more and again there was no answer. Now the slight worry he'd had in his chest bloomed into a full-fledged concern. He wished he was still in Vegas so he could go to her apartment to see if she was there and just not answering or if it was something worse.

Bosch got himself another beer from the refrigerator and went out to the back deck. The new deck was larger than its predecessor and offered a deeper view into the Pass. It was dark and peaceful out. The usual hiss of the Hollywood Freeway far below was easily tuned out. He watched

the spotlights from Universal Studios cut across the starless sky and finished his beer, wondering where she was.

On Wednesday morning, Bosch got to the station at eight and typed out
reports detailing his moves and investigation in Las Vegas. He made copies
and put them in the lieutenant's mailbox and then clipped the originals
into the already inch-thick murder book that Edgar had started. He filed
no report on his conversations with Carbone and Fitzgerald or his review
of the tapes OCID had made off Aliso's office phone. His work was only
interrupted by frequent walks to the watch office for coffee.

     He had completed these chores by ten o'clock but waited another five
minutes before calling the department's gun shop. He knew from experience that he should not call before the time the report on the bullet
comparisons was to be finished. He threw in the extra five minutes just
to make sure. It was a long five minutes.

     As he called, Edgar and Rider gravitated toward his spot at the homi-
cide table so that they could immediately get the comparison results. It
was a make-or-break point in the investigation and they all knew it.
Bosch asked for Lester Poole, the gun tech assigned the case. They had
worked together before. Poole was a gnomish man whose whole life re-
volved around guns, though as a civilian employee of the department he
did not carry one himself. But there was no one more expert at the gun
shop than he. He was a curious man in that he would not acknowledge
anyone who called him Les. He insisted on being called Lester or even
just Poole, never the diminutive of Lester. Once he confided to Bosch
that this was because he feared that if he became known as Les Poole, it
would only be a matter of time before some smartass cops started calling
him Cess Poole. It was his intention never to let that happen.

     "Lester, it's Harry," Bosch said when the tech picked up. "You're the
man this morning. What have you got for me?"

     "I've got good and bad news for you, Harry."

     "Give me the bad first."

     "Just finished with your case. Haven't written the report yet but this
is what I can tell you. The gun has been wiped clean of prints and is not
traceable. Your doer used acid on the serial and I couldn't bring it up
with any of my magic tricks. So that's that."

"And the good?"

"I *can* tell you that you've got yourself a match between the weapon and the bullets extracted from your victim. It's a definite match."

Bosch looked up at Edgar and Rider and gave the thumbs-up sign. They exchanged a high five and then Bosch watched as Rider gave Lieutenant Billets the thumbs-up through the glass of her office. Bosch then saw Billets pick up her phone. Bosch presumed she was calling Gregson at the DA's office.

Poole told Bosch that the report would be finished by noon and shipped through intradepartmental courier. Bosch thanked him and hung up. He stood up smiling and then walked with Edgar and Rider into the lieutenant's office. Billets spent another minute on the phone and Bosch could tell she was talking to Gregson. She then hung up.

"That's a very happy man there," she said.

"He should be," Edgar said.

"All right, so now what?" Billets asked.

"We go over there and drag that desert dirtbag's ass back here," Edgar said.

"Yes, that's what Gregson said. He's going to go over to babysit the hearing. It's tomorrow morning, right?"

"Supposed to be," Bosch said. "I'm thinking of heading over there today. There are a couple loose ends I want to square away, maybe take another shot at finding the girlfriend, and then I want to make the arrangements so we can get out of there with him as soon as the judge says go."

"Fine," Billets said. Then to Edgar and Rider, she asked, "Did you two decide who is going with Harry?"

"Me," Edgar said. "Kiz is more plugged in on the financial stuff. I'll go with Harry to get this sucker."

"Okay, fine. Anything else?"

Bosch told them about the gun being untraceable, but this didn't seem to dent the euphoria engendered by the ballistics match. The case was looking more and more like a slam dunk.

They left the office after a few more self-congratulatory statements and Bosch went back to his phone. He dialed Felton's office at Metro. The captain picked up right away.

"Felton, it's Bosch in L.A."

"Bosch, what's up?"

"Thought you might want to know. The gun checks out. It fired the bullets that killed Tony Aliso."

Felton whistled into the phone.

"Damn, that's nice and neat. Lucky ain't going to feel so lucky when he hears about that."

"Well, I'm coming out in a little while to tell him."

"Good. When you going to be here?"

"Haven't set it up yet. What about the extradition hearing? We still on for tomorrow morning?"

"Absolutely, as far as I know. I'll have somebody double-check to make sure. His lawyer might be trying to make waves but that won't work. This added piece of evidence will help, too."

Bosch told him that Gregson would be coming out in the morning to aid the local prosecutor if needed.

"That's probably a wasted trip but he's welcome just the same."

"I'll tell him. Listen, if you've got a spare body, there's still one loose end bugging me."

"What?"

"Tony's girlfriend. She was a dancer at Dolly's till she got fired by Lucky on Saturday. I still want to talk to her. She goes by the name Layla. That's all I have. That and her phone number."

He gave Felton the number and the captain said he'd have somebody check into it.

"Anything else?"

"Yeah, one other thing. You know Deputy Chief Fitzgerald out here, don't you?"

"Sure do. We've worked cases together."

"You talked to him lately?"

"Uh, no . . . no. Not in—it's been a while."

Bosch thought he was lying but decided to let it go. He needed the man's cooperation for at least another twenty-four hours.

"Why do you ask, Bosch?"

"No reason. Just thought I'd ask. He's been advising us from this end, that's all."

"Good to hear that. He's a very capable individual."

"Capable. Yeah, that he is."

Bosch hung up and then immediately set about making travel arrangements for himself and Edgar. He booked two rooms at the Mirage. They were above the department's maximum allowance for hotel rooms but he was sure Billets would approve the vouchers. Besides, Layla had called him once at the Mirage. She might try again.

Last, he reserved round-trip tickets for himself and Edgar out of Burbank. On the Thursday afternoon return he reserved one more seat for Goshen.

Their flight out left at three-thirty and got them into Las Vegas an hour later. He figured that would give them plenty of time to do what they had to do.

Nash was in the gatehouse and came out to greet Bosch with a smile. Harry introduced Edgar.

"Looks like you guys've got yourself a real whodunit, eh?"

"Looks that way," Bosch said. "You got any theories?"

"Not a one. I gave your girl the gate log, she tell you that?"

"She's not my girl, Nash. She's a detective. Pretty good one, too."

"I know. I didn't mean nothing."

"So, is Mrs. Aliso home today?"

"Let's take a look."

Nash slid the door of the gatehouse back open, went inside and picked up a clipboard. He scanned it quickly and flipped back to the prior page. After scanning it he put the clipboard down and came back out.

"She should be there," he said. "Hasn't been out in two days."

Bosch nodded his thanks.

"I gotta call her, you know," Nash said. "Rules."

"No problem."

Nash raised the gate and Bosch drove through.

Veronica Aliso was waiting at the open door of her house when they got there. She was wearing tight gray leggings beneath a long loose T-shirt with a copy of a Matisse painting on it. She had on a lot of makeup again. Bosch introduced Edgar and she led them to the living room. They declined an offer for something to drink.

"Well, then, what can I do for you men?"

Bosch opened his notebook and tore out a page he had already written on. He handed her the page.

"That's the number of the coroner's office and the case number," he said. "The autopsy was completed yesterday and the body can be released to you now. If you are already working with a funeral home, just give that case number to them and they'll take care of it."

She looked at the page for a long moment.

"Thank you," she finally said. "You came all the way up here to give me this?"

"No. We also have some news. We've arrested a man for your husband's murder."

Her eyes widened.

"Who? Did he say why he did this?"

"His name is Luke Goshen. He's from Las Vegas. Have you ever heard of him?"

Confusion spread across her face.

"No, who is he?"

"He's a mobster, Mrs. Aliso. And your husband knew him pretty well, I'm afraid. We're going to Las Vegas now to get him. If all goes well, we will be coming back with him tomorrow. Then the case will proceed through the courts. There will be a preliminary hearing in municipal court, and then if Goshen is bound over for trial as we assume he will be, there will be a trial in Los Angeles Superior Court. It is likely you will have to testify briefly during the trial. Testify for the prosecution."

She nodded, her eyes far off.

"Why did he do it?"

"We're not sure yet. We're working on that. We do know that your husband was involved in business dealings with this man's, uh, employer. A man named Joseph Marconi. Do you recall if your husband ever mentioned Goshen or Joseph Marconi?"

"No."

"What about the names Lucky or Joey Marks?"

She shook her head in the negative.

"What business dealings?" she asked.

"He was cleaning money for them. Washing it through his film business. You sure you did not know anything about this?"

"Of course not. Do I need my lawyer? You know he already told me not to talk to you people."

Bosch gave an easy smile and held his hands up.

"No, Mrs. Aliso, you don't need your lawyer. We're just trying to get to the facts of the case. If you knew something about your husband's business dealings, it might help us build a case against this man Goshen and possibly his employer. You see, right now we've got this Goshen character pretty well tied up for this. We're not sweating that. We've got ballistics, fingerprints, hard evidence. But he wouldn't have done what he did if Joey Marks didn't tell him to. Joey Marks is who we'd really like to get. And the more information I have about your husband and his business, the better the chance we have of getting to Joey Marks. So if there is anything you can help us with, now is the time to tell us."

He was silent and waited. She looked down at the now folded piece of paper in her hand. She finally nodded to herself and looked at him.

"I know nothing about his business," she said. "But there was a call last week. It came here on Wednesday night. He took it in the office and closed the door but . . . I went to the door and listened. I could hear his side of it."

"What did he say?"

"He called the caller Lucky. I know that. He did a lot of listening and then he said he'd be out there by the end of the week. He then said he'd see the caller at the club. And that was it."

Bosch nodded.

"Why didn't you tell us this before?"

"I didn't think it was important. I . . . you see, I thought he was talking to a woman. The name Lucky, I thought it was a woman's name."

"Was that why you were listening through the door?"

She averted her eyes and nodded her head.

"Mrs. Aliso, have you ever hired a private investigator to follow your husband?"

"No. I thought about it but I didn't."

"But you suspected he was having an affair?"

"Affairs, Detective. I not only suspected, I knew. A wife can tell."

"Okay, Mrs. Aliso. Do you remember anything else about the telephone conversation? Anything else that was said?"

"No. Just what I told you."

"It might help us with the court case, as far as questions of premeditation go, if we could isolate this call. Are you sure it was Wednesday?"

"Yes, because he left the next day."

"What time did the call come in?"

"It was late. We were watching the news on Channel 4. So it was after eleven and before eleven-thirty. I don't think I can narrow it down any further."

"Okay, Mrs. Aliso, that's good."

Bosch looked over at Edgar and raised his eyebrows. Edgar just nodded. He was ready to go. They stood up and Veronica Aliso led them to the door.

"Oh," Bosch said before he got to the door. "There was a question that came up about your husband. Do you know, did he have a regular doctor that he went to?"

"Yes, on occasion. Why?"

"Well, I wanted to check to see if he suffered from hemorrhoids."

She looked like she was about to laugh.

"Hemorrhoids? I don't think so. I think Tony would've complained loud and often if he did."

"Really?"

Bosch was standing in the doorway now.

"Yes, really. Besides, you just told me that the autopsy was completed, wouldn't that doctor be able to tell you the answer to that question?"

Bosch nodded. She had him there.

"I guess so, Mrs. Aliso. The only reason I ask is that we found a tube of Preparation H in his car. I was wondering why it was there if, you know, he didn't need it."

She smiled this time.

"Oh, that's an old performer's trick."

"A performer's trick?"

"You know, actresses, models, dancers. They use that stuff."

Bosch looked at her, waiting for more. She didn't say anything.

"I don't get it," he said. "Why do they use it?"

"Under their eyes, Detective Bosch. You know, shrinks the swelling? Well, you put it under your eyes and the bags from all that hard living get shrunk, too. Probably half the people who buy that stuff in this town use it under their eyes, not what it's supposed to be used for. My husband . . . he was a vain man. If he was going to Las Vegas to be with some young girl, I think he would have done this. It was just like him."

Bosch nodded. He thought of the unidentified substance under Tony Aliso's eyes. You learn something new every day, he thought. He would have to call Salazar.

"How do you think he would have known about that?" he asked.

She was about to answer but hesitated, then she just hiked her shoulders.

"It's a not-so-secret Hollywood secret," she said. "He could've learned it anywhere."

Including from you, Bosch thought but didn't say. He just nodded and stepped through the door.

"Oh, one last thing," he said before she closed it. "This arrest is probably going to hit the media today or tomorrow. We'll try to contain it as much as possible. But in this town, nothing's ever sacred or secret for long. You should be prepared for that."

"Thank you, Detective."

"You might want to think about a small funeral. Something inside. Tell the director not to give information out over the phone. Funerals always make good video."

She nodded and closed the door.

On the way out of Hidden Highlands, Bosch lit a cigarette and Edgar didn't object.

"She's a cold piece of work," Edgar said.

"That she is," Bosch answered. "What do you think of the phone call from Lucky?"

"It's just one more piece. We got Lucky by the balls. As far as he's concerned, it's over."

Bosch took Mulholland along the crest of the mountains until it wound down to the Hollywood Freeway. They passed without comment the fire road down which Tony Aliso had been found. At the freeway, Bosch turned south so he could pick up the 10 in downtown and head east.

"Harry, what's up?" Edgar asked. "I thought we were leavin' outta Burbank."

"We're not flying. We're driving."

"What are you talking about?"

"I only reserved the flights in case somebody checked. When we get to Vegas, we let on that we flew in and that we're flying out right after the hearing with Goshen. Nobody has to know we're driving. You okay with that?"

"Yeah, sure, fine. I get it. Precautions, settin' a smoke screen in case somebody checks. I can dig it. You never know with the mobsters, do you?"

"Or with the cops."

IV

Averaging over ninety miles an hour, including a fifteen-minute stop at a McDonald's, they got to Las Vegas in four hours. They drove to Mc-Carran International Airport, parked in the garage and took their brief-cases and overnighters out of the trunk. While Edgar waited outside, Bosch went into the terminal and rented a car at the Hertz counter.

It was almost four-thirty by the time they got to the Metro building. As they walked through the detective bureau, Bosch saw Iverson sitting at his desk and talking to Baxter, who stood nearby. A thin smile played on Iverson's face but Bosch ignored it and went straight to Felton's office. The police captain was behind his desk doing paperwork. Bosch knocked on the open door and then entered.

"Bosch, where ya been?"

"Taking care of details."

"This your prosecutor?"

"No, this is my partner, Jerry Edgar. The prosecutor isn't coming out until the morning."

Edgar and Felton shook hands but Felton continued to look at Bosch.

"Well, you can call him and tell him not to bother."

Bosch looked at him a moment. He knew now why Iverson had smiled. Something was going on.

"Captain, you're always full of surprises," he said. "What is it this time?"

Felton leaned back in his chair. He had an unlit cigar, one end soggy with saliva, on the edge of the desk. He picked it up and clenched it between two fingers. He was playing it out, obviously trying to get a rise out of Bosch. But Bosch didn't bite and the captain finally spoke.

"Your boy, Goshen, is packing his bags."

"He's waiving extradition?"

"Yeah, he got smart."

Bosch took the chair in front of the desk and Edgar took one to the right. Felton continued.

"Fired that mouthpiece Mickey Torrino and got his own guy. Not that much of an improvement, but at least the new guy's got Lucky's best interest in mind."

"And how did he get smart?" Bosch asked. "You tell him about the ballistics?"

"Sure, I told him. Brought him over, told him the score. I also told him how we broke his alibi down to shit."

Bosch looked at him but didn't ask the question.

"Yeah, that's right, Bosch. We haven't been exactly sitting over here on our asses. We went to work on this guy and we're helping to pound him into the ground for you. He said he never left his office Friday night until it was time to go home at four. Well, we went over and checked that office out. There's a back door. He could've come in and gone out. Nobody saw him from the time Tony Aliso left until four, when he came out to close the club. That gave him plenty of time to go out there, take down Tony and hop the last flight back. And here's the kicker. Girl that works over there goes by the name of Modesty. She got into it with another dancer and went to the office to complain to Lucky. She said nobody answered when she knocked. So she tells Gussie she wants to see the boss and he tells her the boss ain't in. That was about midnight."

Felton nodded and winked.

"Yeah, and what did Gussie say about that?"

"He isn't saying shit. We don't expect him to. But if he wants to get on the stand and back up Lucky's alibi, you can tear him apart easy. He's got a record goin' back to the seventh grade."

"All right, never mind him. What about Goshen?"

"Like I said, we brought him over this morning and told him what we got and that he was running out of time right quick. He had to make a decision and he made it. He switched lawyers. That's about as clear a sign as you're going to get. He's ready to deal, you ask me. That means you'll get him and Joey Marks, a few of the other douche bags in town. We'll take the biggest bite out of the Outfit in ten years. Everybody's happy."

Bosch stood up. Edgar followed suit.

"This is the second time you've done this to me," Bosch said, his voice measured and controlled. "You're not going to get a third. Where is he?"

"Hey, cool down, Bosch. We're all working for the same thing."

"Is he here or not?"

"He's in interview room three. Last I checked, Weiss was in there with him, too. Alan Weiss, he's the new lawyer."

"Has Goshen given you any statement?"

"No, of course not. Weiss gave us the particulars. No negotiating until you get him to L.A. In other words, he'll waive and you take him home. Your people will have to work out the deal over there. We're out of it after today. Excepting when you come back to pick up Joey Marks. We'll help with that. I've been waiting for that day for a long time."

Bosch left the office without further word. He walked through the squad room without looking at Iverson and made his way to the rear hallway that led to the interview rooms. He lifted the flap that covered the door's small window and saw Goshen in blue jail overalls sitting at the small table, a much smaller man in a suit across from him. Bosch knocked on the glass, waited a beat and opened the door.

"Counselor? Could we speak for a moment outside?"

"Are you from L.A.? It's about time."

"Let's talk outside."

As the lawyer got up, Bosch looked past him at Goshen. The big man was handcuffed to the table. It was barely thirty hours since Bosch had seen him last but Luke Goshen was a different man. His shoulders seemed slumped, as if he was closing in on himself. His eyes had a hollow look, the kind of stare that comes from a night of looking at the future. He didn't look at Bosch. After Weiss stepped out, Bosch closed the door.

Weiss was about Bosch's age. He was trim and deeply tanned. Bosch wasn't sure but thought he wore a hairpiece. He wore glasses with thin gold frames. In the few seconds he had to size the lawyer up, Bosch decided that Goshen had probably done well for himself.

After introductions Weiss immediately got down to business.

"My client is willing to waive any challenge to extradition. But, Detectives, you need to act quickly. Mr. Goshen does not feel comfortable or safe in Las Vegas, even in Metro lockup. My hope was that we would have been able to go before a judge today but it's too late now. But at nine A.M. tomorrow, I'll be in court. It's already arranged with Mr. Lipson, the local prosecutor. You'll be able to take him to the airport by ten."

"Slow down a second, Counselor," Edgar said. "What's the hurry all of a sudden? Is it 'cause Luke in there heard about the ballistics we got or because maybe Joey Marks has heard, too, and figures he better cut his losses?"

"I guess maybe it's easier for Joey to put the hit out on him in Metro than all the way over in L.A., right?" Bosch added.

Weiss looked at them as if they were some form of life he had not previously encountered.

"Mr. Goshen doesn't know anything about a hit and I hope that statement is just part of the usual intimidation tactics you employ. What he does know is he is being set up to take the fall for a crime he did not commit. And he feels the best way to handle this is to cooperate fully in a new environment. Someplace away from Las Vegas. Los Angeles is his only choice."

"Can we talk to him now?"

Weiss shook his head.

"Mr. Goshen won't be saying a word until he's in Los Angeles. My brother will take the case from there. He has a practice there. Saul Weiss, you may have heard of him."

Bosch had but shook his head in the negative.

"I believe he has already contacted your Mr. Gregson. So, you see, Detective, you're just a courier here. Your job is to get Mr. Goshen on a plane tomorrow morning and get him safely to Los Angeles. It will most likely be out of your hands after that."

"Most likely not," Bosch said.

He stepped around the lawyer and opened the door to the interview room. Goshen looked up. Bosch stepped in and moved to the table. He leaned over it and put his hands flat on the table. Before he could speak, Weiss had moved into the room and was talking.

"Luke, don't say a word to this man. Don't say a word."

Bosch ignored Weiss and looked only at Goshen.

"All I want, Lucky, is a show of faith. You want me to take you to L.A., get you there safe, then give me something. Just answer one question. Where—"

"He has to take you anyway, Luke. Don't fall for this. I can't represent you if you don't listen to me."

"Where's Layla?" Bosch asked. "I'm not leaving Vegas until I talk to her. If you want to get out of here in the morning, I've got to talk to her tonight. She's not at her place. I talked to her roommate, Pandora, last night and she says Layla's been gone a couple of days. Where is she?"

Goshen looked from Bosch to Weiss.

"Don't say a word," Weiss said. "Detective, if you step out, I'd like to confer with my client. I think, actually, that might be something I won't have a problem with him answering."

"Hope not."

Bosch went back into the hallway with Edgar. He put a cigarette in his mouth but didn't light it.

"Why's Layla so important?" Edgar asked.

"I don't like loose ends. I want to know how she fits."

Bosch didn't tell him that he knew from the illegal tapes that Layla had called Aliso and asked, at Goshen's request, when he'd be coming out to Vegas. If they found her, he would have to draw it out of her during the interview without giving away that he already knew it.

"It's also a test," he did tell Edgar. "To see how far we can get Goshen to go with us."

The lawyer stepped out then and closed the door behind him.

"If you try that again, talking to him when I specifically said he would not respond, then we will have no relationship whatsoever."

Bosch felt like asking what relationship they already had but let it go.

"Is he going to tell us?"

"No. I am. He said that when this person Layla first came to work at the club, he gave her a ride home a few nights. On one of those nights she asked him to drop her at a different place because she was trying to avoid somebody she was dating at the time and she thought he might be waiting at her apartment. Anyway, it was a house in North Las Vegas. She told him it was where she grew up. He doesn't have the exact address but said the place was at the corner of Donna Street and Lillis. The northeast corner. Try there. That's all he had."

Bosch had his notebook out and wrote the street names down.

"Thank you, Counselor."

"While you have the notebook out, write down courtroom ten. That's where we will be tomorrow at nine. I trust you will make secure arrangements for my client's safe delivery?"

"That's what a courier is for, right?"

"I'm sorry, Detective. Things are said in the heat of the moment. No offense."

"None taken."

Bosch went out to the squad room and used the phone at an empty desk to call Southwest and change the reservations on the return flight from three in the afternoon to a ten-thirty morning flight. Bosch didn't look at Iverson but could tell the detective was watching him from a desk fifteen feet away.

When he was done Bosch stuck his head in Felton's office. The captain was on the phone. Bosch just mock-saluted him and was gone.

Back in the rental car, Edgar and Bosch decided to go over to the jail and make arrangements for the custody transfer before trying to find Layla.

The jail was next to the courthouse. A discharge sergeant named Hackett gave the detectives a rudimentary rundown on how and where Goshen would be delivered to them. Since it was after five and the shifts had changed, Bosch and Edgar would be dealing with a different sergeant in the morning. Still, it made Bosch feel more comfortable seeing the routine ahead of time. They would be able to put Goshen into their car in an enclosed and safe loading-dock area. He felt reasonably sure that there wouldn't be trouble. At least not there.

With directions from Hackett, they drove into a middle-class neighborhood in North Las Vegas and found the house where Goshen had once dropped Layla off. It was a small bungalow-style house with an aluminum awning over each window. There was a Mazda RX7 parked in the carport.

An older woman answered the door. She was mid-sixties and well preserved. Bosch thought he could see some of the photo of Layla in her face. Bosch held his badge up so she could see it.

"Ma'am, my name is Harry Bosch and this is Jerry Edgar. We're over from Los Angeles and we are looking for a young woman we need to talk to. She's a dancer and goes by the name Layla. Is she here?"

"She doesn't live here. I don't know what you're talking about."

"I think you do, ma'am, and I'd appreciate it if you'd help us out."

"I told you, she's not here."

"Well, we heard she's staying here with you. Is that right? Are you her mother? She's tried to contact me. There's no reason for her to be afraid or to not want to talk to us."

"I'll tell her that if I see her."

"Can we come in?"

Bosch put his hand on the door and firmly but slowly started to push it open before she could reply.

"You can't just . . ."

She didn't finish. She knew what she was going to say would be meaningless. In a perfect world the cops couldn't just push their way in. She knew it wasn't a perfect world.

Bosch looked around after he entered. The furnishings were old, having to last a few more years than they were intended to and she probably thought they would have to when she bought them. It was the standard couch and matching chair setup. There were patterned throws on each, probably to cover the wear. There was an old TV, the kind with a dial to change the channels. There were gossip magazines spread on a coffee table.

"You live here alone?" he asked.

"Yes, I do," she said indignantly, as if his question was an insult.

"When was the last time you saw Layla?"

"Her name's not Layla."

"That was my next question. What is her name?"

"Her name's Gretchen Alexander."

"And you are?"

"Dorothy Alexander."

"Where is she, Dorothy?"

"I don't know and I didn't ask."

"When'd she leave?"

"Yesterday morning."

Bosch nodded to Edgar and he took a step back, turned and headed down a hallway leading to the rear of the house.

"Where's he going?" the woman asked.

"He's just going to take a look around, that's all," Bosch said. "Sit down here and talk to me, Dorothy. Faster we get this over with, the faster we're out of here."

He pointed to the chair and remained standing until she finally sat. He then moved around the coffee table and sat on the couch. Its springs were shot. He sank so low in it that he had to lean forward and even then it felt like his knees were halfway up to his chest. He got out his notebook.

"I don't like him messing around in my things," Dorothy said, looking back over her shoulder toward the hallway.

"He'll be careful." Bosch took out his notebook. "You seemed to know we were coming. How'd you know that?"

"I know what she told me, is all. She said the police might come. She didn't say anything about them coming all the way from Los Angeles."

She said *Angeles* with a hard G.

"And you know why we're here?"

"Because of Tony. She said he went and got himself killed over there."

"Where did Gretchen go, Dorothy?"

"She did not tell me. You can ask me all the times you like but my answer's always going to be the same. I don't know."

"Is that her sports car in the carport?"

"Sure is. She bought it with her own money."

"Stripping?"

"I always said money was the same whether it was made one way or the next."

Edgar came in then and looked at Bosch. Harry nodded for him to report.

"Looks like she was here. There's a second bedroom. Ashtray on the nightstand's full. There's a space on the rod in the closet where it looks like somebody had hung up some clothes. They're gone now. She left this."

He held his hand out and cradled in his palm was a small oval picture frame with a photograph of Tony Aliso and Gretchen Alexander. They had their arms around each other and were smiling at the camera. Bosch nodded and looked back at Dorothy Alexander.

"If she left, why'd she leave her car here?"

"Don't know. A taxi came for her."

"Did she fly?"

"How could I know that if I don't know where she was going?"

Bosch pointed a finger at her like a gun.

"Good point. Did she say when she'd be back?"

"No."

"How old is Gretchen?"

"She'll be twenty-three."

"How'd she take the news about Tony?"

"Not well. She was in love and now her heart's broken. I'm worried about her."

"You think she might do something to hurt herself?"

"I don't know what she might do."

"Did she tell you she was in love, or did you just think that?"

"I just didn't think it up, she told me. She confided in me and it was the truth. She said they were going to get married."

"Did she know Tony Aliso was already married?"

"Yes, she knew. But he told her, he said that it was over and it was just a matter of time."

Bosch nodded. He wondered if it was the truth. Not the truth that Gretchen might have believed, but the truth that Tony Aliso believed. He looked down at the blank page of his notebook.

"I'm trying to think if there is anything else," he said. "Jerry?"

Edgar shook his head, then spoke.

"I guess I'd just like to know why a mother would let her daughter do that for a living. Taking her clothes off like that."

"Jerry, I—"

"She has a talent, mister. Men came from all over the country and when they see her they keep coming back. Because of her. And I'm not her mother. I might as well have been, her own went and left her with me a long time ago. But she has a talent and I'm not talking to you two anymore. Get out of my house."

She stood up, as if ready to physically enforce her edict if she needed to. Bosch decided to let her have her say and stood up, putting his notebook away.

"I'm sorry for the intrusion," he said as he dug a business card out of his wallet. "If you hear from her, would you give her this number? And tonight she can get me at the Mirage again."

"I'll tell her if I hear from her."

She took the card and followed them to the door. On the front step Bosch looked back at her and nodded.

"Thanks, Mrs. Alexander."

"For what?"

They were quiet for a while driving back to the Strip. Eventually, Bosch asked Edgar what he thought of the interview.

"She's a crusty old bitch. I had to ask that question. Just to see how she'd react. Other than that, I think this Layla or Gretchen is just a dead end. Just some stupid girl Tony was leading on. You know, it's usually the strippers that are working the angles. But this time I think it was Tony."

"Maybe."

Bosch lit a cigarette and dropped back into silence. He was no longer thinking of the interview. As far as he was concerned, the work for the day was over and he was now thinking about Eleanor Wish.

When he got to the Mirage, Bosch swung the car into the circle in front and pulled to a stop near the front doors.

"Harry, man, what are you doing?" Edgar said. "Bullets might pop for the Mirage, but she isn't going to dig into the company wallet for valet parking."

"I'm just dropping you off. I'm going to go switch the cars tonight. I don't want to go anywhere near that airport tomorrow."

"That's cool, but I'll go with you, man. Nothin' to do here but lose money on the machines."

Bosch reached over and opened the glove box and pushed the trunk-release button.

"No, Jed, I'm going on my own. I want to think about some things. Grab your stuff outta the trunk."

Edgar looked at him a long moment. Bosch had not called him Jed in a long time. Edgar was about to say something but apparently thought better of it. He opened the door.

"Okay, Harry. You want to grab dinner or something later?"

"Yeah, maybe. I'll call you in your room."

"You're the man."

After Edgar slammed the trunk, Bosch drove back out onto Las Vegas Boulevard and then north to Sands. It was dusk and the day's dying light was being replaced with the neon glow of the city. In ten minutes he pulled into a parking space in front of Eleanor Wish's apartment building. He took a deep breath and got out of the car. He had to know. Why had she not answered his calls? Why had she not responded to his message?

When he got to the door, he felt his guts seize as if gripped in a huge fist. The note he had carefully folded and squeezed into the doorjamb two nights before was still there. Bosch looked down at the worn door-mat and then squeezed his eyes shut. He felt a tremendous wave of the guilt he had worked so hard to bury come forth from inside. He had once made a phone call that got an innocent man killed. It had been a mistake, something he could not possibly have seen coming, but it happened just the same and he had worked hard to put it not behind him but, at least, in a place where he could live with it. But now Eleanor. Bosch knew what he would find behind the door. Asking Felton for her number and address had sent things into motion, a terrible motion that ended with her being hauled into Metro and her fragile dignity and belief that bad things were behind her being crushed.

Bosch kicked over the doormat on the off chance she had left a key. There was none. His lock picks were in the glove compartment of the car parked at the airport. He hesitated a moment, focused on a spot over the doorknob, then stepped back, raised his left leg and drove his heel into the door. It splintered along the jamb and flew open. Bosch slowly stepped into the apartment.

He noticed nothing amiss in the living room. He moved quickly into the hallway and then down into the bedroom. The bed was unmade and empty. Bosch stood there for a moment, taking it all in. He realized he hadn't taken a breath since he had kicked in the door. He slowly exhaled and began breathing normally. She was alive. Somewhere. At least he thought so. He sat down on the bed, took out a cigarette and lit it. His feeling of relief was quickly crowded by other doubts and nagging questions. Why hadn't she called? Hadn't there been something real about what they had shared?

"Hello?"

A man's voice came from the front of the apartment. Bosch assumed it was someone who had heard him pop the door. He stood up and headed out of the bedroom.

"Yeah," he said. "I'm back here. I'm with the police."

He stepped into the living room and saw a man impeccably dressed in a black suit with a white shirt and black tie. It wasn't what Bosch expected.

"Detective Bosch?"

Bosch tensed and didn't answer.

"There's someone outside who would like to talk to you."

"Who?"

"He'll tell you who he is and what his business is."

The man walked out the front door, leaving it up to Bosch whether to follow. He hesitated a moment and did.

There was a stretch limousine in the parking lot, its engine running. The man in the black suit walked around and got into the driver's seat. Bosch watched this for a moment and then walked toward the limo. He brought his arm up instinctively and brushed it against his coat until he felt the reassuring shape of his gun beneath it. As he did this, the rear door closest to him opened and a man with a rough, dark face beckoned to him. Bosch showed no hesitation. It was too late now.

Bosch ducked into the big car and took a seat facing the rear. There were two men sitting on the plushly padded backseat. One was the rough-faced man, who was casually dressed and slouching in his luxurious spot, and the other an older man in an expensive three-piece suit, the tie pulled tight to his neck. Sitting between the two men on a padded armrest was a small black box with a green light glowing on it. Bosch had seen such a box before. It detected electronic radio waves emitted by eavesdropping devices. As long as that green light glowed they could talk and be reasonably assured they wouldn't be overheard and recorded.

"Detective Bosch," the rough-faced man said.

"Joey Marks, I presume."

"My name is Joseph Marconi."

"What can I do for you, Mr. Marconi?"

"I thought we'd have a little conversation, that's all. You, me and my attorney here."

"Mr. Torrino?"

The other man nodded.

"Heard you lost a client today."

"That's what we want to talk to you about," Marconi said. "We've got a problem here. We—"

"How did you know where I was?"

"I've had some fellows watching it for me. We kind of figured you'd be back. Once you left that note, especially."

They had obviously followed him and he wondered when that had started. His mind then jumped to another conclusion and he suddenly knew what the meeting was all about.

"Where's Eleanor Wish?"

"Eleanor Wish?" Marconi looked at Torrino and then back at Bosch. "I don't know her. But I suppose she'll turn up."

"What do you want, Marconi?"

"I just wanted this chance to talk, that's all. Just a little calm conversation. We've got a problem here and maybe we can work it out. I want to work with you, Detective Bosch. Do you want to work with me?"

"Like I said, what do you want?"

"What I want is to straighten this out before it gets too far out of hand. You are going down the wrong road here, Detective. You are a good man. I had you checked out. You've got ethics and I appreciate that. Whatever you do in life, you need a code of ethics. You have that. But you are on the wrong road here. Tony Aliso, I had nothing to do with that."

Bosch smirked and shook his head.

"Look, Marconi, I don't want your alibi. I'm sure it's airtight but I could care less. You can still pull a trigger from three hundred fifty miles away. It's been done from farther away, know what I mean?"

"Detective Bosch, there is something wrong here. Whatever that rat bastard is telling you, it's a lie. I'm clean on Tony A., my people are clean on Tony A., and I'm simply giving you this opportunity to make it right."

"Yeah, and how do I do that? Just kick Lucky loose so you can pick him up outside the jail in your limo here, take him for a ride out into the desert? Think we'll ever see Lucky again?"

"You think you'll ever see that lady ex-FBI agent again?"

Bosch stared at him a moment, letting his anger build up until he felt a slight tremor tick in his neck. Then, in one quick move, he pulled his gun and leaned across the space between the seats. He grabbed the thick gold braided chain around Marconi's neck and jerked him forward. He pressed the barrel deep into Marconi's cheek.

"Excuse me?"

"Easy now, Detective Bosch," Torrino said then. "You don't want to do something rash."

He put a hand on Bosch's arm.

"Take your hand off me, you asshole."

Torrino removed his hand and raised it along with his other one in a surrendering gesture.

"I just want to calm things down a little here, that's all."

Bosch leaned back into his seat but kept his gun in his hand. The muzzle had left a ring of skin indentation and gun oil on Marconi's cheek. He wiped it away with his hand.

"Where is she, Marconi?"

"I just heard she wanted to get away for a few days, Bosch. No need to overreact like that. We're friends here. She'll be back. In fact, now that I know you're so, uh, attached to her, I'll personally guarantee she'll be back."

"In exchange for what?"

Hackett was still on duty at the Metro jail. Bosch told him he had to talk to Goshen for a couple of minutes in regard to a security issue. Hackett hemmed and hawed about it being against regulations to set up an after-hours visit but Bosch knew it was done on occasion for the locals, against the rules or not. Eventually Hackett gave way and took Bosch to a room lawyers used to interview clients and told him to wait. Ten min-

utes later, Hackett waltzed Goshen into the room and cuffed one wrist
to the chair he was placed in. Hackett then folded his arms and stood
behind the suspect.

"Sergeant, I need to talk to him alone."

"Can't do it. It's a security issue."

"We're not going to talk anyway," Goshen interjected.

"Sergeant," Bosch said. "What I tell this man, whether he chooses to
talk to me or not, could put you in danger if it becomes known you have
this knowledge. Know what I mean? Why add that potential danger to
your list? Five minutes. It's all I want."

Hackett thought a moment and without a word left them alone.

"Pretty smooth, Bosch, but I'm not talking to you. Weiss said you
might try a backdoor run. He said you'd want to try to get into the
candy jar before it's time. I'm not playing with you. Get me to L.A., sit
me in front of the people who can deal, and then we'll deal. Everybody
will get what they want then."

"Shut up and listen, you stupid fuck. I don't give a shit about any deal
anymore. The only deal I'm worried about now is whether to keep you
alive or not."

Bosch saw he had his attention now. He waited a few moments to
turn the squeeze up and then began.

"Goshen, let me explain something to you. In all of Las Vegas there is
exactly one person I care about. One. You take her out of the picture and
the whole place could dry up and blow away and I really wouldn't worry
about it. But there's that one person I care about. And out of all the people in this place, she's the one that your employer decides to grab and
hold against me."

Goshen's eyes narrowed in concern. Bosch was talking about his people. Goshen knew exactly what was coming.

"So the deal I'm talking about is this," Bosch said. "You for her. Joey
Marks said if you never get to L.A., then my friend comes back. And vice
versa. You understand what I'm telling you?"

Goshen looked down at the table and slowly nodded.

"Do you?"

Bosch pulled his gun and pointed it three inches from the big man's
face. Goshen went cross-eyed looking at the barrel's black hole.

"I could blow your shit away right here. Hackett would come in here and I'd tell him you made a move for my gun. He'd go along. He set the meeting up here. It's against the rules. He'd have to go along."

Bosch withdrew the gun.

"Or tomorrow. This is how it goes tomorrow. At the airport we're waiting for our flight. There's a commotion over at the machines. Somebody's won a big fucking jackpot and my partner and I make the mistake of looking over there. Meantime, somebody—maybe it's your pal Gussie—puts a six-inch stiletto in your neck. End of you, my friend comes home."

"What do you want, Bosch?"

Bosch leaned across to him.

"I want you to give me the reason not to do it. I don't give a shit about you, Goshen, dead or alive. But I'm not going to let any harm befall her. I've made mistakes in my life, man. I once got somebody killed that shouldn't have been killed. You understand that? It's not going to happen again. This is redemption, Goshen. And if I have to give a piece of shit like you up to get it, I'll do it. There's only one alternative. You know Joey Marks, where would he have her?"

"Oh, Jesus, I don't know."

Goshen rubbed a hand over his scalp.

"Think, Goshen. He's done this kind of thing before. It's routine for you people. Where would he hold somebody he doesn't want anyone to find?"

"There was . . . there's a couple of safe houses he uses. He'd, uh, . . . I think for this he'd use the Samoans."

"Who are they?"

"These two big fuckers he uses. Samoans. They're brothers. Their names are too hard to say. We call them Tom and Jerry. They've got one of the safe houses. Joey would use their place for this. The other place is mostly for counting cash, putting up people from Chicago."

"Where is the house with the Samoans?"

"It's in North Vegas, not too far from Dolly's, actually."

On a piece of notebook paper Bosch gave him, Goshen drew a crude map with directions to the house.

"You've been there, Goshen?"

"A few times."

Bosch turned the piece of paper over on the table.

"Draw the layout of the house."

Bosch pulled the dusty detective car he had picked up at the airport into the valet circle at the Mirage and jumped out. A valet approached but Bosch walked past him.

"Sir, your keys?"

"I'll only be a minute."

The valet was protesting that he couldn't just leave the car there when Bosch disappeared through the revolving door. As he crossed through the casino toward the lobby, Bosch scanned the players for Edgar, his eyes stopping on every tall black man, of whom there were few. He didn't see Edgar.

On a house phone in the lobby he asked for Edgar's room and then breathed an almost audible sigh of relief when his partner picked up the phone.

"Jerry, it's Bosch. I need your help."

"What's up?"

"Meet me out front at the valet."

"Now? I just got room service. When you didn't call I—"

"Right now, Jerry. And did you bring your vest from L.A.?"

"My vest? Yeah. What's—"

"Bring your vest with you."

Bosch hung up before Edgar could ask any questions.

As he turned to head back to the car, he came face to face with someone he knew. At first, because the man was well dressed, Bosch thought it was one of Joey Marks's men, but then he placed him. Hank Meyer, Mirage security.

"Detective Bosch, I didn't expect to see you here."

"Just got in tonight. Came to pick somebody up."

"You got your man then?"

"We think so."

"Congratulations."

"Listen, Hank, I gotta go. I've got a car blocking traffic in the front circle."

"Oh, that's your car. I just heard that on the security radio. Yes, please move it."

"I'll talk to you later."

Bosch made a move to pass him.

"Oh, Detective? Just wanted you to know we still haven't had that betting slip come in."

Bosch stopped.

"What?"

"You asked if we'd check to see if anyone cashed the bet your victim put down Friday night. On the Dodgers?"

"Oh, yeah, right."

"Well, we went through the computer tapes and located the sequence number. I then checked the number on the computer. No one has collected on it yet."

"Okay, thanks."

"I called your office today to let you know but you weren't there. I didn't know you were coming here. We'll keep an eye out for it."

"Thanks, Hank. I gotta go."

Bosch started walking away but Meyer kept talking.

"No problem. Thank *you*. We look forward to opportunities to cooperate with and hopefully help our law enforcement brethren."

Meyer smiled broadly. Bosch looked back at him and felt like he had a weight tied to his leg. He couldn't get away from him. Bosch just nodded and kept going, trying to remember the last time he had heard the phrase *law enforcement brethren*. He was almost across the lobby when he glanced back and saw that Meyer was still behind him.

"One more thing, Detective Bosch."

Bosch stopped but lost his patience.

"Hank, what? I've got to get out of here."

"It will just take a second. A favor. I assume your department will go to the press with this arrest. I'd appreciate it if you kept any mention of the Mirage out of it. Even our help, if you don't mind."

"No problem. I won't say a word. Talk to you later, Hank."

Bosch turned and walked away. It was unlikely the Mirage would have been mentioned in any press release anyway, but he understood the concern. Guilt by association. Meyer was mixing public relations with casino security. Or maybe they were the same thing.

Bosch got to the car just as Edgar came out, carrying his bulletproof vest in his hand. The valet looked at Bosch balefully. Bosch took out a five and handed it to him. It didn't do much to change his disposition. Then Bosch and Edgar jumped in the car and took off.

The safe house Goshen told Bosch about looked deserted when they drove by. Bosch pulled the car to a stop a half block away.

"I still don't know about this, Harry," Edgar said. "We should be calling in Metro."

"I told you. We can't. Marks has to have somebody inside Metro. Or else he wouldn't have known to snatch her in the first place. So we call Metro, he finds out and she's dead or moved somewhere else before Metro even makes a move. So we go in and we call Metro afterward."

"If there is an afterward. Just what the hell are we going to do? Go in blasting? This is cowboy shit, Harry."

"No, all you're going to do is get behind the wheel, turn the car around and be ready to drive. We might have to leave in a hurry."

Bosch had hoped to use Edgar as a backup but after he'd told him the situation on the way over, it was clear that Edgar wasn't going to be solid. Bosch went to plan B, where Edgar was simply a wheel man.

Bosch opened his door and looked back at Edgar before getting out.

"You're going to be here, right?"

"I'll be here. Just don't get killed. I don't want to have to explain it."

"Yeah, I'll do my best. Let me borrow your cuffs and pop the trunk."

Bosch put Edgar's cuffs into his coat pocket and went to the trunk. At the trunk, he took out his vest and put it on over his shirt and then put his coat back on to hide his holster. He pulled up the trunk liner and lifted up the spare tire. Below it was a Glock 17 pistol wrapped in an oily rag. Bosch popped the clip on it, checked the top bullet for corrosion and then put the weapon back together. He put it in his belt. If there was going to be any shooting on this mission, he wasn't going to use his service gun.

He came up alongside the driver's window, saluted Edgar and headed down the street.

The safe house was a small concrete-block-and-plaster affair that blended in with the neighborhood. After jumping a three-foot fence,

Bosch took the gun from his belt and held it at his side as he walked along the side of the house. He saw no light emitted from any of the front or side windows. But he could hear the muffled sound of television. She was here. He could feel it. He knew Goshen had told the truth.

When he got to the rear corner, he saw there was a pool in the backyard as well as a covered porch. There was a concrete slab with a satellite dish anchored to it. The modern Mafia crash pad, Bosch thought. You never knew how long you'd have to hole up, so it was good to have five hundred channels.

The backyard was empty but as Bosch turned the corner he saw a lighted window. He crept down the back of the house until he was close. The blinds were drawn on the window, but by getting close and looking between the cracks he could see them in there. Two huge men he immediately assumed were the Samoans. And Eleanor. The Samoans sat on a couch in front of a television. Eleanor sat on a kitchen chair next to the couch. One wrist and one ankle were handcuffed to the chair. Because the shade of a floor lamp was in the way, he could not see her face. But he recognized her clothes as those she had worn on the day they had dragged her into Metro. The three of them were sitting there watching a rerun of a Mary Tyler Moore show. Bosch felt the anger building in his throat.

Bosch crouched down and tried to think of a way to get her out of there. He leaned his back against the wall and looked across the yard and the shimmering pool. He got an idea.

After taking one more glimpse through the blinds and seeing that no one had moved, Bosch went back to the corner of the house to the slab where the satellite dish sat. He put his gun back in his belt, studied the equipment for a few moments and then simply used two hands to turn the dish out of alignment and point its focus toward the ground.

It took about five minutes. Bosch figured most of this must have been spent with one or the other of the Samoans fiddling with the TV and trying to get the picture back. Finally, an outdoor floodlight came on, the back door opened and one of them stepped out onto the porch. He wore a Hawaiian shirt as big as a tent and had long dark hair that flowed over his shoulders.

When the big man got to the dish, he clearly wasn't sure how to proceed. He looked at it for a long moment, then came around to the other side to see if this afforded him a better angle. He now had his back to Bosch.

Bosch stepped away from the corner of the house and came up behind the man. He placed the muzzle of the Glock against the small of the man's back, though even the small of his back wasn't small.

"Don't move, big man," he said in a low, calm voice. "Don't say a word, 'less you want to spend the rest of your life in a wheelchair with your piss sloshing around in a bag."

Bosch waited. The man did not move and said nothing.

"Which are you, Tom or Jerry?"

"I'm Jerry."

"Okay, Jerry, we're going to walk over to the porch. Let's go."

They moved to one of two steel support beams that held up the porch roof. Bosch kept the gun pressed against the man's shirt the whole time. He then reached into his pocket and pulled out Edgar's cuffs. He handed them around the girth of the man and held them up.

"Okay, take 'em. Cuff yourself around the beam."

He waited until he heard both cuffs click, then came around and checked them, clicking them tightly around the man's thick wrists.

"Okay, that's good, Jerry. Now, do you want me to kill your brother? I mean I could just walk in there and waste him and get the girl. That's the easy way. You want me to do it that way?"

"No."

"Then do exactly what I tell you. If you fuck up, he dies. Then you die 'cause I can't afford to leave a witness. Got it?"

"Yes."

"Okay, without saying his name, because I don't trust you, just call to him and ask if the picture's back on the TV. When he says no, tell him to come out here and help. Tell him she'll be fine, she's handcuffed. Do it right, Jerry, and everybody lives. Do it wrong and some people aren't going to make it."

"What do I call him?"

"How 'bout 'Hey, Bro?' That oughta work."

Jerry did as he was told and did it right. After some back-and-forth banter, the brother stepped out onto the porch, where he saw Jerry with his back to him. Just as he realized something wasn't right, Bosch came from the blind spot to his right rear and put the gun on him. Using his own cuffs this time, he locked the second brother, who he guessed was slightly larger than the first and had on a louder shirt, to the porch's other support beam.

"Okay, take five, boys. I'll be back in a minute. Oh, who has the key to the cuffs on the woman?"

They both said, "He does."

"That's not smart, guys. I don't want to hurt anybody. Now who has the cuff key?"

"I do."

The voice came from behind him, from the porch door. Bosch froze.

"Slowly, Bosch. Toss the gun into the pool and turn around real slow like."

Bosch did what he was told and turned around. It was Gussie. And Bosch could see the delight and hate in his eyes, even in the dark. He stepped onto the porch and Bosch could see the shape of a gun in his right hand. Bosch immediately became angry with himself for not casing the house further or even asking Jerry if there was anyone other than his brother and Eleanor in the house. Gussie raised the gun and pressed its barrel against Bosch's left cheek, just below the eye.

"See how it feels?"

"Been talking to the boss, huh?"

"That's right. And we're not stupid, man, you're stupid. We knew you might try something like this. Now we gotta call him and see what he wants to do. But first off, what you're gonna do is unhook Tom and Jerry. Right the fuck now."

"Sure, Gussie."

Bosch was contemplating reaching into his coat and going for his other gun but knew it was suicide as long as Gussie held his gun at point-blank range. He started slowly reaching into his pocket for his keys when he saw the movement to his left and heard the shout.

"Freeze it up, asshole!"

It was Edgar. Gussie didn't move an inch. After a few moments of this stand-off, Bosch reached into his coat, pulled his own gun and pushed the muzzle up into Gussie's neck. They stood there staring at each other for a long moment.

"What do you think?" Bosch finally said. "You want to try it? See if we both get one off?"

Gussie said nothing and Edgar moved in. He put the muzzle of his gun against Gussie's temple. A smile broke across Bosch's face and he reached up and took Gussie's gun from him and threw it into the pool.

"I didn't think so."

He looked over at Edgar and nodded his thanks.

"You got him? I'll go get her."

"I got him, Harry. And I'm hoping he does something stupid, the big fat fuck."

Bosch checked Gussie for another weapon and found none.

"Where's the cuff key?" he asked.

"Fuck you."

"Remember the other night, Gussie? You want a repeat performance? Tell me where the fucking key is."

Bosch figured his own cuff key would fit but he wanted to make sure he got one away from Gussie. The big man finally blew out his breath and told Bosch the key was on the kitchen counter.

Bosch went inside the house, his gun out, his eyes scanning for more surprises. There was nobody. He grabbed the cuff key off the kitchen counter and went into the back den where Eleanor was. When he stepped into the room and her eyes rose to his, he saw something that he knew he would always cherish. It wasn't something he believed he could ever put into words. The giving way of fear, the knowledge of safety. Maybe thanks. Maybe that was how people looked at heroes, he thought. He rushed to her and knelt in front of her chair so that he could unlock the cuffs.

"You okay, Eleanor?"

"Yes, yes. I'm fine. I knew, Harry. I knew you would come."

He had the cuffs off and he just looked up at her face. He nodded and pulled her into a quick hug.

"We gotta go."

They went out the back, where the scene did not look as if it had changed at all.

"Jerry, you got him? I'm going to find a phone and call Felton."

"I got—"

"No," Eleanor said. "Don't call them. I don't want that."

Bosch looked at her.

"Eleanor, what are you talking about? These guys, they abducted you. If we hadn't come here, there's a good chance they would've taken you out into the desert tomorrow and planted you."

"I don't want the cops. I don't want to go through all of that. I just want this to end."

Bosch looked at her a long moment.

"Jerry, you got him?" he asked.

"I got him."

Bosch went to Eleanor and grabbed her arm and led her back into the house. When they were in the alcove by the kitchen and far enough away that the men outside could not hear them, he stopped and looked at her.

"Eleanor, what's going on?"

"Nothing. I just don't want—"

"Did they hurt you?"

"No, I'm—"

"Did they rape you? Tell me the truth."

"No, Harry. It is nothing like that. I just want this to end here."

"Listen to me, we can take down Marks, his lawyer and those three assholes out on the porch. That's why I'm here. Marks told me he had you."

"Don't kid yourself, Harry. You can't touch Marks on this. What did he really tell you? And who's your witness going to be? Me? Look at me. I'm a convicted felon, Harry. Not only that, I used to be one of the good guys. Just think what a mob lawyer can do with that."

Bosch didn't say anything. He knew she was right.

"Well, I'm not going to put myself through that," she said. "I got a dose of reality when they jerked me out of my home and took me down to Metro. I'm not going to go to bat for them on this. Now can you get me out of here?"

"As long as you are sure. You can't change your mind once we're out of here."

"I'm as sure as I'll ever be."

Bosch nodded and led her out to the porch.

"It's your lucky day, boys," he said to the three thugs. Then to Edgar he said, "We're pulling out of here. We'll talk about it later."

Edgar just nodded. Bosch went one by one to the Samoans and put their own cuffs on their wrists and then took off the others. When he was done, he held the key up in front of the smaller of the two giants and then tossed it into the pool. He went over to the fence that ran behind the pool and took down a long pole with a net attached to the end of it. He fished his gun off the bottom and handed it to Eleanor to hold. He then returned to Gussie, who was dressed completely in black. Edgar was still standing to his right, holding the gun against his temple.

"Almost didn't recognize you without the tux, Gussie. Will you give Joey Marks a message?"

"Yeah. What?"

"Fuck you. Just tell him that."

"He's not going to like that."

"I don't really care. He's lucky I don't leave him three bodies here as a message."

Bosch looked over at Eleanor.

"Anything you want to say or do?"

She shook her head.

"Then we're outta here. Only thing is, Gussie, we're one set of cuffs short. That's too bad for you."

"There's rope in the—"

Bosch hit him on the bridge of the nose with the butt end of his gun, crushing whatever bone had not been broken in their earlier scuffle. Gussie dropped heavily to his knees, then pitched forward, his face making a thud on the porch tile.

"Harry! Jesus!"

It was Edgar. He looked shocked by the sudden violence.

Bosch just looked at him a moment and said, "Let's go."

When they got to Eleanor's apartment, Bosch backed the car up nearly to the door and popped the trunk.

"We don't have a lot of time," he said. "Jerry, you stay out here, watch for anybody coming. Eleanor, you can fill the trunk with whatever you can fit in there. That's about all you can take."

She nodded. She understood. Las Vegas was over for her. She could no longer stay, not with what had happened. Bosch wondered if she also understood that it was all because of him. Her life would still be as it had been if he had not wanted to reach out to her.

They all got out of the car and Bosch followed Eleanor into the apartment. She studied the broken door for a moment until he told her he had done it.

"Why?"

"Because when I didn't hear from you I thought . . . . I thought something else."

She nodded again. She understood that, too.

"There's not a lot," she said, looking around the place. "Most of this stuff I don't care about. I probably won't even need the whole trunk."

She went into the bedroom, took an old suitcase out of the closet and started filling it with clothes. When it was full, Bosch took it out and put it in the trunk. When he came back in, she was filling a box from the closet with her remaining clothes and other personal belongings. He saw her put a photo album in the box and then she went to the bathroom to clear the medicine cabinet.

In the kitchen all she took was a wine bottle opener and a coffee mug with a picture of the Mirage hotel on it.

"Bought this the night I won four hundred sixty-three dollars there," she said. "I was playing the big table and I was way in over my head but I won. I want to remember that."

She put that in the top of the full box and said, "That's it. That's all I have to show for my life."

Bosch studied her a moment and then took the box out to the car. He struggled a bit, getting it to fit in next to the suitcase. When he was done, he turned around to call to Eleanor that they must go and she was already standing there, holding the framed print of *The Nighthawks*, the Edward Hopper painting. She was holding it in front of her like a shield.

"Will this fit?"

"Sure. We'll make it fit."

At the Mirage, Bosch pulled into the valet circle again and saw the chief valet frown as he recognized the car. Bosch got out, showed the man his badge quickly so that he might not notice it wasn't a Metro badge, and gave him twenty dollars.

"Police business. I'll be twenty-thirty minutes tops. I need the car here because when we leave we're going to have to really book."

The man looked at the twenty in his hand as if it were human feces. Bosch reached into his pocket, pulled out another twenty and gave it to him.

"Okay?"

"Okay. Leave me the keys."

"No. No keys. Nobody touches the car."

Bosch had to take the picture out of the trunk to get to Eleanor's suitcase and a gun kit he kept there. He then repacked the trunk and lugged the suitcase inside, waving off an offer of help from a doorman. In the lobby, he put the case down and looked at Edgar.

"Jerry, thanks a lot," he said. "You were there, man. Eleanor's going to change and then I'm going to shoot her out to the airport. I probably won't be back until late. So let's just meet here at eight o'clock tomorrow and we'll go to court."

"Sure you don't need me for the airport run?"

"No, I think we're fine. Marks won't try anything now. And if we're lucky, Gussie won't be waking up for another hour or so anyway. I'm going to go check in."

He left Eleanor there with him and went to the desk. There was no wait. It was late. After giving the clerk his credit card, he looked back at Eleanor saying her good-bye to Edgar. He put out his hand and she shook it but then she pulled him into an embrace. Edgar disappeared into the crowd of the casino.

Eleanor waited until they were in his room before she spoke.

"Why am I going to the airport tonight? You said you doubted they would do anything."

"Because I want to make sure you're safe. And tomorrow I won't be able to worry about it. I've got court in the morning and then I'm driving Goshen to L.A. I have to know you're safe."

"Where am I going to go?"

"You could go to a hotel but I think my place would be better, safer. You remember where it is?"

"Yes. Up off Mulholland?"

"Yeah. Woodrow Wilson Drive. I'll give you the key. Take a cab from the airport and I'll be there by tomorrow night."

"Then what?"

"I don't know. We'll figure it out."

She sat down on the edge of the bed and Bosch came around and sat next to her. He put his arms around her shoulders.

"I don't know if I could live in L.A. again."

"We'll figure it out."

He leaned in and kissed her on the cheek.

"Don't kiss me. I need to take a shower."

He kissed her again and then pulled her back onto the bed. They made love differently this time. They were more tender, slower. They found each other's rhythm.

Afterward, Bosch took the first shower and then while Eleanor bathed he used oil and a rag from his gun kit to clean the Glock that had been thrown into the pool. He worked the action and trigger several times to make sure the weapon was working properly. Then he filled the clip with fresh ammunition. He went to the closet and took a plastic laundry bag off the shelf, put the gun inside it and shoved it beneath a stack of clothes in Eleanor's suitcase.

After her shower Eleanor dressed in a yellow cotton summer dress and twined her hair into a French braid. Bosch liked watching her do it with such skill. When she was ready, he closed the suitcase and they left the room. The head valet came up to Bosch as he was putting the suitcase into the trunk.

"Next time, thirty minutes is thirty minutes. Not an hour."

"Sorry 'bout that."

"Sorry doesn't cut it. I could've lost my job, man."

Bosch ignored him and got in the car. On the way to the airport he tried to compose his thoughts into articulate sentences that he could recite to her but it wasn't working. His emotions were too much of a jumble.

"Eleanor," he finally said. "Everything that's happened, it's my fault. And I want to try to make it up to you."

She reached over and put her hand on his thigh. He put his hand on top of hers. She didn't say anything.

At the airport, Bosch parked in front of the Southwest terminal and got her suitcase out of the trunk. He locked his own gun and badge in the trunk so he could go through the airport's metal detector without a problem.

There was one last flight to L.A., leaving in twenty minutes. Bosch bought her a ticket and checked her bag. The gun would cause no problem as long as the bag was checked. He then escorted her to the terminal, where there was already a line of people making their way down the jetway.

Bosch took the key to his house off his keychain, gave it to her and told her the exact address.

"It's not the same as you might remember it," he said. "The old place got wrecked in the earthquake. It's been rebuilt and it's not all the way done. But it will be all right. The sheets, uh, I probably should've washed them a few days ago but didn't have time. There's fresh ones in the hallway closet."

She smiled.

"Don't worry, I'll figure everything out."

"Uh, listen, like I said before, I don't think that you've got anything to worry about anymore but just in case, you've got the Glock in your suitcase. That's why I checked it."

"You cleaned it while I was in the shower, didn't you? I thought I smelled the oil when I came out."

He nodded.

"Thanks, but I don't think I'll need it anyway."

"Probably not."

She looked over at the line. The last people were boarding. She had to go.

"You're being very good to me, Harry. Thank you."

He frowned.

"Not good enough. Not enough to make up for everything."

She went up on her toes and kissed him on the cheek.

"Good-bye, Harry."

"Good-bye, Eleanor."

He watched her hand in her ticket and go through the door to the jetway. She didn't look back and there was a whisper in the back of his mind telling him he might never see her again. But he shut it off and walked back through the nearly deserted airport. Most of the slot machines stood mute and ignored. Bosch felt a deep sense of loneliness engulf him.

The only hitch in Thursday morning's court proceedings occurred before they started, when Weiss came out of lockup after conferring with

his client and quickly went into the hall to find Bosch and Edgar conferring with Lipson, the local prosecutor who would handle the extradition hearing. Gregson had not made the trip from the L.A. County DA's
office. Weiss and Lipson had given him their assurances that Luke
Goshen was going to waive any objection to being brought back to California.

"Detective Bosch?" Weiss said. "I was just in with my client and he
asked me to get him some information before the hearing. He said he
wanted an answer before he gave any waiver. I don't know what it's
about, but I hope you haven't been in contact with my client."

Bosch put a concerned yet puzzled look on his face.

"What's he want to know?"

"He just wanted to know how last night worked out, whatever that
means. I'd like to know what is going on here."

"Just tell him everything is fine."

"What is fine, Detective?"

"If your client wants to tell you, he can tell you. Just deliver the
message."

Weiss stalked away, heading back toward the lockup door.

Bosch looked at his watch. It was five till nine and he figured the
judge wouldn't come out to the bench at the crack of nine. None of
them ever did. He reached into his pocket for his cigarettes.

"I'm going outside to have a smoke," he told Edgar.

Bosch took the elevator down and went out to the front of the courthouse to have his cigarette. It was warm out and he thought the day
would probably be another scorcher. With Las Vegas in September it was
pretty much guaranteed. He was glad he'd be leaving soon. But he knew
the ride through the desert during the heat of the day would be rough.

He didn't notice Mickey Torrino until the lawyer was a few feet away
from him. He, too, was smoking a cigarette before going in to handle the
day's business of mob-related legal work. Bosch nodded his greeting as
did Torrino.

"I guess you heard by now. No deal."

Torrino looked around to see if they were being watched.

"I don't know what you're talking about, Detective."

"Yeah, I know. You guys never know anything."

"I do know one thing and that's that you are making a mistake on this one. In case you care about things like that."

"I don't think so. At least not in the big picture. We might not have the real shooter but we have the guy who set it up. And we're going to get the guy who ordered it. Who knows, maybe we'll get the whole crew. Who you going to work for then, Counselor? That is, if we don't get you, too."

Torrino smirked and shook his head as if he were dealing with a foolish child.

"You don't know what you're dealing with here. It's not going to play. You'll be lucky if you get to keep Goshen. At best you've got only him. That's all."

"You know, Lucky keeps making noises about being set up. He, of course, thinks it's us putting him in the frame and I know that's bullshit. But I keep thinking, 'What if there is a frame?' I mean, I have to admit that him keeping that gun is hard to figure, though I've seen even dumber moves in my time. But if there is a frame and we didn't do it, who did? Why would Joey Marks frame his own guy when that guy's just going to roll over and put the finger back on Joey? Doesn't make sense. At least, from Joey's point of view. But then I started thinking, What if you were Joey's right-hand man, say his lawyer, and you wanted to be the big shot, the one who makes the calls? See what I'm talking about here? This'd be a nice little way of getting rid of your nearest competitor and Joey at the same time. How would that play, Counselor?"

"If you ever repeat that bullshit story to anyone, you will be very, very sorry."

Bosch took a step toward him so that their faces were only a foot apart.

"If you ever threaten me again, *you* will be very, very sorry. If anything ever happens to Eleanor Wish again, I will hold you personally responsible, asshole, and sorry is not the right word for how you will be then."

Torrino stepped back, loser in the staring contest. Without another word he walked away from Bosch and toward the courthouse doors. As he opened the heavy glass door, he looked back at Bosch, then disappeared inside.

When Bosch got back to the third floor, he met Edgar as he was coming quickly out of the courtroom, followed by Weiss and Lipson. Bosch looked at the hallway clock. It was five after nine.

"Harry, whereya been, smokin' a whole pack?" Edgar asked.

"What happened?"

"It's over. He waived. We've got to bring the car around and get over to the release desk. We'll have him in fifteen minutes."

"Detectives?" Weiss said. "I want to know every detail of how my client will be moved and what security measures you're taking."

Bosch put his arm on Weiss's shoulders and leaned into him in a confidential manner. They had stopped at the bank of elevators.

"The very first security measure we are taking is that we aren't telling anyone how or when we're getting back to L.A. That includes you, Mr. Weiss. All you need to know is that he'll be in L.A. Municipal Court for arraignment tomorrow morning."

"Wait a minute. You can't—"

"Yes, we can, Mr. Weiss," Edgar said as an elevator opened. "Your client waived his opposition to extradition and in fifteen minutes he'll be in our custody. And we're not going to divulge any information about security, here or there or on the way there. Now, if you'll excuse us."

They left him there and loaded onto the elevator. As the doors closed, Weiss shouted something about them not being allowed to talk to his client until his Los Angeles counsel had met with him.

A half hour later the Strip was in the rearview mirror and they were driving into the open desert.

"Say good-bye, Lucky," Bosch said. "You won't be back."

When Goshen didn't say anything, Bosch checked him in the mirror. The big man was sitting sullenly in the back with his arms cuffed to a heavy chain that went around his waist. He returned Bosch's stare and for a brief moment Bosch thought he saw the same look he had let loose for a moment in his bedroom before he managed to drag it back inside like a naughty child.

"Just drive," he said after he had recovered his demeanor. "We're not having a conversation here."

Bosch looked back at the road ahead and smiled.

"Maybe not now, but we will. We'll be talking."

V

As Bosch and Edgar were leaving the Men's Central Jail in downtown Los Angeles, Bosch's pager sounded and he checked the number. He didn't recognize it but the 485 exchange told him the person paging him was in Parker Center. He took the phone out of his briefcase and returned the call. Lieutenant Billets answered.

"Detective, where are you?"

Her use of his rank instead of his name told him she probably wasn't alone. The fact that she was calling from Parker Center rather than the bureau in Hollywood told him that something had gone wrong.

"At Men's Central. What's up?"

"Do you have Luke Goshen with you?"

"No, we just dropped him off. Why, what is it?"

"Give me the booking number."

Bosch hesitated a moment but then held the phone under his chin while he reopened his briefcase and got the number from the booking receipt. He gave Billets the number and once again asked what was going on. She once again ignored the question.

"Detective," she said, "I want you to come over to Parker right away. The sixth-floor conference room."

The sixth floor was administration level. It was also where the Internal Affairs offices were. Bosch hesitated again before finally answering.

"Sure, Grace. You want Jerry, too?"

"Tell Detective Edgar to go back to Hollywood Division. I'll contact him there."

"We've only got the one car."

"Then tell him to take a cab and put it on his expense account. Hurry it up, Detective. We are waiting for you here."

"We? Who's waiting?"

She hung up then and Bosch just stared at the phone for a moment.

"What is it?" Edgar asked.

"I don't know."

Bosch stepped off the elevator into the deserted sixth-floor hallway and proceeded toward the conference room he knew was behind the last door before the entrance to the police chief's office at the end of the hall. The yellowed linoleum had been recently polished. As he walked toward his destiny with his head down, he saw his own dark reflection moving just in front of his steps.

The door to the conference room was open and as Bosch stepped in all eyes in the room were on him. He looked back at Lieutenant Billets and Captain LeValley from the Hollywood Division and the recognizable faces of Deputy Chief Irvin Irving and an IAD squint named Chastain. But the four remaining men gathered in chairs around the long conference table were strangers to Bosch. Nevertheless, he guessed from their conservative gray suits that they were feds.

"Detective Bosch, have a seat," Irving said.

Irving stood up, ramrod straight in a tight uniform. The dome of his shaven head shone under the ceiling fluorescents. He motioned to the empty seat at the head of the table. Bosch pulled the chair out and sat down slowly as his mind raced. He knew that this kind of showing of brass and feds was too big to have been caused by his affair with Eleanor Wish. There was something else going on and it involved only him. Otherwise, Billets would have told him to bring Edgar along.

"Who died?" Bosch asked.

Irving ignored the question. When Bosch's eyes traveled across the table to his left and up to Billets's face, the lieutenant glanced away.

"Detective, we need to ask you some questions pertaining to your investigation of the Aliso case," Irving said.

"What are the charges?" Bosch responded.

"There are no charges," Irving replied calmly. "We need to clear some things up."

"Who are these people?"

Irving introduced the four strangers. Bosch had been right, they were feds: John Samuels, an assistant U.S. Attorney assigned to the organized crime strike force, and three FBI agents from three different field offices. They were John O'Grady from L.A., Dan Ekeblad from Las Vegas and Wendell Werris from Chicago.

Nobody offered to shake Bosch's hand, nobody even nodded. They just stared at Bosch with looks that transmitted their contempt for him. Since they were feds, their dislike of the LAPD was standard issue. Bosch still couldn't figure out what was going on here.

"Okay," Irving said. "We're going to get some things cleared up first. I'm going to let Mr. Samuels take it from here."

Samuels wiped a hand down his thick black mustache and leaned forward. He was in the chair at the opposite end of the table from Bosch. He had a yellow legal tablet on the table in front of him but it was too far away for Bosch to be able to read what was on it. He held a pen in his left hand and used it to hold his place in his notes. Looking down at the notes, he began.

"Let's start with your search of Luke Goshen's home in Las Vegas," Samuels said. "Exactly who was it who found the firearm later identified as the weapon used in the killing of Anthony Aliso?"

Bosch narrowed his eyes. He tried looking at Billets again, but her eyes were focused on the table in front of her. As he scanned the other faces, he caught the smirk on Chastain's face. No surprise there. Bosch had hooked up with Chastain before. He was known as Sustained Chastain by many in the department. When departmental charges are brought against an officer, an Internal Affairs investigation and Board of Rights hearing result in one of two findings: the allegations are either sustained or ruled unfounded. Chastain had a high ratio of sustained to unfounded cases—thus the departmental moniker which he wore like a medal.

"If this is the subject of a departmental investigation, I think I'm entitled to representation," Bosch said. "I don't know what this is about but I don't have to tell you people anything."

"Detective," Irving said. He slid a sheet of paper across the table to Bosch. "That is a signed order from the chief of police telling you to cooperate with these gentlemen. If you choose not to, you will be suspended without pay forthwith. And you'll be assigned your union rep then."

Bosch looked down at the letter. It was a form letter and he had received them before. It was all part of the department's way of backing you into the corner, to the point that you had to talk to them or you didn't eat.

"I found the gun," Bosch said without looking up from the order. "It was in the master bathroom, wrapped in plastic and secreted between the toilet tank and the wall. Somebody said the mobsters in *The Godfather* did that. The movie. But I don't remember."

"Were you alone when you supposedly found the weapon there?"

"Supposedly? Are you saying it wasn't there?"

"Just answer the question, please."

Bosch shook his head in disgust. He didn't know what was going on but it was looking worse than he had imagined.

"I wasn't alone. The house was full of cops."

"Were they in the master bathroom with you?" O'Grady asked.

Bosch just looked at O'Grady. He was at least ten years younger than Bosch, with the clean-cut looks the bureau prized.

"I thought Mr. Samuels was going to handle the questioning," Irving said.

"I am," Samuels said. "Were any of these cops in that bathroom with you when you located this weapon?"

"I was by myself. As soon as I saw it, I called the uniform in the bedroom in to take a look before I even touched it. If this is about Goshen's lawyer making some beef to you people about me planting the gun, it's bullshit. The gun was there, and besides, we've got enough on him without the gun. We've got motive, prints . . . why would I plant a gun?"

"To make it a slam dunk," O'Grady said.

Bosch blew out his breath in disgust.

"It's typical of the bureau to drop everything and come after an L.A. cop just because some sleezeball gangster drops a dime. What, are they givin' annual bonuses now if you guys nail a cop? Double if it's an L.A. cop? Fuck you, O'Grady. Okay?"

"Yeah, fuck me. Just answer the questions."

"Then ask them."

Samuels nodded as if Bosch had scored a point and moved his pen a half inch down his pad.

"Do you know," he asked, "did any other police officer enter that bathroom before you entered to search it and subsequently found the gun?"

Bosch tried to remember, picturing the movements of the Metro cops in the room. He was sure no one had gone into the bathroom other than to take a quick look to make sure no one was in there hiding.

"I don't know for sure about that," he said. "But I doubt it. If somebody did go in, there wasn't enough time to plant the gun. The gun was already there."

Samuels nodded again, consulted his legal pad and then looked at Irving.

"Chief Irving, I think that's as far as we want to take it for the moment. We certainly appreciate your cooperation in this matter and I expect we'll be talking again soon."

Samuels made a move to stand up.

"Wait a minute," Bosch said. "That's it? You're just going to get up and leave? What the fuck is going on here? I deserve an explanation. Who made the complaint, Goshen's lawyer? Because I'm going to make a complaint right back at him."

"Your deputy chief can discuss this with you, if he chooses to."

"No, Samuels. You tell me. You're asking the questions, now you answer a few."

Samuels drummed his pen on his pad for a moment and looked at Irving. Irving opened his hands to show it was his choice. Samuels then leaned forward and looked balefully at Bosch.

"If you insist on an explanation, I'll give you one," he said. "I'm limited, of course, in what I can say."

"Jesus, would you just tell me what the hell is going on?"

Samuels cleared his throat before going on.

"About four years ago, in a joint operation involving the FBI offices in Chicago, Las Vegas and Los Angeles, the strike force instituted what we called Operation Telegraph. Personnel-wise it was a small operation but it had a large goal. Our goal was Joseph Marconi and the remaining tentacles of the mob's influence in Las Vegas. It took us more than eighteen months but we managed to get someone inside. An agent on the inside. And in the two years since that was accomplished, that agent was able to rise to a level of prominence in Joseph Marconi's organization, one in which he had the intended target's complete confidence. Conservatively, we were four to five months from closing the operation and going to a grand jury to seek indictments for more than a dozen high-ranking members of the Cosa Nostra in three cities, not to mention an assortment of burglars, casino cheats, bust-out artists, cops, judges, lawyers and even a few Hollywood fringe players such as Anthony N. Aliso. This is not to mention that, largely through the efforts of this undercover agent and the wiretaps authorized with probable cause gathered through him, we now have a greater understanding of the sophistication and reach of organized crime entities such as Marconi's."

Samuels was talking as if he were addressing a press conference. He let a moment pass as he caught his breath. But he never took his eyes off Bosch.

"That undercover agent's name is Roy Lindell. Remember it, because he's going to be famous. No other agent was underground for so long and with such important results. You notice that I said *was*. He's no longer under, Detective Bosch. And for that we can thank you. The name Roy used undercover was Luke Goshen. Lucky Luke Goshen. So I want to thank you for fucking up the end of a wonderful and important case. Oh, we'll still get Marconi and all the others with what Roy's good work got us, but now it's all been marred by a . . . by you."

Bosch felt anger backing up in his throat but tried to remain calm and he managed to speak in an even voice.

"Your suggestion then is—no, your accusation is—that I planted that gun. Well, you are wrong about that. Dead wrong. I should be angry and offended, but given the situation I understand how you made the mistake. But instead of pointing at me, maybe you folks ought to take a look at your man Goshen or whatever the hell his name is. Maybe you should question whether you left him under too long. Because that gun wasn't planted. You—"

"Don't you dare!" O'Grady blurted out. "Don't you dare say a word about him. You, you're nothing but a fucking rogue cop! We know about you, Bosch, all your baggage. This time you went too far. You planted evidence on the wrong man this time."

"I take it back," Bosch said, still calm. "I am offended. I am angry. So fuck you, O'Grady. You say I planted the gun, prove it. But first I guess you gotta prove that I was the one who put Tony Aliso in his trunk. Because how the hell else would I have the gun to plant?"

"Easy. You could've found it there in the bushes off the goddamned fire road. We already know you searched it by yourself. We—"

"Gentlemen," Irving interjected.

"—will put you down for this, Bosch."

"Gentlemen!"

O'Grady closed his mouth and everyone looked at Irving.

"This is getting out of hand. I'm ending this meeting. Suffice it to say, an internal investigation will be conducted and—"

"We are doing our own investigation," Samuels said. "Meantime, we have to figure out how to salvage our operation."

Bosch looked at him incredulously.

"Don't you understand?" he said. "There is no operation. Your star witness is a murderer. You left him in too long, Samuels. He turned, became one of them. He killed Tony Aliso for Joey Marks. His prints were on the body. The gun was found in his house. Not only that, he's got no alibi. Nothing. He told me he spent all night in the office, but I know he wasn't there. He left and he had time to get over here, do the job and get back."

Bosch shook his head sadly and finished in a low voice.

"I agree with you, Samuels. Your operation is tainted now. But not because of me. It was you who left the guy in the oven too long. He got cooked. You were his handler. You fucked up."

This time Samuels shook his head and smiled sadly. That was when Bosch realized the other shoe hadn't dropped. There was something else. Samuels angrily flipped up the top page of his pad and read a notation.

"The autopsy concludes time of death was between eleven P.M. Friday and two A.M. Saturday. Is that correct, Detective Bosch?"

"I don't know how you got the report, since I haven't seen it myself yet."

"Was the death between eleven and two?"

"Yes."

"Do you have those documents, Dan?" Samuels asked Ekeblad.

Ekeblad took several pages folded lengthwise from the inside of his jacket and handed them to Samuels. Samuels opened the packet and glanced at its contents and then tossed it across the table to Bosch. Bosch picked it up but didn't look at it. He kept his eyes on Samuels.

"What you have there are copies of a page from an investigative log as well as an interview report prepared Tuesday morning by Agent Ekeblad here. There are also two sworn affidavits from agents Ekeblad and Phil Colbert, who will be with us here shortly. What you'll find if you look at those is that on Friday night at midnight, Agent Ekeblad was sitting behind the wheel of his bureau car in the back parking lot at Caesar's, just off Industrial Road. His partner Colbert was there next to him and in the back seat, Agent Roy Lindell."

He waited a beat and Bosch looked down at the papers in his hands.

"It was Roy's monthly meeting. He was being debriefed. He told Ekeblad and Colbert that just that night he had put four hundred and eighty thousand dollars cash from Marconi's various enterprises into Anthony Aliso's briefcase and sent him back to L.A. to have it put in the wash. He also, by the way, mentioned that Tony had been in the club drinking and got a little out of line with one of the girls. In his role as enforcer for Joey Marks and manager of the club, he had to get tough with Tony. He cuffed him once and jerked him around by his collar. This, I think, you might agree, would account for the fingerprints recovered from the deceased's jacket and the antemortem facial bruising noted in the autopsy."

Bosch still refused to look up from the documents.

"Other than that, there was a lot to talk about, Detective Bosch. Roy stayed for ninety minutes. And there is no fucking way in the world he could have gotten to Los Angeles to kill Tony Aliso before two A.M., let alone three A.M. And just so you don't leave here thinking all three of these agents were involved in the murder, you should know that the meeting was monitored by four additional agents in a chase car also parked in the lot for security reasons."

Samuels waited a beat before delivering his closing argument.

"You don't have a case. The prints can be explained and the guy you said did it was sitting with two FBI agents three hundred and fifty miles away when the shooting went down. You've got nothing. No, actually, that's wrong. You do have one thing. A planted gun, that's what you've got."

As if on cue the door behind Bosch opened and he heard footsteps. Keeping his eyes on the documents in front of him, Bosch didn't turn around to see who it was until he felt a hand grip his shoulder and squeeze. He looked up into the face of Special Agent Roy Lindell. He was smiling, standing next to another agent who Bosch assumed was Ekeblad's partner, Colbert.

"Bosch," Lindell said, "I owe you a haircut."

Bosch was dumbfounded to see the man he had just locked up standing there but quickly assimilated what had happened. Irving and Billets had already been told about the meeting in the parking lot behind Caesar's, had read the affidavits and believed the alibi. They had authorized Lindell's release. That was why Billets had asked for the booking number when Bosch had returned her page.

Bosch looked away from Lindell to Irving and Billets.

"You believe this, don't you? You think I found the gun out there in the weeds and planted it just to make the case a slam."

There was a hesitation while each one left space for the other to answer. Finally, it was Irving.

"The only thing we know for sure is that it wasn't Agent Lindell. His story is solid. I'm reserving judgment on everything else."

Bosch looked at Lindell, who was still standing.

"Then why didn't you tell me you were federal when we were in that room together at Metro?"

"Why do you think? For all I knew, you had already put a gun in my bathroom. You think I'm just going to tell you I'm an agent and everything would be cool after that? Yeah, right."

"We had to play along, Bosch, to see what moves you'd make and to make sure Roy got out of the Metro jail in one piece," O'Grady said. "After that, we were two thousand feet above you and two thousand behind you all the way across the desert. We were waiting. Half of us were betting you made a deal with Joey Marks. You know, in for a pinch, in for a pound?"

They were taunting him now. Bosch shook his head. It seemed to be the only thing he could do.

"Don't you people see what is happening?" he said. "You're the ones who made a deal with Joey Marks. Only you don't know it. He is playing you like a symphony. Jesus! I can't believe I'm sitting here and this is actually happening."

"How is he playing us?" Billets asked, the first indication that she might not have gone all the way across to the other side on him.

Bosch answered, looking at Lindell.

"Don't you see? They found out about you. They knew you were an agent. So they set this all up."

Ekeblad snorted in derision.

"They don't set things up, Bosch," Samuels said. "If they thought Roy was an informant, they'd just take him out to the desert and put him under three feet of sand. End of threat."

"No, because we're not talking about an informant. I'm talking about them knowing specifically he was an agent and knowing that because of that they couldn't just take him out to the desert. Not an FBI agent. If they did that, they'd have more heat on them than the Branch Davidians ever felt. No, so what they did was make a plan. They know he's been around a couple years and knows more than enough to take them all down hard. But they can't just kill him. Not an agent. So they've got to neutralize him, taint him. Make him look like he crossed, like he's just as bad as they are. So when he testifies, they can take him apart with Tony Aliso's hit. Make a jury think that he'd carry out a hit to maintain his cover. They sell a jury that and they could all walk away."

Bosch thought he had planted the seeds of a pretty convincing story, even having pulled it together on the fly. The others in the room looked at him in silence for a few moments, but then Lindell spoke up.

"You give them too much credit, Bosch," he said. "Joey's not that smart. I know him. He's not that smart."

"What about Torrino? You going to tell me he couldn't come up with this? I just thought of it sitting here. Who knows how long he had to come up with something? Answer one question, Lindell. Did Joey Marks know that Tony Aliso had the IRS on his back, that an audit was coming?"

Lindell hesitated and looked to Samuels to see if he could answer. Bosch felt the sweat of desperation breaking on his neck and back. He knew he had to convince them or he wouldn't walk out of the room with his badge. Samuels nodded to Lindell.

"If he knew, he didn't tell me," Lindell said.

"Well maybe that's it," Bosch said. "Maybe he knew but he didn't tell you. Joey knew he had a problem with Aliso and somehow he knew he had a bigger problem with you. And he and Torrino put their heads together and came up with this whole thing so they could kill two birds with the one stone."

There was another pause, but Samuels shook his head.

"It doesn't work, Bosch. You're stretching. Besides we've got seven hundred hours of tapes. There's enough on them to put Joey away without Roy even testifying one word."

"First of all, they might not have known there were tapes," Billets said. "And secondly, even if they did, it's fruit of the poison tree. You wouldn't have the tapes without Agent Lindell. You want to introduce them in court, you have to introduce him. They destroy him, they destroy the tapes."

Billets had clearly shifted to Bosch's side of the equation and that gave him hope. It also made Samuels see that the meeting was over. He gathered up his pad and stood up.

"Well," he said, "I can see we aren't going any further with this. Lieutenant, you're listening to a desperate man. We don't have to. Chief Irving, I don't envy you. You have a problem and you have to do something about it. If on Monday I find out that Bosch is still carrying his badge, then I'm going to go to the sitting grand jury and get an indictment against him for evidence tampering and violating the civil rights of Roy Lindell. I will also ask our civil rights unit to look into every arrest this man has made in the last five years. A bad cop never plants evidence once, Chief. It's a habit."

Samuels made his way around the table toward the door. The others got up and were following. Bosch wanted to jump up and throttle him but he remained outwardly calm. His dark eyes followed Samuels as the federal attorney moved to the door. He never looked back at Bosch. But before stepping out, he took one last shot at Irving.

"The last thing I want to have to do is air your dirty laundry, Chief. But if you don't take care of this, you'll leave me no choice."

With that, the federals filed out and those remaining sat in silence for a long moment, listening to the sound of the steps tracking down the polished linoleum in the hallway. Bosch looked at Billets and nodded.

"Thanks, Lieutenant."

"For what?"

"Sticking up for me at the end there."

"I just don't believe you'd do it, is all."

"I wouldn't plant evidence on my worst enemy. If I did that I'd be lost."

Chastain shifted in his seat while a small smile played on his face, but not small enough to pass Bosch's notice.

"Chastain, you and I have hooked up a couple times before and you missed me both times," Bosch said. "You don't want to strike out, do you? You better sit this one out."

"Look, Bosch, the chief asked me to sit in on this and I did that. It's his call, but I think you and that story you just wove out of thin air are full of shit. I agree with the feds on this one. If it was my choice, I wouldn't let you out of this room with a badge."

"But it's not your choice, is it?" Irving said.

When Bosch got to his house, he carried a bag of groceries to the door and knocked but there was no answer. He kicked over the straw mat and found the key he had given Eleanor there. A feeling of sadness came over him as he bent to pick it up. She was not there.

Upon entering he was greeted by the strong smell of fresh paint, which he thought was odd because it had now been four days since he had painted. He went directly into the kitchen and put away the groceries. When he was finished, he took a bottle of beer from the refrigerator and leaned against the counter drinking it slowly, making it last. The smell of paint reminded him that now he would have plenty of time to finish all the work the house needed. He was strictly a nine-to-fiver at the moment.

He thought of Eleanor again and decided to look to see if there was a note from her or whether her suitcase might be in the bedroom. But he went no farther than the living room, where he stopped and looked at the wall he had left half-painted after getting the call to the crime scene on Sunday. The wall was now completely painted. Bosch stood there a long moment, appraising the work as though it were a masterpiece in a museum. Finally he stepped to the wall and lightly touched it. It was fresh but dry. Painted just a few hours before, he guessed. Though no one was there to see it, a broad smile broke across his face. He felt a jolt of happiness break through the gray aura surrounding him. He didn't need to look for her suitcase in the bedroom. He took the painted wall as a sign, as her note. She'd be back.

An hour later, he had unpacked his overnighter and the rest of her belongings from the car and was standing in the darkness on the rear deck. He held another bottle of beer and watched the ribbon of lights moving along the Hollywood Freeway at the bottom of the hill. He had no idea how long she had stood in the frame of the sliding door to the deck and watched him. When he turned around, she was just there.

"Eleanor."

"Harry . . . I thought you wouldn't be back until later."

"Neither did I. But I'm here."

He smiled. He wanted to go to her and touch her, but a cautious voice told him to move slowly.

"Thanks for finishing."

He gestured toward the living room with his bottle.

"No problem. I like to paint. It relaxes me."

"Yeah. Me, too."

They looked at each other a moment.

"I saw the print," she said. "It looks good there."

Bosch had taken her print of Hopper's *Nighthawks* out of the trunk and hung it on the freshly painted wall. He knew that how she reacted to seeing it there would tell him a lot about where they were and where they might be headed.

"Good," he said, nodding and trying not to smile.

"What happened to the one I sent you?"

That had been a long time ago.

"Earthquake," he said.

She nodded.

"Where'd you just come from?"

"Oh, I went and rented a car. You know, until I can figure out what I'm going to do. I left my car in Vegas."

"I guess we could go over and get it, drive it back. You know, get in and out, not hang around."

She nodded.

"Oh, I got a bottle of red wine, too. You want something? Or another beer?"

"I'll have what you're having."

"I'm going to have a glass of wine. You sure you want that?"

"I'm sure. I'll open it."

He followed her into the kitchen and opened the wine and took down two glasses from a cabinet and rinsed them. He hadn't had anyone who liked wine over in a long time. She poured and they touched glasses before drinking.

"So how's the case going?" she asked.

"I don't have a case anymore."

She creased her brow and frowned.

"What happened? I thought you were bringing your suspect back."

"I did. But it's no longer my case. Not since my suspect turned out to be a bureau agent with an alibi."

"Oh, Harry." She looked down. "Are you in trouble?"

Bosch put his glass on the counter and folded his arms.

"I'm on a desk for the time being. I've got the squints investigating me. They think—along with the bureau—that I planted evidence against the agent. The gun. I didn't. But I guess somebody did. When I figure out who, then I'll be okay."

"Harry, how did this—"

He shook his head, moved toward her and put his mouth on hers. He gently took the glass out of her hand and put it on the counter behind her.

After they made love, Bosch went into the kitchen to open a bottle of beer and make dinner. He peeled an onion and chopped it up along with a green pepper. He then cleared the cutting board into a frying pan and sautéed the mixture with butter, powdered garlic and other seasonings.

He added two chicken breasts and cooked them until the meat was easy to shred and pull away from the bone with a fork. He added a can of Italian tomato sauce, a can of crushed tomatoes and more seasonings. He finished by pouring a shot of red wine from Eleanor's bottle in. While it all simmered, he put a pot of water on to boil for rice.

It was the best dinner he knew how to cook in a kitchen. He would have preferred grilling something on the deck, but the grill had been hauled away when the original house was demolished after the earthquake. While he had replaced the house, he had not yet gotten around to getting a new grill. He decided as he mixed rice into the boiling water that if Eleanor chose to stay for a while, he would get the grill.

"Smells good."

He turned and she was standing in the doorway. She was dressed in blue jeans and a denim shirt. Her hair was damp from the shower. Bosch looked at her and felt the desire to make love to her again.

"I hope it tastes good," he said. "This is a new kitchen, but I don't really know how to use it yet. Never did much cooking."

She smiled.

"I can tell already it will be good."

"Tell you what, will you stir this every few minutes while I take a shower?"

"Sure. I'll set the table."

"Okay. I was thinking we'd eat out on the deck. It doesn't smell like paint out there."

"Sorry."

"No, I mean it will be nice out there. I'm not complaining about the paint. In fact, that was all a ruse, you know, to leave the wall half painted like that. I knew you wouldn't be able to resist."

She smiled.

"A regular Tom Sawyer, detective third grade."

"Maybe not for long."

His comment ruined the moment and she stopped smiling. He silently chastised himself on the way back to the bedroom.

After his shower, Bosch put the last part of his recipe into the frying pan. He took a handful of frozen peas and mixed them into the simmering chicken-and-tomato stew. As he brought the food and wine out to the picnic table on the deck, he told Eleanor, who was standing at the railing, to have a seat.

"Sorry," he said as they settled in. "I forgot about a salad."

"This is all I need."

They started the meal in silence. He waited.

"I like it a lot," she finally said. "What do you call this?"

"I don't know. My mother just called it Chicken Special. I think that's what it was called in a restaurant where she first had it."

"A family recipe."

"The only one."

They ate quietly for a few minutes during which Bosch surreptitiously tried to watch her to see if she really enjoyed the food. He was pretty sure she did.

"Harry," Eleanor said after a while, "who are the agents involved in this?"

"They're from all over; Chicago, Vegas, L.A."

"Who from L.A.?"

"Guy named John O'Grady? You know him?"

It had been more than five years since she had worked in the bureau's L.A. field office. FBI agents moved around a lot. He doubted she would know O'Grady and she said she didn't.

"What about John Samuels? He's the AUSA on it. He's from the OC strike force."

"Samuels I know. Or knew. He was an agent for a while. Not a particularly good one. Had the law degree and when he figured out he wasn't much of an investigator, he decided he wanted to prosecute."

She started laughing and shook her head.

"What?"

"Nothing. Just something they used to say about him. It's kind of gross."

"What?"

"Does he still have his mustache?"

"Yeah."

"Well, they used to say that he could sure put a case together for prosecution, but as far as investigating it out on the street went, he couldn't find shit if it was in his own mustache."

She laughed again—a little too hard, Bosch thought. He smiled back.

"Maybe that's why he became a prosecutor," she added.

Something occurred to Bosch then and he quickly withdrew into his thoughts. Eventually he heard Eleanor's voice.

"What?"

"You disappeared. I asked what you were thinking. I didn't think it was that bad a joke."

"No, I was just thinking about what a bottomless hole I'm in. About how it doesn't really matter whether Samuels actually believes I'm dirty on this. He needs me to be dirty."

"How so?"

"They've got cases to make with their undercover guy against Joey Marks and his crew. And they've got to be ready and able to explain how a murder weapon got to be in their guy's house. Because if they can't explain it, then Joey's lawyers are going to shove it down their throats, make it look like their guy is tainted, is a killer worse than the people he was after. That gun has reasonable doubt written all over it. So the best way to explain away the gun is to blame it on the LAPD. On me. A bad cop from a bad department who found the gun in the weeds and planted it on the guy he thought did it. The jury will go along. They'll make me out to be this year's Mark Fuhrman."

He saw the humor was long gone from her face now. There was obvious concern in her eyes but he thought there was also sadness. Maybe she understood, too, how well he was boxed in.

"The alternative is to prove that Joey Marks or one of his people planted the gun because they somehow knew Luke Goshen was an agent and needed to discredit him. Though that's the likely truth, it's a harder road to follow. It's easier for Samuels just to throw the mud on me."

He looked down at his half-finished dinner and put his knife and fork on the plate. He couldn't eat any more. He took a long drink of wine and then kept the glass in his hand, ready.

"I think I'm in big trouble, Eleanor."

The gravity of his situation was finally beginning to weigh on him. He'd been operating on his faith that the truth would win out and now clearly saw how little truth would have to do with the outcome.

He looked up at her. Their eyes connected and he saw that she was about to cry. He tried to smile.

"Hey, I'll think of something," he said. "I might be riding a desk for the time being, but I'm not taking both oars out of the water. I'm going to figure this out."

She nodded but her face still looked distraught.

"Harry, remember when you found me in the casino that first night and we went to the bar at Caesar's and you tried to talk to me? Remember what you said about doing things differently if you had the chance to go back?"

"Yes, I remember."

She wiped her eyes with her palms, before any tears could show.

"I have to tell you something."

"You can tell me anything, Eleanor."

"What I told you about me paying Quillen and the street tax and all of that . . . there's more to it."

She looked at him with intensity now, trying to read his reaction before going further. But Bosch sat stone still and waited.

"When I first went to Vegas after getting out of Frontera, I didn't have a place or a car and I didn't know anyone. I just thought I'd give it a shot. You know, playing cards. And there was a girl I knew from Frontera. Her name was Patsy Quillen. She told me to look up her uncle—that was Terry Quillen—and that he'd probably stake me after he checked me out and saw me play. Patsy wrote him and gave me an introduction."

Bosch sat silently, listening. He now had an idea where this was going but couldn't figure out why she was telling him.

"So he staked me. I got the apartment and some money to play with. He never said anything about Joey Marks, though I should have known the money came from somewhere. It always does. Anyway, later, when he finally told me who had really staked me, he said I shouldn't worry because the organization he worked for didn't want me to pay the nut back. What they wanted was just the interest. Two hundred a week. The tax. I didn't think I had a choice. I'd already taken the money. So I started paying. In the beginning it was tough. I didn't have it a couple times and it was double the next week plus that week's regular tax. You get behind and there's no way out."

She looked down at her hands and clasped them on the table.

"What did they make you do?" Bosch asked quietly, also averting his eyes.

"It's not what you're thinking," she said. "I was lucky . . . they knew about me. I mean, that I had been an agent. They figured they could use my skills, as dormant as they were. So they had me just watch people. Mostly in casinos. But there were a few times I followed them outside. Most of the time I didn't even know exactly who they were or why they wanted the information, but I just watched, sometimes played at the same tables, and reported to Terry what the guy was winning or losing, who he was talking to, any nuances of his game . . . you know, things like that."

She was just rambling now, putting off the meat of what she had to tell him, but Bosch didn't say anything. He let her go on.

"A couple days I watched Tony Aliso for them. They wanted to know how much he was dropping at the tables and where he was going, the usual stuff. But as it turned out, he wasn't losing. He actually was quite good at cards."

"Where did you watch him go?"

"Oh, he'd go out to dinner, to the strip club. He'd run errands, things like that."

"You ever see him with a girl?"

"One time. I followed him on foot from the Mirage into Caesar's and then into the shopping arcade. He went to Spago for a late lunch. He was alone and then the girl showed up. She was young. I thought at first it was like an escort thing, but then I could tell, he knew her. After lunch they went back to his hotel room for a while and when they came out, they took his rental and he took her to get a manicure and to buy ciga-rettes and to a bank while she opened an account. Just errands. Then they went to the strip club in North Vegas. When he left, he was alone. I fig-ured then she was a dancer."

Bosch nodded.

"Were you watching Tony last Friday night?" Bosch asked.

"No. That was just coincidence that we ended up at the same table. It was because he was waiting to go to the high-stakes table. I actually hadn't done anything for them in a month or so, other than pay the weekly tax, until . . . Terry . . ."

Her voice trailed off. They were finally at the point of no return.

"Until Terry what, Eleanor?"

She looked toward the fading horizon. The lights across the Valley were coming on and the sky was pink neon mixed with gray paint. Bosch kept his eyes on her. She spoke while still watching the end of the day.

"Quillen came to my apartment after you took me home from Metro. He took me to the house where you found me. They wouldn't tell me why and they told me not to leave. They said nobody would get hurt if I just did what I was told. I sat around that place for two days. They only put the handcuffs on me that last night. It was like they knew you'd be coming then."

She let a beat of silence follow. It was there if Bosch wanted to use it but he didn't say a word.

"I guess what I'm trying to tell you is that the whole thing was something less than an abduction."

She looked back down at her hands now.

"And that's obviously why you didn't want us to call out Metro," Bosch said quietly.

She nodded.

"I don't know why I didn't tell you everything before. I'm really sorry, Harry. I . . ."

Now Bosch felt his own words sticking in his throat. Her story was understandable and believable. He even felt for her and understood that she was in her own bottomless pit. He saw how she had believed she had no choices. What he couldn't see, and what hurt him, was why she couldn't tell him everything from the start.

"Why couldn't you tell me, Eleanor?" he managed to get out. "I mean right away. Why didn't you tell me that night?"

"I don't know," she said. "I wanted . . . I guess I hoped it would just go away and you would never have to know."

"Then why are you telling me now?"

She looked right at him.

"Because I hated not telling you everything . . . and because while I was there at that house I heard something that you need to know now."

Bosch closed his eyes.

"I'm sorry, Harry. Very sorry."

He nodded. He was, too. He washed his hands over his face. He didn't want to hear this but knew he had to. His mind raced, jumping between feelings of betrayal and confusion and sympathy. One moment his thoughts were of Eleanor and the next they were on the case. They knew. Someone had told Joey Marks about Eleanor and him. He thought of Felton and Iverson, then Baxter and every cop he had seen at Metro. Someone had fed Marks the information and they used Eleanor as bait for him. But why? Why the whole charade? He opened his eyes and looked at Eleanor with a blank stare.

"What was it that you heard and that I need to know?"

"It was the first night. I was kept in that back room, where the TV was, where you came and got me. I was kept in there and the Samoans were there, in and out. But from time to time there were people in other parts of the house. I heard them talking."

"Gussie and Quillen?"

"No, Quillen left. I know his voice and it wasn't him. And I don't think it was Gussie. I think it was Joey Marks and someone else, probably the lawyer, Torrino. Whoever it was, I heard the one man call the other Joe at one point. That's how come I think it was Marks."

"Okay. Go on, what did they say?"

"I couldn't hear all of it. But one man was telling the other, the one he called Joe, what he had learned about the police investigation. About the Metro side of things, I think. And I heard the one called Joe get very angry when he was told the gun had been found at Luke Goshen's house. And I remember his words. Very clearly. He was yelling. He said, 'How the hell did they find the gun there when we didn't do the goddamned hit?' And then he said some more things about the cops planting the gun and he said, 'You tell our guy that if this is some kind of shakedown, then he can fuck off, he can forget it.' I didn't hear much after that. They lowered their voices and the first guy was just trying to calm the other guy down."

Bosch stared at her for a few moments, trying to analyze what she had overheard.

"Do you think it was a show?" he asked. "You know, put on for your benefit because they figured you'd turn around and tell me what you heard?"

"I did at first, and that's another reason I didn't tell you this right away," she said. "But now I'm not so sure. When they first took me, when Quillen was driving me out there and I was asking a lot of questions, he wouldn't answer them. But he did say one thing. All he would tell me was that they needed me for a day or two to run a test on some-body. He would explain no further. A test, that's all he said."

"A test?"

Bosch looked confused.

"Listen to me, Harry. I've done nothing but think about this since you got me out of there."

She held up a finger.

"Let's start with what I overheard. Let's say it was Joey Marks and his lawyer, and let's say it wasn't a show but what they said was true. They didn't put the hit on Tony Aliso, okay?"

"Okay."

"Look at it from their perspective. They had nothing to do with this, but one of their in-close guys gets picked up for it. And from what they hear from their source in Metro, it's looking like a slam-bang case. I mean, the cops have fingerprints and the murder weapon found right there in Goshen's bathroom. Joey Marks has to be thinking either it's all been planted by the cops or maybe Goshen went and did this on his own for some unknown reason. Either way, what do you think his immediate concern would be?"

"Damage control."

"Right. He has to figure out what is going on with Goshen and what's the damage. But he can't because Goshen has gone and gotten himself his own attorney. Torrino has no access to him. So what Joey does instead is he and Torrino set up a test to see if the reason Goshen's gotten his own attorney is because he's going to talk."

"Make a deal."

"Right. Now, let's say that from their source in Metro they know that the lead cop on the case has a relationship with someone they know of and have their hooks in. Me."

"So they just take you to the safe house and wait. Because they know that if I find out where the safe house is and show up to get you, or if I call up Metro and say I know where you are, then they know Goshen is the only one who could have told me. It means he's talking. That was the test Quillen was talking about. If I don't show, they're cool. It means Goshen is standing up. If I *do* show up, then they know they've got to get to Goshen in Metro right quick and put a hit on him."

"Right, before he can talk. That's how I figured it, too."

"So that would mean that Aliso wasn't really a hit—at least by Marks and his people—and that they had no idea Goshen was an agent."

She nodded. Bosch felt the surge of energy that comes with making a huge step through the murky darkness of an investigation.

"There was no trunk music," he said.

"What?"

"The whole Las Vegas angle, Joey Marks, all of that, it was all a diversion. We went completely down the wrong path. It had to be engineered by someone very close to Tony. Close enough to know what he was doing, to know about the money washing, and to know how to make his killing look mob connected. To pin it on Goshen."

She nodded.

"And that's why I had to tell you everything. Even if it meant we . . ."

Bosch looked at her. She didn't finish the line and neither did he.

Bosch took a cigarette out of his pocket and put it in his mouth but didn't light it. He leaned across the table and picked up her plate and his own. He spoke to her as he slid off the bench.

"I don't have any dessert, either."

"That's okay."

He took the plates into the kitchen and rinsed them and put them into the dishwasher. He had never used the new appliance before and spent some time leaning over it and trying to figure out how to operate it. Once he got it going, he started cleaning the frying pan and the pot in the sink. The simple work began to relax him. Eleanor came into the kitchen with her wineglass and watched him for a few moments before speaking.

"I'm sorry, Harry."

"It's okay. You were in a bad situation and you did what you had to do, Eleanor. Nobody can be blamed for that. I probably would have done everything you did."

It was a few moments before she spoke again.

"Do you want me to go?"

Bosch turned off the water and looked into the sink. He could make out his dark image reflected in the new stainless steel.

"No," he said. "I don't think so."

· · ·

Bosch arrived at the station at seven Friday morning with a box of glazed doughnuts from the Fairfax Farmers Market. He was the first one in. He opened the box and put it on the counter near the coffee machine. He took one of the doughnuts and put it on a napkin and left it at his spot on the homicide table while he went up to the watch office to get coffee from the urn. It was much better than what came out of the detective bureau's machine.

Once he had his coffee, he took his doughnut and moved to the desk that was behind the bureau's front counter. His assignment to desk duty meant that he would handle most of the walk-ins as well as the sorting and distribution of overnight reports. The phones he wouldn't have to worry about. They were answered by an old man from the neighborhood who donated his time to the department.

Bosch was alone in the squad room for at least fifteen minutes before the other detectives started to trickle in. Six different times he was asked by a new arrival why he was at the front desk, and each time he told the detective who asked that it was too complicated to get into but that the word would be out soon enough. Nothing remained a secret for long in a police station.

At eight-thirty the lieutenant from the A.M. watch brought the morning reports in before going off shift and smiled when he saw Bosch. His name was Klein and he and Bosch had known each other in a surface way for years.

"Who'd you beat up this time, Bosch?" he kidded.

It was well known that the detective who sat at the desk where Bosch now sat was either there by fate of the bureau rotation or on a desk duty assignment while the subject of an internal investigation. More often than not it was the latter. But Klein's sarcasm revealed that he had not yet heard that Bosch actually was under investigation. Bosch played off the question with a smile but didn't answer. He took the two-inch-thick stack of reports from Klein and gave him a mock salute back.

The stack Klein had given him constituted nearly all crime reports filed by Hollywood Division patrol officers in the last twenty-four hours. There would be a second, smaller delivery of stragglers later in the morning, but the stack in his hands constituted the bulk of the day's work in the bureau.

Keeping his head down and ignoring the buzz of conversations around him, it took Bosch a half hour to sort all the reports into piles according to crimes. Next he had to scan them all, using his experienced eye to possibly make connections between robberies and burglaries or assaults and so on, and then deliver the individual piles to the detective tables assigned to that particular classification of crime.

When he looked up from his work, he saw that Lieutenant Billets was in her office on the phone. He hadn't noticed that she had come in. Part of his desk job would be to give her a morning briefing on the reports, informing her of any significant or unusual crimes or anything else she should be aware of as the detective bureau commander.

He went back to work and weeded through the auto-theft reports first because they made up the largest pile he had culled from the stack of reports. There had been thirty-three cars reported stolen in Hollywood in the last twenty-four hours. Bosch knew that this was probably a below-average tally. After reading the summaries in the reports and checking for other similarities, he found nothing of significance and took the pile to the detective in charge of the auto-theft table. As he was heading back to the front of the squad room, he noticed that Edgar and Rider were standing at the homicide table putting things into a cardboard box. As he approached, he realized they were packing up the murder book and the ancillary files and evidence bags relating to the Aliso case. It was all being sent to the feds.

"Morning, guys," Bosch said, unsure of how to start.

"Harry," Edgar said.

"How are you doing, Harry?" Rider said, genuine concern in her voice.

"I'm hangin' in. . . . Uh, listen, I just . . . I just want to say that I'm sorry you guys have been pulled into this, but I wanted you to know there is no way I—"

"Forget it, Harry," Edgar said. "You don't have to say one damn thing to us. We both know the whole thing is bullshit. In all my years on the job you are the most righteous cop I know, man. All the rest is bullshit."

Bosch nodded, touched by Edgar's words. He didn't expect such sentiments from Rider because it had been their first case together. But she spoke anyway.

"I haven't worked with you long, Harry, but from what I do know I agree with what Jerry says. You watch, this will blow over and we'll be back at it again."

"Thanks."

Bosch was about to head back to his new desk when he looked down into the box they were packing. He reached in and pulled out the two-inch-thick murder book that Edgar had been charged with preparing and keeping up to date on the Aliso case.

"Are the feds coming here or you just sending it out?"

"S'posed to have somebody come pick it up at ten," Edgar said.

Bosch looked up at the clock on the wall. It was only nine.

"Mind if I copy this? Just so we have something in case the whole thing drops into that black hole they keep over there at the bureau."

"Be my guest," Edgar said.

"Did Salazar ever send over a protocol?" Bosch asked.

"The autopsy?" Rider asked. "No, not yet. Unless it's in dispatch."

Bosch didn't tell them that if it was in transit, then the feds had somehow intercepted it. He took the murder book to the copy machine, unhooked the three rings and removed the stack of reports. He set the machine to copy both sides of the original documents and put the stack into the automatic feed tray. Before starting he checked to make sure the paper tray was filled with three-hole paper. It was. He pressed the start button and stood back to watch. There was a copying franchise chain in town that had donated the machine and regularly serviced it. It was the one thing in the bureau that was modern and could be counted on to work most of the time. Bosch finished the job in ten minutes. He put the original binder back together and returned it to the box on Edgar's desk. He then took a fresh binder from the supply closet, put his copies of the reports on the rings and dropped it into a file cabinet drawer that had his business card taped to it. He then told his two partners where it was if they needed it.

"Harry," Rider said in a low voice, "you're thinking of doing a little freelancing on it, aren't you?"

He looked at her a moment, unsure of how to answer. He thought about her relationship with Billets. He had to be careful.

"If you are," she said, perhaps sensing his indecision, "I'd like to be in on it. You know the bureau isn't going to work it with any due diligence. They're going to let it drop."

"Count me in, too," Edgar added.

Bosch hesitated again, looked from one to the other and then nodded.

"How 'bout we meet at Musso's at twelve-thirty?" he said. "I'm buying."

"We'll be there," Edgar said.

When he got back to the front of the bureau, he saw through the glass window of her office that Billets was off the phone and looking at some paperwork. Her door was open and Bosch stepped in, knocking on the doorjamb as he entered.

"Good morning, Harry." There was a wistfulness to her voice and demeanor, as if maybe she was embarrassed that he was her front-desk man. "Anything happening I should know about right away?"

"I don't think so. It looks pretty tame. Uh, there's a hot prowler working the strip hotels again, though. At least it looks like one guy. Did one at the Chateau and another at the Hyatt last night. People never woke up. Looks like the same MO on both."

"Were the vics anybody we should know and care about?"

"I don't think so but I don't read *People* magazine. I might not recognize a celebrity if they came up and bit me."

She smiled.

"How much were the losses?"

"I don't know. I'm not done with that pile yet. That's not why I came in. I just wanted to say thanks again for sticking up for me like you did yesterday."

"That was hardly sticking up for you."

"Yes it was. In those kinds of circumstances what you said and did was sticking your neck way out. I appreciate it."

"Well, like I said, I did it because I don't believe it. And the sooner IAD and the bureau get on with it, the sooner they won't believe it. When's your appointment, by the way?"

"Two."

"Who is your defense rep going to be?"

"Guy I know from RHD. Name's Dennis Zane. He's a good guy and he'll know what to do for me. You know him?"

"No. But listen, let me know if there is anything else I can do."

"Thanks, Lieutenant."

"Grace."

"Right. Grace."

When Bosch went back to his desk he thought about his appointment with Chastain. In accordance with departmental procedures, Bosch would be represented by a union defense rep who was actually a fellow detective. He would act almost as an attorney would, counseling Bosch on what to say and how to say it. It was the first formal step of the internal investigation and disciplinary process.

When he looked up, he saw a woman standing at the counter with a young girl. The girl had red-rimmed eyes and a marble-sized swelling on her lower lip that looked like it might have been the result of a bite. She was disheveled and stared at the wall behind Bosch with a distance in her eyes that suggested that a window was there. But there wasn't.

Bosch could have asked how he could help them without moving from his desk, but it didn't take a detective to guess why they were there. He got up, came around the desk and approached the counter so they could speak confidentially. Rape victims were the people who evoked the most sadness in Bosch. He knew he wouldn't be able to last a month on a rape squad. Every victim he had ever seen had that stare. It was a sign that all things in their lives were different now and forever. They would never get back to what they had had before.

After speaking briefly to the mother and daughter, Bosch asked if the girl needed immediate medical attention and the mother said she didn't. He opened the half door in the counter and ushered them both back to one of the three interview rooms off the hallway to the rear of the bureau. He then went to the sex crimes table and approached Mary Cantu, a detective who had been handling for years what Bosch knew he couldn't handle for a month.

"Mary, you've got a walk-in back in room three," Bosch said. "She's fifteen. Happened last night. She got too curious about the pusher who works the nearby corner. He grabbed her and sold her and a rock to his next customer. She's with her mother."

"Thanks, Bosch. Just what I needed on a Friday. I'll go right back. You ask if she needed medical?"

"She said no, but I think the answer is yes."

"Okay, I'll handle it. Thanks."

Back at the front desk, it took Bosch a few minutes to clear his thoughts about the girl from his mind and another forty-five to finish reading through the reports and deliver them to the appropriate detective squads.

When he was done, he checked on Billets through the window and saw she was on the phone with a pile of paperwork in front of her. Bosch got up and went to his file cabinet and took out the copy of the murder book he had put there earlier. He lugged the thick binder back to his desk at the front counter. He had decided that in his free time between his duties at the front desk he would begin reviewing the murder book. The case had taken off so quickly earlier in the week that he had not had the time he usually liked to spend reviewing the paperwork. He knew from experience that command of the details and the nuances of an investigation was often the key to closing it out. He had just started turning through the pages in a cursory review when a vaguely familiar voice addressed him from the counter.

"Is that what I think it is?"

Bosch looked up. It was O'Grady, the FBI agent. Bosch felt his face burn with embarrassment that he'd been caught red-handed with the file and with his growing dislike for the agent.

"Yeah, it's what you think it is, O'Grady. You were supposed to be here a half hour ago to pick it up."

"Yeah, well, I don't run on your time. I had things to do."

"Like what, get your buddy Roy a new ponytail?"

"Just give me the binder, Bosch. And all the rest."

Bosch still had not gotten up and made no move to now.

"What do you want it for, O'Grady? We all know you're going to let the thing drop. You people don't care who killed Tony Aliso and you don't want to know."

"That's bullshit. Give me the file."

O'Grady reached over the counter and was reaching around blindly for the release button on the half door.

"Hold your fucking horses, man," Bosch said as he stood up. "Just wait there. I'll get it all."

Carrying the binder, Bosch walked back to the homicide table and, using his back to shield O'Grady's view, placed the binder on the table and picked up the box containing the original binder and the ancillary reports and evidence bags that Edgar and Rider had put in with it. He carried it back and dropped it on the counter in front of O'Grady.

"You gotta sign for it," he said. "We're extra careful about how we handle evidence and who gets to handle it."

"Yeah, right. The whole world knows that from the O.J. case, don't they?"

Bosch grabbed O'Grady's tie and jerked his upper body down over the counter. The agent could not find a purchase with his hands that would give him the leverage to pull back. Bosch bent down so that he was talking directly into his ear.

"Excuse me?"

"Bosch, you—"

"Harry!"

Bosch looked up. Billets was standing in the door of her office. Bosch let go of the tie and O'Grady's body sprang backward as he straightened up. His face was crimson with embarrassment and anger. As he jerked his tie loose from around his neck he yelled, "You're certifiable, you know that? You're a fucking asshole!"

"I didn't know you agents used that kind of language," Bosch said.

"Harry, just sit down," Billets commanded. "I'll take care of this."

She had come up to the counter now.

"He's got to sign the receipt."

"I don't care! I'll handle it!"

Bosch went back to his desk and sat down. He stared dead-eyed at O'Grady while Billets dug through the box until she found the inventory list and receipt Edgar had prepared. She showed O'Grady where to sign and then told him to go.

"You better watch him," he said to Billets as he picked the box up off the counter.

"You better watch yourself, Agent O'Grady. If I hear anything else about this little disagreement here, I'll file a complaint against you for inciting it."

"He's the one who—"

"I don't care. Understand? I don't care. Now leave."

"I'm leaving. But you watch your boy there. Keep him away from this."

O'Grady pointed to the contents of the box. Billets didn't answer.

O'Grady picked the box up and made a move to step away from the counter but stopped and looked once more at Bosch.

"Hey, Bosch, by the way, I got a message from Roy."

"Agent O'Grady, would you please leave!" Billets said angrily.

"What is it?" Bosch said.

"He just wanted to ask, who's the meat now?"

With that he turned around and headed down the hall to the exit. Billets watched him until he was gone and then turned around and looked at Bosch with anger in her eyes.

"You just don't know how to help yourself, do you?" she said. "Why don't you grow up and quit these little pissing wars?"

She didn't wait for his reply because he didn't have one. She walked quickly back into her office and shut the door. She then closed the blinds over the interior window. Bosch leaned back with his hands laced behind his neck, looked up at the ceiling and exhaled loudly.

After the O'Grady incident Bosch almost immediately became busy with a walk-in case involving an armed robbery. At the time, the entire robbery crew was out on a carjacking that had involved a high-speed chase, and that meant Bosch, as the desk man, had to interview the walk-in victim and type up a report. The victim was a young Mexican boy whose job it was to stand on the corner of Hollywood Boulevard at Sierra Bonita and sell maps to the homes of movie stars up in the hills. At ten that morning, shortly after he had set up his plywood sign and begun waving down cars, an old American-made sedan had pulled up with a man driving and a woman in the passenger seat. After asking how much the maps cost and whether he had sold very many of them, the woman had pointed a gun at the boy and robbed him of thirty-eight dollars. He had come in to report the crime with his mother. As it turned out, he had sold only one map that day before the robbery, and nearly all of the money taken from him was his own—he had brought it with him to make change. His loss was about what he made for a whole day of standing on the corner and waving his arm like a windmill.

Because of the small take and sloppy method used by the robbers, Bosch immediately thought the suspects were a couple of hypes looking for a quick score to buy their next balloon of heroin. They had not even

bothered to hide the car's license plate, which the boy had spotted and
memorized as they drove away.

After he was finished with the boy and his mother, he went to the
teletype machine and put out a wanted on the car with a description of
the suspects. He found when he did this that there was already a wanted
out on the vehicle for its use in two prior robberies in the last week. A lot
of good that did the kid who lost a day's pay, Bosch thought. The robbers
should have been picked up before they got to the boy. But this was the
big city, not a perfect world. Disappointments like that didn't stay long
with Bosch.

By this time the squad room had pretty much cleared out for lunch.
Bosch saw only Mary Cantu at the sex crimes table, probably working on
the paper from that morning's walk-in job.

Edgar and Rider were gone, apparently having decided it would be
better to go separately to Musso's. As Bosch got up to leave, he noticed
that the blinds were still drawn over the window to the lieutenant's office. Billets was still in there, he knew. He went to the homicide table and
put the copy of the murder book into his briefcase and then went and
knocked on her door. Before she could answer, he opened the door and
stuck his head in.

"I'm going to go catch some lunch and then go downtown for the
IAD thing. You won't have anybody out on the counter."

"Okay," she said. "I'll put Edgar or Rider up there after lunch.
They're just waiting around for a case, anyway."

"Okay then, I'll see you."

"Uh, Harry?"

"Yes?"

"I'm sorry for what happened earlier. Not for what I said. I meant
what I said, but I should have taken you in here and spoken to you. Doing it out there in front of the others was wrong. I apologize."

"Don't worry about it. Have a nice weekend."

"You, too."

"I'll try, Lieutenant."

"Grace."

"Grace."

Bosch got to Musso and Frank's Restaurant on Hollywood Boulevard at exactly twelve-thirty and parked in the back. The restaurant was a Hollywood landmark, having been on the Boulevard since 1924. In its heyday it had been a popular destination for Hollywood's elite. Fitzgerald and Faulkner held forth. Chaplin and Fairbanks once raced each other down Hollywood Boulevard on horseback, the loser having to pick up the dinner tab. The restaurant now subsisted mostly on its past glory and faded charm. Its red leather padded booths still filled every day for lunch and some of the waiters looked and moved as if they had been there long enough to have served Chaplin. The menu hadn't changed in all the years Bosch had been eating there—this in a town where the hookers out on the Boulevard lasted longer than most restaurants.

Edgar and Rider were waiting in one of the prized round booths, and Bosch slid in after they were pointed out by the maître d'—he was apparently too old and tired to walk Bosch over himself. They were both drinking iced tea and Bosch decided to go along with that, though privately he lamented that they were in the place that made the best martini in the city. Only Rider was looking at the menu. She was new in the division and hadn't been to Musso's enough times to know what the best thing was to order for lunch.

"So what are we doing?" Edgar asked while she looked.

"We've got to start over," Bosch said. "The Vegas stuff was all misdirection."

Rider glanced over the top of the menu at Bosch.

"Kiz, put that down," he said. "If you don't get the chicken pot pie you're making a mistake."

She hesitated, nodded and put the menu aside.

"What do you mean, misdirection?" she asked.

"I mean whoever killed Tony wanted us to go that way. And they planted the gun out there to make sure we stayed out there. But they screwed up. They didn't know the guy they planted the gun on was a fed who would have a bunch of other feds as an alibi. That was the screwup. Now, once I learned that our suspect was an agent, I thought Joey Marks and his people must have figured out he was a fed and set the whole thing up to taint him."

"I still think that sounds good," Edgar said.

"It does, or it did until last night," Bosch said as an ancient waiter in a red coat came to the table.

"Three chicken pot pies," Bosch said.

"Do you want something to drink?" the waiter asked.

Hell with it, Bosch decided.

"Yeah, I'll have a martini, three olives. You can bring them some more iced tea. That's it."

The waiter nodded and slowly glided away without writing anything on his pad.

"Last night," Bosch continued, "I learned from a source that Joey Marks did not know the man he thought was named Luke Goshen was a plant. He had no idea he was an informant, let alone an agent. In fact, once we picked Goshen up, Joey was engaged in a plan to try to find out whether Goshen was going to stand up or talk. This was because he had to decide whether to put a contract on him in the Metro jail."

He waited a moment to let them think about this.

"So, you can see with that information in the mix now, the second theory no longer works."

"Well, who's the source?" Edgar asked.

"I can't tell you that, guys. But it's solid. It's the truth."

He watched their eyes float down to the table. He knew they trusted him, but they also knew how informants were often the most skilled liars in the game. It was a tough call to base everything from here on out on an informant.

"Okay," Bosch said. "The source was Eleanor Wish. Jerry, have you told Kiz about all of that?"

Edgar hesitated, then nodded.

"Okay, then you know who she is. She overheard all of what I told you while they had her in that house. Before we got there, both Joey and the lawyer, Torrino, were there. She overheard them and from what she heard, they didn't know about Goshen. See, that whole abduction was part of the test. They knew the only way I could find out where the safe house was would be to get it from Goshen. That was the test, to see if he was talking or not."

They sat in silence for a few minutes while Edgar and Rider digested this.

"Okay," Edgar finally said. "I see what you're saying. But if Vegas was one big fucking red herring, how does the gun get over there in the agent's house?"

"That's what we have to figure out. What if there was someone outside of Tony's mob connections but close enough to him to know he was washing money and the reason why he made all the trips to Vegas? Someone who either had personal knowledge or maybe followed Tony to Vegas and watched how he worked, how he picked up the money from Goshen, everything? Someone who knew exactly how he did it, who knew Goshen could be set up to take the fall, and that Tony'd be coming back on Friday with a lot of money in his briefcase?"

"They would be able to set the whole thing up, as long as they could get into the agent's house to plant the gun," Edgar answered.

"Right. And getting into the house would be no problem. It's out in the middle of nowhere. He was away at the club for long stretches at a time. Anybody could get in, plant the gun, and get out. The question is who?"

"You're talking about either his wife or his girlfriend," Edgar said. "Both could have had that kind of access."

Bosch nodded.

"So which one do we set up on? The three of us can't do both, not on a freelance like this."

"We don't need to," Bosch said. "I think the choice is obvious."

"Which?" Edgar said. "The girlfriend?"

Bosch looked at Rider, giving her the chance to answer. She saw his look and then her eyes narrowed as she went to work.

"It . . . it can't be the girlfriend because . . . because she called Tony on Sunday morning. On the voice mail. Why would she call the guy if she knew he was dead?"

Bosch nodded. She was good.

"Could have been part of a setup," Edgar said. "Another misdirection."

"Could be but I doubt it," Bosch said. "Plus, we know she worked Friday night. That would make it kind of tough for her to be over here whacking Tony."

"So then it's the wife," Edgar said. "Veronica."

"Right," Bosch said. "I think she was lying to us, acting like she didn't know anything about her husband's business when she knew everything. I think this whole thing was her plan. She wrote the letters to the IRS and to the OCID. She wanted to get something going against Tony, then when he ended up dead it would point toward a mob hit. Trunk music. Planting the gun on Goshen was just icing. If we found it, fine. If we didn't, then we'd be sniffing around Vegas until we shelved the case."

"You're saying she did this all on her own?" Edgar asked.

"No," Bosch said. "I'm just saying I think this was her plan. But she had to have had help. An accomplice. It took two to do the actual hit and she sure didn't take the gun to Vegas. After the kill, she stays at the house and waits while the accomplice goes to Vegas and plants the gun while Luke Goshen's at the club."

"But wait a minute," Rider said. "We're forgetting something. Veronica Aliso had it very cushy in her existing life. Tony was raking in the bread with his washing machine. They had the big house in the hills, the cars . . . why would she want to kill the cash cow? How much was in that briefcase?"

"According to the feds, four hundred and eighty thousand," Bosch said.

Edgar whistled softly. Rider shook her head.

"I still don't see it," she said. "That's a hell of a lot of money, but Tony was making at least that much a year. In business terms, killing him was a short-term gain/long-term loss for her. Doesn't make sense."

"Then there is something else running through all of this that we don't know about yet," Bosch said. "Maybe he was about to dump her. Maybe that old lady in Vegas who said Tony was going to go away with Layla was telling the truth. Or maybe there's money somewhere we don't know about. But for now I can't see anybody else fitting into this picture but her."

"But what about the gatehouse?" Rider said. "The log shows she never left Friday, the whole night. And she had no visitors."

"Well, we've got to work on that," Bosch said. "There had to have been a way for her to get in and out."

"What else?" Edgar asked.

"We start over," Bosch said. "I want to know everything about her. Where'd she come from, who are her friends, what does she do in that house all day long and what did she do and who did she do it with all those times Tony was away?"

Rider and Edgar nodded.

"There's got to be an accomplice. And my guess is that it's a man. And I'll bet we'll find him through her."

The waiter came up with a tray and put it down on a folding cart. They watched silently as he prepared the meal. There were three separate chicken pot pies on the tray. The waiter used a fork and spoon to take the top crust off each and put it on a plate. Next he scooped the contents of each pie out and put it on the crust, served the three cops their dishes and put down fresh glasses of iced tea for Edgar and Rider. He then poured Bosch's martini from a small glass carafe and floated away without a word.

"Obviously," Bosch said, "we have to do this quietly."

"Yeah," Edgar said, "and Bullets also put us on the top of the rotation. Next call comes in, me and Kiz get it. And we hafta work it without you. That's going to take us away from this."

"Well, do what you can. If you get a body you get a body, nothing we can do about that. Meantime, this is what I propose. You two work on Veronica's background, see what you can find. You got any sources at the *Times* or the trades?"

"I know a couple at the *Times*," Rider said. "And there's a woman I once had a case with—she was a vic—who's a receptionist or something at *Variety*."

"You trust 'em?"

"I think I can."

"See if they'll pull a search on Veronica for you. She had a brief flash of fame a while back. Her fifteen minutes. Maybe there were some stories about her, stories that would have names of people we could talk to."

"What about talking to her again?" Edgar asked.

"I don't think we should do it yet. I want to have something to talk to her about."

"What about neighbors?"

"You can do that. Maybe she'll look out the window and see you, give her something to think about. If you go up there, see if you can take another look at the gate log. Talk to Nash. I'm sure you can turn him without needing another search warrant. I'd like to take a look at the whole year, know who has been going in to see her, especially while Tony was out of town. We have Tony's credit records and can construct his travel history. You'll be able to know when she was in that house alone."

Bosch raised his fork. He hadn't had a bite of food yet, but his mind was too full of the case and what needed to be done.

"The other thing is we need as much of the case file as we can get. All we've got is the copy of the murder book. I'm going down to Parker Center for my little chat with the IAD. I'll swing by USC and get a copy of the autopsy. The feds already have it. I'll also go talk to Donovan in SID and see if he came up with anything we pulled out of the car. Also, he's got the shoe prints. I'll get copies, hopefully before the feds come in and take everything. Anything else I'm missing?"

The other two shook their heads.

"You want to see what we get and then put our heads together after work?"

They nodded.

"Cat and Fiddle, about six?"

They nodded again. They were too busy eating to talk. Bosch took his first bite of food, which was already getting cold. He joined them in their silence, thinking about the case.

"It's in the details," he said after a few moments.

"What?" Rider asked.

"The case. When you get one like this, the answer is always in the details. You watch, when we break it, the answer will have been sitting in the files, in the book. It always happens."

The interview with Chastain at Internal Affairs began as Bosch expected it would. He sat with Zane, his defense rep, at a gray government table in one of the IAD interview rooms. An old Sony cassette player was turned on and everything said in the room was recorded. In police parlance, Chastain was locking up Bosch's story. Getting his words and explanation in as much detail as possible down on tape. Chastain really wouldn't begin his investigation until after Bosch's story was locked in. He would then hunt for flaws in it. All he had to do was catch Bosch in a single lie and he could take him to a Board of Rights hearing. Depending on the size and import of the lie, he could seek a penalty ranging from suspension to dismissal.

In a dull and laborious drone, Chastain read prepared questions from a legal pad and Bosch slowly and carefully answered them with as few words as possible. It was a game. Bosch had played it before. In the fifteen minutes they had before reporting to IAD, Zane had counseled Bosch on how it would go and how they should proceed. Like a good criminal defense lawyer, he never directly asked Harry if he had planted the gun. Zane didn't really care. He simply looked at IAD as the enemy, as a group of bad cops with the sole purpose of going after good cops. Zane was part of the old school who thought all cops were inherently good and though sometimes the job turned them bad, they should not be persecuted by their own.

Everything was routine for a half hour. But then Chastain threw an unexpected pitch at them.

"Detective Bosch, do you know a woman named Eleanor Wish?"

Zane reached out a hand in front of Bosch to stop him from answering.

"What is this shit, Chastain?"

"Who have you been talking to, Chastain?" Bosch added.

"Wait a minute, Harry," Zane said. "Don't say anything. Where's this going, Chastain?"

"It's very clear from the orders from the chief. I'm investigating Bosch's conduct during this investigation. As far as who I have been talking to or where I get my information, you are not privy to that at this point in the process."

"This is supposed to be about a supposedly planted gun that we all know is bullshit. That's what we are here to answer."

"Do you wish to read the order from the chief again? It's quite clear."

Zane looked at him a moment.

"Give us five minutes so we can talk about this. Why don't you go get the points of your teeth filed?"

Chastain stood up and reached over and turned the tape recorder off. As he stepped to the door, he looked back at them with a smile.

"This time I got you both. You won't get out from under this one, Bosch. And, Zane, well, I guess you can't win them all, can you?"

"You ought to know that better than me, you sanctimonious asshole. Get out of here and leave us alone."

After Chastain was gone, Zane bent over the tape recorder to make sure it was off. He then got up and checked the thermostat on the wall to make sure it wasn't a secret listening device. After he was satisfied their conversation was private, he sat back down and asked Bosch about Eleanor Wish. Bosch told him about his encounters with Eleanor over the past few days but left out mention of the abduction and her subsequent confession.

"One of those cops over there in Metro must've told him you shacked up with her," Zane said. "That's all he's got. He's going for an associating beef. If you admit it here, then he's got you. But if that's all he gets, then it's a slap on the wrist at best. As long as he gets nothing else. But if you lie about it and say you weren't with her when you were, and he can prove you were, then you've got a problem. So my advice is that you tell him, yeah, you know her and you've been with her. Fuck it, it's nothing. Tell him it's over, and if that's all he's got, then he's a chickenshit asshole."

"I don't know if it is or it isn't."

"What?"

"Over."

"Well, don't tell him nothin' about that unless he asks for it. Then use your best judgment. Ready?"

Bosch nodded and Zane opened the door. Chastain was sitting outside at a desk.

"Where ya been, Chastain?" Zane complained. "We're waiting in here."

Chastain didn't answer. He came in, turned the recorder back on and continued the Q and A.

"Yes, I know Eleanor Wish," Bosch said. "Yes, I've spent time with her over the last few days."

"How much time?"

"I don't know exactly. A couple of nights."

"While you were conducting the investigation?"

"Not *while* I was conducting it. At night, when I was done for the day. We all don't work around the clock like you, Chastain."

Bosch smiled at him without humor.

"Was she a witness in this case?" Chastain asked with a tone that denoted that he was shocked that Bosch would cross that line.

"Initially, I thought she might be a witness. After I located her and talked to her, I learned pretty quickly that she was not an evidentiary witness of any kind."

"But you did initially encounter her while you were in your capacity as an investigator on this case."

"That's correct."

Chastain consulted his pad for a long moment before asking the next question.

"Is this woman, that's the convicted felon Eleanor Wish I am still talking about, is she living in your home at this time?"

Bosch felt the bile rising in his throat. The personal invasion and Chastain's tone were getting to him. He struggled to remain calm.

"I don't know the answer to that," he said.

"You don't *know* if someone is *living* in your house or not?"

"Look, Chastain, she was there last night, okay? Is that what you want to hear? She was there. But whether she'll be there tonight I don't know. She's got her own place in Vegas. She may have gone back today, I don't know. I didn't check. You want me to call and ask her if she is officially *living* in my home at this time, I will."

"I don't think that's necessary. I think I have everything I need for the time being."

He then went directly into the standard IAD end-of-interview spiel.

"Detective Bosch, you will be informed of the results of the ongoing investigation into your conduct. If departmental charges are filed, you will be informed of the scheduling of a Board of Rights hearing in which three captains will hear evidence. You will be allowed to choose one of those captains, I will select a second and the third will be chosen at random. Any questions?"

"Just one. How can you call yourself a cop when all you do is sit up here and conduct these bullshit investigations into bullshit?"

Zane reached over and put a hand on Bosch's forearm to quiet him.

"No, that's okay," Chastain said, waving off Zane's effort to calm things. "I don't mind answering. In fact, I get that question a lot, Bosch. Funny, but it always seems I get it from the cops I happen to be investigating. Anyway, the answer is that I take pride in what I do because I represent the public, and if there is no one to police the police then there is no one to keep the abuse of their wide powers in check. I serve a valuable purpose in this society, Detective Bosch. I'm proud of what I do. Can you say the same?"

"Yeah, yeah, yeah," Bosch said. "I'm sure that sounds great on tape for whoever listens to it. I get the feeling you probably sit alone at night and listen to it yourself. Over and over again. After a while, you believe it. But let me ask you this, Chastain. Who polices the police who police the police?"

Bosch stood up and Zane followed. The interview was over.

After leaving IAD and thanking Zane for his help, Bosch went down to the SID lab on the third floor to see Art Donovan. The criminologist had just come back from a crime scene and was sorting through evidence bags and checking the material against an evidence list. He looked up as Bosch was approaching.

"How'd you get in here, Harry?"

"I know the combination."

Most detectives who worked RHD knew the door-lock combo. Bosch hadn't worked RHD in five years and they still hadn't changed it.

"See," Donovan said. "That's how the trouble starts."

"What trouble?"

"You coming in here while I'm handling evidence. Next thing you know some wiseass defense lawyer says it got tainted and I look like an asshole on national TV."

"You're paranoid, Artie. Besides, we're not due for another trial of the century for at least a few years."

"Funny. What do you want, Harry?"

"You're the second guy who said I was funny today. What happened with my shoe prints and all the rest of the stuff?"

"The Aliso case?"

"No, the Lindbergh case. What do you think?"

"Well, I heard that Aliso wasn't yours anymore. I'm supposed to have everything ready for the FBI to pick up."

"When is that?"

Donovan looked up from what he was doing for the first time.

"They just said they'd send somebody by five."

"Then it's still my case until they show up. What about the shoe prints you pulled?"

"There's nothing about them. I sent copies to the bureau's crime lab in D.C. to see if they could ID the make and model."

"And?"

"And nothing. I haven't heard back. Bosch, every department in the country sends shit to them. You know that. And last I heard, they don't drop everything they're doing when a package from the LAPD comes in. It will probably be next week sometime before I hear back. If I'm lucky."

"Shit."

"It's too late to call the East Coast now, anyway. Maybe Monday. I didn't know they suddenly became so important to you. Communication, Harry, that's the secret. You ought to try it sometime."

"Never mind that, do you still have a set of copies?"

"Yup."

"Can I get a set?"

"Sure can, but you're going to have to wait about twenty minutes or so till I'm done with this."

"Come on, Artie, it's probably just sitting in a file cabinet or something. It'll take you thirty seconds."

"Would you leave me alone?" Donovan said with exasperation. "I'm serious, Harry. Yes, it's sitting in a file and it would only take me half a minute to get it for you. But if I leave what I'm doing here, I could get crucified when I testify in *this* case. I can see it now, some shyster all righteous and angry and saying, 'You are telling this jury that while in the middle of handling evidence from this case you got up and handled evidence from *another*?' And you don't have to be F. Lee Bailey anymore to make it sound good to a jury. Now leave me alone. Come back in a half hour."

"Fine, Artie, I'll leave you alone."

"And buzz me when you come back. Don't just come in. We gotta get that combination changed."

The last line he said more to himself than to Bosch.

Bosch left the way he had come in and took the elevator down to go outside and have a smoke. He had to walk out to the curb and light up because it was now against departmental rules to stand outside the front door of Parker Center and smoke. So many cops working there were addicted to cigarettes that there had often been a crowd outside the building's main doors and a permanent haze of blue smoke had begun to hang over the entrance. The chief thought this was unsightly and instituted the rule that if you left the building to smoke, you had to leave the property as well. Now the front sidewalk along Los Angeles Street often looked like the scene of a labor action, with cops, some even in uniform, pacing back and forth in front of the building. The only thing missing from the scene was picket signs. The word was that the police chief had consulted with the city attorney to see if he could outlaw smoking on the sidewalk as well, but he was told that the sidewalk was beyond the bounds of his control.

As Bosch was lighting a second cigarette off the first, he saw the huge figure of FBI agent Roy Lindell waltzing leisurely out of the glass doors of the police headquarters. When he got to the sidewalk, he turned right and headed toward the federal courthouse. He was coming directly toward Bosch. Lindell didn't see Bosch until he was a few feet away. It startled him.

"What is this? Are you waiting for me?"

"No, I'm having a cigarette, Lindell. What are you doing?"

"None of your business."

He made a move to pass but Bosch stopped him with the next line.

"Have a nice chat with Chastain?"

"Look, Bosch, I was asked to come over and give a statement and I obliged. I told the truth. Let the chips fall."

"Trouble is you don't know the truth."

"I know you found that gun and I didn't put it there. That's the truth."

"Part of it, at least."

"Well, it's the only part I know, and that's what I told him. So have a good day."

He passed by Bosch and Harry turned around to watch him go. Once again he stopped him.

"You people might be satisfied with only part of the truth. But I'm not."

Lindell turned around and stepped back to Bosch.

"What's that supposed to mean?"

"Figure it out."

"No, you tell me."

"We were all used, Lindell. I'm going to find out by who. When I do, I'll be sure to let you know."

"Look, Bosch, you don't have the case anymore. We're working it and you better stay the fuck away from it."

"Yeah, you guys are working the case, all right," Bosch said sarcastically. "I'm sure you're pounding the pavement on this one. Let me know when you figure it out."

"Bosch, it's not like that. We care about it."

"Give me one answer, Lindell."

"What?"

"In the time you were under, did Tony Aliso ever bring his wife over there to make a pickup?"

Lindell was quiet a moment while he decided whether to answer. He finally shook his head.

"Not once," he said. "Tony always said she hated the place. Too many bad memories, I guess."

Bosch tried to remain cool.

"Memories of Vegas?"

Lindell smiled.

"For somebody who supposedly has all the answers, you don't know much, do you, Bosch? Tony met her in the club something like twenty years ago. Long before my time. She was a dancer and Tony was going to make her a movie star. Same story he was using on 'em to the end. Only, after her I guess he got wise and learned not to marry every one of them."

"Did she know Joey Marks?"

"Your one question is now up to three, Bosch."

"Did she?"

"I don't know."

"What was her name back then?"

"That's another one I don't know. I'll see you around, Bosch."

He turned and walked away. Bosch threw his cigarette into the street and walked back toward the Glass House. A few minutes later, after being properly buzzed through the door into the SID offices, Bosch found Donovan at his desk again. The criminalist lifted a thin file from the desk and handed it to Harry.

"You got copies in there," he said. "Same thing I sent the bureau. What I did was shoot a copy of the negative and then shot the new negative and printed it in black-and-white contrast for comparison purposes. I also blew it up to actual size."

Bosch didn't understand what Donovan had just said except for the last part. He opened the file. There were two pages of copy paper with the shoe prints in black. Both were partial prints of the same right shoe. But between the two partials almost all of the shoe was there. Donovan got up and looked at the open file. He pointed to a tread ridge on one of the copies. It was a curving line on the heel. But the line was broken.

"Now, if you find the shooter and he still has the shoes, this is where you'll get him. See how that line is broken there? That does not appear to be a manufacturer's design. This guy stepped on glass or something at some point and it cut the tread there. It's either that or a flaw in manufacturing. But if you find the shoe, we'll be able to make an ID match that should send the boy away."

"Okay," Bosch said, still looking at the copies. "Now, did you get anything even preliminary from the bureau on this?"

"Not really. I've got a guy I go to pretty regularly with this kind of stuff. I know him, seen him at a couple of the SID conventions. Anyway, he called just to let me know he got the package and he'd get on it as soon as he could. He said that off the top of his head he thought it was one of those lightweight boots that are popular now. You know, they're like work boots but they're comfortable and wear like a pair of Nikes."

"Okay, Artie, thanks."

Bosch drove over to the Country-USC Medical Center and around to the parking lot by the railroad yard. The coroner's office was located at the far end of the medical center property, and Bosch went in through the back door after showing his badge to a security guard.

He checked Dr. Salazar's office first but it was empty. He then went down to the autopsy floor and looked in the first suite, where the lowered table that Salazar always used was located. Salazar was there, working on another body. Bosch stepped in and Salazar looked up from the open chest cavity of what looked like the remains of a young black man.

"Harry, what are you doing here? This is a South Bureau case."

"I wanted to ask about the Aliso case."

"Kind of got my hands full at the moment. And you shouldn't be in here without a mask and gown."

"I know. You think you could have your assistant dub off a copy of the protocol for me?"

"No problem. I heard the FBI took an interest in the case, Harry. Is that true?"

"That's what I hear."

"Funny thing, those agents didn't bother talking to me. They just came in and got a copy of the protocol. The protocol only has conclusions, none of the ruminating we doctors like to do."

"So what would you have ruminated about with them if they had talked to you?"

"I would have told them my hunch, Harry."

"Which is?"

Salazar looked up from the body but kept his rubber-gloved and bloody hands over the open chest so they wouldn't drip on anything else.

"My hunch is that you're looking for a woman."

"Why's that?"

"The material in and below the eyes."

"Preparation H?"

"What?"

"Nothing, never mind. What did you find?"

"The substance was analyzed and it came back oleo capsicum. Found it on the nasal swabs, too. Know what oleo capsicum is better known as, Harry?"

"Pepper spray."

"Shit, Harry, you ruin my fun."

"Sorry. So somebody sprayed him with pepper spray?"

"Right again. That's why I think it's a woman. Someone who was either having problems controlling him or afraid of problems. That makes me think it's a woman. Besides, all these women around here, they all carry that stuff in their purses."

Bosch wondered if Veronica Aliso was one of those women.

"That's good, Sally. Anything else?"

"No surprises. Tests came back clean."

"No amyl nitrate?"

"Nope, but that has a short retention. We don't find it that often. Did you get anywhere with the slugs?"

"Yeah, we did all right. Can you call your guy?"

"Take me to the intercom."

While Salazar held his hands up in front of himself so they wouldn't touch anything, Bosch pushed his wheelchair to the nearby counter, where there was a phone with an intercom attachment. Salazar told Bosch which button to push and then ordered someone to make a copy of the protocol immediately for Bosch.

"Thanks," Bosch said.

"No problem. Hope it helps. Remember, look for a woman who carries pepper spray in her purse. Not mace. Pepper spray."

"Right."

The end-of-the-week traffic was intense and it took Bosch nearly an hour to get out of downtown and back to Hollywood. When he got to the Cat & Fiddle pub on Sunset it was after six, and as he walked through the gate he saw Edgar and Rider already sitting at a table in the open-air courtyard. There was a pitcher of beer on their table. And they weren't alone. Sitting at the table with them was Grace Billets.

The Cat & Fiddle was a popular drinking spot with the Hollywood cops because it was only a few blocks from the station on Wilcox. So Bosch didn't know as he approached the table whether Billets happened to be there by coincidence or because she knew of their freelance operation.

"Howdy, folks," Bosch said as he sat down.

There was one empty glass on the table and he filled it from the pitcher. He then held the glass up to the others and toasted to the end of another week.

"Harry," Rider said, "the lieutenant knows what we've been doing. She's here to help."

Bosch nodded and slowly looked at Billets.

"I'm disappointed that you didn't come to me first," she said. "But I understand what you are doing. I agree that it might be in the bureau's best interest to let this lie and not endanger their case. But a man was murdered. If they're not going to look for the killer, I don't see why we shouldn't."

Bosch nodded. He was almost speechless. He'd never had a boss who wasn't a rigid by-the-book man. Grace Billets was a major change.

"Of course," she said, "we have to be very careful. We screw this up and we'll have more than just the FBI mad at us."

The unspoken message was that their careers were at stake here.

"Well, my position's already pretty much shot," Bosch said. "So if anything goes wrong, I want you all to lay it on me."

"That's bullshit," Rider said.

"No, it's not. You all are going places. I'm not going anywhere. Hollywood is it for me and all of us here know it. So if this thing hits the fan, back out. I'll take the heat. If you can't agree to that, I want you to back out now."

There was silence for a few moments, and then one by one the other three nodded.

"Okay, then," he said, "you may have told the lieutenant what you've been doing, but I'd like to hear it myself."

"We've come up with a few things, not a lot," Rider said. "Jerry went up the hill to see Nash while I worked the computer and talked to a friend at the *Times*. First off, I ran Tony Aliso's TRW credit report and got Veronica's Social Security number off that. I then ran that through the Department of Social Security computer to try and get a work history and found out that Veronica is not her real name. The Social comes back to Jennifer Gilroy, born forty-one years ago in Las Vegas, Nevada. No wonder she said she hated Vegas. She grew up there."

"Any work history?"

"Nothing until she came out here and worked for TNA Productions."

"What else?"

Before she could answer, there was a loud commotion near the glass door to the interior bar. The door opened and a large man in a bartender's jacket pushed a smaller man through. The smaller man was disheveled and drunk and yelling something about the lack of respect he was getting. The bartender roughly walked him to the courtyard gate and pushed him through. As soon as the bartender turned to go back to the bar, the drunk spun around and started back in. The bartender turned around and pushed him so hard he fell backward onto the seat of his pants. Now embarrassed, he threatened to come back and get the bartender. A few people at some of the outside tables snickered. The drunk got up and staggered out to the street.

"They start early around here," Billets said. "Go ahead, Kiz."

"Anyway, I did an NCIC run. Jennifer Gilroy got picked up twice in Vegas for soliciting. This is going back more than twenty years. I called over there and had them ship us the mugs and reports. It's all on fiche and they have to dig it out, so we won't get it till next week. There probably won't be much there, anyway. According to the computer, neither case went to court. She pleaded out and paid a fine each time."

Bosch nodded. It sounded like a routine disposal of routine cases.

"That's all I've got on that. As far as the *Times* goes, there was nothing on the search. And my friend at *Variety* didn't do much better. Veronica Aliso was barely mentioned in the review of *Casualty of Desire*. Both she and the movie were panned, but I'd like to see it anyway. Do you still have the tape, Harry?"

"On my desk."

"Does she get naked in it?" Edgar asked. "If she does, I'd like to see it, too."

He was ignored.

"Okay, what else?" Rider said. "Uh, Veronica also got a couple mentions in stories about movie premieres and who attended. It wasn't a lot. When you said she had fifteen minutes, I think you confused minutes with seconds. Anyway, that's it from me. Jerry?"

Edgar cleared his throat and explained that he had gone up to the gatehouse at Hidden Highlands and run into a problem when Nash insisted on a new search warrant to look at the complete gate log. Edgar said he then spent the afternoon typing up the search warrant and hunting for a judge who hadn't left early for the weekend. He eventually was successful and had a signed warrant which he planned to deliver the next morning.

"Kiz and I are goin' up there in the morning. We'll get a look at the gate log and then we're probably going to hit some of the neighbors, do some interviews. Like you said, we're hopin' the widow will look out her window and catch our act, maybe get a little spooked. Maybe panic, make a mistake."

It was then Bosch's turn, and he recounted his afternoon efforts, including his run-in with Roy Lindell and the agent's recollection that Veronica Aliso had started her show business career as a stripper in Vegas. He also discussed Salazar's finding that Tony Aliso had been hit in the face with a blast of pepper spray shortly before his death and shared the deputy coroner's hunch that it might have been a woman who sprayed him.

"Does he think she could have pulled this off by herself after hitting him with the pepper spray?" Billets asked.

"It doesn't matter, because she wasn't alone," Bosch answered.

He pulled his briefcase onto his lap and took out the copies of the shoe prints Donovan had recovered from the body and the bumper of the Rolls. He slid the pages to the middle of the table so the three others could look.

"That's a size eleven shoe. It belongs to a man, Artie says. A big man. So the woman, if she was there, could have sprayed him with the pepper, but this guy finished the job."

Bosch pointed to the shoe prints.

"He put his foot right on the victim so he could lean in close and do the job point-blank. Very cool and very efficient. Probably a pro. Maybe someone she knew since her Vegas days."

"Probably the one who planted the gun in Vegas?" Billets asked.

"That's my guess."

Bosch had been keeping his eye on the front gate of the courtyard, just in case the drunk who had been tossed out decided to come back and make his point. But when he glanced over now, he didn't see the drunk. He saw Officer Ray Powers, wearing mirrored glasses despite the lateness of the day, entering the courtyard and being met halfway across by the bartender. Waving his arms in an animated fashion, the bartender told the big cop about the drunk and the threats. Powers glanced around at the tables and saw Bosch and the others. When he had disengaged from the bartender he sauntered over.

"So, the detective bureau brain trust takes five," he said.

"That's right, Powers," Edgar said. "I think the guy you're looking for is out there pissing in the bushes."

"Yes, suh, I'll jus' go out there 'n' fetch him, boss."

Powers looked around the table at the others with a satisfied smirk on his face. He saw the copies of the shoe prints on the table and pointed at them with his chin.

"Is this what you dicks call an investigative strategy session? Well, I'll give you a tip. Those there are what they call shoe prints."

He smiled at his remark, proud of it.

"We're off duty, Powers," Billets said. "Why don't you go do your job and we'll worry about ours?"

Powers saluted her.

"Somebody's got to do the job, don't they?"

He walked away and out through the gate without waiting for a reply.

"He's got one hell of a bug up his ass," Rider said.

"He's just mad because I told his lieutenant about the fingerprint he left on our car," Billets said. "I think he got his ass chewed. Anyway, back to business. What do you think, Harry? Do we have enough to take a hard run at Veronica?"

"I think we almost do. I'm going to go up there with these guys tomorrow, see what's on the gate log. Maybe we'll pay her a visit. I just wish we had something concrete to talk to her about."

Billets nodded.

"I want to be kept informed tomorrow. Call me by noon."

"Will do."

"The more time that goes by on this, the harder it will be to keep this investigation among just us. I think by Monday we're going to have to take stock and decide whether to turn what we have over to the bureau."

"I don't see that," Bosch said, shaking his head. "Whatever we give them, they're just going to sit on. If you want to clear this, you've got to let us alone, keep the bureau off us."

"I will try, Harry, but there will come a point where that will be impossible. We're running a full-scale investigation off the books here. Word's going to get out. It has to. And all I'm saying is that it will be better if that word comes from me and can be controlled."

Bosch nodded reluctantly. He knew she was right but he had to fight her suggestion. The case belonged to them. It was his. And all that had happened to him in the last week made it all the more personal. He didn't want to give it up.

He gathered up the copies of the shoe prints and put them back in his briefcase. He finished the last of his glass of beer and asked who and what he owed for it.

"It's on me," Billets said. "The next one, after we clear this, is on you."

"It's a deal."

When Bosch got to his house he found the door locked, but the key he had given Eleanor Wish was under the front mat. The first thing he checked when he got inside was the Hopper print. It was still there on the wall. But she was gone. He made a quick scan of the rooms and found no note. He checked the closet and her clothes were gone. So was her suitcase.

He sat on the bed and thought about her leaving. That morning they had left things open. He had risen early and, while she was still in bed, watching him get ready for the day, he'd asked her what she was going to do during the day. She had told him she didn't know.

Now she was gone. He rubbed a hand over his face. He was already beginning to feel the loss of her and he replayed in his mind their conversations of the night before. He had played it wrong, he decided. It had cost her something to tell him of her complicity. And he had only evaluated it in terms of what it meant to him and to his case. Not to her. Not to them.

Bosch leaned back until he was lying across the bed. He spread his arms and stared up at the ceiling. He could feel the beer working inside him, making him tired.

"Okay," he said out loud.

He wondered if she would call or if another five years would go by before he saw her again by happenstance. He thought about how much had happened to him in the past five years and how long a wait that had been. His body ached. He closed his eyes.

"Okay."

He fell asleep and dreamed about being alone in a desert with no roads and miles of open, desolate country ahead of him in every direction he looked.

VI

Bosch picked up two containers of coffee and two glazed doughnuts from Bob's in the farmers market at seven Saturday morning, then drove to the clearing where Tony Aliso's body had been found in the trunk of his car. As he ate and drank, he looked out on the marine layer shrouding the quiet city below. The sun rising behind the towers of downtown cast them as opaque monoliths in the haze. It was beautiful but Bosch felt as though he were the only one in the world seeing it.

When he had finished eating, he used a napkin he had wet in the water fountain at the farmers market to clean the sticky residue of sugar off his fingers. He then stuffed all the papers and the first empty coffee cup back into the doughnut bag and started the car.

Bosch had fallen asleep early Friday evening and awakened in his clothes before sunrise. He felt the need to get out of the house and do something. He had always believed that you could make things happen in an investigation by staying busy and with hard work. He decided that he would use the morning to try to find the spot where Tony Aliso's Rolls-Royce was intercepted and pulled over by his killers.

He concluded for a couple of reasons that the abduction had to have taken place on Mulholland Drive near the entrance to Hidden Highlands. First, the clearing where the car had been found was off Mulholland. If the abduction had taken place near the airport, it was likely the car would have been dumped near the airport, not fifteen miles away. And second, the abduction could be done more easily and quietly up on Mulholland in the dark. The airport and the surrounding area were always congested with traffic and people and would have presented too much of a risk.

The next question was whether Aliso had been followed from the airport or his killers simply waited for him at the abduction spot on Mulholland. Bosch decided on the latter, figuring that it was a small operation—two people, tops—and a tail and vehicle stop would be too iffy a proposition, particularly in Los Angeles, where every owner of a Rolls-Royce would be acutely aware of the danger of carjackings. He thought that they had waited on Mulholland and somehow created a trap or scene that made Aliso stop his car, even though he was carrying $480,000 in cash in his briefcase. And Bosch guessed that the only way Aliso would make such a stop was if that scenario involved his wife. In his mind Bosch saw the headlights of the Rolls-Royce sweeping around a curve and illuminating a frantically waving Veronica Aliso. Tony would stop for that.

Bosch knew that the waiting spot had to be on a place on Mulholland they were sure Tony would pass. There were only two logical routes from the airport to Mulholland Drive and then to the gatehouse at Hidden Highlands. One way would be to go north on the 405 freeway and simply take the Mulholland Drive exit. The other way would have been to take La Cienega Boulevard from the airport north to Laurel Canyon and up the hill to Mulholland.

The two routes had only a one-mile stretch of Mulholland in common. And since there was no way of knowing for sure which route Aliso would take home that night, it seemed obvious to Bosch that the car stop and abduction would have been somewhere along that one mile of road. It was here that Bosch came, and for nearly an hour he drove back and forth along the stretch, finally settling on the spot he would have chosen for the abduction if it had been his plan. The location was at the bend in a hairpin curve a half mile from the Hidden Highlands gatehouse. It was in an area with few homes and those that were there were built on the south side on a promontory well above the road. On the north side, the undeveloped land dropped steeply away from the road into a heavily wooded arroyo where eucalyptus and acacia trees crowded one another. It was the perfect spot. Secluded, out of sight.

Once again Bosch envisioned Tony Aliso coming around the curve and the lights of his Rolls coming upon his own wife in the road. Aliso stops, confused—what is she doing there? He gets out and from the north side of the road her accomplice emerges. She hits her husband with the spray, the accomplice goes to the Rolls and pops the trunk. Aliso's hands are clawing at his eyes when he is roughly thrown into the trunk and his hands tied behind him. All they had to worry about was a car coming around the curve and throwing its lights on them. But at that late hour on Mulholland, it didn't seem likely. The whole thing could have been done in fifteen seconds. That's why the spray was used. Not because it was a woman, but because it would make it fast.

Bosch pulled off the road, got out and looked around. The spot had the right feel to him. It was as quiet as death. He decided that he would come back that night to see it in darkness, to further confirm what he felt in his gut to be true.

He crossed the street and looked down into the arroyo where her accomplice would have hidden and waited. Looking down he tried to find a spot just off the road where a man could have ducked down and been concealed. He noticed a dirt trail going into the woods and stepped down to it, looking for shoe prints. There were many prints and he squatted down to study them. The ground here was dusty and some of the prints were fully recognizable. He found prints from two distinctly different sets of shoes, an old pair of shoes with worn heels and a much newer pair with heels that left sharp lines in the dirt. Neither pair was what he was looking for, the work-shoe pattern with the cut in the sole that Donovan had noticed.

Bosch's eyes looked up from the ground and followed the trail into the brush and trees. He decided to take a few more steps in, lifted a branch of an acacia and ducked under it. After his eyes adjusted to the darkness under the canopy of foliage, they were drawn to a blue object he could see but not identify about twenty yards farther into the dense growth. He would have to leave the trail to get to it, but he decided to investigate.

After slowly moving ten feet into the brush, he could see that the blue object was part of a plastic tarp, the kind you saw on roofs all over the city after an earthquake knocked down chimneys and opened up the seams of buildings. Bosch stepped closer and saw that two corners of the tarp were tied to trees and it was hung over the branch of a third, creating a small shelter on a level portion of the hillside. He watched for a few moments but saw no movement.

It was impossible to come up on the shelter quietly. The ground was covered with a thick layer of dead and dried leaves and twigs that crackled under Bosch's feet. When he was ten feet from the canvas tarp, a man's hoarse voice stopped him.

"I've got a gun, you fuckers!"

Bosch stood stock-still and stared at the tarp. Because it was draped over the long branch of an acacia tree, he was in a blind spot. He could not see whoever it was who had yelled. And the man who yelled probably couldn't see him. Bosch decided to take a chance.

"I've got one, too," he called back. "And a badge."

"Police? I didn't call the police!"

There was a hysterical tinge to the voice now, and Bosch suspected he was dealing with one of the homeless wanderers who were dumped out of mental institutions during the massive cutbacks in public assistance in the 1980s. The city was teeming with them. They stood at almost every major intersection holding their signs and shaking their change cups, they slept under overpasses or burrowed like termites into the woods on the hillsides, living in makeshift camps just yards from million-dollar mansions.

"I'm just passing through," Bosch yelled. "You put down yours, I'll put down mine."

Bosch guessed that the man behind the scared voice didn't even have a gun.

"Okay. It's a deal."

Bosch unsnapped the holster under his arm but left his gun in place. He walked the final few steps and came slowly around the trunk of the acacia. A man with long gray hair and beard flowing over a blue silk Hawaiian shirt sat cross-legged on a blanket under the tarp. There was a wild look in his eyes. Bosch quickly scanned the man's hands and the surroundings within his immediate reach and saw no weapon. He eased up a bit and nodded at the man.

"Hello," he said.

"I didn't do nothin'."

"I understand."

Bosch looked around. There were folded clothes and towels under the shelter of the tarp. There was a small folding card table with a frying pan on it along with some candles and Sterno cans, two forks and a spoon, but no knife. Bosch figured the man had the knife under his shirt or maybe hidden in the blanket. There was also a bottle of cologne on the table, and Bosch could tell that it had been liberally sprinkled about the shelter. Also under the tarp were an old tar bucket filled with crushed aluminum cans, a stack of newspapers and a dog-eared paperback copy of *Stranger in a Strange Land*.

He stepped to the edge of the man's clearing and squatted like a baseball catcher so they could face each other on the same level. He took a look around the outer edge of the clearing and saw that this was where the man discarded what he didn't need. There were bags of trash and remnants of clothing. By the base of another acacia there was a brown-and-green suit bag. It was unzipped and lying open like a gutted fish. Bosch looked back at the man. He could see he wore two other Hawaiian shirts beneath the blue one on top, which had a pattern of hula girls on surfboards. His pants were dirty but had a sharper crease in them than a homeless man's pants would usually have. His shoes were too well polished for a man of the woods. Bosch guessed that the pair he wore had made some of the prints up on the trail, the ones with the sharp-edged heels.

"That's a nice shirt," Bosch said.

"It's mine."

"I know. I just said it was nice. What's your name?"

"Name's George."

"George what?"

"George whatever the hell you want it to be."

"Okay, George whatever the hell you want it to be, why don't you tell me about that suit bag over there and those clothes you're wearing? The new shoes. Where did it all come from?"

"It was delivered. It's mine now."

"What do you mean by delivered?"

"Delivered. That's what I mean. Delivered. They gave it all to me."

Bosch took out his cigarettes, took one and offered the pack to the man. He waved them away.

"Can't afford it. Take me half a day to find enough cans to buy a pack of smokes. I quit."

Bosch nodded.

"How long you been livin' up here, George?"

"All my life."

"When did they kick you out of Camarillo?"

"Who told you that?"

It had been an educated guess, Camarillo being the nearest state institution.

"They did. How long ago was that?"

"If they told you about me, then they would've told you that. I'm not stupid, you know."

"You got me there, George. About the bag and the clothes, when was it all delivered?"

"I don't know."

Bosch got up and went over to the suit bag. There was an identification tag attached to the handle. He turned it over and read Anthony Aliso's name and address. He noticed the bag was lying on top of a cardboard box that was damaged from a tumble down the hill. Bosch tipped the box with his foot and read the markings on the side.

SCOTCH STANDARD HS/T-90 VHS 96-COUNT

He left the box and the suit bag there and went back to the man and squatted again.

"How's last Friday night sound for the delivery?"

"Whatever you say is good."

"It's not what I say, George. Now if you want me to leave you alone and you want to stay here, you've got to help me. If you go into your nut bag, you're not helping me. When was it delivered?"

George tucked his chin down on his chest like a boy who'd been chastised by a teacher. He brought a thumb and forefinger up and pressed them against his eyes. His voice came out as if it were being strangled with piano wire.

"I don't know. They just came and dropped it off for me. That's all I know."

"Who dropped it off?"

George looked up, his eyes bright, and pointed upward with one of his dirty fingers. Bosch looked up and saw a patch of blue sky through the upper limbs of the trees. He blew out his breath in exasperation. This wasn't going anywhere.

"So little green men dropped it down from their spaceship, is that right, George? Is that your story?"

"I didn't say that. I don't know if they were green. I didn't see them."

"But you saw the spaceship?"

"Nope. I didn't say that, neither. I didn't see their craft. Only the landing lights."

Bosch looked at him a moment.

"Perfect size," George said. "They got an invisible beam that measures you from up there, you don't even know it, then they send down the clothes."

"That's great."

Bosch's knees were beginning to ache. He stood up and they painfully cracked.

"I'm getting too old for this shit, George."

"That's a policeman's line. I watched 'Kojak' when I had the house."

"I know. Tell you what, I'm going to take this suit bag with me, if you don't mind. And the box of videotapes."

"Help yourself. I'm not going anywhere. And I don't have no video machine, either."

Bosch walked toward the box and bag, wondering why they had been discarded and not just left in the Rolls. After a moment he decided they must have been in the trunk. And in order to make room for Aliso in there, the killers had yanked them out and thrown them down the hill out of sight. They were in a hurry. It was the kind of decision made in haste. A mistake.

He picked up the suit bag by a corner, careful not to touch the handle, though he doubted there would be any prints on it other than George's. The box was light but bulky. He would have to make a second trip for it. He turned and looked at the homeless man. He decided not to ruin his day yet.

"George, you can keep the clothes for now."

"Okay, thanks."

"You're welcome."

As he climbed back up the hill to the road, Bosch was thinking about how he should declare the area a crime scene and call out SID to process everything. But he couldn't do that. Not without announcing he had been continuing an investigation he had been ordered away from.

It didn't bother him, however, because by the time he got up to the road, he knew he had a new direction. A plan was coming together. Quickly. Bosch was jazzed. When he stepped onto level ground he punched his fist in the air and walked quickly to his car.

Bosch worked out the details in his head while he was driving to Hidden Highlands. The Plan. He had been like a cork floating in a great wide ocean that was the case. Bouncing with the currents, not in control of anything. But now he had an idea, a plan that would hopefully draw Veronica Aliso into the box.

Nash was in the gatehouse when Bosch pulled up. He stepped out and leaned down on Bosch's door.

"Morning, Detective Bosch."

"Howzit going, Captain Nash?"

"It's going, I gotta say your people are creating a bit of a stir already this morning."

"Yeah, well, that can happen. Whaddaya gonna do?"

"Go with the flow, I guess. You going in to catch up with them or you heading to Mrs. Aliso's?"

"I'm going to see the lady."

"Good. Maybe that'll get her off my back. I gotta call, you know."

"Why's she on your back?"

"She's just been calling up wondering why you people have been talkin' to the neighbors all morning."

"What did you tell her?"

"I told her they got a job to do and a murder investigation requires them to talk to a lot of people."

"That's good. I'll see you."

Nash waved him off and opened the gate. Bosch drove to the Aliso house, but before he got there he saw Edgar walking from the front door of the home next door to his car. Bosch stopped and waved him over.

"Harry."

"Jerry. Get anything yet?"

"Nah, not really. Thing about these rich neighborhoods, it's like working a shooting in South Central. Nobody ever wants to talk, nobody saw nothing. I get tired of these people."

"Where's Kiz?"

"She's working the other side of the street. We met at the station and took one car. She's on foot down there somewhere. Hey, Harry, what do you think about her?"

"Kiz? I think she's good."

"No, I don't mean as a cop. You know . . . what do you think?"

Bosch looked at him.

"You mean like you and her? What do I think?"

"Yeah. Me and her."

Bosch knew Edgar was six months divorced and starting to pull his head out of the sand again. But he also knew something about Kiz that he didn't have the right to tell him.

"I don't know, Jerry. Partners shouldn't get involved."

"I suppose. So you going to see the widow now?"

"Yeah."

"Maybe I better go with you. You never know, if she figures out we think she's it, then she's liable to wig out, maybe try to take you out."

"I doubt it. She's too cool for that. But let's go find Kiz. I think both of you should come. I've got a plan now."

Veronica Aliso was waiting for them at her door.

"I've been waiting for you people to come by to explain just what is going on."

"Sorry, Mrs. Aliso," Bosch said. "We've been kind of busy."

She ushered them in.

"Can I get you something?" she asked over her shoulder as she led them in.

"I think we're fine."

Part of the plan was for Bosch to do all the talking, if possible. Rider and Edgar were to intimidate her with their silence and their cold-eyed stares.

Bosch and Rider sat where they had sat before and so did Veronica Aliso. Edgar remained standing on the periphery of the seating section of the living room. He put his hand on the mantel of the fireplace and the look on his face said he would rather be anywhere else on the planet on this Saturday morning.

Veronica Aliso was wearing blue jeans, a light blue Oxford shirt and dirty work boots. Her hair was pulled back and pinned up in the back. She was still very attractive though obviously dressing down. Through her open collar Bosch could see a scattering of freckles that he knew from her video went all the way down her chest.

"Are we interrupting something?" Bosch asked. "Were you about to go out?"

"I wanted to go to the Burbank stables sometime today if I could. I keep a horse there. My husband's body was cremated and I want to take his ashes up the trail into the hills. He loved the hills . . ."

Bosch somberly nodded.

"Well, this won't take too long. First off, you've seen us in the neighborhood this morning. We're just conducting a routine canvass. You never know, maybe someone saw something, maybe somebody watching the house or a car here that shouldn't have been here. You never know."

"Well, I think I'd be the one who would know about any car that shouldn't be here."

"Well, I mean if you weren't here. If you were out and someone was here, you probably wouldn't know."

"How could they get in past the gate?"

"It's a long shot, we know, Mrs. Aliso. It's all we've got right now."

She frowned.

"There's nothing else? What about what you told me the other day? About this man in Las Vegas?"

"Well, Mrs. Aliso, I hate to tell you this, but we went down the wrong path on that. We gathered a lot of information about your husband and initially it looked like that was the way to go. But it didn't work out. We do think we're moving in the right direction now, and we're going to make up for the lost time."

She seemed genuinely stunned.

"I don't understand. The wrong path?"

"Yes, well, I can explain it to you, if you want to hear it. But it involves your husband and some unsavory things."

"Detective, I've prepared myself over the last few days for anything. Tell me."

"Mrs. Aliso, as I think I indicated to you on our last visit, your husband was involved with some very dangerous people in Las Vegas. I think I mentioned them, Joey Marks and Luke Goshen?"

"I don't recall."

She kept the look of bewilderment on her face. She was good. Bosch had to give that to her. She might not have made it in the film business but she could act when she needed to.

"To put it bluntly, they're mobsters," Bosch said. "Organized crime. And it looks like your husband had been working for them for a long time. He took mob money from Vegas and put it into his films. Laundered it through. Then he gave it back to them, after taking out a fee. It was a lot of money and that's where we went down the wrong path. Your husband was about to get audited by the IRS. Did you know that?"

"Audited? No. He didn't tell me anything about an audit."

"Well, we found out about the audit, which likely would have revealed his illegal activities, and we thought maybe these people he did business with became aware of it, too, and had him killed so he wouldn't be able to talk about their business. Only we don't think that anymore."

"I don't understand. Are you sure of this? It seems obvious to me that these people had some involvement."

She faltered a little bit there. Her voice was a little too urgent.

"Well, like I said, we thought that, too. We haven't fully dropped it, but so far it doesn't check out. The man we arrested over there in Vegas, this Goshen fellow I mentioned, he looked pretty good for it, I have to say. But then his alibi turned out to be a rock we couldn't break. It couldn't have been him, Mrs. Aliso. It looks as though somebody went to great lengths to make it look like it was him, even planted a gun in his house, but we know it wasn't."

She looked at him with dull eyes for a moment and then shook her head. Then she made her first real mistake. She should have said that if it wasn't Goshen, then it was probably the other one Bosch had mentioned or some other mobster associate. But she said nothing and that instinctively told Bosch that she knew of the setup on Goshen. She now knew the plan hadn't worked and her mind was probably scrambling.

"So then what will you do?" she finally asked.

"Oh, we already had to let him go."

"No, I mean about the investigation. What's next?"

"Well, we're sort of starting from scratch. Looking at it like maybe it was a planned robbery."

"You said his watch wasn't taken."

"Right. It wasn't. But the Las Vegas angle wasn't a total waste. We found out that your husband was carrying a lot of money with him when he landed here that night. He was taking it back here to run through his company. To clean it up. It was a lot of money. Nearly a million dollars. He was carrying it for—"

"A *million* dollars?"

That was her second mistake. To Bosch, her emphasis on *million* and her shock betrayed her knowledge that there had been far less than that in Tony Aliso's briefcase. Bosch watched as her eyes stared blankly and all her movement was interior. He guessed—and hoped—she was now wondering where the rest of the money was.

"Yes," he said. "See, the man who gave your husband the money, the one we first thought was a suspect, is an FBI agent who infiltrated the organization your husband worked for. That is why his alibi is so solid. Anyway, he told us that your husband was carrying a million dollars. It was all in cash and there was so much that he couldn't fit it all into his briefcase. He had to put about half of it in his suit bag."

He paused for a few moments. He could tell the story was playing in her internal theater. Her eyes had that faraway look in them. He remembered that look from her movie. But this time it was for real. He hadn't even finished the interview, but she was already making plans. He could see it.

"Was the money marked by the FBI?" she asked. "I mean, could they trace it that way?"

"No, unfortunately their agent did not have it long enough to do that. There was too much of it, frankly. But the transaction did take place in an office with a hidden video camera. There is no doubt, Tony left there with a million dollars. Uh . . ."

Bosch paused to open his briefcase and quickly consult a page from a file.

". . . actually, it was a million, seventy-six thousand. All in cash."

Veronica's eyes went down to the floor as she nodded. Bosch studied her but his concentration was interrupted when he thought he heard a sound from somewhere in the house. It suddenly occurred to him that maybe there was someone else there. They had never asked.

"Did you hear that?" Bosch asked.

"What?"

"I thought I heard something. Are you alone in the house?"

"Yes."

"I thought I heard a bump or something."

"You want me to look around?" Edgar offered.

"Oh, no," Veronica said quickly, ". . . uh, it probably was just the cat."

Bosch didn't remember seeing any sign of a cat when he had been in the house before. He glanced at Kiz and saw her almost imperceptibly turn her head to signal she didn't remember a cat either. He decided to let it go for the time being.

"Anyway," he said, "that's why we're canvassing and that's why we're here. We need to ask you some questions. They might go over some of the same ground we've covered before but, like I said, we're kind of starting over. It won't take too much longer. Then you'll be able to go to the stables."

"Fine. Go ahead."

"Would you mind if I have a drink of water first?"

"No, of course not. I'm sorry, I should have asked. Anybody else want something?"

"I'll pass," Edgar said.

"I'm fine," Rider said.

Veronica Aliso stood up and headed toward the hallway. Bosch gave her a head start and then stood up and followed.

"You did ask," he said to her back. "But I turned it down. I didn't think I'd get thirsty."

He followed her into the kitchen, where she opened a cabinet and took down a glass. Bosch looked around. It was a large kitchen with stainless-steel appliances and black granite countertops. There was a center island with a sink in it.

"Tap water'd be fine for me," he said, taking the glass from her and filling it at the island.

He turned and leaned against the counter and drank from it. He then poured the rest out and put the glass on the counter.

"That's all you want?"

"Yes. Just needed something to wash the dust down, I guess."

He smiled and she didn't.

"Well then, should we go back to the living room?" she asked.

"That'd be fine."

He followed her out of the kitchen. Just before he entered the hallway, he turned back and his eyes swept across the gray-tiled floor. He didn't see what he thought should be there.

Bosch spent the next fifteen minutes asking mostly questions that had been asked six days earlier and that had little bearing on the case now. He was going through the motions, the finishing touches. The trap was baited and this was his way of quietly stepping back from it. Finally, when he thought he had said and asked enough, Bosch closed the notebook in which he had been scribbling notes he'd never looked at again and stood up. He thanked her for her time and Veronica Aliso walked the three detectives to the door. Bosch was the last one out, and as he stepped over the threshold she spoke to him. He somehow knew that she would. There were parts to her act that had to be played as well.

"Keep me informed, Detective Bosch. Please keep me informed."

Bosch turned and looked back at her.

"Oh, I will. If anything happens, you'll be the first to know."

Bosch drove Edgar and Rider back to their car. He didn't speak about the interview until he pulled in behind it.

"So what do you think?" he asked as he got out his cigarettes.

"I think we sunk the hook but good," Edgar said.

"Yeah," Rider said. "It's going to be interesting."

Bosch lit a cigarette.

"What about the cat?" he asked.

"What?" Edgar asked.

"The noise in the house. She said it was the cat. But in the kitchen there were no food bowls on the floor."

"Maybe they were outside," Edgar offered.

Bosch shook his head.

"I think people who keep cats inside feed them inside," he said. "In the hills you're supposed to keep 'em in. Coyotes. Anyway, I don't like cats. I get allergic to them. I can usually tell when somebody has a cat. I don't think she has a cat. Kiz, you didn't see a cat in there, did you?"

"I spent all Monday morning in there and I never saw a cat."

"You think maybe it was the guy then?" Edgar asked. "Whoever she worked this with?"

"Maybe. I think somebody was in there. Maybe her lawyer."

"Nah, lawyers don't hide like that. They come out and confront."

"True."

"Should we watch the place, see who comes out?" Edgar asked.

Bosch thought a moment.

"No," Bosch said. "They spot us and they'll know the money thing is just bait. Better we let it go. Better just to get out of here, go get set up. We gotta get ready."

VII

During his time in Vietnam, Bosch's primary assignment had been to fight the war in the tunnel networks that ranged beneath the villages in the Cu Chi province, to go into the darkness they called the black echo and to come back alive. But the tunnel work was done quickly, and between those missions he spent days in the bush, fighting and waiting under the jungle canopy. One time he and a handful of others got cut off from their unit and Bosch spent a night sitting in the elephant grass, his back pressed against the back of an Alabama boy named Donnel Fredrick, listening as a company of VC fighters moved through. They sat there and waited for Charlie to stumble onto them. There was nothing else they could do and there were too many to fight. So they waited and the minutes went by like hours. They all made it through, though Donnel was later killed in a foxhole by a direct mortar hit—friendly fire. Bosch always thought that night in the elephant grass was the closest he'd ever come to experiencing a miracle.

Bosch remembered that night sometimes when he was alone on a stakeout or in a tight spot. He thought about it now as he sat cross-legged against the base of a eucalyptus tree ten yards from the tarp the homeless man, George, had erected. Over his clothes, he wore a green plastic poncho he always kept in the trunk of his work car. The candy bars he had with him were Hershey's chocolate with almonds, the same kind he had taken with him into the bush so long ago. And like that night in the tall grass, he had not moved for what seemed like hours. It was dark, with only a glimmer of moonlight making it down through the overhead canopy, and he was waiting. He wanted a cigarette but couldn't afford to open a flame in the blackness. Every now and then he thought he could hear Edgar make a move or readjust himself twenty yards to his right, but he couldn't be sure that it was his partner and not a deer or maybe a coyote passing through.

George had told him there were coyotes. When he had put the old man into the back of Kiz's car for the ride to the hotel they were putting him up in, he had warned Bosch. But Bosch wasn't afraid of coyotes.

The old man had not gone easily. He was sure they were there to take him back to Camarillo. And the truth was, he should have been going back there but the institution wouldn't have him, not without a government-punched ticket. Instead he was going to be treated to a couple of nights at the Mark Twain Hotel in Hollywood. It wasn't a bad place. Bosch had lived there for more than a year while his house was being rebuilt. The worst room there beat a tarp in the woods hands down. But Bosch knew George might not see it that way.

By eleven-thirty the traffic up on Mulholland had thinned down to a car every five minutes or so. Bosch couldn't see them because of the incline and the thickness of the brush, but he could hear them and see the lights wash through the foliage above him as the cars made the curve. He was alert now because a car had slowly gone by twice in the last fifteen minutes, once each way. Bosch had sensed that it was the same car because the engine was over-throttled to compensate for a skip in the engine stroke.

And now it was back for a third time. Bosch listened intently as he heard the familiar engine, and this time there was the added sound of tires turning on gravel. The car was pulling off the road. In a few moments the engine stopped and the following silence was punctuated only by the sound of a car door being opened and then closed. Bosch slowly got up on his haunches, as painful as it was on his knees, and got ready. He looked into the darkness to his right, toward Edgar's position, and saw nothing. He then looked up the incline, toward the edge, and waited.

In a few moments he could see the beam of a flashlight cut through the brush. The light was pointed downward and was moving in a back-and-forth sweeping pattern as its holder slowly descended the hill toward the tarp. Under his poncho Bosch held his gun in one hand and a flashlight in the other, his thumb paused on the switch and ready to turn it on.

The movement of the light stopped. Bosch guessed that its holder had found the spot where the suit bag should have been. After a moment of seeming hesitation the beam was lifted and it swept through the woods, flicking across Bosch for a fraction of a second. But it didn't come back to him. Instead, it held on the blue tarp as Bosch guessed it probably would. The light began advancing, its holder stumbling once as he or she went toward George's home. A few moments later, Bosch saw the beam moving behind the blue plastic. He felt another charge of adrenaline begin to course through his body. Again, his mind flashed on Vietnam. This time it was the tunnels that he thought of. Coming upon an enemy in the darkness. The fear and thrill of it. It was only after he had left that place safely that he acknowledged to himself there had been a thrill to it. And in looking to replace that thrill, he had joined the cops.

Bosch slowly raised himself, hoping his knees wouldn't crack, as he watched the light. They had placed the suit bag in underneath the shelter after stuffing it first with crumpled newspaper. Bosch began to move as quietly as he could in behind the tarp. He was coming from the left. According to the plan, Edgar would be coming from the right, but it was still too dark for Bosch to see him.

Bosch was ten feet away now and could hear the excited breathing of the person under the tarp. Then there was the sound of a zipper being pulled open followed by the sharp cut-off of breath.

"Shit!"

Bosch moved in after hearing the curse. He realized he recognized the man's voice just as he came around the open side of the tarp and raised both his weapon and his flashlight from beneath his poncho.

"*Freeze! Police!*" Bosch yelled at the same moment he put on his light. "All right, come out of there, Powers."

Almost immediately Edgar's light came on from Bosch's right.

"What the . . . ?" Edgar started to say.

Crouched there in the crossing beams of light was Officer Ray Powers. In full uniform, the big patrol cop held a flashlight in one hand and a gun in the other. A look of utter surprise played across his face. His mouth dropped open.

"Bosch," he said. "What the fuck are you doing here?"

"That's our line, Powers," Edgar said angrily. "Don't you know what the fuck you just did? You walked right into a—what are *you* doing here, man?"

Powers lowered his gun and slid it back into its holster.

"I was—there was a report. Somebody must've seen you guys sneaking in here. They said they saw two men sneaking around."

Bosch stepped back from the tarp, keeping his gun raised.

"Come out of there, Powers," he said.

Powers did as he was commanded. Bosch put the beam from his light right in the man's face.

"What about this report? Who called it in?"

"Just some guy driving by up on the road. Must've seen you going in here. Can you get the light out of my face?"

Bosch didn't move the focus of the light an inch.

"Then what?" he asked. "Who'd he call?"

Bosch knew that after Rider had dropped them off, her job was to park on a nearby street and keep her scanner on. If there had been such a radio call, she would have heard it and called off the patrol response, telling the dispatcher it was a surveillance operation.

"He didn't call it in. I was cruising by and he waved me down."

"You mean he claimed he just saw two guys going into the woods?"

"Uh, no. No, he waved me down earlier. I just didn't get a chance to check it out until now."

Bosch and Edgar had gone into the woods at two-thirty. It was full daylight then and Powers hadn't even been on duty yet. And the only car that had been in the area at the time was Rider's. Bosch knew Powers was lying, and it was all beginning to fall into place. His finding the body, his fingerprint on the trunk, the pepper spray on the victim, the reason the bindings were taken off the wrists. It was already there, in the details.

"How much earlier?" Bosch asked.

"Uh, it was right after I came on duty. I can't remember the time."

"Daylight?"

"Yeah, daylight. Can you put the fuckin' light down?"

Bosch ignored him again.

"What was the citizen's name?"

"I didn't get it. Just some guy in a Jag, he waved me down at Laurel Canyon and Mulholland. Told me what he saw and I said I'd check it when I got the chance. So I was checking it out and saw the bag here. I figured it belonged to the guy in the trunk. I saw the bulletin you people put out about the car and the luggage, so I knew you were looking for it. Sorry I blew it, but you people should've let the watch commander know what you were doing. Jesus, Bosch, I'm going blind here."

"Yeah, it's blown all right," Bosch said, finally lowering the light. He lowered his gun to his side also but didn't put it away. He kept it ready there, under the poncho. "Might as well pack it in now. Powers, go on up the hill to your car. Jerry, grab the bag."

Bosch climbed up the hill behind Powers, careful to keep the light up and back on the patrol cop. He knew that if they had cuffed Powers down by the tarp, they'd never get him up the hill because of the steep terrain and because Powers might fight them. So he had to scam him. He let him think he was clear.

At the top of the hill, Bosch waited until Edgar came up behind them before making a move.

"Know what I don't get, Powers?" he said.

"What, Bosch?"

"I don't get why you waited until dark to check out a complaint you got during the day. You're told that two suspicious-looking characters went into the woods and you decide to wait until it's late and it's dark to check it out by yourself."

"I told you. Didn't have the time."

"You're full of shit, Powers," Edgar said.

He had either just caught on or had played along with Bosch perfectly.

Bosch saw Powers's eyes go dead as he went inside to try to figure out what to do. In that instant Bosch raised his gun again and aimed it at a spot between those two vacant portals.

"Don't think so much, Powers," he said. "It's over. Now stand still. Jerry?"

Edgar moved in behind the big cop and yanked his gun out of its holster. He dropped it on the ground and jerked one of Powers's hands behind his back. He cuffed the hand and then he did the other. When he was done, he picked up the gun. It seemed to Bosch that Powers was still inside, still staring blankly at nothing. Then he came back.

"You people, you have just fucked up big time," he said, controlled rage in his voice.

"We'll see about that. Jerry, you got him? I want to call Kiz."

"Go ahead. I got his ass. I hope he does make a move. Go ahead, Powers, do something stupid for me."

"Fuck you, Edgar! You don't know what you've just done. You're goin' down, bro. You're going *down!*"

Edgar remained silent. Bosch took the Motorola two-way out of his pocket, turned it on and keyed the mike.

"Kiz, you there?"

"Here. I'm here."

"Come on over. Hurry."

"On my way."

Bosch put the two-way back and they stood there in silence for a minute until they saw the flashing blue light lead Rider's car around the bend. When it pulled up, the lights swept repeatedly through the tops of the trees on the incline. Bosch realized that from below, down in George's shelter, the lights on the trees might look as if they were coming from the sky. It all came to Bosch then. George's spacecraft had been Powers's patrol car. The abduction had been a traffic stop. The perfect way to get a man carrying nearly a half million in cash to stop. Powers had simply waited for Aliso's white Rolls, probably at Mulholland and Laurel Canyon, then followed and put the lights on when they approached the secluded curve. Tony probably thought he had been speeding. He pulled over.

Rider pulled off the road behind the patrol car. Bosch came over and opened the back door and looked in at her.

"Harry, what is it?" she asked.

"Powers. Powers is it."

"Oh my God."

"Yeah. I want you and Jerry to take him in. I'll follow with his car."

He walked back over to Edgar and Powers.

"Okay, let's go."

"You people have all lost your jobs," Powers said. "You fucked yourselves up."

"You can tell us about it at the station."

Bosch jerked him by the arm, feeling its thickness and strength. He and Edgar then hustled him into the back of Rider's car. Edgar went around and got in the other side next to him.

Looking in through the open rear door, Bosch went over what would be the procedure.

"Take all his shit away and lock him in one of the interview rooms," he said. "Make sure you get his cuff key. I'll be right behind you."

Bosch slammed the door and knocked twice on the roof. He then went to the patrol car, put the suit bag in the back seat and got in. Rider pulled out and Bosch followed. They sped west toward Laurel Canyon.

It took Billets less than an hour to come in. When she got there, the three of them were sitting at the homicide table. Bosch was going through the murder book with Rider while she took notes on a legal pad. Edgar was at the typewriter. Billets walked in with a force and look on her face that clearly showed the situation. Bosch hadn't talked to her yet. It had been Rider who had called her in from home.

"What are you doing to me?" Billets asked, her piercing eyes clearly fixed on Bosch.

What she was really saying to him was that he was the team leader and the responsibility for this potential fuckup rested squarely on him. That was okay with Bosch, because not only was that right and fair, but in the half hour he'd had to go through the murder book and the other evidence, his confidence had grown.

"What am I doing to you? I'm bringing in your killer."

"I told you to conduct a quiet and careful investigation," Billets responded. "I didn't tell you to conduct some kind of half-assed sting operation and then drag a cop in here! I can't believe this."

Billets was now pacing behind Rider's back without looking at them. The squad room was deserted except for the three of them and the angry lieutenant.

"It's Powers, Lieutenant," Bosch said. "If you'd calm down, we—"

"Oh, it's him, is it? You have the evidence of that? Great! I'll call a DA in here right now and we'll write up the charges then. Because you really had me worried there for a minute that you three jerked this guy off the street with just enough probable cause to charge him with jaywalking."

Now she was looking at Bosch with the angry eyes again. She had even stopped her pacing to level them at him. He responded as calmly as he could.

"First of all, it was my decision to take him off the street. And you're right, we don't have enough to call out a DA yet. But we'll get it. There's no doubt in my mind he's the man. It's him and the widow."

"Well, I'm glad there's no doubt in *your* mind but you're not the DA or the goddamned jury."

He didn't respond. It was no use. He had to wait for her anger to ebb and then they could talk sensibly.

"Where is he?" Billets asked.

"Room three," Bosch said.

"What did you tell the watch commander?"

"Nothing. It happened at the end of shift. Powers was going to grab the suit bag and then go punch out. We were able to bring him in while most everybody else was still up in roll call. I parked his car and dropped the key at the watch office. I told the watch lieutenant we were using Powers for a little while on a warrant, that we wanted a uniform with us when we knocked on a door. He said fine and then I expect he went off shift. As far as I know, nobody knows we have him back there."

Billets thought for a moment. When she spoke, she was calmer and more like the person who normally sat behind the desk in the glass office.

"Okay, I'm going to go back there and get some coffee, see if I get asked about him. When I come back, we'll go over all of this in detail and see what we have."

She walked slowly to the hallway at the rear of the squad room that led to the watch office. Bosch watched her go and then picked up the phone and dialed the number of the security office of the Mirage hotel and casino. He told the officer who answered who he was and that he needed to speak with Hank Meyer immediately. When the officer mentioned that it was after midnight, Bosch told him it was an emergency and that he was sure that if Meyer was informed who needed to speak with him, he would return the call. Bosch gave him all the numbers he could be reached at, beginning with his number at the homicide table, and hung up. He went back to his work with the murder book.

"Did you say he's in three?"

Bosch looked up. Billets was back, a cup of steaming coffee in her hand. He nodded.

"I want to have a look," she said.

Bosch got up and walked with her down the hallway to the four doors leading to the interview rooms. Doors marked one and two were on the left, three and four on the right. But there was no fourth interview room. The room marked four was actually a small cubicle with a one-way glass window that allowed for observation of room three. In three, the other side of the glass was a mirror. Billets entered four and looked through the glass at Powers. He sat ramrod straight at a table in a chair directly opposite the mirror. His hands were cuffed behind his back. He still wore his uniform but his equipment belt had been removed. He stared straight ahead at his own reflection in the mirror. This created an eerie effect in the fourth room because it appeared that he was looking right at them, as if there were no mirror or glass between them.

Billets said nothing. She just looked back at the man staring at her.

"There is a lot hanging in the balance tonight, Harry," she said quietly.

"I know," he said.

They stood there silently for a few moments until Edgar opened the door and told Bosch that Hank Meyer was on the phone. Bosch headed back, picked up the phone and told Meyer what he needed. Meyer said he was at home and that he'd have to go into the hotel, but he would call back as soon as possible. Bosch thanked him and hung up. Billets had now taken one of the empty seats at the homicide table.

"Okay," she said, "one of you tell me exactly how this went down tonight."

Bosch remained in the lead and took the next fifteen minutes to recount how he found Tony Aliso's suit bag, set up the sting through Veronica Aliso and then waited in the woods off Mulholland until Powers showed up. He explained how the story Powers had offered for his being there did not make sense.

"What else did he say?" Billets asked at the end.

"Nothing. Jerry and Kiz put him in the room and that's where he's been ever since."

"What else have you got?"

"For starters, we have his print on the inside of the trunk lid. We also have a record of association with the widow."

Billets raised her eyebrows.

"That's what we were working on when you came in. On Sunday night when Jerry ran the victim's name through the computer, we got a hit on a burglary report from back in March. Somebody hit the Aliso house. Jerry pulled the report but it looked unconnected. Just a routine burglary. And it was, except the officer who took the initial report from Mrs. Aliso was Powers. We think the relationship started with the burglary. That's when they met. After that, we have the gate records. Police patrols of Hidden Highlands are recorded on the gate logs by the car's roof number. The logs show the car assigned to Powers—the Zebra car—has been going in there two, three nights a week on patrol, always on the nights we know from credit card records that Tony was out of town. I think he was poppin' over there to see Veronica."

"What else?" the lieutenant asked. "So far all you've got is a bunch of coincidences strung together."

"There are no coincidences," Bosch said. "Not like this."

"Then what else have you got?"

"Like I said, his story about why he came down into the woods doesn't check out. He came down looking for the suit bag and the only way he would have known that it was worth coming back for was through Veronica. It's him, Lieutenant. It's him."

Billets thought about this. Bosch believed the facts he was giving her were beginning to have a cumulative effect in convincing her. He had one thing left with which to nail her down.

"There's one other thing. Remember our problem with Veronica? If she was involved in this, how did she get out of Hidden Highlands and not have it noted on the gate log?"

"Right."

"Well, the gate log shows that on the night of the murder, the Zebra car cruised through on patrol. Twice. He was in and out both times. First time he was logged in at ten and out at ten-ten. Then back in at eleven-forty-eight and out four minutes later. It was noted as just routine patrol."

"Okay, so?"

"So on the first time, he cruises in and picks her up. She gets down on the floor in the back. It's dark out, the gate guy only sees Powers heading back out. They go and wait for Tony, do the deed and then Powers takes her back home—the second set of entries on the log."

"It works," Billets said, nodding her approval. "The actual abduction, how do you see it?"

"We've figured all along it took two people to do this job. First off, Veronica had to know from Tony what flight he was taking. So that set the time frame. Powers picks her up that night and they go to Laurel Canyon and Mulholland and wait for the white Rolls to go by. We figure that happens about eleven or so. Powers follows until Tony is close to the curve through the woods. He puts on the lights and pulls him over, like a routine traffic stop. Only he tells Tony to step out and go to the back of the car. Maybe he makes him open the trunk, maybe he does that himself after he cuffs him. Either way, the trunk is opened and Powers has a problem. Tony's suit bag and a box of videos are in the trunk and that doesn't leave much room for him. Powers doesn't have much time. A car could come around the bend any moment and light up the whole thing. So he takes the suit bag and the box out and throws them down the hill into the woods. He then tells Tony to get in the trunk. Tony says no or maybe he struggles a bit. Either way, Powers takes out his pepper spray and gives him a shot in the face. Tony is then real manageable, easy to throw into the trunk. Maybe Powers pulled his shoes off then to stop him from kicking around in there, making noise."

"That's when Veronica pops out," Rider said, picking up the story. "She drives the Rolls while Powers follows in the squad car. They knew where they were going. They needed a spot where the car wouldn't be found for a couple days, giving Powers time to get over to Vegas on Saturday, plant the gun and lay down a few more clues like the anonymous call to Metro. That call was what was supposed to put the finger on Luke Goshen. Not the fingerprints. That was just luck for them. Anyway, that's getting ahead of the story. Veronica drives the Rolls and Powers follows. To the clearing over the Bowl. She pops the trunk and Powers leans in and does the job. Or maybe he puts one cap in Tony and he makes Veronica do the second. That way they're partners for good, partners in blood."

Billets nodded, a serious look on her face.

"It seems kind of risky. What if he had to take a radio call? The whole plan would go down the drain."

"We thought of that and Jerry checked with the watch office. Gomez was the CO Friday night. He says he remembers that Powers had such a busy shift he didn't take a dinner break until ten. He doesn't recall hearing from him until just before end of watch."

Billets nodded again.

"What about the shoe prints recovered? Are they his?"

"Powers got lucky there," Edgar said. "He's wearing brand-new boots in there. Looks like he maybe just bought 'em today."

"Shit!"

"Yeah," Bosch said. "We figure he saw the shoe prints on the table last night at the Cat and Fiddle. He went out and got new ones today."

"Oh, man . . ."

"Well, maybe there's still a chance he didn't get rid of the old ones. We're working on a search warrant for his place. Oh, and our luck ain't so bad, either. Jerry, tell her about the spray."

Edgar leaned forward on the table.

"I went back to the supply post, took a look at the sheet. On Sunday Powers signed out an OC cartridge. Only I then went and looked at the fifty-one list in the watch loo's office. No use-of-force reported by Powers in this deployment period."

"So," Billets said, "he somehow used his pepper spray, because he had to get a refill cartridge but he never reported using the spray to his watch commander."

"Right."

Billets thought about things for a few moments before speaking again.

"Okay," she said, "what you've come up with quickly is all good stuff. But it's not enough. It's a circumstantial case and most of this can be explained away. Even if you could prove he and the widow have been meeting, it doesn't prove murder. The fingerprint on the trunk can be explained by sloppy work at the crime scene. Who knows, maybe that's all it really was."

"I doubt it," Bosch said.

"Well, your doubts aren't good enough. Where do we go from here?"

"We still have some things in the fire. Jerry's going for a warrant based on what we've got so far. If we get inside Powers's house, maybe we find the shoes, maybe we find something else. We'll see. I also have an angle in Vegas working. We figure that for them to have pulled this off, Powers had to have followed Tony over there once or twice, you know, to know about Goshen and pick him to hang it all on. If we're lucky, Powers would've wanted to stay right on Tony. That would mean staying at the Mirage. You can't stay there without a trail. You can pay cash but you've got to give a legit credit card imprint to cover room charges, phone calls, things like that. In other words, you can't register under any name you don't have on a credit card. I've got a guy checking."

"Okay, it's a start," Billets said.

She nodded her head, cupped a hand over her mouth and lapsed into a contemplative silence for a long moment.

"What it all comes down to is that we need to break him, don't we?" she finally asked.

Bosch nodded.

"Probably. Unless we get lucky with the warrant."

"You're not going to break him. He's a cop, he knows the angles, he knows the rules of evidence."

"We'll see."

She looked at her watch. Bosch looked at his and saw it was now one o'clock.

"We're in trouble," Billets said solemnly. "We won't be able to contain this much past dawn. After that I will have to make proper notification of what we've done and what we've got going. If that happens, you can count on us not being involved, and worse."

Bosch leaned forward.

"Go back home, Lieutenant," he said. "You were never here. Let us have the night. Come back in at nine tomorrow. Bring a DA back with you if you want. Make sure it's somebody who will go to the edge with you. If you don't know one, I can call somebody. But give us till nine. Eight hours. Then you come in and we either have the complete package tied up for you or you go ahead and do what you have to do."

She looked carefully at each one of them, took a deep breath and exhaled slowly.

"Good luck," she said.

She nodded, got up and left them there.

Outside the door to interview room three, Bosch paused and composed his thoughts. He knew that everything would turn on what happened inside the room. He had to break Powers and that would be no easy task. Powers was a cop. He knew all the tricks. But somehow Bosch had to find a weakness he could exploit until the big man went down. He knew it was going to be a brutal match. He blew out his breath and opened the door.

Bosch stepped into the interview room, took the chair directly across from Powers and spread out the two sheets of paper he carried with him in front of Powers.

"Okay, Powers, I'm here to tell you what's what."

"You can save it, asshole. The only one I want to talk to is my lawyer."

"Well, that's what I'm here for. Why don't you take it easy and we'll talk about it?"

"Take it easy? You people arrest me, hook me up like a goddamn criminal and then leave me in here for a fucking hour and a half while you sit out there and figure out how fucked up this is, and you want me to take it easy? What planet are you on, Bosch? I'm not taking anything easy. Now cut me loose or give me the goddamn phone!"

"Well, that's the problem, isn't it? Deciding whether to book you or cut you loose. That's why I came in, Powers. I thought maybe you could help us out on that."

Powers didn't appear to pick up on that. His eyes dropped to the center of the table and they were working—small, quick movements, looking for the angles.

"This is what is what," Bosch said. "If I book you now, then we call the lawyer and we both know that is going to be that. No lawyer is gonna let his client talk to the cops. We'll just have to go to court and you know what that means. You'll be suspended, no pay. We'll go for no bail and you'll sit in the can nine, ten months and then maybe it gets straightened out in your favor. And maybe not. Meantime, you're all over the front page. Your mother, father, neighbors . . . well, you know how that goes."

Bosch took out a cigarette and put it in his mouth. He didn't light it and he didn't offer one to Powers. He remembered offering one to the big cop at the crime scene and being turned down.

"The alternative to that," he continued, "is that we sit here and try to get this straightened out right now. You've got two forms there in front of you. The good thing about dealing with a cop like this is I don't really need to explain this stuff to you. The first one's a rights form. You know what that is. You sign that you understand your rights and then you make your choice. Talk to me or call your lawyer after we book you. The second form is the attorney waiver."

Powers stared silently down at the pages and Bosch put a pen down on the table.

"I'll take the cuffs off when you're ready to sign," Bosch said. "See, now the bad thing about dealing with a cop is that I can't bluff you. You know the game. You know if you sign that waiver and talk to me, you'll either talk yourself out of this or right into it. . . . I can give you more time to think about it, if you want."

"I don't need any more time," he said. "Take off the cuffs."

Bosch got up and went around behind Powers.

"You right or left?"

"Right."

There was barely enough room between the back of the big man and the wall to work on the cuffs. It was a dangerous position to be in with most suspects. But Powers was a cop and he probably knew that the moment he became violent was the moment he lost any chance of getting out of this room and back to his life. He also had to assume someone was watching and ready behind the glass in room four. Bosch unhooked the right cuff and closed it around one of the metal slats of the chair.

Powers scribbled signatures across both forms. Bosch tried to give no indication of his excitement. Powers was making a mistake. Bosch took the pen from him and put it in his pocket.

"Put your arm behind you."

"Come on, Bosch. Treat me like a human. If we're going to talk, let's talk."

"Put your arm behind you."

Powers did as he was told and blew out his breath in frustration. Bosch recuffed his wrists through the metal slat at the back of the chair and then took his seat again. He cleared his throat, going over the last details in his mind. He knew his mission here. He had to make Powers believe he had the edge, that he had a chance to get out. If he believed that, then he might start talking. If he started talking, Bosch thought he could win the fight.

"Okay," Bosch said. "I'm going to lay it out for you. If you can convince me that we have it wrong, then you'll be out of here before the sun's up."

"That's all I want."

"Powers, we know you have a relationship with Veronica Aliso predating her husband's death. We know you followed him to Vegas on at least two occasions prior to the killing."

Powers kept his eyes on the table in front of him. But Bosch was able to read them like the needles of a polygraph machine. There had been a slight tremor in the pupils when Bosch mentioned Las Vegas.

"That's right," Bosch said. "We've got the records from the Mirage. That was careless, Powers, leaving a record like that. We can put you in Vegas with Tony Aliso."

"So I like goin' to Vegas, big deal. Tony Aliso was there? Wow, what a coincidence. From what I heard, he went there a lot. What else you got?"

"We've got your print, Powers. Fingerprint. Inside the car. You got a refill of pepper spray on Sunday, but you never filed a use-of-force report explaining how you used it."

"Accidental discharge. I didn't file a use-of-force because there wasn't any. You haven't got shit. My fingerprint? You're right, you've probably got prints. But I was in that car, asshole. I'm the one who found the body, remember? This is a joke, man. I'm thinking I better just get my lawyer in here and take my chances. No DA is going to touch this bullshit with a ten-foot pole."

Bosch ignored the baiting and went on.

"And last but not least, we have your little climb down the hill tonight. Your story is for shit, Powers. You went down there to look for Aliso's suit bag because you knew it was there and you thought it had something you and the widow overlooked before. About a half million dollars. The only question I really have is whether she called you up and told you or if that was you in her house this morning when we dropped by."

Bosch saw the pupils jump again slightly but then they went flat.

"Like I said, I'll take that lawyer now."

"I guess you're just the errand boy, right? She told you to go and get the money while she waited at the mansion."

Powers started laughing in a fake way.

"I like that, Bosch. Errand boy. Too bad I barely know the woman.

But it's a good try. Good try. I like you, too, Bosch, but I gotta tell you something."

He leaned across the table and lowered his voice.

"I ever run across you again on the outside, you know, when it's just me and you, head to head, I'm going to seriously fuck you up."

He straightened up again and nodded. Bosch smiled.

"You know, I don't think I was sure until now. But now I'm sure. You did it, Powers. You're the man. And there is never going to be an outside for you. Never. So tell me, whose idea was it? Was she the first one to bring it up or was that you?"

Powers stared sullenly down at the table and shook his head.

"Let me see if I can figure it out," Bosch said. "I guess you went up there to that big house and saw all that they had, the money, maybe heard about Tony and his Rolls, and it just went on from there. I'm betting it was your idea, Powers. But I think she knew you would come up with it. See, she's a smart woman. She knew you would come up with it. And she waited. . . .

"And you know what? We've got nothing on her. Nothing. She played you perfect, man. Right down the line. She's going to do the walk and *you*"—he pointed at Powers's chest—"are going to do the time. Is that how you want it?"

Powers leaned back, a bemused smile on his face.

"You don't get it, do you?" Powers said. "You're the errand boy here, but look at yourself. You've got nothin' to deliver. Look at what you've got. You can't tie me to Aliso. I found the body, man. I opened the car. If you found a print, then that's when I left it. All the rest is a bunch of bullshit adding up to nothing. You go in to see a prosecutor with that, they're going to laugh your ass out onto Temple Street. So go get me the phone, errand boy, and let's get it on. Just go get me the phone."

"Not yet, Powers," Bosch said. "Not just yet."

Bosch sat at his spot at the homicide table with his head down on his folded arms. An empty coffee cup was near his elbow. A cigarette he had perched on the edge of the table had burned down to the butt, leaving one more scar on the old wood.

Bosch was alone. It was almost six and there was just the hint of dawn's light coming through the windows that ran high along the east wall of the room. He'd gone at it for more than four hours with Powers and had gained no ground. He hadn't even made a dent in Powers's cool demeanor. The first rounds had assuredly gone to the big patrol cop.

Bosch wasn't asleep, though. He was simply resting and waiting and his thoughts remained focused on Powers. Bosch had no doubts. He was sure that he had the right man sitting handcuffed in the interview room. What minimal evidence they had certainly pointed to Powers. But it was more than the evidence that convinced him. It was experience and gut instinct. Bosch believed an innocent man would have been scared, not smug as Powers had been. An innocent man would not have taunted Bosch. And so what still remained now was to take away that smugness and break him. Bosch was tired but still felt up to the task. The only thing that worried him was time. Time was against him.

Bosch raised his head and looked at his watch. Billets would be back in three hours. He picked up the empty cup, used his palm to push the dead cigarette and its ashes into it and dropped it into the trash can under the table. He stood up, lit another cigarette and took a walk down the aisle between the crime tables. He tried to clear his mind, to get ready for the next round.

He thought about paging Edgar to see if he and Rider had found anything yet, anything at all that could help, but decided against it. They knew that time was important. They would have either called or come back if they had something.

As he stood at the far end of the squad room and these thoughts traveled through his mind, his eyes fell on the sex crimes table, and he realized after a moment that he was looking at a Polaroid photo of the girl who had come into the station with her mother on Friday to report that she had been raped. The photo was on the top of a stack of Polaroids that were paper-clipped to the outside of the case envelope. Detective Mary Cantu had left it on the top of her pile for Monday. Without thinking about it, Bosch pulled the stack of photos from beneath the clip and began to look through them. The girl had been badly mistreated and the bruises documented on her body by Cantu's camera were a depressing testament to all that was wrong with the city. Bosch always found it easier to deal with victims who were no longer living. The live ones haunted him because they could never be consoled. Not fully. They were forever left with the question why.

Sometimes Bosch thought of his city as some kind of vast drain that pulled all bad things toward a spot where they swirled around in a deep concentration. It was a place where it seemed the good people were often outnumbered by the bad. The creeps and schemers, the rapists and killers. It was a place that could easily produce someone like Powers. Too easily.

Bosch put the photos back under the clip, embarrassed by his thoughtless voyeurism of the girl's pain. He went back to the homicide table, picked up the phone and dialed his home number. It was nearly twenty-four hours since he had been to his house, and his hope was that Eleanor Wish would answer—he had left the key under the mat—or there might be a message from her. After three rings the line was picked up and he heard his own voice on tape tell himself to leave a message. He punched in his code to check for messages and the machine told him he had none.

He stood there a long moment thinking about Eleanor, the phone still at his ear, when suddenly he heard her voice.

"Harry, is that you?"

"Eleanor?"

"I'm here, Harry."

"Why didn't you answer?"

"I didn't think it would be for me."

"When did you get there?"

"Last night. I've been waiting for you. Thanks for leaving the key."

"You're welcome. . . . Eleanor, where'd you go?"

There was a beat of silence before she answered.

"I went back to Vegas. I needed to get my car . . . clear out my bank account, things like that. Where have you been all night?"

"Working. We have a new suspect. We're holding him here. Did you go by your apartment?"

"No. There was no reason to. I just did what I had to do and drove back."

"I'm sorry if I woke you."

"That's okay. I was worried about where you were, but I didn't want to call you there in case you were in the middle of something."

Bosch wanted to ask her what came next for them, but he felt such a sense of happiness that she was there in his home that he didn't dare to ruin the moment.

"I don't know how much longer I'll be tied up," he said.

Bosch heard the heavy doors in the station's rear hallway open and bang shut. Footsteps were coming toward the squad room.

"Do you have to go?" Eleanor asked.

"Um . . ."

Edgar and Rider walked into the squad room. Rider carried a brown evidence bag with something heavy in it. Edgar carried a closed cardboard box across which someone had stenciled *Xmas* with a Magic Marker. He also had a broad smile on his face.

"Yeah," Bosch said, "I think I better go."

"Okay, Harry, I'll see you."

"You'll be there?"

"I'll be here."

"Okay, Eleanor, I'll see you as soon as I can."

He hung up and looked up at his two partners. Edgar was still smiling.

"We got your Christmas present here, Harry," Edgar said. "We got Powers right here in this box."

"You got the boots?"

"No. No boots. We got better than boots."

"Show me."

Edgar lifted the lid off the box. Off the top he took out a manila envelope. He then tilted the box so that Bosch could look in. Bosch whistled.

"Merry Christmas," Edgar said.

"You count it?" Bosch asked, his eyes still on the stacks of currency with rubber bands around them.

"Each bundle has a number on it," Rider said. "You add them all up, it equals four hundred eighty thousand. It looks like it's everything."

"Not a bad present, eh Harry?" Edgar said excitedly.

"No. Where was it?"

"Attic crawl space," Edgar said. "One of the last places we looked. Box was just sitting there in front of me as soon as I stuck my head up."

Bosch nodded.

"Okay, what else?"

"Found these under his mattress."

From the envelope Edgar withdrew a stack of photos. They were six by four in size and each had the date of the photograph digitally printed on the bottom left corner. Bosch put them on the table in front of them and looked through them, carefully picking them up by the corners. He hoped Edgar had handled them the same way.

The first photo was of Tony Aliso getting into a car at the valet stand in front of the Mirage. The next was of him walking to the door of Dolly's. Following that was a series of shots of him outside Dolly's talking to the man Aliso knew as Luke Goshen. It was dark outside in these shots and they were taken from a distance, but the neon-glutted entrance of the club was lit as brightly as daylight and Aliso and Goshen were easily recognizable.

Then there were photos from the same location but the date at the bottom corner had changed. They showed a young woman leaving the club and walking to Aliso's car. Bosch recognized her. It was Layla. There were also pictures of Tony and Layla poolside at the Mirage. The last shot was of Tony leaning his deeply tanned body over Layla's lounge chair and kissing her on the mouth.

Bosch looked up at Edgar and Rider. Edgar was smiling again. Rider wasn't.

"Just like we thought," Edgar said. "He cased this guy over there in Vegas. That shows he had the knowledge to set this whole thing up. Him and the widow. We got 'em, Harry. This shows premeditation, lying in wait, the works. We got 'em both, nine ways to Sunday."

"Maybe." He looked at Rider. "What's up with you, Kiz?"

She shook her head.

"I don't know. It just seems too easy. The place was very clean. No old boots, no sign that Veronica ever even set foot in that place. Then we find these so easy. It was like we were supposed to find it all. I mean, why would he take the time to get rid of the boots but leave the photos under the mattress? I can see him wanting to hang on to the money, but putting it in the attic seems pretty lame."

She moved her hand toward the photos and the cash in a dismissive gesture. Bosch nodded his agreement and leaned back in his chair.

"I think you're right," he said. "He's not that stupid."

He thought about the similarity to the gun being planted on Goshen. That, too, turned out to be too easy.

"I think it's a setup," Bosch said. "Veronica did this. He took the photos for her. He probably told her to destroy them, but she didn't. She hung on to them just in case. She probably snuck them back in under his bed and put the cash up in the attic. Was it easy to get to?"

"Easy enough," Rider said. "Fold-down ladder."

"Wait a minute, why would she set him up?" Edgar asked.

"Not from the start," Bosch said. "It was like a fall-back position. If things started to go wrong, if we got too close, she had Powers out there ready to take the fall. Maybe when she sent Powers after the suitcase she went to his place with the photos and the cash. Who knows when it started? But I bet when I tell Powers we found this stuff in his house, his eyes are going to pop. Whaddaya got in the bag, Kiz, the camera?"

She nodded and put the bag on the table without opening it.

"Nikon with a telephoto on it, credit card receipt for his purchase of it."

Bosch nodded and his thoughts strayed a bit. He was trying to think about how he was going to work the photos and money with Powers. It was their shot at breaking him. It had to be played right.

"Hold on, hold on," Edgar said, a look of confusion on his face. "I still don't get this. What makes you say it was a setup? Maybe he was holding the cash and the photos and they were going to split it all after the heat died down. Why does it have to be that she set him up?"

Bosch looked at Rider and then back at Edgar.

" 'Cause Kiz is right. It's too easy."

"Not if he thought we didn't have a clue, if he thought he was clear right up to the moment we jumped out of the bushes up there in the woods."

Bosch shook his head.

"I don't know. I don't think he would have played it the way he did when I was just talking to him. Not if he knew he had this stuff back at his place. I go with it being a setup. She's putting it all on him. We pull her in and she'll feed us some story about the guy being obsessed with her. Maybe, if she's any kind of actress, she tells us, yes, she had an affair with him but then she broke it off. But he wouldn't go away. He killed her old man so he could have her all to himself."

Bosch leaned back and looked at them, waiting for their response.

"I think it's good," Rider said. "It could work."

"Except we don't believe it," Bosch said.

"So what's she get out of this?" Edgar asked, refusing to drop his disagreement. "She's givin' up the money puttin' it in his pad. What's that leave her?"

"The house, the cars, insurance," Bosch said. "Whatever's left of the company—and the chance to get away."

But it was a weak answer and he knew it. A half million dollars was a lot of cash to use to set somebody up. It was the one flaw in the theory he had just spun.

"She got rid of her husband," Rider said. "Maybe that was all that was important to her."

"He'd been screwing around on her for years," Edgar said. "Why now? What was different this time?"

"I don't know," Rider said. "But there was something different or something else we don't know about. That's what we have to find out."

"Yeah, well, good luck," Edgar said.

"I've got an idea," Bosch said. "If anyone knows what that something else is, it's Powers. I want to try to scam him and I think I know how. Kiz, you still got that tape, the one with Veronica in it?"

"*Casualty of Desire*? Yeah. It's in my drawer."

"Go get it and set it up in the lieutenant's office. I'm going to grab some more coffee and I'll meet you there."

Bosch stepped into interview room three with the box of cash turned so that the side that said *Xmas* on it was held against his chest. He hoped it looked like any common cardboard box. He watched Powers for a sign of recognition and got none. Powers was sitting just as Bosch had left him. Ramrod straight, his arms behind him as if by choice. He looked at Bosch with deadpan eyes that were ready and waiting for the next go-round. Bosch put the box on the floor where it would be shielded from view, pulled out the chair and sat across from him again. He then reached down, opened the box and took out a tape recorder and a file folder. He put them on the table in plain sight.

"I told you, Bosch, no taping. If you got the camera on the other side of the glass going, then you're ripping off my rights, too."

"No camera, no tape, Powers. This is just to play you something, that's all. Now, where were we?"

"We were to the point of put up or shut up. You cut me loose or you get my lawyer in here."

"Well, actually, a couple of things have come up. I thought you might want to know about them first. You know, before you make a decision like that."

"Fuck that. I'm through with this shit. Get me the phone."

"Do you own a camera, Powers?"

"I said get—a camera? What about it?"

"Do you own a camera? It's a pretty straightforward question."

"Yes. Everybody owns a camera. What about it?"

Bosch studied him for a moment. He could feel the momentum and control start to maybe shift just a bit. It was coming across the table from Powers. He could feel it. Bosch played a thin smile on his face. He wanted Powers to know that from this point on it was slipping away from him.

"Did you take the camera with you when you went to Vegas last March?"

"I don't know. Maybe. I take it on all my vacations. Didn't know it was a crime. The fucking legislature, what will they think of next?"

Bosch let him have his smile but didn't return it.

"Is that what you called it?" he said quietly. "A vacation?"

"Yeah, that's exactly what I called it."

"That's funny, because that's not what Veronica is calling it."

"I don't know anything about that or her."

His eyes momentarily looked away from Bosch. It was the first time, and again Bosch felt the balance shifting. He was playing it right. He felt it. Things were shifting.

"Sure you know about it, Powers. And you know her pretty good, too. She just told us all about it. She's in the other room right now. Turns out she was weaker than I thought. My money had been on you. You know the saying, the bigger they are the harder they fall, all of that. I thought you'd be the one but it was her. Edgar and Rider broke her down a little while ago. Amazing how crime scene photos can work on somebody's guilty conscience. She told us everything, Powers. Everything."

"You're so full of bullshit, Bosch, and it's getting pretty old. Where's the phone?"

"This is how she tells it. You—"

"I don't want to hear it."

"You met her when you went up there that night to take the burglary report. One thing led to another and pretty soon you two were having a little romance. An affair to remember. Only she came to her senses and broke it off. She still loved ol' Tony. She knew he traveled a lot, strayed a lot, but she was used to that. She needed him. So she cut you off. Only, and this is according to her, you wouldn't be cut off. You kept after her, calling her, following her when she'd leave the estate up there. It was getting scary. I mean, what could she do? Go to Tony and say this guy I had an affair with is following me all the time? She—"

"This is so much bullshit, Bosch. It's a joke!"

"Then you started following Tony. You see, he was your problem. He was in the way. So you did your homework. You followed him to Vegas and you caught him in the act. You knew just what he was up to and how to put him down in a way that we'd go down the wrong path. Trunk music, they call it. Only you couldn't carry the tune, Powers. We're on to you. With her help, we're going to put you down."

Powers was looking down at the table. The skin around his eyes and his jawline had drawn tight.

"This is so much crap," he said without looking up. "I'm tired of listening to it and to you. She's not in the other room. She's sitting up there in that big house on the hill. This is the oldest trick in the book."

Powers looked up and a twisted smile cracked his face.

"You try to pull this shit on a cop? I can't believe it. This is really weak, man. You're weak. You're embarrassing yourself here."

Bosch reached over to the tape recorder and pushed the play button. Veronica Aliso's voice filled the tiny room.

"It was him. He's crazy. I couldn't stop him until it was too late. Then I couldn't tell anyone because it . . . it would look like I—"

Bosch turned it off.

"That's enough," he said. "It's out of line for me to even play *that* for you. But I thought, cop to cop, you should know where you stand."

Bosch silently watched Powers as he did a slow burn. Bosch could see the anger boiling up behind his eyes. He didn't seem to move a muscle, yet he seemed all at once to become as hard as a stack of lumber. He finally was able to hold himself back, though, and compose himself.

"It's just her word," he said in a quiet voice. "There's no corroboration of anything. It's a fantasy, Bosch. Her word against mine."

"It could be. Except we have these."

Bosch opened the file and threw the stack of photos in front of Powers. Then he reached across and carefully fanned them on the table so they could be seen and recognized.

"That backs up a good part of her story, don't you think?"

Bosch watched as Powers studied the photographs. Once again Powers seemed to go to the edge with an interior rage, but once more he contained it.

"It doesn't back up shit," he said. "She could've taken these herself. Anybody could have. Just because she gives you a stack of . . . She's got you people wrapped up, doesn't she? You're buying every line she feeds you."

"Maybe that would be so, only she didn't give us the photos."

Bosch reached into the file again and pulled out a copy of the search warrant. He reached over and put it on top of the photos.

"Five hours ago we faxed that to Judge Warren Lambert at his home in the Palisades. He faxed it back signed. Edgar and Rider have been in your little Hollywood bungalow most of the night. Among the items seized was a Nikon camera with telephoto lens. And these photos. They were under your mattress, Powers."

He paused here to let it all sink in behind Powers's darkening eyes.

"Oh, and one other thing we found." Bosch reached down and brought the box up. "This was in the attic with the Christmas stuff."

He dumped the contents of the box on the table and the stacks of cash tumbled every which way, some falling to the floor. Bosch shook the box to make sure it had all come out and then dropped it to the floor. He looked at Powers. His eyes were wild, darting over the thick bundles. Bosch knew he had him. And he also knew in his gut that he had Veronica Aliso to thank for that.

"Now, personally, I don't think you are this stupid," Bosch said quietly. "You know, to keep the pictures and all this cash right in your house. Of course, I've seen crazier things in my time. But if I was betting, I'd bet that you didn't know all of this was there because you didn't put it there. But, hey, either way it works fine for me. We've got you and we'll clear this one, that's all I care about. It would be nice to grab her, too, but that's okay. We'll need her for you. With the photos and her story and all the other stuff we've talked about here, I think we got you for the murder easy. There's also lying-in-wait to tack on. That makes it a special circumstances case, Powers. You're looking at one of two things. The needle or LWP."

He pronounced the last acronym *el-wop*, knowing that any cop, just as any criminal in the system, would know it meant life without parole.

"Anyway," Bosch continued, "I guess I'll go get that phone brought in here so you can call your lawyer. Better make it a good one. And none of those grandstanders from the O.J. case. You need to get yourself a lawyer who does his best work outside of the courtroom. A negotiator."

He stood up and turned to the door. With his hand on the knob he looked back at Powers.

"You know, I feel bad, Powers. You being a cop and all, I was sort of hoping you'd catch the break instead of her. I feel like we're hitting the wrong person with the hammer. But I guess that's life in the big city. Somebody's got to be hit with it."

He turned back to the door and opened it.

"*Bitch!*" Powers said with a quiet forcefulness.

Then he whispered something under his breath that Bosch couldn't hear. Bosch looked back at him. He knew enough not to say a word.

"It was her idea," Powers said. "All of it. She conned me and now she's conning you."

Bosch waited a beat but there was nothing else.

"Are you saying you want to talk to me?"

"Yeah, Bosch, have a seat. Maybe we can work something out."

At nine Bosch sat in the lieutenant's office, Billets behind the desk, bringing her up to date. He had an empty Styrofoam cup in his hand, but he didn't drop it in the trash can because he needed something to remind him that he needed more coffee. He was beat tired and the lines beneath his eyes were so pronounced they almost hurt. His mouth tasted sour from all the coffee and cigarettes. He'd eaten nothing but candy bars in the last twenty hours and his stomach was finally protesting. But he was a happy man. He had won the last round with Powers and in this kind of battle the last round was the only one that mattered.

"So," Billets said, "he told you everything?"

"His version of it," Bosch said. "He lays everything on her and that's to be expected. Remember, he thinks she's in the other room laying everything on him. So he's making her out to be the big bad black widow, like he never had an impure thought in his life until he ran across her."

He brought the cup up to his mouth but then realized it was empty.

"But once we get her in here and she knows he's talking, we'll probably get her version," he said.

"When did Jerry and Kiz leave?"

Bosch looked at his watch.

"About forty minutes ago. They should be back with her any time."

"Why didn't you go up to get her?"

"I don't know. I figured I took Powers, they should have her. Spread it around, you know?"

"Better be careful. You keep acting like that and you'll lose your rep as a hardass."

Bosch smiled and looked down into his cup.

"So what's the gist of his story?" Billets asked.

"The gist is pretty much how we figured it. He went up there to take a burglary report that day and it went from there. He says she put the moves on him and next thing you know they had a thing going. He started taking more and more patrol swings through the neighborhood and she was stopping by his bungalow in the mornings after Tony went to work or while he was in Vegas. The way he describes it, she was reeling him in. The sex was good and exotic. He was hooked up pretty good."

"Then she asked him to tail Tony."

"Right. That first trip Powers took to Vegas was a straight job. She asked him to tail Tony. He did and he came back with a bunch of photos of Tony and the girl and a lot of questions about who Tony was meeting with over there and why. He wasn't stupid. He could tell Tony was into something. He says Veronica filled him in, knew every detail, knew all the OC guys by name. She also told him how much money was involved. That was when the plan came together. She told Powers that Tony had to go, that it would be just them afterward, them and a lot of money. She told him Tony had been skimming. Skimming off the skim.

For years. There was at least a couple million in the pot plus whatever they took off Tony when they put him down."

Bosch stood up and continued the story while pacing in front of her desk. He was too tired to sit for very long without being overcome with fatigue.

"Anyway, that was what the second trip was for. Powers went over and watched Tony one more time. It was research. He also tailed the guy Tony made the pickups from. Luke Goshen, who he obviously had no idea was an agent. They decided Goshen would be the patsy and worked out the plan to make it look like a mob hit. Trunk music."

"It's pretty complicated."

"Yeah, that it is. He says the planning was all hers, and I kind of think he might be telling the truth there. You ask me, Powers is smart but not that smart. This whole thing was Veronica's plan and he became a willing player. Only she had a back door built into it that Powers didn't know about."

"He was the back door."

"Yeah. She set him up to take the fall, but only if we got too close. He said he'd given her a key to his place. It's a bungalow over on Sierra Bonita. She must've gone over there sometime this week, shoved the photos under the mattress and stuck the box of money in the attic. Smart woman. Nice setup. When Jerry and Kiz get her in here, I know just what she'll say. She's going to say it was all him, that he became infatuated with her, that they had an affair and that she broke it off. He went ahead and knocked off her husband. When she realized what had happened, she couldn't say anything. He forced her to go along with it. She had no choice. He was a cop and he told her he could pin it all on her if she didn't go along."

"It's a good story. In fact, it still might work with a jury. She could walk on this."

"Maybe. We still have some things to do."

"What about the skim?"

"Good question. Nothing like the kind of money he's talking about showed up on Aliso's bank accounts. Powers said she said it was in a safe deposit box but she never told him where. It's got to be somewhere. We'll find it."

"If it exists."

"I think it does. She planted a half million in Powers's place to put him in the frame. That's a lot of money to spend on setting him up, unless you happen to have a couple million more stashed someplace. That's what we—"

Bosch looked through the glass into the squad room. Edgar and Rider were walking toward the lieutenant's office. Veronica Aliso was not with them. They came into the office with urgent looks on their faces and Bosch knew what they were going to say.

"She's gone," Edgar said.

Bosch and Billets just stared at them.

"Looks like she split last night," Edgar said. "Her cars are still there but there was nobody at the house. We slipped in a back door and it's empty, man."

"She take her clothes, jewelry?" Bosch asked.

"Doesn't look like it. She's just gone."

"You check the gate?"

"Yeah, we checked at the gate. She had two visitors yesterday. First was a courier at four-fifteen. Legal Eagle Messenger Service. Guy was there about five minutes, in and out. Then a visitor last night. Late. Guy gave the name John Galvin. She had already called the gate and given the same name and told them to let him through when he showed up. They took his plate down and we ran it. It's Hertz out of Vegas. We'll put a call in. Anyway, Galvin stayed until one this morning. Just about the time we were in the woods hooking up Powers, he split. She probably went with him."

"We called the guard on duty at the time," Rider said. "He couldn't remember if Galvin left alone or not. He doesn't specifically remember seeing Mrs. Aliso last night, but she could have been down in the backseat."

"Do we know who her attorney is?" Billets asked.

"Yes," Rider said, "Neil Denton, Century City."

"Okay, Jerry, you work the trace on the Hertz rental and, Kiz, you try to run down Denton and see if you can find out what was so important that he had to messenger it over to her on Saturday."

"All right," Edgar said. "But I got a bad feeling. I think she's in the wind."

"Well, then we have to go into the wind to find her," Billets said. "Go to it."

Edgar and Rider went back out to the homicide table and Bosch stood silent for a few moments, thinking about this latest development.

"Should we have put people on her?" Billets asked.

"Well, looking back, it seems that way. But we were off the books. We didn't have the people. Besides, we didn't really have anything on her until a couple hours ago."

Billets nodded, a pained expression on her face.

"If they don't get a line on her in the next fifteen minutes, put it out on the air."

"Right."

"Listen, getting back to Powers, you think he's holding anything back?"

"Hard to say. Probably. There's still the question about why this time."

"What do you mean?"

"I mean Aliso had been going over to Vegas for years and bringing back suitcases full of money. He'd been skimming for years, according to Powers, and also had been having his share of the women over there. Veronica knew all of this. She had to. So what was it that made her do it now, rather than last year or next year?"

"Maybe she just got fed up. Maybe this was just the right time. Powers came along and it clicked."

"Maybe. I asked Powers and he said he didn't know. But I think maybe he was holding back. I'm going to take another run at him."

Billets didn't respond.

"There's still some sort of secret we don't know about," Bosch continued. "There's something there. I'm hoping she'll tell it. If we find her."

Billets dismissed it with a wave of her hand.

"You have Powers on tape?" she asked.

"Audio and video. Kiz was watching in room four. As soon as he said he wanted to talk she started it all rolling."

"Did you advise him again? On the tape?"

"Yeah, it's all on there. He's sealed up pretty good. You want to watch it, I'll get the tape."

"No. I don't even want to look at him if I can help it. You didn't promise him anything, did you?"

Bosch was about to answer but stopped. There was the sound of muffled yelling that he could tell was coming from Powers, still sequestered in room three. He looked through the glass of the lieutenant's office and saw Edgar get up from the homicide table and go down the hall to check it out.

"He probably wants his lawyer now," Bosch said. "Well, it's a little late for that. . . . Anyway, no, I made no promises. I did tell him I'd talk to the DA about dropping special circs, but that's going to be tough. With what he told me in there, we can take our pick. Conspiracy to commit, lying in wait, murder for hire maybe."

"I guess I should get a DA in here."

"Yeah. If you don't have anyone in mind or anybody you owe a hot case to, put in a request for Roger Goff. This is his kind of case and I've owed him one for a while. He won't blow it."

"I know Roger. I'll ask for him. . . . I have to call out the brass, too. It's not every day you get to call a deputy chief and tell him not only have your people been running an investigation they were specifically told to stay away from, but that they've arrested a cop to boot. And for murder, no less."

Bosch smiled. He would not relish having to make such a call.

"It's really going to hit the fan this time," he said. "One more black eye for the department. By the way, they didn't seize any of it because it's not related to this case, but Jerry and Kiz found some scary stuff in Powers's place. Nazi paraphernalia, white-power stuff. You might alert the brass about that, so they can do with it what they want."

"Thanks for telling me. I'll talk to Irving. I'm sure he won't want that to see the light of day."

Edgar leaned in through the open door.

"Powers says he's got to take a leak and can't hold it any longer."

He was looking at Billets.

"Well, take him," she said.

"Keep him hooked," Bosch added.

"How's he gonna piss, his hands behind his back? Don't be expecting me to be taking it out for him. No way."

Billets laughed.

"Just move the cuffs to the front," Bosch said. "Give me a second to finish in here and I'll be right there."

"Okay, I'll be in three."

Edgar left and Bosch watched him through the glass as he walked to the hallway leading to the interview rooms. Bosch looked back at Billets, who was still smiling at Edgar's comical protest. Bosch put a serious look on his face.

"You know, you can use me when you make that call."

"What do you mean?"

"I mean, if you want to say you didn't know about any of this until I called you this morning with the bad news, that's cool with me."

"Don't be ridiculous. We cleared a murder and got a killer cop off the street. If they can't see that the good in this outweighs the bad, then . . . well, fuck 'em if they can't take a joke."

Bosch smiled and nodded.

"You're cool, Lieutenant."

"Thanks."

"Anytime."

"And it's Grace."

"Right. Grace."

Bosch was thinking about how much he liked Billets as he walked down the short hallway to the interview rooms and into the open door of room three. Edgar was just closing the cuffs on Powers's wrists. His hands were in front of him now.

"Do me a favor, Bosch," Powers said. "Let me use the can in the front hallway."

"What for?"

"So nobody'll see me in the back. I don't want anybody to see me like this. Besides, you might have a problem if people don't like what they see."

Bosch nodded. Powers had a point. If they took him to the locker room, then all the cops in the watch office would likely see them and there would be questions, maybe even anger from some of the cops who didn't know what was going on. The bathroom in the front hallway was a public rest room, but this early on a Sunday morning it would likely be empty and they could take Powers in and out of there without being seen.

"Okay, let's go," Bosch said. "To the front."

They walked him past the front counter and down the hallway past the administration offices, which were empty and closed for the day. While Bosch stayed with Powers in the hall, Edgar checked the rest room out.

"It's empty," he said, holding the door open from inside.

Bosch followed Powers in and the big cop went to the farthest of three urinals. Bosch stayed by the door and Edgar took a position on the other side of Powers by the row of sinks. When Powers was finished at the urinal, he stepped toward one of the sinks. As he walked, Bosch saw that his right shoelace was untied and so did Edgar.

"Tie your shoe, Powers," Edgar said. "You trip and fall and break your pretty face, I don't want any cryin' 'bout *po*-lice brutality."

Powers stopped and looked down at the shoelace on the floor and then at Edgar.

"Sure," he said.

Powers first washed his hands, used a paper towel to dry them and then brought his right foot up on the edge of the sink to tie his shoe.

"New shoes," Edgar said. "Laces on 'em always come undone, don't they?"

Bosch couldn't see Powers's face because the cop's back was turned toward the door. But he was looking up at Edgar.

"Fuck you, nigger."

It was almost as if he had slapped Edgar, whose face immediately filled with revulsion and anger. He looked over at Bosch, a quick glance to judge whether Bosch was going to do anything about his plan to hit Powers. But it was all the time Powers needed. He sprang away from the sink and threw his body into Edgar, pinning him against the white-tiled wall. His cuffed hands came up and the left one grabbed a handful of the front of Edgar's shirt while the right pressed the barrel of a small gun into the stunned detective's throat.

Bosch had covered half of the distance to them when he saw the gun and Powers began to shout.

"Back off, Bosch. Back off or you got a dead partner. You want that?"

Powers had turned his head so that he was looking back at Bosch. Bosch stopped and raised his hands away from his body.

"That's it," Powers said. "Now this is what you're going to do. Take your gun out real slowly and drop it in that first sink there."

Bosch made no move.

"Do it. Now."

Powers spoke with measured force, careful to keep his voice low.

Bosch looked at the tiny gun in Powers's hand. He recognized it as a Raven .25, a favored throw-down gun among patrol cops going back to at least his own time in a uniform. It was small—it looked like a toy in Powers's hand—but deadly and it fit snugly into a sock or boot, virtually unseen with the pants leg pulled down. As Bosch came to the realization that Edgar and Rider had not completely searched Powers, he also knew that a shot from the Raven at point-blank range would certainly kill Edgar. It was against all his instincts to give up his weapon, but he saw no alternative. Powers was desperate and Bosch knew desperate men didn't think things out. They went against the odds. They were killers. With two fingers he slowly removed his gun and dropped it into the sink.

"That's real good, Bosch. Now I want you to get on the floor underneath the sinks."

Bosch did as he was told, never taking his eyes off Powers as he moved.

"Edgar," Powers said. "Now your turn. You can just go ahead and drop yours on the floor."

Edgar's gun hit the tile.

"Now, you get under there with your partner. That's it."

"Powers, this is crazy," Bosch said. "Where're you going to go? You can't run."

"Who's talking about running, Bosch? Take out your cuffs and put one on your left wrist."

After Bosch had complied, Powers told him to loop the cuffs through one of the sink trap pipes. He then told Edgar to put the free cuff around his right wrist. He did so and then Powers smiled.

"There, that's good. That ought to hold you guys for a few minutes. Now, give me your keys. Both of you, throw 'em out here."

Powers picked Edgar's set up off the floor and unlocked the cuffs around his wrists. He quickly massaged them to get the circulation go-ing. He was smiling but Bosch wondered if he even knew it.

"Now, let's see."

He reached into the sink and grabbed Bosch's gun.

"This is a nice one, Bosch. Nice weight, balance. Beats mine. Mind if I borrow it for a couple minutes?"

Bosch knew then what he was planning to do. He was going for Veronica. Bosch thought of Kiz sitting at the homicide table, her back to the front counter. And Billets in her office. They wouldn't see him until it was too late.

"She's not here, Powers," he said.

"What? Who?"

"Veronica. It was a scam. We never even picked her up."

Powers was silent as the smile dropped away and was replaced with a serious look of concentration. Bosch knew what he was thinking.

"The voice came from one of her movies. I taped it off the videotape. You go back to those interview rooms and it's a dead end. There's no-body back there and no way out."

Bosch saw the same tightening of skin around Powers's face that he had seen before. His face grew dark with blood and anger, then, inexpli-cably, the smile suddenly creased across it.

"You smart fucker, Bosch. Is that so? You 'spect me to believe she's not there? Maybe this is the con, and not before. See what I'm saying?"

"It's no con. She isn't there. We were going to pick her up with what you told us. Went up the hill an hour ago but she's not there either. She left last night."

"If she's not already here, then how . . ."

"That part was no scam. The money and pictures were in your house. If you didn't put them there, then she did. She's setting you up. Why don't you just put the gun down and let's start this over? You apologize to Edgar for what you called him and we drop this little incident."

"Oh, I see. You drop the escape but I still get hit with the murder."

"I told you, we're going to talk to the DA. We got one coming in right now. He's a friend. He'll do right by you. She's the one we really want."

"You fucking asshole!" Powers said loudly. He then brought his voice

back into check. "Don't you see that I want her? You think you beat me?
You think you broke me down in there? You didn't win, Bosch. I talked
because I wanted to talk. I broke you, man, but you didn't know it. You
started trusting me because you needed me. You should've never moved
the cuffs, brother."

He was silent a moment, letting that sink in.

"Now I've got an appointment with that bitch that I'm going to keep
no matter what. She ain't here, then I'll go find her."

"She could be anywhere."

"So could I, Bosch, and she won't see me coming. I have to go."

Powers grabbed the plastic bag out of the trash can and emptied it on
the floor. He put Bosch's gun into the bag, then turned the faucets in all
three sinks on full blast. The cascading water created a cacophony as it
echoed off the tile walls. Powers picked up Edgar's gun and put it in the
bag. He then wrapped the bag around itself several times, concealing the
two guns inside. He put the Raven in his front pocket for easy access,
threw the handcuff keys into one of the urinals and flushed each one.
Without even looking at the two men handcuffed under the sink, he
headed to the door.

"Adios, dipshits," he threw over his shoulder and then he was gone.

Bosch looked at Edgar. He knew that if they yelled, it was likely they
wouldn't be heard. It was a Sunday, the administration wing was empty.
And in the bureau there were only Billets and Rider. With the water
running, their shouts would probably be unintelligible. Billets and Rider
would probably think it was the normal yelling from the drunk tank.

Bosch swiveled around and braced his feet on the wall beneath the
sink counter. He grabbed the trap pipe so that he could use his legs as
leverage in an attempt to pull the pipe free. But the pipe was burning hot.

"Son of a bitch!" Bosch yelled as he let go. "He turned the hot water on."

"What are we going to do? He's getting away."

"Your arms are longer. See if you can reach up there and turn off the
water. It's too hot. I can't grab the pipe."

With Bosch feeding his arm almost up to the elbow through the pipe
loop, Edgar was barely able to touch the faucet. It took him several seconds to turn the water down to a trickle.

"Now turn on the cold," Bosch said. "Cool this thing down."

It took another few seconds, but then Bosch was ready to try again. He grabbed the pipe and pushed against the wall with his legs. As he did this, Edgar squeezed his hands around the pipe and did the same. The added muscle broke the pipe free along the seal beneath the sink. Water sloshed down on them as they threaded the cuffs' chain through the pipe break. They got up and slid along the tile to the urinal, where Bosch saw his keys on the bottom grate. He grabbed them up and fumbled with them until he had the cuff off. He handed the keys to Edgar and ran toward the door, sloshing through the water that had completely spread across it.

"Turn off the water," he yelled as he hit the door.

Bosch ran down the hallway and vaulted over the detective bureau front counter. The squad room was empty and through the glass he saw the lieutenant's office was vacant. He then heard a loud pounding and the muffled shouts of Rider and Billets. He ran down the hallway to the interview rooms and found all the doors open but one. He knew Powers had checked for Veronica Aliso anyway after locking Billets and Rider in room three. He opened the door to three and then quickly ran back through the squad room into the station house's rear hallway. He slammed through the heavy metal door and into the back parking yard. Instinctively reaching to his empty shoulder holster, he scanned the parking lot and the open bays of the garage. There was no sign of Powers, but there were two patrol officers standing near the gas pumps. Bosch focused on them.

"You seen Powers?"

"Yeah," said the older of the two. "He just left. With our fucking car. What the fuck's going on?"

Bosch didn't answer. He closed his eyes, bowed his head and cursed silently to himself.

Six hours later, Bosch, Edgar and Rider sat at the homicide table, silently watching the meeting taking place in the lieutenant's office. Huddled in the small office like people on a bus were Billets, Captain LeValley, Deputy Chief Irving, three IAD investigators including Chastain, and the

chief of police and his administrative aide. Deputy District Attorney
Roger Goff had been consulted on the speaker-phone—Bosch had heard
his voice through the open door. But then the door was closed and Bosch
was sure the group was deciding the fate of the three detectives sitting
outside.

The police chief stood in the middle of the cramped room with his
arms folded and his head down. He was the last to arrive, and it looked as
if he was getting the run-down from the others. Occasionally he nodded,
but it didn't look to Bosch as though he was saying much at all. Bosch
knew that the main issue they were discussing was how to handle the
problem with Powers. There was a killer cop on the loose. Going to the
media with that would be an exercise in self-flagellation, but Bosch saw
no way around it. They had looked in all the likely places for Powers and
had not found him. The patrol car he had commandeered had been
found abandoned up in the hills on Fareholm Drive. Where he had gone
from there was anyone's guess. Surveillance teams stationed outside his
bungalow and the Aliso house, as well as the lawyer Neil Denton's house
and office, had produced nothing. It was now time to go to the media, to
put the rogue cop's picture on the six o'clock news. Bosch guessed that
the reason the police chief had showed up was that he planned to call a
press conference. Otherwise he would have left the whole thing for Irving to deal with.

Bosch realized Rider had said something.

"Excuse me?"

"I said what are you going to do with your time?"

"I don't know. Depends on how much we get. If it's just one DP, I'll
use it to finish work on my house. If it's longer than two, I'll have to see
about making some money somehow."

A DP, or deployment period, was fifteen days. Suspensions were usually
handed out in such increments when the offense was serious. Bosch was
pretty sure the chief wouldn't be handing out minor suspensions to them.

"He isn't going to fire us, is he, Harry?" Edgar asked.

"Doubt it. But it all depends on how they're telling it to him."

Bosch looked back at the office window just as the chief was looking
out at him. The chief looked away, not a good sign. Bosch had never met
him and never expected that he would. He was an outsider brought in to

appease the community. Not because of any particular police administrative skills, but because they needed an outsider. He was a large black man with most of his weight around his waist. Cops who didn't like him, and there were many, often referred to him as Chief Mud Slide. Bosch didn't know what cops who liked him called him.

"I just want to say I'm sorry, Harry," Rider said.

"Sorry about what?" Bosch asked.

"About missing the gun. I patted him down. I ran my hands down his legs but somehow I missed it. I don't understand it."

"It was small enough that he could fit it in his boot," Bosch said. "It's not all on you, Kiz. We all had our chances. Me and Jerry fucked up in the rest room. We should've been watching him better."

She nodded but Bosch could tell she still felt miserable. He looked up and saw that the meeting in the lieutenant's office was beginning to break up. As the police chief and his aide, followed by LeValley and the IAD dicks, filed out, they left the bureau through the front entrance. It would make for an out-of-the-way walk if their cars were parked in the station lot out back, but it meant they didn't have to walk by the homicide table and acknowledge Bosch and the others. Another bad sign, he thought.

Only Irving and Billets remained in the office after it cleared. Billets then looked out at Bosch and signaled the three of them into her office. They got up slowly and headed in. Edgar and Rider sat down but Bosch stayed on his feet.

"Chief," Billets said, giving Irving the floor.

"Okay, I'll give it to you the way it was just given to me," Irving said.

He looked down at a piece of paper on which he had taken a few notes.

"For conducting an unauthorized investigation and for failure to follow procedure in searching and transporting a prisoner, each of you is suspended without pay two deployment periods and suspended *with* pay for two deployment periods. These are to run consecutively. That's two months. And, of course, a formal reprimand goes into each of your jackets. Per procedure, you can appeal this to a Board of Rights."

He waited a beat. It was heavier than Bosch had expected, but he showed nothing on his face. He heard Edgar audibly exhale. As far as the appeal went, disciplinary action by the police chief was rarely

overturned. It would require two of the three captains on the Board
of Rights to vote against their commander in chief. Overruling an
IAD investigator was one thing, overruling the chief was political
suicide.

"However," Irving continued, "the suspensions are being held in
abeyance by the chief pending further developments and evaluation."

There was a moment of silence while the last sentence was computed.

"What does he mean, abeyance?" Edgar asked.

"It means the chief is offering you a break," Irving said. "He wants to
see how things fall out over the next day or two. Each of you is to come
to work tomorrow and proceed with the investigation where you can.
We talked with the DA's office. They're willing to file on Powers. Get
the paperwork over there tomorrow first thing. We've put the word out
and the chief will take it to the media in a couple hours. If we're lucky,
we'll get this guy before he finds the woman or does any other damage.
And if we're lucky, you three will probably be lucky."

"What about Veronica Aliso, aren't they going to file on her?"

"Not yet. Not until we have Powers back. Goff said that without
Powers, the taped confession is worthless. He won't be able to use it
against her without Powers on the stand to introduce it or her being able
to confront a witness against her."

Bosch looked down at the floor.

"So without him, she walks."

"That's the way it looks."

Bosch nodded his head.

"What's he going to say?" he asked. "The chief, I mean."

"He's going to tell it like it is. You people will come out okay in some
parts, not so okay in others. Overall, it's not going to be a good day for
this department."

"Is that why we're getting hit for two months? Because we're the
messengers?"

Irving looked at him a long moment, his jaw clenched, before answering.

"I'm not going to dignify that with a reply."

He looked at Rider and Edgar and said, "You two can go now. You're
finished here. I need to discuss another matter with Detective Bosch."

Bosch watched them go and prepared for more of Irving's ire about the last comment. He wasn't sure why he had said it. He knew it would bait the deputy chief.

But after Rider closed the door to the office, Irving spoke of another matter.

"Detective, I wanted you to know that I've already talked to the federal people and we're all squared away on that."

"How is that?"

"I told them that with today's developments it has become pretty clear—make that crystal clear—that you had nothing to do with planting evidence on their man. I told them it was Powers and that we were terminating that particular aspect of our internal investigation of your conduct."

"Fine, Chief. Thanks."

Thinking that was it, Bosch made a move toward the door.

"Detective, there is one other thing."

Bosch turned back to him.

"In discussing this matter with the chief of police, there is still one other aspect that bothers him."

"And what is that?"

"The investigation started by Detective Chastain brought in ancillary information about your association with a convicted felon. It's troubling to me, too. I'd like to be able to get some assurance from you that this is not going to continue. I'd like to take that assurance to the chief."

Bosch was silent a moment.

"I can't give you that."

Irving looked down at the floor. He was working the thick muscles of his jaw again.

"You disappoint me, Detective Bosch," he finally said. "This department has done a lot by you. So have I. I've stood by you through some tough spots. You've never been easy, but you have a talent that I think this department and this city certainly need. I suppose that makes you worth it. Do you want to possibly alienate me and others in this department?"

"Not particularly."

"Then take my advice and do the right thing, son. You know what that is. That's all I'm going to say on that."

"Yes, sir."
"That's all."

When Bosch got to his house, he saw a dusty Ford Escort parked at the curb out front. It had Nevada plates. Inside the house, Eleanor Wish was sitting at the table in the small dining room with the classified ads section of the Sunday *Times*. She had a lit cigarette in the ashtray next to the paper and she was using a black marker to circle want ads. Bosch saw all of this and his heart jumped into a higher gear. What it meant to him was that if she was looking for a job, then she might be digging in, staying in L.A. and staying with him. To top it all off, the house was filled with the aroma of an Italian restaurant, heavy on the garlic.

He came around the table and put his hand on her shoulder and tentatively kissed her on the cheek. She patted his hand. As he straightened up, though, he noticed she was looking at ads for furnished apartments in Santa Monica, not the employment section.

"What's cooking?" he asked.

"My spaghetti sauce. You remember it?"

He nodded that he did but he really didn't. His memory of the days he had spent with her five years before were all centered on her, the moments they were intimate, and what happened afterward.

"How was Las Vegas?" he asked, just to be saying something.

"It was Vegas. The kind of place you never miss. If I never go back that will be fine with me."

"You're looking for a place here?"

"I thought I might as well start looking."

She had lived in Santa Monica before. Bosch remembered her apartment with the bedroom balcony. You could smell the sea and if you leaned out over the railing, you could look down Ocean Park Boulevard and even see it. He knew she couldn't afford a place like that now. She was probably looking at the listings east of Lincoln.

"You know there's no hurry," he said. "You can stay here. Nice view, it's private. Why don't you . . . I don't know, take your time."

She looked up at him but decided not to say what she was about to say. Bosch could tell.

"Do you want a beer?" she asked instead. "I bought some more. They're in the fridge."

He nodded, letting her escape from the moment, and went into the kitchen. He saw a Crock-Pot on the counter and wondered if she had bought it or brought it back with her from Las Vegas. He opened the refrigerator and smiled. She knew him. She had bought bottles of Henry Weinhard's. He took two out and brought them back to the dining room. He opened hers and gave it to her, then his own. They both started to speak at the same time.

"Sorry, go ahead," she said.

"No, you."

"You sure?"

"Yeah, what?"

"I was just going to ask how things went today."

"Oh. Well, they went good and bad. We broke the guy down and he told us the story. He gave up the wife."

"Tony Aliso's wife?"

"Yeah. It was her plan all along. According to him. The Vegas stuff was just a misdirection."

"That's great. What's the bad part?"

"Well, first of all, our guy is a cop and—"

"Oh, shit!"

"Yeah, but it's even worse. He got away from us today."

"Got away? What do you mean got away?"

"I mean he escaped. Right out of the station. He had a pistol, a little Raven, in his boot. We missed it when we hooked him up. Edgar and me took him into the can, and he must've stepped on his shoelace while we were going over. You know, on purpose. Then, when Edgar noticed it and told him to tie his shoe, he came up with the Raven. He got away from us, went into the back lot and just took a squad car. He was still in uniform."

"Jesus, and they didn't find him yet?"

"That was about eight hours ago. He's in the wind."

"Well, where could he go in a patrol car and in a uniform?"

"Oh, he dumped the car—they already found that—and I doubt, wherever he is, he's in the uniform. It looks like he was into the far-right, white-supremacy thing. He probably knew people who'd get him clothes, no questions asked."

"Sounds like a helluva cop."

"Yeah. It's funny. He was the guy who found the body, you know, last week. It was on his beat. And because he was a cop, I didn't give him a second thought. I knew that day he was an asshole, but I didn't even look at him at all as anything other than the cop who found the stiff. And he must've known that. And he timed it so that we'd be in a rush out there. He was pretty smart about it."

"Or she was."

"Yeah. More likely it was her. But, anyway, I feel more, I don't know, upset or disappointed about that first day, that I didn't take a look at him, than I do about letting him get away today. I should've looked at him. More often than not the one who finds the body is the one. His uniform blinded me to that."

She got up from the table and came over to him. She put her arms around his neck and smiled up at him.

"You'll get him. Don't worry."

He nodded. They kissed.

"What were you going to say before?" she asked. "When we both talked at once."

"Oh . . . I don't remember now."

"Must not have been important, then."

"I wanted to tell you to stay here with me."

She put her head down against his chest so that he couldn't see her eyes.

"Harry . . ."

"Just to see how it works. I feel like . . . it's almost like all this time hasn't gone by. I want—I just want to be with you. I can take care of you. You can feel safe and you can have all the time you need to make a new start here. Find a job, whatever you want to do."

She stepped back from him and looked up into his eyes. The warning Irving had given him was the furthest thing from his mind. Right now all he cared about was keeping her close and doing whatever it took to accomplish that.

"But a lot of time has gone by, Harry. We just can't jump in like this."

Bosch nodded and lowered his eyes. He knew she was right but he still didn't care.

"I want you, Harry," she said. "Nobody else. But I want to take it slow. So that we're sure. Both of us."

"I already know I'm sure."

"You just think you are."

"Santa Monica is so far away from here."

She smiled and then laughed and shook her head.

"Then you're just going to have to sleep over when you come visit."

He nodded again and they embraced for a long moment.

"You can make me forget a lot of things, you know that?" he whispered into her ear.

"You, too," she said back.

While they made love the phone rang, but whoever was calling did not leave a message when the machine picked up. Later, after Bosch got out of the shower, Eleanor reported that another call had come in but no message was left.

Finally, while Eleanor was boiling water for the pasta, the phone rang a third time and Bosch got it before the machine picked up.

"Hey, Bosch?"

"Yeah, who's this?"

"It's Roy Lindell. Remember me, Luke Goshen?"

"I remember. Was that you who called a couple times before?"

"Yeah, why didn't you pick up?"

"I was busy. What do you need?"

"So, it was the bitch, huh?"

"What?"

"Tony's wife."

"Yeah."

"Did you know this guy Powers?"

"Not really. Just to see around."

Bosch didn't want to tell him anything he didn't already know.

Lindell exhaled in a bored way loudly into the phone.

"Yeah, well, Tony once told me that he was more afraid of his wife than he was of Joey Marks."

"Yeah?" Bosch said, suddenly interested. "He said that? When?"

"I don't know. One night we were talking in the club and he just said it. I remember the place was closed. He was waiting for Layla and we were talking."

"Lindell, thanks a lot for telling me this. What else did he say?"

"Hey, I'm telling you now, Bosch. Anyway, I couldn't before. I was in character, man, and in that character you don't tell the cops shit. And then after, I . . . well, then I thought you were trying to fuck me over. I wasn't going to tell you shit then, either."

"And now you know better."

"Yeah, right. Look, Bosch, most guys you would've never heard from. But I'm calling. You think you'll hear from anybody else from the bureau saying maybe we made a mistake about you? No way. But I like your style. I mean, you get pulled off the case and what do you do, you turn around and get right back on it. Then you solve the fucker. That takes balls and style, Bosch. I can dig that."

"You can dig it. That's great, Roy. What else did Tony Aliso tell you about his wife?"

"Nothing much. He just said she was cold. He said that she had him by the short hairs. Hooked and snooked and that was that. He couldn't get a divorce from her without losing half his wad and then having her running around out there with all that she knew about his business and his business associates. If you know what I mean."

"Why didn't he just go to Joey Marks and ask for a whack on her?"

"I think on account that she knew Joey from way back and he liked her. It was Joey who introduced her to Tony way back when. I think Tony knew that if he went to Joey, it would get KO'd pretty quick and it might get back to her. And if he went to somebody else, he'd have to answer to Joey. Joey had the final say on that kind of stuff, and he wouldn't want Tony getting involved in a freelance job like that and possibly endangering the wash operation."

"How well do you think she knew Joey Marks? You think she could've gone back to him now?"

"No way. She killed the golden goose. Tony made Joey legitimate money. His first allegiance is always to the money."

Bosch was quiet for a few moments and so was Lindell.

"So what happens with you now?" Bosch finally said.

"You mean with my thing? I go back to Vegas tonight. I sit down in front of the grand jury in the morning. I figure I'll be talking to them at least a couple weeks. I've got a pretty good story to tell 'em. We should have Joey and his crew tagged and bagged by Christmas."

"Hope you're bringing your bodyguards."

"Oh, yeah. I'm not alone."

"Well, good luck, Lindell. All the bullshit aside, I like your style, too. Let me ask you something, why'd you tell me about the safe house and the Samoans? That wasn't in keeping with your character."

"I had to, Bosch. You scared me."

"You thought I'd actually clip you for them?"

"I wasn't sure, but that didn't really worry me. I had people watching over me that you didn't know about. But I *was* sure that they'd clip her. And I'm an agent, man. It was my duty to try to stop that. So I told you. I was surprised you didn't guess I was undercover right then."

"Never crossed my mind. You were good."

"Well, I fooled the people I had to fool. I'll see you around, Bosch."

"Sure. Oh, Lindell?"

"Yeah."

"Did Joey Marks ever think that Tony A. was skimming off him?"

Lindell laughed.

"You don't give up, do you, Bosch?"

"I guess not."

"Well, that information would be part of the investigation and I can't talk about it. Officially."

"What about unofficially?"

"Unofficially you didn't hear it from me and I never talked to you. But to answer your question, Joey Marks thought everybody was skimming off him. He trusted no one. Every time I wore a wire with the guy, I was sweating bullets. Because you never knew when he was going to put his hand down your chest. I was with him more than a year and he was still doin' that every now and then. I had to wear the bug in my armpit, man. You try pulling tape out of your armpit sometime, man. It hurts."

"What about Tony?"

"That's what I'm getting at. Sure, Joey thought Tony was skimming. He thought I was, too. And you gotta understand, a certain amount of that was permissible. Joey knew everybody had to make a buck to be happy. But he mighta felt Tony was taking more than his share. He never told me that's what he thought, but I know he had the boy followed a couple times over here in L.A. And he got to somebody in Tony's bank in Beverly Hills. Joey was being copied on the monthly statements."

"Yeah?"

"Yeah. He would've known if there were any deposits that were outta line."

Bosch thought a moment but couldn't think what else to ask.

"Why'd you ask that, Bosch?"

"Oh, I don't know, something I'm workin' out. Powers said the wife told him Tony had a couple million he skimmed. It's hidden somewhere."

Lindell whistled over the line.

"Seems like a lot to me. Seems like Joey would've caught that and put the hammer down on Tony pronto. That's not what you call permissible."

"Well, I think it accrued over the years, you know. He could have piecemealed it. Also, he was washing money for some of Joey's friends in Chicago and Arizona, remember? He could've skimmed them, too."

"Anything's possible. Listen, Bosch, let me know how it all shakes out. I have to catch a plane."

"One more thing."

"Bosch, I gotta get to Burbank."

"You ever heard of anybody in Vegas named John Galvin?"

Galvin was the name of the man who had last visited Veronica Aliso on the night she disappeared. There was a beat of silence before Lindell finally said the name was not familiar. But that silence was what Bosch really heard.

"You sure?"

"Look, I never heard of the guy, okay? I gotta go."

After hanging up, Bosch opened his briefcase on the dining room table and took out a notebook so he could write down a few notes about what Lindell had said. Eleanor came out of the kitchen with utensils and napkins in her hands.

"Who was that?"

"Lindell."

"Who?"

"The agent who was Luke Goshen."

"What did he want?"

"I guess to apologize."

"That's unusual. The bureau usually doesn't apologize for anything."

"It wasn't an official call."

"Oh. Just one of those macho male bonding calls."

Bosch smiled because she was so right.

"What's this?" she asked as she put the silverware down and took the tape of *Casualty of Desire* out of his briefcase. "Oh, was this one of Tony Aliso's movies?"

"Yeah. Part of his Hollywood legacy. It's one of the ones Veronica was in. I was supposed to give it back to Kiz."

"You already saw it?"

Bosch nodded.

"I would've liked to see it. Did you like it?"

"It was pretty bad, but we can put it on tonight if you want."

"You sure you wouldn't mind?"

"I'm sure."

During dinner Bosch updated her in detail about the case. Eleanor asked few questions and eventually they lapsed into a comfortable quiet. The Bolognese sauce and linguini Eleanor had made was fantastic and Bosch broke the silence to tell her so. She had opened a bottle of red wine and that tasted good, too. He told her about that as well.

Afterward, they left the dishes in the sink and went out to the living room to watch the movie. Bosch sat with his arm on the back of the couch, his hand lightly touching Eleanor's neck. He found it boring to watch the film again and his mind quickly drifted away as he thought over the day's events. The money was what held his attention the longest. He wondered if Veronica already had it in her possession or if it was in a place where she had to go to get it. Not a local bank, he decided. They had already checked the local bank accounts.

That left Las Vegas, he concluded. Tony Aliso's travel records showed that in the last ten months he had not been anywhere but Los Angeles and Las Vegas. If he had been operating a skim fund, he'd have to have had access to it. If the money wasn't here, then it was over there. And since Veronica had not left the house before today, Bosch also concluded that she didn't have the money yet.

The phone rang and interrupted these thoughts. Bosch climbed up from the couch and answered the phone in the kitchen so he wouldn't disturb Eleanor's viewing of the movie. It was Hank Meyer calling from the Mirage but it didn't sound like Hank Meyer. It sounded like a scared boy.

"Detective Bosch, can I trust you?"

"Sure you can, Hank, what's the matter?"

"Something's happened. I mean, something's come up. Uh, because of you I know something I don't think I should know. I wish this whole thing . . . I don't know what to—"

"Hold on, hold on, Hank. Just calm down and tell what it is that's wrong. Be calm. Talk to me and we'll fix it. Whatever it is, we'll fix it."

"I'm at the office. They called me at home because I had a flag on the computer for that betting slip that belonged to your victim."

"Right."

"Well, somebody cashed it tonight."

"Okay, somebody cashed it. Who was it?"

"Well, you see, I put an IRS flag on the computer. Meaning that the cashier was supposed to request a driver's license and get a Social Security number, you know, for tax purposes. Even though this ticket was worth only four thousand I put the flag on it."

"Okay, so who cashed the slip?"

"A man named John Galvin. He had a local address."

Bosch leaned over the counter and pressed the phone tightly to his ear.

"When did this happen?" he asked.

"At eight-thirty tonight. Less than two hours ago."

"I don't understand, Hank. Why is this upsetting to you?"

"Well, I left instructions on the computer for me to be contacted at home as soon as this slip was cashed. I was contacted. I came in and got the information on who cashed the slip so I could get it to you ASAP and then I went directly to the video room. I wanted to see this John Galvin, you know, if we got a clear picture of him."

He stopped there. It was like pulling teeth getting the story out of him.

"And?" Bosch said. "Who was it, Hank?"

"We got a clear picture. It turns out I know John Galvin but not as John Galvin. Uh, as you know, one of my duties is to interface with law enforcement, maintain relations and help when I can whenever there—"

"Yes, Hank, I know. *Who* was it?"

"I looked at the video. It was very clear. John Galvin is a man I know. He's in Metro, a captain. His name is—"

"John Felton."

"How'd—"

"Because I know him, too. Now listen to me, Hank. You didn't tell me this, okay? We never talked. It's best that way. Safest for you. Understand?"

"Yes, but . . . but what is going to happen?"

"You don't have to worry. I'll take care of it and no one at Metro will ever know about this. Okay?"

"Okay, I guess. I—"

"Hank, I've got to go. Thanks, and I owe you a favor."

Bosch hung up and called information for the number of Southwest Airlines at the airport in Burbank. He knew Southwest and America West handled most of the flights to Las Vegas and they both flew out of the same terminal. He called Southwest and had them page Roy Lindell. While he waited, he looked at his watch. It had been more than an hour since he had talked to Lindell, but he didn't think the agent was in as much of a hurry as he had intimated on the phone. Bosch thought he had just said that to get off the phone.

A voice came on the line and asked who he was holding for. After Bosch repeated Lindell's name, he was told to hold and after two clicks Lindell's voice was on the line.

"Yeah, this is Roy, who's this?"

"You son of a bitch."

"Who is this?"

"John Galvin is John Felton and you knew it all the time."

"Bosch? Bosch, what are you doing?"

"Felton is Joey's man in Metro. You knew that from being on the inside. And when Felton does things for Marks, he uses the name John Galvin. You knew that, too."

"Bosch, I can't talk about this. It's all part of our in—"

"I don't give a shit about your investigation. You have to figure out whose side you're on, man. Felton has got Veronica Aliso. And that means Joey Marks has got her."

"What are you talking about? This is crazy."

"They know about the skim, don't you see? Joey wants his money back and they're going to squeeze it out of her."

"How do you know all of this?"

"Because I know."

Bosch thought of something and looked out through the kitchen door to the living room. Eleanor was still watching the movie and she looked over at him and raised her eyebrows in a question. Bosch shook his head to show his dissatisfaction with the person on the other end.

"I'm going to Vegas, Lindell. And I think I know where they'll be. You want to get your people involved? I sure as hell can't call Metro on this."

"How are you so sure she's even there?"

"Because she sent up a distress signal. Are you in or out?"

"We're in, Bosch. Let me give you a number. You call it when you get over there."

After Bosch hung up, he went into the living room. Eleanor had already turned off the tape.

"I can't watch any more of that. It's terrible. What's going on?"

"That time you followed Tony Aliso around in Vegas, you said he went to a bank with the girlfriend, right?"

"Right."

"Which bank? Where?"

"I, uh . . . it was on Flamingo, east of the Strip, east of Paradise Road. I can't remember the name. I think it was Silver State National. Yes, that's it. Silver State."

"The Silver State on Flamingo, are you sure now?"

"Right, yes."

"And it looked like she was opening an account?"

"Yes, but I can't be sure. That's the problem with a one-man tail. It's a small branch bank and I couldn't hang around inside too long. It looked like she was signing account papers and Tony was just watching. But I had to go out and wait outside until they were done. Remember, Tony knew me. If he even saw me, the tail would be blown."

"Okay, I'm going."

"Tonight?"

"Tonight. I have to make some calls first."

Bosch went back into the kitchen and called Grace Billets. While filling her in on what he had learned and his hunch about what it all meant, he got a pot of coffee going. After getting her approval to travel, he next called Edgar and then Rider and made arrangements to pick them up at the station in one hour.

He poured himself a cup of coffee and leaned against the counter in deep thought. Felton. There was a contradiction, it seemed to Bosch. If the Metro captain was the Joey Marks organization's inside man, why had he moved so quickly to go after Goshen when he got the match on the fingerprints Bosch had provided? Bosch played with this for a while and finally decided that Felton must have seen an opportunity in moving Goshen out of the way. He must have believed that his position in the Las Vegas underworld would rise if Goshen were out of the picture. Perhaps he even planned to arrange Goshen's assassination, thereby ensuring the indebtedness of Joey Marks. Bosch realized that for this plan to work, Felton either didn't know that Goshen knew he was the organization's inside man, or he planned to get rid of Goshen before he got a chance to tell anyone.

Bosch took a sip of the scalding coffee and put these thoughts aside. He went back into the living room. Eleanor was still on the couch.

"Are you going?"

"Yeah. I've got to pick up Jerry and Kiz."

"Why tonight?"

"Got to be there before the bank opens tomorrow."

"You think Veronica is going to be there?"

"It's a hunch. I think Joey Marks finally figured out just like we did that if he didn't whack Tony, then somebody else did and that person had to have been close to him. And that that person now has his money. He knew Veronica from way back and would figure she was up to it. I think he sent Felton over to check into it and to get his money back and take care of her if she was dirty on it. But she must've talked him out of it somehow. Probably by mentioning she had two million in skim in a safe deposit box in Vegas. I think that's what stopped Felton from killing her and instead made him take her with him. She's probably only alive until they get into that box. I think she gave Felton her husband's last betting slip because she knew he might cash it and we'd be watching for it."

"What makes you think it's at the bank where I saw him go?"

"Because we know about everything he had over here, all his accounts. It's not over here. Powers told me Veronica had told him that Tony dropped the skim into a safe deposit box that she wouldn't have access to until he was dead. She wasn't a signatory on it. So my guess is that it's in Vegas. It's the only place he's been outside of L.A. for the last year. And that if one day he was taking his girlfriend to open a bank account somewhere, he'd just go ahead and take her to the same bank he used."

Eleanor nodded.

"It's funny," Bosch said.

"What is?"

"That what all of this really came down to was a bank caper. It's not really about Tony Aliso's murder, it's about the money he skimmed and hid. A bank caper with his murder sort of a side effect. And that's how you and I met. On a bank job."

She nodded, her eyes going far off as she thought about it. Bosch immediately wished he hadn't brought the memory up.

"Sorry," he said. "I guess it's not really that funny."

Eleanor looked up at him from the couch.

"Harry, I'm going with you to Las Vegas."

VIII

The Silver State National Bank branch where Tony Aliso had taken his girlfriend while Eleanor Wish had watched was in the corner of a small shopping plaza between a Radio Shack and a Mexican restaurant called La Fuentes. The parking lot was largely empty at dawn on Monday morning when the FBI agents and LAPD detectives came to set up. The bank didn't open until nine and the other businesses would follow beginning at ten.

Because the businesses were closed, the agents had a problem in locating their surveillance points. It would be too obvious to stick four government cars in the lot. They would be too noticeable because there were only five other cars in the entire block-long parking lot, four parked on the outer fringes and an old Cadillac parked in the first row nearest the bank. There were no license plates on the Caddy, which had a spider web crack in the windshield, its windows left open and the trunk sprung and held closed by a chain and padlock through one of its many rusted-out spots. It had the sad appearance of having been abandoned, its owner probably another Las Vegas casualty. Like someone lost in the desert and dying of thirst just a few feet from an oasis, the Caddy had stopped for the final time just a few feet from the bank and all the money inside it.

The agents, after cruising by the location a few times to get the lay of the land, decided to use the Caddy as a blind, by popping the hood and sticking an agent in a greasy T-shirt under it and ostensibly working on the dead engine. They complemented this agent with a panel van parked right next to the Caddy. Four agents were in the van. At seven that morning they had taken it to the federal utilities shop and had a painter stencil *Las Fuentes Mexican Restaurant—Established 1983* on the side panels in red paint. The paint was still drying when they drove the van into the lot at eight.

Now at nine, the lot was slowly beginning to fill, mostly with employees of the stores and a few Silver State customers who needed to take care of business as soon as the bank opened its doors. Bosch watched all of this from the backseat of a federal car. Lindell and an agent named Baker were in the front seat. They were parked in the service bay of a gas station across Flamingo Road from the shopping center where the bank was located. Edgar and Rider were in another bureau car parked farther up Flamingo. There were two other bureau cars in the area, one static and one roving. The plan was for Lindell to move his car into the bank parking lot once it became more crowded with cars and the bureau car would not stand out. This plan included a bureau helicopter making wide arcs around the shopping center.

"They're opening up," a voice from the car radio reported.

"Gotcha, Las Fuentes," Lindell said back.

The bureau cars were each equipped with a radio pedal and overhead mike on the windshield visor, meaning the driver of each car simply depressed the foot pedal and spoke, avoiding having to raise a microphone to his mouth and possibly being noticed and identified as law enforcement. Bosch had heard that the LAPD was finally getting such equipment, but the narcotics units and specialized surveillance teams were getting it first.

"Lindell," he said, "you ever go to talk on the radio and slam on the brakes by mistake?"

"Not yet, Bosch. Why?"

"Just curious how all this fancy equipment works."

"It's only as good as the people who work it."

Bosch yawned. He couldn't remember the last time he had slept.

They had driven through the night to get to Las Vegas and then spent the rest of the time planning for the bank surveillance.

"So what do you think, Bosch?" Lindell asked him. "Sooner or later?"

"This morning. They'll want their money. They don't want to wait."

"Yeah, maybe."

"You think it's later?"

"If it was me, I'd do it later. That way if there were people out there watching and waiting—whether it's the bureau or LAPD or Powers or whoever—they'd get cooked in the sun. Know what I mean?"

"Yeah. We sit out here all day and we aren't going to be very sharp when the time comes."

Bosch was quiet for a little while after that. From the backseat he studied Lindell. He noticed that the agent had gotten a haircut. There was no sign of the spot where Bosch had hacked off his ponytail.

"You think you're going to miss it?" Bosch asked.

"Miss what?"

"Being under. The life, I mean."

"No, it was getting old. I'll be happy to go straight."

"Not even the girls?"

Bosch saw Lindell's eyes take a quick swipe at Baker and then look at Bosch in the rearview mirror. That told Bosch to let that subject go.

"Whaddaya think about the lot now, Don?" Lindell said, changing the subject.

Baker scanned the lot. It was slowly filling up. There was a bagel shop on the far end from the bank, and that was responsible for most of the autos at the moment.

"I think we can take it in, park it by the bagel place," Baker said. "There's enough cover now."

"Okay, then," Lindell said. He tilted his head slightly so that he was projecting his voice toward the visor. "Uh, Las Fuentes, this is Roy Rogers. We're going to take our position in now. We'll check ya from the bagel shop. That will be to your posterior, I believe."

"Roger that," came the return. "You always wanted to be on my tail end, didn't you, Roy?"

"Funny guy," Lindell said.

.   .   .

An hour went by while they watched from their new position and nothing happened. Lindell was able to move their car in closer, parking in front of a card-dealing school about half the parking lot's length from the bank. It was class day and several would-be dealers had been pulling in and parking. It was good cover.

"I don't know, Bosch," Lindell said, breaking a long silence. "You think they're going to show or not?"

"I never said it was anything more than a hunch. But I still think it all fits. It even fits better since we got here. Last week I found a matchbook in Aliso's room at the Mirage. It was from Las Fuentes. Whether they show or not, I say Tony's got a box in that bank."

"Well, I'm thinking about sending Don here in to ask about that. We might be able to call an end to this and stop wasting our time if we find out there's no box."

"Well, it's your call."

"You got that right."

A couple more minutes of tense silence went by.

"What about Powers?" Lindell asked.

"What about him?"

"I don't see him here, either, Bosch. When you got here this morning, you were all hot and heavy about him comin' out here to find her and blast her full of holes. So where is he?"

"I don't know, Lindell. But if we're smart enough to figure this out, so is he. I wouldn't doubt it if he knew from tailing Tony where the box was all along and just left that out of our little conversation."

"Wouldn't surprise me, either. But I still say it'd be stupid for him to come here. He's got to know we have a fix on this."

"Stupid isn't the word. It's suicidal. But I don't think he cares. He just wants her to go down. And if he takes a bullet, too, then that's the way it goes. Like I told you before, he was ready to do the kamikaze scene at the station when he thought she was there."

"Well, let's just hope he's cooled down a little since—"

"There!" Baker barked out.

Bosch followed his pointing finger toward the far corner of the lot, where a white limousine had just pulled in and was moving slowly toward the bank.

"Jesus," Lindell said. "Don't tell me he is this stupid."

All limos looked basically the same to Bosch but somehow Lindell and Baker had recognized the car.

"Is that Joey Marks?"

"It's his limo. He likes those big whitewalls. It's the wop in him. I just can't—he can't be in there. He's not going to waste two years of my fucking life making this pickup, is he?"

The limo stopped in the lane in front of the bank. There was no further movement.

"You got this, Las Fuentes?" Lindell asked.

"Yeah, we got it," came a whispered reply, though there was clearly no way anyone in that van could be overheard by someone in the limo.

"Uh, one, two and three, standby," Lindell continued. "Looks like we might have the fox in the henhouse. Air Jordan, you take five until further. I don't want you swinging over and spooking anybody."

This brought a chorus of rogers from the three other ground units and the helicopter.

"On second thought, three, why don't you come on up by the southwest entrance and stand by there for me?" Lindell said.

"Roger that."

Finally, the door to the limo opened, but it was on the side blocked from Bosch's view. He waited, not breathing, and after a beat Captain John Felton emerged from the limo.

"Bingo," the whisper came over the radio.

Felton then leaned back into the open door and reached in. Veronica Aliso now emerged, Felton's hand tightly around her arm. Following her, another man emerged at the same time the trunk opened automatically. While this second man, who was wearing gray pants and a shirt with an oval name tag sewn above the breast pocket, went to the trunk, Felton bent down and said something to someone still inside the limo. He never took his hand off Veronica's arm.

Bosch caught only a glimpse of Veronica's face then. Though he was an easy thirty yards from her, he could see the fear and weariness. It had probably been the longest night of her life.

The second man pulled a heavy red toolbox from the trunk and followed behind as Felton walked Veronica toward the bank, his arm still gripping her and his head swiveling as he looked about. Bosch saw Felton's focus linger on the van and then finally look away. The paint job had probably been the deciding factor. It had been a nice touch.

As they walked alongside the old Cadillac, Felton bent down to look at the man working under the hood. Satisfied he was not a threat, Felton straightened up and went on to the glass doors of the bank. Before they disappeared inside, Bosch saw that Veronica was clutching a cloth bag of some kind. Its dimensions were not discernible because it appeared to be empty and folded over on itself.

Bosch didn't breathe again until they were no longer in sight.

"Okay," Lindell said to the visor. "We've got three. Felton, the woman, and the driller. Anybody recognize him?"

The radio was silent for a few seconds and then a lone voice answered.

"I'm too far away but I thought it looked like Maury Pollack. He's a safe-and-lock man who's worked for Joey's crew before."

"Okay," Lindell said. "We'll check him later. I'm sending Baker in now to open a new account. Wait five and then, Conlon, you go in next. Check your sets now."

They went through a quick check of the radio sets Baker and Conlon were wearing under their clothes with wireless earpieces and wrist mikes. They checked out and Baker got out of the car and walked briskly along the sidewalk in front of the other stores toward the bank.

"Okay, Morris," Lindell said. "Take a walk. Try the Radio Shack."

"Roger."

Bosch watched as an agent he recognized from the pre-dawn meeting started crossing the lot from a car parked near the southwest entrance to the lot. Morris and Baker crossed paths ten feet apart but didn't acknowledge each other or even glance at the limo, which still sat with its engine idling in the lane in front of the bank.

It took about an hour for the next five minutes to go by. It was hot out but Bosch was mainly sweating from the anxiety of waiting and wondering what was going on. There had been only one transmission from Baker once he was inside. He had whispered that the subjects were in the safe deposit vault.

"Okay, Conlon, go," Lindell ordered at the five-minute mark.

Bosch soon saw Conlon walking along the storefronts from the direction of the bagel shop. He went into the bank.

And then there was nothing for the next fifteen excruciating minutes. Finally, Lindell spoke just to break the silence.

"How we doin' out there? Everybody chipper?"

There was a chorus of microphone clicks signaling an affirmative response. Just as the radio had gone silent again, Baker's voice came up in an urgent whisper.

"They're coming out, coming out. Something's wrong."

Bosch watched the bank doors and in a moment Felton and Veronica came out, the police captain's hand still firmly on her arm. The driller followed behind, lugging his red toolbox.

Felton didn't look around this time. He just walked with purpose toward the limo. He carried the bag now and it did not appear to Bosch to have grown in size. If Veronica's face looked fearful and tired before, it now looked even more distorted by fright. It was hard for Bosch to tell at this distance, but it looked like she was crying.

The door to the limo was opened from within as the threesome retraced their path alongside the old Cadillac and were getting near.

"All right," Lindell said to the listening agents. "On my call we go in. I'll take the front of the limo, three, you are in behind me. One and two, you got the back. Standard vehicular stop. Las Fuentes, I want you people to come up and clear the limo. Do it quick. If there's shooting, everybody watch the cross fire. Watch the cross fire."

As the rogers were coming in, Bosch was watching Veronica. He could tell she knew she was going to her death. The look on her face was vaguely reminiscent of what Bosch had seen on her husband's face. That certain knowledge that the game was up.

As he watched, he suddenly saw the trunk of the Cadillac spring open behind her. And from it, as if propelled by the same taut steel, jumped Powers. In a loud, wild-animal voice that Bosch heard clearly and would never forget, Powers yelled one word as he hit the ground.

"Veronica!"

As she, Felton and the driller turned to the origin of the sound, Powers raised his hands, both of them holding weapons. In that instant Bosch saw the glint of his own gun, the satin-finished Smith & Wesson, in the killer cop's left hand.

"Gun!" Lindell yelled. *"Everybody in! Everybody in!"*

He jerked the car into gear and slammed his foot on the gas pedal. The car jerked forward and started screaming toward the limo. But Bosch knew there was nothing they could do. They were too far away. He watched the scene unfold with a grim fascination, as if he were watching a slow-motion scene from a Peckinpah movie.

Powers began firing both guns, the shells ejecting and arcing away over both his shoulders as he stepped toward the limo. Felton made an attempt to go inside his jacket for his own gun but he was cut down in the fusillade, the first to drop. Then Veronica, standing perfectly still, facing her killer and making no move to run or shield herself, was hit and went down, dropping to the pavement, where Bosch couldn't see her because the limo blocked his view.

Powers kept coming and firing. The driller dropped his toolbox, raised his hands and started stepping backward away from the line of fire. Powers apparently ignored him. Bosch couldn't tell if he was shooting at Veronica's fallen body or into the open door of the limo. The limo took off, its tires spinning at first without purchase before it finally started to move, the rear door still open. But almost immediately, its driver failed to negotiate the left turn in the parking lane and the big car crashed into a row of parked cars. The driver jumped out and started running in the direction of the bagel shop.

Powers seemed to pay the fleeing driver no mind. He had reached the spot where Felton had fallen to the ground. He dropped Bosch's gun on the police captain's chest and reached down for the bag, which was on the ground next to Felton's hand.

It seemed that Powers did not realize the bag was empty until he had actually picked it up off the ground and held it. And as he was making this discovery, the doors of the van behind him were opened and four agents carrying shotguns were coming out. The agent in the T-shirt was coming around the side of the Cadillac, the handgun he had hidden in the engine compartment now pointed at Powers.

A squealing tire from one of the approaching bureau cars drew Powers's attention away from the empty duffel bag. He dropped it and turned on the five agents behind him. He raised both his hands again, though he only had one gun this time.

The agents opened fire and Bosch watched as Powers was literally lifted off the ground by the force of the impact and onto the front hood of a full-sized pickup truck that probably belonged to a bank customer. Powers landed on his back. His hand lost its grip on the remaining gun and it clattered off the hood to the ground. As loud as the eight seconds of shooting had been, the silence that followed the gun falling to the ground seemed even louder.

Powers was dead. Felton was dead. Giuseppe Marconi, aka Joseph Marconi, aka Joey Marks, was dead—his body sprawled and awash in blood on the soft leather seats in the back of his limousine.

When they got to Veronica Aliso, she was alive but dying. She had been hit with two rounds in the upper chest, and the bubbles in the froth of blood in her mouth indicated her lungs had been shredded. While the FBI agents ran about securing and containing the scene, Bosch and Rider went to Veronica.

Her eyes were open but losing their moisture. They were moving all around as if searching for someone or something that wasn't there. Her jaw started to work and she said something but Bosch couldn't hear. He crouched down over her and turned his ear to her mouth.

"Can you . . . get me ice?" she whispered.

Bosch turned and looked at her. He didn't understand. She started to speak again and he turned his ear to her mouth again.

". . . the pavement . . . so hot. I . . . I need ice."

Bosch looked at her and nodded.

"It's coming. It's coming. Veronica, where's the money?"

He bent over her, realizing that she was right, the pavement was now burning the palms of his hands. He could barely make out her words.

"At least they don't . . . they don't get it."

She started coughing then, a deep wet cough, and Bosch knew her chest was full of blood and it wouldn't be long before she drowned. He couldn't think of what to do or say to this woman. He realized they were probably his own bullets in her and that she was dying because they had fucked up and let Powers get away. He almost wanted to ask her to forgive him, to say she understood how things could go so wrong.

He looked away from her and across the lot. He could hear sirens approaching. But he had seen enough gunshot wounds to know she wasn't

going to need the ambulance. He looked back down at her. Her face was
very pale and going slack. Her lips moved once more and he bent to listen. This time her voice was no more than a desperate rasp in his ear. He
could not understand her words and he whispered in her ear to say it
again.

". . . et my gergo . . ."

He turned his head to look at her, the confusion in his eyes. He shook
his head. An annoyed expression crossed her face.

"Let," she said clearly, using the last of her strength. "Let . . . my
daughter go."

Bosch kept his eyes locked on hers as that last line ran through his
mind. Then, without thinking about it, he nodded once to her. And as he
watched, she died. Her eyes lost their focus and he could tell she was gone.

Bosch stood up and Rider studied his face.

"Harry, what did she say?"

"She said . . . I'm not sure what she said."

Bosch, Edgar and Rider stood leaning against the trunk of Lindell's car,
watching as a phalanx of FBI and Metro people continued to descend on
the crime scene. Lindell had ordered the entire shopping center closed
and marked off with yellow tape, a move that prompted Edgar to comment, "When these guys throw a crime scene, they really throw a crime
scene."

Each of them had already given a statement. They were no longer
part of the investigation. They were merely witnesses to the event and
now observers.

The special agent in charge of the Las Vegas field office was on the
scene directing the investigation. The bureau had brought in a motor
home that had four separate interview rooms in it and agents were taking
statements in them from witnesses to the shooting. The bodies were still
there, now covered in yellow plastic on the pavement and in the limo.
That splash of bright color made for good video for the news helicopters
circling overhead.

Bosch had been able to pick up pieces of information from Lindell
on how things stood. The ID number on the Cadillac in which Powers

had hidden for at least the four hours it was under observation by the FBI was traced to an owner in Palmdale, California, a desert town northeast of Los Angeles. The owner was already on file with the bureau. He was a white supremacist who had held antigovernment rallies on his land the last two Independence Days. He was also known to have sought to contribute to the defense funds of the men charged with bombing the federal courthouse in Oklahoma City two years before. Lindell told Bosch that the SAIC had ordered an arrest warrant for the owner on charges of conspiracy to commit murder for his role in helping Powers. It had been a nice plan. The trunk of the Caddy was lined with a thick carpet and several blankets. The chain and padlock used to hold it closed could be unhooked from the inside. Through rusted-out spots on the fenders and trunk it had been possible for Powers to watch and wait for the right moment to come out, guns ready.

The driller, who it turned out was indeed Maury Pollack, was only too happy to cooperate with the agents. He was just happy he wasn't one of the ones wearing a yellow plastic blanket. He told Lindell and the others that Joey Marks had picked him up that morning, told him to wear a working-man's outfit and to bring his drill. He didn't know what the situation was because there was little talking in the limo on the ride over. He just knew the woman was scared.

Inside the bank Veronica Aliso had presented a bank officer with a copy of her husband's death certificate, his will and a court order issued Friday in Las Vegas Municipal Court granting her, as sole heir to Anthony Aliso, access to his safe deposit box. Access was approved and the box was drilled because Mrs. Aliso said she had not been able to locate her husband's key.

The trouble was, Pollack said, when he drilled the box open, they found it was empty.

"Can you imagine that?" Lindell said as he related this information to Bosch. "All of this for nothing. I was hoping to get my hands on that two mil. Of course, we'd've split it with L.A. Right down the middle, Bosch."

"Right," Bosch said. "Did you look at the records? When was the last time Tony went into his box?"

"That's another thing. He was just in on Friday. Like twelve hours before they killed him, he went in and cleared the box. He must've had a premonition or something. He knew, man. He knew."

"Maybe."

Bosch thought about the matchbook from Las Fuentes that he had found in Tony's room at the Mirage. Tony didn't smoke but he remembered the ashtrays at the house where Layla had grown up. He decided that if Tony had cleared his box out on that Friday and eaten at Las Fuentes while he was here, the only likely reason he would have ended up with matches from the restaurant in his room was that he had been at the restaurant with someone who needed them.

"Now the question is, where's the money?" Lindell said. "We can seize it if we can find it. Ol' Joey's not going to need it."

Lindell looked over at the limo. The door was still open and one of Marconi's legs stuck out from under the yellow plastic. A powder blue pants leg, a black loafer and white sock. That was all Bosch could see of Joey Marks now.

"The bank people, are they cooperating or do you need a warrant for every move you make?" Bosch asked.

"No, they're on board. The manager's in there shaking like a leaf. Not every day you get a massacre outside your front door."

"Then ask them to check their records and see if there's a box in there under the name Gretchen Alexander."

"Gretchen Alexander? Who's that?"

"You know her, Roy. It's Layla."

"Layla? Are you fuckin' kidding me? You think he'd give that bimbo two million ducats while he goes off and gets himself killed?"

"Just check, Roy. It's worth a shot."

Lindell went off toward the bank doors. Bosch looked at his partners.

"Jerry, you going to want your gun back? We should tell them now so they don't destroy them or file them away forever."

"My gun?"

Edgar looked at all of the yellow plastic with a pained look on his face.

"No, Harry, I don't think so. That piece is haunted now. I don't ever want it back."

"Yeah," Bosch said. "I was thinking the same thing."

Bosch brooded about things for a while and then heard his name be-

ing called. He turned and saw Lindell beckoning him from the door of
the bank. He headed over.

"Bingo," Lindell said. "She's got a box."

They walked back into the bank and Bosch saw several agents conducting interviews with the branch's stunned employees. Lindell led him
to a desk where the branch manager sat. She was a woman of about
thirty with brown curly hair. The nameplate on her desk said Jeanne
Connors. Lindell picked up a file that was on her desk and showed it to
Bosch.

"She has a box here and she made Tony Aliso a signatory on it. He
pulled the box at the same time he pulled his own on the Friday before
he got nailed. You know what I'm thinking? I think he emptied his and
put it all in hers."

"Probably."

Bosch was looking at the safe deposit entry records in the file. They
were handwritten on a three by five card.

"So," Lindell said, "what we do is we get a warrant for her box and
drill the sucker—maybe get Maury out there to do it, since he's being so
cooperative. We seize the money and the federal government is that
much ahead. You guys'd get a split, too."

Bosch looked at him.

"You can drill it, if you've got the probable cause, but there isn't going to be anything in it."

Bosch pointed to the last entry on the box card. Gretchen Alexander
had pulled the box herself five days earlier—the Wednesday after Tony
Aliso was killed. Lindell stared at it a long moment before reacting.

"Jesus, you think she cleared it out?"

"Yeah, Roy, I do."

"She's gone, isn't she? You've been looking for her, haven't you?"

"She's in the wind, man. And I guess so am I."

"You're leaving?"

"I gave my statement, I'm clear. I'll see you, Roy."

"Yeah, okay, Bosch."

Bosch headed to the door of the bank. As he opened it, Lindell came
up behind him.

"But why'd he put it all in her box?"

He was still holding the box card and staring at it as if it might suddenly answer all his questions.

"I don't know but I've got a guess."

"What's that, Bosch?"

"He was in love with her."

"Him? A girl like that?"

"You never know. People can kill each other for all kinds of reasons. I guess they can fall in love with each other for all kinds of reasons. You gotta take it when it comes, no matter if it's a girl like that or . . . someone else."

Lindell just nodded and Bosch stepped through the door.

Bosch, Edgar and Rider took a cab to the federal building and picked up their car. Bosch said he wanted to stop by the house in North Las Vegas where Gretchen Alexander had grown up.

"She isn't going to be there, Harry," Edgar said. "Are you kidding?"

"I know she won't be there. I just want to talk to the old lady for a minute."

He found the house without getting lost and pulled into the driveway. The RX7 was still there and didn't look like it had moved.

"This will only take a minute, if you want to stay in the car."

"I'll go in," Rider said.

"I'll stay and keep the AC going," Edgar said. "In fact, I'll drive the first leg, Harry."

He got out as Bosch and Rider exited and came around and took Bosch's place behind the wheel.

Bosch's knock on the front door was answered quickly. The woman had heard or seen the car and was ready.

"You," she said, looking through the two-inch crack she had allowed in the door. "Gretchen still isn't here."

"I know, Mrs. Alexander. It's you I want to talk to."

"Me? What on earth for?"

"Would you please let us in? It's hot out here."

She opened the door with a resigned look on her face.

"Hot in here, too. I can't afford to put the thermostat lower than eighty."

Bosch and Rider entered and moved into the living room. He introduced Rider and all three of them sat down. This time Bosch sat on the edge of the sofa, remembering how he had sunk in last time.

"All right, what's this about? Why do you want to talk to me?"

"I want to know about your granddaughter's mother," Bosch said.

The old woman's mouth went slack and Bosch could tell Rider wasn't much less confused.

"Her mother?" Dorothy asked. "Her mother's long gone. Didn't have the decency to see her own child through. Never mind her mother."

"When did she leave?"

"Long time ago. Gretchen wasn't even out of diapers. She just left me a note saying good-bye and good luck. She was gone."

"Where'd she go?"

"I have no earthly idea and I don't want to know. Good riddance, is what I say. She turned her back on that beautiful little girl. Didn't have the decency to ever call or even send for a picture."

"How did you know she was even alive?"

"I didn't. She could be dead all these years for all I know or care."

She was a bad liar, the type who got louder and indignant when she lied.

"You know," Bosch said. "She sent you money, didn't she?"

The woman looked sullenly down at her hands for a long moment. It was her way of confirming his guess.

"How often?"

"Once or twice a year. It wasn't near enough to make up for what she did."

Bosch wanted to ask how much would have been enough but let it go.

"How did the money come?"

"Mail. It was in cash. I know it came from Sherman Oaks, California. That was always the postmark. What does this have to do with anything now?"

"Tell me your daughter's name, Dorothy."

"She was born to me and my first husband. My name was Gilroy back then and that was hers."

"Jennifer Gilroy," Rider said, repeating Veronica Aliso's true name.

The old woman looked at Rider with surprise but didn't ask how she knew.

"We called her Jenny," she said. "Anyway, you see, when I took over with Gretchen I was remarried and had a new name. I gave it to

Gretchen so the kids at school wouldn't bother her about it. Everybody always thought I was her momma and that was fine with the both of us. Nobody needed to know diff'rent."

Bosch just nodded. It had all come together now. Veronica Aliso was Layla's mother. Tony Aliso had gone from the mother to the daughter. There was nothing else to ask or say. He thanked the old woman and touched Rider on the back so that she would go through the door first. Out on the front step, he paused and looked back at Dorothy Alexander. He waited until Rider was a few steps toward the car before speaking.

"When you hear from Layla—I mean, Gretchen—tell her not to come home. Tell her to stay as far away from here as she can."

He shook his head.

"She shouldn't ever come home."

The woman didn't say anything. Bosch waited a couple moments while looking down at the worn welcome mat. He then nodded and headed to the car.

Bosch took the backseat behind Edgar, Rider sat in the front. As soon as they were in the car and Edgar was backing out of the driveway, Rider turned around and looked at Bosch.

"Harry, how did you ever put that together?"

"Her last words. Veronica's. She said, 'Let my daughter go.' I just sort of knew then. There's a resemblance there. I just didn't place it before."

"You've never even seen her."

"I've seen her picture."

"What?" Edgar said. "What's going on?"

"Do you think Tony Aliso knew who she was?" Rider asked, ignoring Edgar.

"Hard to say," Bosch said. "If he did, it makes what happened to him easier to understand, easier to take. Maybe he was flaunting it with Veronica. Maybe it's what sent her over the edge."

"And Layla-slash-Gretchen?"

Edgar's head was swiveling back and forth between them and the road, a look of confusion on his face.

"Something tells me she didn't know. I think if she did, she would have told her grandmother. And the old lady didn't know."

"If he was just using her to get to Veronica, why'd he move all the money into her box?"

"He could've been using her but he also could've been in love with her. We'll never know. Might've just been coincidence that it happened on the day he got killed. He could've just transferred the cash because he had the IRS on him. Maybe he was afraid they'd find out about the box and freeze his access to it. It could've been a lot of things. But we'll never know now. Everybody's dead."

"Except for the girl."

Edgar made a hard stop, pulling to the side of the road. Coincidentally, they happened to be across the street from Dolly's on Madison.

"Is somebody gonna tell me what the hell is going on?" he demanded. "I do you people a favor and keep the car cool while you two go inside for a chat and then I'm left in the dark. Now what the hell are you two talking about?"

He was looking at Bosch in the rearview mirror.

"Just drive, Jed. Kiz will tell you when we get to the Flamingo."

They drove into the front circle of the Hilton Flamingo and Bosch left them there. He moved quickly through the football field–sized casino, dodging rows of slot machines, until he reached the poker room, where Eleanor had said she would be when they were done. They had dropped her at the Flamingo that morning after she had shown them the bank she had once seen Tony Aliso going into with Gretchen Alexander.

There were five tables going in the poker room. Bosch quickly scanned the faces of the players but did not see Eleanor. Then, as he turned to look back across the casino, she was there, just as when she had appeared on the first night he'd gone looking for her.

"Harry."

"Eleanor. I thought you'd be playing."

"I couldn't play while thinking about you out there. Is everything okay?"

"Everything is fine. We're leaving."

"Good. I don't like Las Vegas anymore."

He hesitated for a moment before saying anything. He almost faltered but then the resolve came back to him.

"There is that one stop I'd still like to make before we leave. The one we talked about. That is, if you've decided."

She looked at him for a long moment and then a smile broke across her face.

IX

Bosch walked across the polished linoleum on the sixth floor of Parker Center, purposely driving his heels down with each step. He wanted to put scuff marks on the carefully tended finish. He turned into the alcove entrance to the Internal Affairs Division and asked the secretary behind the counter for Chastain. She asked if he had an appointment and Bosch told her he didn't make appointments with people like Chastain. She stared at him a moment and he stared back until she picked up a phone and punched in an extension. After whispering into the line, she held the phone to her chest and looked up at Bosch and then eyed the shoebox and file he held in his hands.

"He wants to know what it's about."

"Tell him it's about his case against me falling apart."

She whispered some more and then Bosch was finally buzzed through the counter's half door. He went into the IAD squad room, where several of the desks were occupied by investigators. Chastain stood up from behind one of these.

"What are you doing here, Bosch? You're on suspension for letting that prisoner escape."

He said it loudly so that the others in the squad room would know that Bosch was a guilty man.

"The chief cut it down to a week," Bosch said. "I call that a vacation."

"Well, that's only round one. I still got your file open."

"That's why I'm here."

Chastain pointed to the interview room Bosch had been in the week before with Zane.

"Let's talk in there."

"No," Bosch said. "We're not talking, Chastain. I'm just showing."

He dropped the file he was carrying on the desk. Chastain remained standing and looked at it without opening it.

"What is this?"

"It's the end of the case. Open it."

Chastain sat down and opened the file, exhaling loudly, as if he were embarking on a distasteful and worthless chore. On top was a copy of a page from the department's manual of procedure and officer conduct. The manual was to IAD dicks what the state penal code was to the rest of the officers and investigators in the department.

The page in the file pertained to officers associating with known criminals, convicted felons and members of organized crime. Such association was strictly forbidden and punishable by dismissal from the department, according to the code.

"Bosch, you didn't need to bring me this, I've got the whole book," Chastain said.

He was trying out some light banter because he didn't know what Bosch was doing and was well aware that his peers were watching from their desks while trying to act as if they weren't.

"Yeah? Well, you better get your book out and read the bottom line there, pal. The exception."

Chastain looked down at the bottom of the page.

"Says, 'Exception to this code can be established if the officer can show to the satisfaction of superior officers a family relationship through blood or marriage. If that is established, officer must—' "

"That's enough," Bosch said.

He reached down and took the page so that Chastain could see what was in the rest of the file.

"What you have there, Chastain, is a marriage certificate issued in Clark County, Nevada, attesting to my marriage to Eleanor Wish. If that's not good enough for you, beneath it are two affidavits from my partners. They witnessed the marriage. Best man and maid of honor."

Chastain kept his eyes on the paperwork.

"It's over, man," Bosch said. "You lose. So get the fuck out of my life."

Chastain leaned back. His face was red and he had an uncomfortable smile on his face. Now he was sure the others were watching.

"You're telling me you got married just to avoid an IAD beef?"

"No, asshole. I got married because I love somebody. That's why you get married."

Chastain didn't have a reply. He shook his head, looked at his watch and shuffled some papers while trying to act as though this was just a minor interruption in his day. He did everything but look at his nails.

"Yeah, I thought you'd run out of things to say," Bosch said. "I'll see you around, Chastain."

He turned to walk away but then turned back to Chastain.

"Oh, and I almost forgot, you can tell your source our deal is done with, also."

"What source, Bosch? Deal? What are you talking about?"

"I'm talking about Fitzgerald or whoever you get your information from at OCID."

"I don't—"

"Sure you do. I know you, Chastain. You couldn't have come up with Eleanor Wish on your own. You've got a pipeline over there to Fitzgerald. He told you about her. It was him or one of his people. Doesn't matter to me who. Either way I'm out of a deal I made with him. You can tell him that."

Bosch held the shoebox up and shook it. The videotape and audiotapes rattled inside it, but he could tell Chastain had no idea what was in the box or what it meant.

"You tell him, Chastain," he said again. "See you around."

He finally left then, pausing only at the counter to give the secretary a thumbs-up sign. In the hallway, rather than turn left toward the elevators, he took a right and headed through the double doors of the chief of police's office suite. The chief's adjutant, a lieutenant in uniform, sat behind the reception desk. Bosch didn't know him, which was good. He walked up and put the shoebox down on the desk.

"Can I help you? What's this?"

"It's a box, Lieutenant. It's got some tapes the chief will want to watch and listen to. Right away."

Bosch made a move to leave.

"Wait a minute," the adjutant said. "Will he know what this is about?"

"Tell him to call Deputy Chief Fitzgerald. He can explain what it's about."

Bosch left then, not turning around when the adjutant called after him for his name. He slipped through the double doors and headed down to the elevator. He felt good. He didn't know if anything would come of the illegal tapes he had given the police chief, but he felt that all decks were cleared. His show with the box earlier with Chastain would ensure that the word got back to Fitzgerald that this was exclusively Bosch's play. Billets and Rider should be safe from recriminations by the OCID chief. He could come after Bosch if he wanted, but Bosch felt safe now. Fitzgerald had nothing on him anymore. No one did.

X

It was their first day on the beach after spending two days almost exclusively in their room. Bosch couldn't get comfortable on the chaise lounge. He didn't understand how people did this, just sit in the sun and bake. He was covered with lotion and there was sand caked between his toes. Eleanor had bought him a red bathing suit that he thought made him look foolish and that made him feel like a target. At least, he thought, it wasn't one of those slingshot things some of the men on the beach were wearing.

He propped himself up on his elbows and looked around. Hawaii was unbelievable. So beautiful it was like a dream. And the women were beautiful, too. Especially Eleanor. She lay beside him on her own lounge. Her eyes were closed and there was a small smile on her face. She wore a one-piece black bathing suit that was cut high on her hips and showed off her tanned and nicely muscled legs.

"What are you looking at?" she said without opening her eyes.

"Nothing. I just . . . I can't get comfortable. I think I'm going to take a walk or something."

"Why don't you get a book to read, Harry? You have to relax. That's what honeymoons are about. Sex, relaxation, good food and good company."

"Well, two out of four isn't bad."

"What's wrong with the food?"

"The food's great."

"Funny."

She reached out and hit him in the arm. Then she, too, propped herself up on her elbows and gazed out at the shimmering blue water. They could see the spine of Molokini rising in the distance.

"It's so beautiful here, Harry."

"Yes, it is."

They sat in silence for a few moments, watching the people walking by at the water's edge. Bosch brought his legs up, leaned forward and sat with his elbows on his knees. He could feel the sun burning into his shoulders. It was beginning to feel good.

He noticed a woman walking languidly along the edge. She had the attention of every man on the beach. She was tall and lithe and had long brownish-blond hair that was wet from the sea. Her skin was copper and she wore the smallest of bathing suits, just a few strings and triangles of black cloth.

As she passed in front of him, the glare dropped off Bosch's sunglasses and he studied her face. The familiar lines and tilt of the jaw were there. He knew her.

"Harry," Eleanor whispered then. "Is that . . . it looks like the dancer. The girl in that photo you had, the one I saw Tony with."

"Layla," Bosch said, not answering her but just to say the name.

"It's her, isn't it?"

"I didn't used to believe in coincidences," he said.

"Are you going to call the bureau? The money's probably right here on the island with her."

Bosch watched the woman moving away. Her back was to him now and from that angle it was almost as if she were naked. Just a few strings from her suit were visible. The glare came back on his glasses at this angle and his vision of her was distorted. She was disappearing in the glare and the mist coming in from the Pacific.

"No, I'm not calling anybody," he finally said.

"Why not?"

"She didn't do anything," he said. "She let some guy give her money. Nothing wrong with that. Maybe she was even in love with him."

He watched for another moment, thinking about Veronica's last words to him.

"Anyway, who's going to miss the money?" he said. "The bureau? The LAPD? Some fat old gangster in a Chicago suburb with a bunch of bodyguards around him? Forget it. I'm not calling anybody."

He took one last look at her. She was far away now and as she walked she was looking out to sea, the sun holding her face. Bosch nodded to her, but of course she didn't see this. He then lay back down on the lounge and closed his eyes. Almost immediately he felt the sun begin penetrating his skin, doing its healing work. And then he felt Eleanor's hand on top of his. He smiled. He felt safe. He felt like nobody could ever hurt him again.